Dedication

This story is written for, and with the great encouragement and help of my very best, dearest Friend and Confidante, the Lord Jesus Christ.

Disclaimer

Writers on writing often say that one writes best at what one knows best, so I have created a main character who shares many of my own interests and traits. In fact, I reached a point where I stopped trying to please all other categories and wrote a book to appeal to my own tastes. Aside from the Lord Jesus, and chunks of myself, it is filled with characters that are figments of my imagination, but have become quite real to me. I borrowed traits from people I know as seemed useful to this story. They are in no way accurate or complete portraits of them. Otherwise, all the characters, events and circumstances described are totally fictitious. I hope you enjoy them as much as I did.

Story Summary

Caring, imaginative, Ruthe supports her family as a telephone operator, using her free time to rescue others from evil but dares not tell her prairie hometown Mennonite family. Trapped by her deception, Ruthe must find a creative solution for her own torment.

Wish a miracle-working angel would rescue you from your family problems? Wouldn't a friend be great who knows what to say or do in every crisis? Ruthe is that kind of miracle-working friend. But having so many friends creates a few problems for her, especially since she doesn't want her family back in her prairie Mennonite hometown to know about her wonderful city friends.

How can Ruthe be totally devoted to Christ, winning friends, and helping them to live holy lives, and to be so blind to her own short-comings? Watch as her deception and double-life sets a trap for Ruthe, and the creative way she finally deals with it.

Preface

At age 12 I dreamed vividly that I would one day write a book that would win many friends to my Best Friend, Jesus Christ. I did not believe my family or friends would think I could ever do it, so for many years I worked at it in secret, sometimes setting it aside in discouragement, and then at His gentle prompting I came back to it. Since I couldn't afford to go to college to learn to write, I told Him that He would have to teach me, and in the many re-writes and by my reading of library books on writing, He did just that. I owe all I am or have become to the patient work of the Lord in me by His dear Spirit. Therefore, I have long ago promised to give away all the profits from this book, and its sequels, as He guides and prompts me. That will be a new adventure, I'm sure, but I look forward to it. My goal is to be a generous giver, like God.

For a number of important years in my life I worked with children's ministries, particularly with girls' clubs. My best rapport was with young teen girls. They often were already whispering secret prayers to God, and hungry to know Him more intimately - exactly what I wanted to teach them out of my life. The crafts and outings were just ways to bring us together more often.

This novel will be like rich, delicious cream to such girls wherever you are.

Naturally, I like to think there are women, and even men, and kids too, who also crave an intimate relationship with the Lord; one where they sense His loving presence, where they may pray conversationally, and see God act in response to their prayers. I hope you'll all read this book and be delightfully affected by Ruthe and her friends.

Anticipating certain questions, let me answer them ahead of time. I have put in some dialogue with the Mennonite Grosz'mama in Low German or Plaut Deutsch language to honour my grandmother and heritage. Playing with written dialogue as I hear it proved to be great fun, for my ears tend to hear such nuances. I hope it does not get in the way of your reading and enjoyment of the story. Just take them phonetically, as the letters sound to you. Do the same with the Low German (Plaut Deutsch) words if you want to try them. Remember, the translations are always in the endnotes.

ONE

"Please, Dad! Wear your tie tonight!" Ruthe clicked into the living room with her first ever high heels. The mismatched, second-hand furniture looked worse against the pink lace shirt-dress swirling around her knees. But with nervous self-examination her eyes were on her skirt edges.

"Or what?"

"I won't go to my own graduation!" Ruthe's threat rang high-noted, hollow and desperate.

"He will. He will." Ruthe's mother pacified from the bedroom where she was dressing. Anna Veer began to nag and prod Ben to put on the tie she'd bought for their wedding. He saved it for extremely high and holy occasions.

"Kids get disrespectful once they've some education–" Her Dad strolled back into the living room in a hunting pose, pausing to watch his eldest checking herself nervously in one mirror then another.

She caught his glance and turned away as she realized her undemonstrative father was rather proud of her. He would wear that despised tie for her. A long tense whoosh of air expelled from her trembling rib cage. *Lord, they don't understand me or life... I've got to protect and take care of the folks.*

Now she threw herself back into analyzing her appearance. Ruthe straightened the wide belt with the square rhinestone buckle, pulling in her breath and again, slowly twirling the rustling skirt around her knees. There. That flat, undecorated bodice reminded her with a fresh crush that the other girls had ordered real flower corsages. She patted the spot on her left side where deep pink roses with an iridescent bow should be, and sighed silently, *no one can tell this is a second-hand dress, can they? Thanks then, Lord, for this good find.*

Gingerly she poked into the mass of light brown curls and waves that tumbled down and beyond her shoulders. She had far more hair than her delicate features warranted. Now she swung the whole mass of sprayed hair like she had seen others do in the school washroom. She spotted a few stray wisps on top and tucked them down a bit.

More waiting? Ruthe took off her glasses and rubbed them vigorously with a tissue for the third time, then studied her nails critically. Her dad would not allow nail polish, but Maelyn had lent her clear nail strengthener in school, and so far he had not spotted it. She had even worn it to work the last two nights at the telephone office in the city.

The phone shrilled. Ruthe nearly tripped on her seven-year old sister, Sharri, as she dashed into the kitchen just fast enough to beat thirteen-year old Suzanne to the receiver. "Hello?"

She ignored Brandt, grinning from his perch on the counter, swinging his lanky legs, eyeing the comedy. "Yes. Speaking."

For a long attentive minute she froze in a listening pose, weighing, deciding. Suddenly the gold flecks in her teal eyes jumped with life. "I'm coming right in. It's okay. Hold on– I'm on my way."

In one motion Ruthe hung up, swooped the car keys from the kitchen windowsill, and her new white patent purse from the table. As she tore through the porch doors, she called over her shoulder, "matter of life and death! Go ahead without me. I'll be back soon's I can!"

In those same split seconds her parents had appeared in the kitchen, Suzanne had bounced back downstairs from their bedroom, and Sharri screamed Ruthe's name. But their dressed up graduate jumped into the old brown '59 Pontiac, backed out into the gravel street and spun away, hearing none of them.

Ruthe breathed deep trembling breaths as she steered nimbly around the familiar corners of Kleinstadt and onto the highway to Saskatoon. She was now an adult on a serious mission.

Abruptly she giggled a tiny taut giggle. What a crazy reprieve from the fussy banquet and public ceremonies and speeches, the anticipation of which had tied her in knots all day. This was exhilarating; speeding down the highway in the magic of an early evening hour in May. The sun shone warmly, a welcome surprise after a long winter of cold and very short days.

Just when she was beginning to unwind a new nervousness washed over Ruthe. What could she possibly do for the O'Briens when she got there?

On the phone Muriel had said that her mother was dying and asking for her, and her older sister had vanished. "Ruthe, you've got to come help me find Cathy before Mom dies!" her new teen friend had sobbed.

"I've never been at a deathbed before," Ruthe worried. "I was not really at Grandpa's last year. Not right when he died.' What will the rest of the O'Briens think, me barging in like this?"

Swiftly her thoughts went into a soundless but high-charged dialogue with God, a habit developed in her lonely preteen years. *What will I do, Lord? I'm only that mousy bookworm who reads too much and is scared of strangers. Just look at what I've got myself into now!*

Vivid scenes from the last two weeks washed in like tidewater to remind her how she stumbled into this double life.

Her dad had been out of work all winter. He was a strong, healthy man who was not afraid of strenuous outdoor labour. It was the first time ever that he had been unable to find work. Her mother had been in poor health almost as long as Ruthe could remember, and had suffered several big surgeries in recent years, but when she, with rash pride, began to threaten to go washing floors for others, Ruthe knew it was time to step in to help. Her parents had promised she could stay in school as long as they could afford it, but before they would go on welfare, she would be expected to do what all good Mennonites, at least of her parents' generation, had done; work to help the family pull through hard times.

Ruthe was observant enough to know if she dropped out of grade twelve, chances of finishing would get slimmer with time. After much deliberation and prayer and quiet inquiries, she wrote a letter she had polished daily for three weeks. It won her a special interview in the city with the Chief Operator at SaskTel, the provincial telephone company. She got a fine arrangement to work weekend night shifts in the telephone office, with extra shifts in any week when she notified the scheduling clerk she was available.

The Chief Operator had been so understanding and amenable to help Ruthe this way until she could take full-time shifts, because she had done it herself in the fifties, in a small town not far from Kleinstadt. Since the late sixties, operators were now to have their high school completed. It was a coup, yet Ruthe did not brag.

Her parents did when she announced the job to them. They told everyone they knew. Her mother worried about her commuting to and from the city those forty minutes at night and again at so early in the morning. At the same time, they were both clearly relieved that Ruthe had found a way to support the family and stay in school until after her June finals.

City life held a unique fascination for Ruthe. Characters and intrigues she had experienced vicariously in books percolated and blended in her imagination. She couldn't keep from staring at people in the streets, and at the huge buildings, which held so many unrelated individuals at once. Each face, each voice she heard in her headset hinted at volumes of personal stories.

Tenderhearted, Ruthe soon began to have physical cramps of empathetic ache at the human suffering she sensed. A month ago she began to come earlier or stay a while after a shift to drive up and down the streets, sub-consciously hoping to be in the right place at the right time to help someone, she supposed.

"Dear God!" she moaned now, as she brushed her damp hands on the pink lace and gripped the wheel tighter, unaware that her foot pressed down as she thought of Muriel and her mother, waiting. *You did a miraculous thing the night You directed me to Muriel. You even put words in my mouth. Do it again! Please Lord! I cannot turn around now! Ple-as-e. I've promised.*

Two weeks earlier Ruthe drove down one of the more run down business streets when she spied a narrow, weather-beaten building, held upright by a cafe

5

on one side and an over-stuffed pawn shop on the other. An eye-straining sign flickering over the door proclaimed it to be Rona's DanceSpot. She knew she was too naive about this, but felt one thing instinctively; there had to be some unhappy kids there, never mind what Arlene at school said about the fun of modern dancing.

Cold clammy fear touched her neck. Some of those people might be hiding their misery under a false gaiety, but which ones would admit it in there right now? And, what would the plain, conservative people of Kleinstadt say if she set foot in that place? A few of her classmates would be willing to dance there, but would sure be selective in whom they would tell about it.

Still driving steadily toward the city, and away from her own graduation banquet in the streamer-decorated basement of the biggest church in Kleinstadt, Ruthe's mind was reliving how she had driven around and around the block two weeks ago. She had stopped across the street and stared at the door, which seemed to open and close with each colour change of the sign above. With great turmoil, she had distorted and drawn out the sleeves of her old white cardigan sweater draped over her shoulders.

Fears taunted her after a fresh surge of compassion came, "Wow, you're schizo! Know something? You're too naive for words!"

Oh-h Lord! another part of her whimpered, *I'm sorry, but, unless You give me the courage, I can't do it! Should I really go in there?*

"Ach-h, you silly country bumpkin," her fears taunted her again, "Drive yourself to Emergency. There's St. Paul's hospital just up the street."

"Will you shut up!" Ruthe cried out. "The Lord God Almighty is with me. If He wants me to go in there He'll give me the courage."

For a stunned moment she considered the echo of those words. The battle eased for her some, but she drove around the block once more.

Three tears dribbled down her cheeks as she prayed with a fresh conviction that there was someone God wanted her to rescue in that place. She vowed to go in. Abruptly, she parked in front of the door and dashed in. Fast.

The throbbing, thumping music deafened her as she entered. That, and the purple-brown haze of the psychedelic lights flashing on and off through a cloud of suffocating smoke promptly numbed her good intentions. Ruth froze as bodies shook and shimmered before her. Suspended in space like a speck of dust, she was about to call herself a daydreamer and worse, when she heard a muffled sob behind the door handle she was still clutching.

Ruthe about-faced, ducked some flailing limbs, and looked under the coats on a coat rack. There was someone with tousled auburn hair on her white knees, with white arms hugging her thin white legs to herself. Ou-p. Ruthe's heart jumped into her mouth, as she blinked to clear her quickly smarting eyes from the smoke.

You've been wanting to help someone, whispered her silent companion, *how about her?*

That flesh has to be covered! Ruthe whipped her cardigan off her shoulders and onto those creamy white ones, whispering urgently, "hey, com'on. Let's get out'a here."

A white swollen face lifted under the auburn mop. "–Like a game! Two guys fought over me. Then-n, wh-when I split a seam, they tor-e my dres-s! God! I can't go home. Ever!" Her head dropped on her knees again. "I wanna die!"

"Let's go fast." Ruthe urged briskly. "My car is at the door."

"They threw my dress away!" the young teen wailed.

"Com'on." Ruthe coaxed, feeling desperate for fresh air herself.

Slowly the redhead got up out of the coats and stood on wobbly platforms, stretching the bottom of Ruthe's sweater down past her panties, and attaching herself to Ruthe's arm slunk out with her.

The redhead had begun to cry aloud in the car, and Ruthe, not sure what to do with an unhappy soul now that she had found one, simply pulled away and drove out of that area. She decided that what was needed next, was to talk it out, and let this girl spill her trauma. If in her place, she knew she would not want to be taken to the police, or other strangers, but now that she had begun, Ruthe was ready to die before she would bail out of helping this girl. Whatever it took, she was in this one hundred percent, plus.

When she saw that they were on a quiet residential avenue parallel to the riverbank, beautifully canopied with shade trees, Ruthe decided it would be okay to park in a hidden spot.

"Ahm? My name's Ruthe. What's yours?"

"Mu'riel–l." Embarrassed, she cried again, "Oh– my-God, Ruthe! I can never face my mother and dad!"

Glancing in the back seat to be sure, Ruthe apologized that she had nothing more to offer for a covering. Nervous at first, then growing more tender, she got Muriel to talk more coherently.

Muriel told how it happened that certain new boyfriends that she had tried to impress had persuaded her to try that DanceSpot.

In reply to a question about why she had come to rescue her, Ruthe opted for the truth. That led her to explain some things about her family, and her own feelings about people. How her parents took the family to every service at their small Mennonite church, but they were reluctant to care about strangers, while on the other hand, she had a great hunger and ache for people with problems. Since about nine, when she invited Christ to save her, Ruthe said, she had found

Him to be a great personal Friend to whom she could confide all her thoughts. "I always capitalize words or pronouns related to Jesus. He's that precious to me. Only, I'm not greedy, Muriel. I want everyone else to have this same wonderful Friend. He died to save every person in the whole world, and wants to be close to everybody!"

Muriel drank it up. Her family were good Catholics, but she had never met anyone willing to discuss religious stuff informally with her. She had never presumed that she might be able to talk directly with the great Creator Himself.

Rapt in this conversation Muriel forgot for a bit that she was curled up sideways, in just her black bikini underwear and still stretching Ruthe's sweater like a blanket around herself. "I'd love to talk to God," she said wistfully. "Show me how."

Ruthe demonstrated her informal chattering style with her invisible Friend, and bubbled enthusiastically as she introduced Muriel to Him. "She's anxious to meet You, Lord, tho' I bet You've been looking forward to this much longer than we can guess. –Go ahead, you talk to Him now, Muriel."

"Oh sweet Jesus; I've never done this, but my new friend talks to You as if You understand ordinary English... an' have feelings. Oh–ho-o God!" Muriel dissolved in tears again. "How I wish it had never-ever happened! Can You forgive me? An' please, can You make my life okay to live again?"

Ruthe smiled at an oncoming car as she remembered those prayers.

Nearly three in the morning they had rolled up in the O'Briens' quiet drive, just a few blocks further. The car stopped between lovely lawns and landscaped trees in the pearl grey moonlight. Muriel's brick home was all dark and solemn. The clinging ivy rustled. Ruthe watched Muriel slip up to the large oak door, find it unlocked, and slip through, still stretching the old sweater all about her.

In her ears rang an invitation to come visit soon.

Ruthe smiled with dimples now as she checked her graduation hairdo in the rear view mirror and recalled how she had felt driving back to Kleinstadt that night. A six to midnight shift plus another two hours spent with this new friend meant she had robbed herself of sleep, but she didn't care. She sang at the top of her lungs, praising God and venting the extra adrenalin energy that had built up.

Over and over she had exclaimed, "Oh Lord-but-I love You! I love You! Oh-ew-how I love You!" Then she worried that there would be such a shine on her face the next day that people would make her tell what happened. That she resolved not to do. This night would always be a secret between Muriel, the Lord, and herself.

A glance at her watch; she could be at Mrs. Pearl O'Brien's bedside in another ten minutes.

When her mother had asked where her sweater was, Ruthe said, "In the city," correctly guessing her mother would think she meant her operator's locker. Her mom warned her sternly about leaving temptation lying around for strangers to steal. "Don't trust anyone in the city, no matter how nice they talk to you." Grateful not to be quizzed further, Ruthe accepted the warning with a nod.

The following Monday Ruthe had stopped at the O'Brien house to pick up her cardigan. Mostly she was curious to find out if her new friend was still traumatized. Had she told her parents? What if Muriel pretended not to recognize her today?

A poised woman in a tweed and cream ruffles ensemble, wearing her thick auburn curls in a smart coiffure, answered the door's chimes.

"My name-um-m," suddenly Ruthe was the painfully shy Mennonite girl others in her hometown thought she was. "Ah. Is Muriel home please?"

"No. But do come in, Ruthe. She'll be home from her music lesson shortly." Mrs. O'Brien drew her in with both hands and closed the handsome door behind Ruthe.

"I'm so glad you came." She motioned the gulping guest into an elegant living room. "My daughter told me all about... well, what happened on Friday night, and the kindness you showed. I told her she ought to have taken your number and address so we could thank you properly."

Panic hit Ruthe at the idea of her parents meeting these people. "Oh-no. That's all right. No need!" She made a mental memo to impress on Muriel never to call her at home. Leave a number with the operators' clerk instead. Nerves knotted her neck and between her shoulder blades as Ruthe glanced about the room. It was perfectly appointed in a navy blue, white and gold French Provincial decor.

With a gracious wave of her hand, Mrs. O'Brien had offered her the blue brocade chair, and perched on the edge of the brocade sofa nearby. "Just today I've been wishing I could talk with you, alone. So this is timely." Twisting her hands fiercely, she went on to tell Ruthe what a wonderful thing she had done to help Muriel escape that wild hangout, and how good her attitude was now about life. "You saved our family from an awful scandal." And more. "Of course," she interjected a couple of times, "that's the first time any of our children have ever been involved with such crude young people."

Abruptly her shoulders sagged. "I just wanted to thank you, Ruthe."

Intuitively, Ruthe sensed that Mrs. O'Brien had just lost the courage to say something. Looking at the tense face and the fingers twisted into pretzels, compassion rose in Ruthe like warmed mercury and she found herself suddenly sitting beside the tight woman, her hand gently on the twitching back, "Okay. What's really wrong?"

The woman's face dropped into her hands. "I– went to my do-doc-tor's th-this morning an'-and the tests sh-show advanced ca-cancer of my cer-vix!"

Ruthe tried to explain that before this became serious, the doctors would help her.

"No-no. You don't under-s-stand! I hid it too long! The doctor said this morning-g that I have only a few days. At most th-three weeks! Ouh, Ruthe!" she wailed. "I'm so scared! I've been stumbling around all day fee-ling icy... with f-fear. How will I ever tell Ian tonight? What will become of my children?"

Now she clung desperately to Ruthe. "An-what of me? I don't want to die! I can't! I jus-won't!" Realizing she had no power over death, her voice trailed in anguish, "Oh-h God-d, must I!?"

Though death had never worried Ruthe much; she had heard so many sermons on the glories awaiting believers in eternity; this woman's fear was catching, and Ruthe shivered with cold. She could not think of anything appropriate to say, so she patted Mrs. O'Brien's back and let her cry herself into exhaustion. That took some minutes. During that time Ruthe did what was her habit whenever she didn't know what to do next. Her thoughts became a dialogue with her Friend who always listened and often prompted her with ideas what to do next.

After a time Ruthe felt impressed to whisper to Mrs. O'Brien, "Do you feel God loves you? Specifically you?"

The tweed shoulders grew quieter and a muffled answer agreed. "Yes, God loves us all."

"Since He is perfectly holy, do you think He might ever make a mistake and let a sickness or death slip by Him to a person, and then say, 'Oops. Didn't mean that to happen!'?"

Sniffling into her ruffled wrist, Mrs. O'Brien raised her head and dried her eyes. "No. He's got to be reliable, or He is not worth calling God. Or regarding as one. But–"

"Exactly." Ruthe warmed up. "If we understood everything we could run for His office. We need to trust Him and see His view on things. Sometimes He tells people– in fact, the Bible teaches that He always warned people and told them what He was doing, especially if they were His followers."

"I wish I could ask Him about so many things!" she interrupted. "Muriel sa-id you– you talk with Him personally."

Ruthe's favourite subject. She was so relieved that prayer was the key to helping this woman. They knelt then on the ivory broadloom and she had taught Mrs. O'Brien to pray in her own frank and intimate way. They took turns for half an hour. Then the city woman began to believe that God had heard her, and that He felt very tenderly towards her.

"Oh Ruthe!" she beamed. "He says He loves me! He's even willing to forgive me for being unfaithful to Ian. An-an the reason He let these things happen– was so I could end my long search for Him. It's just as if He's kneeling here on the other side of me. I just know I've met Him at last!"

That was when Muriel came in. Mrs. O'Brien was all over her daughter, excitedly telling of her encounter with God. Next both of them were handling Ruthe with hugs and kisses. She felt embarrassed and tried to leave for work, but they were loath to let her go.

Floating on secret clouds, Ruthe had made two more visits since. One in the hospital just after a hasty hysterectomy was performed, but Mrs. O'Brien's surgeon had found her bladder and lower bowels perforated and filled with cancer too. The specialist offered no hope and let her go home when she insisted she meant to die in her own bed. The other visit, at their home, had given Ruthe a passing glance at Muriel's brother, Ross, but not the rest of the family.

Ross was eighteen, and like Ruthe, graduating from high school. His class ceremonies were to come at the end of June. He was red haired like his mother and sister Muriel, and Ruthe was warned that he considered himself a captivating ladies' man.

Cathy, seventeen, was described by her mother and sister as a well-proportioned blonde looking twenty-seven; a jet-set party animal. Until that other Friday night, fifteen-year old Muriel had envied her sister's many adoring boyfriends who bet each other for turns at dates with Cathy.

Keith, three years younger than Muriel, was more like her, though blond like Cathy. "He's creative and brave," Muriel had explained. A few twelve-year old boys tagged after her brother into whatever projects he thought up. His mother felt he was hiding his real brains because of peer pressure.

It usually took Ruthe thirty-five minutes to make the trip into the city, but this night she arrived in twenty-five as she turned in at the curved driveway and stopped before the brick two-story house.

Muriel was in the doorway. "Oh Ruthe! What are we going to do?" she cried, running around the car front and directly into her friend with arms outstretched.

11

TWO

"What's happening? Found Cathy yet?" Ruthe asked briskly.

Muriel locked arms with her and led her inside as she described how a few hours earlier her mother's pain had become unbearable. "Daddy got the doctor to come out, but he agreed with Mom. So he gave her morphine. However, it won't delay the end. He said there's nothing else he can do unless Mom changes her mind and wants to die in the hospital."

She stopped. "My Mom is dying!"

"I know." Ruthe moaned sympathetically. "What about Cathy?"

"She told me she was eloping with her boyfriend, Lloyd, tonight from a party they were both invited to."

"When was that?"

"About four. She was dressing. But I didn't know Mom was dying right now until just a bit later. I went to tell Cathy but she had slipped out the back way."

Muriel's voice once more leaped to a helpless crescendo. "Oh Ruthe! What are we going to do?"

In her hidden thoughts Ruthe was praying. Until an idea came, she would keep Muriel talking. "Have you told your Mom? Or Dad?"

"I told her that Cathy is out on a date. I haven't had the heart yet to tell her Cathy doesn't plan to be back. If only we could find her real quick. She'll kill herself if she comes back from a weekend honeymoon and finds it too late to say good bye to Mom!"

Ruthe wondered how she would persuade Cathy, if they did find her. They might miss them by minutes, and it would take even the police days to find Cathy. But Muriel was counting on her for some action. Brimming with reckless compassion, Ruthe hugged Muriel. "Okay, where's that party suppost to be?"

The rust-flecked olive green eyes shone with new hope. "She didn't say, but with her set, most likely at her friend Ida's, or, as it's a weekend night, at Harold's Club on Cumberland."

They had neared the top of the stairs.

A boy sat in the doorway of the bedroom, looking glum and mixed up. Like he was afraid to leave and uncomfortable staying. Must be Keith, Ruthe decided, and smiled at him as they stepped over his legs.

Ross had been pacing noisily up and down the carpeted stairs with a soft thud-thud, and in fierce circles in the living room and kitchen. Just then he was thud-thudding back up into the bedroom behind the girls. He stared hard at

Ruthe, then marched down to pace and smoke some more, swearing under his breath and billowing clouds like an old locomotive.

The bedroom drapes were drawn though it was still quite light outside, and Mr. O'Brien was wandering aimlessly about the room, a tall, gaunt shadow in the pale pink and blue light of the lamps.

Ruthe hesitated near the door, watching.

He had just broken some petals from an enormous bouquet of deep pink long stemmed roses on the night table. He was shredding them as he begged plaintively, "I don't understand you, Pearl! Why? I know you liked Father Inglis a lot, but why won't another priest do while he is out of town?"

Struggling to answer, she saw Muriel and Ruthe entering. A relief broke out on the chalky white face.

Quickly now, Ruthe moved closer.

Mrs. O'Brien laid a cold, damp hand over Ruthe's and gasped between breaths of pain, "Ruthe dear!.. I'm so glad.. you've come. You know... I doubted... Him for a bit... yesterday. But I found.. in... the Testa-ment..." She paused to groan as a stab of pain deepened. As it lifted a smile of confidence crept over her. "You're right!" She nodded at Ruthe. "God does not... make mistakes!"

Ruthe blinked hard. Her throat constricted. She had said that so confidently to this woman a few days ago. Was it true now?

Muriel's arm over her shoulder helped Ruthe to kneel. She stroked the cold, clinging fingers through another extremely strong wave of pain. Gritting her teeth, Mrs. O'Brien said, "Ruthe, my husband... my family... they're so distraught!"

"Of course. Because they love you. They're going to miss you a lot." Tears were quivering on her own lids. Trying to regain her composure, Ruthe quipped weakly, "they can't take off their feelings like a coat and lay them in a trunk like souvenirs."

The woman, lying flat, gaunt white, smiled back.

"Don't worry about your family." Ruthe said with more assurance than she felt. Inwardly she suspected she would have a big job to comfort them. "Just trust them to God's love and care like you did with your own soul. He loves each of them as much as He loves you, and will draw them to Himself too."

"Isn't He... marv-el-ous?" she sighed. "I'm counting on you to help them learn to love... His voice. Like you did me. Soon I'll see... His face!" Her smile faded as she poked her white fingers around her unusually tousled hair. "Where is Cathy? Maybe we could... pray? All together?"

"Sure. Tell you what. You save your strength." Ruthe got to her feet. "Muriel and I will go find her."

13

The woman drew a deep breath. "So sweet..." She bit her lip apologetically. "You're... all dressed up. Grad night?"

"Don't worry about that," Ruthe said expansively. "I was hoping to get out of my speech somehow."

Impatiently Muriel took her arm and said, "Mom, we will be back as quick as we can. You rest."

"Ken I go?" Keith muttered as he got up to let them exit.

"Sure," Ruthe whispered as she and Muriel began tripping down the soft stairs. "But let's hurry or she may be in Banff soon."

First they drove past Ida's home. All they saw was a woman in a lawn chair sipping a tall drink, and a man in Bermuda shorts, practicing golf swings. No party, Muriel decided.

However, there certainly was a party at Harold's Club. It wasn't seven yet and the parking lot was full. The building looked large and fairly new. It obviously catered to a more formal society, judging by the elegantly dressed people arriving and leaving. The band music swirled in the air around the building. *It was not quite as primitive as that at the party Muriel had been at two weeks earlier*, Ruthe thought. *This has a lively, gracious swing to it.*

She drove slowly around to the back of the club restaurant as they tried to pool ideas for finding Cathy with the least attention to themselves.

Both Keith and Muriel screamed at the same time, "There she is!"

Ruthe looked up at the balcony and the natural-rock stairs coming down the back of the building. Sure enough, there was a lovely blonde in a red raw silk gown and stole. The belt and borders of the stole were encrusted with tiny diamond-like stones. She was followed closely by a handsome escort, wielding a wrapped bottle over his head.

A stray dog had been barking insults and demands around the corner at the service door. He became aware of the two, and came bounding to the foot of the stairs, barking even more furiously.

It was clear that Cathy was afraid of strange dogs and just now, this one.

"Run for my car, Cath!" they heard the gallant Lloyd shout. "I ain't scart of no dog. I'll kill 'im!"

"Quick," said Ruthe, pulling closer to the bottom step. "You and Keith pull her in as soon–"

Cathy was so terrified she didn't think about whose car she had jumped into until Ruthe was glancing past her face, left and right at the street.

Keith crowded the rear window. "Hey, Lloyd kicked the dog! He's going to have to pay for that Tux now! The dog's taking off with one leg of the pants!"

Cathy began to squirm and scream in her tight space between Ruthe and Muriel on the front seat. This upset Muriel.

"Whoa-there, Cathy." Ruthe said sharply, though still a bit bug-eyed at how she had clambered right over her sister. "Your mother wants to see you before she dies."

"I know she's got cancer," Cathy retorted. "*This* your *new friend*, Mur? Anyway. She's still dragging around the house; I want Lloyd!"

"Listen, Cath! Please!" Muriel begged. "Mom told the doctor she wanted to die at home. With us. He was over after you left. Cathy, Mom is really truly dying! Tonight!"

The teen in the sparkling evening wear stared at her younger sister as if trying to discern a trick.

"She's right," helped Ruthe. "Could be in hours, or minutes."

Cathy fumed and pouted the rest of the drive home, but showed signs of fearing the truth, and not having the resources to cope.

Muriel explained that she had not told their mother about Cathy's elopement. She only promised to bring her home as quickly as possible.

Once she sighted her mother's heaving form in the softly lit bedroom, Cathy flung herself across her mother's body and burst into the loudest, most frightened sobs Ruthe had ever heard in her life. "No! No-o-o! Mom-m-my! You can't die! You can't! I need you-ouh-h-eo!"

Mrs. O'Brien tired to lift her face from underneath Cathy, but she had grown too weak to speak. Her eyes searched the air until they met Ruthe's. With them she pled for Cathy's sake.

Gently, Ruthe took hold of Cathy's shoulders and tugged and lifted, until she turned around and clung to her, weeping uncontrollably. Next thing she knew, Ruthe was crying, Muriel and her Dad were sobbing on the other side of the bed, and even Ross and Keith were hiccupping helplessly somewhere in the room.

Ruthe ached. This family's wife and mother was fading from this life and there was nothing any one of them could do to keep her. She couldn't think of anything appropriate to say, so she just stroked Cathy's back over and over and let her own tears drip into the red silk. A half-glance away she saw Mr. O'Brien making the sign of the cross over and over.

Mrs. O'Brien tried once more to speak to her family, but when she found she could not, she gave up and simply looked wistfully from one to another in a circle. Her eyes stopped. Her smile shortened ever so slightly as the muscles in her face relaxed, and with a tiny sigh, the spirit of Mrs. Pearl O'Brien slipped away to heaven.

Ruthe burrowed her face in Cathy's bejeweled shoulder. For some time they all remained as they were and went on with their weeping. *Lord*, she prayed, *thanks for helping us find her in time.*

15

Cathy's sobs were the most wrenching, and after a while Ruthe motioned Muriel to help her take Cathy out of the room. They steered her into her own bedroom across the hall.

Though Ruthe knew in her mind, she need not sorrow for their mother, her goneness now left her with a cold, amputated feeling. As if one of her own arms or legs had been abruptly cut off.

Cathy, the socialite, now shrunken and childlike, clung to Ruthe's arm as if she were the last ray of warmth from her mother. Even while all three applied gobs of tissues to their faces, Cathy wouldn't ease her grip on Ruthe.

"Y'know– both Muriel and Mom tried to t-tell me about the x-citing things that happened when they met you. Sounded like religious talk, S-so I...."

"That's okay," Ruthe soothed.

"No-but, but now it's different. Here you– you cry with me–" She began to hic with fresh sniffles. "Af-after seeing how much you c-care about us, about me– I want to love you back!"

"Oh Cath!" exclaimed Muriel.

"@#$%@!" Cathy grabbed Ruthe tighter. "God must think I'm a terrible phoney. Spoilt, selfish! I hate myself too! Listen; can you get God to forgive me?"

Suddenly Ruthe knew what was happening. A tiny giggle burped out, and she hugged Cathy's head, rubbing her nose in the silky blonde hair. "Cathy-O-Cathy! God loves you already! He knows exactly how you feel. He can tell you are truly sorry, and He knows just how bad you are. Better than you do. The important thing is to admit it, and ask Him to forgive you. Then you just let Him do whatever He thinks best to change you, and, of course, obey His Word."

"Does He ever!" added Muriel encouragingly. "I find something new about Him, and me, almost every day now."

"What I want is the kind of quietness He gave you and Mom about dying. I was scared out'a my tree! I still am. It's so for-ev-er!"

Cathy was about to start crying again, so Ruthe and Muriel encircled her with their arms and led the talk to prayer. It would make Jesus become real; they urged her to listen, and then try it.

Ruthe and Muriel found words to express their grief, however, confidence in God flowed in once they got started.

Cathy was hesitant, then broken, then touched in a holy way too.

After that, they had ever so much more to talk about.

Abruptly, Muriel remembered. "O-no! The Chief Operator said this was your grad night when I persuaded her to put my call through!"

"Ruthe," she moaned contritely, "I'm sorry we ruined it for you!" Cathy wanted to know why a May grad instead of June or September, so Ruthe told the story of the class decision to beat the pressures of finals and grad preparations at the same time, and some were leaving the province the day after the last exam.

Suddenly Cathy stood up and took charge. "It's 8:20," she said as Ruthe and Muriel picked themselves up from the candy pink fake fur carpet. "When were the ceremonies to begin? Eight? How long a drive?"

Ruthe said lightly, "I might make it for the scroll presentations and the candlelight march if I hurried." She honestly wasn't in a mood for a graduation after all this, but the girls insisted. They were so sincere, even when she added, "the diplomas are only blank sheets that another girl and I had to antique with tea and tie with ribbons. It's all just symbolic."

"Wait a sec." Cathy cried, dashing out into the hall. She rushed into the room where her mother lay motionless and straight, and her father knelt just as still, his head buried under his arms. She paused an instant. She tiptoed to the bedside stand and broke out three roses and two rosebuds from the pink bouquet.

As she returned to the hall, Muriel seemed to see what Cathy wanted to do, and ran off ahead down the stairs to fetch a roll of green floral tape and a few short wires from the sun room. With quick, efficient twists of her fingers and wrists, Cathy wired the roses and their leaves, while Muriel was off for ribbon and a corsage pin. In another minute the sisters had put it all together and Cathy was deftly attaching the large fragrant corsage to Ruthe's shoulder. "Something Mom would probably have thought to do for you. She wore flowers to everything. Myself, I prefer lights."

"B-ut-t!" Ruthe stuttered with admiration. "How did you learn to do that? It's beautiful! The one thing I thought was missing!"

"Watching Mom, I guess." Cathy's calm smile was amazingly sunny.

At the car, Ruthe promised to stop in the next day to ask about funeral arrangements, then exchanging assurances that God loved them for their profuse expressions of gratitude, she left.

"What an evening!" she sighed. "Not just a vicarious adventure in a book; I lived this!"

Almost immediately she ransacked her mind for a good explanation of her disappearance. She could never tell an outright lie. How could she skirt all the questions that would be asked? Horror of horrors, what if the principal asked her publicly?

No, Lord! she groaned with a lightened sensation as if in a falling dream. *Is this going to force my secrets out into the open after all? What will Mom say? She might draw the line and consider letting us go on welfare after all rather than let me work in the city!*

She fell silent, utterly deflated.

In a moment more Ruthe laughed aloud. She knew the answer to all this frightened drivel. *If You're as loving and great as I told Cathy tonight, You won't be any different when I reach Kleinstadt, will You? You never make a mistake!*

Ruthe was breathless and more than nervous as she reached the school auditorium. It was too late for her toast to the teachers. By now the banquet was over and the ceremonies, to be held here, almost done. *Good. It's almost over, Lord.* In one sweeping motion she glided through the side entrance behind the piano, through the swinging door to the backstage area, and up a few dark steps.

She recognized the familiar drone of the principal, Mr. Logan's voice on the platform and glanced at the darkened auditorium with its sea of shadowy faces and figures. Pausing behind the curtain to catch her breath, she saw that the grads on the platform were rising. Now the gap at her chair was a little less obvious; she would be able to pull it back to step into her place.

Melinda walked to the centre of the platform to accept her scroll and shake the principal's hand, just as they had been coached. Ruthe stood breathing heavily in her spot. *Well. I missed the guest speaker even.*

While Melinda rustled her chiffon skirts back to her chair, Mr. Logan read from his list, "Ruth Veer–." He stopped to look up, remembering her absence. Surprise and relief flooded his face as he saw her coming for the scroll in his hand. Right on cue. He beamed as he pumped her hand. He sounded as if he truly meant the congratulatory bit he parroted to each of them. Other than that, he carried on as if nothing had gone amiss all evening.

Ruthe appreciated that. At the same time she was overcome with a profound feeling that this pomp and ceremony was quite insignificant in the light of the real life she had just tasted.

Fuss and formality out in this sleepy village, she thought to herself as she fell in line with the others to light their candles, *while out there in the world are exciting things to do, like rescuing Muriels and Cathys, comforting dying people. Probably lots more that naive little me, I've never heard about yet.*

Oh God, she prayed, hardly noticing anyone as she stepped into the rehearsed marching line with her candle flickering gingerly. *Some would call this youthful idealism, but I don't want to just exist. I want to do important, meaningful things in my life, for others, together with You!*

In this cloud of her own, it took time for Ruthe to notice that people were turning to stare after her, whispering. When she did, Ruthe began to scheme her escape. Next time near that door....

But she miscounted while marching. The lights came up and there they stood in their prearranged reception line. The crowd was thickest at her end as people milled around, asking both sincere and snide questions all at once.

"–A matter of life and death, your parents said."

18

"Yes, a matter of life and death." She repeated it another time or two, as she realized it was a dramatic but evasive answer.

"Sorry, I can't break a confidence," nonplussed a few inquiries.

"Why can't you tell?"

"What kind of emergency would....?"

"That stupid telephone company! I would've told them off!"

However, there were so many others talking at Ruthe that she only shook her head and laughed helplessly. Then she saw a fresh wave of people coming. Seconds later she saw a small rift in the human mass. Ducking and veering sharply, Ruthe disappeared.

Without waiting for the rest of her family at the car, she drove the four odd blocks home and didn't relax until she was in the drive. *No sign of the kids,* she sighed. She was glad Brandt and her sisters had gone to the ceremonies, though only parents were invited to the banquet at six.

Ruthe was also glad she had got away before her classmates tried to wheedle her to come along to the all night grad party and breakfast a few miles up the river. They would have had fun tormenting her to tell all they wanted to know, or wanted to believe.

She opened the car doors on both sides and stretched out her full five feet and seven inches (1.5m) on the front seat. She looked up at the deepening blue way up in the sky and for several minutes simply breathed her lungs full of the delicious evening air. The only sounds, a cricket chorus in a muddy dugout a diagonal block away over a vacant lot of willow bushes, and the hum of the highway traffic shuttling past the little town. Closing her eyes, Ruthe yawned contentedly. A cooling breeze visited and went on.

Her mind cleared so she could see her life in perspective again. As she replayed the evening in her mind, she noticed things she had been too absorbed to see before, and saw questions to ask and consider. She was eager to work them all out with her most intimate Friend.

Hearing the shrill voices of her sisters up the street, she shifted herself and sat up. More urgent now was to pray for calm and wisdom in talking with her own family members in the next few minutes. Ruthe drew in spiritual strength with a deep breath.

THREE

Once her sisters sighted the car, they ran up, with demanding questions. "Why didn't you wait at the aud-a-torium?!" her pet sister cried, wrapping strong bony arms around Ruthe's waist as she got out of the brown sedan. "We looked– and looked– all over! No you. No car!"

"What were you up to?" demanded Suzanne. "We had no car to pick up Grosz'mama. She couldn't come."

"Oh!" Ruthe gasped. But she knew her demure grandmother would not have complained, only worried about her safety. And prayed.

"Had to work, huh?" teased Brandt in his deepening voice as he loped up behind them. He came between Ruthe and Suzanne in age.

With exaggerated calm Ruthe commanded, "Hold it. Keep your shirts on."

Their parents arrived next, panting heavily from a hurried trot. "W– wh're on earth were you, Ruthe!" exclaimed her mother showing tremendous anxiety.

"What kind of emergency'd be more important than your own graduation?" raged her stout father, his stomach quivering.

"Okay, okay," Ruthe soothed as she marshalled them into the small white house. "Let's not set up outdoor broadcasting."

"Now Ruthe. What happened?" insisted her mother, taking off her Sunday floral kerchief, and trying to regain her usual authority in the home.

"Someone was dying and asking for me." Ruthe blinked once. *What a nice, short answer. Thanks, Lord.*

"Why you? Couldn't she ask for another operator?"

"Because–" Ruthe hesitated. How little could she get away with? "She liked me, and she didn't know any other operator. So I did what I could, and came back as soon as I could. But, Mom. Having just been at a deathbed, I didn't feel like visiting around at the auditorium."

A flicker of sympathy lit in her mother's eyes.

"But we have a right to know!" shouted her dad, yanking loose his tie and shedding his suit jacket with the permanent wrinkles in his elbows.

Ruthe ignored him, knowing that if she got past her mom, she would take care of dad for her. "As a matter of fact, I still don't feel much like talking. So I'm going to bed."

"Me too," announced Sharri, taking her hand like a loyal nine year old sister. "I'm going with you."

"Yes– but," said her mother dolefully, dying to know more. "Don't you trust us any more? You've become so secretive lately, as if–"

"As if you're a stuck up city girl now!" finished her dad vehemently.

"Oh Dad! Mom!" Ruthe moaned in exasperation. She knew just where this conversation cycle was going.

Ruthe respected her mother's practical mind, but saw her as a worrier, and the things she did and thought about these days would only give her more to worry about. She looked on her secrecy as a kindness to her mother. Instead she reached for her intense sense of justice. "Mom, when another person trusts me, isn't it Christian and fair that she be able to count on me to keep that confidence?"

Though her mother was reluctant to let go, Ruthe could see that her logic was hitting its mark. For this moment.

Her dad, who knew nothing of keeping secrets, was opening his mouth to press for a total confession, so Ruthe added hastily, "I assure you, your little Ruthe didn't get into any trouble or do anything to be ashamed of, so how about all of you trusting her for a change?"

Turning, she added with an enhanced yawn, "I've had a long, hard day, and I've promised to work extra hours tomorrow. You know we need the money."

"Yeah. Think you're indispensable," muttered Suzanne.

It was delicate work negotiating understandings with this budding teenage sister, so Ruthe let that remark go, and turned to make her escape.

"*Mijall! Houl stell!*" [1]

Ruthe froze at the anger in her dad's voice.

With a raised fist and a speech more nimble in his mother tongue, her father stood before her and told her that graduate or not, she was still his daughter, and was going to tell the truth, or he would pound it out of her.

"Ben! Ben!" suddenly her mother was pulling down his upraised arm and urging him to control himself. He jerked his arm away and sputtered some dirty words in Low German.

"Ruthe," her mother now turned on her with authority. "You're too big to spank, but if you are doing anything to be ashamed of, getting bad friends in Saskatoon, then I am going to phone up the telephone office and tell them– you quit! You no longer work there. I have always said I would never go on welfare, but I will do that before I will let you throw your life into the gutter! Hear me?!"

"Yeah, y' hear that?" yelled her dad, coming back, dangerously close.

In the back of Ruthe's mind, deep in her thin body dressed in the pink lace with the corsage of deep velvety roses that now seemed to find it too hot and humid here, came a tiny whisper, "They don't understand! And see? They're too blind to notice the roses." However, her stronger, normal spirit seemed to blink and come to its senses, and knew that she loved her parents too much, despite all their faults to turn on them in revenge. Ruthe gulped, turned, not answering, and

21

with scalding tears washing down her face, stumbled up the narrow wooden stairs for the bedroom under the eaves that she shared with her two sisters.

Sharri came running along behind, trying to catch Ruthe's hand. When they were nestled on the old, opened sofa bed that they shared, together with a roll of toilet paper that Ruthe kept handy for such occasions of nose-blowing and weeping, the little sister said to big sister, "I know you didn't do anything bad, Wuffie. Why didn't you just tell 'em what you did?"

Ruthe blasted into a wad of paper first. "Because, other people have a right to their secrets. If they can't trust me, then I don't deserve to be their friend. Besides, God knows the truth. The Bible says He will defend me."

"So? You're crying."

"Because my feelings are hurt doesn't make it okay to hurt back."

Suzanne came into the room and threw herself on her own cot, but Sharri knew better than to beg for Ruthe's secret adventure when this middle sister was there. So they sniffled, and Ruthe got Sharri to describe the graduation instead.

Here Suzanne jumped in and corrected or expanded on the junior's view, until their parents hollered that they should get ready for bed properly. Suzanne suddenly saw the roses, and wanted an answer.

Ruthe reminded her they were to be quiet, and just stared wistfully at the roses in her hand. She tried to memorize the colour and curl of the petals. Then her mind leaped into fantasy gear for a split moment and saw long hedges just dripping with roses of many shades.

If only they weren't so blindly afraid of other ethnic people, Ruthe thought to herself as she tucked her corsage away in a cast off box and hid it to dry. They often heard sermons in church on witnessing to the lost; rescuing the perishing. Her parents enjoyed missionary reports as much as she did, so why did they work so hard to spend time with only their own relatives and kind? Why did they run down any English or foreign types they saw or heard of in town? What was there to fear?

Ruthe mulled on these questions and others, discussing them with her Companion until asleep, and again at six the next morning, as she sauntered through the vegetable garden, and across a dirt road into an unkempt willow bush and rough pasture on the edge of town. She sat on a fallen log and watched the sun rise higher. The twittering birds, the rustling leaves, the cool dew all refreshed her. The masses of moving colours in the eastern sky filled her with awe for the Creator. It was easy then to talk to the Lord and imagine His replies.

Because of an old hymn she had heard, she thought of these walks and talks as her trysts in the garden of prayer, with Jesus, her Friend. She hummed, not aloud, but in the back of her mind;

"*I come to the garden alone*[2]
while the dew is still on the roses;
and the voice I hear, falling on my ear;
the Son of God discloses."
Ruthe sighed with satisfaction. She was loved and understood by this unseen Friend. Forty-five minutes later she turned and headed back to the house, some of her questions unanswered, yet it didn't matter. She almost swung His hand as her mind sang the chorus:
"*And He walks with me,*
and He talks with me,
And He tells me I am His own,
And the joy we share as we tarry there,
None other has ever known."
Her parents and Suzanne tried to bother more information out of her that morning before Ruthe left for work in the city, but she felt she had survived the worst battle. She found she could suffer and weep and hold her tongue at the same time. Ruthe wasn't totally sure God approved of secrecy and deception, but He did seem to be helping her avoid the clash with her parents that could put an end to her extra life in the city. No doubt there would be other scenes, and one day they might find out about the strange people she was meeting in the world. That hung over her like an axe on a thin rope, and she hoped she would be sufficiently brave when that day came.

Everyone was busy when she got back in the evening, so she didn't have to tell them about stopping in at the O'Briens again.

Ruthe took another early Sunday morning walk. The glow of that was with her right through breakfast, and the usual dressing up for church hassle, and as she taught a class of eight primaries in Sunday School.

As Pastor Ewert preached in the worship service, Ruthe gained a new insight into a comforting passage she could share with bereaved sisters, perhaps after the funeral that afternoon.

Ruthe eased the family home after church and sped up the noon meal, ready in the roaster, so that she could get away in time for Pearl O'Brien's funeral without having to let on.

Handing her mother the apron after she had done most of the dishes by herself, Ruthe said quietly that she felt like a drive. "If I'm not back by faspa[3] I've gone on to my evening shift."

For a moment she thought her mom would say something about how hard it was to lose a friend to death, or ask what to say to Grosz'mama if she didn't show up for their usual Sunday afternoon visit. Instead she warned Ruthe to eat properly on her supper-break, "and lock your doors while driving. Remember, you promised Grosz'mama and me that you'd never pick up a hitchhiker."

Promising again, Ruthe slipped out before her mother remembered more questions, and before Sharri could notice her absence. She was always begging to come along for a ride. Not that Ruthe liked to refuse her, but right now she was not sure how well little Sharon Rose could keep a secret.

She smiled at her sister's name. When this baby sister had arrived, Ruthe had just discovered another name for Jesus in the Bible, Rose of Sharon, so when her mother asked for a modern, instead of the usual Mennonite name, that had been her nomination. Her practical mother had changed it to Sharon Rose. Changing her diapers, Ruthe and Brandt had called her Sharri and it was still used.

Ruthe wasn't sure what this Catholic funeral would be like, but she did look forward to being with her new girlfriends. *Muriel is so sweet and seems to look up to me. While Cathy is almost a whole year younger than me, she seems older; 'cause she's sophisticated.* Ruthe felt quite naive compared to her. Both sisters needed her. That felt nice, though the responsibility weighed on her a bit. *Lord, help me to transfer their dependency to You,* she prayed as she drove. *To depend on humans is to ask for trouble.*

FOUR

When she walked in on the soft carpets and the sympathetic organ music, Ruthe found the girls waiting impatiently in the foyer for her. They insisted that she come sit with them.

While Muriel, in a short-skirted suede suit of burgundy, squeezed one of her hands, and Cathy, in a tight and stunning black and white linen dress, hugged her other arm, Ruthe glanced about the compact, grey and blue funeral chapel. This was a first for her and she could hardly hide her curiosity. She noticed the modern shaped pews were honey-brown, which she liked, but how the decorator fell on gold, purple and green stained windows and accent pieces puzzled her.

Glancing down at her own simple cotton dress in nubby light blue plaid with pink rosebuds, she felt like a country lass from another era.

Mr. Ian O'Brien, and his sons, Ross and Keith, sat in the first short pew on the right. The two sisters and Ruthe were on the left. A number of people were scattered through the rest of the pews, including four or five ladies, each sobbing gently, quietly, under her gauzy black veil. Fascinated, because none of the ladies in Kleinstadt ever dressed like that, Ruthe asked Cathy who they were. She whispered back that they were some of her mother's bridge friends. "I refuse to wear those veils," Cathy added. "This's the seventies, for G#$%– oops."

Surrounding the ivory velvet casket at the front were banks and tiers of flowers, many of them in huge white wicker baskets with high arching woven handles. Some had wide ribbons wound artistically across them with gold letters stapled to them that said, "Mother," "Darling Wife," and "Pearl."

Wow, Lord. Nice flowers! Yet she sighed. Ruthe was used to packed out churches and long lines of people filing soberly past the open coffin, either before or after the service. Here it was closed. She got no farewell peek at her friend of three short weeks.

Looking around even after the priest began to speak, the odd colour combinations grew on her. Parts of the service Ruthe didn't understand at all, but she allowed for that. It seemed only right that Mr. O'Brien had called their priest, Father Inglis, back from a trip, to conduct this service as a Catholic one. Mrs. O'Brien had spent much time over the years bothering him for answers in her search to be accepted in God's sight. What comforted Ruthe was that Pearl had met God personally and knew she was forgiven and loved. She hoped the girls remembered that.

During the solemn trip, for which the girls insisted she come with them in the big black limousine to the sunny cemetery, Ruthe began to feel like an intruder. A fresh sobbing at the lowering of the coffin was inevitable, and she joined with the family. She had always found tears catching. When they regained control and stumbled back to the long car, Cathy and Muriel begged her to come home with them. Tea was to be served on the lawn.

Ruthe expressed concern about having her car there so she could leave for her shift at four, so Cathy instructed the driver to drop her off at her car at the funeral home, and she followed them.

A catering maid was ready to serve tea on a white lawn table with a glass top. Sandwiches and cookies were arranged on doily-lined silver platters. Controlled and polite now, the family stood about with their guests in the afternoon sunshine, sipping at tea, and nibbling at the dainties.

Several ladies asked Ruthe to introduce herself. Which she did.

For all their politeness and round of sympathy kisses to each of the O'Briens, Ruthe noticed that they did not stay long. Soon there were only the O'Briens, Father Inglis and Ruthe left.

Come to think, Ruthe glanced over the lovely green grounds, surrounded by carefully chosen and placed background plants and trees, *Ross is not in sight any more. And, I bet those rosebushes are going to bloom next week!*

The priest had conducted the service without personal comment. Now he stood facing one of his favourite parishioners, and drew him into conversation about his deceased wife. He wanted to know more of the spiritual experience the girls had mentioned about their mother. Ruthe froze in her pose, wondering how Mr. O'Brien would answer, and whether she ought to go round the table to join them.

What if he gets hostile and tries to pick apart all your innocent theology? tormented her enemy, pleased to find her in a quandary again. *You don't want to start a quarrel. So what if it works in your simple little life? You've got to be able to explain it if you are up against a priest.*

Turning aside to the rosebush, Ruthe moaned silently, *Now what do I do?* A snatch of a Bible verse came to mind, and she knew she didn't have to rely on herself for tact or wise words. She turned around and drew closer to the two men.

"...So this is my first opportunity to talk with you, Ian. Come, did Pearl really find a new way to pray? Tell me about her beautiful experience."

"I'm not sure I understand all of it myself. But Pearl says– Excuse me." He caught his forehead with the heel of his hand, rearranged himself, and continued, "she read in the Bible that, when anyone claims Christ's sacrifice and resurrection as completed for oneself– then the Holy Spirit, or maybe God...." His voice trailed as he looked about.

"Maybe one of the girls, or their new friend, can explain it better."

26

Ruthe, standing behind him, was opening her mouth to volunteer when Keith appeared at her side, tapping her shoulder.

She turned to see him put his hands behind his back, with his shoulders squirming nervously under his best blue suit. "Could I talk with you?"

"Sure." As she moved away with Keith, she had a sudden premonition that he wanted to meet God too.

"Let's take a walk around the far end of your house," she suggested lightly. "I haven't seen your back yard yet."

Keith nodded assent.

As they rounded the far corner of the glassed sunroom, Keith's self-control broke and slipping his arms around Ruthe's waist he began to cry with a whimper. Poking her fingers into his thick strawberry blond hair, she waited.

In a moment or two he pulled back as if he'd just remembered he was supposed to be too old for this. He dried his cheeks on the sleeve of his suit jacket while Ruthe scrounged in her purse for a tissue that was not too wrinkled and balled up.

Suddenly he could talk. "I– I guess you've been thinking I didn't care about losing my Mom. Well, maybe my brother doesn't care, but I– I do! I– ouh-h, I miss my Mom! I need my Mom!"

"I know you do," and Ruthe wrapped him to herself again.

"I feel so... so cold and naked without her!"

"I know. On Friday night I felt like.... It's like someone has chopped off one of your arms or legs, isn't it?"

Hiccupping with emotion, he tried to tell her all his feelings at once. He couldn't talk to anyone else in his family because they wouldn't believe he ever thought such serious, grownup things. He was sorry about breaking up like this, but he'd seen how his sisters had cried on her shoulder and found a friend in her. He wished he could have a friend who really understood him properly. And, would she mind?

"Of course not, Keith. I'm only so glad you want to be my friend. I'm glad too, that you had enough nerve to come and ask me, because I've lost mine to ask you, several times."

Keith smiled a bit. They moved over to sit on the thick blue-green grass in the shade of the two metre high hedge of Chinese elm. It was a perfectly smooth, leafy wall except for one shady gap, from which emerged a narrow footpath in the luscious lawn.

Keith was looking earnestly into her face and blurted, "This– this business of having God live inside you?"

"Yes?" Ruthe began to grin with anticipation.

"Well, I don't understand how it is possible, but if you explain it to me slowly, could I try it too?"

"Sure you can! I'd love to!" Though she was feeling eager, she paused for a moment to think. He was different from his mother and sisters. From other kids his age too. *Lord, how do I begin?*

Just like that she recalled an illustration that Pastor Ewert had used only a Sunday or two ago. One she'd heard a number of times as a child. Keith would identify with this story. "There was this boy, who had created from almost nothing, from scratch, a masterpiece of a model ship. It was a beauty. All the sails and ropes and everything done in realistic miniature."

"One day," she went on, "when this happy fella was trying it out for the first time on an ocean beach some distance from his home, it sailed away on the tide and he lost it. The poor kid was heartbroken. He'd put so much work and tender care into that particular ship."

Keith leaned forward, drinking in every word.

"Some time later, he spied that very same model in a local shop window and immediately ran inside to claim it. The proprietor had bought the ship and insisted the boy could only get it by paying the full price."

Ruthe saw Keith reacted as intently to every nuance of a story as she did.

"So," she continued, "that desperate, determined kid went to his hiding place at home, and taking out every last cent he owned, he hurried back to buy his own little ship! On the way home, someone overheard him whispering to his precious model, 'There, little ship. Now you are twice mine. First I made you and then I paid everything I had for you!"

Keith understood. "I love to make things too; I know how he felt."

"That must be a bit like God's feelings about us," Ruthe explained. "First He made you and me. But we became lost. Our sins, like selfishness and our stubborn wills, took us far away. That broke His heart. But by sacrificing Himself, through Jesus (who was God in human form), He paid the price to get us back to enjoy His precious companionship."

Ruthe raved about the thrill of having Jesus as an intimate Friend.

Keith wanted to know, "About getting this; are kids allowed in? How do I get initiated?"

"Remember the story of Pentecost?" Ruthe asked, wondering if Keith had ever had some equivalent of Sunday School classes on the Bible.

"Sort'a. I go to a Catholic Separate school, and I don't always skip the religious instruction classes."

"Good. That was when the Holy Spirit arrived after Jesus had gone back to heaven. Well, He has been present with each one who believes that Jesus died for him or herself. This is what makes Jesus so close and easy to talk to at any time. All you have to do is choose to believe that Jesus is God's Son, and that when He died on the cross and rose again from the dead, Jesus did that for you. You promise to walk with Him all your life, and He comes to live with you by His Spirit."

"That's all Mom and Muriel did?"

"Right. And just Friday night, Cathy did too."

Keith shook his head. "I couldn't figure it. Something sure got into them!" His voice lowered. "Mom took me into her bedroom just last Sunday and tried to tell me all about this. But– it sounded like nun talk. I guess I didn't pay attention to Mom then."

His face puckered with regret. "Wish I had."

"No doubt your Mom did too. She wanted all of you to have the same wonderful experience. However, I think God can still let her know today. What I can't guarantee is that you will have another week to make up your mind."

"It sounds good," Keith answered carefully, "but, what if the kids at school find out? Won't they think I'm kind'a queer?"

"Do you think," Ruthe leaned forward and spoke gently, "anything your friends could say might make God a liar? He is far bigger and better than they. Your friends need to hear about this fabulous friendship too!" Even as she said these words her conscience twinged at her own reticence in sharing her Saviour with school friends. She was always afraid they would laugh and say, "We know you; you're just that mousy bookworm, Ruthe Veer."

Keith grinned. "They're the ones to pity. Not me."

"Exactly. As soon as you choose to believe, God will forgive you for Jesus' sake, and the Spirit of God will live with you always. Maybe slowly at first, you will begin to have new attitudes. You'll see people the way God does. In fact, I bet you will be eager to share Jesus with all your friends."

Keith plucked some grass. "What do I do first? Pray?"

"That's best. You just talk to Him as though He is sitting right here." Ruthe patted the grass in front of them. "Just tell Him what you've decided and ask Him to do what He promised."

"Me? Does He promise me anything in there?" He pointed to Ruthe's Bible on her knees.

"He sure did! Let me show you." Ruthe picked it up very quickly, suddenly glad she took her Bible with her to any kind of church service she attended, and opened it to First John, scooting around sideways so Keith could read.

"This promise says, *'If we confess our sins, he is faithful and just and to forgive us our sins and to cleanse us from all unrighteousness.'*[4] And here," she flipped a page and pointed to a line shaded in red pencil. "You read this, Keith."

"'Whosoever shall confess that Jesus is the Son of God, God dwelleth in him, and he in God.'[5] Hey, I'm reading it; like you said!"

Excitedly, Keith read a few more verses at random. "De-cen-t! I'd love to have a Bible! I've often wondered what secrets are in it."

"Shouldn't be too hard to arrange," Ruthe assured him, making a mental note to tell his sisters.

He asked again if Ruthe would show him how to talk to Jesus, so she bowed her head, thanking Him for Hiss love, and for drawing Keith to Himself in the middle of his loneliness for his mother. "Please make this loss up to Keith with Your extra-great friendship."

Keith said a few words of greeting, apologized briefly for his past, and ended with, "So long, Lord-Jesus-God. Be seein' You later." His head bobbed up, sparkling with dewy cinnamon spots.

"I feel sort'a bathed."

He grabbed Ruthe's hand as they got up. "Let's go tell the girls, eh?"

His sisters saw them coming around the corner of the house and met them half way. "So that's where the two of you are!"·

"Cathy. Mur!" Keith blurted out his news in a rush.

The four of them formed a circle, linking arms, and passed around hugs.

Their huddle worked towards the lawn table where Father Inglis and Mr. O'Brien sat watching and discussing them.

Ruthe studied Mr. O'Brien as Keith sprinted toward his father. The man could hardly be more than forty-eight, even with those greying temples in the sunshine. Yet now the haggard, forsaken look on his face made him appear to be sixty-five and failing. So little seemed to hold up his tall, thin frame, that Ruthe found herself wishing he would stay seated. His loneliness ached vicariously in her heart, just as it had for the others, although she was aware that she really did not know it as deeply as he did.

She believed that simply trusting God and learning to discuss his most intimate cares with the Lord would solve much of his problem, or at least do wonders in easing his pain. But how could she explain that to a man as deep and inquiring as Mr. O'Brien? He was looking for very complicated answers. Ruthe squashed the idea of going behind the house with him the instant it entered her mind. This would have to happen differently if Pearl was to get all her prayers answered this day.

"Ah-ha, here she is," said Father Inglis gallantly as they came nearer. "Young lady, we've been waiting to talk to you. Our girls have been telling us about the new prayer practices you put forth. Are you a charismatic, my dear?"

"No-o," Ruthe said slowly. "I don't think so, Sir. I've heard the word, but I'm your basic, garden-variety, Bible-believing Christian. If I'm different, it's only that I get so excitable about seeing Christ do things in my daily life. I can't help but share it. I don't mean to offend."

The elderly priest gathered his black jacket snugly around his middle, and settled down in his lawn chair as if ready to debate.

"Girls," said Mr. O'Brien in a quiet aside to Cathy and Muriel. "We need more chairs." They hurried off to bring some nearer from the other side of the deserted tea table.

Keith drew up one of the closest chairs for Ruthe, but after a moment's hesitation she suggested he offer it to his father. She longed to sit on the cool grass again. It would impart some calm.

Mr. O'Brien offered it to Ruthe once more. He accepted it back only after she said shyly, questioningly, ""I really admire your luscious lawn, and if it's not rude or impolite, I'd rather sit on it. May I?" When he nodded, she got down and spread her gingham and floral printed dress skirt around her knees in a circle.

Father Inglis leaned toward her, eager to start.

Keith dropped cross-legged, as far as his suit allowed, at his dad's feet and looked up eager to see if this were a good moment to tell what had transpired behind their house.

Mr. O'Brien glanced from Keith to Ruthe, and both saw that he had caught on. He laid a long hand on Keith's head and swallowed his adam's apple with great care.

Oh-h-ew dear Lord! Please choose my words! Ruthe's limp, worn Bible lay open on her knees, and now her downcast eyes fell on a heavily underlined part in First Thessalonians, with the words, *"We which are alive and remain...."* Yes. Her eyes whisked over to the beginning of the passage. This was the one to share.

She looked up again to catch what Father Inglis was saying to her.

"–What you've been telling these people? One should think you would be offering hope that their mother may be in heaven some day. Instead, the girls are saying, you've talked about forgiveness and chatting informally with God."

"But you see, Sir, they already know that their mother's in heaven. God promises eternal life to all who trust Christ. The problem is to make sure they will be there to meet her."

"Of course, dear." The priest harrumped as if putting something aside.

"The Lord Jesus told us," she patted her old Bible, "that whatever we ask of our Heavenly Father, believing we receive it, we shall have. Mrs. O'Brien asked with faith for forgiveness and assurance of that forgiveness. She got it!"

Ruthe looked kindly at Mr. O'Brien, hoping to draw him in on her side. "Her confidence was beautiful on Friday night, wasn't it?"

He spoke carefully, she realized, to avoid hurting her feelings as he answered, "Yes, but there is more to obtaining divine and eternal grace than simply believing you have it because you asked. Isn't there?"

Ruthe took a deep breath. "God has the best of love and meaning in mind for our lives, right? However, we can't experience it as we are, because– well, just as a spot of darkness cannot stay near a light, so our souls cannot come directly into His Holy presence. Except that God loved us so much that He came up with the only solution. He became human. He became me, and took my death sentence for sin. Since He arose again in a new, glorified body, so will I! By faith we may live a new spiritual kind of life now, before we even get our new glorified bodies. Doesn't your Bible teach that, Father Inglis?"

She forgot her fears as her voice rose in joyous enthusiasm. "Every part of the Bible declares it to be this way, and the fact that I see its results in my own life and in others, proves it!"

"Another Martin Luther." Father Inglis cleared his throat. "Uhk-um. I grant you all that for the moment. However, you've also been saying that God speaks audibly to you?"

"Audibly? No." Ruthe was cautious now, watching for a trap. Still, she wanted to be honest and polite. "Though I have experienced God's Spirit speaking in my conscience to reprove me, and in my intuition to guide me. That's a knowing." She smiled a tiny smile. "My imagination, which loves words, can easily supply those."

The girls had pulled up chairs for themselves on either side of Ruthe, and everyone seemed to be waiting for her to continue.

"Mind you, God does speak in other ways. Frequently He may grant us specific signs we've prayed for. Sometimes He'll show us by the advice and example of Bible characters or more mature Christians. Usually, we have good clues from the circumstances we find ourselves in, but we can always know His opinion and plan by earnestly studying His Word, the Bible. Least-ways, if we are prepared to obey."

Ruthe had said quite a mouthful. Maybe it sounded like a sermonette. She stopped and waited.

The priest sat doubled forward on his wooden slat chair, chin on his fist, staring right through Ruthe, into his thoughts.

Mr. O'Brien was lost in thought too, as if weighing each phrase of her statements against some inner scale.

Suddenly Ruthe remembered the passage from First Thessalonians. "Cathy, Muriel?" she said softly, trying not to disturb the two men digesting her words. "Let me show you something."

They moved closer. Keith leaned nearer too.

She read in a lowered voice, beginning at, *"But I would not have you to be ignorant brethren, concerning them which are asleep, that ye sorrow not, even as others which have no hope...."* and ending with, *"Then we which are alive and remain shall be caught up together with them in the clouds to meet the Lord in the air: and so shall we ever be with the Lord. Wherefore comfort one another with these words."*[6]

Muriel looked up into the sky with anticipation.

"I didn't even realize that was in the Bible!" exclaimed Cathy. "That's when we'll see Mom again!"

Father Inglis spoke, "All quite commendable, m'dear. I used that passage this afternoon myself. But be careful when you're reading the Scriptures so freely. Not everything is meant to be taken literally, you know."

"I understand your point, Sir. False doctrines have come from taking a verse out of context; but this passage means just what it says and it becomes clearer when it is studied with other related chapters." *Oh Lord, am I too bold to talk like this?* Ruthe whispered on another level.

She turned the thin pages, trying to think of good examples. While she did, she found herself saying, "God also tells us His Word is spiritual and can only be understood through His Spirit. We must first have that indwelling of His by faith before we can grasp these– well, more profound truths."

"Meaning," asked Cathy, "Only those who walk and talk with Him, in that garden walk you told us about, can understand the Bible?"

"Yes, we could say that. If, as Christians, we refuse to read God's Word because we're afraid of misinterpreting it, we are as badly off as a certain little old lady who refused to eat foods of all kinds when she learned she could be poisoned by certain sorts of mushrooms."

Keith snickered mildly, "Sounds like our Granny."

This took everyone off on a tangent while Cathy and Muriel explained about their Granny O'Brien living in that tall grey stone building on the other side of that elm hedge.

Ruthe's eyes followed the path that disappeared in the gap. For a split second she expected a humpbacked old woman with a pointed chin to come through waving a gnarled stick.

"She fought with Mom for years," said Muriel. "I wonder who she will pick on now?"

Mr. O'Brien stirred uncomfortably in his chair. "Come now, girls, that is no way to talk about your grandmother."

In an effort to bring the conversation back to theological matters, he turned to Ruthe. "I don't see how you can have Christ, or as you like to say, the Holy

Spirit, living within you and communing with you all day, when they are members of the Triune God."

Oh-oh, Lord; help! Ruthe prayed, blinking her eyes for a moment, before she said, "I'm afraid I don't understand the physics of it either." She smiled and cocked her head in a friendly manner. "I do know that God manifests or shows Himself in three Persons, all equal. Take a man: he can be a son, a husband, and a father all at the same time. I don't know, Mr. O'Brien; this is one of those areas where we have to trust God, let's Him be the One who knows all things, and exercise spiritual faith. If we have physical evidence, we can only exercise physical faith, right?"

"My child, how long have you believed all this?" asked the priest.

"Oh, I've known these Bible facts all my life. However, I was about nine when I prayed and asked the Lord Jesus to forgive me. It's only just been in the last few years that I've begun to realize what that really meant. I've spent many hours trying to understand myself, and God. He seems very friendly and willing to teach me."

Ruthe glanced at Muriel, who was drinking in each word. "I still struggle with new truths, but a lot of them have started to fit together for me." She gripped her Bible tightly. "It's all in here, if one takes time to read, and think, and ask for understanding."

Just thinking about these growing stages flooded her with memories. The little group was so attentive, Ruthe found herself rambling on. There was the time she had learned to vanquish jealousy and love Greta, her sister, or Suzanne, as she wanted to be called. She digressed to explain; one day as her sister complained about her old-fashioned name, Ruthe looked up from a magazine borrowed from a school friend. She suggested Greta ask everyone to call her something new, like Suzanne, which she saw there on the page. Greta had been doing it ever since. Their parents couldn't understand trading one good Mennonite name for another, but now they called her Suzanne.

"The bigger miracle is; I'm learning to love my prettier sister as she is. Without trying to make her over."

Ruthe didn't notice she had slipped into a storyteller mode. She just knew that she was able to talk about things she thought, and nobody was cutting her off. "A couple of weeks back," she went on, "The Lord showed me that He could supply courage as well as the desire to help someone. He gave me action when I was frozen with panic. As a result I met Muriel. Since then," she smiled around, "all of you."

The next instant, Ruthe had a sinking feeling that it was late in the afternoon. Glancing at her watch, she blushed, but avoided sighing with relief. She might still make it to work!

"Ack-um. You both confirm and blow up what I know of Mennonites," said the man in black, stiffly. He rose and straightened his cramped back. "May God always bless you, m'child." With a courteous nod to the family, he about-faced and marched to his car in the drive.

"He has long looked for live saints who live exactly as they believe," murmured Mr. O'Brien.

Ruthe gazed kindly at the speaker. His own face showed wrenching decision-making.

Cathy and Muriel saw it too, and went to either side of him. Keith went to hug his dad's knees. "Oh Daddy," whispered Muriel, encircling his neck from behind. "It's all true. If you could feel it for a minute you'd know!"

Cathy stood bent at his other side. With long fingers that reminded one of her mother, she lifted his chin. Without a word, but with her mother's eyes, she pled with him to join them in this venture.

"Oh-h– girls," he said hoarsely. He turned to stare into the west where the sun was just dipping behind the tops of the trees. But all his concentration could not keep tears from blurring his vision.

Ruthe held her breath, not wanting to break the spell as he made his momentous decision.

"All right," he said very deliberately. "Al-l ri-right. Why put it off?" Three pairs of arms tangled around him.

Blushing, Ruthe scrambled up, looking at her watch. At the same time recalling she had not seen Ross since– well, since the funeral. Where was he?

She tapped Cathy's shoulder and whispered, "Listen; I'm glad with you. But I've got to run to skid into the toll room on time. And, maybe you ought to check around for Ross."

35

FIVE

Graduation behind them, the Kleinstadt grade twelve class buckled down to study for June finals. Daily routine returned, except that two or three classmates teased Ruthe with different stories they cooked up as to what kept her from their grad banquet. She tried to ignore them but couldn't hide her tiny smiling blushes. They were more intrigued.

Mr. Logan, the principal,, as an after-thought, or because he became aware of the teasing, called Ruthe into his office late on Monday, for an explanation.

With utmost sincerity she said, "A friend in the city was dying and calling for me. What could I do, Sir, but rush to her bedside? I was fortunately, able to bring a wayward daughter to say her last good bye as well."

The portly man, who often laughed alone at his own jokes, was sensitive enough not to clown at this. He accepted it and told Ruthe that he had a high regard for her compassionate ways. "You really live up to the meaning of your name, toward your family, and your friends," he said. "What is more, even with your part-time job, you have created an advantage for yourself, in that you disciplined yourself to study all through the year. These finals should present no problem to you."

She marveled that he knew of her study habits, but she thanked him and left quickly before he asked more questions. She breathed ecstatic love notes to the Lord all the way back to her classroom.

Her family tried to worm more of the story out of her for a few days. Eventually they resigned themselves to her silence. They did not notice that Ruthe sighed often, as if she had escaped by some happy fluke. Whenever she prayed though, she gave God the credit.

As Mr. Logan had pointed out, her rigorous studying paid off. She could still work her late evening shifts, and manage to stop in at the O'Briens about once or twice a week. Their friendship was opening up a new world to Ruthe.

Muriel informed her that Ross had gone to commiserate with Granny in the old Greystone next door. While they were having tea, he was pointing Ruthe out from her bedroom window. But Granny out-complained and out-whined him. Ross had been bitter and angry when he returned. No one could reason with him. Mostly, he stayed out now. His sisters didn't know where or what he was doing.

The girls made Ruthe feel welcome and special. With Keith and their dad making her out a heroine, when they were in, Ruthe blushed a lot.

Cathy wanted to know; "What kind of boyfriend do you have?"

She pinked up still more as she admitted for the first time to another person that she had a private arrangement with God. Muriel was eager to know about this too, so the sisters worked together to draw it out of Ruthe.

"Sex loses its beauty and holiness when it's sprayed about like cheap cologne. God meant it as a special friendship for marriage, something private and unique." Ruthe scrunched up her face in a smile that brought out her hidden dimples. It was plain she was unused to such conversations, aloud no less. "The Lord has been my dearest Friend since I was a child, and I respect His Word and ways of doing things. So I've promised to keep out of relationships where I'm in danger of being talked into a try at sex. It's no new soft drink, y'know."

Muriel just had to interrupt. "You mean, you don't want any romance or marriage? Like a nun?"

"Sure I want romance and marriage!" Ruthe returned quickly. "I look forward to that. But I've promised the Lord, I'll avoid rushing into that territory. I'll let Him choose the perfect husband for me. In fact, I'll let Him first make me into a woman worthy of him."

Cathy said, "You are weird!" But she was full of questions and shared some experiences of her own that confirmed in Ruthe's mind she was on the right track. Casual sex was not worth it. Their mother's cancer was a solemn warning to all three girls.

Muriel was eager to make a similar vow. When Ruthe prayed with her, to make it formally with their Lord, Cathy became moody and jealous.

Later, at another visit, Ruthe told Cathy that she had just read about a chastity vow that could be made by those who had lost their virginity. Cathy listened carefully.

Ruthe revelled in the girls' sophistication and their elegant home. Yet, when they tried to give her some of their mother's wardrobe, and her mouth watered at the lovely ivory blouses, rust-coloured suits and dresses, and pink silks– Ruthe refused. "I'd never be able to explain them at home! Can you imagine these at the MCC Thrift store? I better wait for Aunt Agnes' next parcel."

Muriel and Cathy coaxed Ruthe to tell them more about her family.

Mostly she talked of her own thoughts and dreams so she could steer clear of downgrading anyone else. "I have a little day dream that if I took this correspondence dress designing course I saw in a magazine, I could learn to sew and make my own lovely outfits." Ruthe caressed a silky sleeve as Muriel folded yet another blouse to lay away in a box. "Then I'd make something like this!"

"Don't you sew now?" asked Muriel. "Aren't all Mennonite girls born with such talents?"

"Oh no. Mom's been too sickly most of the years. Besides, she says that, me, being a lefty, I'd be hard to teach."

"Why don't we just lay these aside until you have started that course," offered Cathy, "Then when you can start adding these things to your wardrobe, you gradually pretend that you have made them."

"No. That wouldn't be honest...." Ruthe's voice trailed off.

She did allow Cathy to persuade her to write away for information on the designing and sewing course.

In these brief, intense visits to their home, Keith and Ruthe became better friends too. He often skidded to the front door, as eager as Cathy and Muriel to tell her all that had happened since he last saw her.

Keith reported that he was telling everyone at his school about the marvellous relationship he had started having with God the same weekend that his mother died. "Two of my buddies joined up!"

Ruthe had no problem getting excited at such news. She hugged Keith and asked him all kinds of questions to hear what had transpired.

When their dad was home he greeted her warmly as well. Their encounters were usually brief, but Ruthe was observant enough to see that he still pined away nobly, for his wife. At least she thought so, until one day, he made a quiet, caustic remark that made Ruthe remember a cold hard truth; Pearl's cancer came from sexual encounters with someone other than her husband. Yet, this devastating thought was what made him keen to learn more about forgiveness. Ruthe believed that besides reading and praying, the tall lawyer with the silver temples was likely weeping behind the door of his den.

Occasionally he asked Ruthe what she thought a certain Bible verse or phrase meant, but in the main he seemed to be working out most of his questions on his own. Or, perhaps with Father Inglis, whom she met, another time or two, coming out of the den.

One thing Mr. O'Brien asked Ruthe was, whether they ought to be attending an evangelical, Protestant church like hers.

"Why? Do you feel uncomfortable in yours?"

Lord, this could be delicate. I know some folks back home would urge them to come out of Catholicism, but I don't know how big this issue is with You.

She added, "I thought Father Inglis was a good friend of yours."

"He is. We've discussed this. But I read in the New Testament that believers are to have a close fellowship with others of like precious faith; to function together as members of the living Church. I see a vacuum for that kind of working relationship in our parish. There is a tie to traditions, so it's not likely to happen. Father Inglis agrees, however reluctantly."

This caught her off guard. She sent up silent prayers for guidance while she offered some tentative suggestions. Aware that there were evangelical denominations for every temperament, she advised that they spend a few weeks trying out different ones. Maybe they could even interview the pastors during the week to find out which ones believed and followed the Bible most closely. If they prayed about it and had a humble, teachable attitude, she was sure God would help them sense which was the right church for them. "If I were looking," she added, "I'd want one where the preaching and teaching would help me to know and love God still more, and where they would let me get involved in special projects to help others."

Over the next number of Sundays the O'Briens followed this plan fairly closely. All except Ross, of course.

Ross was not about to be a silhouette in the door of a church. He kept himself aloof from his immediate family when he wasn't snapping at them. They all knew something was eating him, but he would not discuss it. Defiantly, Ross did as he pleased, and could not be held accountable to even his dad, never mind his sisters, who wished he would at least show up on time for their meals.

If Ross was at home when Ruthe dropped by, he put on a totally different persona. He would try to race his sisters to her, and put on a flirtatious air. Ross wanted her to be his date at his graduation at the end of June. She declined. He tried to lure her into his new red Mustang for a ride more than once. Other times he clowned and goofed, and interrupted Ruthe's serious conversations with Cathy and Muriel, making sarcastic quips and digs. Ruthe's first impression was that Ross was acting like a puppy needing to be petted. She had to smile at some of his antics.

He crowed when he saw that he was frustrating them beyond their self-control. When their tempers showed he would exhort them with an exaggerated, "Oh-oh, Christians can't get angry! Ya' have to love your enemies, remember?"

The three young women found a fine line between controlling themselves and ignoring his petty behaviour. One minute he was funny, the next he was vexation personified. Ruthe wanted to be fair, so sometimes she tried to carry on a sincere dialogue with Ross, but he made it next to impossible with his jokes when she was saying something in earnest. On one hand, she knew he needed to become friends with the Lord, but she also worried that if she worked too hard at convincing him it would look like she was chasing Ross socially.

He is not my type! she reminded the Lord. *I know I asked You to be my matchmaker, but pl-ease, not Ross!*

To avoid running into him more often than necessary, she started to stay away from the O'Brien home a bit more, even when she had extra time before or after a shift. One Saturday, after a full day at the telephone office, instead of going straight home, she drove up and down the streets of Saskatoon again. Ruthe did not know what she was looking for, but she felt compelled to search.

SIX

It was early evening, and she ought to be home finishing up the Saturday house cleaning that Suzanne most likely had not completed. However, Ruthe ended up on one of the few narrow streets in the downtown, hemmed on both sides by old brick buildings converted into apartment complexes. *Oh, for the days when these were new and the best houses in town,* she thought. *They look so ashamed and defeated.* She visualized bits of the misery that these dejected old structures might be seeing and hearing. One apartment might watch a succession of different lovers every night. Another could be shuddering daily to sounds of a quarrelsome family. Yet another taciturn old apartment might know of a crippled, neglected person, who never felt a ray of sunlight, or friendship.

Hundreds of variations, aren't there, Lord? she prayed. *Behind those dirty windows and tattered curtains, a dozen unhappy people must be having the worst kind of day. While here I sit, perfectly snug and safe in our ol' car, with no bigger problem than figuring Ross out.*

With her imagination she tried on the feeling of living here on a permanent basis. It was a caged feeling. She wanted to feel the backyard, Ruthe suddenly decided, so she headed to the end of the block and around into the back alley.

She peered at the back fire escapes and the little metal balconies, some of which were cluttered with laundry and rugs hung out to air. The small front yards had looked bad, but the muddy, messy patches in the back were worse.

Just about out at the street again, she heard a blood-curdling scream. Ruthe froze. *A woman being molested? Or killed?* Then it came again, from the second last old building along the alley.

She put the car into Park, ready to jump into action, then was unable to move for fear. *Ought I do something? Lord, I'm scared! Anyhow, by the time I get to a pay phone she'll be murdered, or whatever —so what's the use? I'm too late!* Her compassion and fears wrestled in the pit of her stomach.

Suddenly a pillow came hurtling through the open door at the top of the second floor fire escape. With a numb plop it landed in a puddle beside some soggy newspapers.

If there's a murderer loose, neither Mom, nor Grosz'mama want me here. But this is not about hitchhikers. What if I were that poor woman?

"Oh Lord!" she cried aloud. "Nobody would blame me for running, but if I don't go to help, I'll always hate myself. You do want me to go, don't You? You'll protect me?"

Ruthe leaped out of the car and zipped up the fire escape. Gripping the rail she could do two steps at a time. Momentarily she paused, puffing in the half open doorway, trying to make out what was happening in the unlit room.

Slowly they focused. He was a big, hairy man with only a pair of brown print shorts on, and he was deliberately tightening a towel around her throat. Her thick black hair covered most of her face, but her faded, light-green nylon housecoat hung wide open.

Uh-gh-ch-h! Vomit climbed in her throat as Ruthe realized what he was doing to the nearly undressed woman. Something inside her boiled up and threw the lid. Without a second thought, she bounced up behind the man, landing her knuckled left fist as it arrived, just above his ear and around the corner from his eye. He fell over to his right. Slowly, but yes, he was falling.

In that split instant Ruthe recalled all the times she and Brandt had wrestled and fooled around on the floor until her mother had insisted she was too old for that game. How often had mom warned them to stop, saying that if they continued they might "hit someone on the temple" and that child would be as dead as Goliath.

Idon'tcareifheis! Ruthe viciously ground her teeth. *Had it comin'!*

The woman crumpled as his hold on the towel eased at the beginning of the man's fall. Quickly, Ruthe snatched at the towel and threw it behind her, stepping over the man's foot to halt the woman's fall with her own body. Her grasp wasn't right. All she could do was guide the victim's slump to the floor.

Ruthe drew the lustrous black hair out of the eyes as the purple seeped from the smooth, olive face. She patted the cheeks. *Are you alive? You have to be!*

Her Goliath moaned. –Lord! Ruthe squealed in silent panic. *He's coming to?! I thought he was dead! Let's get her out'a here!*

But the woman was unconscious, and it would be hard work to drag her down those cruel, metal stairs.

Ruthe had heard before how city people refused to become involved with their neighbours. It was no use calling for help, she decided, when she needed every breath she had left. Standing over him, hands on her hipbones, she glanced about, and thought while she took a deep gulp of air. He moaned again, and she knew when he came to he would be an offended bull.

Then she noticed; the bed was a high old brass-like affair with a pilled sheet over a lumpy mattress; against the wall beside it stood a big steel trunk about the same height as the bed frame. Her memory flitted back to a creative childhood game of cave-making.

Whoosh. Pushing with both hands and feet, Ruthe rolled her Goliath over so he was underneath the bed frame. Then she turned to the trunk. Crouching at an angle, pushing with a foot and both hands, she gave it all she had until it scraped to a stop beside the bed. *There. He'll be wide awake before he does much else!*

The little black-haired woman was moaning now. Though Ruthe panted urgently, the semiconscious heaving of her prisoner in his cave egged her on in her work. *Dear– Lord*! her anxious spirit gasped, *You've given me more strength than I've ever had. Keep pouring it in! We're not done yet!*

Lifting her in such a way that the olive-tanned arms and head fell over her shoulder, Ruthe dragged, or pushed in front of herself, the shorter woman to the door and balcony, where she had entered about sixty seconds ago. She paused to expel a long shaky breath. There had to be a better way to carry a body, but no one had ever shown her.

On the top step, Ruthe turned the body draped on her shoulder around, and sat her down on the metal platform. The sharp grilled metal work made the darker woman wince aloud.

If it wakes you up, good, thought Ruthe, and put the bare feet down a step, then lifting and tugging, sat down with her on the step below their bottoms. She put both feet down again, and pausing only to button the other's housecoat while she panted, Ruthe moved the body down onto the next one.

Lord! her heart and soul and back all screamed, *Help! We've got to get– to a– hoss-abul, I su– ppose– but away– fore he–!*

Just then her protege began to make bewildered grunts.

"Sh-sh– jus' sh-s-sh!" Ruthe gasped, still putting her down one step at a time with frantic urgency.

Fortunately, the limp body seemed to sense that they were escaping, and lifted a bit more of her own weight when Ruthe raised her.

At last the ground.

Ruthe now suspected the victim she was rescuing might be younger than she had first assumed. She pulled her up, and with the woman tilting at an angle, stumbled to the car in the alley. Ruthe put her in on the right side and hurried around to the left, just as the air above them tore with a roar, a thumping, bumping, and then a shattering crash. Ruthe's spine experienced a violent cramp as she visualized him raising the bed with his back and throwing it across the room. She noticed her knuckles twitched as she gripped the steering wheel and bent on getting far out of sight.

The university hospital over the bridge took the victim in, of course, but she was in no shape to answer questions. All Ruthe could tell was what she had seen, and what she imagined happened just before that.

The intern who quizzed her was a handsome young man with a very conscientious manner about him. His name was Dr. David Pollock, and when he allowed himself a smile, he dimpled so sweetly that Ruthe was ready to call him Davie. She just stopped herself in time.

The moment she described the strangler and how she had left him, or heard him, Dr. Davie grabbed a phone and punched in the short code for the police, briskly telling them to look for a strangler at–, Ruthe gave the street name and identified the building, which the doctor echoed.

This intern had asked her two and a half pages of questions when they were joined by a uniformed police officer, who said he had been sent to get the facts. Minutes later they were joined by a second who reported missing the strangler.

There were no more chairs in the cubicle, so they stood in a space between some polyester curtains, and looked down at Ruthe. They excused Dr. Davie when he asked. Giving their names as officers Aubrey and Ginter, they cross-examined Ruthe. She feared that they suspected her of making it all up. At the same time, they kept interrupting each other to tell her to relax.

Since there wasn't much to tell but her own actions, the quiz soon degenerated into a discussion on people who get emotionally involved and those who remain aloof. Ruthe got confused, and longed to drive off to pray, but she made a heated retort about being glad she could still get involved instead of being a cold professional when people needed help. They praised her again, and she realized they were giving her a backhanded compliment, so she backed away and left for home as soon as she could excuse herself.

She couldn't pray right away. Mentally she argued with the officers all the way home, defending her bleeding heart kind of social action. *It was my faith in action. Their clinical detachment? No thanks!*

Still moody when she arrived home, Ruthe got scolded from both Suzanne and her mother for not hurrying home to help with the Saturday cleaning chores. Not wanting to tell the truth about this adventure, she felt exceedingly glum and persecuted. After a brief nibble at the leftovers, she washed up supper dishes and set to doing the floors, the part Suzanne hated the most and had left undone for her. The unfairness didn't help, but Ruthe had found balm for her emotions before in vigorous floor scrubbing, so she threw herself into it, knowing her grunts and energy would work out her foul mood. Towards the end she was telling her Friend, Jesus, about it all.

Anyway, Ruthe decided as she was pouring the bucket of dirty water down the onion row in the garden, *I did my part, didn't I? There is no need for that woman to find out who her rescuer was. So I'll stay away. What am I? Conceited? No way! There are others who can help this woman far better now than I ever could dream of doing. This country bumpkin is going to stop interfering in the lives of others.*

SEVEN

By Monday morning, on her private early dawn walk, Ruthe still considered backing off this new adventure trail, however, she knew with a growing insight, that she had to go check on that woman. At least once.

What if she has no home to go to? What if she was scared out of her wits? All morning, as she wrote her chemistry exam, these questions haunted her.

Lord, I'm scared of him too, but I have an advantage; I can pray and expect You to deliver me. That short young woman with the shiny black hair probably can't. The reasonable, mature thing to do was to check out the aftermath of Saturday evening, perhaps even with the police. Ruthe winced, but she knew that sometimes doing right costs.

As soon as her exam was done, Ruthe could leave. She threw her resolve to remain anonymous away, and her tightly budgeted studying time too. She told her mother she had to drive into Saskatoon a couple of hours before her evening shift. She did not say why.

When she was thirteen, Ruthe had stumbled on a profound thought. If she hid from one crisis, there would be sure to be others to cow her into a corner. That was not how she meant to live her life. On that premise she had begged her dad not to pick up and move just because he felt the neighbours did not like him in Kleinstadt. He had never said she had changed his mind, but Ruthe was relieved when he dropped the idea. This connected in her mind. She was going to follow through on what she had started the previous Saturday.

The woman sitting on the hospital bed did not recognize her, so Ruthe made a self-conscious face and introduced herself as, "the person who brought you here on Saturday night." She added offhandedly, "early evening, actually."

That olive complexion looked paler against the blue pillow and sheets. Now that Ruthe looked closer, the woman seemed much younger. But the expression was hard and old.

"By the way, my name's Ruthe. Yours?" she asked, shifting her weight back to her left foot uneasily.

"That's the idea," said the conscientious intern, swinging through the door on rubber soles. "Get her personal data and next of kin, will you? She's refused to help us out. Not a word."

Ruthe gave a startled look at the dimple man. She turned back to the woman.

"A–, I wasn't sure– what happened. What did I do? Them #@$%& cops don't need nothin' on me!"

Ruthe turned to show Dr. Davie her own dimpled left cheek. "Would you excuse us a bit," she asked softly, "while I censor the facts?"

44

He dimpled right back. "Sure, Angel o' Mercy. I trust you. D'sooner d'better." He left with a good-natured whistle.

Ruthe pulled up the cheap guest chair beside the bed. "Now, I'm just an ordinary, rather naive country girl, who cares about people." The patient turned to face her directly. "Yeah. Y'look like a softy. Y'don't want to know the @#$ #$%& mess."

"You matter to me. Maybe more than you'll ever know."

"The cops said you bopped ol' Beresford on the head and rolled him under the bed, then you dragged me down those @#$* #$%@ stairs. Did you really?"

Ruthe grinned sheepishly, moving her chin around as if undecided on an expression to wear. "It was hard on the nerves. But we got away, didn't we?"

"Then it's true? You saved my life? I remember him tying a towel around my neck." She motioned dramatically as if yanking something tighter around her throat. Now the patient wanted to know all the details again from Ruthe, especially if the cops had anything to put herself in jail.

"As far as I know, they see you only as a victim of a strangler. Privately they may think you were dumb to be there in the first place, but no, I don't think they put you in jail for being the victim."

There was a deep sigh, so Ruthe asked for her name again.

"Okay. My name is Darlene. Darlene Bonne Barrett to be exact. I'm sixteen. I, –okay, so it was sort'a my fault. I was workin' my way through all the Johns in school, from Z to A, when this little Jamie runt sic-ed his big brother on me. How was I to know he was psycho?"

Ruthe listened in growing amazement as Darlene spilled out the ugly story of her life. Despite her broad-minded reading, she had never come across anything quite so awful. *Do people really do such things? Does a prostitute mother really not know better than to show her daughter such vile, immoral acts?*

No wonder Darlene was afraid she might have done something to put her in jail. *Lord, now that I know all this, do I have to report her?* Immediately Ruthe felt reassurance within her spirit that she had only to care and help as opportunity might arise. She decided what Darlene needed most was to experience God's forgiveness in Jesus Christ.

"I hate my life!" Darlene ended her story. "I sort of wish that #$@%@& #$%*+ pervert had killed me."

A slight gasp escaped Ruthe's lips. She ached, how she ached for this girl. Their eyes locked a moment, but Darlene pulled hers away.

"@#$%@! It feels like you're pourin' maple syrup on me!"

"Sorry– I...." Ruthe wished she wouldn't swear so; it made her feel dirty.

"The #$% school counsellor broke into a @#$ @#$%@#$% when I told her a bit of my @#$ @#$$@@#$."

"I might be different," Ruthe answered slowly. "I hurt as if all that stuff has just happened to me. But I wonder how much you would change if you gave the Lord Jesus a chance to re-make your life."

"Oh, I tried to turn over a new leaf," she said hastily. "@$$#, I've tried a million times! Nobody ever believes me! An' before I know it, there I am, my old $%#& self again."

A stab of pain hit the left half of Ruthe's chest. How hopeless it must feel.

Darlene swore viciously again and snorted threatening tears back up her nose. "It's all no #$$ use!"

"I know," agreed Ruthe. "It's perfectly impossible to start our life over without slipping back into the old wicked ways. None of us can do it. But listen, Darlene, I do know of a fool proof way to get help. If you don't mind trusting someone bigger and far better, you can live a new life and keep it for good."

"You're kiddin'! There's no way. Nobody...." but her voice trailed off as she studied Ruthe's face intently.

"People are always telling me that I look twenty-five. Some say thirty. My life's flushed down the %&& hole. It's too late." The tone of her voice indicated she wanted to be contradicted.

Which of course, Ruthe quickly did. Fishing her little Gideon's Testament out of her purse, she insisted that it was not too late, and her thoughts were a rushing undercurrent of prayer. She began. "Jesus promises you, Him that cometh to me I will in no wise cast out."[7]

"Jesus?" Darlene asked, scratching herself. "You said that like a name."

"You've never heard of Jesus before?!" Ruthe was incredulous.

No, Darlene thought it was an oral exclamation mark.

So Ruthe tried to explain what she thought every literate person in Canada must know. Who God was, and Jesus Christ, His Son. Ruthe opened her New Testament while speaking. Glancing down she saw it was at the Gospel of John, and suddenly knew what to look for. She scanned the tops of the pages until she found it. Turning sideways, hitching closer to the bed, she showed Darlene the page. "Here in God's Word, or Record, we have a story of a woman who was an adulteress, a prostitute. She was brought to face Jesus while He was on earth."

Darlene nodded, listening.

"You see, this woman sensed that Jesus was the Son of God, as I have just explained, and she believed He had the power to wipe out her wicked past. Do you know what Jesus said to her? 'Your sins are forgiven. Go, and sin no more.'"

Darlene wanted to read that for herself. She hesitated at most of the words, but when she finished she looked at Ruthe and stared. "You mean, He could forgive my past like that? Even if I've done much worse muck?!"

"Yes, this minute if you ask Him. He's done it many, many times for others."

"$%#@$%!" She was in a daze. "I bet she found it easy not to sin again. Not after talking person-to-person with the Son from God, eh?"

Ruthe agreed. "When we sincerely ask Him to forgive us, and when we believe He does, the innocent blood Jesus shed is counted as if it spilled for our personal sins, and all our guilt. It makes us just as pure as He is in God's sight."

Darlene concentrated on that idea.

"You see, Darlene, Jesus has finished everything that needed doing for our forgiveness. It's all like a wrapped gift. All we have to do is reach out our faith and take it as ours."

"Fantastic!"

"Right." Ruthe broke into a slight giggle. She knew they were on the brink of something truly fantastic. "It's as if I handed you a thousand dollar bill; it could be yours as soon as I decided to give it, but it wouldn't do you any good until you took it and spent it."

Darlene's eyes riveted on Ruthe's. "Get me to wherever this Jesus is. I want to see Him in person too."

Ruthe explained that Jesus, by the Holy Spirit, could hear their very thoughts, and each word they spoke. He was God, and therefore everywhere, they could talk to Him as if He was right in the room. Because He was.

Darlene was eager to try that. She accepted Ruthe's outstretched hands, and bent her head when she did. Ruthe told the Lord she was bringing a new friend to Him. Then she squeezed Darlene's hands and whispered, "Go ahead."

"Hi Jesus. You can hear me clear?" Darlene plunged in with gusto, following Ruthe's example. "Sorry I didn't know You were around 'til now. I hear You've known all along about me, and still You went ahead and died for me before I was even born. #$%, You didn't know what crap I was going to do, did You? I really have tried to stop, eh, lots of times. But it never lasted. From now on will You clean up the mess I am, and start my life over? Help me catch on from this Ruthe. I'm so clueless. Please and thank You, Sir."

There was so much Ruthe could think to teach Darlene, but it was high time she raced off to work. As she got up and tried to say a gentle good bye, Darlene surprised her by pulling down her face for a kiss. "Back tomorrow then?" With still more feeling she added, "$%$@! Am I ever glad you heard me scream Saturday night!"

Various emotions washed through Ruthe after she gave Darlene's name, age and address at the desk, then left for work. For herself she felt like shouting and singing. Thinking of Darlene, she wondered what would happen next. Would old surroundings and acquaintances soon draw her back into old habits? She knew God could change her, but what if she was too deeply set in her old ways?

What if she changed her mind? Were God's new life promises stronger; or human nature?

Should she suggest Darlene leave that bad example mother? Would that solve anything, and was Darlene mature enough to live alone?

Ruthe was at it most of her shift, pestering the Lord for answers to all these questions.

Besides, Lord, Ruthe sighed several times as the shift wore on, *If You don't help me keep this from my family I'm in hot water! They would disown me if they knew I was friends now with an ex-prostitute! Never mind assaulting a would-be murderer!* She cringed at this look at her life from their perspective.

EIGHT

At two-thirty the next day, Ruthe hurried off to the city once more, relieved at the ease with which she was beginning to come and go with no quizzing. Was it was true that folks think more of themselves than others?

Entering the hospital room, she found Darlene upset and pacing impatiently. "That cute guy called my ol' lady. So Marie comes by this afternoon. Even brings a present; a pack of cigarettes."

Ruthe bit her lip, afraid of what this new curve meant.

"Guess what happened." Darlene sounded puzzled.

"What?" the country girl asked cautiously.

"I thought I heard Jesus whisper, inside me sort'a, *Don't. Let those dirty things be.*"

"You mean you didn't take them after all?"

"Uh uh. I told her about your visit. Y'know, Jesus forgiving me, 'n all that."

"What did your mother say?"

"Marie was furious. Said I hadn't done wrong. Her feminist spiel; the world has sinned against us, an' on and on. When I told her about the prostitute or adulter- that hooker, in the Bible, well, she blew her @#$%#$~ guts! Marie said if I was going to get religious I'd better stay out of her sight. If I dare come to the apartment she'll kick me #$%#-less!"

Ruthe stared, dumbfounded.

"You said it was fool-proof, Ruthe. It's got'a work! I'm not quittin' on Jesus after He died for all my- that filthy goop of my life." Darlene burst into tears. "I was so happy last night. I was humming and giddy, and I had a long, long chat with Jesus, an' y'know, He doesn't hate me, He likes me!"

This melted Ruthe's heart. With tears she opened her arms and Darlene walked into them. "It's okay, Darlene. Moms sometimes lose their tempers. She will get over it."

"Oh no, she meant it. She's beat me to a pulp before."

Darlene blew her nose angrily. "Hah. That's $%#%& fine with me. I'll manage without her. I can move in with you, right?"

"You're sure she won't–?"

"Dead sure. Marie wants all her Johns to herself."

"What about your Dad?" Ruthe was reaching panic-stricken for another answer. "Maybe–"

"Haven't any, remember?" She sat back on the edge of the bed with a bounce that made the springs ping and squeak, and motioned to the guest chair. "Sit."

Whew, Lord, let's think of something fast! Ruthe sat down.

"Ahm, Darlene. Let's pray. My home situation is very different in that my parents tend to block out strangers, anyone that is not of or like themselves. So we're going to need an alternative plan."

They bowed their heads, as she'd explained the day before, in deference to their divine Friend. "Lord, I thank You for the love and patience You have already shown us, and the wonderful future I know You have mapped out for each of us. We're totally dependent on You, Father-God. You have said that You take a special interest in widows and the fatherless, and Darlene here is certainly fatherless, and now it appears, also motherless. We are at wit's end, Lord. We sure need clear ideas for our next move."

Then Darlene prayed, telling the Lord how she had hoped to share His forgiveness with her mom, and at school, she had meant to apologize to the girls she had tormented by systematically stealing their boyfriends. Now she had no home from which to go to school. What should she do?

After a short silence, they raised their heads. Ruthe patted Darlene's knee for comfort, and started to question her about her favourite subjects and special interests. Maybe she could land a part-time job and get an apartment.

Darlene admitted that because of her extra-curricular activities she had done very poorly in school. She was repeating grade ten and still not able to pass. Besides, the teachers all hated her and would never believe her if she said she was going to study now. "The Ol' Dragon especially, would swear I was cheating."

Final exams started the following week, so Ruthe knew there was no point in trying to help her study a whole year's worth of work. In her observant judgment, Darlene was probably mature enough to handle a job and be independent. But wouldn't her lack of education hinder her? What exactly was there she could do?

"Maybe you could get me in at the telephone office?" Darlene asked, remembering what Ruthe had told her about her arrangement.

"No. they insist on a diploma now. A couple of my school friends got turned away recently, so I know I got in by a miracle."

Ruthe chewed at the inside of her cheek, trying to think. Her thoughts darted about like bees in a blossoming plum tree. *She is bright, despite what she says about low grades, has a shrewd head... hey, a business head. Bet two cents she could run a business!*

Excited, Ruthe rummaged around in her purse while a student nurse came to take Darlene's temperature and blood pressure. "Have you ever done any sewing?" she asked mysteriously, as she groped with both hands in her cracked vinyl purse.

Darlene went blank, and mumbled over the thermometer, "Why?"

"We can both learn from the bottom up," Ruthe said recklessly. "I've always wanted to, but I'm left-handed and Mom says, I'm hopeless to teach. Some new friends have encouraged me to send away for this correspondence course." She came up with the envelope she was looking for; waving it and opening it at the same time, she said, "I had this secret crazy dream of learning dress designing and maybe setting up a shop. So I wrote for information on this course by mail. They take nothing for granted; sewing, designing, sketching, advertising, bookkeeping, it's all included. Only; even I will admit that I don't have a good business head, so I was ready to drop the idea."

She spread the leaflets and papers over the bed, but bumped into the student nurse who was still fussing around. "Oops. Excuse me," the nurse apologized as Ruthe stepped on her white shoe.

"My fault," Ruthe responded instantly. "You have your job to do."

But in her enthusiasm, Ruthe forgot the nurse promptly. "This offers lessons in designing, drafting new patterns, fitting, fashion sketching, sewing, and even shows how to set up a shop. The whole bit! Now, if we took this course during the summer, we might be able to set up a place for you by September where you could live and work."

"#@$%@!" Darlene screeched, catching on immediately. She stopped short as she realized she had just used the name of her Saviour as an expletive.

Ruthe saw the look, and blurted as an aside, patting Darlene's hand, "Very soon we are going to discuss swearing."

"However," she went on in a stage whisper, completely wound up in her brain wave. "We have to make this a unique, only-one-in-the-world kind of place. You'd tell all your clients, while you are sewing for them, what Jesus means to you, and invite them to become friends with Him too. I suspect you understand many different types of people, more than I do, and you would do well at this. If we find you have a good business head, why, there you go; a home and a job!"

"You mean I can be a designer and business woman? Without my high school?" Darlene grabbed Ruthe's shoulders. "I love it! I love it!"

"I mainly need to learn to sew darts and seams, and how to put in sleeves and zippers. But if you are creative, Darlene, you might really go places."

The two rehashed various aspects of this idea, and sometimes repeated themselves, but both became convinced it could come to pass.

For the moment, Ruthe shoved aside the question festering at the back of her mind; how to explain such a project at home. "I've only tried to sew a bit," she confessed, "but I'm sure if we push ourselves and polish our techniques we might get to where we zip together an outfit as we chat with a client, and an hour or two later she could wear it out of the shop."

"That fast? Oh Ruthe!" She grabbed Ruthe's head and almost shook it. "This is God's answer to our talk with Him, isn't it?" Darlene sat back and squirmed with anticipation. "All I need now is a house big enough for a shop, huh?"

"Sort of. I see this as a small house on a quiet street with the main floor converted into informal but efficient sewing rooms, and the basement made into a neat, modern little apartment for you."

"Sounds good enough. Who's got the money? You don't have much, eh?" She was looking at Ruthe's thrift store, slightly out-dated, beige polyester slacks and bronze/gold floral top, and the well-worn white cardigan sweater.

"Nope. Afraid I don't," she confessed with an embarrassed laugh. This reference to money brought her spirit down with a thump. All at once Ruthe could talk slower and more matter-of-factly again.

"I guess money is the first miracle we have to talk to the Lord Jesus about. Like you said, you might pass for twenty-five, but on the legal forms you'd have to show up as an honest sixteen, and that might present problems. I'm only eighteen myself, but we can see some bank managers, and maybe a few finance companies, to find out if we can borrow some under my name." Her conscience twitched at this, for her parents avoided debts like a plague. *But modern city people do this all the time*, she reasoned. Mr. O'Brien came to mind, but it wasn't right to approach a new friend for money. *One shouldn't beg!* Ruthe knew her mother and Grosz'mama would both say that.

"First we've got to find you a place to stay when you get out of here," she said, trying hard to be practical, and to close her mind to the deep waters she might be entering.

"A shrink is to see me in the morning," Darlene informed her soberly, "but the cute one wants to let me go after that."

Ruthe smiled. "The one I want to call Davie?"

"Guess so. He says I'm sterile; likely from my three abortions. Not good surgeries! Otherwise, I guess I survived a @#$%@ murder."

Getting up to go, Ruthe moved closer and slipped an arm around Darlene.

"I'd make a lousy mother any ways!" but Darlene leaned against Ruthe and a few tears squeezed past her bunched up eyes.

Ruthe hugged her and whispered a prayer into her shoulder, "Lord, please heal and comfort Darlene tonight." Then she scooted away.

That evening at work, she worried that she had promised too much. *Of all the nerve! It would take a country bumpkin like me! This was only the second time I talked with her, but... Oh God, I can't back out after all I said, can I?*

The only people she dared take Darlene to, even temporarily, were the O'Briens. The girls would be compassionate. Maybe they would give some of their mother's clothes to Darlene. If she'd wear that type. Ruthe found herself mulling over Darlene's story as she prayed and puzzled about helping her. Again, she felt convinced this was of God. He had brought them together, had set her up with this dream idea, and Darlene liked it too. A lot. While she felt that way, she was relieved and at peace. As soon as she worried that her silly imagination had gone wild, she had a terrible unsettled, hollow grow inside. Since she knew her job like a parrot, this went on all evening. However, the strain of thinking about one thing and talking about another gave her a headache in a couple of hours.

Towards the last hour she reminded herself several times that James warned Christians in the New Testament, if they toss between faith and doubt they should not expect to get anything. Only those who believe will receive.[8]

Okay, what do I know for sure? God loves me a lot, and He loves Darlene too, even if we are different. Therefore, I believe He will bring good things to pass, even if my dreams are foolishly off beam. She hung on to that, repeating it a number of times until the end of her shift.

And then she had an idea for step one.

NINE

Though it was late after her shift, Ruthe dared to stop at the O'Briens. The two sisters were still up and eager to tell her all about the church they had found.

"There's just about two hundred people, and are they ever warm and outgoing!" exclaimed Cathy.

Muriel added, "Different ones come up and introduce themselves. They make us feel like we've finally come home."

They described the minister, Pastor Monty Teaon, as a mid-thirties man with an enthusiastic, boyish personality. "He preaches simple, captivating sermons on Bible truths."

"His wife is very hospitable and cheerful. She invited us over after the evening service last Sunday. So we went twice in one day." Muriel held both of Ruthe's hands. "You have to come meet them and tell us what you think."

Cathy seconded this invitation.

When Ruthe asked how their dad saw this pastor and the church, Cathy answered, "Dad's very impressed with the man's knowledge and Bible interpretations."

Keith joined in his pyjamas. "What I love is his sense of humour in his illustration stories."

She promised to come for a service when she could work it in during the summer, and then explained Darlene's situation.

Muriel offered to bag some of her clothes. Ruthe squinted at Muriel, and confirmed that she was likely the same size as Darlene. Together they went to Muriel's room and gathered a bright kelly green skirt, a white cotton shirt, and several loose t-shirts, a pair of jeans, a few undies, and a pair of sandals and also some hardly used runners. "Someone at school laughed at them, so I never wore them again," Muriel apologized.

"Would your dad mind," Ruthe turned to Cathy, "If I brought her here a few days until I can find a place for Darlene to live?"

She was assured there would be no problem.

Ruthe's head was throbbing on the way home, her studying time was all used up, and she was feeling too weary to pray, so she put it all off and aimed her body for her side of the open couch on which Sharri slept.

She slept in too late for a dawn walk, and had to cram for an exam at nine, while the headache lingered. When she got home at noon it was worse, so she finally took something for it, and wandered off to go sit on her log beyond the willows.

Her knees tucked up tight under her chin, she stared into the pink petals of the first wild rose of the summer, and asked the Lord to sort out her thoughts according to His perfect will. As she relaxed, she smiled, anticipating a summer of stolen hours, learning with Darlene. Ruthe resolved not to be cowed into corners by fear. She would be open, check out all the options, and feel free to adjust her plans when more light came.

I've often cried on Your dear shoulder when I thought I had no friends. Now I have a few, and I need You more than ever. Help me to be the kind of friend You are. Stop us if You think this dress designing shop is a wrong idea! If it pleases You, then give us a hand, and work out all the little details, okay? For one, my family better not know. For another, Darlene needs the right kind of house for a shop and home combined, soon! Since those aren't free, how about a big bunch of money?

Feeling much better, and remembering that Darlene needed that bag of Muriel's clothes in the car trunk if she was to be released today, she slowly stood, walked back, got changed and headed into the city.

Darlene was waiting. Quickly, she put on Muriel's clothes; Ruthe suggested the skirt and blouse for going to see bank managers, and they headed downtown. She herself was wearing a longer, fitted suit skirt in dusty rose linen that was a hand-me-down sent from her Aunt Agnes in Ontario, and a beige crepe blouse with ruffles, that she had bought at the MCC thrift story for a dollar-eighty. Ruthe felt like quite the young career woman.

Ruthe cleared her throat as they crossed the road to her car and pointed out, tactfully she hoped, that she would only be involved indirectly in this business for family reasons. "This venture will be your responsibility, Darlene." She added just as fast, "Of course, I'll help you whenever I can."

Darlene smiled amiably and threw herself into the front seat with a light bounce.

The loans manager of the bank where Ruthe had cashed her cheques since she got her job in spring refused to have another word with them when he discovered their ages. He showed them to his door, amazed at their audacity.

They visited a finance company around the corner. "They might make an exception to this legal age fuss in return for a higher interest rate," Darlene said.

Ruthe caught herself sighing a couple of times. *Lord, two of us means two minds, doesn't it?* but she went along with her friend.

This manager was considerate enough to listen to their plan, and since he seemed to really hear them, they got a bit carried away with some of its special aspects. When he thought they were done, he became very jolly.

"I hear a great many reasons for borrowin' in this 'ere office," he drawled. "Howsome-ever, your story is so original–" He paused to shift his more barrel-like parts in the black vinyl chair. "Ahm. I have a suggestion, gals. Now don't get me wrong; I think you're fine, well-meanin' wimen, but that– that idea of talking to all your customers? Yaha-well, see, I'm a businessman, eh? Owned a successful store for many years...."

They nodded.

"Right. So I should know about running a business, eh? Anyways. Let me tell you, you can't run one for long, restricting yourselves to people interested in your religion. The Salvation Army is for that." His tone became almost wheedling. "Besides, you're too intelligent for that Sally Ann approach. Why don't you go for some training, and get some work experience first? Your dreams will come."

Darlene stared steadily into his eye.

Ruthe sighed and prayed anxiously within, *Lord, he's right! We can't expect a loan big enough to support Darlene while she takes the course and provide a building– and everything! What ailed me? We're no candidates....*

Suddenly the huge man was impersonal and detached. "Well, (Har-um-ph-h) exactly how much did you ladies plan to borrow? I'm no banker, but I do like to see a business plan too."

A glance at Darlene convinced Ruthe that she might just twist his arm and make him give them money. Suddenly she wanted to get them out of there. Urgently. "You see, Sir," Ruthe said rising and trying to make her voice sweet and professional. "We only came to see what our financial options might be."

"Thanks for your time," Darlene said coolly, taking her cue from Ruthe and standing too. "We'll call you if we need you."

"Hey; that's suppost to be my line!" His hearty laugh sounded phony. He lifted himself out of his chair by pressing his palms on his desk. "Oh, one other thing I should mention. The most we could lend you here is three– four hundred. If you have collateral, maybe a thousand. At twenty percent."

They thanked him again as they backed out the door.

In the car they did some mental and oral math. But Ruthe silently kicked herself for not having a clue what these things cost. What was really needed to start a business? Even if the tiny little house she had pictured in her mind cost just ten thousand, say, it would take at least another three or four thousand to furnish it and buy a couple of cheap sewing machines, never mind a starting supply of fabrics and notions. Fifteen to twenty thousand, minimum. It was hopeless. It was impossible.

Darlene asked about collateral. Ruthe explained that this was something like her dad's car, which the finance company would take if they didn't keep up the monthly payments. No way could she offer it. "The most expensive thing I own are my new twenty-five dollar white grad shoes."

Feeling snubbed and emotionally tired, they headed to the O'Brien place where Ruthe told Darlene, she could stay a few days.

The girls graciously welcomed Ruthe's new friend as their guest and crowded close to listen while they described their naive attempts to get a loan.

"We'd gladly give you the money. Your shop sounds like a great idea," Cathy said solicitously. "But we get just enough for an allowance and our education until we're of age. I'm only seventeen."

"I'm only fifteen!" moaned Muriel.

The big front door opened and Mr. O'Brien stepped through. "All that bad?" he asked playfully, seeing their long kitten faces right there in the entrance.

Muriel dashed to him, and dangling lovingly from his neck, she told him what had happened to Ruthe and Darlene.

Hearing her tell and embellish it, embarrassed Ruthe, since she had never meant to come across as a whining beggar.

While Muriel was still going on about how terribly they had been treated, her father tilted his head and looked thoughtfully at Ruthe. He sized up the petite but mature looking Darlene, and then studied Ruthe again.

Giving Muriel a tender squeeze, he came a couple of steps nearer. "In the weeks we've known you, Ruthe, I haven't ever thought of you in connection with business. Now that I do, I see your high personal standards and that colourful mind of yours as a combination. You're capable of doing anything you set your will to do."

Warm thrills shot up and down through Ruthe's body. No one had ever expressed such confidence in her. Now she wanted to prove Mr. O'Brien right; do something wonderful so it would tie a big bow on his insight about her.

He continued, smiling very kindly at her. "I would be honoured to be your business counsellor, to help you start out. One day it will be my claim to fame."

"Oh-ah-h!" Springing to life, Ruthe insisted that her idea was for Darlene to manage the business and live in it. "My friend has the business head. I merely suggested it, and offered to help out as much as possible. Still–" she choked, "I thank you for your very high regard."

Struck with an idea of his own, Mr. O'Brien turned to his daughters, "Cathy? Muriel? Remember those paintings your mother was madly buying up a few years ago for creative posterity?"

"Sure Dad," they chorused.

"Fred Monks was asking about them today. I'd meant to leave them alone a while longer I guess, in case their value increased. They are up in the attic, aren't they? If you want to bring them down, I'll call Fred. I imagine he'll be willing to pay at least the ten or fifteen thousand your mother put into them at one time."

All four girls burst into cries of surprise and gratitude, but the tall man just smiled, picked up his mail from the hall table and went to his den, saying over his shoulder, "don't be shy, Ruthe, when you run into your next problem."

Her Cinderella hour had come. Ruthe said her good byes and made exit too.

On her break Ruthe phoned the O'Briens and heard how the art collector had written a cheque for twenty thousand. Mr. O'Brien had explained to Darlene that he would hand it to Ruthe as an investment loan, which would insure that Ruthe had to be a part of all her business decisions. As partners they could set a goal of paying it back, but he had just found several verses in the book of Proverbs that advised lending money to the poor without interest, so he would ask for none.

Ruthe was so astonished she stuttered and stammered a lot the rest of her shift. Even in her nimble mind, she fumbled for words.

When she tried to thank Mr. O'Brien properly the next day, he murmured, "just picture Pearl wanting to help you. I'm trying to let her know I forg–" She could tell he was choked up this time as he advised them to open a business account in a bank he recommended, and then go on to their next steps. "I'm sure you'll pray a lot," he added, "But take time to think your basic principles through and put them on paper. Operating on intuition alone can be painful."

Ruthe promised on her honour, that Darlene and she would pay it all back as soon as possible. She was already imagining the shop would be ready to open by the end of summer. But now that final exams were upon her, she wouldn't be able to do much at all for a few days.

Mr. O'Brien spent some time with Darlene, showing her how to use the bookkeeping ledgers he bought for them. He explained a few business laws too.

Muriel and Darlene decided to get along for Ruthe's and Jesus' sake. For Darlene this was a time of learning to participate in simple friendships, now that she no longer wanted to be spiteful. Knowing these folks loved her, and that Jesus cared about the details of her life did much to soothe her need for acceptance. In fact, Darlene seemed to have a better grasp of the stupendous new direction Ruthe had brought her than Ruthe did.

Ruthe had to smile when Darlene observed that Mr. O'Brien was not open to sex on the side, like most. "And Ross?" she asked, wondering how he would be read. "Met him yet?"

"Yeah. He's ready all right. Funny thing– now I'm not."

It was hard for Darlene not to kick herself for her past. Until Cathy suggested she might get over it easier if she tried apologizing to some of those she had hurt. "I did that to my previous boyfriends, and now I have peace about my past. I even have fun with some now."

It took several days of catching city buses going this way and that way over the city, for Darlene to follow that advice. When Muriel thought she could study for her next exam on the bus, she went along to give Darlene moral support.

At her mother's, Darlene got kicked in the thigh in the apartment hallway, without even getting inside. A few old friends lashed at her with strong language, but as these visits progressed, Darlene grew free emotionally from her past. She discovered that her repentant reputation was preceding her like electrical currents. This news added polish to Darlene's persona for it proved that her *leaf was turned for good,* and that from now on she was starting out as a vivacious young woman in a whole new life.

Going to the O'Brien's newly discovered church, she learned to sing and hum, "Jesus is mine, mine, mine!" and a medley of choruses that followed.

Cathy used endearments freely. She couldn't resist calling Darlene, Darlin' at times. Muriel picked it up, and Ruthe caught herself copying them. Darlene liked the pet name, and asked if they would call her Darlin' Bonne, to give others the impression her second name was her first.

That helped Ruthe settle on a name for the shop. "How about Darlin' Bonne's Shop?" she asked. They all loved it.

Then, for nearly a week she cut back her visits, and Ruthe tried to focus on her exams. The Chief Operator was trying to schedule her for less shifts so as not to interfere with her finals. However, the suspense of wondering what they would use as Darlin' Bonne's Shop nearly crowded out her well-studied grade twelve knowledge. When she saw a shift and a German exam coming up that she usually handled with intuitive guesses anyway, and a whole weekend to study for the literature exam the following Monday, Ruthe discarded her carefully budgeted studying schedule to race to the city. This afternoon she would go house hunting with Darlin' Bonne. "Who knows," she cried out excitedly in the car, "we might be lucky on the first day!"

They saw four houses at outrageous prices, and began to feel hot and tired. *What an impatient mistake,* Ruthe chided herself.

Out of the blue, the man who had shown them the last house turned and said, "I think a better place for you would be the one called in this morning. It isn't on our listing yet, just going into paperwork, but it is supposed to be a rush sale. Kind'a tiny, but would you young ladies care to see it?"

"Sure. Might as well."

"As long as I can get to work by six."

It was a smaller house all right, with a pretty traffic-light green wood siding. "I adore greens!" sang out Darlin' Bonne.

It was on a quiet avenue as he had said, but not more than two blocks from a business intersection that everyone in the city knew well, and it happened to be in the right zone for converting easily to business purposes. The detached garage would do for storage. The house boasted a fully furnished basement suite, completely self-contained with a kitchen, bath, bedroom and living room.

"The previous owners rented the basement to university students for the winter, but school's out now. Just last week the couple was killed in an accident out east. Their married children are trying to sell it all quickly to cover funeral costs."

Ruthe and Darlin Bonne barely heard all the agent said as they explored. The main floor had a living room at the front and a corridor with three smaller rooms on each side and a bath at the end. Between the kitchen on the front left and the bedroom on the left was a narrow passage leading to the side entrance and the stairs into the basement.

"This house, pre-fab garage, furniture; eighteen thousand cash," said the agent while the girls rushed from room to room, planning changes they would like to make for a shop, and of course, the new decor they would work in. The agent raised his voice as they disappeared around a corner, "The lot is two thousand because it is so narrow."

Suddenly both registered what he had said. "Twenty thous–?!" Grabbing each other they jumped up and down. "We can do it! We can!"

The location was perfect. A well-known and easy to find street, with meter-free parking for the clientele. They chattered at the agent, generating more ideas as they talked. "If we sold the kitchen appliances, and the bedroom furniture from the main floor we might get enough to have special sewing tables and shelves made, right?"

They called Mr. O'Brien to join them at the Peerless Real Estate office to give the purchase papers a look, and to tell them if they had found a good deal.

Ruthe spent her break on the lounge phone, talking to Darlin' Bonne to discuss the next steps. Cathy and Muriel volunteered to advertise and help sell the extra furniture as their exams were done. Ruthe should concentrate on her last few finals. "Okay, but pack up the personal papers, photos and things of the owners and set them in the garage," she urged. "Their children may come looking for them yet."

When they mentioned the carpentry work wanted, she heard Keith begin to ask questions in the background. While Ruthe had to hang up, she could well imagine the girls continue to discuss with Keith what they thought was needed. He probably showed them plans from his magazines. Her mind swirled. *And I'm supposed to study literature all weekend?!*

TEN

Ruthe had another shift on Sunday night. When she stopped by, Mr. O'Brien suggested that because Keith had never tried such a big woodworking project before, she and Darlin' Bonne hire one or two professionals, and let Keith help them to keep costs down. The girls accepted it as sensible advice.

Talk turned to Granny O'Brien.

The sisters described their eccentric grandmother as a narrow-minded, self-centred, and rude. She lived in her bed, surrounded with antiques, many of them, ornamental clocks that she had gilded, secluded with only a grumpy maid in the mansion of grey rocks next door.

All Ruthe had seen of it so far was a wide sweeping drive looping around a small, neglected lily pool near the street. At the right side a short gravelled drive led to the wide handsome door of a carriage house, with heavy black wrought iron carriage lamps on either side. The house itself, made of large irregular grey rocks, rose mystically behind a number of very tall blue spruce and shady maples. By ducking down in the car she could see under a tree branch; the entrance was up three large curved steps to an arched doorway like some old cathedral. It had two grey, steel doors within the arch. The second floor had rows of windows, all with mossy, grey-blue shutters, and they were closed. The third floor seemed to have two or three gable windows jutting out from the roof. At least from the east side. On the street she had not known for sure, but thought the south and north sides might have gables too.

"Course," Cathy conceded with a pang of conscience, new to her, as she darted about the kitchen trying to find her mother's stew spices. "It's hard to remember if Granny became so miserable before or after we as a family started hating and ignoring her."

"Mom went over and tried to apologize," Muriel explained, "just a couple of days before she died. I remember her saying how she felt she ought to ask Granny's forgiveness. Granny wouldn't listen. Mom tried to tell her that she knew God had forgiven her, but Granny just hooted like she always does."

Bedridden, the elderly Mrs. O'Brien had excuse not to come to the funeral. The girls and Keith assured Ruthe that she would not have come even if she had been able.

Her only son, Ian, after he encountered Christ also felt it necessary to apologize for his part in the prolonged quarrel between his mother and his family. He suspected that bringing her to Canada just after her husband died had been unwise. She had too many adjustments to make. He had met furious bitterness, which made him think he had hit upon the root nerve. However, it was impossible to discuss a thing with her.

Cathy and Muriel didn't know how to approach her.

That evening Keith showed Ruthe a verse which says, if we hate someone we have as good as murdered him. "I can't help but hate Granny," he confessed. "That's all we've done around here. But nor do I want to be a murderer. How can I love her when I can't think of a single nice thing about her?"

Darlin' Bonne piped up, "I want to hear the answer to this too!"

Ruthe suggested that he might have been conditioned to hate her by the attitudes of the family. She told again of how she had disliked her sister Suzanne, but begged the Lord to lend her a bit of His love. "Now I sometimes catch myself feeling real concern for her. I hope one day we become friends."

While Ruthe was back in Kleinstadt writing her last two exams, Keith followed her example in prayer, and tried a few more visits to his Granny. She lectured him in angry tirades for all their sudden overtures of kindness.

After her last exam, her class had a three-day break before they returned for their marks and diplomas. By the afternoon Ruthe was at the O'Briens again. Cathy and Darlin' Bonne were out selling items of furniture from the shop-to-be, and Muriel had run upstairs for something. That left Ross with Ruthe in the kitchen.

"Aw-w, @#$%&!" Ross made a grotesque face as he wiped half a dozen cookies into his mouth. "You know, all this praying, rejoicing, and weeping, makes a full time job watching you."

Then you're fired, she wanted to say. There wasn't a civil answer to such silliness, so Ruthe tried to reprimand him for swearing.

"I'm Catholic. All Catholics swear."

"They do not!"

"Yeah. Even the terribly devote ones like Father Inglis. Except you, my sweeet Ruthe. You're perfect. Hey, and how about that Darlin' Bonne of yours? I've heard her blaspheme–!"

Ruthe started to explain she had recently discussed those words with Darlin' Bonne, and she had since made sincere efforts to stop. However, Ross changed the subject by slipping his arm around Ruthe, grinning boyishly into her face, and cajoled her to come with him for a ride in his mint-condition red Mustang.

"No thanks," and Ruthe stepped deliberately away from him.

Ross froze a second, then his face softened. He came up close and grew very tender. "Ruthe, I'm sorry for being so mean. I 'm so full of sin I can't help myself. Let's go sit in the living room. Maybe you can help me break through my pride and all these bad habits?"

This rang like truth. Ruthe hesitated, then shook her head as the doorbell chimed.

"Aw– pretty please, with sugar on top?"

Muriel had just come down the stairs. She went straight on to the door. In the kitchen again, she handed a note to Ruthe, and turned on Ross, pleading with him to stop haunting Ruthe. He just sauntered to the corner counter where the teddy bear cookie jar stood, whistling, hoping to annoy Ruthe and Muriel.

Ruthe opened the note. It read, *Miss Ruth; Come see me at once.* Signed, *Kate O'Brien.* With a trembling hand she held it out to Muriel.

"I wondered why Bessie brought a note for you. It's usually a summons for Daddy when Granny needs something."

"@#$%@!" cried Ross, crowding over Muriel's shoulder to read. "#$@ #@$@&@! The old witch is goin'a boil ya!" He threw back his head and crowed with glee. "See, it pays to be like me! Stay out'a her hair!"

"Will you shut up, Ross!" Muriel cried, and almost in the same breath, "Ruthe, what are you going to do?"

Ah-ha, laughed a cruel voice only Ruthe could hear. *Thought you got rid of your shyness, huh? You're not cured!*

"Guess I'll go see her," Ruthe said aloud, pursing her lips firmly, determined to keep the upper hand over the Evil One.

At the same time her spirit sailed through the ceiling in prayer. *Lord, this is the first persecution I've ever faced. Unless we count Ross. No, I'm not afraid of him. Now this bitter old Granny is going to– I don't know!* All at once Ruthe was disgusted with herself. *Afraid of a bedridden, helpless old lady? What next!*

"Granny has a phobia about phones," Muriel apologized, "but her cryptic notes send us into spasms too."

The footpath Ruthe had seen disappearing into the Chinese elm hedge continued beyond, across an unkempt rockery and berry garden, a tennis court overgrown with hay-like grass between the square tiles, around to the front, and underneath several gigantic shade trees that guarded the door of the neglected house. Another, fainter path crossed over the tennis court down to some gnarled apple trees at the rear. *An orchard? What an estate this must've been.* Ruthe walked cautiously, alertly, down the path, up through the ragged garden. Pausing at the court to glance about, and noticing she had just passed several untrimmed raspberry rows and a current bush or two. She ignored the back door, went around the rear south corner and under the big trees, then up to the east or street side, to the massive old double doors.

Dropping the knocker with a startling clang, Ruthe turned to look up the long curved drive with still frost-killed flower border debris and patchy, uncut and yellowing lawn.

Bessie was a large, overweight woman in a navy blue dress with a white collar. It was the first time Ruthe had ever met a live-in maid. As she was led up the winding, hand-carved staircase, she looked at Bessie from the back and decided that maids were ordinary people. *There's a dozen women like this around Kleinstadt.*

Ruthe's darting eyes snapped pictures as she followed Bessie up to the second floor. *Is this Victorian?* They passed underneath an enormous chandelier in the almost empty entrance space. Looking straight ahead was a living room or parlour big enough, Ruthe thought, for fifty people if standing or dancing at a party. *This furniture is terribly old, though,* she commented to herself. *Overstuffed burgundy chairs and sofas; nice wood, but really out of date.*

Next they passed through one end of the huge dining room, dominated by an oval banquet table that must seat twenty-four, easily. *Now that thing gleams!* she told herself with awe. The stairs, banisters, newel posts, and even the baseboards were of carved wood and looked like they had been lovingly oiled with a cloth. Not recently, however. An old musty air hung about like a box of some yellowed novels in an attic.

At the top of the stairs she was surprised to find herself looking down a great gaping opening that overlooked the shining dining table. The opening was fenced around with carved posts. Around that fence was a hallway with doors off in every direction. *How many rooms can there be?* Ruthe wondered.

Bessie turned right, huffed to a stop and opened a door.

Looking in, Ruthe saw, right beside the window, the biggest, highest old canopy bed she had ever– no, she had never– dreamed of seeing. Sunk chest deep into its ballooning cloud of goose down quilts, sat a tiny, wrinkled woman. The outline of her skull and jaw showed clearly through her thin skin, and almost transparent halo of short white hair. The window provided secondary light for the bed area, but the rest of the room seemed crowded with masses of shadowy antique shapes that she couldn't begin to classify. Just a lot of things cluttered on lots of cabinets and chests, some of those stacked two or three high.

"Ar' ye afraid o' me?" called a strong but cracking voice.

"Go on in," urged Bessie, and Ruthe found herself moving closer.

"Wal, an' yer sartainly a young lass," the small woman said, rolling a steady gaze down Ruthe's suddenly chilly body.

"Ah-yes, Ma'm. Everyone says I look younger than my age." She worked hard now at sounding cheerful and at ease, yet she tossed her thick brown mass of wavy hair back over her shoulder self-consciously, and smoothed down her beige slacks. She hoped the wet underarms of her red cotton blouse weren't showing. She didn't dare glance down, knowing it would draw attention to them.

"Har-rr-um. Ta 'er me gran'chil'n yer a maricle worker 's wise 's Elija'."

"No, I'm not–" Ruthe stopped. That sounded rude, abrupt. She better take time to think before she said much. *Oh dear, I was going to forget the unkind things I'd heard about her and speak graciously!*

"Wal-then," and she harrumped again. "Le'me 'ear y'tell it."

Bessie left, scraping the door back on its threshold.

Pulling up a big tapestry footstool, Ruthe gingerly sat down by the bed. *Lord, she can't kill me with words, can she?*

Forcing a bit of ingenue naturalness, Ruthe began to tell her about herself. Granny should understand, she at least, held nothing against her. Maybe, if she did some meek listening she would learn clues the other O'Briens had missed.

Granny interrupted, then urged Ruthe on with terse questions. Soon she had loosened up a bit and was rambling on almost intimately. She tried to explain her loneliness in her early teens, and the comforting friendship she had discovered possible with God.

Ruthe pointed out that she had no experience with drugs or street life, "but I'm beginning to realize that I have good news for lonely people. I watch for them now." Since Granny nodded vigorously to all this, Ruthe even shared how she felt when she thought of all the lonely people in the city. This pretty prairie city had quite a few. In her imagination she suffered along with such people. Little Mrs. O'Brien vouched that she was right about lonely folks.

Ruthe suspected that it pleased old Granny to have someone confide in her like this. No one else did. *But Lord, how do I switch to a helping mode?*

She went on to tell about commuting to the city and her naive but burdened longing to help somebody, anybody, somehow. "I drove up and down the streets, looking for trouble," she said frankly.

The old woman nodded her sparse, feathery white hair energetically, "Go git'm, Buster! At's wha' I al'ays says. No one's goina han' ye' wha' ye wants."

Ruthe hadn't meant to sound like a go-getter. She was thankful that Granny was still listening though, not telling her off as Ross had predicted. She tried to be careful to avoid details as she explained that as a result of her search one night, the Lord had led her directly to Muriel, and now they were good friends.

"So the gurl di' mean it when she said ye'd res-cued 'er from shame n 'ell."

Not wanting to dwell on Muriel's embarrassment, she quickly moved the conversation on to meeting Mrs. Pearl O'Brien, and how she had found that special something she had searched for all her life in social service and great philosophical thought. After all that, it was hers simply for taking God at his promise to forgive sins and abide in us.

The wizen Irish woman really began to quiz Ruthe about this. "Naow. That Pearl had 'er sins. My son do'na knaow the half! Wha' makes ye sa' sure we're all bad? Y'r sayin' I'm not goin' ta 'eaven?" And, "why d'ye think the gud Fath'r allows sickness and suffer'n? Tell me that naow, ye clev'r Coll'en."

Com'on, com'on. You're stuck now, whispered the mocker, *you can't fool her with a flimsy answer.*

Ruthe took a deep breath. "We're all bad because the Bible says so, and when we listen to our conscience in true honesty, it tells us the same thing. Unless, of course," she added as an after thought, feeling on shaky ground as to Granny's conscience, "we've sinned so much that our conscience has been seared or calloused."

Hey, this Granny might not be beyond hope! Whipping a small New Testament out of her purse, she said, "The Bible tells us, *'For all have sinned and come short of the glory of God.'*[9] And back in Isaiah, although I don't have that part here, it says, *'All we like sheep have gone astray, we have turned everyone to his own way.'*[10]"

As for sickness and suffering; that question had bothered Ruthe at times too. There was a Scriptural answer she had heard, but for the life of her she couldn't recall the reference just now. So she took another deep breath and tried to explain it in her own words. "God never meant for us to be sick or suffer pain, or even the least unhappiness, originally. As a human race we brought it upon ourselves. That is, as we are represented in Adam and Eve, the first people, when they deliberately disobeyed God."

Granny was opening her mouth to protest, but Ruthe was quick. "Nor can we complain about suffering for their sin, because absolutely anyone of us put in their place would sooner or later have committed that historic first sin too. As humans we just have not got the power to be holy like God." Ruthe's eyes narrowed in concentration. "Mrs. O'Brien, do you remember hearing how when God made them leave Eden, He warned that henceforth it meant death and decay and they would have to fight weeds and wild animals to eke out a living? Our bodies and the whole world is in a process of decay and degeneration, of which hunger, sickness and suffering in all kinds, are only the symptoms."

"Bu-t if God rea'lly love us, why do'na He stop us from goin' our fool'esh ways?"

"Because He loves us too much to demand obedience against our wills. Besides, He did arrange the one and only way by which it is possible for us to come back to what He intended us to be. He honour-bound Himself to wait for our decision. We have to want it first."

"Tha' cross," Granny sighed. "Och-h, dearie, wha' a gamb'l He took. Most folks do'na wan' tha'."

"Yes,"Ruthe sighed too, ready to cry over it. "That sacrifice Jesus made was for everyone. But not everyone accepts it, so in their cases Jesus' precious blood seems wasted." She paused, overwhelmed again at God's tremendous love for mere mortals. "Isn't His love fathomless?!"

Mrs. O'Brien had followed intently. Her eyes were still riveted on Ruthe as she said, "Y' knaow, the yong lad we'r right. Ye do commune wi' God. Ye preach a movin' sermon."

"Anyone can communicate with God!" Ruthe cried quickly, rising involuntarily and coming closer. Suddenly she ached for Granny to try it too. "Why, my life proves it! If a shy Mennonite girl like me, a country bumpkin sort, can get to know Him personally and talk with Him all day long– then surely, you can do it!"

Granny struggled to sit more upright and gripped her thick quilt with both hands. "Do y'– ye think it's na' ta' late for an ol' witch likes o' me? This mar'cle in the 'heart?" Before Ruthe could answer, she continued in a torrent of loneliness and fears. "Och-h, I'm an ol' woman. Doc'ter says if I wer'na sa' stubborn, I 'ould die. I d'na wan'na die! I jus' can'a un'erstan' it; my 'ead says God cou'na see me ta' 'ell, an' my 'eart knaows I jus' cou'na stan' in His 'oliness!"

Ruthe could have burst into tears, except for shock. She had to be reading this? *Is this actually happening?* It seemed the Lord was in this shadowy room. She reached across the bulky old quilt, wrapping her arms around the trembling, wiry woman. "Don't you see," she soothed, "the very fact that we are so unworthy shows up the greatness of His love. Yes, including for me and you!"

For several minutes they just clung to each other and cried.

Then Ruthe prayed. It was beginning to feel like an old, comfortable pattern.

Granny's pride was levelled. Having an example to follow, she burst into a humble and penitent prayer too. She confessed to peace as years of brittle glass seemed to tinkle and melt away inside her.

A flash of consciousness of time led Ruthe to glance at her watch and beg to be excused. The wispy woman gripped Ruthe's wrists and implored her to come back. "Y'er the only one ever ta' talk wi' me as if I had a soul!"

Ruthe promised she would as often as she could, and then, possessed by a terrible fear she would lose her job for being late, escaped in record time. So fast it scared the O'Brien girls when she drove off without coming in to tell them of her experience with their Granny.

Ruthe was damp with perspiration but walked into the toll room only seconds after the rest of her shift. Her heart seized with fright when a supervisor promptly relieved her and sent her to the Clerk's desk.

"Please explain to your friends that we can only call you to take a personal call in a true emergency," said the Chief Operator politely.

It was Cathy, with Muriel on an extension, in a panic to know what Granny had done to her.

"Go over and find out for yourselves," Ruthe urged, but knew her voice sounded unreal and cryptic from her hurrying.

"Keith just went," they said, and begged to know, "are you okay?"

"On second thought," Ruthe advised, trying hard to calm herself and think. "Give her until tomorrow to absorb her big decision. She made the same one you both did." Ruthe scratched her face then covered it with her hand to hide her expression from the Chief Operator, while Cathy and Muriel shrieked with questions and amazement. In the background Keith was confirming the news. "Listen, I'm on duty. I'll call you later," and with that she brashly hung up.

Ruthe had to do Saturday cleaning until two the next day, then eased away early to check on her friends and Granny O'Brien. She heard all about how the three girls went to see Granny in the morning for them selves. Her cheery civility had stunned the granddaughters, who had no memory of her like that. Shock kept them from any deep conversations, but all three girls urged Ruthe to give Granny a quick pop-in visit whenever she could.

She did. Not quite every day, but just about every other time she had a shift.

After picking up her marks on Monday morning she was free to start on the full-time shift schedule the Chief Operator assigned Ruthe. It had a range of days, splits and evening hours. Squeezing in a quick trip to Granny in a longer lunch break made her feel guilty for not visiting her own beloved Grosz'mama much these days. Especially after she told Granny about her, Ruthe realized how fortunate she was to have such a pure role model.

Driving home, Ruthe imagined telling Grosz'mama about that Irish Granny in the city. She had to smile. Grosz'mama had a very tender heart and loved to read and hear human interest stories. Yep, Ruthe nodded emphatically, *Grosz'mama would be glad Granny has accepted God's love. She would even be proud of me for going to talk to her like I did.*

But at home there were family tensions, and Ruthe tried to settle a peace between her Dad and her brother Brandt, who wanted a job as a farmhand. Forget going to tell Grosz'mama.

Sometimes her visits to Granny O'Brien were only ten or fifteen minutes, but they meant so much to the old invalid, it got easy to do. She became almost nonchalant about darting in and out of the mansion. Ruthe got used to Granny's bird-like movements, her attachment to that eiderdown quilt, and her very personal accent.

They discussed everything from the O'Brien grandchildren, whom Granny privately adored but did not know how to praise, to the meaning of Ruthe's favourite hymns and choruses, which she had to sing over and over despite Ruthe's protests that she did not read or understand music. Granny, brash and snoopy, soon had a play-by-play account of all that was happening with Darlin'

Bonne and now, the purchase and renovations of the little green house into a dress shop. The place where Ruthe tried to be when not visiting Granny. It tore her to decide sometimes.

Granny admitted that with her low blood pressure, she ought to be in a bedroom with windows east or south, but she had taken this one, with just a north window, because it was the only one from where she could look over a low spot in the Chinese elm hedge to watch her son's driveway. "I've be'n af'er an af'er Ian to get that 'edge cut. E' will n'a do it! Pearl n' the chil'en likes priv'cy, 'e said."

Ruthe joined Granny in laughing at herself.

In stages, Ruthe told Granny about an operator at work who seemed to want to reach out in friendship, but was shy. At times she felt guilty for telling Granny so much, but it helped, as did her secret garden chats with the Lord, and it did wonders for Granny to be taken vicariously out of her room.

"Each friend is like a rose. My dearest Friend and I admire them as we walk and talk together. We discuss how to culture more love into each friendship," Ruthe explained.

Granny was tickled at Ruthe's comparison of her new city friends to various types of roses in her garden of friends. When she discovered that Ruthe knew next to nothing about roses, familiar mainly with wild prairie roses in the ditches, Granny sent Bessie on a hunt for several days through certain rooms for books and magazines on growing roses. These she gave Ruthe to feed her imagination. They were a unique prize and Ruthe worked hard to figure out how to get them home and hidden.

"Keep up yer frien'ship wi' m'gurls," Granny advised, thumbing next door. "I train' Pearl in roses when she wer'a bride, an' I see Mur'l is still look'n af'er the green'ouse at back. A'times Cat'leen do as well." Ruthe must have looked puzzled, for Granny added, "so's they ken giv' ye real roses onc'a while." They laughed together again.

Mr. O'Brien praised Ruthe for the visits to his mother, and thanked her sincerely. So she made time, though some days she had an airy feeling in her stomach like she was on skis going fast down a slope with no horizon.

ELEVEN

Ruthe had talked to June Johnson only a few times in the Operator's Lounge through the winter. She appeared to be a self-possessed career girl. Since June didn't seem to need her, Ruthe was too shy to pursue get-acquainted conversations. In the beginning they were only polite and nodded to each other as they passed in and out of the toll room. That did not keep Ruthe from studying her, however, as she did most of the women with whom she worked.

June reminded her of a Sear's catalogue model in her deliberate and regal bearing and her ever-perfect grooming. They were about the same height, but June had a clear, faultless face, while Ruthe was convinced hers was flawed. June wore her dark brown hair long too, but where Ruthe's was light brown and wavy, and rippled in a warm feathery mass over her shoulders, June's was cut bluntly and hung straight to just short of her shoulders. Her thick shiny bangs came down to her eyebrows accentuating her soft, chocolate-coloured eyes. Mostly, Ruthe's were teal flecked with gold. Sometimes a hesitant blue.

Once or twice Ruthe wondered if June might not be just as shy as she was. She noticed June took pains to sit near her at the switchboard when she could, even though she did not initiate much chat. A number of other operators were far more outgoing. It was June though who made the first move, and invited Ruthe to her home one Saturday during the exam weeks, when they happened to work the same day hours.

Ruthe had meant to go help Darlin' Bonne a while at the shop, but decided to snap up this opportunity to make a new friend. She offered June a ride in the family's brown sedan since June usually came downtown by bus.

On the way June warmed up and said that she was the oldest of six, had graduated from high school the previous year, and, that her father had run away. Her family subsisted on her pay cheques and Welfare.

"I'm an oldest too!" As for the rest, Ruthe was surprised; June did not wear expensive clothes but she always was so nicely groomed. Spotless. But as soon as Ruthe saw her mother, she realized by contrast what good personal habits can accomplish.

Mrs. Johnson was pretty too, in a wild, natural way. She was barefoot and in blue jeans with an oversized man's cotton shirt, and her long corn silk hair straggled all over her back like a pre-teen's. *Maybe it's her attitude that makes her look younger than June by three or four years*, thought Ruthe.

The youngest two girls, both pre-school, were also barefoot and scampered about with hardly any clothes on.

Their subsidized housing unit, though new, had only a few odd pieces of junk for furniture. From the wood floor of the living room, to the tile floor of the kitchen was woven a sticky mat of syrup threads, peanut butter and bread crumbs. "Phew-he-ee!" whistled June in disgust. "Looks like I'll have to clean our pigsty all over again tonight! Can't you kids keep it clean for one day?"

"Linnet and Byron did it!"

"Where are they?" June roared.

"I don't know," snapped the saucy Gilda who was five, but ducked as June moved in on her, and managed to call "time" by grabbing Ruthe's hands and walking familiarly up her legs and stomach like a monkey, to Ruthe's laughing astonishment.

June had not finished introducing Ruthe to her mother when the two little sisters crowded Ruthe onto the threadbare car seat, serving as a couch, and played quite affectionately with her face and hair. Ruthe would have insisted that she loved all children on sight, and Gilda and Cheryl were cute, but she was grateful when June snatched them up, one under each arm, and took them into the bathroom. Despite their winsome friendliness, they were sticky to the touch.

"Into-the-tub!" shouted June. "This instant!"

"Why?" hollered one, while the other got as far as the bathroom door in her escape.

"Cause I said so!" June snapped Cheryl up in her arms again, and slammed the door so that the building shuddered.

Silently Ruthe recognized that June was covering up her shame.

While June was furiously scolding and scrubbing, her mother sat close to Ruthe to chat blithely. "Junie is so wonderful with the kids," she informed her as though sharing with another mother. "I simply couldn't manage without her."

"You have other children besides June and these two?" Ruthe inquired, making polite conversation Then she listened while Cindy Johnson raved about Wesley, Linnet and Byron and how smart and cute they were.

It was difficult to decide if she were just so simple-minded, or whether she really had faith that her husband would be back soon's he had the wild oats out of his pants, as she said. On the other hand, Ruthe thought, trying to be fair, this may be a front she puts up to keep her courage going. Ruthe had no category for Mrs. Johnson, never having met this type before. She found it unreal, listening to her chatter so cheerfully about making the best of life as it comes to each of us, while she seemed oblivious to the mess around her. She did not know whether to feel sorry for her, or admire her. Ruthe's own mother would have insisted on cleanliness as the least she could do in the interim, no matter what. Couldn't Mrs. Johnson do that much?

Ruthe did feel tremendous empathy with June. Underneath that bearing she had been so shy of, was pride and a real ambition to work up to a different life. June's heartache throbbed vividly in her own. There had been times when she was ashamed of her family. In Kleinstadt too, Ruthe always knew they were on the wrong side of the tracks.

Over the previous year or two Ruthe had felt convicted of her critical attitude while having her more frequent long walks or garden talks with the Lord. She had found that honesty there had led to changes in her view of her family. With a surge of hope, Ruthe knew that if June would listen, she had a great message to share. But this was not the right time or place.

Ruthe had meant to check on Darlin' Bonne, and knew that Granny was expecting her, but as she waited for June, her conscience troubled her that her mother would be impatient for her to come home in time for supper. At the rate time was slipping away she had better hurry straight home, or she would have a crisis of her own. She excused herself from Mrs. Johnson in mid-sentence, popped her head in the bathroom door, and said, "I'll have to go. Sor–ry. I'll see you at work soon, and then we can plan another get together, okay?"

June left the girls in the tub, followed her to the door, and was profuse with apologies for her home, her sisters, and everything. Ruthe stopped in the door a few more minutes to soothe June and tell her not to fret about it. "Our place is a mess some days too," she added. "It's just a sign that people live here. I know it's out of your control."

June caved in with a sigh.

Two days later, they met in the corridor at work. Immediately June apologized again for her family's lazy, primeval ways. But it was a momentary meeting.

The following day they spent their break together in the cafeteria. June was still ashamed of her home, but because Ruthe now knew about it, she was anxious to tell all her secrets. "You saw what a basket case my mother is? Well, the kids don't care one iota more about sitting in their own mess! Oh," she moaned unhappily, "I wanno get out!"

"Running away doesn't strike me as the best idea, but I–"

"I've got a plan," June said. "How would you like to share an apartment with me? You wouldn't have to drive home late at night, like I heard Dottie tell Gretchen, and I'd be able to live in a clean, nicely furnished place for once. What do you say?"

"Wel-l..." Ruthe began cautiously. "You don't know how super-poor I am; I have to support my family too. But your family needs you even more. If you desert them, they'll never know a better life. You can't leave those kids to the mercy of your–" Quickly, Ruthe bit her lower lip. She hated it when others degraded her parents, even if she was well aware of their faults.

June's shyness was all gone. "Ruthe! I've tried! They don't change for me. Nothing works! Honestly, the best thing I can do for the kids is earn as much money as fast as I can and try to get custody of them later. They'll change in a different environment."

Ruthe clutched her hands together under her chin and moaned gently. "By that time it'll be too late, June. It would take too long. Besides, environment doesn't necessarily change folks, nor does it guarantee a certain kind of destiny. Take you and me for example."

"If I let them live on Welfare while I spend my money taking this Interior Decorating course I know of, I'm sure I'll get a higher paying job and–"

"I've cooked up plans like that myself," Ruthe said as kindly as she could. "Only there are a hundred and one things that can go wrong. Many things over which we have no control. Those cute little imps would resent you if you walked out of their lives and then tried to come back later as if you still loved them."

Reaching out with a deep breath, Ruthe touched her arm firmly. "June, I know of a different way. Guaranteed to change at least you, and then through you it has potential to bring miraculous changes to the rest of your family. One day you would see something much better has taken place. Want to hear it?"

"What is it?" June asked warily.

In as few sentences as possible, Ruthe explained how her relationship with Jesus Christ had changed her, and assured her that it could transform her life too.

June held back. She clung to her little dream plan tightly. She did not refuse to consider Ruthe's suggestion, but her mind was so absorbed with the disappointment of having Ruthe reject her plan that she could not take her mind out of *Park*.

How can I blame her? Ruthe thought later. Intuitively, she sensed that it had cost June lots of built-up nerve to open up to a friendship with her, and to share her dream plan. June's dilemma and deep pain crept into every spare moment of Ruthe's time as she finished the last of her exams and school days. She threw out more creative ideas for helping June than she could remember or count afterwards.

TWELVE

It's a good thing Dad can walk to his new temporary job in Kleinstadt, Ruthe thought, *he sure isn't getting much use of his car.* But she heard him mumble more often about her superior attitude. She balanced out her tiny guilt feelings by speaking with extra kindness and consideration to her parents, asking permission and advice about wee detail things. She denied it when they suggested that getting her high school diploma made her feel too self-important. Ruthe was not about to tell them that she thought her air was more due to knowing she was a secret partner in Darlin' Bonne's Shop, for it was really coming to pass; the renovations had started. Besides that, she revelled in a number of city friends who admired her.

Poor Mom, Ruthe mused. *She's our levelheaded organizer, but my irregular comings and goings have upset her sense of being in charge.* By now her mother often made Suzanne clear off a meal, and let Ruthe raid the fridge whenever she got home. Ruthe could jump in the car just about any day of the week, and her mother thought she was hurrying to work. "Didn't I warn you?" she explained, "As soon as my exams were done I would be getting all kinds of regular and split shifts." She tried to be softer and patient. "Besides, there is plenty of overtime available if I want it. At time-and-a-half, you'll want me to take as many overtime hours as I can handle."

Her parents could only agree. Her pay cheques covered their groceries and utility bills. Sometimes it had to do for their clothes and shoes as well as her gas to and from the city.

At last the Monday morning when Ruthe received her final marks and school was out at last. After lunch and dishes she raced to the city with a new plan. She would take June to meet Darlin' Bonne at the shop, where she was moved in and supervising the renovations. Darlin' Bonne was such a vibrant example of what she had tried to tell June; it had occurred to her that June might be persuaded if she met the dynamo.

Happy to find June home, Ruthe invited her to come meet someone special. June came along quietly, politely. So quietly that Ruthe changed her mind about suggesting that June might find a potential roommate in this visit.

From the street they could hear Darlin' Bonne over the carpentry tools that shrieked and pounded lustily. *What are the neighbours thinking?* Ruthe wondered. However, hot with curiosity she picked her way over the threshold and into a world of sawdust, fresh lumber and power tools.

June looked around gingerly, and followed.

Immediately they came upon the two hired carpenters who said, "Howdy," and "Hi girls!" and then Keith and two of his friends. Ruthe responded warmly as she studied what had been the kitchen a week ago. All cabinets and appliances were removed and one of the men was going in to put together a table with a huge folding surface. Up along three walls were brand new and sappy-smelling supply shelves.

Ruthe jumped over a stack of wood planks in the hall and turned to watch June do it, when suddenly, "Hi-i-ya! Ruthe-darlin'!" As quickly as Darlin' Bonne erupted from one of the other rooms she was all about Ruthe in a hug. Lithely, they ducked in unison as one of Keith's young friends came by with a two-by-four held at an awkward angle.

Nudging Ruthe, she bubbled, "Did Cath tell you I've moved in this weekend? O-but-I've missed you, Ruthe! School all done? Hey, guess what! The first lesson package arrived this morning! And Mr. O'Brien was here a couple of minutes ago with our new business lic– excuse me; you brought somebody?"

"Yes," Ruthe laughed, feeling proud of Darlin' Bonne. She introduced June, adding, "She isn't so sure God would ever do anything special for her."

"But Junie-darlin', He can! He would!" Darlin' Bonne turned all her emotional forces onto June. "He'd love to do some miracles for you! Our Heavenly Father and our handsome Lord Jesus enjoy miracles– they *love* people who are ready for 'em!"

Too much was going on to stand still, so Darlin' Bonne wrapped a tugging arm around June and another around Ruthe, and started to lead them away, touring the house. With examples fresh from her most recent experiences, Darlin' Bonne tried to prove to June that God loves the most hopeless and most unlovable. "Junie, He cares about every detail of our lives. What we wear, how we do our hair, whether we eat well. Everything!"

Ruthe felt tickled through and through. Darlin' Bonne was behaving just as she had hoped and known she would. She beamed and seconded all Darlin' Bonne said, sure that June would have to be affected.

It was also a thrill to notice evidence of Darlin' Bonne's business foresight. She'd had Keith and his buddies remove some walls and re-section the spaces with floor to ceiling shelves. Thus the same fabric could be at her fingertips from two different rooms. *Or the fingertips of others we will take in as employees later on,* Ruthe told herself with a confident smile that wouldn't stop.

June didn't say much in response to Darlin' Bonne, so they stood watching Keith at work. He stuck out the tip of his tongue in concentration, then there was a terrific look of satisfaction as he put down the electric saw and fitted the panels of a small drawer together.

"Wouldn't you like to learn to sew with us?" Darlin' Bonne and Ruthe asked June. She shook her head tentatively, restlessly.

Ruthe allowed a few more quiet moments, then, since June still did not say much, she turned to Darlin' Bonne to discuss when to start the correspondence lessons. Ruthe promised to try a daily or at least alternate days' visit.

Still nothing from June. Though there was time to spare, after a bit more planning with Darlin' Bonne, Ruthe took June to the telephone office.

Both of them had early evening shifts that day. However, their breaks were staggered and they didn't get to sit close together at the switchboard. Ruthe spent her free moments trying to figure June out. How could she have resisted that enthusiastic and personal invitation from Darlin' Bonne?

Granny O'Brien clucked and couldn't understand it either, when Ruthe popped by after 10:30, and told her of the disappointment. She promised to clutch Jesus' feet and wait for an answer the next day. It made Ruthe smile.

Two days later at work, June beckoned Ruthe to step behind some lockers with her, out of sight of other operators. "Ruthe, please say you'll move into an apartment with me. Please?"

"I'm terribly sorry, June. I promised Mom I'll be home to help her as often as I can, and I'm already sneaking time for myself. Besides, then I couldn't afford to pay for my family's groceries. Dad is just digging a couple of wells, and that certainly doesn't pay much. I'm so sorry, June, but I just can't!"

In the windows of June's eyes, Ruthe watched something die. "Guess you are right," June said slowly. "A wonderful dream, but it can't be done. I need a friend to make it come true."

"Now now. With enough determination one can make most dreams come to pass. Only, it would be an awful struggle, I doubt you'd be happy in the end."

Looking crushed, June turned to go.

"Com'on, June," Ruthe blurted, seeing her chance going. "Let Jesus have all your life and your dreams. Your family too. He'll work out something much better than you can ever imagine."

"Oh-Ruthe—" June began to sniff, trying to control herself. "I was hoping you'd ask me again! I didn't know how to bring it up, but I haven't stopped thinking of what Darlin' Bonne said about her life!"

Whoa, she was listening after all!?

June was just leaving on her lunch break, and Ruthe was on her way in to start her split shift, so they didn't finish their conversation until later that night.

What she had just heard though made Ruthe so happy she could hardly contain herself. Several operators and a supervisor noticed her mood and asked "Got a new boyfriend?" At that Ruthe blushed and made negative comments that sounded like lies because she kept grinning self-consciously.

June's shift finished first, so she waited in the lounge. When Ruthe came out of the toll room and put away her headset, June put down the magazine she was curling and uncurling, and they went together down to the brown Pontiac. Ruthe drove around while they talked.

After they had hashed over the problems of June's family, Ruthe's home situation, Darlin' Bonne's past and brand new personality, other stories Ruthe had heard of God helping people in desperate circumstances, and after several efforts to steer the conversation to how trusting Jesus Christ would affect her, June did pray. She expressed her desire very simply, "I want to trust You to be my Saviour. Amen."

That sentence prayer did nothing miraculous for June. She only felt more mixed up. It seemed all her orderly pigeonholed emotions were flying about her head now; she didn't know their names, never mind filing or stuffing them away.

Ruthe felt more taut herself. June's rebirth was more difficult than anyone's so far, and she had no wild and wonderful ideas for fixing June's life. She suggested living and working with Darlin' Bonne, but sewing and talking in a counselling with people did not appeal to June. On the other hand, completely deserting her family was advice Ruthe didn't want to give, although she understood June's feelings.

When they got to the Johnson duplex June's mother was sitting on her bare feet, still in blue jeans, watching a late movie. She sat so close to the old second-hand TV that she wasn't aware that Linnet, eleven, and Byron, seven, were up and quarrelling in the kitchen. Wes shut them up with threats.

As Ruthe had suggested, June told her mother that she had asked Christ to take over her life and help her live it. Her mother only glanced up a second, nodded and said, "Sure, Honey. You're a smart kid. You know what to do."

At that June seemed to fall together physically. She had been so sincere, and it had cost her so much to come to this decision. How could her mother be so unobservant? "R-r-uth-e!" June whispered in anguish, "What next?"

Ruthe wanted a good cry, but she tried to comfort June. "Things don't always clear up instantly. Let the Lord worry about it. Believe He has accepted the problem and is working on it right now for you." She hugged June and smiled at her with a face griped in sympathetic pain, "Because He really loves you!"

For the next couple of days Ruthe favoured June with more of her time, and she discussed the matter with Jesus whenever she got a few minutes. She stopped on the shoulder of the highway to watch a sunset, and asked the Lord, *is that the shade of rose June is in our garden?* She tried to plot various solutions. Expressing her frustrations and insights helped narrow down her grasp of the basic factors. Ruthe felt the Lord answered her when she remembered a Scripture passage which showed how He felt about such dilemmas.

THIRTEEN

She shushed her fresh twinge of guilt about visiting Grosz'mama less, by recalling that she had spent an hour there on Sunday afternoon. However, Ruthe had not been able to tell her anything confidentially. There was always someone else from her family hanging around there, or other guests. Even if she were to tell the demure woman she had always revered stories about her city friends, her secrets would be hard to keep from her family. Ruthe kept a finger in the door of this possible secret sharing, but there was no right moment.

Granny O'Brien on the other hand, constantly begged Ruthe to come again. She asked prying questions to draw out Ruthe's secrets, even her dreams. Granny had time to listen and did not trust anyone else enough to tell them the things Ruthe told her. She had earnestly begged God to put June on a right path with Him, and to help her do right by her siblings; still Granny was not sure God had heard that prayer. Ruthe explained that He had.

"Xecpting Ross, the gran'chil'en come off'ner naow," she commented, "But th're not the same as ye ar', lass. Me' ol'ness an' strang'ness do na put ye off?"

Ruthe managed to avoid a whole yes, and lightly changed the topic.

This got them talking about Ross and his need of a transformation. Becoming believers in Jesus had affected the girls and Keith so well that Granny was convinced Ross would be stupendously revolutionized once he had such an experience. A prize husband too.

Ruthe shared about some of her encounters with Ross, and how his sisters pleaded with him to become a Christian. "He seems to have hardened his heart like Pharaoh. So it puzzles me that he hangs around and goads us into talking about spiritual things; I like to think that means there's hope."

Granny seized on the hope and made it an obsession; Ross would one day be transformed. Ruthe noticed it grow in each subsequent visit.

One day Granny sent Ruthe down to the china cabinet in the dining room to bring up a huge family Bible. Ruthe got a wet cloth to wipe the dust off the covers before she left and Granny settled down in her quilts to, as she put it, "Mark a few spots fer m' fav'r'ite heir."

Telling the wiry Irish woman about June's dream and her disappointment brought Ruthe around to talking about her own dreams for her family before she could stop herself. Like June, she was able to love her family while being misunderstood. They were not demonstrative with their affection, but Ruthe longed to do something spectacular for them so they would know how much she loved them. "I'd like to send the whole family away on their first real vacation.

While they're gone, I'd secretly build a new house on our big yard, right in front of the old one. Later the old one could be sold or broken down. But our new house would be fully furnished and the yard all landscaped by the time they came home, just like those contractor's sketches in the ads."

"I do love my parents!" Ruthe insisted emphatically to Granny, as if all the world doubted it. "I ache when I think how Mom has been poor all her life and disappointed that we've always had to live in half-finished excuses for houses. Each time we've moved, Mom and Dad start remodelling, but the money or time runs out and it dribbles to an end. First it was the farmhouse, now we are on our third second-hand house in town. Each one is a slight improvement but nowhere like other peoples'."

"Why do'na they finish an' stay put?" Granny probed.

"Cause Dad either, suddenly has a job and no time, or he has time and no money. Mom keeps sketching her dream home on the back of old calendar pages, but I feel like I'm forever sweeping up sawdust in the corners on Saturday, so some rooms will be clean enough to walk in on Sunday." Her voice trailed off with the hopelessness of it. She moped on, reviewing how she couldn't afford to send them on a holiday, and if she could, she needed a car for her job, so how could they travel?

"Mom is a worrier, so she probably would raise half a dozen more impossibles. Like, she'd refuse to leave me behind, or say that Sharri is too young." Ruthe grimaced with a blush at the white-haired lady as she realized how amusing she must sound. "At times I guess I live right through it all."

Granny crackled with delight and reached out to hold Ruthe's wrist with a wiry grip. "Naow, naow, dear'e. Wha' was't ye sa'd aboot havin' faith fer the impos'bl? Ar' it the Mast'r's ain words ye read ta' me? *What's things ye desi're, when ye pray, belie' ye rece've 'em, and ye shall hav' em.*"

Ruthe blushed again. Her steps of faith were proving so successful with Darlin' Bonne and the Shop idea. She ought to apply them consistently to all areas of her life. Feeling rebuked she looked down and found her eyes filling with tears.

But Granny gripped her arm again and prompted her to pray about it right away, and aloud. Once Granny had joined and humbly pleaded for God to act on Ruthe's behalf, she felt encouraged. She resolved to stop wishing; to start asking and trusting far more.

Moments later they were back to June and her dreams. While talking, pieces of an idea came to Ruthe. "Mom recently hinted that we'll soon need a second car." She began to think aloud. "Though I can't share rent with June, maybe she'd be willing to buy a car with me. Used, of course! Then as soon as Dad's well-digging is finished, the rest of the family could go on a trip, and June could come spend a while with me. We might have to trade shifts with others to be on the same hours for a couple of weeks, but that should give June a break, no?" Ruthe grinned at Granny. "Think she might see her place is with her brothers and sisters again?"

Granny had listened closely. "Ye'r par-nts wo'd ap'prove o' her?"

Ruthe paused, doing a quick mental inventory of June, cross-referencing those traits against her parents' attitudes. Yes, Ruthe felt she could introduce June as a new friend from the office, and the family would never liken her to any of the other friends. She nodded, "June is a secret-keeper. And she has perfect manners."

"June might help ye dec'orate the new house!" Granny volunteered, getting into Ruthe's new positive fever.

Ruthe lit up, then her eyes dimmed as she said, "If there is no money there will be no house. Still. I'd have a couple of weeks where I could spend extra time with Darlin' Bonne, studying the designing lessons with her. That would be worth something."

The next morning when Suzanne wondered aloud what the other telephone operators were like, Ruthe said tentatively, "I've met one quite friendly girl named June Johnson. She's an oldest too, and is helping to support her mother and five younger kids."

Her mother overheard, and soon both parents were curious about June and wanted to meet her. Later at the office, Ruthe tried out this idea on her new friend, wondering what to tell her family if June refused.

But June jumped at the car and move to Kleinstadt plot. "Shall I come for supper tonight?" Discovering they both had the next day off, they decided to fetch June's overnight things, tell her mother, and make it a sleepover.

On the way Ruthe realized that she had made another decision quite abruptly. She got nervous. *One of these days, Lord, I'll stumble into a trap I've set for myself, right?* Still, it seemed natural after hers and Granny's prayer the day before.

The Veers thought June was citified, but nice. As Ruthe had expected, her parents were impressed with her friend's shy and polite ways.

Ben Veer asked June bluntly, "You a Christian?"

June nodded, "Just recently." Ruthe knew her family could have jumped to that conclusion because of June's neat, conservative appearance in her white blouse, brown corduroy skirt, and blue blazer.

Suddenly bold, Ruthe pretended to be hesitant and unsure as she raised the idea of buying a car together with June, and sharing it for the summer. Once paid for, one might want to buy it from the other.

Her parents debated this earnestly and looked for things that could go wrong, while June looked on amazed at adults hashing something over so frankly. Ruthe caught the look, shrugged lightly, and waited until her parents were repeating themselves and running out of steam.

"So? What's the final verdict?" she asked.

"If you find a used one that is drivable," said her mother. "It would be nice to have our own car back for our use."

"Yeah, we don't get to go on any holidays or rides, or anything as things stand now!" inserted Suzanne, busy paging a Sears catalogue.

Her Dad, of the old miser school, thought a car priced more than a thousand dollars was far to expensive. "It better be a good bargain, or I'll put my foot down!" he insisted with loud warnings.

"I'll sign up for a driver training course tomorrow," June said, showing a willingness to do her share.

The rest of the evening they discussed how much money they both could spare for car payments. When it came out that neither comfortably could give up more than fifty dollars a month, Ruthe began to have misgivings. What if they found some rattletrap that gobbled money every trip? Ruthe longed to go to her favourite spot beyond the willows to pray. But she had company.

Then her parents prepared for bed, and realizing that this was the month of June and the sun was not going to be fully set until after ten, Ruthe decided to take June out for a dusk walk before they went to bed. They agreed that June would not move in until they had found their car, and only if Ruthe's parents decided to go on the trip she hoped they would take with the old car. "To listen to your parents discuss things like that," admitted June, "Would be hard on me."

They bought a city newspaper at the convenience store. Then veered around the long way to Ruthe's favourite praying spot early in the mornings. However, it didn't seem to make a big impression on June. She put aside the idea of introducing her to Grosz'mama, (besides, she would be in bed already, Ruthe told herself), and took June around the outer streets of Kleinstadt to see the newest, most expensive houses in town. Now that impressed the city girl.

Back home they marked ads to phone in the morning.

Early the next morning Ruthe's mother was pushing them to get on with their search. Now that she had made up her mind she wanted to see it done. By mid-morning Ruthe and June had lined up several places and were on their way to the city.

One elderly gentleman in the Mayfair area advertised a white '65 Rambler for $500 dollars. Ruthe's father didn't think it could be worth anything at that age, but he liked the price. After listing all the things for which she should refuse to consider it, he had urged them to go there first.

The old man's wife had won it in a bingo back when it was new, but she had been ill a lot and recently her diabetes was worse, so they were moving into a seniors' home. The car had only one hundred and ninety-one miles on it. Ruthe thought it only fair to point out to the talkative man that this car in his shed was in mint condition. "Surely it is worth much more than five hundred."

He stood by his figure. It had cost them nothing in the first place, and they had only spent that much in license and insurance over the years. "The Mrs. and I agreed that if we got anybody inquiring, who looked like we'd like 'em to be our granddaughters or grandsons, and if they agreed to come pay us visits, even for small monthly pays on the car, thems the ones we'll sell it to."

Since her visits to Granny O'Brien were so easy now, Ruthe beamed. She leaned on June and whispered, "See? God is in this!"

June stared back, her eyes enormous chocolates. "God's doing this?"

"Sure. Isn't this exactly the car we need? And we can easily be their granddaughters! We could never invent a better deal."

Ruthe befriended and blessing the elderly couple with kind words as they went inside to complete the paperwork. While they chattered, and the woman in the wheelchair made coffee and set out the donuts she had warmed while they were outside, the old man laboriously wrote out their agreement on three sheets of paper with carbon papers between. When he and Ruthe and June had all signed, he separated the sheets and gave them each their own copy. This took an hour and a half. Although the girls were anxious to get to the Government insurance office to buy the license they restrained themselves.

When they brought out a lap full of photo albums, Ruthe crouched beside the wheelchair and asked as tenderly as if speaking to her Grosz'mama, "Can we save those for our next visit? You see, we need to go make arrangements for our first instalments on the car, and the transfer of license, and insurance in our names, and then I have to go back to my hometown for my Dad because June doesn't have her driver's license yet."

"Oh yes. Go! Go! We don't mean to steal your day," the couple urged. Ruthe and June left with many thanks for the lunch of donuts.

They hatched a quick itinerary on the way to the SGI office. Ruthe would write a cheque for the insurance. While June made appointments for her learners' and driving course, and took a bus home to fetch her cash, then go back to the couple's home to visit and wait, Ruthe would drive home to bring in her Dad to drive his Pontiac back so she and June could come away with the Rambler.

On the way back into the city again, her father grew boyish. "You know, I'm wondering if it might be a good summer for a fruit-picking trip to B.C. My well-digging job is just about done, and I have nothing lined up until harvest when I 'xpect I'll have more offers than I can take."

Ruthe pinched her face muscles tight to contain her surprise and the dancing in her eyes as she vouched that he could be right. "But you'll have to work on Mom."

"Mom and I earned good money in B.C. on our honeymoon, just picking cherries and other fruit. We could do that again!"

Ruthe's hopes began to soar. *Hey Lord, are You going to grant all my wishes in a row this summer?*

It really was her father who wore down her Mom's hesitation with all his vivid suggestions for making the trip worthwhile. She finally yielded on two conditions; Ruthe should get that nice girl, June, to come stay with her, (in case someone tried to break into the house, so she wouldn't have to fight off a man alone), and, Sharri should stay at home with Ruthe and June. "Seven is too young for serious fruit-picking. She'll just whine and get in the way."

"She's nearly eight! But what if June and I both have the same shifts?" Ruthe cried out. Everything had clicked into place so well until this moment. "In fact, we can't use the same car if we have different shifts!"

Her mother thought it was all very easy. "Take Sharri over to Grosz'mama's when you girls both have to be in the city. She can help Grosz'mama with weeding and raspberry picking."

Sharri was put out that she was too young for fruit picking in B.C., but could help Grosz'mama in the same boring way. She pouted and threw herself around.

"My original plan called for Sharri to go too," Ruthe confided in a rush to Granny O'Brien during a quick ten-minute visit. "However, I can see the other aspects working out. Mom's mind is settled, so I've decided to give in. It's the only way that's worked in the past," she declared with a firm grip in her jaw. Then she softened and thanked Granny for her prayers just a few days earlier.

Granny was thrilled to pieces that God had answered her prayers for June. She bared her forearms to do more real work in partnership with Him.

For two days Sharri cried and flounced all over their house.

Ruthe tackled her comforter role now. She and her baby sister had more than just their resemblance bonding them. She had rocked and fed this baby, and held and carried her for long spells when their mother had been ill. Ruthe knew Sharri adored her, so she took her aside and promised dramatically, "I'll let you in on a wonderful secret once the rest of the family is gone, Mietze[11]."

"I wan'a go to Saskatoon with you!" she howled.

"Okay. But that depends on how you behave. Also, if you can keep the secret I want to tell you," Ruthe repeated mysteriously, with her arms wrapped familiarly around her little sister with the elbow-length brown wavy hair, and rocking slightly left-right, left-right.

Sharri continued to pout a few more minutes, but with less energy. She accused her big sister, "You're just sayin' that to shut me up."

Ruthe repeated her promises convincingly.

"Okay." Sharri submitted at last. "You got'a promise me one other thing; some day we'll go on a holiday too. Just us. Nobody else from this stinky ol' family!"

"Us two will do oodles of special stuff!" Ruthe promised.

FOURTEEN

In the week that followed, while the Veer family prepared for their trip west to visit relatives and pick fruit, June moved in with three cardboard boxes of personal things and an armful of hangered clothes. Sharri had to sleep on the living room couch for two nights, which she did not like much, and Suzanne kept laying down rules not to touch her things while she would be away in B.C. It had been agreed that June would use Suzanne's cot for the next two weeks, but Suzanne seemed afraid that all her personal possessions would disappear.

The two working girls were home very little those two days. Ruthe supervised June in cautious highway driving trips in their tidy white Rambler with the zippy red vinyl interior. She gladly did this as an excuse to get to the city more often. She caught on that their shift differences would often give her extra hours in the city, which would in turn allow her to join Darlin' Bonne in her lessons more often.

Meanwhile, June found that she really missed her two brothers, Wes and Byron, and her sisters, Linnet, Gilda and Cheryl now that she was not constantly scolding and watching them. She was ready to squeeze in a morning or afternoon with them when she could.

A close look at the loose-leaf pages in the first package of the correspondence course convinced Ruthe that they could only gain from this designing course if they applied strict self-discipline and demanded more of themselves than the assignments did. It had basic information laid out in simple English, but it would be easy to cheat and get a diploma for nothing. Lord, she prayed with a deep breath, *Help me to be a loving but firm whipcracker!*

Both she and Darlin' Bonne had their interest whetted as they worked through the first lesson. It was on the ideal figure and how different types of real women compare, and how various silhouettes of clothes can disguise these variations.

They studied that first lesson in the basement apartment and suffered the noise of the hammers and power tools above them. But they could stand it because they knew the men would be finished in just another day or so. Then they could move upstairs and use the whole house, and set up the sewing machines that had arrived.

Even Darlin' Bonne saw that the instructions were simple enough for a twelve-year-old, which was where she placed her reading comprehension, so she was going to read and study one lesson for each morning the rest of July and August. Then she would do the assignments. As often as Ruthe could drop in she would check them over, try the assignment too, and together they would prepare their efforts for mailing. The rest of the time, except Sundays, was to be spent in practice sewing, from the simple to the more complex garments.

Ruthe had to leave to pick up June; when they came upstairs Keith and his friends announced that the woodwork was ready. One of the carpenters was packing away tools, and the other was gathering up the newspapers and drop sheets they had walked on in the various rooms.

"Sure glad you took the advice to divide up the rooms and get them all ready for your future expansions," said the head carpenter. "Got my wife in hospital and two jobs backed up, waiting. You're lucky you caught me in a slack period."

Ruthe joined Darlin' Bonne in thanking them all heartily. Darlin' Bonne gave them all hugs and reminded them to always trust God. As they choked up and accepted her love, Ruthe felt confirmed in her original faith that Darlin' Bonne was right for this plan.

They stole a few moments to go look through all the rooms where the dust was settling. Each of the five workrooms had a large, built-to-suit worktable or island in the middle, with recessed shelves and compartments underneath it. This was surrounded by sleek new counters along at least one or two walls, with a built-in desk for the sewing machine placed right in front of a window. Recessed lights flooded that work area too for overcast days and dark nights. Below the counters were many tray-like drawers for the countless notions they were bound to collect over time.

"Maybe we'll stock just one room at a time, eh, Ruthe darlin'?"

Ruthe thought that was sensible. Then she pointed out, "Actually, first the whole house needs a thorough scrubbing and shine. Guess we'll have to break the tight schedule we just made to dust the ceilings, wash the walls and vinyl floors, and put out the things we have already."

"Afraid I don't know a thing about such cleaning," confessed Darlin' Bonne.

Ruthe sighed. "I'm off tomorrow, and my parents are packing to leave day after, but June is scheduled to work. She's still driving with learner's so I'll have to come with her." She brightened as she looked into her friend's eyes. "I'll teach you spring cleaning."

It rained all the next morning, but by mid-afternoon, using Ruthe's spring cleaning approach, she and Darlin' Bonne cleaned from the back of the house to the front door. Ruthe opened the door wide, wanting to show the world they were not afraid of it.

"Yes!" Darlin' Bonne laughed. "Let's let in the sunshine and fresh air." She was teetering atop the back of the long curved sofa in the reception room, looking like a cartoon lemon character as the sun suddenly streamed in through the door and caught her neon yellow cotton shirt with a blinding brightness.

Ruthe had just landed with a running leap astride the high back of the lazy-boy chair, trying to help Darlin' Bonne re-hook part of the drapes on the track, when their beam of sunlight was broken by a figure in the doorway.

"Uhk-hum-m. Good afternoon. My name is Betty...."

They stared down at her. She had a suitcase in each hand and was wearing a grey suit skirt with a smartly pleated front slit, and a pale pink blouse with shoulder pads. Her white stockings and shoes also caught Ruthe's eye.

Hesitantly, Betty stepped further into the house. "Remember me? I worked in the hospital when you were there." She was looking at Darlin' Bonne. Her next glance included them both. "I overheard when you were planning this shop. And, I'd like to join you. That is, may I?"

Both young women came down to the floor as Betty introduced herself. "See," she directed this at Ruthe, "I come from a Christian family. My parents farm a couple of hours south west of the city. As for me; I've sewn all my life. Make all my own clothes and– well, I just love to sew!"

Her voice dropped a couple of octaves. "Mom and Dad wanted me to be a nurse. They were afraid I might lose my Christian faith working in the fashion industry. They persuaded me to go into this RN course." The light brunette, with the remarkably royal blue saucers for eyes swallowed with difficulty in her eagerness to have them understand. "Though I had no trouble with the classes, I got sick whenever I was put on Emergency rotation. Those mangled and sometimes bloody patients get to me. I haven't got the stomach for it!"

With a bit more control she added, "I wanted to quit, but I knew it would break my parents' hearts. I just didn't know what to do until I overheard you girls making plans for this shop. A place to meet the needs of spiritually starved women and girls while sewing? That's the place for which God made me!"

Now the lights came on in Ruthe's memory. This was the student nurse who had fumbled about the bed as she was spilling her idea on Darlin' Bonne. "I stepped on your foot, didn't I?" she exclaimed. "But look; we had none of this back then. How did you track us here?"

Betty's face had a hint of mischief. "Afraid that was my biggest hurdle. Our course started summer recess a few weeks ago, but my dorm mate and I stayed on in the housekeeping department of the hospital. Mainly because I wanted to find you before I went home to my folks. Information had no phone number for either of your names. Nor did Dr. Pollock know. Then, last night, quite by accident– or in answer to my prayers, I overheard a visiting husband tell his wife who was a patient, about the job he had just finished, putting huge shelves and sewing tables in a small house. When he described the vivacious young ladies who supervised the project, I knew it had to be you girls. So I asked him, and he gave me this address."

"Darlin', you can't stand the sight of blood?" asked Darlin' Bonne. She was already stretching a sympathetic arm around Betty.

Betty shook her head. "Yesterday I got hysterical when an accident victim passed me on a stretcher. Two doctors threatened to get me thrown out!"

She looked at Ruthe with fascinating blue eyes. "Please forgive me for begging. Could I join you? Today? I– I quit my job this morning."

Ruthe moved closer to Betty, but looked at Darlin' Bonne. They had buoyantly talked of expanding when their reputation grew, but they could not afford to hire employees yet. "Nursing isn't going to do you any good if you're not suited to it, Betty," Ruthe began, trying to be kind. "The thing is, we have to budget even our pennies until we can open for business, and then we want to pay back our loan first. We'd love to have a Christian like you join us, especially since you're experienced at sewing, and we're just learning."

"Oh I'm prepared to work for nothing too, if I may sleep on the floor and help make a meal once a day. I'm not after money. I want to do something meaningful with my life. That's all."

"Can you cook?" asked Darlin' Bonne with a sudden pounce.

Betty hid a giggle. "Like a farmer's daughter."

Darlin' Bonne impulsively jumped on Ruthe with both arms. "She can stay with me in the apartment downstairs. I'm getting sick and tired of canned tuna, and you did say my groceries would be cheaper if I cooked from scratch."

Ruthe broke up in laughter. "Okay. I want her to stay too!"

Betty's beautiful eyes enlarged with joy and relief. She was gathered in a mutual welcoming hug, and then taken in to to see the whole house.

After a bit they remembered to take her suitcase down to the basement, and all three chatterers had to compete evenly for a chance to speak as they made lunch and ate together. Then they finished the main floor spring-cleaning.

When Ruthe had to leave to pick up June for the driving lesson going home, her mind hummed with happy insights and evaluations that confirmed what her heart already knew. *Betty is a fine Christian with a good Bible upbringing; she'll be able to teach Darlin' Bonne when I'm not around. Another thing, sewing is an art best learned with over-the-shoulder coaching from an experienced guide; as a lefty I have to have time to figure out my own backward steps. Betty can teach both of us how to follow patterns and operate the machines! At the same time, she looks forward to the drafting and designing lessons.*

Ruthe's faith enlarged to believe other business principles could be ironed out as they came along, and the Lord would see that the girls would have food. *I'll bring them stuff out of our garden after Mom and Dad are gone tomorrow.*

FIFTEEN

Before sunup Ben and Anna Veer and their two middle children drove off in the old brown car. In the eerie stillness of dawn Brandt and Suzanne sounded loud as they shouted and waved good byes until they were off the driveway and out of sight.

"I wanna go too!" Sharri sobbed, leaning on Ruthe. Both Ruthe and June assured her that she would have a good time with them. Soon all three felt limp and yawned a lot, and went back to bed.

In her doze Ruthe felt vaguely guilty. She felt as if she had promised to produce her dream house out of a hat for Sharri and she had no idea how to pull it off. So far she had not told Sharri of the dream. Now she felt like she ought to throw some hindrance off her legs and go for a walk to tell the Lord she was ready for a miracle.

About ten o'clock Ruthe woke to the ringing of the phone. Quickly she stumbled to it in the kitchen.

"Kate O'Brien 'ere. Ru-tie, de'r, yer fo'k is gone?"

"Yes. They left–"

"Wou' ye drive in ta see me quick-like?" Granny had told Ruthe, as had Muriel, that she never used the phone at her bedside if she could avoid it. It was there so Bessie could call her doctor when she got chest pains.

With a stinging lump in her throat, Ruthe asked, "Something wrong?"

"No-o. It's jus' impor'ant I see ye."

Ruthe got no more out of Granny. She hung up slowly. "Weird," she muttered to June who had got up and was putting the kettle on. "Granny sounded as if she'd been running. Does her fear of phones do that? She knew I'll be in later in the day to see her."

"I'll stay here with Sharri. You better go." June urged.

Beginning to worry more by the minute about this city Granny who was so very different from her own Grosz'mama, Ruthe gulped some porridge and literally squeezed the accelerator to the city. A couple of times she let up as she caught herself speeding.

Granny's tomb-like mansion was in a rustle and flurry of activity. All the O'Briens were there. Ruthe was let in by Keith, saw Ross waving possessively at furniture and things in the parlour, and heard Mr. O'Brien talking to Bessie in the kitchen, while taking from the cupboards items that she said she had bought.

Suddenly needing to hurry more, Ruthe ran up the now familiar stairs into the room where she had begun to memorize the indefinite shadows. But the shadows had moved, and some had taken flight. Cathy and Muriel were soberly but efficiently tidying up for the undertaker who was expected directly.

For a moment Ruthe's heart seized up. She wondered if Granny had died and her body been removed. Then she saw; it had sunk so low in the huge bed, and the feather duvet had been fluffed and pulled so high that she could barely see the top of Granny's head.

"Ruthe," said Muriel, noticing her and slipping up to hug her left arm with both of her own. "I'm so glad that she met you, and through you, Granny found peace with God."

"She suffered so long," said Cathy, standing before her with arms cradled full of odds and ends and a waste basket of dirty tissues hooked her on little finger. "We're actually glad for her."

Ruthe looked again at the little head, which made her think of a broken doll some growing girl might have tucked away for the last time years ago. She began to quiver and in another minute she was crying. "I'm– glad fo-her– too," Ruthe hicked. "I don't know– wh-what I'm crying for. What happened?"

Bessie came running to tell us. She brought in Granny's mid-morning tea at ten and found her gagging for air with the telephone in her hands," said Cathy.

"We called the doctor and all came over at once. It was too late," Muriel added, stroking Ruthe's back. "Bessie is already packing in her maid's suite beside the kitchen."

Now it registered. Granny was dead. Still. No more accent.

The girls tenderly did what they could to comfort her, but this time she appeared to be the only one with tears.

Mr. O'Brien came into the room and said something or other very kindly to Ruthe, but the next minute she had no idea what he had said. Keith came in too, and her crying would not let up. She began to feel foolish. They, the family, were comforting her, slipping arms around her, and holding her.

Slowly they moved together into the hall, and gradually down the stairs to the main floor. Even Ross tried to be nice, sincerely nice, when he saw how upset Ruthe was. *Why am I the only one surprised? Caught off guard?* Ruthe thought, but it would be rude to say aloud.

If all that were not enough attention, a Mr. Newton arrived. He was Mr. O'Brien's law partner, (even looked like him in many respects, Ruthe decided), and he had been Mrs. O'Brien's lawyer she now learned.

As soon as he picked her out, he came up and said that he had most especially looked forward to meeting her. "I've heard of you from Ian here, and I understand, Miss Veer, that you were his mother's last close and dear friend, her confidante, is that correct?"

"Oh– ahm. I suppose... well, maybe." His special interest in her was confusing. "I don't know. Yes, we were friends." An O'Brien she was not, but she could concede that much. A hot, itchy, encircled-feeling enveloped her.

Ross came up behind her, his old puckish self. "Aw-w, don't look so worried, Ruthe-babe," he whispered with a pinch at her elbow. "The ol' witch was rather eccentric. Probably left you her old jewels." He glanced around for his sisters to overhear him and get excited. "Granny must've changed her will. That's why Newton wanted to meet you."

She turned instantly in shock to the lawyer.

Mr. Newton was speaking to Mr. O'Brien, but heard Ross and answered with care. "Ross, we might all be in for a surprise. Why don't we all gather in the parlour here, and I'll read her will."

"Before the funeral?" asked Mr. O'Brien, bewildered, "Ken!"

"Those were her orders to me, only this morning. She called me up and made me swear that I'd be sure to read it immediately after her decease. For some strange reason she was fairly sure it would be today. I told her I have to be in court in Regina this afternoon."

"Has the doctor been here yet?" Ruthe asked of no one in particular as she saw an undertaker and his helper come in and follow Muriel up the stairs. Instead of being in charge of this situation she felt like a victim of it. *Who is doing this?!*

"Her doctor was here and left minutes before you came, Ruthe," said Kathy and came over to stand protectively beside her.

Her cold hands began to tremble. Ruthe tried to hold them tight.

Mr. Newton scratched his neck with a well-manicured hand that wore an expensive watch on the wrist. "I have to drive to Regina at noon, and I'm afraid I won't be back until late tomorrow. Since I promised her I would read the will today, may I ask all of you to gather over in this room? If you don't mind?"

Obediently, they moved to the parlour and Keith ran to get Muriel.

A strange thought struck Ruthe. She had told Granny about her family leaving today. *She wouldn't– might she have given up her stubborn will to live so.... Or, would she have prayed to die just so she could leave me a gift toward the dream house?* A thud-like foreboding that she had hit the truth rose like heartburn to scratch her throat with acid. She swallowed with a wince.

Gulping weakly, she sat down where Cathy guided her, pinching and twisting her cold white fingers nervously. *Oh-ew-w. What's going to happen next? What am I doing in these people's lives?*

While they were settling, Cathy lifted a pair of huge thick red drapes aside to their gold-leaf clasps and though it was clouding over outside, her action brought patches of brightness to the dark oriental carpeting and the heavily carved antique furniture. Never having seen this room in light before, Ruthe could not resist looking about here and there.

But after Mr. Newton had read a few paragraphs of the will she sank far back into the recesses of the hard padded wing chair she perched on. *Me? uh-uh. I'm reading this up in our dim attic and my imagination is running away. Uh-Uh-uh!*

Ross found it harder to believe. He jumped up and dashed the length of the room and the entry, calling his late Granny some dreadful names as he went. The steel front door clapped like thunder.

The rest sat in silent shock as Mr. Newton went back to reading the will. Mrs. Kate O'Brien's last will and testament stated first, her lawyer was to be the Executor and instructed him to move as quickly as possible. She went on in glowing and complimentary terms to describe Ruthe, the first person in many decades to recognize a soul in her warped old body. God had sent Ruthe as His special ambassador despite her life-long rejection of Him and all her bitterness towards her own relatives. The minutes she had spent with her had lit up her life with a heavenly sunlight. Because of this, the will read, and because she admired Ruthe's ambitious dreams for her family and others who had no place to go, she wanted Ruthe to have the thirty thousand left in her bank account. Mr. Newton stopped reading to explain that he had told her the will's distribution usually waited for thirty days, so she had written out a cheque for Ruthe to receive today whether she died or not. He had it in hand.

Mr. Newton went back to reading the will; and Ruthe was to receive the old Greystone, as Ruthe had once called her home, in which to keep all her stray city roses. All property and furnishings in and upon the home were to be hers as well, except for the items following, and in the envelopes attached.

Money to build her dream house? This mansion too? Oh Lord! Ruthe could not help herself, her face screwed up; tears came down her cheeks in sheets.

Mr. Newton waited respectfully. while she fumbled in her purse for tissues, then he continued reading. Cathy and Muriel were to divide all the jewellery of her debutante youth, which she had threatened to keep from them since their childhood. With the will, for each granddaughter, were individual, hand-written letters of apology and love. Her only son Ian, and youngest grandson Keith, were designated various heirlooms and some old pieces which had the family emblem or crest on them. Both got personal and private letters of apology too.

Poor Mr. O'Brien, thought Ruthe, *he looks dazed.*

"I told her she didn't have to leave us anything," Ian O'Brien murmured. "She took me literally!"

Ross reappeared at the door as Mr. Newton read the gifts for his father and brother. Then Ross's own bequeath; the large family Bible that lay locked in the china closet in the dining hall. Ross turned purple around his nose and under his jaw.

Knowing how proudly she had doted on Ross, who was the most like his Granny, Ruthe stopped thinking of herself in stunned shock. Why, Granny and she had discussed Ross often. She had confessed quite candidly once, that though he was attractive and winsome, she thought him very immature. Granny saw great possibilities in Ross too, so they had pacted together in prayer, pleading with God for the salvation of his soul. It dawned on Ruthe that this change in her will had cost Granny, but showed her confidence that God would one day answer their prayers. Granny closed her will by saying God had promised her the day would surely come when Ross would raise a large family on the good words of that Book.

Hey, Granny, cheered a wee tiny voice inside. *You're some lady of faith!*

Ross left like a bolt of lightening.

A numb silence hung over the rest.

Ruthe was still looking into space, trying to grasp it all, when Cathy and Muriel focused before her eyes. "Granny did the right thing. Really, she did. We treated her so badly, and never gave her a chance to say all she felt like you did."

"We don't even deserve the jewels!" cried Muriel, kneeling in front of Ruthe.

"Bu-t, Cathy, Muriel; she idolized your girls! She never had the courage to tell you. Sure, she was terribly proud. Too proud to suddenly be demonstrative. But she loved you dearly. Every single thing that happened to you touched her. She quoted things you said as girls, and loved to join me in praying for you!"

Mr. O'Brien shook his head, then said kindly with only a hint of strain, "It's quite all right, Ruthe. She told me she might do this. I'm just so glad you could bring my mother a brief time of happiness after all those wasted years."

Keith stepped forward, nodding in agreement and about to speak similarly. At this point Ruthe dropped her face onto her knees and sobbed openly. Afterwards what she remembered fondly was that they all touched her and let her weep. It was permitted in this circle.

Because Mr. O'Brien and the sisters egged her on, Ruthe took the special blue-green cheque that Mr. Newton placed on the palm of her hand, and deposited it in a new account she opened downtown. He had explained that there were waiting periods for the rest of her inheritance and forms and procedures to be followed, so it could be several months before she had the title to the property free and clear.

My parents will be back in two weeks, flooded her mind. She said, "Granny liked my idea of building Mom's dream house while they are away on holidays. May I take Mom's sketches to a contractor and get started?"

"Today, if you wish," answered Mr. Newton, positioning himself for his own quick take-off.

There were so many new things for Ruthe to do that she didn't have time to weep much. In fact, she felt like a battery-operated toy that raced back and forth between two walls, bouncing off one to go to the other, her two walls being Kleinstadt and Saskatoon. She went home for the sketches, and picked a contractor from the Yellow Pages.

Mr. Jacobs was an enthusiastic, take-charge man. "Yep. Can adjust one of our pre-fabs to suit that plan perfectly. You get a building permit 'cause we'll be there Monday bright 'n early."

Meantime, Granny O'Brien's funeral the next day, was smaller than her daughter-in-law's. Ross absolutely refused to attend. Bessie complained that she could not help it that the old lady had not eaten in the last two days, and moved to her next employer's house. Only her son, three of the grandchildren, and Ruthe mourned her passing.

The death surprised the family. Though eighty-one, Granny's weak heart and nervous condition had been at the serious end of the spectrum for fifteen years, so they had come to accept it as normal for her. Granny's doctor claimed that the cause of death was a relaxing of her intense concentration on staying alive; she had simply picked a day when she would release her will, stop her pills, and die.

The fact that Ruthe felt the loss of their visits so sharply now caught her unawares. She had not realized she was so fond of the old woman. *To think, Lord, she was ready to die so she could give us our dream house!*

Over the weekend she slipped away for a solitary walk. Her shoes got wet with dew, tight and warped, as she walked around Kleinstadt and out to the cemetery a ways out of town. Ruthe needed to unload her mixed up feelings about the will. *I'm flattered that she wanted to do this, but is it fair to the O'Briens, Lord? The gracious thing would be for me to turn the mansion and stuff over to them, right? I really would rather be friends at peace than have what belongs to them.*

In the end, once unwound enough to listen to her Confidant, Ruthe sensed an urging to accept it humbly. She had not asked for this. It was all a gift. Nor had she lost her friendship with the O'Briens. *There comes a time to learn to say a lovely 'Thank you.' It is an art too. Sometimes saying 'No' is more pride than true humility.*

Ruthe sighed. *Yes-but, Ross...."*

To give in to Ross plays into his selfish hands. Do not let him disorient you.

Okay, Ruthe conceded, *But what can I do to handle Ross? He is so disappointed, so very angry!* If there was an answer to that she didn't hear it.

SIXTEEN

The local Kleinstadt authority came to quiz Ruthe Monday morning before he filled out a building permit. He chortled genially when she described her planned surprise for her parents.

It was at this point she finally told her pet sister the big secret surprise. Ruthe made quite a production of it, and was pleased to see Sharri get so excited. Like a puppy she wanted to be in and about the construction site, but with the extra trips to take June to work and spend her free hours at the shop instead of waiting, Sharri had to be coaxed to go to Grosz'mama's house nearly every day.

Ruthe meant to invest quality time with her own Grosz'mama, the time she used to give Granny O'Brien but felt scattered and unprepared yet.

The contractor's men were soon there and lost no time in digging the basement where Ruthe pointed, and framing the walls and foundation. Her parents had often pointed to the small knoll on the large front yard of their corner acreage, across the street from the railway tracks, as the very best spot for their brand new house.

Watching the framers, she smiled. The new house would hide the old one completely, which would add a wonderful dimension to the surprise when the family pulled up. The old driveway came from the side street so that lot could be cut off and sold later on. Ruthe became satisfied that the contractor and his men knew what they were doing. She could get on with her dressmaking schedule.

She was not at the shop as often as she had hoped, but marvelled at God's timing in bringing Betty to help Darlin' Bonne learn to sew. They were in full production whenever she dropped in.

There had been enough money left in Pearl's art gift account to order more machines, and Darlin' Bonne had already phoned some textile firms, who sent out salesmen. All were helpful, and one in particular. He offered to immediately ship at freight costs, a dozen bales or so, of remnants and millends for their practice sewing during the summer.

By the time Ruthe stopped in again, Betty and Darlin' Bonne were sorting the heaps of material with zest. There were lovely lengths of all kinds of material. Some of it even experimental. Betty could not remember a Christmas better than seeing all this fabric. Because she had experience, she could explain why she was ecstatic over this, or what that was wonderful for making, and what the cautions are when working with this rare and expensive stuff, and so on.

Although Ruthe could not be with them every day, she knew their daily routine and fell in eagerly when she could join them. As soon as Darlin' Bonne and Betty had completed the day's lesson they polished up their speed and creative finesse at the sewing machines. Each day they chose a different basic style, such as the shift or chemise, and made it in as many variations as they could. At each try they would work a little faster, smoothed out the procedures, and finished with a new, smarter look than the last.

The next day they would take something like the proportional basic-fit pattern and make it in as many looks as possible, and in as many kinds of fabrics and sizes as they dared without becoming ridiculous.

One afternoon while Ruthe was there they made A-line skirts until they had twenty-one lying all over the furniture.

Most of the clothes were in their own or one another's sizes. Naturally, they gave a number to Cathy and Muriel, and to June and her sisters, but Ruthe didn't dare take any home.

Some of the more experimental designs flopped, of course, but this happened less frequently as the days passed, and they discovered what worked and what looked repugnant, or just blah.

Betty glowed as a sewing teacher. While they worked, she told Bible stories to Darlin' Bonne. The younger novice was getting a condensed version of hundreds of hours of Sunday School lessons.

The second week in July they planned to graduate to the use of the fitted french sloper for princess lines, form-fitting suits and the like. Ruthe looked forward to that, but knew with Betty to guide Darlin' Bonne, she would not absolutely have to be there. Sharri did not like it that she was dropped off at Grosz'mama's every day, *and what if I'm needed when the house is nearly done?*

Ruthe was pulled over on the highway's shoulder, gazing at a sunset. Ostensibly it was to show June how beautiful it looked over a green wheat field. However, June was leaning back, dozing.

Lord, she asked, *would there be any harm in bringing Sharri in to the shop? She wouldn't be in the way. She'd gobble it all up with big eyes!* She decided, the problem was that Sharri might not keep the secret when their family got back. Though she was not sure what exactly her parents could do to ruin her life, they had warned and threatened so often to stay away from *different* people that Ruthe believed they could destroy her.

The sun's left-behind glory very gradually faded all over the wide table-top horizon of tidy grain fields, and far-flung farms and hamlets, so she rolled back onto the highway and headed home. However, her mind continued to work over every possible way of guaranteeing that Sharri would not tell. The plan that appealed most to Ruthe was to gradually train her with little tests and rewards if she did not repeat details or tidbits of secrets. *So, Lord, if I wait to see how much she blurts out about this house, I can't take her along to the shop just yet, can I?*

At home, seeing the progress on the construction site, she became obsessed with the need to have it completed before her parents got back. If she could just do that, everything else would turn out right. Sharri would somehow be satisfied, Darlin' Bonne's Shop would be a big success when it opened, Ross would calm down and become a rational young man, June would be able to look after her brothers and sisters sensibly in a good place, and all the world would get along.

"Aren't we going to get Sharri?" asked June rousing from her nap.

"Oh yes!" Ruthe turned back the blocks she had gone too far.

Little opportunities to talk with her Grosz'mama were popping up almost daily. This unworldly paragon was always poised and dignified, with a quiet self-possession, and a reverence for anyone or anything with life.

She had explained for June's benefit, "So many times, when Mom was sick, we kids were taken to Grosz'mama's. It's almost a ritual too, that on Sundays we go there for faspa[12]. And if any of our uncles and aunts or cousins show up, we all troop over to get in on the visiting. While Grosz'papa was alive, obeying him and promoting his wishes seemed to be Grosz'mama's constant pleasure. I wonder if he didn't adore her so much he ended up doing things her way too."

"Lucky people," June murmured, "If you can get it to go both ways."

Grosz'mama dreams too, Ruthe told herself as she parked in that familiar driveway, *but only as high as she knows she can reach. More practical than I,. She lays plans and follows through with quiet determination, thinks nothing of letting others count on her, yet never takes for granted they ought to help her.*

At the door Ruthe toyed with the idea of confiding her city adventures to Grosz'mama. It had helped when she told Granny O'Brien things. Sort of guided her to understand her situations and options better, and here she had an even more noble woman already in her life. However Sharri was noisy with impatience. "I've waited long enough for you!"

Maybe tomorrow?

The next day was much like the ones before. Ruthe spent the morning with Sharri, but mostly in the garden, then took her to Grosz'mama's. After dropping June at her mother's housing unit for a couple of hours before their evening shifts, she treated herself to another afternoon at the shop.

The three of them, Darlin' Bonne, Betty and Ruthe, had just brought their machines into the front sewing room, the one that used to be the kitchen and dining area, so that they could all work together.

Betty had recently had the rest of her personal things forwarded from her former apartment, and among them was a lovely stereo and tape collection. "A bribe of sorts, from my parents," she told them. That morning Keith and an older friend had wired it up in such a way that it provided gentle background music throughout the house. The three chattered merrily above the music and their purring machines.

About the middle of this progressively hotter and more humid afternoon, they heard a sudden rap at the side door.

Darlin' Bonne bounced up and dashed around the corner. In seconds she brought back two teens. "Hey, a delegation from our neighbours," she announced impishly. "They've heard such a racket from here the last few weeks that we scared 'em. Two have finally braved all kinds of invisible goblins to see what we're doing."

"I'm Donalda McPherson; Donnie, if you will," said the one with the dark and downy soft curls. "From next door." Her head tossed slightly in the direction of the taller, older stucco house on their right.

"I'm Louise Nunweiller," said the willowy girl with the carroty pixie head and the orange juice freckles on the softest, daintiest face Ruthe had ever seen. "I live across the street in that brick house."

They looked about seventeen, maybe eighteen, and good friends judging by the way how their arms draped over one another's shoulder.

The seamstress-designers introduced themselves and explained what they were doing. They added that they hoped to be finished with this self-training program in time to open up their shop in September when everyone usually bought school clothes and fall and winter outfits.

"We'd better be ready," laughed Betty, "Our patrons can't afford to pay us grocery money much longer for the outfits we give them."

"#@$%+! Cool! Dec–cent!"

"What a set up!" The visitors were intrigued by the discoveries.

"Can we join you?" Donnie piped up in her bird-like voice. "We finished school the other week and still haven't found a job."

"Yes," said Louise raising her foot behind her to rub her ankle. "We combed the downtown stores for six hours steady last week."

"In heels, can you believe?" laughed Donnie.

Ruthe sat back in astonishment, which caused her to prick herself. She couldn't make this out and stared ahead to think. *We've told them we are Christians and this shop is not going to be just another dressmaking place. We expect to help some people, but I was braced for those who would laugh at us. These two don't think we are funny.* She glanced at Darlin' Bonne and Betty. *Starting our faith, according to the church saints I've heard, is suppost to be difficult.*

Darlin' Bonne's eyes flicked recklessly, as she grinned at Ruthe. Since Ruthe was not answering, she turned to the newcomers and explained fluidly that this shop was going to specialize in helping women and girls become new and different by believing and trusting in Jesus Christ. "As manager, I can't very well take on anyone has not experienced this for herself. She'd soon feel out of place here."

"So?" asked Donnie with a saucy toss of her curls, "How long does it take to believe in Him? To qualify?"

"If you won't be opening until September you'll have almost two months to help us become like you, right?" asked Louise with a quizzical, yet eager look on her delicate face.

Ruthe expelled a deep, nervous breath. *Say Lord, what's going on here? Are we to encourage them to become Christians just so they can work here?*

That matters? He whispered gently into her conscience.

"We'd love to have you meet Jesus and share Him with us," Darlin' Bonne told them enthusiastically. She turned on Ruthe and Betty, "Wouldn't we?"

"Of course!" they chimed in.

Darlin' Bonne turned back to the new girls. "You realize God's love cost Him a lot. We can't treat it lightly, okay? After forgiving us everything and living in us, He deserves honesty and complete obedience from us. Without strings or conditions."

The newcomers looked at each other.

"Okay," said Donnie carefully. "I always thought spirits and such sorta spooky, but this doesn't seem to scare you three. I've been trying to talk Louise here into sex– but I was feeling guilty about it anyway. Your relationship– you all look real happy, but it's not the same, is it? Like as if, as if you're in love, all with the same man, and not a bit jealous?"

"We are in love with Jesus Christ," said Betty warmly. "You are right, Donnie, in that this is a higher, nobler relationship. Because of His holy love and wonderful sacrifice on the cross for our sins and shortcomings, we care for each other in kind, respectful ways. Jealousy fades out of the picture. We are humans, so we may have to fight it down from time to time in the future."

"I listened to a Billy Graham speech on TV, and want to know that kind of God," Louise said wistfully. "If yours is the same One, I'm ready for it."

"Great!" cried Darlin' Bonne, reaching for her Bible. "I've only been a Christian for a couple of months myself– not like these old hands, but I'd be thrilled to show you what I know about it." She paused to look back at the other two. "May I? For practice?"

Ruthe and Betty nodded, their hands still working at their sewing, but slower now, ready to stop as soon as needed.

Darlin' Bonne did a fine job explaining salvation in Christ Jesus, and how it could be had for believing and thanking Him. The new girls were willing, so Darlin' Bonne prayed a prayer of introduction as Ruthe had done, let them each pray their own prayer of coming to Christ, and then she closed in another short prayer of thanksgiving.

Ruthe was impressed, and a little nonplussed at how Darlin' Bonne copied her example. Betty followed with another prayer of welcome, and so she did too.

After a few minutes of talking about prayer, they all got up for a tour of the whole shop. They were just back to show them the lessons, and how their designing plan worked, when they heard a shrill whistle outside.

"No!" cried Donnie, "My supper signal. Got'a go."

Louise glanced at her watch just as Ruthe did, and said she was expected to have dinner on the table in half an hour for her mother.

Ruthe realized with a guilty thud that she would have to skip her meal as a consequence for not watching the time. She had to rush to pick up June in time for their evening shift.

From that day on Donnie and Louise were part of the group that Ruthe thought of as *Darlin' Bonne and the girls*. Later, at Louise's suggestion, that same group cheerfully made it their business to find out upon her arrival, when Ruthe needed to leave, so as to share the responsibility of clock watching.

The new girls were content to wait for wages just as the others, however, they continued to live at home, which meant they slept there. All their waking hours were soon spent at the shop. In no time Betty was cooking for four or five, or six, if Ruthe and June dropped in at the right time. It was a running miracle how there was always food.

Ruthe was expected to pick peas and the other vegetables as they ripened in the garden, get them cleaned and into their freezer. Several times she had bigger pickings than she could finish before time to leave for the city so she brought a bucket of this or that to the shop to help out with the groceries.

The girls attended the same church as the O'Briens. Once they mentioned these treats of garden produce in the foyer chats, other women began to bring them extras, even fresh preserves. The more they praised God, the more food came in.

Betty shopped frugally for their staples, and began to bake at night to avoid the heat. Since transporting bags of groceries by city bus was a problem, she trained her shop sisters to co-operate in a search and gather method that raked in the best deals in a fraction of the time she needed to shop alone.

When they got a ride to the Farmer's Market Betty would sigh, "If only my family would accept my career change. They always give away so much from the garden to the less organized neighbours."

While Ruthe was busy back at home a few days, Darlin' Bonne and Betty taught Donnie and Louise until they were all caught up at about the same place. When she came back again, all were taken with how well Donnie did at the sketching lessons. She had not known she was an artist. Louise, they had found, had a fine sense of colours. If in doubt they could always check with her rather than the colour wheel.

Ruthe was pulled in various directions. The house under construction gave her a heavy sense of responsibility, and a vague foreboding. What if her parents didn't like it? Sharri wasn't getting enough time. Grosz'mama deserved more of her attention as well. Her job as an operator was taking on an incidental aspect. The empty Greystone might soon be attracting vandals; when and how should she care for it? But at the little green shop on Lindsay she was greeted with soothing melodies, merry laughter, and sisterly hugs. She couldn't imagine sleeping here, but it was a happy hideout. For the smallest excuse, even a few moments, she would detour and make a stop there.

When Ruthe came for Sharri at Grosz'mama's she was greeted with, "What took you so long? You were suppost to be off duty hours ago!"

SEVENTEEN

By Wednesday, the foundation and basement cement were considered hard enough, and the skeleton of the house went up fast. Mr. Jacobs put extra men on the job so the walls and roof were completed by the end of the first week.

At that point Ruthe felt the world was on her side. She grew whole units of confidence as she watched with Sharri, who darted all over the yard and around the workmen like a puppy trying to experience it all at once. Because Grosz'mama asked such sincerely interested questions, they out did each other to tell their grandmother what progress was being made each day. Sometimes if Ruthe and June were gone too many hours, Sharri and Grosz'mama would walk over in the late afternoon for another look as the workmen packed up their tools.

June watched the sisters jealously. "I wish we girls could share that kind of innocent happiness. Especially Linnet and I."

"Tell me more about Linnet," Ruthe urged. "I did see her in the kitchen the night you tried to tell your Mom you were a Christian. She disappeared right away though."

"She stays out as much as she can. Linnet hates our family and what it means for her. Instead of bettering herself, as I try to do, she's growing hard and cruel."

"How old is she?"

"Twelve, going on forty-two," answered June, getting sadder. "I have got angry calls from her teacher, and twice the police brought her home when she was caught shoplifting."

Ruthe dropped her eyelashes and prayed silently. Then she reached for June's hands and held them as she prayed aloud for Linnet to give June hope. She also made a mental note to seek Linnet out.

The other operators had picked up that Ruthe was willing to work their evening shifts. The whole week felt wrong for her if she had to work a Sunday morning, so she would do all kinds of trades for others if they would take that one off her hands. She was getting to be popular for shift trades. As was June, who wanted the same hours. It meant that Ruthe could get the garden produce looked after in the mornings, see what progress the men were making on the house, and waiting a bit after lunch so Grosz'mama could have time for her afternoon nap, Ruthe and June took Sharri over and visited briefly, inspected and tasted from her raspberry patch, and then were off to the city until late at night. It seemed to work better to come wake up and take the limp, sleepy Sharri home, then to be gone all day and resist her accusations all evening.

June was amazed that Ruthe's Grosz'mama never complained that she had to stay up late for them. Rather, she would smooth down her cotton print apron over her dark dress as she laid aside her big German Luther Bible and welcomed them back. "You gurls mus' be gettin' dizzy wit all dis drivin' back un forth," she would marvel. "I pray every day dat our Loving Heavenly Fadder keep you both safe."

"And He does, Grosz'mama," Ruthe was always quick to assure her.

She did not realize that she had formed that habit because her mother worried so much, until June pointed out some observations. "Your Grosz'mama shows a lot of respect and trusts that we know how to cope in the city. Why do you brush off and hide the extras you do besides your job there? You make the operator work sound so complicated. She would be proud of all you're doing at that dress shop."

"I'd like to tell her," Ruthe conceded, "I know she wouldn't gossip but if Mom and Dad ever questioned her– she wouldn't cover up for me."

"Wish I were so lucky..." murmured June.

"Hasn't she been adopting you?" returned Ruthe.

June blushed happily. "Yes, Grosz'mama remembers everything I say or do. I think she likes me. She said she prays for me."

Because Sharri bragged on the dream house every day, Grosz'mama liked to ask about its progress from Ruthe and June. After their answer she often shook her head, "You young wimen wit education sure make lots of money nowadays! Dat you have courage to build a brand new house is somethin' to wonder at. In my day, men mostly decided tings like that."

"City girls learn lots of things," Ruthe tossed off. Her conscience bothered her the next moment, so she added that they really did not make very much.

"How do you afford a house-present?" Grosz'mama asked, "You don't borrow from bank, no?"

"Oh no. No, the Lord has wonderfully provided for it. I'm not in debt for this new house!" She belaboured the point, hoping that by focusing on praising God, the matter could be dropped. Her Grosz'mama let it go without further comment, but after that Ruthe worried about explaining how she got the money to her parents. They would not just drop it.

Oh Lord, give me the right answer! Keep them from being angry! was her constant, repetitive prayer every moment she was alone from then on. *I can't tell them about Granny, nor the inheritance. What can I say without lying?*

By the middle of the second week the contractor's men had the walls finished inside and out, and the shingles were on the roof. Painters were now working at a pace that Ruthe thought might be a little fast even for professionals. She had told Mr. Jacobs they had two weeks and was pleased that they would be done by then. She began to think about what furniture her Mom would like to find inside as she walked through the new rooms.

"Who did ya give the landscaping contract to?" asked one the painters as she passed him.

Ruthe stopped in her tracks. "That's not included?"

"Not in this contract," said the man. "Jacobs is sending a cat today to level the ground, but that's all."

Ruthe grew frenzied. She believed she had to get the house ready by the weekend. She hurried back to the old house, and rushed June and Sharri through the pea-shelling and preparations for the freezer, all the while chattering about needing to buy furniture at least, if she couldn't seed a lawn, and plant flowers all around it.

June reminded her that they both had the day off. "Or did you have other plans?"

"Hallelujah! That's right!" With relief, Ruthe tried to narrow down the list of furniture stores to try. "And we need some groceries too!"

Sharri rolled her eyes, and made funny faces for June's benefit at her sister's hysteria. Just in case, she made a stab at asking to go along to the city.

Ruthe paused a second. What could go wrong if they were just going shopping? "Okay, Mietz, today you get to come along." She prided herself on her ability to be generous even under pressure.

With a quick light lunch she had all three of them in the car and on the highway. A few miles down the road, Ruthe recalled that her new account was getting very low. She'd written that one cheque to Mr. Jacobs, and there was only about three hundred, or three-fifty left. She couldn't furnish a single room on that. Her eyes narrowed at a spot on the white line ahead on the highway and threw herself heavenward in panic, *Lord, I'm desperate! I've walked into a corner and I don't know how to get out. We can drag some of our old furniture into the new house, but now I more or less had my heart set on nice new stuff. Dare I ask for a miracle? Please? –Or. Do You want me to say, 'Sorry, I forgot I have no money,' and turn around to go home?* She lifted her foot slightly from the accelerator as she prepared to–

"Are you thinking of taking any pieces out of that big place?" June asked in a soft, low voice.

For a second Ruthe was confused. What big place? She glanced at her friend and caught the furtive look meant to keep Sharri out of this conversation. "Oh," she said. "The Gre–" and she cut herself off.

Lord, is this a prompting from You? But the furniture in the Greystone is so humumgus. It wouldn't look right in our new house, and it would be still harder to explain. For sure I'd have tell about Granny O'Brien's will! Her mind nearly went over a cliff at the thought.

Ruthe had recently promised to show the Greystone to June, knowing she would enjoy it, since she liked interior decorating. How could she now, with Sharri in the car?

Cathy and Muriel had suggested she sell some of the antiques if she needed sudden cash. She had told them to let her know if they heard of anyone interested. But if she stopped to inquire, Sharri would know about them too.

Oh dear God! Ruthe prayed. *Am I ever in a tight place! You know I wanted to teach Sharri to keep secrets, but I hadn't worked out how yet. She's so young and unpredictable.*

Darlin' Bonne passed through her mind as well, but she knew the shop account was very short of cash now. She ought to be raising funds to help the girls eat and pay the power until the end of August. Best to stay away today. *Maybe I could phone the O'Briens from a pay phone?* Just then they neared the city, and slowed for a light at a service station. She spotted a pay phone, turned in suddenly and parked by it.

In just moments she was back in the car, grinning. "I'm going to make a couple of brief stops before we start shopping, okay? Then we will have a good time choosing nice things," she promised.

At the O'Briens, Ross was just getting into his Mustang as Ruthe pulled into the drive beside his car. He stepped out with one foot, "I should sue you!" he yelled at her, shaking his fist violently in the air. "I should sue you!"

Ruthe got out and stared at him, her heart going out to the deep pain she heard in his voice. She shut the Rambler's door. "So why don't you?" she offered, recklessly wanting to give him a chance to win his inheritance all back.

"I'm too mad, jus' way too mad!" he yelled. Then his Mustang spat gravel and tufts of lawn grass as he backed up and tore away.

Cathy came out to join Ruthe, standing in the sunshine on the gravel drive. "Ruthe, Dad and Mr. Newton just got him to agree not to go to court about Granny's will. Ross needs to cool down."

"But–?" Ruthe gulped, moving further away so that June and Sharri couldn't overhear them. She saw they were discussing "that angry man."

"Look, Ross says he's madly in love with you, but I'd keep out of his way until he's more predictable. Here's your key. Mr. Newton and Dad agreed after Ross signed that thing that you could start using Granny's stuff and have this key, even though the paperwork won't be done for a few months yet. They suggested you move in– or have someone else you trust– before vandals discover it vacant."

105

Ruthe accepted the key with a sigh, then a sudden glance towards June. "Where are the people that want to buy the Irish crystal?"

"Muriel is on the phone to the lady."

About then Muriel came rushing out, waving a piece of paper. "Here you go, Ruthe! She says she'll meet you at this bank down town in fifteen to twenty minutes with a certified cheque." They started to chat, but when Ruthe saw Sharri getting out to join them, she got nervous, said a quick thanks and good bye and hurried back to the car.

"You know those ladies?" Sharri asked.

"Get back in, Mietz. Yes. They're my friends, kind'a..."

"Who was that man that yelled at you?"

Ruthe played deaf and busy steering as she went back to the street and right into the next drive, leaving the girls to gasp at this even bigger mansion while she dashed to the door, used the key, and let herself in.

For a full second she froze, and turned chilly and damp as she remembered that Granny was not upstairs any more. "This deathly still mound of stones is suppost to be mine?"

She kept from further thoughts by forcing herself to find the crystal in the china cupboards beyond the huge polished dining oval, then into the kitchen, festooned with yellowing plants hanging from the baskets over the work island. She found a linen towel, wrapped the heavy faceted cream and sugar set in it, then spied a pile of paper bags and snapped one open. She smiled tightly as the whole bundle just slid into the bag.

"I'm busy driving, Sharri," she answered tersely to fend of more questions. Minutes later she was downtown. She parked by a large furniture store, and sent June and Sharri in to start looking around. "I'll join you in just a few minutes." With the brown paper parcel tucked close under her chest with both arms, she walked briskly down the street to the named bank. The right lady spotted her immediately. After a satisfying peek into the bag and linen in a discreet corner, the woman handed her a cheque for two thousand dollars.

Ruthe slipped it into her wallet, planning to hurry across the street and up a block to the bank where she had deposited Granny's gift cheque. The woman suggested she open an account here, naming some services she especially appreciated. Ruthe blinked. *Why not?*

The teller who helped her was wonderfully efficient yet pleasant, giving her a temporary chequebook, promising more and explaining advantages.

Ruthe began to relax and smile to herself. She had never known any one who had accounts in more than one bank, so she felt she had stumbled on something clever.

Their shoes were killing them hours later, when June reminded Ruthe of drapes and curtains. They stepped into a drapery store, but when she saw the prices, she gulped and went into such a coughing fit the clerk brought her a drink of water.

"Three hundred dollars?" Sharri echoed the drapery clerk in a dramatic whisper, the way she'd heard her sister do it in different store. She was walking about on the heels of her shoes because of the blisters by her toes. "Those sheers," Sharri pointed at a display of custom-made voiles, and asked Ruthe, "Are three hundred dollars?"

"As Grosz'mama would say," explained Ruthe hoarsely while the clerk went to answer a phone, "It pays to make our own and keep our money."

"Do you know how?" asked June.

"I'll have to learn," answered Ruthe, expelling all her breath. "I only have two hundred and twenty-three left. We've blown a lot of money this afternoon." She felt grateful that June could quietly go along, helping to decide on colour and style, without asking questions about the money in front of Sharri.

Sharri, bored, swirled quietly on her rubber heels, saying, "I can't wait until they deliver those beds and the mirrors for our girls' room!"

Ruthe bought three rolls of pleater tape instead, and put off the clerk by saying, "We're getting too tired to decide today." In her mind she was already asking the girls at Darlin' Bonne's if she could have some of that sheer stock since she was a partner. Maybe she could sew them right there.

She promised the girls just one more stop before they went for a few groceries in a supermarket and then home. Parking in front of the shop she dashed in, glad that both June and Sharri wanted to sit in the car, and breathlessly explained her predicament to Betty.

"Well, I've helped my mother make drapes before," Betty volunteered. "Why don't I start them for you tonight? Maybe we'll even have them done by Saturday night. Come pick your material."

Gasping with relief, Ruthe did so, then ran out to the car to fetch the pleater tape, saying, "These ladies have offered to make them for us! Isn't God good?!" When she dashed back in Darlin' Bonne was in the room. "Hey, Ruthe Darlin'! Guess what I got for you!" She turned around then held up a new portable sewing machine.

Amid her shrieks of surprise, Ruthe learned that another fabric supplier had heard of the nice deal the other salesman had made; to win more orders from them when the shop opened, he had given them this sewing machine gratis. It was not quite of the industrial stamina of the ones they had purchased, so the girls had agreed they should give it to Ruthe. She should pretend to learn to sew at home, and when she began to sport all kinds of new clothes, everyone would believe she had made them at home.

Ruthe decided to accept. Because of the timing, it would appear she had bought it to stock the house for her mother.

She could not hide her excitement as she carried it to the car, so she explained as they went for groceries, "I know those ladies a bit. They sew a lot. And when I explained about needing drapes they offered to make them! Isn't that marvellous? What's more, they gave me this terrific deal on this brand new sewing machine for Mom. "Course, we girls can all learn to sew on it too!"

Sharri liked that idea. June just listened and smiled.

You know, Lord, tonight I should ask June if she'd like to move into the Greystone with her brothers and sisters. She'd make a great tenant, wouldn't she?

Later that evening, in old comfortable shoes, they walked to the post office. June had been in her element when they tried to match pieces from several different stores; now she was unusually talkative. Her rhapsodic chatter about the colours and style choices they had made that day was abruptly cut when Ruthe read aloud a postcard from her mother. *"Since Gramma wrote to Aunt Lena that you girls are doing good & bcuz we found a new orchard today, where we all get good wage for picking fruit, we are staying here one more week. Will bring car full. So wash all the jars, okay? Love, Mom."*

Ruthe skipped and kicked up her feet as she walked, daring to sing out loud and nearly full volume, "Glory be, glory be! Oh glory be to God! He really, truly never makes a mistake!"

"What's it mean?" asked Sharri.

"It means, Mietz-Kitty, that we have time to arrange for landscaping, if the Lord provides, and the men can finish all the cabinets and shelf arrangements I asked for in the bedrooms.

After Sharri was in bed, Ruthe and June went to sit outside where they could stare at the new house surrounded by brown soil and building scraps, and wait for after dark breezes. There Ruthe told June about the Greystone and needing a tenant so it would not look deserted. Also, ultimately it was to be a place to bring girls in trouble to stay a while. June accepted and grew more relaxed and talkative as she saw her dreams coming true.

The next day the carpenters were packing up and moving out, with none of the cabinets or shelves even begun. Ruthe demanded a reason. They said, "Wasn't in the contract, Miss. Our company builds the house, not the furniture."

"Mr. Jacobs promised me! I showed him all my Mom's sketches and he promised to work it all into his blueprints."

"Miss, the boss found a pre-fab plan that fit those drawings pretty close. What you got here is a popular pre-fab house. Period. It don't come with furniture or shelves an' such. You get a special finishing carpenter for that stuff."

Ruthe stewed and fumed and worried until it was time to get ready to go to work for their evening shifts. June persuaded her to stop in to see her lawyer for advice. Ruthe was afraid he might give her a big bill just for his office time, but her need to know won out.

After some short questions, Mr. Newton told her that since she had paid Mr. Jacobs with a cheque right up front, before he began the work, she had no leverage to insist that she had understood the extra cabinets to be included unless she took him to court. She really ought not to have paid him until she was fully satisfied the job was done right. "Try reasoning with him, in case his workmen just got their instructions wrong."

She called him from there, but the contractor was as innocent as a newborn calf. He insisted that it must have been she who had misunderstood. He was so very, very sorry about it all, but he only built houses. "I've scheduled my men at another work site, a church."

Ruthe sank together in a heap. She'd been had. She was embarrassed. What if others learned of her foolish business move? *Mr. O'Brien will be so disappointed in me!*

"We all learn from our mistakes," Mr. Newton reminded her. "But look, you have all kinds of things in your mansion to turn into cash. Heard you had quite a shopping spree yesterday on one or two pieces of Irish crystal," he said, in a gentle tease.

She looked up in surprise, "How–"

"My sister-in-law is a real antiques hound. Just don't let her loose in that house alone. She won't be able to resist the temptation to steal from you. Here's a couple of insurance appraisers, who can give you a better idea of values before you sell things." He handed her some small cards. "If I were you, Miss Veer, I'd get to know what I have before selling to the first collector who shows interest."

Ruthe listened with attentive nods, thanked him, then asked for her bill.

There was none. "I'm still the executor of the will. I consider counselling you, and seeing Mrs. O'Brien's intentions carried out as part of that job." He smiled, resting his chin on his manicured hands, "Since you spent all the cash in the estate, I'll tell you when you must sell a piece of crystal to pay my percentage." He smiled a bigger smile. "Better yet, save me– if you find it– the gold Meissen snuffbox with gilt and gemstones."

Cheerfully Ruthe agreed, and asked him to write it out. "I've asked my friend June to move in as soon as my parents get home, so that the place will looked lived in. She'll be delighted to sort through the antiques and make lists. June even wants to study up on them now."

Mr. Newton was very happy as he handed her his business card with the snuffbox described on the back. "Ian once showed it to me when I was a kid. I've never forgotten it."

At work Ruthe remembered how Keith had helped to make the shelves at Darlin' Bonne's and began to hope again. When she phoned him on her break, Keith was glad for the challenge. "I'll bring Gregg and Chris, and we'll have Ross drive us out each day."

Ruthe couldn't believe Ross would do it.

When he did, she was astonished. Ross now acted as if there was nothing wrong between them. However, he openly talked of marrying Ruthe, and assumed he would win her over. His self-confidence was up.

Ruthe's went down. She resolved quietly that once Keith knew what was expected of him, she would be gone most of these days.

Besides regular kitchen cabinets, (which Keith said would be cheaper to order in ready-made units, but they would install), her Mom had wanted lots of panty shelves, and extra storage in the bedrooms. She was making the master bedroom the girls' room. For years Suzanne had slept on a cot and she and Sharri had shared a foldout davenport; now each would get a single bed. Ruthe wanted a whole wall of cupboards and built-in vanities like she had seen in a magazine, that she proudly showed to Keith. The wall left of the door was to be a huge walk-in closet covered with mirror panels to give the pink floral beds and fluffy beige rug the look of femininity and spaciousness she had seen in Cathy and Muriel's bedrooms.

Brandt's room would be papered in a very pale plaid, and she had ordered a plain pine bedroom suite. If he ever carried out his threats to drop out of school to go make a life of his own that room could easily be turned over to someone else.

"And in the basement?" asked Keith, taking notes as they toured.

The size of the basement surprised Ruthe. She was used to the hand-dug cold storage cellars her Dad had made so far. "Even with the space given to the furnace room and water heaters, and the laundry corner," she said to Keith, "Do you think there's room for a couple of small spare bedrooms?"

"Why not wall off those two corners for bedrooms," Keith suggested, "And that one maybe for a workshop for your Dad?" The rest, he felt could be used as a family entertainment area or developed otherwise as they had time and funds.

Ruthe responded enthusiastically, and helped Keith and his friends mark out where to add walls, and a future washroom.

Each morning after that, upon the arrival of Keith and his friends, chauffeured by Ross, Ruthe briefly discussed the day's work and the supplies to be ordered, then found reasons to soon be on her way. But Ross nagged for attention, becoming bolder as he saw his time frame shrinking.

Ruthe didn't find his witticisms funny. Sharri did. His one-liners sent her into great fits of giggles. Every time Ruthe made half a turn she seemed to bump into Ross. She got impatient, then stern, and shoo-ed him away. Ross merely spun aside, then back in her way for physical contact, even if only accidental. He followed her around the new house with foolish questions, quips and showy antics.

What does he think he's doing? Ruthe moaned to the Lord more than once. *Trying to marry his lost inheritance? He could just politely ask and I'd be a pushover, right?*

The kitchen cabinets were up late Wednesday afternoon, but Ruthe was concerned at all the woodwork left yet. Thursday morning she tried to apologize and think of a way out if they needed it.

Keith answered firmly, with echoes from Gregg and Chris, "We're the fastest beavers you could get, Ruthe. We'll do our very best. It will go faster now. Count on it." Keith nodded upstairs towards the unseen Ross, "He even helps once you're not around."

Gregg called out as he put down an electric saw, "You treat us like adults; okay, we do adult work."

"Is she backing out?" Chris asked Keith in a horrified whisper from the door of the fast-forming guest bedroom.

"No, no," Ruthe assured them quickly. "I just wanted to make sure I wasn't asking too much of you guys."

Keith's face split in half with a grin. He grabbed her hands and spun Ruthe around so her red floral print blouse billowed as if in some square dance reel.

Ross came into the basement in time to see this. Not to be outdone, he swooped up behind Ruthe, wrapping his arms about her waist with a wolfish growl, ready to dance.

Keith held up his fists and snarled with disgust, "Go look for your skull, Ross. You're out of it!"

Ruthe wriggled out of Ross' grasp and gave him a smart slap on his hand. "Given up being winsome, have you?"

He slunk off to pout.

Meantime, Ruthe gripped her nerves, found Sharri to take her to Grosz'mama's, and then she and June were off to the city, to help make the drapes for one thing.

Mr. O'Brien sought her at the shop. He was not hard on Ruthe at all for paying Mr. Jacobs in advance. "I bet you won't make that mistake again, right?" She confided about paying Mr. Newton with the snuffbox he wanted.

Ian O'Brien stood very still for a moment. "Ken knows the value of that item. You are paying him a generous $75,000 fee with that. I suggest you don't give it to him until all the estate work is done. Or you might be fleeced again."

Ruthe's jaw fell away. *Lord! I've got to be careful with those old things!* she prayed quickly within. Then she softened. Reaching out to touch his arm lightly she asked, "Okay. And what treasures would you like from that house before I make any more foolish mistakes?"

He shook his head, then offered a suggestion. "Since Ken has the estate going into your name at land titles soon, why not get a landscaper to dig up an apple tree or two from the back, where the orchard is too crowded anyway, and have it planted on your parents' place? Or a plum tree if you prefer."

Beaming, Ruthe asked directions, then phoned the business he recommended.

The previous three evenings, June had taught Ruthe what she knew about wallpapering, and they had finished the few walls that were to get that touch. That evening, she and June hung all the drapes and curtains, and dusted the last of the sawdust out the bedroom shelves and closets.

The boys expected to be done the next day. That in mind, Ruthe stayed home, and sure enough, about mid-afternoon, they were loading the last of Keith's tools into Ross' small Mustang trunk. Ruthe sat on the front steps of the new house to calculate what she owed them. She had just crossed off some math work to start over, and was nervous that Ross might hold her up with another approach, when one of Keith's co-operatives shyly stopped beside her on the step to thank her for letting him help with the carpentry.

"At three dollars an hour?" she teased, "You guys did me a big favour."

"Yeah-but," interrupted Chris, "I wouldn't have missed seeing how Christians get along for anything.

"Right," added Gregg, coming back from the car. "Now we know what kind of love Keith was talkin' bout."

Her face stretched and wrinkled in astonishment. Had they seen Christian love here? In spite of all Ross had done to thin down their tempers?

Presently Keith stood behind Gregg and Chris, hardly able to restrain himself. "Com'on ya guys, tell her."

They got shy and shrugged, "Aw... you can."

"They asked Jesus to move in last night," Keith volunteered eagerly for them. "He can make all the renovations He wants!"

"That's terrific!" Suddenly Ruthe rolled backward, trying to suppress a giggle. "Ho-ho, so that is why the contractor got away without doing everything?!"

"You mean," asked Chris, catching on, "You were meant to get gypped? So we'd come?"

Ruthe thought so. That stopped the new believers. God would do miracles for their benefit? They mattered that much to Him?

Only Ross went back to the city disappointed. All his attempts at getting Ruthe's attention had turned sour. Driving the boys was to be his selfish opportunity; now it was his good deed. He had even helped to hold and hammer for Keith.

That evening they vacuumed and cleaned the new house thoroughly and persuaded themselves it was okay to lug in the clothes and bed linens and personal effects, and to start sleeping in the new house.

June and Ruthe had both traded away their shifts for Friday, Saturday and Sunday to have the weekend free. Excitement built with each passing hour. The next morning, Grosz'mama came slowly, carefully walking the shortcut through the back alley, to see the house since Sharri had run over the day before to brag it was all done. They were moving in.

Grosz'mama followed the three girls from room to room, stroking and admiring the woodwork, while they explained about the talented young men and Sharri chattered about that funny guy.

Looking out of their parents' bedroom window, they saw an appliance van back into the new dirt driveway. As they were going to the front door, a bigger furniture truck stopped on the street and started to back in as well.

The men from the first confirmed with Ruthe that they were at the right place, and soon waddled in with appliances strung between them on woven straps or harnesses. June directed traffic, while Ruthe went to meet the workmen on the second truck.

The appliance truck was just gone, and the furniture pieces starting to come in, when a pickup with the name of a landscaper came. He was followed directly by a huge truck with a tree swinging up in a metal claw, and the back loaded with rolls of grassy sod. Again Ruthe darted outside to show them where to put their deliveries and signed another invoice.

When she came puffing into the kitchen through the back door, she found Grosz'mama backed up against the kitchen counters, waiting for permission to slip out somehow and go home so she wouldn't be in the way. "But don't you try to cook in this ruhrei[13]," she stressed to her in-charge granddaughter, "Send Sharri to get your meddach[14]. Yoh?"

Gladly, Ruthe accepted the offer of lunch and escorted her grandmother through the back way, and the garden, to the path through the willows that were a shortcut to her house.

With much cheerful shouting the furniture got into place, the apple tree was planted in a deep hole in the front and closed over again, then surrounded with a slightly sloped green lawn. Flushed with both heat and excitement, Ruthe helped the landscaper dig holes for the flats of flowers and rooted twigs he had in the back of his pickup. "You wait," he promised, "Next year you'll have roses and delicious berries along here." He urged her to water generously all summer.

It turned out that Cathy and Muriel had asked him to dig them up at the Greystone at dawn that morning, and bring them along.

By six o'clock the last of the hectic parade and workmen were gone.

Ruthe's gait was weary, but when June called out to come see the view from the street, she loped down the freshly gravelled driveway to have a look.

A neighbour, one of many who had walked by slowly all day, paused to exclaim, "Eh, look't that!"

Ruthe's eyes swept over the lovely white ranch-style house with royal blue roof and trim. The wide-branching apple tree in front of it, gave it a touch of artistic life and welcome. The bright petunias and greenery around the base of the house framed it. The crushed gravel clearly marked, as if a royal carpet, the way to the double car garage attached at the left of the house. Satisfied, she sighed.

The polite conversation with June and the neighbour about the tree and the pleasant view, was refreshing.

As they were coming back in, Sharri came through the garage from the back, calling, "Ruthe! June!" Spotting them, she bounded to them screaming, "I love the back yard! Come see!" Grasping her sister's hand, "Ruthe, isn't this the greatest day that ever was?"

Her mature sister agreed, "But why you're not hoarse from all your yelling today, I don't know."

"To use Grosz'mama's expression," June said, "I'm a dishrag."

Ruthe smiled. "Me too!"

June had carried groceries and kitchen things into the new house by the box full. Now, with pleasure they opened the new fridge and found a watermelon in it. There were still rollkucken[15] left from the lunch Sharri had brought from Grosz'mama's. That would be supper. They carried their platters of food to the backyard and sprawled on the freshly laid lawn, not far from the ticking sprinkler.

Even so, Sharri leaped up. "One more day! Tomorrow Mommy and Daddy and Brandt and Suzanne will all be back!" Pointing at the new house, she spun in circles, "Won't they ever be surprised?"

Again, Ruthe laughed with satisfaction.

Heaving from her calisthenics, Sharri plopped to the grass. "Can you picture it, Ruthe? What are they gon'a say?"

Ruthe's conscience twitched. She had not given her family's reaction much thought. Only the planning stage. All this work had finally made it seem real. She leaned forward letting the juice from her last slice of watermelon dribble to the ground as she ate. Then she wiped her chin and mouth, and laid backwards on the grass with a long, audible sigh. She rolled her head slightly sideways to stare at the house again. *Very nice! Lord, You really pulled off a beautiful miracle! It's all I hoped for....*

While Ruthe drifted off into her private world, Sharri entertained June by demonstrating the expressions of surprise her family would show and what each one would say. "Suzanne will go, 'Look! Mom's dream house fell out of the sky after all!' She always used to say it would have to fall from the sky if we were ever to get a nice house."

"Daddy will go, 'Huts-drot! Waut bediedt dit?[16]' Brandt won't say anything right away. He'll go like this–" Sharri tilted her head with a bemused smile. "Then he'll scratch or squeeze one of his pimples on his throat, and maybe he'll say.... Oh, I don't know, but it will be funny, like, "I swear; sugar!' Or whatever."

"What about your Mom?" asked June.

Sharri's face tightened and she pursed her lips. Ruthe felt herself tighten up all over too, though but half listening. "That depends," answered Sharri. "If she likes it, she'll check it all out and ask lots and lots of questions. About ev-ver-y little thing."

"If she doesn't like it?" asked June.

Sharri turned to Ruthe. "She'll still ask questions, right? Only somebody will have to cough up the good answers."

A twitching expression crossed Ruthe's face, and she sighed as she turned to look up at the sky. *Those good answers need some working on, Lord. What are they?*

"Too bad no neighbours are popping by tonight, to give you practice," suggested June lightly.

"Oh, they've been asking Grosz'mama every day," said Sharri. "They all know about this house."

Ruthe didn't want to think about reactions just yet. She focused on the world of nature. The sun had slid down to the tops of the trees by the tracks, so they were in shade, but it was another three hours or so until sundown. The air hung still and windless. The hum of traffic on the highway, two blocks away, sounded clear but was lulling. Only a block away to the south, at the edge of Kleinstadt, in a slough or pond, the frogs and crickets were clearing their throats for their evening concert. Sharri stopped talking for a few moments. Ruthe savoured the lovely quietness that now swirled around them like a gentle breeze.

A distinct crunch of car tires was heard on the gravel out front.

June and Ruthe sat up with a start. *They couldn't be arriving stonight! Not until Sunday!*

"Maybe I spoke too soon about neighbours," offered June.

Sharri was up in a flash, and streaked to the corner of the garage. "Hey!" she yelled, "It's Ross! In a convera'bull full of people!"

EIGHTEEN

Ruthe sighed deeply. *What makes that guy tick?* she asked the Lord in frustration. Putting her hands behind her head she fell back to the grass to put off her encounter with Ross.

"Hi, Ruthe," said Cathy, beaming down at her in a summery sleeveless blue dress that Ruthe remembered making at Darlin' Bonne's. "We brought you some visitors."

"Yeah," said Ross, his face suddenly over her air space like a bothersome fly. "Had to, while your folks are away. Else you won't let us near here," he sneered.

Embarrassed, Ruthe was already scrambling to her feet.

Sure enough. There were Cathy, Muriel, Ross, and another girl who was reaching for his arm, plus three strange young guys about eighteen to twenty. All in casual-clean date clothes, with an air of élan, except for the third girl.

"Wha– What's this mean?" she asked, with a panicky thought to protect her new house.

"These are guys I used to hang around with," explained Cathy in a low voice aimed behind Ruthe's shoulder. "I've tried to tell them what happened to me, but they just don't get it. I thought, as your parents aren't home yet, maybe we'd come over. We get to see your lovely new home, and you get to show them what a Christian is really like, okay?"

Muriel helped Cathy make the introductions all around. The giggling brunette on Ross' arm was Ann Mueller. Cathy's men friends were: Lloyd Sherwood, a tall handsome blond, and a tall, dark-looking Scot named Graham McKenzie, with a burr in his voice, and there was Gordon, plain and medium everything, except for dull-steel eyes.

"Just Gordon," added Cathy softly in an aside. "He has no other name."

Ruthe greeted them as pleasantly as she could, and tried not to be too confused by what Cathy expected her to do with them.

Ross offered to show Ann the house. Ruthe thought she heard a note of pride in his voice, as if he had helped. Muriel and Cathy wanted to see it too. They all trooped through it, wandering in and out of the rooms, while Ruthe milled between, to explain or name things.

When all had their curiosity satisfied, they came back to where they had started on the patio stones and lawn in back. Soon they were stretched out in relaxed positions, making themselves at home.

June had disappeared to cut up more watermelon. Now she brought out a platter of juicy slices for the guests.

"Ruthe," begged Cathy a few minutes later, once all the guys were slurping at their refreshment. "Would you like to explain how, or why...(yum-m), you're so different?"

"Uh– how do you mean, different?"

"For one, you really love people. As you told me once, until your heart hurts sometimes. I hate to think what a mess our family would be in if you hadn't stepped in to love us."

Muriel added, "Then there was the way you were able to break in to our Granny's soul when no one else could."

Cathy nodded emphatically. "You changed her outlook so much that she changed her will– and here you are spending it on your family instead of yourself. Like; would I?" Cathy glanced around for confirmation, "Would any of us?"

Sharri tried to distract Lloyd and Graham with a riddle. Tugging at Sharri's shirt and giving her a glare, Ruthe said lamely, "I– just love surprising people. I can't say it any better than you did." Instantly her conscience pricked. This dream house was an answer to prayer. A prayer she had not prayed seriously until Granny O'Brien had egged her to it. She ought to give credit where it was due; not let them think she was so marvellous. Would these fellows laugh?

"Actually, I didn't do anything," Ruthe corrected. "It would never have happened, except for this very good Friend I have."

Cathy and Muriel smiled knowingly.

It occurred to Ruthe like a whiff of an idea, that she might pretend they were all as willing to hear her thoughts and experiences as Cathy and Muriel were. Then she could just let things flow from her rather than agonizing over every word or sentence. She smiled shyly around at them all, and slowly began describing her family and giving thumbnail sketches of each.

"Mom is our perpetual worrier-perfectionist. Dad loves to talk to folks, but since he never learned social graces he doesn't know when to stop and let them have a turn. He could be a more creative type if he'd stayed in school, or had Mom's self-discipline. Though I can't see it, others tell me I have traits from both my parents." Ruthe shook her hair loose and fluffy in a playful but woeful bewilderment. "So I must be an agonizer and a dreamer at the same time."

"Then there is my brother Isbrandt, who likes to go by the more modern non-Mennonite name of Brandt." She sighed, "He has a lot of intelligence– I'm sure of it– but Dad won't hear of taking him to a remedial reading specialist. Doesn't want any of his kids addled by a shrink, he says. I'm afraid he's going to drop out of school, and being shy, he may not get a job. I don't want him a welfare bum.

"Suzanne is our family beauty. I'll leave it at that. Then there is Sharon Rose here, my pet Mietzi." Ruthe saw questioning eyebrows. "It means kitten in Low German."

At this introduction Sharri crept closer, made cute mewing sounds and then curled up with her head and arms on Ruthe's lap to imitate a relaxed kitten. Everyone smiled, indulgently.

June asked softly, "How about Grosz'mama?"

While Ruthe described her grandparents, and some of their history, the over-exhausted Sharri fell sound asleep.

Fingering her sister's soft brown curls and ringlets, damp from the day's perspiration, Ruthe found herself moving right along to describe things she felt deeply about. "Grosz'mama calls it being tenderhearted, but it feels odd to be able to see people's character quite clearly from within. My parents call it *having a runaway imagination.*" In her loneliness she had discovered it possible to have a continuing intimacy with Jesus, her Saviour, just as she had heard in sermons. "I think of my prayer times as walks and talks with Jesus in a lovely garden. When I make a new friend it's as if we come around a bush and discover a beautiful new rose. Jesus and I admire it together."

No one paid attention to the dusk creeping up. Shadows silently reached to each other and united. The visitors listened with hardly a stir. When Ruthe paused, Cathy or someone asked a question, and she was off digging into memories of her carefree childhood on the farm, Grosz'mama's godly example, and her bitterness when her mother was sick for long spells. Especially, she went into how her daily date with Jesus brought her to where she gave Him her fantasies and plots.

"Whenever I read something in a magazine or book about other lonely people, particularly in crowded cities, I yearn for them to discover Christ like I have." Ruthe crossed her arms and concluded, clutching her shoulders in a vicarious hug, "If only I could persuade you He has enough love to be as intimate with you as with me! I get cramps in my heart, just thinking about it!"

It was harder to see one another now, though June had slipped up to turn on the kitchen light. That cast a dim glow over the tops of their heads, but it was next to impossible to read faces. A chilly breeze swept down over them. This stirred the guests. They got to their feet, murmuring about it being time to go.

Cathy darted back after the others were out of earshot, "Thanks, Ruthe," she whispered, bending down. "I think they understand. I'll talk to them as soon as I get a good chance. Tell you what happens next time you drop by, k?"

Ruthe had Sharri sleeping in her lap and could not get up quickly enough to follow them to Lloyd's convertible. She sat listening as their footsteps, then the tires faded in sound. *Should I have invited them to accept Christ too? Oh no, I've lost the moment!*

After Sharri was in her own brand new bed, June and Ruthe talked a bit longer with more and more yawns as they made up the other two beds. They evaluated Lloyd, Graham and Gordon, of course, but Ruthe wanted to sort out the dilemma she had just run into; did sharing one's faith mean one had to make a sales pitch for a decision to trust Christ every time one met a new person?

"I hate imposing on people," June said with a grimace, "Nor can I tell stories like you do. I don't think I should try to witness. I just turn people off."

"I'm scared too," Ruthe answered quickly, "But are you sorry I imposed on you? Remember, I just told you what I thought the Lord would do for you?"

"No, you did the right thing." June admitted. "Though the first time you brought it up I was terribly disappointed. My mind was not in gear to hear. The guys that sat back there, were listening tonight. Deep down, they heard you."

June got starry-eyed as she tried to decide if she liked Lloyd or Graham better. She felt the rich one was still on Cathy's leash, so she was ready to settle for Graham. She turned on Ruthe, "Unless you go for him first."

She shook her head. "I'm not chasing anyone, remember?" Ruthe reviewed briefly her agreement with God to let Him be her matchmaker. After a long stretch and yawn, she added, "God can see far more and better choices than I can, all around the world. This way I'm not limited to my field of vision."

June changed the subject and drooled about moving into the Greystone. She was full of questions.

Ruthe was already putting her head down on her pillow between answers. Now she assured June again that they would go explore it as soon as her family was home, and they'd check out the rest then.

They took their time getting up the next morning, knowing they had the same Saturday evening shift. However, by noon they were organizing for another shopping trip. Groceries mainly. They would bring the groceries back to their freezer, so Sharri was allowed to come along.

Driving off, they glanced back to admire the new house. Sharri asked, "Hey, Ruthe, what are you going to do with the old house?"

"Mietz; it's still Mom and Dad's. They can sell it, rent it, or whatever."

"I hope they sell it." Sharri wiggled dramatically.

"Why?" asked June innocently.

"So Mom and Dad can afford our groceries and then Ruthe can use her money to buy me nice new clothes."

Ruthe spied into the rear view mirror to watch Sharri. "How about if I sew you some?"

"You can't. You're left-handed."

"Oh?" Ruthe drawled mysteriously, "You might be surprised at what lefties can learn to do."

"Mom says lefties sew backwards," she recited blandly.

On the highway, Ruthe was overcome with an irresistible desire to drop in on the O'Brien sisters. After a few minutes of silence, Ruthe was praying, *Lord, I feel this urge to see the girls. I hope You are in this, 'cause if Sharri tells Mom and Dad about this fancy address where I've stopped twice—* June signalled that she'd stay with Sharri in the car.

Ruthe nodded her gratitude and thanked the Lord. Then she explained to Sharri that it pleased Jesus to keep promises, and sometimes that included keeping secrets. Sharri was already convinced.

Both Cathy and Muriel appeared in the doorway when she rang. They were on their toes immediately. "Guess— just guess what happened last night!" shrieked Cathy, hugging Ruthe wildly and lifting her over the threshold into their home.

"Wh-what? I...."

Cathy was laughing so hard she was crying. "Last night, after we left your place? Well, Ross started to mock you and joke about something you had said."

"He was uncomfortable," Muriel put in breathlessly, having her go at hugging Ruthe, "Because everyone else in the car was so quiet."

Cathy continued, "Anyhow. Suddenly Lloyd says, 'Dry up, Ross. You are not funny. So this Ruthe does her thing; believes in God and talks to Him. It works for her. She doesn't wake up in the mornings and hate herself like I do.'"

Ruthe stared at Muriel for confirmation, who nodded vigorously.

Cathy couldn't wait to tell more. "Next thing we know, Lloyd was stopping the car and saying, 'Cath, I'm pulling over here and I'm going to sit here until I get this— whatever it is that you and that girl have got.'"

"No!" Now Ruthe began to feel excited.

"Yeah, he pulled onto the shoulder right there!" echoed Muriel.

Cathy rushed on, "You should'a heard him. He says, 'I don't want that phony sissy stuff. I want to be transformed in and out.'"

"You led him to the Lord?" Ruthe leaped at Cathy with a wild hug.

"I did! First time since I became a Christian, I helped.... Oh, I'm so happy, Ruthe!"

Muriel shut the door and crowded them into the kitchen. "That's only how it started. I was talking to Ann in the back seat all the while, and she said she felt rebellious and wretched all the time, even though she loves her family, just like you had described your-self. Ann wanted new attitudes too."

"So you—?" Ruthe couldn't believe this much had happened so soon after they left Kleinstadt.

Muriel beamed. "Prayed with her an' everything."

"Then, all of a sudden," Cathy interrupted again, "Graham and Gordon announced that they wanted to pray like that."

Ruthe's jaw dropped.

"There we were on the shoulder of the highway, sitting in the dark, for at least an hour or more!" repeated Muriel, elation fracturing their story.

"Ross too?" Ruthe was ready to believe anything.

Cathy's smile vanished. She shook her head sadly, "Even Lloyd and Graham asked him if he would, but he refused and got madder and madder all the way home."

"He rather took it out on poor Ann," said Muriel, "Although at first he just turned his back on her and wouldn't speak to her."

"Dad was reminding us this morning," added Cathy, "How the fact that Ross is upset shows he's still reacting. To Christ, that is. If he were indifferent it might be another story."

Sharri was impatiently honking the horn. Ruthe had to go, but the three promised each other not to give up on Ross, and that they would get together with the others as soon as they could work it out.

Between reassuring Sharri and distracting her by pointing out new things to see in the supermarket aisles, Ruthe hummed to herself. She said to the Lord more than once, *Just think! Not only is our family getting a new house, but strangers have come to love You through this. Oh-h, I praise and thank You, my wonderful Lord and God!*

While her cup of joy was so full, she didn't allow herself to think about the little dark bumps crowding the edges of her consciousness, the thoughts that this was all too good to last, and that she had not figured out yet how to explain the dream house to her family. Ruthe chose to revel in all the good happenings since Granny O'Brien and she had prayed and asked God to bring her dreams, and June's, to pass.

The next morning, Ruthe, Sharri and June went to Sunday School and the worship service at the small white church in Kleinstadt. As they had the last two Sundays, they enjoyed extra attention and compliments as friends asked about the new house, and when the folks would arrive.

"Later today? Oh-my. I'm sure they'll be thrilled to pieces!"

Sharri was artless and unselfconscious as she bragged about the beauties of their new home, while June stood quietly nearby, trying to adjust to all the chattering before and after the more serious, holy part of the morning.

Ruthe thought she put on a fairly good act herself, chattering about how pleased her parents would be, and covering the growing tension in her deeper spirit that they might over-react negatively.

After lunch the three of them lounged about like the idle rich, while Ruthe grew more and more absorbed inwardly. Ruthe helped June move her things into one of the new spare bedrooms downstairs, where they had dragged Suzanne's old cot. They joined Sharri on the front entrance steps, watching and waiting.

At long last, at quarter to five, the old brown car slowly turned into the new driveway, with wide-eyed stares. As Ruthe had expected, a hysterically happy Sharri flew at the car doors.

Just like that Ruthe jumped up, turned into the house, darted up the hallway to the bedrooms, then back toward the kitchen, paused, then through and whirled down the stairs into the basement with the spaces for extra rooms that Keith had divided off. Ruthe started into June's room, then backed up and veered behind the furnace into a low crawl space under the stairs.

She heard them come in, making a terrible to-do about everything they saw. "Where's Ruthe?" they demanded of Sharri, then of June.

Neither of them knew. "She's right– here! Somewhere!"

"How did all this get here?"

"Who did this?"

"Somebody has to have an explanation for this!" Her mother stamped her foot. "Where is that daughter of mine? She must be ashamed of herself. I want to get to the bottom of this!"

The emotional knot in Ruthe's throat grew into a huge hippopotamus. How could she tell them about Granny O'Brien, or her deep prayers of faith, when her parents still recited memorized prayers? How could she say she had done this because she loved them, when they never said they loved her? It wouldn't come out of her throat. "Oh-h-h... dear God!" she wept as scalding tears wet her knees and her shoulder heaved with sobs. "De-a-r-r God!"

NINETEEN

June made an attempt to defend Ruthe to the Veers, without giving away about the inheritance from Granny O'Brien. She pointed out, "All this is evidence of Ruthe's love for you. It proves how highly she thinks of her family." June appealed to Sharri for confirmation, "She worked hard to get this wonderful surprise ready, didn't she?"

Sharri gladly seconded it, but drowned out her words with her giddy laughter and jumping around so Ruthe couldn't hear each word.

"You mean," her dad asked June, "That God just reached down from heaven and set this house down on our yard? With all this furniture and stuff?"

"Does it seem that way?" June's voice was shy and low so that Ruthe could hardly make it out.

More confusion. Then June must have pointed out the deed and new insurance papers on the kitchen counter. "...It's added there to your property."

Her mother read parts aloud. Then she interrupted herself, "It's plain the girls are not upset. Nobody held a gun to your heads while this house was built?"

"No way!" Sharri shrieked and tumbled around as she yelled, "Never-ever!"

"Nobody can build a house so fast," exclaimed her dad. "What were we gone? Just a couple of weeks?"

"Wake up, Dad," retorted Suzanne, "This is not the old days any more. Folks do so build houses real fast. Like in pre-fabs, n' all–"

"Oh. You mean like a barn-raising?"

"I bet I know why Ruthe went to hide and cry," announced Sharri. "Cause she knew you wouldn't say 'thank you.' You'd just argue about little things. Like she said once, 'In this house the dust never settles until somebody gets the blame.'"

A fresh sheet of hot tears came down on Ruthe's knees as she heard that. She had been just about ready to dry her face and go up to join the battle. Now she had to wait a while longer.

"Don't you like this house?" asked June, puzzled. "Aren't you grateful for a lovely new home?"

Thank You Lord! Ruthe sniffed, *June knows I'm listening. She's trying to get them to say they love it. Isn't she sweet?*

She was stunned to hear her mother choke as she said, "It's exactly what I've been dreaming and begging for ever since we got married. I just can't believe it's true! Only Ben never–"

Her dad's roar of self-defence was matched by Sharri's shouting, "Okay. You love it? Then let's all be happy and live here!"

June added, "Give God the credit if you don't want to give it to Ruthe. She'll settle for that."

Brandt came in the back door, slamming it. He admired the backyard which he had just checked out, and commented on what he thought was a fine crabapple tree out front. "It'll take our biggest ladder to reach the little green ones on top."

Their parents went out to look, and then to bring in their cases of fresh fruit and their luggage.

Suzanne asked what was downstairs.

"Come with me!" cried Sharri, "I'll show ya!"

Ruthe grew quiet and waited in her undiscovered hiding place.

Suzanne excitedly wanted to claim the bedroom Ruthe had just helped June move her things into for this last night. She listened as June softly explained the advantages of the larger girls' room upstairs and took Suzanne up to see it again.

When the sisters were busy there, June came back down to rearrange her already boxed clothes. Ruthe slipped in then to thank her, but ended up having another cry on her friend's shoulder.

"Let's slip out and go to the city, maybe to your mansion, until they all go to bed," offered June in sympathy. "You are in no shape to talk to your parents today."

Ruthe nodded. First she had to go to the girls' room to get her purse and better quality shoes. Suzanne and Sharri were exploring Brandt's room, so they didn't notice her.

Her mother spotted Ruthe as she came out of the sisters' bedroom with her purse and sweater over her arm, and the shoes in her hands. "Hold it! Where are you going, my gurl?" she commanded curtly.

Ruthe dropped her shoes and sighed. Then she gulped. "Just away to the city. My happiness from preparing all this has evaporated."

Her mother came and stood in front of her and stared steadily at her for a minute. "How come," she accused in a low voice, "You never tell us anything any more?"

Ruthe sniffed as tears brimmed up dangerously again, "I meant it as a surprise love-gift." She knew her mother despised her weakness for tears. "But I guess, just like you, Mom, I'm tired of being hurt and disappointed, so I hide." Instantly, Ruthe was shocked at what she had just said, and also recognized it as true. *How did I know that?*

She spied June watching tenderly beyond her mother, and stepped automatically into her shoes. Her mother seemed stunned too. Chewing both her lips between her teeth to keep from bursting into sobs, Ruthe managed to say, "I'll help you tomorrow with the canning, okay?" With that she whisked right past her mother, who, she noticed, now looked stronger and healthier than in years, and managed to get away with June before anyone else was aware.

They had just started to walk around from room to room in the huge Greystone house, giggling at the echo of their voices in the high ceilings, and beginning to make lists as they cooed freely over various things. Suddenly the doorbell rang. It was Keith. He had noticed the white Rambler in that drive, and had come to tell them that Cathy was waiting for an opportunity to take Ruthe to meet Lloyd and his buddies again.

Ruthe looked at June, knowing that she much preferred to be doing what they had just begun. "You might get to pick; Lloyd or Graham."

June shrugged and declined, so Ruthe graciously left her to enjoy her redecorating dreams and decide what room she would live in when they brought her things in the next day.

Cathy drove her to a posh twelfth story apartment. It had, until just months ago, belonged to Lloyd's bachelor uncle who was a travelling furrier and seldom home. Even before, whenever the uncle flew away, Lloyd had the use of the vintage convertible, as well as his own red Triumph. He had been out of school a year, but Cathy didn't know if he had ever graduated.

"Graham lives with his widowed mother," Cathy chattered on. "He says she's been a Christian for years. She has a tiny stucco cottage, the kind you used to see on old postcards of Scotland? With a darling picket fence holding together a garden wildly bursting with colours.

"Because Graham thought it smart to take part in Lloyd's escapades," Cathy confided, "He played down the fact that he is a wizard with figures. He told us so Friday night."

She didn't know much about Gordon. Just that he presently boarded with an elderly couple, the Adams. Mr. Adams had an auto wrecking concern in an industrial section. "I don't know if it's true, but I heard he found Gordon one morning sleeping in a wreck on his lot and invited him home."

Cathy was on a roll and hard to stop. "I also heard that he has a photographic memory. Lloyd says if Gord once sees a car or motor he has it memorized. Guess that's why he picked him up as a friend; he can get customizing and tune ups as often as he wants."

Ruthe, her emotions, still rather raw and tender from the home crisis, was a bit nervous about this totally new adventure. *Lord*, she sighed in prayer as Cathy talked, *Sort out and give me a clear mind. I'm willing to help if I can, but I feel like a big nothing. These guys got saved on Friday night. What more can I possibly do for them now?*

Lloyd answered the intercom when they buzzed. Also the door when they got up to the highest floor.

Ruthe had to smile at the handsome figure and face before her. This could be a new development in her life. By contrast the boys in her school had been shy, rather average farmhands, or very physical hockey fiends. There was intelligence and a sensitive light in Lloyd's eyes.

Cathy and Lloyd each took a hand and pulled her inside, and as Ruthe glanced around it became clear why others would be flattered to be his friends. *Evidence of money? Whow-whe! Such modern– black and white geometric– decor!*

"You guys feel at home here?" she asked Graham and Gordon, fumbling for something to say, but judged they must be by the way they were sprawled on the white shag. Tapes, vinyl records, magazines and posters were messed all around them.

Lloyd was clearing a spot for her and Cathy on the black Spanish style sofa, and coughed. She guessed that it was dawning on him that the room was messier than it should be.

"Hi," greeted Graham from the floor, "How'r you?"

"Fine, thanks. And you?" Cathy answered cheerily as they sat down.

"Hello Gordon. Enjoying some music?"

"Hel-low," said Gordon in a low rumble, turning off the TV and turning down the stereo some.

Cathy's example helped Ruthe through the greetings.

A brief awkwardness followed. Ruthe supposed they all looked different from their first meeting in the twilight.

Their tall blond host coughed again and made as if to get right to the point. "Ahm-mm, Ruthe...." But his voice trailed off as he became dissatisfied with the words he had chosen.

He walked over to the huge window, which overlooked the downtown area. She watched him tense and relax and tense up again as he stared out, seeing nothing. Then, very suddenly, he spun around. "See this elegant purple martin nest? Everything th-e very best?"

Ruthe nodded and held her breath.

"Nothing's too good for Ol' Uncle George's poor orphaned nephew!" He expelled his breath bitterly and swore. "@#$%#, none of it's a blame thing to me! My uncle– ach-h-h, what was the use? He never talked to me! It didn't heal his hurts and loneliness either. He committed suicide in March. Over in Europe. By #$@+, Ruthe, I'd chuck it all after him through this window if it would get me that old-fashioned family upbringing you told us about Friday night!"

"All this," said Ruthe reflexively, "For a family on the wrong side of the tracks? One that can hardly make ends meet? Everybody on their own wavelength?"

"Don't know your luck," growled Gordon without moving a muscle.

"Sorry," said Ruthe quickly, raising her hand in defense towards Gordon. With all her might she wished she had not said that, and began to pray in a panic for wisdom to speak wisely. She felt stupid. There had to be something better to say. The trauma from home was still raw behind her swollen sinuses. She looked at Cathy, who was unusually quiet now. Cautiously she looked at the three young men. *Lord, are they leading up to something? Save this situation!*

Lloyd continued, "I've been doin' some serious thinking since I heard your story the other night. Cathy told you what happened on the way back, right?"

"Oh-yes, the girls told me all about it the next day. I'm so glad for you, all three of you!" Ruthe was about to rave on, but Lloyd had more to say.

"We've been talking it over. We realize our past is suppost to be like water under a bridge, flowin' out'a sight. But we need something worthwhile and exciting to live for, like you."

"But you do! You've got Jesus Christ!" Right away she remembered that they didn't know Him yet the way she did. How could they appreciate what a worthy purpose He brought into one's life. "Just wait. Once you grow to love the Lord more, and see Him at work in your lives; why you'll find hundreds of things to do. Sometimes you won't know where to begin!"

All three made polite momentary attempts at smiles.

Lloyd dropped himself onto the black sofa between Ruthe and Cathy. "What I'm trying to say, Ruthe, is— we can't think of anything good to do. Until now we just bombed around all day taking on anything that looked wild enough. Or risky. Now those things seem silly; tearing like mad in my Triumph to scare the girls on the street corners, or using my uncle's convertible to impress chicks like–" he paused to look embarrassed as Cathy made a face at him, "It's mere juvenile delinquency compared to your life."

Huh? Ruthe was flabbergasted.

Graham helped Lloyd out. "Yesterday we drove up north of P.A. towards Shell Lake for Adams. Took us all day to look for some rare auto part in far off wreckers' lots. We went to church with the girls this morning. That killed some time. We have hashed over all we saw and heard, now we're bored again."

Lloyd put his hand on Ruthe's knee. "See? Cathy and Muriel told us how you got involved with them. You rescued them, risking all kinds of scummy stuff. Cath even says you set up a girl, whom you yanked from a strangler, in a specially designed business. You dreamed up this tailoring shop to give her a job and a home, just 'cause she got kicked out by her Mom for turning Christian."

Ruthe's eyes popped in amazement. *Was it that big?* "Maybe Cathy exaggerated a bit," she murmured softly, suddenly aware that a masculine face with long blond eyebrow hairs, was very close to hers. The lines in his haircut around his ear looked rather smart.

Ruthe began to pray earnestly again as Lloyd turned his face away to sigh and say, "I don't know, Ruthe. Maybe I'm not saying this right. Let me try once more. We're asking for suggestions. Something to do all day. We're out of school, and bored."

Graham tried to help by rephrasing the question. "You have a way of finding adventure while you share all you know about Jesus, your close Friend. So what would be a unique way for us to share our experience? We just want you to brainstorm with us."

Ruthe was almost afraid to speak for fear she would blurt out something wrong. They waited while she took a couple of deep breaths. "I don't have any secret formula." She swallowed dryly as she tried to pray, think and talk all at the same time.

"Okay. The first thing I ought to tell you is that Christians have to learn not to depend on anyone but the Lord. Have you tried praying about this?"

"Yes," answered Lloyd, "Nothing happened. We don't know how to hear His voice."

"We're so new at it," added Graham gravely, "We thought you might hear, if He's talking in this room."

Cathy spoke up. "Could be a problem with the subliminal message of that rock music you got in the Box. What do you think, Ruthe?"

She nodded thoughtfully. It made her feel crowded, hemmed in.

Gordon reached out and turned it off.

As quiet sank into the soft furnishings and carpeting, Ruthe found her spirit could pray easier, and her mind wasn't thinking in such choppy jerks. She nodded again, "That was part of your problem. Jesus is always present where His Believers are, but if you get clashing messages from the atmosphere where Satan has been reigning freely, you will have difficulty hearing His still small voice in your conscience.

"Have you started reading a Bible? Anybody teach you to pray yet?"

"I took them shopping for Bibles last night," volunteered Cathy. "I showed them the ones you said were the easier-to-read translations."

"We're suppost to stop to think and pray after each verse, like you taught her, right?" Lloyd asked.

"We tried that with verses all over the Bible today," Graham pointed out. "We stumbled on the story of Daniel this afternoon– that was good– but so far nothing to tell us what to do here in Saskatoon."

Oh-dear-Lord! Ruthe closed her eyes, put her hands over her face and tried to concentrate. *Whatever shall I say to them? They're asking me to spell out what You want them to do. Sure, the answer to Darlin' Bonne's problem came to me rather suddenly, but I have no guarantee it will happen now. I've never been asked point-blank.... Com'on Lord, what shall I say?*

She worried it might seem a light-year to them, watching her with her palms pressed into her eye sockets, which still throbbed, she noticed, but now felt parched from her earlier crying jag. She tried to become still, to pick up how the Lord felt about these young men.

Slowly, gently He reminded her that He had spoken through prophets in the Old Testament times to nations and individuals. It was reasonable that He might speak to them through her. All she needed to do was ask and believe.

Still, it's so far-fetched for an unimportant girl like me from Kleinstadt to—

Now, Ruthe, He chided ever so softly.

I'm sorry! You're right. It's not true faith if I want the answer before I'll believe. I'm sorry. But in Darlin' Bonne's case, all I had was my imagination, and a feeling... a feeling she could meet a need—

What are all those magazines on the floor about? Ruthe peeked between her fingers to make sure. Yes, there was a red car on a black background shining across two pages of a magazine on the floor. Cathy had said that Gordon was a brain when it came to cars. A strange surge went through Ruthe. A confidence. She'd been miffed a few weeks ago about the poor service on Dad's old car, before they left on their trip. Recently, while teaching June to drive on the highway, she had got some firm opinions as to how people ought to be taught.

Aware again of their wait, she opened her eyes. "What interests all three of you? I take it you want to stick together, right?"

"I suppose we... we're all crazy about cars. Not your scholastic jocks," said Lloyd with a shrug. He was mystified.

"It's all I can think of," added Graham.

"But in what way?" Ruthe had to stall for time, since her big brain wave had not arrived. "Is it driving them, working on them, or what?"

"I'm your driving devil," said Lloyd cheerfully as he tried to figure her angle. "Gord here, he knows all there is to know about the innards of any car. He's lived on auto graveyards all his life and has memorized every nut and bolt in thousands of cars; haven't ya', Gord?"

Lloyd leaned forward towards Ruthe, "You should see a couple of the old heaps he's revived at Adams' Place. Why, they are better'n when they first came off the assembly line in the fifties and sixties. Even one from the early forties!"

Gordon shrugged his shoulders together in a slight show of embarrassment. "Adams' been show'n me how to rebuild 'em."

130

"And what parts," Graham added generously, "Can be swapped with other models. Useful stuff."

Lloyd gave Graham an affirming clap on the back, "Meanwhile, ol' Gra is your bookkeeping type. He carries my credit cards and keeps track of my allowance. Else Judge Tomas wants the pleasure of my presence."

"No inspiration, are we?" asked Graham dryly.

"Oh-mm," drawled Ruthe with a touch of melodrama, "I don't know about that...."

She studied them with a frank, deliberate gaze, as she tried to lay out the facts. Another business with goals like the shop. Lloyd; obviously a natural leader. People sensitive. Could learn to be tactful. She could see him rise to the challenge, taking charge. Graham; every business needed at least one terrific bookkeeper who keeps at it until the books balance. *Then he's also likely to be a practical sceptic, isn't he, Lord?* Gordon; appeared so expressionless, lying there on the floor, listening like a fence post. Was he as great a mechanic as they said? *Lord, he can't possibly be more than 17 or 18. The success of any car business could hang on the quality of his work.*

Ruthe lifted her gaze through the huge picture window and said with dramatic impishness, "I see an enterprise. You have the manager-salesman, the accountant or comptroller, and the service wizard, all right here in this room."

"Wha're ye talkin' aboot?" demanded Graham with a sudden accent.

Lowering her eyes with a flourish to meet his, she grinned, "Buying and recycling old cars. Maybe you could throw in a fantastic but really tough Driver Training Track."

More earnestly then, she told them about the problems they'd had with her dad's car just before the rest of the family went west, and how dissatisfied she was with the service they got. If Gordon was so great, people needed him. But he could only succeed if Lloyd and Graham were prepared to pool their talents as well.

"This's fantastic!" Cathy raved. As she went on, the young men had a chance to decide whether they liked the idea.

Lloyd rolled his eyes, "@#$%, when you have an idea, Ruthe, you leave the ground!"

"Originality itself," she quipped giddily.

Deep down within her something practical was rising out of the waters and about to glare at her. This idea was so reckless, and the pride she had just detected in her voice made her feel queasy. *Oh Lord, help! I'm floundering!* She gasped, under a breath.

"How'd this be diff'rent 'n another car lot?" asked Gordon.

Ruthe couldn't tell if he was truly interested or sarcastic. She pretended he was sincere. "Simply because the three of you are different. That's what makes the shop Darlin' Bonne is going to open soon so unique. Because those girls are one hundred percent Christ's, their clients will get loving, conscientious attention and workmanship. Each one will hear, at least once, in the most tender way, that Jesus loves her and wants to be her Saviour, Lord, and Friend."

Graham looked shocked now. "You mean combine good ethics and personal soul winning with business?"

"Sorry. That's the kind of ideas I get." More emphatically Ruthe added, "You'll find in the epistles that all Christians are supposed to be doing that. As part of our new lifestyle."

A grimace came to his face. "How many actually do?"

Ruthe sighed with deep, long nods. "So I've decided to buck the mainstream and obey the Lord. It costs, but it has its rewards too."

"We asked her," reminded Lloyd, kicking Graham's ankle.

Cathy echoed with a laugh, "You asked!"

"Okay, thanks-but–" Lloyd shifted to sit down on the floor at Ruthe's feet. His forehead was puckered. "I'm still so new at this myself. I don't know enough of the Bible. It's a thick book. How would I answer all kinds of questions that strangers might throw at me?"

"You could always take a couple or three years to go to a Bible college first." Even while she said that, Ruthe doubted these guys could sit still at desks so long; they had asked for action.

She digressed for a minute to tell them about Donnie and Louise and how eager they had been to accept Christ. She admitted to being surprised at how easily. "You're learning too, aren't you? God's done something wonderful for you and you are quite sure, right? So like a court witness, just report what you know personally. If they want more information, you refer them to others. Get a list of ministers and counsellors ready, or whatever."

Cathy pointed out that they could keep on learning a bit more every day. "Besides, it's exciting if the Holy Spirit prompts you sometimes, just like He does Ruthe. I'm learning to listen to His inner hints myself this summer."

Lloyd wanted to know more about that, so Ruthe found herself giving a short lesson on the presence and guidance of God's Spirit.

Other questions steered her back to her new idea. They wanted it developed more. It became more visual to her as she talked. "Hey, you could buy some land on the outskirts of the city. Maybe beside the highway coming in from the north. Around your main building you could have a small village-sized layout of painted streets and intersections for driver training courses. With little touches, like a brook, or gardens, a pretty walkway here or there. Maybe you could simulate various road and weather conditions in a covered section. Naturally, you would hire only instructors with a real good knack for teaching."

Ruthe digressed again to mention how hard she had drilled June when she was practice-driving, and what a good driver June was now.

Lloyd's smile became a grin. He liked her extravagance. He turned to Gordon, "I'd buy them, and you'd tune up all those old clappers and paint them so's they look and behave like they're coming off a line–" Lloyd interrupted himself with a burst of enthusiastic laughter, "Make 'em purr, make 'em shine, and give 'em away at a profit."

He winked at Graham, "Green industry, eh?"

"I'm to oil this kit'n kabudle?" asked Graham.

Lloyd gave his dark-haired, dark-eyebrowed buddy a mighty whack on his back, "Man, wasn't it you that said earlier today that now that you got a conscience you won't let me blow my inheritance on gambling? You told me about boring church folks, so we stayed away from them. Until we met Ruthe. If we want her kind of life, we got'a throw ourselves into her kind of projects, don't you think?"

Graham nodded apologetically, "Or turn into hypocritical deacons."

Ruthe had a pressure headache building up behind her eyes, but she waited until Lloyd had confirmed that Graham and Gordon were gung ho for this business venture. When they started talking about a name, and drawing up a financial goal plan, she glanced questioningly at Cathy.

The good byes were full of thanks to Ruthe, but the broad-shouldered young men were so eager to work on their plans this did not hold them up long. Their heads were bent together once more before the door shut behind the girls.

"June will be waiting," said Ruthe in the elevator, leaning wearily against the wall. *And it is late enough to miss the battle at home.*

TWENTY

June drove their Rambler home so Ruthe could slouch against the passenger door, and mostly press her cold fingers over her eyeballs. For a not-so-talkative person, June kept up a steady chatter, reassuring Ruthe that her family liked the new house and would not give her a hard time over it. "Like I said, I'm sure your Mom loves it. Once they get used to it, they'll accept it. Maybe they'll never thank you, but it could be worse.

"Listen, you did say I could move into the Greystone tomorrow, right?" June asked. "Why not move in with me? You need a break from your family too."

Ruthe shook her head resolutely. "A vow is vow. God will move me out when it's the right time."

Her brain got paralysing cramps at the thought of her parents finding out she had inherited that old mansion in the city. She refused to give that idea two seconds of her time. However, she sensed that June was eager to get on with the next stage of her life. The prospect of cataloguing the antiques and maybe redecorating parts of that huge old home had sure drawn June out of her shell.

"She raised her head to explain to June, "I'll have to help with the canning tomorrow, but you pack your stuff, and as soon as we can leave, you can move into that old mansion. I may not charge you rent... or not until I own it legally."

June was warm with gratitude and compliments, and offered Ruthe her half of this car. "I can take buses again if I'm living in the city."

Ruthe murmured, "I'll ask that old couple if I can extend the payments for ten months," and wondered, *In that case, should I charge rent?*

"You get into those visits more than I," responded the driver.

June glanced a couple of times at Ruthe, tilted silently at the window, letting a few minutes of silence pass before she said, "Cathy thought you had performed a miracle for those boyfriends of hers tonight. Do you always go to mountain tops with your city friends, and slump into the valley as you head home?"

"I don't know," Ruthe replied from under her hand splayed over her face. "This is just a 'soggy head' catching up to me from before when I cried so much. It'll be gone tomorrow. Usually is."

After a pause, realizing that June was kind, "You know, June. I've got to train myself to say thanks when friends are special to me. Thank you for standing by me in all this." Fresh tears rolled down her quivering chin. She had not expected to reap such kindnesses in return for helping June out.

In the morning Ruthe learned that her family had gone to Grosz'mama's the previous evening. Her grandmother's effervescent compliments to Ruthe's hard work at preparing the great surprise house convinced them that all was well. Since they had never learned to express positive affirmation, they were sure Ruthe would understand if they just acted normal from now on, as if nothing was wrong.

When Ruthe woke her mother was already washing peaches and plums and cutting out pits, all the while calling out for her girls to get dressed and bring over her sealer jars from the old house. Suzanne and Sharri were already up and soon were bringing in one box full after another. However, the younger girls were easily distracted and wandered off to explore and move into other things as soon as their mother thought she had enough jars.

Only gulping a week-old muffin, Ruthe calmed her mother by filling the sinks and earnestly washing and rinsing four dozen glass jars. Her mother settled quietly at the table with her paring knife, surrounded by huge basins of fruit, as Ruthe hurried to place sterilized ones at her right hand. Next she cooked a huge pot of syrup water, ladled it over the fruit in jars, and sealed lids. She knew the way to please was to stay in the kitchen, briskly do what was urgent, or her mother called for, and forget personal agendas until the fruit was cleaned up.

June came to look, then went to pack for an hour. About ten, when she saw that Ruthe was plodding along in the steamy kitchen heat, June offered to help. Anna Veer was not used to giving outsiders orders, so she ignored June except to motion to Ruthe when she thought June was doing something not precisely as it had always been done.

Ruthe's feet and back ached, but she tried to remember to be tactful as she explained how this must be cut, or that wiped.

Because there was so much fruit, and some truly over ripe, Anna Veer soon figured out how to get more done at once by using the old stove in their former home as well as the new one. She had three jam pots going after she sent Sharri to Grosz'mama's to borrow a big, heavy pot, and Suzanne to the store for a brand new one. By three o'clock they had two canners rocking away at full steam, each filled with seven jars, and three foaming, boiling jam pots. When the timer rang it was tricky remembering to which element it applied.

Suzanne was supposed to watch and stir the ones in the old house, but when they spied her outside chasing Sharri, Ruthe volunteered.

Bringing back the second pot of finished jam, she was met at the sink by her mother. "When we can sell or rent out that old house, we will see you get some money back. Right now it's useful!"

"No, Mom," she replied, pushing hair off her forehead with the back of her hand. "You keep it as a cushion, in case Dad's unemployed again over the winter." She named a neighbour who had expressed interest to Grosz'mama.

The old cure of hard work was like a familiar, strong-smelling salve to Ruthe's soul. No further discussion took place. She doubted it would, but it didn't matter so much today. Just seeing her mother accept and use this kitchen helped. When she remembered the switches for the ceiling fan, and the fan sucking heat out from above the stove, she had satisfaction in hearing her mother say, "What an improvement that breeze makes! Makes all this hard work pleasanter."

By two o'clock the canners were silent, row upon row of sealed jars gleamed on the counters, and the dishes were done, and the pile of wet tea towels gathered for the washing machine.

"Mom," Ruthe followed her mother to the living room where she was ready to throw herself down, exhausted, ready for a nap, "June has found a great chance to be housesitter in the city. That means she is supposed to live in someone's home so it will look lived in, so it doesn't tempt any thieves. We both have an evening shift today, but I'm going to help her move in there before we start, okay?"

Mrs. Veer nodded, sinking into the couch. She turned to June just behind Ruthe, "You be sure to lock the doors there. I'd hate to hear you got to any harm." Then she folded her hands, laid her cheek on them, and was asleep almost instantly.

Ruthe and June shrugged at each other. "She means well," Ruthe added.

They chose the master suite at the rear of the main floor for June's new home. Bessie had used it and cleaned it more recently than the smaller maid's room beside the kitchen. It didn't take long to hang June's clothes.

Later that week, sandwiched between visits to the shop, and to June at the Greystone, Ruthe squeezed in time to see the boyfriends. That was what Cathy and Muriel called them at first, though Keith described them as drones switching allegiance to a new queen bee.

Ruthe did turn the possibility of romance over in her mind a few times. Especially, when she noticed Lloyd had a habit of coming quite close to her and putting his hand on her back, or touching her in a friendly way. It gave her an electric thrill, but was disconcerting at the same time. Her ideals and convictions got a scathing going over from her most pitiless critic. What would she stand up for if caught in an emotionally charged situation? What if she had to make a split-second decision? What image did she want to project to men generally? Did they sense a come-on from her?

Most of the men in her life treated her with respect. Probably because she was such an open Christian, she realized. Some thought her an unusual character. *Good. I want to start there,* she told the Lord, *but what else do I really want to be known for?*

From past discussions like this with her Friend, Jesus, Ruthe knew that any friend allowed close enough to become a potential husband had to be at least as intimate with the Lord as she. He had to care very much about people, and not hold her back from reaching out to them. She wanted rather, a partnership, which would increase the effectiveness for both of them with people. A minister or missionary had often seemed like good prospects. At least her parents might approve; if she didn't move to a scary foreign land.

These guys looked on her as a counsellor or religious big sister. Ruthe decided she would befriend and advise them, but romance was out of the picture. *These boys are lapping it up; they need mothering. I will make an invisible fence around myself.* From watching her parents, she had decided long ago that she did not want to mother a husband the rest of her life. *I'll nip it before others lock me in.*

Arming herself with a mentally prepared answer, Ruthe boldly raised the issue at their third visit. She explained, "I don't see this as a boy-girl relationship we have here. We have Christ and business interests in common, but if you begin to chase me– with romantic notions– you'll find me backing out of your lives very quickly."

Lloyd saluted her. "*Comprehende.* None of us will take advantage of you. I'll see to that." End of conversation.

Ruthe referred to them as Cathy's friends. Cathy, in fact, often took the initiative to invite them over to her home, sometimes with other new friends for she was always making fresh and renewed social contacts. That was where Ruthe met up with them most often.

Ross was the biggest complication in this social milieu. The sight of those three handsome men gathered around Ruthe, lapping up every word she said, made him see red. He would go from rude to angry and obscene. A few times Ruthe thought it wise to excuse herself and leave just to keep Ross from going overboard.

Lloyd's Uncle George had been trustee and guardian of all that belonged to him after his parents' accidental death, and it was set up so he was not to get control of any of that money until he was twenty-five. However, since March, when his uncle had jumped from a high building in Europe, Lloyd was the sole heir to his fur business and stocks with no age restriction. The delays came with searching for the best buyer. Lloyd knew the fur market was shrinking. He might end up giving away the whole thing for peanuts, if not careful. He was getting some crash lessons from the company agents in selling stocks, sales territories, and *customer good will.*

Meantime, Graham tried to find financial backers on their Bright City venture. Their inexperience and delinquency records were against them. They learned, that though the Lord is gracious to forgive and forget, some sins do leave scars and blots.

"I've heard that God can take those sin scars and turn them into the most beautiful features of one's life," Ruthe told them. She was at Adams' Place to see how they were coming with her dad's old car.

She was relieved that Bright City was not her responsibility. If she had the money, she would gladly have handed them a huge lump sum. But she was glad they were doing their own business research and fundraising. She only need ask how it was coming.

Graham pointed out that the money-logjam seemed to worry her more than them. "Lloyd has the money," he assured her. "It just takes time to get it moved at some stages."

Ruthe glanced aside at Gordon who was hard at work on the brown family car. His head came up grinning just then. "Got it."

Lloyd and Graham, even Gordon, when not under a car, were more preoccupied with their inner discoveries. They prayed for something; only hours, perhaps minutes later, it was there. They acted as if landing on a new continent, and Ruthe was cheered to hear them talk of prayer. For so long she had felt like the only one who knew this secret.

On Sundays they met the O'Briens at church, and as they met the church people, the three were impressed with the Christians' concern for each other and for them. "Even the old fogies make nice friends once you get to know them individually," exclaimed Lloyd. "Last week one elderly couple we never noticed before invited us home for lunch. No dummies, them! Had a lot of class, in fact. Been to different parts of the world."

Ruthe's dimples twinkled as she tried to tame back her smile. "Some of my most favourite people are old folks."

Graham had attended Sunday School and church as a young boy and thought he knew what to expect, but he was just as excited about their Bible study in a class for young adults called, College and Careers.

It was the same church to which Darlin' Bonne regularly brought Betty, Donnie and Louise. Betty urged them all to join the choir so they could have one totally different activity each week. They suggested only once to the three fellows that the choir director would like some more male voices in fall.

The day after their first choir practice Lloyd phoned about leaving messages for Ruthe to call him back. She found notes on the bulletin board at work, June had a huge note on the memo board by the kitchen phone at the Greystone, Darlin' Bonne was waiting to tell her, and so were Muriel and Keith. She called Lloyd's apartment from the O'Briens'.

"Irvin expects the best, but he takes time to teach how to read the notes. Those kids, including the pianist and the peppy organist, all are so easy-goin'— so much fun!" Lloyd raved. "I just couldn't wait to tell you."

"When our church has one, I love choir singing too," she laughed. "And when my shifts don't interfere." Then she added a tease about other attractions.

"No," Lloyd said earnestly, not picking up the innuendo. "It's a new kind of people. Grown up but witty. Not cruel. We have clean fun."

Ruthe accepted an invitation to an evening service when the choir would be singing, and when she thought she could sneak in a couple of hours after her shift before going home.

At that service she warmed with pride in several instances when she observed Lloyd talking to someone, enthusiastically sharing some great truth he discovered in the last day or two. He noticed and remembered individuals, and they drew toward him, not knowing they were walking.

Graham was not far behind as a facilitator with people. He told a young couple with a baby and two older widows what a step of faith it had been for him to sign up for a night course in accounting.

Only Gordon stood around like a suited mannequin in church. He moved when he saw Lloyd and Graham easing to another area, and he answered in monosyllables when people spoke to him. These ethereal things one could not pinch between one's fingers or grab with a strong greasy hand were invisible butterflies to him. He wanted to see them too, but it often took sessions after a church service, rehashing a sermon for him to understand those spiritual beauties. The figures of speech in the hymns made problems for him intellectually as well, though he rather liked the feel of the tunes, he confessed.

Ruthe sensed his frustration, and several times urged the others to make a habit of discussing these things more simply to help Gordon catch on. Sometimes she, or Cathy, got in on these private lessons.

Mid-August, the week of Lloyd's birthday, he was more sensitive, pre-occupied, and later Cathy said, depressed. He found old letters from his parents to his uncle and was stunned to learn his parents had rejected a clear invitation to accept Christ and made sarcastic jokes about God, daring Him to kill them in an accident. His uncle had felt the same way. Lloyd believed this led to his uncle's extreme sense of hopelessness. That he had headed the same way before he accepted Christ as his Saviour gave Lloyd cause to suck in his breath.

Graham called Cathy, and Cathy called Darlin' Bonne's Shop to ask for prayer. By the time Ruthe and Cathy converged the next day to confront Lloyd and see what could be done, he had just got word that his inheritance was now all his, all two hundred and fifty thousand.

"I could've managed," Lloyd told them uncomfortably, as he slumped together, "If only they had not spat in God's face."

"But a quarter of a million!" whistled Graham. "With a little nursing that could stretch to put us on the map for aye and aye."

"Well, ol' boy,"said Lloyd blandly, "Nurse it. I've never learned anything about money except to spend it. It's safer with you. Unless, if you prefer; give the job to Ruthe."

In panic, Ruthe shook her head. "Nope. Graham is your man!"

Drawn out with questions, Ruthe quoted some thoughts about God using negative happenings to make positive things for His praise and the good of those that love Him. She felt out of her element but she wanted to help bring Lloyd out of his blue funk.

Driving away together, Ruthe and Cathy agreed that Lloyd might seem the charismatic leader to others, but they might have to pull him out of the pit of despair again.

"Would you like to marry Lloyd," Cathy asked, "And help him spend that quarter mil wisely?"

"No way!" retorted Ruthe. "Please; the idea frightens me."

Cathy promised not to tease her any more about Lloyd. "Instead, you can pray for me that I don't get jealous. I wish they looked up to me like they do to you, Ruthe." She added quickly, "Right now those guys needs your friendship. I'm not about to chase you off."

Ruthe's head and stomach churned with taut nerves until she went for a long walk at dusk, all around Kleinstadt, and talked it over with her Friend.

Even if Lloyd was no accountant or budget man, he might be called a creative engineer. When he took their plans, which he had redrawn seventeen times, to an architect for the final layout, he received warm compliments for the innovative ideas.

Bright City called for lots of space. They were bidding on a large acreage on the highway at the city's north gateway. A yard of disintegrating buildings, and a small junk heap of rusting cars and farm machinery would be cleared away for a huge concrete driving circle. This would surround a showroom-service tower with an entrance coming under the driving track. Directly behind the tower complex, inside the track, was to be a flat area for student drivers to learn to handle a car without running into anything but lines painted in the pavement. Later, under parts of the circle another track was to be built with special simulating devices to train people to drive in any weather condition, from blinding snow to sheets of rain and glare ice.

Lloyd bought a few wrecks from Mr. Adams, and Gordon, along with a couple of new friends met at church, were repairing, or rather, almost re-making those cars. They were going to be in business long before their contractor got started on the new property.

Graham raved about buying up some great deals for $50 or $200, and how after they were rebuilt as good as new, they expected to sell for ten times that or more. One fifty-dollar heap, Mr. Adams had assured them, would net $40,000 if they could just come up with the missing parts, and re-do the old upholstery, and a good paint job on the body. They had lots to learn yet, but they offered to do one over for Ruthe.

"You got a great deal in that Rambler," Lloyd complimented her, "Excellent condition!"

She told how she had just managed to convert her payment plan to twenty visits with fifty dollars each time, and how she was making friends of the elderly couple in the retirement home.

"Great," Lloyd soothed, "But if you ever need another car, I'll fill your bill."

Ruthe blushed and flashed him a big dimpled smile, not knowing why.

Later, driving home, she wondered, *Could I– should I buy a car for Darlin' Bonne? She doesn't have time, but she could be Lloyd's first driving student. A car would be such a great asset to those girls. It would certainly be easier for the four of them to get around by car than by bus. But the shop opens next week. They haven't got time....*

TWENTY-ONE

Towards the end of August, thanks to Muriel and Keith's calligraphy and tracing, the words *Darlin' Bonne's Shop* graced the glass pane in the front door of 73 Lindsay Avenue, in fancy gold Park Avenue script.

The last week before their Labour Day opening the girls were putting in eight or more hours of practice each day, just to polish up their needlecraft speed. More shipments of fabrics were arriving, sending them trotting in and out of the garage and the sewing rooms carrying armloads of colours and weights.

One evening Ruthe walked in to see party clothes of all kinds laying about in layered spreads in the waiting room. She touched some of the new materials and had a few ideas for new outfits to design too. The girls moved up and down the hall, in and out of the side door, too busy to greet her with their usual hugs and eagerness to show and tell.

Betty grabbed her hand as she passed and whisked Ruthe to the side entrance. "Here. The driver plunked all these bundles on the landing. You can help divide it for the shelves in the rooms. That pile goes to the garage for later."

Ruthe got right into it. "I'm too big for the china cabinet," she said to Darlin' Bonne, as she passed her in the doorway of the rear sewing room.

When she came back to the landing for her third armload, panting, she met Betty again, who commented earnestly, "You know, Ruthe, I still haven't heard a word from my parents. I wonder about their feelings about me being here."

"Maybe they are tied up with harvest."

"Not every day of the summer. Surely they should have clattered in on the half-ton by now– to check this place out for themselves."

Ruthe hitched a load on her hip and paused to pay attention to Betty with another reassuring excuse.

"Dad never combines or bales on Sundays," Betty replied. "But Mom hasn't written either since I left the Residence. She wrote faithfully every week."

"Hi, Louise," Ruthe tossed off a quick greeting, before giving her load another hitch and asking, "Did you write before you moved?"

"Yes. The night before. Soon's I made up my mind to come here."

They had to keep moving and the conversation ended there.

That work done, they gathered in twos or threes in the sewing rooms to organize their equipment and new notions. Darlin' Bonne distributed a pressing iron and three padded hams to each room, after Betty showed how to use them for pressing sleeve caps and small curved corners. She was sorting button cards, laces and ribbons into their drawer compartments. Donnie filed away patterns and muslin slopers, while Louise and Ruthe laid up a supply of needles, threads and zippers, trying to keep sizes and types together. They ended up carrying the drawers into the same room, so that while they worked they could all talk about this and that.

Out of this, or maybe it was that, Darlin' Bonne suddenly had an idea. "How would it be if we had cameras? Then we could take pictures of our clients modelling their clothes right after we've made 'em."

"Terrific!" several chorused.

"We'd have a perfect file of everything we ever design or sew," added Darlin' Bonne.

"Why not–" Ruthe jumped on the brain wave, "Publish them in a book with glossy pages 'n all that? Bet the clients would love to see themselves in this album... or catalogue."

"Or fancy magazine," said Donnie.

"Maybe once a year," said Betty, "Or once a season, once we get enough business."

"Call it *Darlin' Bonne's Album*," offered Louise, eager to get in on it. "Or is that too cute?"

Donnie shrieked happily, "It'll sell like ice cream!"

Ruthe began to see that a bunch of girls having ideas together could get swept away, but she laughed just as heartily when Betty volunteered as a joke, "Let's make it huge, like a pattern catalogue," as she lifted two hefty ones.

Darlin' Bonne tried to summarize; "A record of our designs, maybe extra income, and a treat for our regulars." Then she whirled over to Ruthe to give her a hug of sheer exuberance.

Donnie chirped in her high voice, "Our European peers will send spies to our printer to see where the hemline is supposed to be!"

When the laughter died down Ruthe asked if they had worked out their routines for the big opening on Monday. All the girls helped to describe it.

"Think in terms of a beauty salon. Individual service to a client from one designer who will not desert her the whole time." Since they all wanted to sew, they would take turns as receptionist, or hostess, greeting the clients and making appointments. As soon as available, one of the designers would take a client off to a private room. The patron would describe her desires and choose material from the wall of shelves. Next, she would be fitted with a muslin sloper, which would be labelled and filed for future visits. The designer-seamstress would chat with the client as she cut and sewed. If the client could not spare the thirty to sixty minutes wait, she could be excused after the initial fitting and come back for the outfit at a later date.

"A client who knows and can describe what she wants," said Darlin' Bonne, "can expect the same person to cut, fit, and sew it up in an hour or so. We need a test under real conditions before I guarantee it, but most times, at any rate."

If the client didn't know what she wanted, or preferred to trust the designer's judgment, the designer could go with her through dozens of magazines and pattern books for ideas; even draw up quick sketches to show what might be just right. "We're not polished yet on foundation garments and heavy winter coats, but we can do anything from baby layettes to wedding gowns," said Betty. "All we need is praise to get more self-confidence."

"We haven't figured out how to make pantyhose or shoes," Donnie pointed out, "But Darlin' Bonne ordered hundreds of plain white or black pumps to give away on opening day, and later whenever we see a person who needs them."

"I wrote away for that purse and shoe-making book," Louise reminded Donnie. "We're getting ready for expansion and big business."

Ruthe hoped it would remain a small, intimate shop, but agreed that most women she knew preferred to look for clothes in stores because it was faster. Some because they thought they couldn't sew well enough. Those that could, or knew and could afford a good seamstress, preferred the quality fit. In their discussion they figured it took the average woman anywhere from half an hour to two or three hours to try ready-made clothes before she buys one or two. If they could consistently average the same or less time to whip up as good an outfit, but give it a dressmaker's precise fit, they should attract a loyal clientele.

"Word of mouth will bring us enough clients; why advertise?" someone asked. That had been Ruthe's first image of the shop idea. Other ideas had been hashed over through the summer, but she was glad they had latched onto this one again. They had timed themselves as they practiced sewing and chatting all summer. By late August now, a simple skirt took them about thirty minutes, and a dress with a few extra seams a bit more than an hour. an elaborate wedding gown or tailored suit still took the longest, but each of the girls could make a simple one in a day if she had no interruptions or delays.

Ruthe's practice time had been rather sporadic, so her pace was no match for the other girls' but she kept trying simply because she wanted to learn.

Betty, the practical hen, listed lots of things to do yet, so when Ruthe was ready to leave, she promised to be back on Saturday.

It was a grey, rainy Saturday, but after a very hot harvest week everyone was relieved at the cooler, if damper air. Ruthe had been able to persuade June to put down the antiques pricing books and come along for the afternoon. Darlin' Bonne and Betty had prepared a check-list at the reception desk. Each one could look at it, do a job, check it off, and take up another.

In the midst of their genial bustle to clean up every room, arrange displays, and lay supplies ready, there was a long shrill ring on the front doorbell. "Hey, you. Can't you wait? It's only Saturday!" cried Donnie, mocking at imaginary mobs of impatient would-be clients.

Darlin' Bonne made an embarrassed grimace at the still topsy-turvy cluttered reception room. Shrugging her shoulders with a carefree, "Com'on, Ruthe. Let's see what surprise God has for us," she snatched Ruthe's wrist and pulled her along to the door.

Louise's mother, a social worker, stood outside holding a black umbrella over a lovely blonde. She motioned the storybook princess to step in ahead of her as Ruthe and Darlin' Bonne backed up in welcome.

The tall girl's expression was a bit timid, but she had the posture and bearing of royalty, and a complexion with the famous peaches and cream look Ruthe had seen advertised in her box of old English magazines from Granny O'Brien. Her pale yellow hair shone with silkiness. The ends turned into soft generous curls upward where her hair reached her shoulders.

Mrs. Nunweiller was taller yet, and gently pushing her charge in, she made introductions. "Gals, I'd like you to meet Evelyn Hargraves. Evelyn, this is Darlin' Bonne Barrett, Betty Oaks over here, Donnie McPherson from next door, and my daughter Louise. That must be June, I think." Then turning back to where Ruthe had slipped behind Darlin' Bonne, Mrs. Nunweiller exclaimed, " I do believe this is the famous Ruthe." She held out her hand, "I'm thrilled to meet you at last!"

"Famous?" blurted Ruthe. "Why would I be–?"

Everyone was laughing and Darlin' Bonne was hugging her proudly. "Darlin', you know you can't trust a chatterbox to keep many secrets."

Ruthe swallowed her wonderment to look back at the newcomers.

Mrs. Nunweiller wanted to get to business. "Gals, I brought Evelyn here because she has no where else to stay now that her invalid father has passed on. I'm afraid she's not brave enough to live alone like an independent swinger. She needs friends. Evelyn finished a hairstyling course at night school– which the Home Care nurse, wisely I might add, talked her into as a recreational outlet. She's quite good, which will tell you about her creativity."

She looked directly at Darlin' Bonne and Ruthe, "You've been so good to my Louise, I thought, maybe you would have room for Evelyn."

There was a paralysed moment of looking at each other. How to handle this? They had already gambled in taking on this number.

"Mom!" Louise moaned in an embarrassed aside. "You don't understand how this place oper–!"

145

Darlin' Bonne yucked a chuckle, pecked Ruthe's cheek, her arm still around her, and looked for Betty's face with a merry wink, "Our heavenly Father must have a crazy debut planned for us on Monday. He can see we'll need reinforcements."

Ruthe's reserve dissolved on Darlin' Bonne's shoulder with a lopsided hug. "Okay," she nodded with full eyes very close to her dark-haired friend's face, "Why don't we get to know her and see if Evelyn won't soon qualify? We'll take her on faith."

As if signalled, the rest converged on Evelyn, drawing her further in, taking her coat, and speaking kind, welcoming words.

Over the hubbub, Mrs. Nunweiller called out, "I have to be going. It's my day off, and I do have a home to look after." She tilted her umbrella and disappeared into the damp outdoors.

June sidled up to Ruthe, "We have to leave soon, if we are to keep our jobs as operators."

Sure enough, it was time to go. Ruthe regretted she would not be on hand for the rest of the day. She would have to hear about the absorption of Evelyn into the knit of the family later. However, she was confident it would all work out.

Sunday was a busy day at home, with some relatives gathering at Grosz'mama's in the afternoon. Ruthe could not excuse herself to go to the city early enough to find out about Evelyn before her shift. Instead, she phoned Darlin' Bonne from the office lounge on her break.

Darlin' Bonne caught her up on the past twenty-four hours while the others started walking to Spadina Park at the river. In her report, she said that there were several attempts made to explain the shop policies about being Believers and wanting to share the good news of Jesus Christ as a Saviour and Friend. Evelyn had listened politely to everything, but responded to nothing until bedtime. Donnie and Louise were gone for the night, and Betty was rearranging their bedding to make up a third one on the foldout sofa. "As we settled down for our quiet time and prayers, I told Evelyn what we were doing, and she began to ask questions. You know, Ruthe, she's awfully shy."

Both wondered how she would be able to deal with the public, and Ruthe asked, "But how did she respond? Still nothing?"

"She lapped it up like a kitten. She'd read some stuff about Jesus, deeper books than I have ever touched, and she thought she was the only one in the modern world that knew any of that history stuff. Betty recognized some of those authors, like oh, George McDonald, and C. S. Lewis, and I don't know who all. Betty was able to tell Evelyn that we believe the same theology, and we try to live it here."

Ruthe sighed with relief. Then asked more questions.

Darlin' Bonne told how she and Betty had made sure Evelyn understood Jesus' work of salvation on the cross and how to pray.

"She was willing to pray aloud?" Ruthe was pleased and shocked.

"Slow at first, but she's learnin' like an ice cube in a hot oven. Don't worry, Ruthe, Evelyn's one of us now. She just comes out of one of God's fancier cookie presses. She'll make a lovely hostess."

Ruthe tumbled backward in the lounge chair with laughter. She had to get back to the switchboard, but she could hardly wait for the next day. "I traded it off. I plan to be at our big opening tomorrow!"

"We're all going to burn out," prophesied Darlin' Bonne.

TWENTY-TWO

The McPhersons and Nunweillers had told a few friends and neighbours that this was a quick, while-you-wait dressmaking shop, and it was going to open on Labour Day. The O'Brien sisters had called all their friends. Of course, the shop girls told the choir and all their church friends. A number had promised to come try them out. Many had repeated it to still others. There was no telling what to expect the first day, technically a legal holiday.

Half a dozen teens arrived at nine o'clock with sketches or torn out ads in hand, wanting custom-made school clothes for the next day.

When Ruthe arrived about ten, the reception room was full, and the seamstresses were in the four sewing rooms, each with a client. A stranger had the telephone receiver pinched between her cheek and shoulder and was scribbling notes at the little wall desk by the door. She was also waving and motioning welcomes in sign language to the waiting ladies and girls crowded two to a chair at places. When she introduced herself, the stranger blessed her loudly, and held out her hand. "Dot McPherson here. Donnie recruited me to help out– 'Til Ruthe gets here,' she said."

"That's me." Ruthe tried to take it in.

"What happened to Evelyn?"

"Evelyn started answering the phone and such, but the others needed an assistant so often by turns, to fetch or hold, that Donnie pressed me into service. Frees Evelyn to help with fittings and pinning. Whoever sings out her name loudest gets her help next."

Ruthe turned to stare and listen down the hall. Exactly what was happening? She worried about Darlin' Bonne feeling panicky, but realized that was probably because she was feeling overwhelmed herself.

Mrs. McPherson was back on the phone. Ruthe motioned she was at home here, and went to look for Darlin' Bonne. She tapped softly on the first door.

Darlin' Bonne pulled her by the arm into her sewing room, whispering crisply, "Ruthe darlin', we've got one free at the end of the hall. You know what to do, okay?"

Ruthe nodded soberly. Then she found herself pulled up close to Darlin' Bonne again. "Just be your Jesus-filled self. If you can't find something, sing out for Evelyn. She glides around like a princess until she finds what you need."

Gulping to swallow a frog, Ruthe went back to the reception area to get her first customer, and led her to the room at the end of the hall where the door was open.

Smiling broadly to first put herself in a cheerful, friendly frame, Ruthe sat down with the high school student. It turned out she wanted a new blouse to go with the old plaid skirt her mother wanted her to wear. She was already late for something else and worried in the manner of an intense, bookish type with no social skills. Soon Ruthe could see that it would do no good to chat lightly, and then steer to spiritual topics, so she decided to give her best at her fastest and hope the girl would be back some other time. It took her a little more than half an hour.

The client had asked at the beginning how much it would cost, and Ruthe explained it would be ten dollars. As Ruthe shook out the cut off threads and ironed it, the girl pulled out a crumpled bill, popped the blouse on, still warm, and stuffed her old blouse into a homemade denim backpack. Ruthe led her to the front desk to ask Mrs. McPherson to make out a receipt.

Her next client was an old lady with a cane and hips that humped to the right. As she was also hard of hearing, it took a long time to discuss what she wanted her new dress to look like, and still longer to fit because of her modesty.

Ruthe sighed softly to herself, *it's a lot of work, this success.*

They had a steady flow of clients that morning, mostly neighbours and friends of Donnie's and Louise' who had been invited personally. Around noon the O'Brien sisters arrived with some of their friends, but they were polite enough to insist that the seamstresses pause to eat the sandwiches Evelyn had made and brought up. An hour or two later it looked as if all the women and young girls for two or three blocks in each direction were marching on 73 Lindsay, as if to a garage sale. A number commented that they had noticed the gold lettering on the door and had been waiting for news of its opening.

The sewing designers hardly dared break away from their eager customers for even a washroom stop. When they met in the hallway they remarked on understanding why the Lord had brought Evelyn just when He did. By the end of the afternoon, they discovered that she was a great bookkeeper besides.

Ruthe found the whole day too fast-paced, and the tension knot in between her shoulder blades too distracting to keep up her normal inner dialogue with the Lord. She was operating on automatic pilot as a headache built between her eyes. However, in the snatches of conversation she had with the others, she was relieved to note they were not forgetting their goal of suggesting Jesus to everyone they sewed for. They tried. Naturally, not all were ready to have a personal encounter with Him, but each listened politely to what her designer shared of her own experience with the Saviour.

There were those clients, from the girls' church mostly, who already were Christians. Ruthe had two such women in her day. One admitted frankly that

149

hers was an up and down kind of joy in the Lord. She often wondered if it had to be like that. "Do some people live on a more stable plane?" she asked.

Ruthe was happy to tell her that she had found constant joy and peace by practicing a more or less continuous dialogue with God. By the time Ruthe had finished that woman's outfit, she was ready to try out such praying with Ruthe.

At five-thirty Darlin' Bonne went to the front room to tell the waiting clients, "Sorry. we will not be able to serve you today. My staff are all exhausted and can only finish with the clients they have right now. We have to call this a day—but oh God, what a day!"

They promised to try again. Some made appointments.

As they finished, from six on, the girls drifted down to the apartment and collapsed in sprawls over the furniture. But all wanted to talk and tell stories. They counted up thirty-eight clients for the day. Twelve had either become Christians or become more excited about Jesus. This news inspired enough strength so that a couple got up to help Betty with the tuna casserole and table setting, and making a pitcher of punch.

Ruthe stayed as late as her conscience allowed on her day off, and finally pulled herself away just when a lively discussion started on a pricing policy and whether to take Mondays or Saturdays off for recreation. All could see that to sew for fifty to sixty hours a week was going to ruin their health if they kept it up.

"But folks will come even on our days off," Ruthe heard someone remark after she had said farewell and was exiting. "We'll need to go on day trips to get away from here."

Ruthe nodded to herself in her Rambler. *And they'll need a car. I'll talk to our Bright City guys.*

TWENTY-THREE

A couple of days later Ruthe stopped after work at Adams' Place. She found only Gordon there. Conversations with him were usually brief, but this turned interesting.

Gordon had just rebuilt the motor of a station wagon, and needed a few more days to redecorate the interior. Ruthe liked the look of it and inquired, "How much?" Gord thought Lloyd might sell it for ten thousand. Ruthe examined it thoughtfully and went from there straight to the Greystone to see how June was doing with sorting the antiques.

On the way Ruthe had a pang of conscience. *Lord, if that will does not make it through those probate stages, or whatever this process is called, I'll have to reimburse Granny's estate with anything I make off the antiques, won't I? I shouldn't have even sold that crystal.*

June wasn't at the mansion. Ruthe prowled through some of the rooms at the back where she had gathered, sorting into heaps or shelves the smaller antique items from all over the house. But by now her conscience troubled her so much that she left and went through the hedge to the O'Briens' home.

It seemed no one was home there either. After ringing the doorbell twice, she turned to go. Then Mr. O'Brien opened the door. He apologized for being alone, then invited her in, sensing her depression. "What is the matter?"

It was all too much near the surface. "I want to give a gift to Darlin' Bonne to help out with the Shop. They need a car, and Gord is fixing up an old wagon from the early sixties. But suddenly I feel guilty about selling the antiques," she confessed in a rush. "I guess I need to know where I stand with that will of Granny's, and what is right and fair about all those fancy things. June is so excited. She thinks there is a lot of money in them."

Mr. O'Brien had her sit down in a leather chair in his office. He went behind his desk and explained all about wills and the processes they go through. It was more complicated than Ruthe had realized, but he assured her that neither he, nor his children were going to contest the will, so it would be all hers soon.

"Doesn't Ross have any say in the matter?"

"Technically, if he could afford the legal battle, he could try. However, I have persuaded him that Granny would come out as perfectly sane and in her right to change her will. I have earnestly hunted in case there was a different, more recent will," Mr. O'Brien said wryly. "This is it."

He promised to tug the ear of Ken, his partner, in case he was dragging his toes, to speed the will from checkpoint to checkpoint.

That seemed to help, for the following week Mr. Newton contacted her through June, for a suitable time to bring her the official documents and title deed. It was done in moments.

"And what is usually your bill for these services?" Ruthe asked.

Mr. Newton named a price between six and seven hundred.

"Just a moment, please." She got up and left the room.

June had determined that a Meissens gold snuff box could be sold for seven to nine thousand, except the one with the gems set in the lid could go for nearly $75,000. Ruthe picked it up, ready to be generous, then suddenly knew that she would rather give that to Mr. O'Brien for Christmas. She picked up another one of handsome quality for Mr. Newton. She spotted and snatched up some tissue to tuck around it as she left the room.

"Now, shall I wait until you make up my bill, or until you have a receipt book with you?" Ruthe asked sweetly, placing the crumpled tissue covered box on the dining table, inches from Mr. Newton's elbow. The gold-trimmed ends shows on either side.

"Oh, I have both with me," the elegant lawyer said, swiftly opening his brief case. In a large flourish he wrote, *Paid in Full,* on the bill and added *w/Thanks,* under his signature on the receipt. Without unwrapping the snuffbox, he slid it into his brief case. Their smiles were all friendly as she saw him to the door.

Ruthe and June went back to survey her riches. The Jacobite wine glasses might bring thousands too, if the right collector were contacted. The hand-gilded french mantel clocks, June told her, since there were so many that Granny had painted and fixed up quite authentically, might be the easiest to sell.

Ruthe tried to remember some of these details and went for a walk all about the mansion and the grounds to pray. It was hard to get a sense of truly owning all this now. She chattered to the Lord silently and told Him she was giving it all to Him. Yet, as she looked about, Ruthe began to see things she wanted fixed or cleaned up. Her upbringing seemed to come to the fore. She did not think she or the Lord wanted to be connected to something so messy and neglected as the gnarled apple orchard out back, and the over-grown tennis court. She saw potential for the rockery and the flowerbeds, but this was going to call for lots of work. Especially the berry garden. *How will I ever bring them home without telling Mom where they came from? Or should I give them all away to my city friends?*

June came out to ask, "What about all the old, ornate furniture?"

Ruthe told June the beds and some furniture could stay in the second floor bedrooms, "But let's clear out all those old expensive antiques, and put in simple department store stuff." If she were to bring in all kinds of stray people, everyone would feel better if the rare things were out of the way. "Besides, we are going to need that money to run the place. I have to start paying utilities and taxes on this big house." *Now, there's a weighty thought!* she added silently.

June wanted to know, "Where do we store them until they sell? In the carriage house?"

Ruthe had forgotten about that. "I've never been in there, have you?"

June had not. They found the key hanging in the kitchen and went to check it out. It smelled faintly of horses or a barn, but a green convertible with *Beaumont* on it, and a decrepid old European car with a bump for a rear end stood there instead. They were pleased to see the double car garage was tidy and orderly with a pegboard wall hung with some tools. The doors were sealed with good locks, both the wide doors at the front and the regular door at the back. However, their eyes were drawn back to the cars and bulged as they stared at them.

The old black, rusted hump reminded her of Granny's stories of travelling about, buying and selling antiques with her father. She had said they sold china out of the boot in back. Only now it looked– if it was the same one– as if it had exploded in a gasoline fire and the rear half was licked clean of even its paint. The front end had patches of black curled-up paint.

The kelly green convertible on the other hand, looked shiny and flawlessly new, if one ignored the layer of dust evenly coating the hood, the dash, and the exposed upholstery.

Ruthe took it in, moving towards the convertible, breathing, "Darlin' Bonne would love this!" The keys were in it. Giving June a mischievous grin, she opened the door and sat down. However, the key would not start the car. Not even a faint groan of the battery. "Well, I'll get the guys to come have a look," she told June as she got out with a sigh, missing the longing survey that June was giving that car.

Together they debated whether this might not be a good place to store the larger pieces of antique furniture until they sold. June agreed. "It would be handy for one or two-day sales open to the public. Then we don't have them tramping all through the big house."

Ruthe phoned around until she caught up with Lloyd. When she described the cars, he offered to come examine them that evening with Gord and Mr. Adams' tow truck. "I won't be here, but June can show them to you."

By the time Ruthe got back to the rooms with the smaller items June had gathered earlier, she felt her choices were plain. Why wait for a more profound solution? *Lord, I'm just a steward of Your possessions. I don't want to clutch them, so I'll just sell them slowly and carefully.* Thinking of the O'Briens, she added, *And some will just be my resource for gift-giving.*

She called three of the collectors on the business cards Mr. Newton had given her in July, and mentioned the snuff box, wine glasses and clocks, naming nine thousand as the price for the snuff box and each of the wine glasses. One eagerly came and made a deal for the glasses. He promised to notify a collector friend in England about the snuffboxes. (He assumed she had more in hiding). The other dealer came a few days later and took a clock for a thousand, then offered the suggestion that they make up a simple stapled catalogue list and distribute copies.

The very next day the collector from England telephoned and after asking questions about it for half an hour, asked them to hold the snuffbox. He would wire the money immediately, and come to pick it up in person in a month. At that time he would see what else she had.

When Ruthe had deposited the cheques in her city account she went to see the finished white station wagon with the wood-grain panel and the newly upholstered interior once more. Lloyd was there. As requested he had her green Beaumont convertible towed in. Ruthe admired it all afresh. "Wow, Darlin' Bonne's favourite colour! And now the girls need to get away on their days off."

"June sure loves it too," Lloyd said matter-of-factly.

As Gordon and Lloyd pointed out all its remarkable features, and how they would revamp it, Ruthe heard the echo of Lloyd's words, "June sure loves it too." *Lord? It's Darlin' Bonne's colour, remember?* The echo came again, *June sure loves it too.*

Is it fair? asked the very low, silent voice.

She sighed deeply and murmured, "One must be practical."

Standing quite still and staring straight away, Ruthe thought on this. She had almost persuaded herself that Darlin' Bonne had to have the green Beaumont, and then she might give June the station wagon. June had invested two payments in the Rambler but wasn't getting any use of it. *I am letting her live in and decorate the Greystone. Do I owe June another favour?*

Oh Lord, I never knew the joy of giving would get so complicated. Her joy was definitely dampened and she knew she had better sort it out before she made a mistake that would be hard to undo. *Look, there's three men all watching me.*

At last she chose and announced her decision, "Since the Shop girls need a car as soon as possible, and the Lord has helped me sell some antiques to raise the money, I better take the wagon as I planned. If you'll tell me how much, maybe I can have you fix this Beaumont too. I believe I'll give it to June."

She opened her purse and slipped a finished cheque out, stretching it in her hand toward Lloyd. "Here. Will this cover it? Gord thought you would be asking ten thousand once it was finished."

"No, no!" Lloyd grabbed her by the shoulders. "That's for a stranger! For our spiritual mother– it's only half!"

Ruthe scraped her lips through her teeth to keep from grinning. *Good thing You sent me shopping, Lord, instead of Darlin' Bonne.*

Suddenly Lloyd's eyes broke into a new twinkle. He turned her shoulders around to face the kelly green convertible. With his arm around her back, he said confidential-like, "No for that price we'll do the Beaumont as well. Give us a month."

She turned to look up at Lloyd's face with a grin she could not repress. "I bet Gord needs cash to buy tools and upholstery fabric, eh? Why don't I give you this now, and we agree that I get the Beaumont back as soon as it's done?"

Lloyd smiled back broadly, "You realize Graham might scold us for such a trusting business deal. Why don't we shake on it, and then you can carry the cheque around until we get Graham in on the act. He can decide whether to take it in advance or not."

Ruthe shook hands with Lloyd, then not to linger, went over to Gordon to ask if he had heard and understood the agreement and would vouch that this conversation had happened.

Gordon's white teeth beamed in his grease-smeared face, but he wiped his right hand on a dirty black rag before he stuck it out to shake Ruthe's. "I heard; both for ten."

As she turned to leave, Mr. Adams came to stand in front of Ruthe. "What d' ya plan to do with the other car, Miss?"

Ruthe shrugged, and looked around puzzled.

Lloyd came up quickly to her side again. "Yeah, over there–," he pointed to the ashy-black heap with a foreign shape two lanes over beyond some other wrecks.

"Can't say 'tow it to a dump' if it is at a dump, can I?" she asked wittily.

Lloyd's eyes were big and earnest as he shook his head.

Mr. Adams spoke; "These young boys have never seen such an old Rolls Royce. It may take years to find all the parts and equipment to rebuild it, but it could be worth a lot to you, restored."

Ruthe blinked, "But I can't affor–"

Mr. Adams held out a greasy hand in a pretend motion that indicated he was putting it around her back. (She noticed Gordon moving closer with great interest on his face). "Tell you what; if you let us work on that Rolls for the practice and joy of it, I'd only charge you for any parts we have to order from overseas. One day you'll have a real show piece there."

Lloyd, whose hands were clean slipped in between and did put his arms around her, repeating the offer persuasively and with more words.

155

Again, Ruthe looked past him to hear her thoughts, and also paced away to study the Rolls, but that was basically to put space between her and Lloyd. It couldn't stand in the carriage house to distract antique shoppers. If she waited for a different offer she might end up with fifty dollars or less; someone else would make the big profit. *So, shall I snap it up?* Ruthe sensed only a huge smile from her dearest Friend, and the fragment of a faint echo that sounded like, *glad you didn't overlook June.*

A new giddy mood broke on her as she looked up into Lloyd's nearby face again. "Tell you what, if you can arrange for some strong young men to help carry old furniture out to the carriage house, where we want to sell it, I'll let you guys have the pleasure of working on that old burned out heap. See what you can make of it."

Minutes later, as she was about to leave, Lloyd got in the station wagon to deliver it. Ruthe circled around to roll down her window and instructed him to inform them that it was an anonymous gift car. His gallant salute assured her that it would go well.

That night Darlin' Bonne was phoning around leaving messages for her to call, so that she could tell Ruthe. "That's hilarious!" she had told Lloyd at the door, "I don't even drive!– 'Allow me to finish;' Lloyd says with a flourish, 'The gift comes with another, free driving lessons– with yours truly!'"

Ruthe did her best to act thrilled and surprised for Darlin' Bonne and the girls at the shop, and she asked if Betty didn't have her own drivers' license, but she was sure glad she was in the lounge at work, and Darlin' Bonne could not see her face. It would have been a far bigger give-away. She even stayed away a few days so everyone could get used to the station wagon.

Instead she went to tell June that she would get the Beaumont when it was repaired, in a few days. It did much to mend their friendship, for June confessed to feeling miffed that Ruthe had not noticed her interest at the time of their discovery, and that she had thought of other friends first. Ruthe explained her reasoning, and together they rebuilt their relationship.

On the way home and for several days after, as June and she, with the help of the Bright City guys, moved antique furniture down to the carriage house, Ruthe thought in images of friendships as burned out rare cars restored to better than mint-condition status and priceless Rolls Royces. *Let those fellas work with steel, metal parts, plastic and grease to rebuild cars, You've called me to restore and rebuild friendships, right?*

However, when they went to look up a lovely, late summer rose of both pink and orange-gold tones behind the carriage house in the selection of reference books, Ruthe returned to image of her friends as rare and precious roses that must be nurtured along.

When she did get back to the shop, and the girls told of the free car with the lessons, Ruthe enthusiastically exclaimed, "That's wonderful! Don't we have a great Heavenly Father?"

They suspected Lloyd of the generous gift and thanked him every time they saw him. He faked a convincing, *Aw shucks, ain't nothin'* attitude.

It gave Ruthe a tremendous charge to know she had got away with this secret, much better than the house for her family. She clapped her hands down on the wheel and hummed with happy chatter to the Lord, whenever by herself, driving to or from the city.

She was not particularly good at remembering tunes, but snatches struck her mind like the stuck needle of an old record player. She sang, then hummed a haphazard second or two before the line was back again. Sometimes they were old Sunday school choruses, sometimes phrases of her own making. That she had a secret cache from which to give gifts to others, while she was still poor for all intents and purposes, gave her a deep satisfaction. This was the kind of rich she had dreamed of as an early teen. Only she had always assumed she would have to be swept off into marriage by a rich man. Apparently not!

The pace of clients at Darlin' Bonne's shop slowed down after the first few hectic days so they could work with less rush and panic. Yet only one or two of the girls were without a customer any given hour of their business day. They put off advertising. Donnie knew all about free publicity by news releases through her father, but they didn't get around to that either. When they had a spell without clients they gladly sat with their feet up, chatting, or just spent more time with individual clients, who were soon all friends.

Betty and Donnie could already drive, so Mondays they supervised Darlin' Bonne's practice driving and had rides all over the countryside, sometimes a museum, or an Indian village for tourists; sometimes lying in a park, sketching each other; sometimes a drive to Regina to window shop for new design ideas. Monday was a lark day, and though they enjoyed their clients, all of them looked forward to this holiday each week. None of them wanted the high pressure of the opening days of the shop as a regular tension.

TWENTY-FOUR

On a windy, blustery day in Kleinstadt, in old jeans and a blue sweater over an old plaid, long-sleeved blouse, Ruthe spaded up the last of the carrot rows for the final garden harvest of the season. Sharri was hanging around, but exploring bugs more than she was helping. Ruthe sent her into the house with the plastic bucket of carrots. Their mother was at the sink cleaning the previous bucket full and was probably ready for this one.

Hooking her wind-blown hair behind her ear, Ruthe casually ducked between the barbed fence wires and headed down the path through the willow woods on a vacant town lot. A fork in the path veered off to the back gate of her Grosz'mama's home. She hesitated a moment, but took the other direction that led past a boarded up little brown house and over the deserted back street into a pasture thick with unkempt willows at the first, lower end. She came to a clearing that sloped up, and there she sat down on a fallen poplar trunk about as thick as her thigh. This was a favourite spot that she visited often.

Right at her feet was the remains of one prairie rose, only two petals still clinging to it. She reached out to touch the under-edge of a petal, but didn't try to pick it. Her cheek on her knee, Ruthe smiled and let her imagination go to pictures she had seen of cultured roses in Granny's books and magazines, then played her mental game of comparing them to her city friends.

The O'Brien sisters were large, full-bloomed yellow roses. *No, Muriel is a smaller, sweetheart type. Darlin' Bonne is a passionate crimson rose, right, Lord?* The other girls at the shop might be various shades of pink.

She recalled a week earlier. June had taken her around the south and west sides of the Greystone mansion and shown her the pink roses still growing untrimmed up against the grey rock foundation of the back of the carriage house. Ruthe, read up now on such things, thought she could identify them, but when Muriel and her Dad came through the hedge, she asked them, and they confirmed that those were tea roses. With trimming, fertilizer, and care they would do even better.

One stood out, and Mr. O'Brien referred to it as a rare Talisman rose. He was amazed that it had survived with so little attention. The one on that stem appealed to Ruthe's imagination because of its delicate blends of yellow with a golden bronze pink, it was not quite orange or yellow or red, but a glorious combination of those shades. Now, sitting by the willow bushes, sheltered from the gusty fall wind, and knowing she couldn't come here so easily in winter, Ruthe pondered which of her new friends could be compared to a Talisman rose.

Maybe I haven't met that person yet. What do You think, Lord? Am I going to meet even more unusual people?
She got no specific answer. She had not exactly expected one. She was just mulling things contentedly in her mind. Relaxing.

Early the next morning though, she caught herself wondering as she drove to the city, what kind of friend would have to come into her life to be most like that golden bronze rose. *Someone stunningly beautiful? Or, more likely, with unusual energy and sparkle?* Ruthe nodded an unconscious smile. God wasn't finished bringing interesting people into her life yet. *My life is just beginning!*

It was Friday. After Ruthe's day shift, she arrived at the Shop just after the closing, after six.

Mrs. McPherson, a taller version of Donnie, known now to the girls as Mama Mac, their receptionist, was shaking with indignation and rattled nerves. "...Like a dog! Like a vicious dog, I tell you!"

"What's happened?" asked Ruthe, looking around the empty room.

Mama Mac shook herself to loosen up her 'anger fur' and her thin, light brown curls fluffed up, making an airy halo about her head. "Ach this dame walked in a few minutes before six and demanded to see Miss Barrett. I says to her, I says, 'Darlin' Bonne is with a client. She should be free shortly, Madam.' – See, I knew I couldn't chase her off until the girls come out with their last clients for the day. 'Please have a seat, Madam,' I says."

"And?" Ruthe's adrenalin was up because of Mama Mac's.

"That prim and righteous spinster barked: 'Use her proper name and call her this minute! I have important things to say to that young lady.'"

Mama Mac understood the Shop rule against being interrupted when with a client. She guarded their privacy as part of her job, so she had refused to fetch Darlin' Bonne.

"This Miss Shulton, (her name, she says)– she told me off in no uncertain terms. Tho' I didn't get half of her hunder-dollar words."

Mama Mac described how she had feared they might come to blows, except, just then Darlin' Bonne had come down the hall with a client. "Soon's the door closed after the client, Miss Shulton pounced on her former student!"

The news in this tirade had Ruthe puzzled. Lost in thought, she scratched her head and arms unconsciously, then offered to take over and let Mama Mac go home, who refused however, until all the designers had heard her eye-witness account.

As the group in the waiting room grew, Donnie remembered Darlin' Bonne had run into some old schoolmates and invited them to come. One had reported that a teacher at their high school was threatening to go after every dropout.

"Would they tell her Darlin' Bonne's name change and new address, and all this?" asked Ruthe.

Donnie shook her head, "To hear them, she's a fire-spitting dragon. But this Shop is hot stuff on all the school campuses this month, so she may have overheard something."

Mama Mac mimicked the high school teacher sarcastically, "'Miss Barrett, what do you think you are doing, dropping out of school to work in a sweat shop? Don't you realize you need an education to get anywhere in today's world?'"

Evelyn's eyes sputtered in shock while several blustered about the surprise this teacher would meet in Darlin' Bonne.

Donnie's mother was ready to go home to set on supper for her family now. Betty and Ruthe urged her to go ahead, "Don't worry!"

Hearing muffled conversation from the first sewing room, Ruthe stood in the hall, trying to imagine what she would say, or what Darlin' Bonne would say to this irate teacher. *Lord, I know I would cry out to You while talking, but that's hard. I'd wish someone was praying for us.*

Ruthe looked about. Betty was locking the door, Evelyn was bent over the accounts ledger, while Donnie and Louise were sorting the cheques and cash into piles. *Lord? This is more serious?* Suddenly she said, with a shepherding motion toward the sofa and chairs, "Come over here, girls. Let's pray. Our dear Darlin' Bonne may be introducing that fire-spitting dragon to the love-breathing Saviour. We can help."

None hesitated. They sat in a knee-tight huddle and poured themselves into fervent prayer. They asked God to give peace and power to Darlin' Bonne this very hour. "...Give her Jesus' mind in all her thoughts and reactions."

"Soften, melt Miss Shulton's heart and will."

"Bring a miracle to pass!"

They prayed around several times, each expressing the same goal in a sentence or two, and after a few turns, Ruthe sensed that all of them were confident that Darlin' Bonne was experiencing these things in the next room. Their prayers grew into exultant praise. A bit past six-thirty Ruthe felt it was okay to stop. While Betty and Evelyn soon drifted back to the day's cash, Donnie and Louise sat telling Ruthe about their clients of the day.

A few minutes more, and Darlin' Bonne came out of the sewing room, lovingly squeezing a tall woman by her slim waist.

Dabbing at her swollen green eyes with one hand, her old-fashioned glasses in the other, the woman suddenly noticed Ruthe and the other girls closing a circle around them. She stiffened upright and tried to sniff away her last tears. "I... I'm afraid I...." Ruthe notice the deep lines pointing inward to the woman's mouth. "I don't know what came over me– but I now feel–" She shrugged as if abandoning an old mask, and resolving to be nakedly honest, "What can I say?"

Ruthe's spirit was warming with sympathy already as she put an arm around Miss Shulton, bumping into Darlin' Bonne's young familiar arm. "There's nothing to be ashamed of, dear," Ruthe said kindly. "Most of us go through some emotional crisis when we meet the Lord for the first time. Afterwards often too."

The woman gave her a grateful look as she put on her glasses.

Darlin' Bonne cheerfully introduced everyone.

"But we use first names here," said Donnie slyly. "What's yours?"

The stiff, other-generation Miss Shulton hesitated, then answered, "Phyllis."

"That was my mother's name," volunteered Evelyn, a little bashfully, yet pleased.

"I always thought Phyllis quite pretty," Louise said.

Like a motherhen Betty broke in with, "Right, ladies. Step this-a-way. Come around the corner and down our grand plateaus into our humble abode."

"Yes, let's!" exclaimed Darlin' Bonne, steering Phyllis along with the eager little throng. "I'm starved!"

Betty had prepared the main dish while on her lunch break and put it in the slow cooker. Now she opened the fridge door and handed a different vegetable to each of the girls to prepare for the salad. She washed and put a pot of apples on to steam and then set the crockpot's thick hot pads in the centre of the table. The others scurried around too, setting places, pouring ice water.

The seamstresses had all had a long day, and now they let themselves go. Darlin' Bonne undid the long barrette holding up her black hair, and swung her hair free. They clowned and kidded with each other like seasoned comediennes with practiced one-liners.

Phyllis couldn't help it. Here she was laughing helplessly at the cute remarks and sassy retorts that flew around her. She looked giddy.

Ruthe caught Darlin' Bonne's eye signalling her to come into the bedroom. She went gliding in after Darlin' Bonne and shut the door.

Darlin' Bonne put her barrette on the dresser and sank into the bed's edge expelling a shaky whistle.

"Yeah-h," Ruthe whispered, "What-ev-er happened?"

Her head full of thick black upturned ends rocked from side to side, "Ruthe Darlin', you won't believe it! You just cannot imagine!"

"Try me."

"I always hated her in school! More'n any of the other teachers," she began, "But so did all the other kids."

She pulled Ruthe to sit down beside her. "Anyways. She starts off by bawling me out for dropping out of school. I was ready to snap at her about how well I was doing, manager of this shop, n' all that, when the Lord reminded me it was a gift from Him, and you, darlin'." She shook her head again. "I've never thought my prayers so fast!"

Ruthe nodded. "She's sort'a scary?"

"No. Not of her. I was scared I'd lose my temper! Is it ever hard to be nice to someone you can only remember hating. Someone who does not have a single good trait to her name!"

"Yes-but, you cried out to the Lord– and He controlled you," countered Ruthe.

"Oh-h-ew, He sure did!"

Darlin' Bonne went on to describe how she had taken Miss Shulton into the sewing room, and firmly asked her to listen to her story first. "I told her about the sexual attack and strangling, but I stressed that best of all, I'm helping people find this friendship with the Son of God who really, truly wipes out sins forever."

"She kept asking me how I knew or could tell God was real, Ruthe. She said, maybe I'd dreamed Him up in a sub-conscious effort to... compensate, or whatever. I don't remember all that. I told her over and over that I'd never heard of God before you came to visit me in the hospital. I was wishing I were dead! Now look at all He has done for me since!"

In school everyone had known Miss Shulton to be an avowed atheist, but Darlin' Bonne got the impression this afternoon that she was checking and double-checking this strange story, in case– just supposing there was a God, a nice, caring, trustworthy God, after all.

Darlin' Bonne had felt a wave of boldness all at once, and had invited the teacher to try talking to God herself, in humble respect, to find out whether or not He would speak to her. Here Darlin' Bonne's eyes rolled upward expressively.

"So she babbled in some other language?" Ruthe asked.

Darlin' Bonne stared at her. "How'd you guess?"

"It seems to be a sign God gives to some. Doesn't happen in Kleinstadt, but I've read about it. Very controversial in some churches, I understand."

"Well, @#$– oops, I prayed first. Then, all of a sudden, she was there, stuttering and lying face down on the floor, crying and I guess jabbering in something Indonesian! It sure sounded like she was face-to-face with Almighty God, the Boss of all the Universe!"

"Hey, you two," Betty called with a light tap at the door. "We're ready to eat."

"Coming," Darlin' Bonne called.

As they passed through the door, Ruthe had a flash vision of this Miss Shulton arriving back at school on Monday morning so transformed that the students wouldn't believe it was her. She turned quickly to whisper with her hand on Darlin' Bonne's shoulder, "What if we re-made her? Wardrobe, face, maybe even her mannerisms? Monday she could tell the kids that the old Miss Shulton had died over the weekend, and she's the new teacher!"

Darlin' Bonne gave a low whistle, hugging Ruthe with impish glee.

TWENTY-FIVE

It didn't take long for the other young women to tell their leaders had a new idea. Throughout the meal's banter, they watched for clues.

Over the dessert of steamed apples Darlin' Bonne urged Phyllis to stay the whole evening. "We'd love to sew a few new clothes for you."

Evelyn spoke up gently, "I think I could give you an elegant hairdo if I might have permission to tint it a stronger shade of red to give your eyes full advantage as emeralds."

Louise, who had become quite adept with cosmetics, chimed in, offering to soften her skin, and to smooth away some of those wrinkles at the corners of her eyes and mouth.

Phyllis couldn't get out a *'no'* so she consented to letting them play *dress-the-doll* with her.

They whipped through the dishes as a team, and hurried back upstairs, oblivious to the weariness they had complained of earlier. The sewing machines from the other rooms were hefted onto the larger table in the first room as if they did this every evening. Which, in fact,, they did more often than not.

Phyllis was over fifty and wore an old charcoal crepe dress with long sleeves, shoulder pads, and below the knee hem. It was well constructed and not cheap, however it made her look lifted out of a 1920s photograph. She had frizzy red hair streaked with grey, knotted in a braided bun, which she kept checking with long dextrous fingers.

They had to coax her to take off the crepe dress. She wanted to keep it on until they had made a new one. Donnie applied her charms, wheedling and begging on one knee until, "I don't know what to say. You are all so nice to me, and I realize I'm being prudish–" With a last glance about, she yielded.

The tall lean formed uncovered was what the designing course had described as rare, the ideal figure. Darlin' Bonne and Ruthe took her measurements and fitted a basic muslin sloper on her before they gave her a dressing gown to wear. While they used the sloper to draft, or by now, simply outline pattern pieces on the tissue paper, Evelyn took her away into the semi-ready hair salon at the end of the hall, where she rinsed Phyllis' hair a bright rust-gold.

Evelyn brought her back so the others could talk with Phyllis too, while she set the hair in short but thick curls with a wave perm. For a time she had to wait in silence, as the increasing birring of five machines, each making a new outfit, meant conversations had to be shouted almost. Once set and rinsed, Evelyn swept the curls up majestically from her forehead, but in and around her thin, high cheeks.

Louise and Evelyn changed places right after so Louise could give Phyllis a facial. when she took that off, she put on a clear, creamy makeup with flourishes and touches and comments that kept the others giggling and laughing.

"Hey ever-y-body," Louise yelled suddenly, "Look at this!"

With a clatter of falling scissors, the others came to see.

"No more than say, thirty-five, is she?" asked Louise dramatically.

Ruthe's mouth popped wide. Phyllis' face did look incredibly younger, smoother. A much better colour too.

Phyllis herself was delighted and bobbed her head foolishly this way and that in front of the mirror in her hand.

"Exactly which miracle cream did you use, Louise?" Donnie teased. "Point it out."

Darlin' Bonne handed Phyllis the emerald satin chemise she had just finished, to try on. Betty produced a brand new set of undies and a pair of black patent high-heeled pumps. They tried to help her dress, yet wanted to let her do it herself.

When she stood up and smoothed down the lovely-to-touch fabric, and the gold braid belt, they all backed off to look. Oo-ing and ahh-ing, they pointed out new details. The new Phyllis was a tall, sophisticated woman with fine taste and intelligence written all over her. She had luscious red-gold curls, and a chin and nose outline to make any fashion artist like Donnie drool. Her eyes. Sad huge emerald eyes that came alive when she laughed. They lit her face like neon lights. The cheeks just below those eyes were ivory and smoothly curved like the lines of a baby's bum.

They praised and pivoted her like a professional model, and even took few pictures for their Album.

"Promise," begged Darlin' Bonne, "That you'll get rid of all your old clothes and wear only the ones we're making for you tonight, okay? Promise?"

Helplessly, Phyllis promised.

Betty made up a coat and dress ensemble in an iced tea colour with a matching hat and purse that shimmered with gold lights.

Donnie zipped together a bright red taffeta plaid with black velvet to make a stunning set of coordinates.

Ruthe managed to sew a pale blue wool suit as her contribution.

After Evelyn finished Phyllis' hair, she had also started to sew, and made a bronze brocade evening gown. Louise went back to her sewing machine too and made another bra and pantie set.

The evening seemed early yet, so they all started second outfits as soon as they had finished the first round. Of course, as they had hoped, and had experienced with many clients over the previous couple of weeks, along with this physical unmasking, Phyllis gradually opened up and told them all about herself.

She was orphaned as a child in Australia. At thirteen she had grown not only withdrawn, but bitter against God and the world when she was raped in a deserted stretch of woods through which she usually walked from school to her foster home.

Afraid to trust anyone, especially men, she had locked herself into a world of books, a safe and private realm where she could have adventure without involvement. Diligent and thorough, she earned degrees in literature and history while still in her twenties.

Then she had to set new goals. She wrote textbooks for elementary schools, and travelled to the States. There she went to another university and got degrees in arts, music, and philosophy. Education, journalism and even political science followed. She drove herself on, only stopping to write another textbook or history tome when she ran low on tuition fees and living expense money. She set higher goals and got doctorates, no matter how long or difficult the courses, as long as she did not have to think of relationships, or her lack of them.

A time had come when there were no more courses that interested her. Realizing she had some responsibility to pass her knowledge on, she decided to come teach in Canada. She chose high school, rather than a professorship, so she could feel superior to her students. They would not notice her shortcomings. (At that Darlin' Bonne turned and raised a quick eyebrow at the others).

"Even with all my credits, I'm a flop. I've just antagonized all of them. The whole school. The whole generation, in fact!"

Though she had written complicated theses to prove it was impossible for God to exist, the girls learned that almost her main argument had been that in all her travels she had never met anyone who was the kind of transformed person prescribed in the New Testament.

Oh Lord, Ruthe moaned silently. *What a shame!* She felt a strange stab of pain in her heart area. She kept still until it eased away.

"Yet tonight I know He is real," Phyllis went on, warming up to her new testimony as she spoke. "It's as though He has taken on your bodies and is present here. In you! And, I felt His Spirit enter me too, when I prayed earlier."

Ruthe moved over, looped an arm around Phyllis, and gave her a squeeze. "That's what this transformation is all about." It had been an emotional journey for Ruthe to see Phyllis relive her past. She was glad they were back to the more positive present.

"What amazes me," answered Phyllis, "Is how He reveals Himself to me at last only after I humble myself, admit He is God after all, and I am only a depraved sinner. Once I was willing to be changed it finally happened. Girls, you would not believe how I have feared God all these years. I was sure if I dropped my guard for a minute He might jump out and kill me. Many a night I've read until daybreak because I was afraid to fall asleep."

To prevent recurrence of such nights, Betty handed her a Bible from their under-the-table stash, and helped her mark a few verses to reassure her of God's loving promises to her, if these fears should come back. She should claim them as her own, given specifically to her.

"Believe me, Phyllis," Ruthe warned, "When you get home, or as soon as the emotional high fades you've got being with us here, Satan is going to try to make you miserable. He's an awfully sore loser; he'll really begin to play dirty. Doubts will probably be his choice weapon in your case, since you are an intellectual."

Phyllis smiled. "You're the thinker in this crowd, aren't you?"

"Aw," Ruthe replied quickly, "I'm just your garden-variety plain dreamer, but I've found that we sometimes have the hardest time hanging onto what we believe. At least until we know we'll never go back. The gospel message is simple so that even mentally handicapped children can believe quite easily. Those of us who want to understand it all so badly are the ones who get tripped up with doubts sometimes."

"Just don't resign," added Darlin' Bonne, "You're on the victor's side. Spend time living around other believers and learn the art of living through Him. Or Him-through-you, as it says in John."

As they talked the new clothes piled up in heaps. Stopping to look around at them, Phyllis wailed, "Tell me, where am I going to wear all these beautiful, elegant clothes? I never go anywhere!"

"Go to school," retorted Donnie innocently, "Where else?"

"Be eccentric. The kids will love it," murmured Louise matter-of-factly, squinting at something in black lace she had just finished and was examining for thread ends.

All at once Phyllis realized something she had not fully comprehended. She had gone too far to go back. She looked new. She felt new. People were certain to react differently to her.

Ruthe saw, vaccumed in her breath, and spoke up about the vision she had seen earlier. How the school kids would think their fire-spitting dragon had died over the weekend and that she was a new teacher.

"Oh, I was quite tired of the old me. But I don't know any other way of teaching. It won't be long before they recognize the old *Fire-spitting Dragon* again!"

"It doesn't have to go like that," said Betty firmly. "You can let the Holy Spirit guide you. Christ is standing by to transform you into a new creature."

"Tell you what," Ruthe said, "I've just had another idea. Why don't we help you plan your dramatic entry and announcement? Your complete first day in your new personality at school? We'll go over every possible aspect, every reaction we think you might get."

Phyllis stared into Ruthe's eyes. "Do you mean that?"

The other girls chorused with her, "Sure!"

While they finished the sewing at hand, Darlin' Bonne told Phyllis just which of her teaching habits irritated the students most. They suggested new attitudes and techniques to replace some of the old habits. The new ones would improve her rapport with the kids three hundred percent.

In Ruthe's Sunday School teaching she had discovered some new tricks for starting a lively discussion. She passed these on to Phyllis for adapting to older students.

"Use more visuals and imaginative displays," said Donnie. "Contrary to general opinion, those apathetic-looking kids are alive. They are interested in things they can see and touch. TV addicts, remember?"

"Try field trips," added Louise. "I still remember vividly things and places I saw on kindergarten trips eons ago. I loved the high school teacher that took us to see some factories."

"Listen," suggested Betty the organizer, "Why don't you bring your books over tomorrow night, and we'll try to show you how the lessons could be taught. A fresh perspective might help."

Phyllis gave Betty a long look, then at the heap of new clothes and the other girls. Tears humped over the nearly invisible lines in her new ivory cheeks. "If only I had met people like you years ago!"

Because Ruthe was nearest just then, Phyllis draped herself over her shoulder for a few moments of tears. In those moments Ruthe realized deep in her soul that this woman was going to be the talisman rose in her garden of friends.

She wasn't able to be with them over the weekend, but heard later by phone how the girls spent Saturday giving Phyllis intense coaching, and took her to church in the morning. By the afternoon she said, "It is time to learn to love back," and took them all out for lunch.

TWENTY-SIX

Minutes after Ruthe arrived late Monday afternoon, at Darlin' Bonne's Shop, Phyllis came in too, bubbling, and with her lean frame jiggling as she walked on her high heels. "Ruthe, it happened! I can't get used to it; I'm a completely new person! The whole school bought it too!"

"Hallelujah!" Ruthe hugged Phyllis back. "That's great!"

"Hallelujah, that's a nice word!" Phyllis hugged her ecstatically again, and then quickly another time, her emerald satin shoulders twitching with excitement, and her costume necklaces doing a soft clicking, sliding dance on her bodice.

"It would never have happened if you young women had not saturated me all weekend with attention and encouragement."

Ruthe suspected that was true, but urged Phyllis, "Give God all the credit. He had so-o much fun making you over, and He's not done yet!"

Mama Mac eyed Phyllis like she ought to know her.

The reception room was empty, so Ruthe gave Mama McPherson permission to go home, without thinking to make introductions.

Mama Mac pointed out protectively, "Each of the girls has a client yet, but you can lock the door now so you don't get new ones."

Doing so as the neighbour left, Ruthe said to Phyllis, "I was about to go down and set the table for supper. Why don't you come too, and tell me all about your day?"

The elegant teacher picked up her purse and leather briefcase to follow, stirring her bent elbows eagerly, "They suggested Saturday night that I tape the more dramatic beginning parts of my school day."

Ruthe saw her tottering on the stairs, so held back to grab her arm and steady Phyllis down the stairs, secretly thankful all of a sudden that her father didn't allow her to use stilts like that. As they entered the lower apartment Ruthe asked to hear the tape.

Standing still, Phyllis promptly obliged, pulled the small dictating device out of her case, and held it up. "There were only a few students in the room when I first turned it on."

"How did they react to you?"

"It was most embarrassing. They had the impression I was a substitute, just as you thought they would. They talked about the Dragon they normally had in the class. Here."

169

Ruthe bent over the little recorder to hear the background voices. "@#$@+! We've got a new sub," one male voice whistled an expletive with a slam of the door.

"#$@@%&! Old Dragon must be sick," laughed another.

"Naw-w. She must'a died. That Fire-Spittin' Dragon ever get sick?" retorted a different young man.

"Haa, she's sick all the time," came a girl's voice. "In her head!"

There was a space of unintelligible noise on the tape as the room filled, so Phyllis took the opportunity to explain with a blush, how some of those students had eyed her and gathered in little clusters to whisper. Meanwhile, she had tried to control herself by busily arranging her desk and trying to pray and ignore them until the bell rang.

On the tape a bell birred loudly and everyone went with tremendous scraping and scuffing to their places. A hush fell over the class, but a girl's voice breathed quite audibly, "Do I ever love that hair!"

A boy, beside or just across from her, replied, "Ah-shoot, her bodd needs more curves."

Phyllis covered her face as she heard that again.

"Get used to it," Ruthe smiled, "It's not the last time you'll hear such backhanded compliments."

"I don't know if I'll ever learn how to handle that, Ruthe!"

"Well. Don't try then either. I've given up, and put the Lord in charge of that department," Ruthe counselled. "Tell Him you'll obey if He will be in charge of your attitudes, reactions– even what you hear others say about you."

They stopped to pay attention to the tape again.

"Ladies and Gentlemen," Phyllis' voice carried rich and husky, "Whether or not you can believe it, this is the same old 'Dragon' you saw last week. Only today I am completely new. A wonderful change has come over me this weekend."

Ruthe could imagine the students staring in disbelief. She heard a catch in Phyllis' voice as she said, "I want to apologize to all of you for the way I've treated you. I promise you a totally different teacher for the rest of this year. The opposite of all I have been."

"You see," she explained, "I went to Darlin' Bonne's Shop this weekend and came face to face with the reality of Jesus Christ. I believe some of you know the place. There is something very magnetic – a holy joy about Darlin' Bonne, and her staff. I'd always thought of her as unwilling to learn, and yes, a girl of bad reputation. Now there she was, a serene and gracious woman. The force of her unusual compassion for me, was... (sigh) it was just irresistible!"

Her voice grew lower on the tape. "I've been bitter at the whole world for a long time. Friday night I realized that I had been taking it out on myself, and on you. I met God and received His forgiveness, His peace. I discovered that He loves me despite all I've done. Now there is nothing left to fear. Perhaps you can't tell, but this is the first morning I'm not afraid, or not quite so much afraid of you. Not of God; He and I are friends now. And you– you all look like interesting people today. People I think I shall enjoy getting to know."

Ruthe could picture her tossing her thick red curls as the voice grew more confident and positive on the recording. "I hope you are ready for adventure; I'm out to win you over as my friends!"

The history lesson, which followed on the tape was almost spellbinding. Not just Phyllis' presentation, but the way the students opened up and entered into the debate on world issues into which she drew them. Towards the end of the period they got bolder and sidetracked her with more curious, personal questions about her weekend experience. She answered gingerly but honestly, which made Ruthe glad.

Surprised as they were at her, Phyllis was every bit as astonished at the degree of rational thinking that she discovered in her class. She never noticed any signs of it before when she spent whole periods writing off her detailed notes for them to copy from the board, expecting them to be memorized for her exams.

"Doesn't your head reel at the challenge?" asked Ruthe, feeling inspired. She remembered how she used to weigh being a missionary and being a teacher in her idealistic mind. Now she was resigned to what incidental influence she could exert in her present life style. "Just imagine what God might make of them, through your influence!"

They counted themselves in as they set the table and discussed the possibilities, and what Phyllis thought would be limitations to her influence.

When Phyllis turned and asked, "What are your goals in life?" Ruthe became abruptly shy and timid.

"Oh– I don't know.... I have too big an imagination, they tell me. I've got to keep pulling in its reins all the time."

Phyllis, still pumped up with confidence, pressed on with more questions where Ruthe would have sensed signals to stop. By degrees Ruthe admitted she had debated from age nine whether she should be a foreign missionary, or a teacher. Or a writer. Or, if possible, all three. Marriage? In her wildest dreams– maybe a doctor or a pastor's wife, where she could help many people as well. Get an education? Ruthe's stomach went queasy with shock. "I'm afraid it's out of the question. My folks can't afford to send me to Bible College." She realized Phyllis was referring to university and added, "They think universities are for people on other planets. No, Phyllis, my main goal now is to earn enough money to keep the family off welfare. Right now I have plenty of friends I can help, so I'm content."

"Why not decide what you really want most, announce your decision, and let them get used to it?" Phyllis asked bluntly. "You can always get loans for education."

"It's not that easy!" exclaimed Ruthe, feeling strangely defensive at this woman she thought was going to be her special friend. "There's other factors. Family loyalty... Um, some of us feel God does not want us to go into debt. Anyway, I've committed my life and future to the Lord and He is going to bring His will to pass. He knows how to overcome' all obstacles in my life, and– well, how to step carefully around everyone's feelings so no one is hurt."

Phyllis pulled her shoulders back puzzled, while they heard steps coming down, "I don't understand your philosophy. I thought it was good to systematically set goals and aim for them."

Ruthe interrupted swiftly, instinctively, "But what did your fear of God do to you at night? Don't you think that fear of what family members think, whom I try to honour, can hold me back?"

Now all the girls came pounding down the stairs, hungry and lively. "Touche," murmured Phyllis to Ruthe and became the pliant student again of these younger women.

In a week or two, Phyllis needed less and less help from the girls at the shop. She was a quick study and caught on to preparing her lessons with the new approach. She applied all her previous learning and experiences to make each class a thorough and fresh adventure. The time involved was immaterial. Phyllis had brand new goals and a drive like never before. However, whenever in her eagerness she blundered and made a mistake, she called or came around again to discuss the underlying Christian way of thinking she needed to firm up.

Before long, a prize technique of hers was a little blue loose-leaf notebook, in which she wrote and to which she referred constantly. Her students were each represented by a stamp-sized miniature photo at the top of a page. It, and the following pages, were covered with finely written notes and observations as she got to know them personally. Plots to assist them were noted in bracketed capitals throughout. Ruthe had suggested the notebook so Phyllis could pray specifically for each student, but it seemed to meet other purposes too.

She often shook her head and marvelled after an encounter with this new teaching dynamo. In some ways Phyllis was brilliant and in some ways quite naive. They didn't always agree, so Ruthe had to learn to hold her own position on certain principles. This friendship took more work.

The end of the week she was to receive the convertible, Lloyd apologized to Ruthe, "That green Beaumont is not ready to give to June. I 'fess up, we've been too busy on the Rolls. But now we are stuck for parts." When she made a woe-be-gone face, he added gallantly, "Can I loan you my MG until we get it done?" Ruthe hesitated. "June is thinking of having her brothers and sisters move in with her. Your itty-bitty car would be too small. The other day I heard June dream of a small van. Got one of those?"

June had landed an interior decorating job while taking her correspondence course. She discovered, Ruthe explained, that she had to take wallpapers and carpet samples to and from the home up the river, never mind the stuff she was gradually bringing into the Greystone as she redecorated room after room.

Lloyd promised to see what he could do, and in a few days had sold his MG and bought a shiny white van. Ruthe delivered it to June, realizing that he had given her a very advantageous trade.

"That green convertible is history!" June trilled at this tailored miracle just for her. "Do you really think it's safe to move the kids into the Greystone?"

Ruthe winced inwardly, knowing those wild kids would likely damage something, but looking at June, she told the Lord, *people are more important than houses.* "I'll come with you to get them, June, and try to be around more for a while so they get house-broken to some rules."

However, there was a problem. Mrs. Johnson became adamant that her husband was coming back any day, and they must be where he had left them. She would not move, and June must not move Wes and Linnet out, else she had no one to look after her.

"But I need Wes and Linnet to help look after the younger ones when I'm away at work!"

June wasn't surprised, but Ruthe was stunned that the mother did not care if the youngest three were taken away from her. Linnet pointed out that they weren't loved either, but had got in the habit of bringing their mother trays at mealtimes. So they had to leave them where they were. Ruthe was all out of ideas, but promised that they would think of something soon.

In her praying she concluded that perhaps Mrs. Johnson needed to be committed to an institution. She got June to call their social worker, but even then it took weeks for any action. Meantime, she advised June to bring them into the Greystone anytime they both had a day or two off, and use that as a transition time.

A couple of weeks later Ruthe was notified that the Beaumont was restored and ready to drive. It took all three men to convince Ruthe it was also hers to give if she wished. The van had been an apology for the delay. Finally she accepted it, and asked Lloyd to bring it to Darlin' Bonne's Shop.

Again, she stayed away from the shop for a while. Her delirious joy in giving such grand gifts was tempered with trying hours holding onto slippery, squirming Johnson kids, and lecturing them on common courtesies.

Her family and coworkers asked if she were in love, else why would she be always smirking to herself? "Your eyes dance and you tilt your head this way and that, as if you hear tunes," said one operator near her at the switchboard.

When she denied being in love at home, Suzanne made cracks about Ruthe being mentally unbalanced. This gave their parents a scare for they could not understand Ruthe, but were horrified at the thought of having to put her away in a mental ward. Her mother lectured her about behaving normally. "Stay away from strangers in the city! Don't have anything to do with them. Or you'll quit your job and stay home!"

The idea of being kept at home to do maid work sobered Ruthe. She thought she ought to be able to prove she was sane to most doctors, but aware of Mrs. Johnson's case made her cautious. She didn't want the rift between her and her parents to deepen, so she spent her off days at home, and less with her city friends. At least for a few weeks until they got other things on their minds. Besides, her mother was whining for help to bring the last of the potato harvest in for the winter, and her Dad had a new farmhand job for a while. Ruthe considered this the price of peace.

Besides that, the days were getting shorter and the nights cooler. It meant she soon had to find nooks and times for her praying indoors rather than the dawn and sunset walks she enjoyed. These days she pondered on honouring or dishonouring one's parents. Was distrusting them a sin? She could bear misunderstanding from anyone else as long as she could count on the Lord listening to her, and caring about the details of her life. He gave no clear yea or nay to her question.

Her mind also constantly drawn to her city friends, Ruthe began to make time for them again when she found herself moping privately over the rose books and magazines Granny had given her, and when the old empathetic heart aches were back. She wept because some hurting soul would die before being introduced to Jesus. She *must* be in the city in case of any new opportunities.

Then her parents were able to sell the old house and Ruthe's mother came to her quietly to slip her a hundred dollars. She tried to refuse it but her mother said, "The minister's wife asked last week at Bible study if you weren't making enough to afford some decent office clothes. So you go see if you can find some bargains for yourself. Are you suppost to wear them fancy high-heels too?"

Ruthe stood very still. She tried to take this in, and at the same time knew where she would find her bargains. It took a minute before she could pull herself together to say a quiet, choked up, "Thanks, Mom. I know a new place to go to."

They were about to part ways, when her mother added, "Dad wanted to buy a better car, but I made him put the money from the house into the bank so we can live on that if he's out of work this winter. Maybe you should save up your pay cheques for something– like when you get married, or anything."

"Okay, Mom." Ruthe turned away, shaking her head ever so lightly at the expected mixed with the mysteries, and smiling to herself.

The shop girls gladly helped her put together a bargain wardrobe, they reported how useful the green convert' proved to be. More often now, they received calls at night from teens or women who had been in the shop and wanted the proffered spiritual help after all, or they needed more of it. Several times both cars had been out at the same time, but in different directions.

Ruthe paced herself for once or twice a week visits, and soon became involved in a couple of these evening trips. Once it was to talk someone out of a suicide. Ruthe had her heartaches and lonely times, but because she could tell it all to Jesus she had never considered taking her life. Happily, Darlin' Bonne was surprisingly adept at persuading the woman that God valued her.

Mostly Ruthe prayed in the background, and echoed what Darlin' Bonne said. *Our precious Darlin' Bonne,* she crooned silently to their mutual Friend. *During the day she's this efficient, constantly moving business woman; dressed the part in those chic black suits–* (just then Ruthe was looking at her in a fitted black velvet blazer over a dark red gathered skirt with black roses, which made her look stunning, but more informal); *Evelyn's taught her to sweep that lustrous black hair up for daytime in that.. what is it, Parisian way?*

Ruthe had no need to compare her simple ingenue look to Darlin' Bonne's elegance and feel small. The uninhibited hugs and cries of delight with which this friend greeted her cancelled any contradiction in their appearance. Because Ruthe had once suggested she try to catch up on missed innocent years, in the evenings, Darlin' Bonne often put on girlish shirts and peasant blouses, and combed her hair into a bouncy flip below her ears, so she was nothing more than a loveable sweet sixteen ready for adventure.

Betty was the mother hen. She looked after practical things and made most meals. She was content in this place, with its creative, loving atmosphere, and the gentle music she made sure was always wafting on the air. It was her dream life, except for the time each day when she checked the mail and bit her lip, or moaned, "What ails my folks not to write?"

Ruthe wasn't sure if Betty had written recently or at all since coming to the shop. She suspected dread of having been disowned kept Betty from phoning to hear it. She couldn't quite imagine Christian parents going that far, but she told the Lord, *I'm not the only one with problems. Some are worse off than I.*

Through that fast and busy summer Donnie had become the group's pet canary. She was always chirping something witty in her high, bird-like voice. At first Ruthe thought it an affectation, but like the others she learned this was Donnie, and loved her as she was.

And Donnie was artistic, though she had not know she could sketch so well until she tried the lesson on fashion illustrating. If, when Ruthe dropped in, she described a dress she had just seen downtown in the Bay window, Donnie would put a few deft strokes on a sheet with a brush or oil crayons, and presto, there was the dress. When she added a few more touches, her artwork scintillated with delicate colours like a bubble in sunlight. It had a gossamer sheerness that Ruthe loved, an exquisiteness of detail that made her think of butterfly wings or almost see-through petals, or– of Louise's delicate features.

From grade one Louise had been Donnie's quiet shadow, letting Donnie say and decide everything for her. Since joining the shop, Louise had discovered her own creative and intuitive talents and begun to speak for herself. Betty confided to Ruthe, "Louise recognizes other timid or smothered souls and gently pulls their hands to Jesus."

Evelyn had learned quickly as well. The others taught her sewing and designing in a laid-back way on alternate evenings to the ones when she taught them hairdressing. In the daytime she took the easiest to please customers, but already everyone noticed that she had a flare for classic lines and excellent stitching. A few clients phoned ahead to reserve her when they wanted something super special.

Ruthe's sister Suzanne heard about Darlin' Bonne's Shop at school and repeated the bits of gossip at mealtimes at home. Because her sister didn't often say what was going on in her mind, Ruthe tried to be uninformed, yet interested. Her ears twitched one day when Suzanne bragged, "Our own young Saskatoon designers have not had a single rude or unhappy customer! Tracey heard it."

"Not one?" Ruthe asked, smiling absently as she recalled the day Phyllis first came to the shop..

"What you grinnin' at?" her Dad asked suspiciously.

"Nothing," Ruthe answered quickly sobering. "Just daydreaming."

"About what?" queried Suzanne.

"Oh... happy roses, seekers of Truth with a capital T...."

"What a dreamer," her mother charged. "Some day Satan will try to trip you right on that worldly mind of yours. You let it run away with you too much."

Ruthe was about to ask, "What if it's a gift from the Lord?" then quickly tucked her lips between her teeth.

TWENTY-SEVEN

Phyllis, the earnest seeker of Truth, began to invite Ruthe to her apartment to answer a growing list of questions about God and how to get her own answers from Him. With concentration Ruthe juggled visits to the O'Briens, the Greystone, the Shop, the Bright City men, and the elderly couple to whom she made car payment visits, and fit in time for Phyllis. Mostly when she came off shift at midnight and was still too hyper and tense to go home to bed.

Ruthe didn't often mention to others her favourite analogy of her prayer life to walking in a garden with Jesus, but Phyllis asked such penetrating and drawing questions that she found herself describing it before she had decided to do so. Then she tried to apologize. "I'm afraid some folks see this as a silly mind game. They say I live in a fantasy world, but my walking and talking with the Lord are happening on a spiritual plane; they are real!"

Catching on quickly, Phyllis explained it back to her with psychological words, until Ruthe realized that they were both talking about *abiding in Christ*, as Jesus Himself described it in John's gospel. She breathed easier as Phyllis convinced her it was okay for a person, gifted with imagination to personalize her spiritual life as a garden.

Their teacher-disciple roles switched back and forth between them quite suddenly at times, making them fairly equal, despite an age gap of more than thirty years. There were moments when this intense friend stirred Ruthe inside, and made her uncomfortable in the very spots she had accepted and rooted down some belief. Other moments her heart ached with identity in Phyllis's searching questions, and she was so glad she already knew whom to trust with the unknowns. There were other questions they had to agree to research.

Long weak on etiquette, (but planning to take a course), Phyllis bored deep and direct with her questions. She wanted to know, "What else are you doing to maximize your life for the glory of God?"

"Huh?" Ruthe's jaw hung slack and dry. "I'm doing all I can in my circumstances, am'n't I?" She looked down at her new wardrobe; she was wearing a pumpkin coloured cotton dress with a snug bodice and flared skirt. *"What do you see in me that I can't?"*

The redhead in the red tartan with black-trimmed white blouse looked fabulous, but was totally unconscious of herself, as she leaned forward, "Dear Heart, you think you are a poor nobody; you have ten times more potential than you are using. You are creative, artistic, imaginative, and are very intuitive with people– and that's just what I have observed the few times I've met–"

177

Ruthe's shoulders seized into a knot as she cried in defence, "I'm already working all night at the office, I've been putting in four to six hours a day at home, with the garden harvest and preserving, plus I'm trying to keep tabs on all my new friends in the city. I have no time for more talents!"

Phyllis lightened up with a laugh, but was earnest. "I didn't mean your current to-do list, Ruthe. I'm talking about your life as a whole. I see the years clicking by and you are on a little treadmill while you have potential for greatness." She folded herself into a pretzel version of a thinker pose, but her eye focused on Ruthe, who sputtered and groped for a response. Taking a dressed up lady pose again, Phyllis added, "I must not rush you. God has your ear, and you are still young. It was my impatience speaking. I'm sorry. I must trust and believe Him as well as You do, and in time He will bring it to pass."

Ruthe shook her head. She didn't know how to answer this stuff. It was time to go home and get some rest for the next day.

"Have you ever watched how slowly God pries open the petals on a rose?" Phyllis asked at the door.

"He doesn't pry them at all."

"In the same way, you are a rose in your own spiritual garden. A slow-opening one, but when you bloom, Ruthe, you will be beautiful."

At the apartment door, and at the elevator door, and down in the lobby of the building, Phyllis trailed Ruthe with what was supposed to be closing comments and good byes. She urged her to consider taking up writing poetry or fiction.

"My thoughts don't rhyme...." But Ruthe could not shrug off or hide the spark of interest that the idea of writing a book elicited in her.

"I'll tutor you. Act as your editor. Get you a typewriter, whatever you need."

Ruthe saw no place in her full schedule, and her mind cramped at the idea of explaining away more blocks of absence at home. Or, for that matter, a typewriter, if she dared bring it home. Feeling very mixed up, Ruthe declined. "Thanks ever so much, Phyllis, but your friendship is enough."

Driving home in the moonlight on the almost deserted highway, her thoughts jumped about, from what a thrilling compliment Phyllis had paid her, to how she had changed in just a few weeks, what new channels her strength of character had found, and how blessed her high school students were, and that Phyllis had offered to tutor her– Suddenly these thoughts bumped into thoughts about her brother Brandt.

"Ha!" she exclaimed aloud. She began to scheme and figure out how to bring Brandt into the city for remedial reading with Phyllis. "Let him have the tutoring she offered me."

Brandt was dropping too far behind his age group. Her brother did not socialize much and being labelled a "slow learner" depressed him. He was threatening to quit school on his October birthday. While still in high school she had reminded her parents that Brandt had been home sick for a month just when he was supposed to be learning to read phonetically. If only he had been caught up with those lessons, he would not have failed. She had suggested professional help.

Her Dad had said, "No kid of mine's going to be addled by a shrink. Then he's mentally ill the rest of his life!" It did not good to explain the titles and functions of various counsellors. "All shrinks believe in shock treatments," was her dad's authoritative conclusion, "And I saw what that did to my cousin."

Phyllis would do perfectly for Brandt, Lord, if only she didn't look so– Ruthe couldn't think of the right word and at the same time knew the teacher's beauty shouldn't hinder. A tremulous smile made her chin wiggle up and down. She didn't know why, but felt like offering a barter; *then, maybe... after that, Lord, if You want to open a petal or two on me....*

TWENTY-EIGHT

It was the end of another day. Sunset came earlier in October. Ruthe was just thinking, *there won't be time for a prayer-walk by the time I get home,* when she caught glimpse of a girl in a pink quilted house coat disappearing into the shadows under some shrubs and a row of gloriously coloured maple trees along the city sidewalk. Her curiosity aroused, she slowed down to peer into the dim of the first hour after sunset. *Was I wrong?*

Once again she had a momentary glimpse of a darting figure as it vanished around the corner at the end of the block. She urged the car faster, then around the corner. Her headlights caught the girl as she was about to cut diagonally across the street. She jumped behind a wide tree trunk and crouched there in a huddle.

Ruthe stepped out and called over the top of the car in a loud but friendly whisper, "It's okay. I'm a girl too. If someone is chasing you, jump in, and I'll hide you."

The invitation was accepted.

Once the girl was in her car, Ruthe took a good look at her, even while she pulled away. *She can't be more than thirteen or fourteen, Lord.* The newcomer had petite, dainty features that reminded Ruthe of Louise, but there was a firm signal of experience with hard work in the girl's manner. "What happened?" asked Ruthe politely.

The girl slid down so her head would not show in the window, and had been giving Ruthe a sideways inspection for a couple of minutes. Now she began to rub her knuckles in her eyes.

Does this mean she trusts me? Ruthe wondered. To help, she asked a few questions.

The girl could not recall her father too clearly, but yes, she had one, somewhere. Her mother had told her that he had not been able to stand employment. Their marriage interrupted his college education, so he returned to single student life. "Daddy wasn't bad," the delicate stray insisted. "He used to come home for Christmas, 'cause he had no other family. Since I started school, he just came at night to be Santa. I've never seen him all these years."

"So where is your mother?"

"She died at Easter."

"Any brothers or sisters?"

She had two younger brothers, Freddie and Gerry, and a baby sister, Michelle, and found comfort in one fact; all three had birthdays one day after another in March, and their mother had lived long enough to celebrate all of them. But no one had known how to reach her father, so the neighbours had arranged the funeral.

Ruthe found this a fascinating story. She pled for more.

None of the neighbours had been close friends and one man in particular had always scared her. At the chapel service she had noticed him standing off, bartering with a wealthy-looking middle-aged couple, people she had never seen before in that area. "By the way they sized me up, I was afraid the neighbour was selling me!"

Ruthe gasped. She was now several blocks away, on a scenic river view street.

"A little later, while different adults drooled over us, calling us dear orphans, and patting our heads, I got separated from my brothers and baby sister. The strange, rich people took me in their car, and told me the other children were coming to the cemetery in another car. I never knew funerals had so much getting in and out of cars."

"Did they come in another car?"

"No. I've never seen them since." That made her cry.

Wispy yellow curls tumbled out of a high switch caught on her head with a rubber band. Ruthe had a sense of looking at photos of her own early teen years. "I worked hard too," she confided to the young stranger, "When my mother was in the hospital a lot. I was constantly afraid she would die and we kids would be handed out to various relatives. Our lives would go different directions."

"That's happened to us!" the girl cried afresh. "I tried more than once this summer to run away from those selfish people. I have to find my family! (sniff) Once I ran to the next door neighbours, and told them I was kidnapped. They called these people, to check out my story, they said, but they gave me back when the woman cried and begged me to love her– and the man scribbled in his cheque book."

"Oh-h-no!" Ruthe sighed sympathetically.

"Another time, (sniff) we went shopping in a mall I'd seen before. I got lost on purpose and took a bus back to our old house. It was all locked up. So I went to a friendly neighbour family. It was nice for a few days, but they bragged on my coming back, so the bad neighbour heard about it. He took me back to the people who gave him money in the first place."

Hmm, what street was I on when I first saw her? Ruthe asked herself. *In case I, or the police want.... Naw, I don't want her to go through that again!*

Finding the hard way that none of the people she had known, or her captors knew could be trusted, the girl had still determined to get away. "I'll never give up until I find my brothers and sister! And Daddy too." Her plan included refusing to give her name or any past address so she could not be returned. The girl was most resolute.

"I have no intention of giving you back to people like that," Ruthe promised. But she knew just as quickly, that if the police got involved, which seemed only right, they would check it all out. *No telling if they'd return her, Lord.* Ruthe's spirit flew upward. *I do believe her, but what am I supposed to do next?*

"Now, the couple who bought you would not go to the police, right?" Ruthe asked, still trying to understand the situation.

"Yes-but!" replied the girl with a teary cough, "If the police talk to them they will believe the beautiful, touching story they'll tell. I just know I'd end up back there!"

"How do you expect to live?" Ruthe asked next, sighing softly, *Please, Lord, what can she do?* "I mean, without money, day clothes, or a name.... Nothing."

"I can't help it! They locked my clothes in their bedroom after the last time I ran away," the girl cried out. "I've just got'a believe somebody somewhere will help me!"

A sinus blockage between Ruthe's eyes seemed to melt. "As for clothes, I can help you out there. I have friends who have a dressmaking shop, and they'll be glad to make you a starter wardrobe."

"For free?"

"Yes, for free." Ruthe smiled and grew serene inside. She had one step of action. Though the girls at the shop had hardly room for the three who lived in the basement suite, they would put their heads together and find some place. *Not a hotel, Lord, okay? And not with Social Services either, all right?* Then she remembered why she had the Greystone.

"I couldn't give up," the girl was saying into the embroidered collar of the housecoat. "I just prayed and prayed to God to help me try over and over until I got away. This time I knew He was going to bring me together with people who are kind and wise. Do you trust God?"

Ruthe swallowed at the damp lump sliding from her sinuses to her throat. "Yes. Thanks for reminding me. Yes, I do love and trust God as well. Whenever I get into a tight place I pray and He has answered me wonderfully many times. Especially this summer!"

The young eyes opened wide at Ruthe as she whispered, awestruck, "See, God is still the Friend of widows and orphans."

At the shop, Ruthe pulled out her special key, unlocked the front door and sang out, "Hi-y' everybody. Come meet my new stray kitten!"

Of course, the Shop family gathered quickly. While some fell to their knees, gushing with concern and questions, Ruthe explained her story in an aside way to Darlin' Bonne and Betty.

When they asked her name, she looked soberly over all the friendly faces, but decided not to trust them. She shook her head respectfully. "You're all very nice, but I am not going to tell you. You might end up having to tell someone else. If you don't know, you have no problem."

"I promised her a new wardrobe while we try to figure out other steps," announced Ruthe. At that the approximately thirteen year old was swept off into the first sewing room for the royal treatment.

Ruthe and Darlin' Bonne hung back to talk.

After a fresh review of the girl's story, they agreed that they had to call the police, or their own relationship with the officers would be tarnished. Ruthe picked up the receiver from the wall desk. The officer she talked to knew of no missing person report of the girl's description, but would send someone over right away to talk to her.

When Ruthe hung up, Louise was standing in front of her. "Call my Mom across the street," she whispered. "I know she's with Social Services, and this girl doesn't want to become a ward, but if you call my mother at home, she'll keep her official mouth shut, and tell you our options."

"Maybe," Darlin' Bonne chimed into the huddle, "she can tell us how to check the girl's background without a name or address."

Mrs. Nunweiller was sympathetic, but said she would get into deep trouble if she didn't report it to the right department. "If she saw this black market adoption happening," the neighbour moaned, "why didn't she speak up?"

Ruthe felt the professional knew the answer well enough but said quickly in the girl's defense, "Without true relatives or good close friends to look out for them, it seems disinterested strangers were in charge. I'm sure she begged to be allowed to look after her younger siblings, but she was ignored."

Mrs. Nunweiller wasn't angry at Ruthe, promised to ask questions, and warned her not to get the girl's hopes too high. "These things seldom have happy endings."

Darlin' Bonne and Ruthe went to join the others in the next room where there was laughter and chatter. The nameless guest was being turned and fitted for several outfits at once.

"This way, sweetheart," Betty called out.

"Look what these colours do for you!" exclaimed Donnie.

"All right," asked Louise, "Does this feel comfortable?"

The slender blonde spun herself as directed. Her eyes were drawn to the array of materials in the shelves, and the sewing machines. Spotting Ruthe, she called out, "I ju-st love it here! Ho-but I thank God you found me."

"You know anything about sewing?" asked Darlin' Bonne.

"Could you lift your arm?" Evelyn asked quietly.

183

The model obeyed happily. "You know, my mother used to take in sewing. Before she got so sick. I always helped her do all the buttonholes. Everyone said I did them so nicely."

"If you mean bound buttonholes," said Betty, "how would you like to like to prepare some for this new coat? Between fittings."

"You'll let me? Really and truly?"

Darlin' Bonne stepped behind Ruthe and whispered into the back of her head, "Maybe, with a bit of makeup, her hair done up on top like mine, maybe she could pass for one of us and we could use her in the shop. The Labour Board need never know, eh?"

"Aw-w-w-you!" Ruthe laughed and nudged her back playfully.

But when Ruthe told the girl that the police were coming to question her, she tensed and quickly volunteered to help out in the shop to pay for the bother she would be if she could stay with them.

"At your age–"

Darlin' Bonne accepted graciously, "If the police will let you, I'll be very glad to have you stay and help us out." She gave Ruthe a deliberately mischievous wink.

"Are you short-staffed again?" Ruthe asked in exaggerated shock.

"Evelyn's looking after clients by herself," Darlin' Bonne took her arm and steered her aside, "And Mama McPherson isn't always available to run errands and stay in the reception room."

Louise had come softly up behind them again. "Why don't I do up her hair and put a dab of makeup on her? See if she doesn't look a bit older?"

Darlin' Bonne picked up a needle and made as if to prick Ruthe. Ruthe backed up smirking helplessly, and nodded at Louise, "Why not?"

Soon their walking, talking doll could have passed for seventeen or eighteen. A petite teen, but not much different from Donnie or Louise. Neither was quite eighteen. "Besides, Darlin' Bonne is only sixteen and no one can tell," Donnie repeated twice.

When the police officer showed up, Ruthe saw it was one of those who had given her such a hard time when she brought Darlin' Bonne into the hospital as a limp victim; the one called Aubrey. They chatted about that day for a few minutes, and Ruthe was relieved at the respect he showed. "A business woman now, eh?" Aubrey turned on Darlin' Bonne with awe. "Terrific!"

He poked his head into all the doors and satisfied his curiosity about the shop and its principle of operation.

As they stopped again in the door of the şewing room where the others were still fitting the model, but working quietly now, Ruthe offered, "We are willing to keep her here at the shop, but I could also take her to my Greystone mansion."

He turned on her with questions until she had explained how she inherited it, and where it was. This officer seemed pleased to hear that and promised to remember it.

"And," Ruthe added, suddenly boring her gaze intently into his eyes, "if you try to take her back to those black market parents," her voice was lo and steel hard, "I may lie down in front of your patrol car to prevent you."

He backed up as if shocked, and saluted.

When the new girl was standing all alone, Aubrey slipped around the cutting table and crouching in front of her asked her to describe what had happened to her. She repeated her story in a few brief sentences, looking down into his face which nodded and nodded.

Ruthe watched apprehensively until he stood up, patted the girl's shoulder and said, "Don't worry. You have fallen into the hands of our Angel d' Mercy. Things will go better for you." Ruthe gulped as Aubrey said farewell to her at the door. "Little Crusader, go ahead, work your magic on this sweetheart. I'll do the detective work."

Ruthe's thoughts and prayers were getting jumbled. She knew she ought to head home, to spend time alone, maybe behind the furnace, since it was too dark by now to go out. Before she got away, one of the girls asked the newcomer again, if she would give them her name.

"May I have a new name?"

Ruthe moved back to listen, hoping for a clue.

"What would you like to be called?"

"Oh, you all make me feel so happy and excited... Joy?"

"Joy suits you perfectly!" exclaimed Darlin' Bonne instantly.

It did. Just then she was modelling a very vogue white wool dress, with a red and navy scarf tied jus-t so around her neck. Her hair was all swept up into a bunch of soft curls on the top of her head, except for a few whimsical tendrils, which fell down in front of her dainty little ears. Her hair was brighter, more golden than Evelyn's, and she was smaller and shorter than Ruthe. Right then and there, the girl who already had won a place in each heart, took up her identity as Joy.

TWENTY-NINE

Ruthe had tried to avoid Ross O'Brien all through the summer. In September he started university and since Cathy and Muriel wanted her to come over more often again, she did. Even so, there were times she ran into Ross because of his irregular class schedule. Much as she wanted to get along with everyone she knew, Ruthe saw Ross as a painful wood sliver under her skin. It made her wince to think about him.

His rudeness was so deliberate that it was harder and harder for his sisters to be patient with him. Each time they lost their tempers Ross, of course, claimed a victory. He nearly jumped up and down as he pointed out that they were not perfect Christians after all. As a result, Ruthe had to remind them a couple of times that they were saved because of their faith in the finished work of Christ on the cross and His resurrection, not by their perfect behaviour.

His father and brother Keith seemed disinterested. Or perhaps they ignored his cries for attention because they looked foolish, Ruthe wasn't sure which. At any rate, Ross concentrated his verbal and emotional attacks on Ruthe and his sisters, ignoring the males.

A time or two Ruthe tried to reason with Ross and told him earnestly about his soul's destiny. She never had thought she would have the courage to speak so bluntly to a man of any age, but his behaviour warmed her ire until it just flowed fluently from her. Ross grew kiddish, making puns with the words she used. One day she used the word doodle; immediately after she couldn't recall the context, for Ross was waddling like a duck in circles all around them, singing, "Doodle, oodle, noodle, noddle, widdle-waddle, piddle-paddle...." She gave up.

Another time she said, "...God, the essence of love." Ross shot popcorn kernels at the ceiling with a rubber band as he nattered, "Essence, shessance, penance, dance, pants, rants, chance."

She had just visited the directors of all the funeral homes and asked them to recall any funeral arranged by neighbours for a poor woman with three children. She was telling Cathy and Muriel about her efforts while they waited for Mr. O'Brien to come from checking other sources regarding private adoptions. Pretending not to hear Ross they moved into the kitchen.

Ross followed like a friendly puppy, drew closer to Ruthe, and tapped her shoulder as he said, "Hi, Soul mate." Then he swung away to the teddy bear cookie jar. In a moment, with his mouth full, he said that he was invited to a great campus party that night. Inspecting the fridge, he tossed over his shoulder at Ruthe, "Eh, Beauty, be my date. Prove that your invisible Friend really goes with you wherever."

It would only prove his power of persuasion, she knew. Afterwards he would use it to sanction his own presence and activities in such environments. She shook her head firmly, "No way."

Mr. O'Brien and Mr. Newton both came in, and Ruthe gladly turned to ask about their efforts for Joy. To her relief, Ross vanished.

"All that's left to do, is spy out the area where I found Joy," she told the lawyers, the corners of her mouth hanging low.

"How about the schools?" Mr. Newton said. "Have you been there?"

"Surely some teacher would recognize your description of this new girl you've found," added Mr. O'Brien.

It was the challenge and encouragement she needed. Saying hasty good byes, Ruthe decided she could visit at least one or two before she had to be at work. The rest she would do over the next few days.

Besides, she'd heard that Aubrey called the Shop and hinted that they should get Joy into some school soon if they didn't want to be charged with breaking the Education Act. She wanted to find people to question on correspondence or home schooling, in case that worked out better.

When she got out to her Rambler, Ross was waiting for her, leaning against her driver's door. She was exasperated. "Excuse me, Ross. I've got things to do."

Sounding suddenly confidential and urgent, Ross said, "I really need to talk to you, Ruthe. Alone." He hiccoughed as if swallowing a sob. "I've decided to turn evangelical, but I have a few serious questions hindering me. Can we talk?"

Ruthe gulped in her delight. This sounded real. Inwardly she almost shouted, *At last what we've waited for!* Before she could answer, Ross opened her door graciously for her, and handed her in like a princess, then he did a hand-spring over the hood of the car and popped in on the passenger side.

Praying quickly for guidance she turned to watch Ross make himself comfortable on the seat beside her and noticed he was having a hard time hiding his impish sense of victory.

Her hand caught his hand coming up to hold hers, but she caught it in such a way that she could dig her fingernails into his wrist. Applying first gentle pressure, then more, she said with her voice taut and low, boring her gaze into his eyes, "Ross, such lying tricks are not going to work. They only ensure that no one comes when you really, truly do have to grapple with a wolf. When you honestly want help, we won't believe you. Now, out! Out of this car!"

Ross swallowed with a faint flush, caught off guard. He didn't move though.

Ruthe didn't know where the idea came from but she added, "I know you need a Mommy figure real bad, but I'm not, repeat NOT applying for the job. Now, get out!" She drove her fingernails straight down hard.

His other hand reached for the door handle then, his expression pouting, "So. How many ways can a guy ask for help? You never believe me anyway!"

"I'm not the counsellor for you. Speak to your Dad."

Ruthe's lungs trembled and she took deep breaths and prayed much while she drove in a daze, with a weird tick in her left armpit, to talk to the first school principal.

This first principal had a teacher who had reported a student missing, and when she was called, their compared descriptions matched. The thirteen year old's name was Pauline Pepper, or Pauli for short. The office record showed her mother's name as Micheline, and the absent father as Dr. Maxwell Pepper.

At the shop the next day Ruthe took Joy downstairs and confronted her with the information and that she must continue her education.

Face awash with tears, the dressed up girl admitted, "Yes– I'm Pauli. But– please, plea-se don't take me away– from here!"

Ruthe worked hard at reassuring her that she wouldn't end up in another foster home. At last she said, "We probably will keep you here unless your family can be reunited. But Joy, or-Pauli, you must continue your education. That's the law. We can't pay the fine for keeping you out of school."

"I want to work—and learn right here!" Pauli sniffed. She seemed to grasp gradually that Ruthe was on her side.

"Listen, we'll ask Phyllis Shulton to set you up with a good home study plan, and to keep checking on you herself. I heard that home studies only work at their lessons an hour or so a day. You should have plenty of time to help with the sewing here."

"I always finished first anyways!" The petite young face came alive with eagerness. "Look. I could sit at the reception desk and do my homework while greeting clients. Donnie's Mom would prefer to come in the afternoons only."

As it happened, Phyllis gladly threw herself into this new project. She set it up so Joy worked on her own in her books at the desk by the door each morning, and she came to check on Joy every few days. Her afternoons and evenings were free for learning to design, cut and sew clothes. Joy, occasionally addressed as Pauli, told clients that she was an apprentice in this castle. Joy especially loved babies and small children and looked over each one that came into the shop.

It worked out well. Joy clipped through the grade eight curriculum. The others teased her about doing grade nine after Christmas, and Joy blushed happily. "I always did feel slowed down in school by others," and bragged on the number of units she got done in a morning.

Phyllis treated her as a gifted student and gave her special work to add depth to some subjects.

Ruthe coveted this kind of help for Brandt, but dared not bring it up at home. Now that she had Joy's surname, she quietly made further efforts to locate the father, Maxwell Pepper, whenever she could think of a new avenue. Joy had said that he wanted to be a rich doctor. Ruthe started by asking Dr. Davie Pollock if he had ever met such a medical student. He promised to check some leads– but they were standing in a hospital corridor so she didn't expect him to remember to do this. She began a tedious correspondence with the Registrar's office, and cat and mouse phone messages.

Next she was distracted by other things going on in her life.

Because of her last encounter with Ross in her car, Ruthe was quite guarded when early the following week he telephoned her at home in Kleinstadt. It was eight in the evening and she had just finished a cold supper left on the table for her. Ross insisted brokenly that he had to see her. Right away.

"No-o-o. I just got home from a full day in the city."

"Ruthe-e! Please come. Ple-ea-se? This no false cry of wolf!"

She'd never heard that much emotional earnest in his voice before. *Dare I give him another chance?* Ruthe wavered. *Is this just a more elaborate trick?*

Suddenly Cathy was on the phone, raving excitedly that Ross truly needed her. "He's just about sick, Ruthe. We've done all we know, short of taking him to Emerg. He hasn't eaten a single bite all day, and I've talked with him for hours on how we miss our mother and our sub-conscious ways of coping. Not a single wisecrack out him. Ruthe, I think this is it. He is really trying to understand about Christ today. Somehow, he can't grasp the believing part. Daddy's talked with him the last four hours, and even he can't help him to catch on. Ross thinks we're all making it out too simple. That he's got to do more. Some magic steps. Come talk to him, Ruthe, okay?"

Ruthe sighed, then murmured between her unmoving teeth so her family wouldn't hear, "If my folks don't take a fit." It occurred to her to leave it with the Lord. If Ross needed her, her parents would be in an easy mood. She would take it as a false alarm if they balked. Her face brightening, Ruthe prayed, *Okay, You're on,* and said to Cathy, "I'll be there shortly, unless the Lord closes the door. And– I think everybody should be present and accounted for."

"Huh?"

Ruthe hung up and turned to clear off the supper table in the now strangely deserted dining area. When she went into the living room to say she was going to have to go back to the city, her parents were discussing how to finish off the basement workshop. Her Dad with his feet up, said, "Sure glad it's not me putting gas in your car."

Her mother was half hidden under an afghan she was crocheting and said warningly, "Ruthe, you'll get sick if you don't slow down!"

"I'll be careful. So don't wait up," and Ruthe whirled away while the getting away was good.

It was Keith who let her in. Ross was pacing in energetic circles and pulling at his thick, auburn thatch of hair when she entered. She saw right into the living room where Cathy and Muriel hovered at Ross' elbows. But both came hurrying to meet her.

"Ru-thh-ee!" Muriel cried pathetically, "I'm praying you can get through to him tonight!"

Mr. O'Brien and Keith seated themselves across the room to watch.

Driving into the city, Ruthe had braced against being used. "Ross," she began sternly, standing before him with her hands on her hips. "Let's have the truth. What is this about?"

Ross reached up and gripped both her arms tightly, his face distorted. "Ru-u-the! I know what you're thinking! Please– please, just listen to me first."

She tried to freeze the expression on her face.

"I wish I could take back every unkind word I've said to you! I'm sorry. I... I'm awf-fully so-rr-y! Oh Ruthe, will you ever forgive me? Is it too late?"

"If—"

He tightened his grip and went on in a rush, "The only reason I've been so mean was– was that I was jealous. And too terribly proud to admit it! I– I thought I was in love with you. I couldn't stand to see you giving the others more attention than me. I wanted you all to myself, to... to show you off to all my friends and yell at them to look at Smiley, the *Wonderful Girl* I'd found! Be– be-cause you were Mom's f-friend."

Ross lowered his head and hid his eyes inside his elbow as his confession poured out. "Besides, when Mom died, I was mad at her! She shouldn't have let go so peacefully! I wanted like crazy for her to struggle more. She could've stayed alive longer, if she'd tried, just for me." All restraint broke and the dams gushed. "She... she had no business dying– and leaving me so suddenly! I wasn't ready!"

"I wasn't either!" Cathy cried out.

"But you got the miracle-worker!" Ross lashed back.

Ruthe winced at his anger, yet deep inside she was relieved. These feelings had festered inside him too long. Nor had she dreamed he was hurting so badly.

"I wanted somebody to cry with me too, but nobody did. You just paid attention to the girls. And I didn't have the nerve to ask for it like Keith did." He doubled up, creeping off the chair and crouching in front of Ruthe on the carpet as if he had a stomach cramp. Ross cried like a cut child. He was still clutching her one arm. Ruthe bent over him, her free hand stroking his heaving shoulders.

Ross tilted his head sideways and hiccoughed, "I... I've wanted to become a Ch-hristian... every time you asked me, Ruthe. Bu-t I was sca-r-ed th-that I'd start to cry."

She was feeling more kindly towards him but still wanted to make sure of his motives. "Tell me, Ross. Why doesn't it matter that you're crying now?"

"You warned me that you wouldn't believe me when I cried wolf..."

Drawing a long shaky breath, he heaved himself back into the chair just behind him. Ross still had not released her arm, so Ruthe had to come too. She perched on the wing of the big ivory-gold chair. "Yo-u remember Ann?" he sniffed, searching his pockets with his other hand.

"The one with the long uncombed dark curls, and the hand-me-down clothes?"

Ross blew his nose and grew more coherent. "I was stopping for gas one evening when I saw her out walking some toddlers. She promised to come for a ride, if I'd wait there until she had put them to bed.

"I don't know why–" he interrupted himself. "I guess I was just mad at you after Mom's funeral. I was mad at everybody! Even Granny got into a rage when I tried to make fun of you!"

He made a *woe-is-me* face. "Funny thing, Ann got a crush on me and wanted more rides. Late at night, cause she had to look after a bunch of brothers and sisters. She has the weirdest parents–"

Hmmm, the back of Ruthe's mind slipped in a gear of critical analysis, *sounds rather aggressive for a big-sister type.*

"One night I brought her home, hoping you'd be here. You weren't but Cathy was taking her old boyfriend and gang to see you, and suddenly I had this dumb old idea; I wanted to take Ann along to show her to you so you'd worry about the cheap girls I was dating. Maybe you would try to keep me away from them. Only– you don't think like I do, Ruthe!"

"Nope," Ruthe laughed, startling herself slightly with her giddiness, "Got that right."

Ross pounded his head down onto his fist. "You never noticed! Oh-gerr! Then to frost it, she became a new Christian on the way home! I was furious!"

Ruthe looked at Cathy and Muriel. Understanding was on their faces too.

"Anyhow," he finished lamely, "I've been sort'a seeing Ann secretly. Taking her for rides mostly. Or I did, until last night. Just when her friendship was helping me to feel better, she puts her foot down and says she won't see me or even talk to me again!"

"Why?"

"Be-cause... I'm not a Christian."

Bravo for Ann, Ruthe thought with a sudden respect for her. To Ross she said lightly, "I thought you said it was she who had a crush on you, Ross."

He hung his head again. "I didn't know 'til today how– how terribly much Ann comforts me, how lonely I am without her."

"So-o, missing someone spells love?" Ruthe's analysis department had fallen behind. She was bewildered.

He grabbed her face, "I haven't been able to think of anything else all day, except– I got'a be with her! I love her. I care about her and her dreams." Apparently he received the impression that Ruthe did not understand or care at all from her puzzled look, for Ross swung around and desperately thumped his forehead on his knees. "I know– what– you are thinking. But it's true. I don't care how it embarrasses me, I've got to get my messy life all cleaned up!"

Stroking his restless back she turned to his sisters and asked, "Have either of you seen Ann or talked to her recently? What's her version?"

"She's come out to talk with me twice," answered Muriel. "She phones me occasionally from a pay phone to talk. But I didn't know any of what Ross just said here."

"All I knew," said Cathy, "Was that because of family problems she couldn't go to church like we told her she ought to, but she was listening to those Christian radio programs you had recommended. She seemed to be learning lots of the Bible that way."

Ross spoke up. "That's where she heard she shouldn't be seeing me, let alone marry me. According to those Bible lessons on that program last week."

"What!? Did you propose?" asked Cathy, incredulously.

"Yes," said Ruthe, showing her own surprise while her mind whirled backwards trying to recall which programs she might have caught on the car radio. "I was under the impression you were in university. You did start, didn't you?"

"I did." He quivered again. "I hoped... you would at least try to understand!"

Suddenly Ruthe knew it was time to go on the offensive, to react. Wrapping her arm around his neck and pulling his red head onto her shoulder, Ruthe poked her fingers into his tight auburn waves and said firmly, "Ross. Listen. We– Cathy, Muriel, and I– even Keith and your Dad, we all love you very much. However, we can't read your mind. We have been stymied trying to reach you. So you have to tell us how you feel before you can expect us to understand and side with you. Where you are right, naturally."

Before she could stop, she also blurted out that she didn't think he was ready or mature enough for marriage. "Still, since you've started to be open and frank tonight, I'm willing to reserve my final opinion until you have explained all this business between you and Ann."

Ross crushed the muscles in her upper arm until she was about to scream. "Ruthe, you're never going to marry me, are you?"

"No. I do lots of favours for friends," she almost snickered as she smiled, and slowly shook her head, "Not that kind though."

He tightened his grip. "See, I knew it! So I let myself fall in love with Ann! I can't face life without her, Ruthe, i simply can't!"

"Do you suppose, Ross," she asked cautiously, "That maybe you're afraid to face life without God? At least without someone close who knows God? Is it possible you are too proud to admit your sinfulness and self-centredness before Him, yet you want to be friends, sort of, with God, so you have tried to win the companionship of someone who does have peace with Him? Maybe, also a mother-figure, Ross?"

He thumped his head on his knees again. Tearfully he said, "I don't know. Could be. Oh-h Ruthe, help me! I hate myself like this!"

Cathy and Muriel crowded closer, breathing a yearning for Ross to have peace in his heart and mind.

In a spare glance Ruthe saw Mr. O'Brien sitting soberly in chairs across the room, in an attitude of prayer, ready to move forward when the time was right.

For a long minute Ruthe gazed at the back of Ross's bowed head, thinking of what he had said, what all this could lead to, and the prayers his Granny and she had prayed for him. Even of the pride Ross and his Granny had in common. Suddenly the moment when Granny had caved in was vivid before her spirit.

She bent down to his ear, "Ross," she asked softly, "Do you feel miserable enough to cry out to God, who is holy and perfect, to say you are sorry to Him, and to hand Him your tangled, messed-up life? Can you do this tonight and mean it forever after?"

"Yea..." Ross lifted his head and nearly shouted it, "Yes! If you will help me talk to Him, so's I can hear Him, I"ll beg– 'll even cry, and ask Him to forgive me! I want to stop being so wicked!"

"Good. Then we're ready to pray. And for proud folks it's quite important to humble our selves. So let's all kneel."

Ross turned about and knelt at his chair. Ruthe was at his one side, and Cathy at the other. Muriel was already praying and sobbing into the arm of the sofa on the left.

"Dear loving, Heavenly Father," Ruthe started. Then, as often happened when she found herself doing this intimate and private thing aloud among others, she laughed and also had to blink away hard at brimming eyes. "Here is Ross at long last! Isn't it wonderful? After all the times we've talked this over and looked forward to this day— here he is. I'm so glad You didn't give up on him! Thank You, Lord, for loving Ross and speaking to him, and wooing him, even though we couldn't see it." Ruthe was overwhelmed. "You're fantastic, Lord! Just too marvellous for words! I love You, Lord Jesus!"

When she stopped on this note of ecstasy Ross began, "I'm sorry God. I'm sorry. I don't know how to start. I... Oh, God, help me say this! Forgive me all my wickedness, all my bad thoughts, and words, and all my dumb habits! An- and stop me from ever doing any of them again!"

Cathy bowed over Ross and prayed softly, praising God for His mercy and patience.

Ruthe was leaning on him too, and in minutes she felt hope surging through Ross's young masculine body. Her voice joined Cathy's in thanking God for his freedom from sin and its power and the guilt. His voice came in too, making them all a happy blur.

Only later, alone again on the highway, able to pray quietly, and to evaluate more objectively, did Ruthe muse, *how come it took me to bring Ross around? Couldn't his sisters, or for that matter, his Dad have counselled him?* She was half afraid that if Ann Mueller had rejected him, Ross would need a new sexual conquest. Christian or not, she doubted that his drive would disappear. *Well, Lord, I'll just have to put on Your armour and stand firm. Right?*

THIRTY

For a while Ruthe spent more time than usual at the O'Briens' home. She did advise Ross, but then politely pulled back some, so he would not get the idea that she was available for romance.

Saturday, almost a week later, it still had not occurred to Ross to have a cigarette. He first realized this when he found a pack in his sport jacket pocket. "Hey, guess what!" he yelled at the household collectively, "God, the Holy Spirit brought along an automatic air-conditioner when He moved into me."

His Dad heard and answered, "I've been wondering how long it would take, Ross. You've gone five days without a withdrawal symptom."

To Ross this was a sure sign that his bad habits could not master him any more. He resolved to give up drinking while his willpower was high. That was easy. It took a bit more effort though to drop a large chunk of his vocabulary.

The way he took to Bible reading thrilled Ruthe. More than once she came into their home to find him pacing from room to room, his new Bible folded back in hand, reading half aloud to himself. When he found some verse or truth he could grasp he would go all through the house to show it to everyone. "Listen to this," he would say, grabbing Ruthe's shoulder, spinning her to face him. Then he read with all the gusto he could muster.

Keith often shook his head. Ross was one weird Christian in his book. He warned his friends that Ross was not typical.

But many of the verses Ross found told him things to do. Things like, apologize to Lloyd for things he'd said, also, to a number of previous dates. He went to pay for some items he had shoplifted. Above all, he was solicitous and kind towards Ruthe. Which tended to throw her off balance. She swung between being glad and on guard.

Keith and his father seemed to have more time to talk with Ross as his petulance disappeared. The O'Brien family was growing closer than they had ever been, so they all said. Muriel loved to point out how happy this would have made their mother.

Two and a half weeks after the initial surprise Ross called long distance to Kleinstadt again, asking for Ruthe. This time, not so frantic. They were able to chat pleasantly. Ruthe was promptly blushing at his compliments, which gave Brandt and Suzanne cause to pounce on her with loudly whispered accusatory questions about her boyfriend.

Ross insisted that he had another crisis. "You have just got to come in tonight, Ruthe. Please?"

It was hard to refuse Ross. However, she resolved that when she saw him face to face, she would speak very firmly to him about not calling her at home any more. If her parents heard her brother and sister teasing her like this they would get upset, think the worst and would not let her go back to the city for any social calls.

"Ruthe!" yelled her dad after she was off the phone, "Don't you dare go and marry one of them for-en-ers in the city. Keep yer'self clean, like we raised you. Hear?"

"I'm not about to marry anyone, Dad!" Ruthe exclaimed in exasperation at Ross, at everyone.

"Are you see'n someone?" asked her mother with panic in her voice.

"No. I've never had a date in my life!"

"Be careful. Girls get raped all the time in the city. I keep telling you, stay away from strangers," she warned. "I wish you didn't have to work night shifts. I'd feel much better if you had a regular day job. Right here in Kleinstadt would be best."

Rolling her eyes to the ceiling in a cry for patience, Ruthe said tensely through her teeth, "I am as safe as can be. The Lord is with me all the time." *Oh-oh, not a good topic here at home.*

"Oh, I don't know;" declared her dad, not satisfied. "Where is He when people have accidents or get knifed or killed in a crash?"

"Probably at church," muttered Ruthe so he could not hear, throwing herself into doing the dishes, "Or wherever you left your faith."

When Suzanne tried to pick up the teasing again, Ruthe turned on her with an intense, low, emphatic voice, "Just take note how much trouble you are going to be in when you want to start dating. You're the one who wants to, not me!"

At that Suzanne clammed up and diligently dried dishes, then vanished with a flourish.

A bit later everyone had scattered to do their own thing, including her parents who went to mid-week Bible Study at church, and Sharri was sleeping over with a friend, so Ruthe got in her Rambler and left too.

When Ruthe got there, Ann Mueller was at the O'Briens', sitting on Ross's knee, both in his favourite chair.

Ruthe hadn't quite greeted each one present when Keith announced, "Ross has another crisis."

"Isn't that almost his lifestyle?" she tossed back.

Turning to the compressed couple she said, "All right. See if I'll faint this time."

Ross grinned helplessly. "Ruthe, I know I promised to wait and talk it over with your girls before I went back to see Ann. Well, I've done a lot of praying and thinking by myself, and last night, I just decided I had to find out if Ann would believe me. Gals," he included his sisters, "sometimes a guy has got to do what he's got to do!"

Ruthe raised her eyebrows. *If this were a real debate on that–*

"But I called Muriel a few days ago," interjected Ann, playing with Ross's ear. "So I knew all about it. All the miracles that have been happening here."

They confused Ruthe a couple of times in the telling, and she had to ask some questions to get it all straight, but it appeared that Ann was quite eager to marry Ross. The new Ross.

Muriel was perched on the arm of the chair where Ruthe sat. She bent down, whispering, "Aren't you a tiny bit disappointed?"

"Disappointed?" she whispered back, turning sharply. She was too loud. Everyone had heard.

Keith muttered, "Yeah. I thought you'd end up in our family. You sort of belong. Even Granny knew that. That's how I got Ross to drive my buddies and me to your place, to make Granny's dream come true."

Ruthe expelled her breath in surprise. "No," Ruthe said with a strong finality to all of them. "I have learned to like Ross, but not in that sense. He's all yours, Ann. Look, I guess you two are in love. Rather young, not quite the way I imagine it ought to be. I wonder though, are you asking or telling me about all this? Why am I here?"

"We'd like your encouragement and blessing," Ann said. "In a way, we also need your help. You see, I'm nearly eighteen, the oldest of twelve. On top of that, on the wrong side of the tracks. Not far from those smelly slaughter houses on Tupence Street. Furthermore, I should tell you...."

She went on to describe her father, Frank Mueller, a terribly shy, insecure man, who spent most of every night downtown bumming drinks, and nearly all the next day trying to find his way home again. Whenever he found it while still mad drunk, he was so aroused at the sight of his wife, a former Indian princess who made it into the Miss Canada finals, that he often took her by force, even when she was asleep.

Her mother felt so ashamed of her foolish marriage that she spent most of her time sleeping away the days and nights. Tranquilizers helped block her pain. "I know," said Ann bluntly, "That the last three children were conceived while Dad was drunk and Momma zonked out on her pills. I saw it all."

Ruthe could taste stomach acid in her throat.

Clearly, Ann was the nurturer to her younger brothers and sisters. Ruthe regarded her with respect for dropping out of school to take on all these responsibilities. She nodded encouragingly, glad Ann was able to be frank as well as shy, while she admitted that even before becoming a Christian, she had been the one who made the younger ones go to school punctually, and who fed them shrewdly but sufficiently, all out of the cheque which the Social Assistance Department now wisely wrote out to her name.

"Since I met Ross and guessed he was from a well-to-do family," Ann confessed, "it has been my dream escape plan to marry him and take all my brothers and sisters to live with us in a nice home with clean surroundings."

"Remember, Ruthe, how you said that night that even the most wonderful, most trustworthy human friends can fail us, but Jesus never misunderstands us, deserts us, or makes any mistake? Well, I believed you. Such a Friend I wanted! Only I couldn't stop seeing Ross because I had such a craving for someone other than the kids to love me. I hungered to be treated kind of special."

"By the time Ross proposed," Muriel helped Ann out, "the Lord gave you the strength to say no?"

Ann nodded fervently. "That was hard. The radio preachers showed me that the Bible says it is wrong to be matched up in marriage with an unbeliever. You pull in different directions. I really wanted to obey God the rest of my life, so I finally had courage to tell Ross I could not see him any more. —But now look! The dream I gave up is happening after all!"

Ross hugged her and kissed her, while they all smiled or laughed.

"My birthday is this Saturday," Ann added wistfully. "My new dream is that we get married that night and pick up the kids on Sunday. Monday morning I can send them off to school again like usual. My parents would never notice our disappearance. Our social worker says, some day I'll have to let them suffer the consequences of their decisions."

Ruthe's mind was torn. Part of her approved of Ann's brave scheme, but she said, "As a Christian, I don't know if you should desert your parents like that. We have obligations to honour them that go beyond what the secular world thinks fair. Even if we are on different wave lengths."

Ann was suddenly intense. "Believe me, Ruthe, I've tried everything else! Everything the social worker suggested, and everything I've heard or read about. They're past hope! Know what? I asked our caseworker before I sent Ross away, what would happen if I did get married and took the kids away. She just smiled and said, 'Then I'll have legal cause to put them into institutions.' She won't as long as they are being looked after by faithful ol' me!"

Ann leaned forward earnestly. "Don't I have a greater responsibility to the kids? Our parents are adults, who chose to waste their lives!"

Ruthe pulled in her breath. The morality of this was an absorbing question. *Lord, there isn't time to think this through to a proper conclusion right now. What shall I say?*

To buy time she turned to Ross. "How do you feel about her plan?"

"Oh, I don-know, I think it's great." He wrapped an intimate arm around Ann. "Saturday's none too soon for me!" His words weren't as quick and impulsive as usual.

Ruthe waited.

"Except– I don't think it would be too smart to move in here, and for the life of me, I can't see how I will get a new house by the end of this week. Guess I'll have to put off university a year or so, and go be a gas jockey."Ross searched Ann's face carefully. "Funny. Suddenly I feel awfully young– and stupid."

Ann's dark eyes went alert and wary. Even her curly dark brunette hair became tense and springy.

Ross stroked her chin upward with his fingers. "My Dad may be a smart lawyer, Honey, but I have to eke out my high style of living on a studying allowance and nice Christmas gifts. He and I have this agreement; if I dare stop school it's discontinued– zip. And my only skill is pumping gas."

Ann's face showed that this was unexpected news. Why, she had thought! It came tumbling out that she had never fully explained to him her plan for the kids to come along.

"Honey," said Ross lamely, "What do I know about raising kids? I'm still such a spoiled brat myself!"

Ann was about to cave in with tears. "I can't leave them!"

"So what are you saying now, Ross?" Ruthe asked as evenly as she could.

"Well– maybe we could wait until I can swing all of Ann's dream plan."

She collapsed in tears on his shoulder. "Honey! I'm sorry! I'm sorry!" Quickly he did his best to soothe her. There were a few minutes of chaos.

Ruthe hunched forward on her folded legs, elbows on her knees, and her face scrunched into her loose fists. *So, Lord? Did You intend for them to break up? Is her idea no good?*

All at once she wanted terribly for Ann's dream to come true. Surely God had good plans for these two, and all those kids. So what if their marriage would be rocky and others had to keep stepping in to help them out?

"Now listen, you two," she said sharply, "Who's to say the Lord isn't planning one big, terrific miracle? You lovebirds could do each other a world of good. A whole bunch of younger kids and their futures are at stake here besides. Jesus said not to stand in their way, but to let the little ones come to Him."

Muriel sighed with such immense relief she fell off the arm of the chair to the floor. When Ruthe looked quizzically at her to determine whether to laugh or be concerned, Muriel said, "I was praying you'd have an answer like that."

Ruthe stretched her face, which wanted to smile, around into an indecipherable, "Hmm-mm."

She felt they needed a good prayer session to sort out the priorities. Which of God's all-wise principles applied? At her urging they stopped for about half an hour of prayer, taking turns every few sentences.

Although Ruthe did not feel a complete solution was presented yet, she closed off with a final prayer when she sensed that God was aware of this situation and was already involved. It would all turn out okay. She was telling the others of her confidence when she noticed Mr. O'Brien standing in the doorway of his den, watching them all. Ruthe couldn't recall if she had noticed him earlier. His finger was pinched in a book he held; he had a momentous expression.

He cleared his throat. Even so there was a catch in his voice as he said, "I don't know why, but I have this singular premonition– that my next move is the answer to your prayers."

Ross, Ann and the girls all kept staring. Keith got up from his corner of the sofa. He motioned his father there.

"What I mean is; I cannot stand idly by while my oldest son discusses marriage, can I?" He sighed and came closer. "I'm afraid I've been too detached lately. I haven't paid attention to family affairs as I should. In fact, I've got trouble concentrating on my work too. I really ought to retire, or at least sell off some of my business investments. Then I think I could see through to letting Ross have part of what is coming to him."

He had hardly spoken this far before Ross had freed himself of Ann and was choking his Dad with a bear hug.

"Son. It's a long time... this!" and he crushed Ross back to his chest.

"You do care about me?!" Ross cried.

"Of course! Haven't I told you lately?"

Ruthe was blinking hard and needed to change the subject. Just as quickly, she had an idea. "Hey, know what? That old Greystone would be an ideal place to raise a large family! Thought of that?"

Ross had thought of it quite a bit, apparently, but now backed off. Mr. O'Brien would not hear of it either.

Nor would the O'Brien sisters, though Ruthe insisted she had only meant to rent it to them.

"Granny gave it to you, Ruthe, for special purposes," cried Muriel. "You've already got June preparing it, and she can hardly wait until the red tape is done, so the welfare will let her take her siblings there."

"You've got to use it for that!" insisted Cathy. "How long before you find another stray kitten like Joy?"

"Yes, but in an emergency.... temporarily, it–"

"Ruthe, dear," said Mr. O'Brien, "Don't let that thought so much as cross your mind again. No. Ross has matured in the last few weeks. I can flex my rules and help him out."

Ross choked his father again with a dazed look.

Is he really glad? Ruthe asked silently. *This is all happening rather lickety-split fast, isn't it, Lord?*

Wow," murmured Keith, "Is the world full of big sisters taking over their families, or am I imagining things?"

THIRTY-ONE

"If there's to be a wedding here this Saturday," said Cathy, endeavouring to get everyone's attention, "We've got lots to do."

Just like that the emotional gears where shifted and they became a creative brainstorming team.

Ross was to see Pastor Teaon and explain all that he and Ann had gone through. "Better still; he'll want to meet both of you. Take Ann with you," Ruthe advised.

As soon as they agreed the ceremony could take place right in this room Keith volunteered to build a lightweight and portable rose arbour. Cathy and Muriel would decorate it romantically, and see about food for a family reception.

Ruthe's assignment was to take Ann to Darlin' Bonne's for a wedding gown and nice new wardrobe. "If Phyllis and that new girl, Joy, can get *Royal Treatment* in one evening," said Cathy, "Surely you can persuade them to do it for Ann too." Ruthe made a little wry smile, knowing how tired the girls were after a full day of sewing, but she knew they would do it, and cheerfully.

It was Ross who brought Ann to the shop after their interview with Pastor Teaon the next night. He picked her up again about midnight. Ruthe met them there and was glad afterwards that she could be there for most of the evening. That was when she got to know Ann better.

When everyone volunteered at once, the bride elected Darlin' Bonne and Ruthe to design and make her dream gown. It took all evening, but while they worked at it, the other girls made about twenty new outfits for Ann. She was doing better, they all said, than many other brides who have six months to shop around.

While they sewed, Ann sat on a stool in a red velour dressing gown, letting Evelyn put perm rollers in her hair. Talking under and around Evelyn's arms, Ann entertained them with fascinating descriptions of her brothers and sisters.

Marion came after Ann, was sixteen, dark, native looking and dreadfully serious. She wanted to be a teacher and Ann wanted to fight for her to have that opportunity.

Pansy, fifteen, was a dark brunette, like Ann, but much prettier, Ann declared. "Pansy's sensitive and thoughtful, so we've nicknamed her 'The Poet.' Her notebooks and scribblers are called 'The Poet's Posy.' She likes to draw and is always trying out big words. What's more, she finds it fairly easy to speak in rhyme."

Glenn was a laconic thirteen, Ruthe gathered. The first strawberry-blond like their father in that family.

"Glenn's pride bothers him a lot," Ann admitted. "He works part time in a supermarket, but he's vowed one day he will own the chain."

Barry was twelve and Ann described him as completely opposite the first ones. His looks matched Marion's like a twin, but he was much more out-going and confident. He had a paper route and dreamed of travelling in an exciting career. "Reporting news from Afghanistan, or something like that," he had told her once.

Ann had another sister, Sara, who was eleven. A blonde like Glenn, but chubby. Which distressed Sara terribly for just now she had her heart set on being a model. Ann predicted that Sara would have a crush on Ross in no time.

Christopher, nine, again a blond, had only one ambition; to have lots of fun every day. He didn't think adults had any fun. Ingeniously, he made and shared laughter wherever he went.

Next was Eldon, a mischievous, redheaded seven. Ann didn't know what side of the family tree the red hair had come. She had never met any of her father's German relatives. Several of the girls, busy at the sewing machines, paused to explain dominant and recessive genes to Ann. She was very interested.

"I expect Eldon and Ross to be naturals together," Ann went on. "Five year old Ella too; a strawberry-haired mischief maker, that is. Which makes three of them. No, four, counting Chris."

Bradley, three, was a big hefty toddler with soft, dark eyes, who cried a lot. Ann knew something was wrong with him, but hadn't found the right doctor yet.

Ruthe paused to lean her face on the fork of her right thumb and fingers, staring into space. Slowly she said, "Do you suppose, besides hair-colours and personalities, a kid can inherit a dump of sorrow and pain from his parents?" A serious period followed as they discussed this possibility.

Ann wanted to know what kind of specialist could fix that.

"Strikes me," chirped Donnie, "That you need a whole flock of doctors, pastors, and therapists, all taking shifts."

Ann tried to put their case in a brighter light. "The Home care nurse is good about checking on us for minor problems, and the mother of the third nurse before the present one that comes, she lives just a few blocks away. She's a nice older woman who came around to show me how to be a live-in midwife for Momma. Most other things I can figure out just by stopping to think."

The girls sighed, or whistled in amazement, and asked her to go on.

Wendy was two and a blonde, curly-haired angel who toddled about lisping whatever anyone else was saying.

Karin, the most recent baby was nearly one. As far as Ann could tell she was going to be like Wendy, and eventually, like the light-hearted, middle children.

"How did your parents–" Darlin' Bonne tore some thread with her teeth, "think of those names when you said they hadn't wanted or planned those children?"

Ruthe turned to look at Darlin' Bonne. *Is she wondering about her abortions again?*

"Oh-h," Ann blushed, and added defensively, "they do love kids. Just—well, Momma let me name them from Christopher on. She said they could be mine. She can't stand the diaper end of things, that's all."

After a pause Ann added, "Momma can't help all the things she has suffered in her lifetime. If only Papa would sober up long enough to land a good job–, then I'm sure, he would quit drinking and throw himself into working hard. He's basically strong...."

Ruthe could tell something unpleasant was brewing in Darlin' Bonne's mind, but she couldn't read it in this crowd.

Joy had enjoyed these descriptions in a special way, so Ruthe concentrated on identifying with her. They both loved meeting people and both knew what it was like to be the oldest with extra responsibility for the younger ones.

"Who looks after your sisters and bothers when you go out?" Joy wanted to know, "Like tonight?"

"Oh, they're all right," Ann assured her. "I've trained the older kids to help look after the little ones. They all know what might happen if we don't stick close together and look out for one another."

Joy well knew what could happen. Her own loss was suddenly fresh in her mind. Ruthe paused to talk comfortingly to Joy, and to pray with her for Freddie, Gerald and Michelle. She felt guilty for having forgotten to pray for them the last few days.

At the same time, something in Ann's happy chatter was sticking in Darlin' Bonne's craw. She would not bring it out, but she could not, it appeared, totally swallow what was bothering her. Ruthe waited for a signal to go off to another room with her, but didn't see one.

All the girls at the shop were impressed that Ann planned to take her brothers and sisters with her to her new home. Evelyn, Donnie and Louise all expressed concern that this might interfere with Ann's relationship with Ross. "He won't want to be added to your list of children," suggested Donnie.

"From what we've heard," Louise added, "I don't think Ross is ready to be a father either."

Ann's eagerness was damped slightly at these warnings, but she insisted that she was fully aware of the dangers.

The wedding gown, about done, was a frothy white cloud, and Ann's dark brown hair was thick with the perm curls, so Evelyn recommended they bring a framing veil around her face on Saturday night when she was to be brought back to be dressed.

This gave Darlin' Bonne the idea for a mantilla style headpiece and veil. The effect was almost an old-fashioned Spanish look. That was how Ann had described her dream wedding gown, and it turned out to suit her beautifully.

"Better than a store-boughten one!" Ann cried as she looked at herself in the long mirrors. "Every bit as good's any rich girl's!"

That same evening Ross and his father worked out a budget. The next day they found a large bungalow between the university and an elementary school, so Ross would not need his Mustang too much. It only sat four, including the driver.

When Ruthe called him to ask for directions so she could go hang Ann's new wardrobe in the closet, Ross eagerly offered to take her on a tour of their home-to-be Friday afternoon, after her shift.

He proudly showed her the kitchen and its appliances, things he expected would really thrill Ann. "I love to surprise people just like you do, Ruthe. I'm saving all this 'til our wedding night!"

Ruthe encouraged him by poking around and ah-ing over each discovery. Seeing the empty rooms, Ruthe resolved to give them at least one old bedroom suite from the Greystone as a wedding gift. She told him.

"Eh! Terrific! Thank you. I'll go borrow a friend's truck to move it in over supper tonight!" Then Ross added, "From which room?"

Ruthe's tongue went up under her lips and around her teeth as she toyed with the idea of sending him up to the third floor of that huge mansion, then she remembered that June had recruited the Bright City guys and some of their choir friends to take all those meant for sale down to the carriage house. Also that some of them would fetch a lot of money. So, instead she promised to join him over there after this tour and pick out a suite with June's help.

This house had an unfinished basement. Ross had already asked Keith to help make additional bedrooms in it, just as he had for Ruthe in Kleinstadt. "It'll take longer than you think," she prophesied.

"Why? Keith and his buddies did yours in a few days."

"Ross, you are in for some adventures, trying to do renovations with a house full of little kids under foot!" Ruthe clucked warningly.

Ross sought Ruthe's approval on the backyard. It had a tiny patio and a small vegetable patch and lawn. He was sure this would please Ann very much for the place where the Muellers lived on Tupence Street had nothing but dirt and gravel around it.

Will it amount to anything if Ann had no experience with gardening? Ruthe wondered, and then saw the four-stall width space covered in a few years with parked cars when the kids grew up and somehow managed to afford their own transportation.

"I love your thoughtfulness of Ann," she laughed kindly, "But who's going to teach Ann to garden if neither of you have done it before?"

Ross came close to her face with a guilty grin, "You?"

Nightfall was coming by eight, Ruthe noticed on Saturday night as she sat in her Rambler at the service station, waiting for Ann. She nearly started when Ann reached the car and jumped in. She only saw her seconds beforehand in that gloomy dusk, but she greeted Ann warmly. "So? Are the kids all excited for you? Bet they wanted to come along–"

"No. I decided to hold off any unexpected problems or fuss by not telling them until it is all over. Like tomorrow afternoon. I want just one night of blissful aloneness with my husband before I take on the young ones again."

They drove over to the shop where all the girls helped dress Ann up in her rustling white gown and veil. While they did that, Ruthe remembered vaguely that she had agreed to be bridesmaid. When she brought it up, Ann emphatically wanted her to dress up as a bridesmaid. The shop girls had laid aside some for Ruthe to *buy as bargains* whenever she felt it was okay to bring another *steal* home to her family. After dithering and eying several offerings laid out before her, Ruthe chose one with seven layers of sheer bronze chiffon in the skirt, with delicate embroidered scalloped edges of gold thread on the luscious ruffles about the V-collar.

"Whoa!" said Darlin' Bonne, tilting back on her heels, "You must've been quite a first class lady in a previous life time!"

Ruthe leaned forward, close to her friend's face and rebuked her in a quiet aside, "The Bible says nothing good of reincarnation. That's a lie from Satan to mix people up."

Shock wiped over Darlin' Bonne's face, then she said, "Okay. But we need to make a date for a good long talk soon. You know that?"

Ruthe nodded. "I'll try to work it in," she promised softly. "Shall we make it for Monday?"

"Yeah. Let's elope together."

After a fresh volley of compliments and good wishes, she put Ann into her Rambler, gathered her own rustling skirts under the steering wheel, careful not to catch any in the door as she closed it, and drove to the brightly lit, stately O'Brien home.

It was almost nine when they arrived, so going up the steps, they joked about Cinderella arriving in time.

Muriel opened the door wide. Immediately Ruthe and Ann spied the white lattice arbour wired with real roses as if they grew there. The living room was softly lit, the stereo was playing airy music, and huge blue vases of red roses and sprays of baby's breath stood about. Graceful candles flickered atop various tables and shelves. *Oh, how romantic!* Ruthe thought.

"Ann, you're lovely!" said Muriel, focusing their attention back on the bride. Muriel's olive green velvet and brocade empress-cut dress rippled beside Ruthe's free floating bronze chiffon as they followed Ann across the muffled floor to inspect Keith's rose arbour more closely. Ann was very taken with it.

"Ann sure is beautiful," Ruthe agreed. "Did you and Cathy ever do a lot of work here! This is all so... dreamy! So romantic!" Then, as she glanced into the dining room, "Oh-h, that buffet is out of this world! When did you prepare all that food?"

"It's just Cathy's imagination and the energy of a good day maid that Mom always called," Muriel answered with a relaxed smile that reminded Ruthe that these girls were accustomed to all this perfection and elegance. *It's Ann and I that are the stray waifs from the street.*

Both newcomers gasped as Muriel handed Ann her bridal bouquet, and Ruthe said, "You girls out-did yourselves on the flower arranging!"

Muriel nodded happily and positioned them in the dimmer hallway, as per her job, and went to tell the others.

Together Ann and Ruthe felt the velvety dark red roses, and checked out the small bright carnations, and counted the love knots.

When Cathy and the men came down the stairs and took their places, Ann swayed and swished eagerly forward, through the bower to stand beside Ross.

Wasn't the bridesmaid suppost to go in first? Ruthe puzzled, biting her lips. *Oh, right. No rehearsal, no signals arranged....* She quietly slipped in and stood with Keith behind them.

Ross and Ann repeated their vows after Pastor Teaon with long, deep looks into each other's faces. It touched Ruthe's romantic nerve so that she prayed, *See, Lord? I'd like something lovely like this... when You've got 'him' ready.* She imagined God smiling tenderly at her and murmuring softly. She knew she ought not to put words in His mouth, so she let that part of the fantasy trail off unspoken. She felt contented, only half listening to the ceremony.

Suddenly Ann turned and handed Ruthe her bouquet. With a start Ruthe deliberately uncrossed her eyes and paid attention to the last part, particularly now that she was aware of Cathy's flashing camera.

The sisters had arranged a small buffet reception in the candle lit dining room, but before they stepped up to fill clear glass plates with ambrosial salads, spiced cold meats, and dainty wee pastries, Ross raised his voice to welcome them and make an announcement.

"To show that I've completely forgiven Granny for saying that I'd some day raise a large family on the Good Book," Ross put his right hand reverently on the huge white volume surrounded by flowers and candles; "As a dramatic gesture of dedicating our newly begun Christian home, I am going to read a few verses from this Bible."

With both hands he carefully lifted and opened the Bible. "If– if I can decipher these hieroglyphics. Why didn't you warn me, Keith? This must be Gaelic!"

Ross bent lower in the dim flickers of the candles to look for a suitable verse. All at once great astonishment spread over his face. He raised his head to look about for Ruthe. "Ruthe, come see this. There's a note in the margin. It says, *You see, Ross, when you humble yourself, God lifts you up. Marry her and you have it all.*"

Ruthe's face dropped into her hands, "Oh no! Oh no-o!"

At that moment the stereo record changer came to a scratching halt. The scene was over as Keith excused his way through the small crowd to go to the living room and switch over to the local FM radio station instead. It happened to be playing piano classics.

Good thing! thought Ruthe. *Turns that discovery into just a wee little joke. Everyone is in a jolly, smiling mood.* She watched carefully as the bridal couple, then Pastor Teaon, and Mr. O'Brien served up their buffet plates from the tiered platters. But then Mr. O'Brien stepped backward to tease Ruthe with a small comment. Ann heard and asked Ross what that joke had been. Going back into the living room to sit down with their food, Ross began a colourful re-telling of the reading of his Granny's will. Deliberately, Ruthe lingered at the buffet so the story would be over by the time she got there.

Noticing she was beside that very big display Bible, she reached over and flipped some pages. All of a sudden they fell open at a tucked in twenty dollar bill. Her eyes grew huge. But she pushed it deeper into the binding and flipped further. When she paused to see if it were truly another language, she noticed the thin page lift a bit. Turning it over, she came to a fifty bill. Ruthe peered down closer, to make sure she saw correctly, then glanced around her. Everyone was busy talking to someone else. *Granny,* she said silently, flipping more pages, and spotting a five and a ten, *you are giving Ross more than just this beautiful Bible, aren't You? but he's going to have to keep his vow to raise his family by this Good Book if he is to get all of his gifts from You.* When she saw a hundred dollar bill within the last few pages, Ruthe decided she had snooped enough. She turned away to smile at Cathy, who was speaking to her.

Ruth Marlene Friesen

Cathy asked Ruthe to be sure to try her black and white cheesecake bites; Ruthe asked her to point them out; and the evening continued smoothly, just as Cathy had planned it.

Ruthe was not used to this standing or roaming around with a plate of food in her hand, so she spied on Cathy and Muriel, and copied them. Soon all had drifted back into the living room, chatting informally as they ate, each sitting down wherever they saw a comfortable place. Ross headed for his favourite wide-armed chair, and in no time Ann, giggling cautiously, was on his lap and they were nestling their plates on her billowing lace skirt.

Pastor Teaon came to sit beside Ruthe for a while, and they got better acquainted. Just when she thought it would be okay to tell him more about herself he moved away for more food, and Keith came to sit by her for a few minutes. Then it was Muriel.

It was nearly eleven o'clock when their chit-chat stopped mid-air. The stereo music had paused for a bulletin. "We interrupt this program to inform our listeners of a serious fire at 1130 Tupence South," the announcer said with an urgency in his resonant voice that was unusual to that program's pace. They all froze, signalling one another to listen. Ann was the last to stop talking.

"Eleven children escaped or were rescued, but it is believed that the sleeping mother perished in the flames. the children told police their father had started the blaze in a drunken stupor. He has been taken into custody. However, the oldest daughter, who turned 18 today, was out at the time. City police are still not able to locate her. Anyone knowing the whereabouts of Ann Mueller are asked to call the police immediately."

Ann turned an ashen face to her new husband. "That's me! Ross! I– we've got to go! Right away!"

Ross agreed of course, but Cathy and Muriel had the presence of mind to insist they sweep Ann upstairs and get her changed out of her wedding gown first. "It'll only take two minutes if we work together," said Cathy, already gripping the bride's arm and steering her, "Then it won't be around your feet to get ruined while you stand by that burning building."

"But-t... Ruthe took my new clothes to our house–"

"Don't worry." Cathy was in charge. "We've got clothes too."

"Ross," Ruthe said, grabbing his limp arm as he was slowly rising from his chair, "You and I are going to call the police and tell them where Ann is."

Three or four minutes later, Ann, in a turquoise pant suit of Cathy's, was tripping down the carpeted stairs at break-neck speed, Ross grabbed her hand and they were leaping into his red sports car.

"Ross just has that small Mustang?" asked Rev. Teaon of the older O'Brien. Immediately both understood the implications and dashed out to the large Lincoln and the pastor's passenger van.

Ruthe hesitated a second, then elected to stay with Cathy and Muriel to help prepare for the new guests. Ann's adrenaline rush had sparked theirs, and for a couple of minutes all three were rushing from room to room, naming things that needed to be done.

First they spread out the rest of the food, still on the kitchen counters, certain that the younger kids would be hungry. "Excitement makes people hungry," someone said.

Ruthe closed the big Bible and handed it to Muriel to put away.

All at once Cathy started emptying the linen closet to make up beds and cots all over the house. A quick finger count and Ruthe knew there would not be enough mattresses, so she volunteered to dash over to the Greystone and make up a couple of those huge four-poster beds.

"It isn't so spooky now, with June living there." Ruthe could tell Cathy wasn't hearing her, so she trailed off to herself, "She has some rooms redecorated already...."

A minute later Muriel offered the same idea. It was all the encouragement Ruthe needed. They bunched up their elegant skirts in their hands as they scooted sideways through the hedge gap on their high heels.

June was not in, so Ruthe used the hidden key.

Keith tagged after them. He was reeling at the prospect of eleven children coming to spend the night. Even though he had been plotting their basement bedrooms at the bungalow, that number of bodies was just beginning to sink in now. "Ross and Ann aren't sleeping with all those kids tonight, are they?" he asked as Ruthe and Muriel snapped a heavy old white cotton sheet over a bed.

Ruthe looked at Muriel. "Ann will probably think she has to stay and comfort the little ones, but they ought to be alone, no?"

"You're right!" Muriel responded fervently, "Why don't we insist they spend tonight at their house, alone? If they don't take this one night, they won't get another chance for– who knows how long."

"Surely the older ones can soothe and look after the little ones for one night," Ruthe affirmed. "Once they know Ann's not missing."

Keith crowded closer with more questions. At one point Ruthe backed into him, stepping on his foot, but he didn't notice. "It would be fun to have so many kids to play with, huh? Don't you wish you came from a large family like that?"

Ruthe laughed, "Keith, you're in for some changes too. Well, every kid needs a very special uncle. You ready to be copied and idolized?"

June arrived from her shift at the telephone office. Ruthe warned her of the impending company, then dashed after Muriel and Keith, who were breathlessly telling Cathy, "Ann and Ross should still go have their one night honeymoon–"

"That's why I've been making all these beds," she answered in surprise, "I didn't want Ann to take them all along tonight. I dare say they'll be restless and cry a lot."

This crew was just running out of things to do, about twelve, when Ross and Ann got back. The old Mustang burst open on both sides, and children swarmed into the house, all talking. They were followed by the teens with Mr. O'Brien.

For a moment Ruthe and the others stared. Some of the newcomers were rather sooty and smelled of smoke, other than that, none of them appeared to be harmed or burned. The wee ones were in faded, threadbare, but what had been clean pyjamas, and the older ones were still wearing blue jeans and sweaters because they had been studying when the fire began. All were visibly hyperactive. The noise was deafening in the so recently romantic living room. Some were explaining the fire, and some immediately roamed around, touching and handling everything.

"But I knew Annie would save us!" Christopher shouted at everyone in general, "I knew it all along." Ruthe recognized the fearless blond from Ann's description at the shop.

Keith bent down to say "Hi," to a little girl, about five with red curls, who answered solemnly with, "We was near burnt."

That's Ella, Ruthe told herself.

"Yeah," added the one who must be Barry, without shame, "All our old garbage burned. Now we'll get brand new stuff from Welfare."

A strawberry blond, a little older than Ella, who had to be Eldon, jiggled first on one foot and then the other to get some attention. "All our homework, an' the picture of Momma as a Princess, an' even our Poet's Posy, all gone up in flames and smoke!" He made a pouf with his mouth and tilted his head back to watch an imaginary cloud of smoke rising.

It must've been Pansy; a dark, lovely girl, patted Eldon's back and said, "Hush, it's okay. That's nothing compared to losing our Momma."

Barry turned on Pansy. "We didn't lose Ann. That's the best."

Ella tugged on Pansy's loose purple sweater. "Ann didn't die. She's alive!" Then she spun herself thoughtfully on one foot, "Oh goodie. Ann's with us. We're with Ann."

All this time the three babies clung to the pretty brunette lady in the turquoise pant suit, who only an hour before had been the misty-eyed bride in the frothy white lace. The boy toddler, clutching the skin of Ann's throat and wailing away unhappily must be Bradley. The baby in her other arm was crying because she needed to be changed and felt uncomfortable. That was Ruthe's guess. The thin girl toddler on the floor with her face buried in a handful of the turquoise material at the knee of Ann's pant leg had to be Wendy.

Ann was darting searching glances about the room while she tried to soothe the little ones. It was Muriel who first caught on that what she was looking for was a diaper, or several. She hurried off and brought the ones her mother had long ago laid away in an old trunk.

Ross tried to help by tweaking Bradley's nose and touching his ears. However, that child would not have anyone but Ann just then, and he grasped at her hair, wailing still louder.

Wendy wrapped an arm around Ann's leg, tugging occasionally on the top to make sure Ann knew she was there, but she was peeking around.

Since Muriel had just come back with an armload of soft white diapers, Ruthe decided to free Ann of Wendy. She picked her up and gently turned her shy face to look at her own. "Hi there," Ruthe said, as friendly as could be.

Ann could now sit down on the couch, but Muriel had to sit beside her and help her change Karin as Bradley would not let go.

"I not scart," Wendy stated bravely to Ruthe, tossing her hair and making her shirley-temple curls bounce, "Annie come back."

"That's very true. Ann had no intention of forgetting you all. She was planning to take you to a new home."

But then Wendy remembered her fright. Her wee curled fists went into her eyes to begin again. Ruthe cuddled her closer and cooed comfortingly, swaying her body in a soft rocking motion, as she surveyed the rest of them, raiding the buffet table back there like a host of bunnies in a garden.

Lord, I thought we ate well, but look– that's Barry, there's Christopher, and Eldon, all ravenous at the sight of so much fancy food. Those must be Marion, Pansy and Glenn, calling for manners and slapping the younger boys' hands as they get too bold. However, Cathy also hovered nearby and urged them to help themselves.

"You want some fancy cake, Wendy?" Ruthe murmured, moving in closer to the table.

Then her eye caught Keith, backed tight up against a tall green plant in the corner. His father a little dazed himself, was encouraging Keith not to be shy.

Ruthe stepped to the tall man's side with ·Wendy in her arms, heaving softly with each breath, to ask him about Mr. Mueller as Keith slipped away.

Sounding baffled, Mr. O'Brien told her Ann's father was being held on charges of arson and manslaughter, and that Ann had refused to let him bail her father out. She insisted that freedom would not change him, and he'd only cause her more work and trouble than the children.

212

"Maybe the police are better equipped to babysit him than she is right now."

"I suppose. It surprised me that she was able to be so decisive. Actually, I admire her stand."

After a pause Ruthe asked, "Didn't Ann tell us that normally she did not expect him to stumble home until early morning?"

"I don't recall. Apparently some well-meaning person picked him up and brought him to his doorstep about ten-thirty."

"Did he set the fire deliberately?"

"It's what the older siblings say. With all their vivid eyewitness accounts and the circumstantial evidence, I'd think he'll get life. Or, he will be committed indefinitely for psychiatric treatment."

Mr. O'Brien and Ruthe shook their heads in unison.

Noticing Ross again, milling around with the kids and nervously looking from face to face, Ruthe went to him. She was concerned that this crisis not overwhelm him, or make him want to bail out of his new marriage to Ann.

"You look too much the part of a worried husband, Ross. Try the firm Dad-figure on for size."

Ross made a woebegone face at Ruthe.

"So-o you se-e," she teased with a musical lilt before he could express his confusion, still swaying with the warm and now quiet Wendy held close to her, "It seems you can't have one without the o-th-er. To resist the whole idea is to invite friction. Embrace this lifestyle and you'll come to love it."

"I know, I know! And I signed up for both, but–"

"Aw-com'on, Ross. You're not going to let this commotion get the best of you, are you? Don't quit at the beginning."

"No," came out hesitantly. "Just, Ann's so efficient, and right now, while she could use some help badly enough, I'm standing here like a zombie. These kids don't even talk to me."

"Ross," she reasoned, lowering her voice, "Would you trust strangers after such trauma? Give'em a chance to discover you. Introduce yourself and show them what a fun character you are. Hey, where's that powerful stubborn will of yours?"

He grinned foolishly.

"I believe you once said it was big enough to rent out parking spaces to others," Ruthe smiled playfully.

He took a deep, shaky breath and straightened his back. "Y'know, Ruthe, you're right. I'm no longer a happy-go-lucky kid," his voice grew strong and his teasing twinkle came back, "I'll have you know, m'deah, I'm a happy-go-lucky Daddy now."

"That's the spirit!"

213

"God helping me, that is," Ross added quickly, with more humility.

Wendy, who was watching, raised a grubby finger to his face. "New Dadday?"

Ross could not resist. A brand new kind of love crashed the gates of his generous heart. He laughed aloud at her tilted, questioning head. Then he reached out, took Wendy from Ruthe, and holding her very carefully, whispered into the tousled side of her forehead, "Yes, I'm going to be your Daddy now. And.. .I love you, just like Ann does!"

Ruthe turned and gulped. Her eyes were swimming away. *Dear Lord, I want a husband and lots of kids too!*

THIRTY-TWO

Clearly, Ann had a devoted maternal-heart for her brothers and sisters, and wanted to deny herself the one night honeymoon with Ross. She couldn't bear to see them crying and reaching for her without gathering them up. Ruthe sized up the next two oldest girls, Marion and Pansy, as capable, given half a chance, so she sidled up to them to explain Ann's plan to bring them into her new home with Ross after just one night alone with him. "It doesn't seem fair to deny them just one night of peace and quiet, does it?" she asked them gently.

They agreed, but didn't know what to do.

Ruthe explained that beds had been prepared right here at the lovely O'Brien home, and next door at an even bigger house. "If you girls can help us persuade Ann that you will look after the younger ones for this one night, Cathy and I will try to shoo them away to their new home by themselves."

Cathy paused in her traffic to and from the kitchen to second the motion.

Glenn had just appeared behind his sisters and overhearing this conversation, said in a low voice, "Done." To his sisters he said, "I'll take our three bullies out'a your hair if you handle the rest.

Marion became brisk now too. "I'll take Bradley, if Sara will sleep with Ella, and you, Pansy, take Wendy and Karin."

Swoosh, Marion was at Ann's side, claiming Bradley, and Pansy went to pick up Karin, who was sitting on the glass coffee table in her diaper like a cheerful model. "Time to leave for your honeymoon with your husband," they told Ann. When she tried to protest, "You'll never believe that you really got married to him if you don't! You deserve at least that much for having your secret wedding spoiled."

"You've told us before; we can do it," said Pansy over her shoulder as she followed Cathy to see where they were to sleep. "Y'got nice in-laws here."

Just as quickly Glenn had rounded up his brothers, Barry, Chris and Eldon, and stopped before Ann to assure her that everything would be under control.

In panic Ann wanted to know, "Where are you going to sleep?"

Keith had told them he'd be giving up his bed to sleep with them at the old Greystone, his Granny's former home. He came bounding down the stairs at this point, with a small suitcase hastily stuffed with most of his pyjamas drawer's contents, ready to share.

While Glenn was talking about the invitation to the mansion next door, Barry, who had his arms around the necks of his brothers, steering them to the front door, made them swirl around as a unit, their left feet in the air, to say,

215

"Have a sexy night with your lover-hubby." Nearly out the door Chris tipped back his head to yell, "Don't worry, you're too excited to get pregnant!"

Ross exploded with laughter. He called out foxly into the darkness, "I'll give you bravery medals in the morning if Granny does not wake you!"

Seeing Eldon hesitate in his tracks, Ruthe scolded Ross briefly as she went to follow and introduce the boys to June, their hostess.

By the time she came back, Ross and Ann were gone, Muriel had taken Sara and Ella to Keith's room, and they were practically in bed. Cathy had shown Pansy to Ross's bedroom, where she had earlier dragged an antique wooden cradle on a rocker stand. Her own bedroom she'd offered to Marion who was pacing with a fussy Bradley.

Mr. O'Brien was carrying dishes back to the kitchen all by himself. "You didn't even get a chance to say good bye to our newlyweds," he said gently as she stood, head cocked, locating the others with her ears.

She smiled happily, "We pulled it off! Ann was willing to go after all?"

"Yes. But that smart alec was right; it's not a good night for virgin sex. I advised them to drop it if it didn't come easy. To force themselves into intercourse tonight could just ruin their way of relating to each other for a long time to come."

Ruthe stared at him. *What sensible advice. How lucky can they be?* Then she blushed as she recalled that no one else had ever spoken to her so matter-of-factly about sexual problems.

Before she was sure whether Mr. O'Brien had caught on, Muriel and Cathy came back down to clean up some. But when Ruthe wanted to help they urged her not to bother. Looking at her watch, she knew that if her mother was up she would have a hard time explaining this all-day and all-night shift of hers, so she yielded, asked for the use of a bathroom to change back into her working slacks and blouse, and left for home.

At the door, when Ruthe commended Cathy for getting everyone bedded down so nicely, she replied, "Hey, I've got beds to spare yet! I had made up a cot in the solarium, and a sofa bed in the TV room, and Dad was willing to give up his double bed for a mat in his den if the newlyweds had stayed."

They laughed together and agreed with yawns that it had been one interesting wedding.

Driving on the highway by moonlight, Ruthe pondered the problems that the young Mr. and Mrs. O'Brien would encounter yet. Suddenly she strongly resented all the books she had read where the hint of wedding bells was the end of all troubles and seemed to guarantee a happily ever after. *This is their first chapter, not the last.*

THIRTY-THREE

Her mother was furious for having had no real help all Saturday, and her father threatened to tie her down, so Ruthe stayed home on Sunday. She went along to church, even taught a Primary class when the regular teacher did not show up, but the rest of the day was quiet and domestic where her family could see her. While they napped for two hours in the afternoon, Ruthe prayed fervently for the ability to forgive them and not let this emotional wound do her permanent damage, but also the re-arranged Mueller kids. She longed to go sit alone in the willow bush, but it was cold, windy and sometimes raining outside.

Finally she announced to all in earshot, "I'm going to Grosz'mama's." Deliberately she walked slow, and the long way around, and was able to think of how everything had come together for Ann and Ross, instead of herself. However, her family had jumped in the car and were at Grosz'mama's moments before she got there. *So much for some private cheering up,* she told herself. Besides, they found that Grosz'mama was not feeling too well.

Ruthe nearly stayed home all of Monday to prove that she wasn't always in the city. She helped with the laundry first, and acted as if she would be home all day. Then she remembered that she had promised to spend time with Darlin' Bonne. While waiting for the right moment she threw it all in the Lord's lap. She admitted that she did not know how to make this come out right.

After she had the ironing done, she asked, "Mom, what else today?"

However, that day her mother was hung up on the idea; Grosz'mama should not live alone this winter. She had harped on it all morning.

Ruthe knew her grandmother didn't want to move in with any of her children scattered across four provinces, and she didn't think she was old enough for the seniors' home. *Lord, Grosz'mama made it plain enough when Mom brought it up yesterday. What does Mom want from me; a better idea?*

"How about if I move out and board with Grosz'mama?" she offered. "At least she would have someone there most of the night."

"No. I need you at home what time you can spare for me," her mother said sharply. "Suzanne is no kitchen maid yet."

"She won't get to be one as long as she knows I'll do it once I get home".

Just then her mother's deafness came on again.

There were several pots of tomato juice to preserve, so Ruthe committed her city friends to the Lord, and threw herself into the domestic work. It was the only way to get her mother to quit nagging.

Yes, Lord, she said two or three times, *I know I'm not quite indispensible.* Yet she had to admit that she had enjoyed being in the thick of things at the O'Brien home Saturday night. In her imagination, as she stirred the red pulp in the enamel pot, she tried to picture what might be happening in Ann and Ross's home right about now.

When the work was done Ruthe washed the heap of pots and pans. Her mother, exhausted, went to lie down for a nap. By the time she hung up the wet towels, Ruthe had decided to take the risk. She was changed and off in a trice.

The others were away on an outing; Darlin' Bonne was alone, stretched out on the reception room sofa, waiting. To avoid the phone they went driving on out of the way country roads, and tried to avoid the clouds of dust raised by combines roaring in the yellowed fields.

Joy and Ann's talk and enthusiasm about babies had stirred up disquieting visions for Darlin' Bonne. "I tell you, right in broad daylight I see dead babies tumbling out of the fabric shelves!"

Ruthe stared in shock. "In your imagination?"

"Whatever. I know they're not, but I feel as if I see them. I thought it was visions. Ruthe, they are revolting! I can hardly mind my manners when customers bring in their babies and Joy goes all ga-gah over them." She squirmed sideways ready to hash out this problem.

Ruthe decided to pull over on a grassy shoulder and deal with it.

First she let Darlin' Bonne describe it over a few times and to express her mixed emotions. Ruthe just asked sympathetic questions. It was all new to her, but she had to agree that it probably had to do with having had abortions in the past. The sight of the babies in the shop made Darlin' Bonne realize those must have been real human lives she had allowed to be cut up and extracted from her. "Ruthe-darlin', I stare at 'em and feel like screamin', 'I killed three of those?!'"

Ruthe felt tight and hot but didn't really know what to say. She had heard mention in church of a new law legalizing abortions since '69 and how it represented increasing wickedness in society, but the members of her church were not the activist type, so everyone felt helpless to do anything about it. She told Darlin' Bonne as much.

"Oh Marie told me to vote for Trudeau the rest of my life; he'd liberated all woman in a big way. I never dreamed he'd opened a garbage chute for women to go into a suffering hell! Ruthe, some day I may lead a big public fight to make a new law to save lives; right now I just want to be forgiven and rid of my shame over this crime. Shall I go turn myself in to the police? Wanna come with me?"

"If there's no law against it, they don't want to hear it. But God does." Suddenly Ruthe brightened. She knew where the exit was to her friend's crisis. "Listen, Darlin' Bonne, I think I've got it! Your suffering in your spirit because your spiritual eyes have opened to the sin of taking those innocent lives. Even though you didn't realize it at the time. So the answer is spiritual too. Let's go to the Father by Jesus Christ, the one and only way, confess that it was wrong, ask for it to be included in that rotten pile of sins Jesus bled and died for on the cross, and then leave it there. No, more than that! Follow Jesus, identify with Him, abide in Him as He rises from the dead, and the sin stays in the grave forever!"

"Okay. Let me grab that. Jesus died in my place for each of those three abortions– 'cause in God's eyes they were illegal, never mind the laws of Canada– and when He rose up on Easter my guilt, my death sentence was done! In God's legal system they don't exist any more, right?" Darlin' Bonne sounded convinced yet needed reassurance.

"Right." Ruthe agreed with intensity. "Unless you keep remembering and accusing yourself, or listening to Satan's accusations against you, God is never going to throw them into your face again!" Then she recalled snatches of verses about God's complete forgetfulness of forgiven sin. They looked them up together in her worn, marked up Bible, then prayed with tears and claimed this victory.

Spent and sweaty in this warm harvest weather, Ruthe returned home in time to peel potatoes for supper. As she drove she praised God that her own home conflicts were so minor. *Lord-God, my problems in being understood by my parents isn't a bean compared to what Darlin' Bonne has gone through. Help me not to complain any more....*

At work the next day Ruthe saw that the young O'Briens' new phone was connected, memorized the number, and called it on her next break.

Ann assured her that they'd had a nice honeymoon night. "The kids came on Sunday afternoon. So did a caseworker with a bundle of clothes. But the girls liked the ones Cathy and Muriel gave them much better. They say you are going to take them to Darlin' Bonne's Shop for something called 'The Royal Treatment'?"

Ruthe had not heard this, but laughed, "Okay, guess I will." Sensing Ann's hesitation she explained, "It's the same as you got; an evening of visiting and getting a whole wardrobe made.

"How are you managing for furniture?"

"Oh, we already got vouchers from Social Assistance yesterday, and we picked out some from that big place that has those sale flyers out. They are suppost to deliver here any minute. I was just making calls now about a memorial service for our Momma. It's tomorrow at two, at Pastor Teaon's church. He promised that the church would give Momma a proper funeral. You don't know how much that means to me."

"Are they paying for the coffin and everything?" Ruthe was thrilled to hear of such generosity.

"Actually, Welfare pays for the cheapest coffin and cemetery plot, but Pastor Teaon said the church would pay for the rest."

"Oh, Ann, I'm so glad. The Lord is looking after you, and I've been praying for you all weekend."

"So many said that in church on Sunday, I could just burst for happiness! Ruthe, all my dreams are coming true! Our case worker assigned me and Ross as guardians to the children."

"Wow. That worked out well."

"The only thing I don't like to think about is our Dad's court case when it comes up. He was arraigned yesterday and stays in jail."

Ruthe promised to pray about that, although Ann was not sure what to hope or pray for.

The funeral was just about over by the time Ruthe got off work the next day and drove to that part of the city. She stood in the foyer on a step, watching the people file out and by their remarks gathered that a few had hoped to see a charred body in an open coffin. When she spotted some folks from Kleinstadt moving in the flow, Ruthe suddenly decided she did not need to be here at all.

She went to join Darlin' Bonne and girls for supper, and then later to visit Ann and Ross, relieved to see no guest vehicles nearby.

Her concern about Ross being able to adjust was eased in the first few minutes. "I should have known," Ruthe exclaimed as she watched him crawl around the living room floor with three laughing little ones riding on his back. He made noises like a whole zoo of animals. Barry, Chris, Sara, and Eldon sat sprawled on the new-smelling furniture, laughing and holding their sides.

Ann came to stand beside Ruthe near the door, and said in a low, confidential tone, "The kids are finding Ross a perfect party animal."

"Good," Ruthe said brightly. "How about the older ones? I notice they are missing right now."

"They've got homework and part-time jobs, but they quizzed Ross until satisfied that he has quit drinking. He told them he is still working at clearing up his swearing."

In the back of her mind, Ruthe remembered that Ross had lots to learn yet about parenting, and what his father had said rang in her memory as a warning not to judge by this impression alone. However, at the moment he was such a hilarious elephant, obviously trying to impress her as well as the children, so she allowed herself to enjoy the fun. A wave of smugness crept over her soul. *What a knack I have for matchmaking, eh?*

With real interest, Ruthe listened as Ann showed off the new furniture in each room, and told about the crowd of people at her mother's funeral, how the church ladies had served a light lunch afterward in the basement, and long lines of people had come by to say they were sorry, and praying for her and the children.

"When almost everyone was gone, the funeral director gave us a briefcase full of papers and sympathy cards," said Ann with widening eyes, "And guess what! Many of them had money! Over two thousand—!

Eldon clutched Ruthe's arm and wanted to tell her about his first ever experience in a cemetery. But Marion and Pansy had come in and edged closer too, wanting to get to know her. Ruthe had wanted to mention that if they needed it, Ross' big Bible had more money, but instead she focused on Eldon and the girls, and then the others, asking them questions, letting them talk, and feeling all the while like quite a wonderful lady.

THIRTY-FOUR

Ruthe still felt extra-confident and talented two days later.

A would-be suicide had just called Darlin' Bonne's Shop when she arrived in the middle of the afternoon. The girls were busy sewing so she volunteered to hurry over. She talked to the lonely, depressed woman with cheerful concern for some time, but when the obese woman fell asleep from her usual medication, Ruthe quietly let herself out of the apartment again. She felt like an efficient counsellor with a trim figure.

As she headed for the stairs she passed a partially open apartment door and overheard part of a quarrel spiced with endearments. Ruthe stopped in mid-step.

A woman was crying. The pacing steps must be the man's. His tender exasperation won Ruthe as she overheard him say, "Honey! Let's learn; marriage is not playing house in a sandbox. I know this place isn't much. That's why we have to organize and budget so we can eat as well as be sheltered."

"I can't, Scottie, I can't!" she screamed. "I simply cannot stay in this box of a place all day, talking to myself, figuring out dinners that are mathematically economic! Your formulas for everything make my back crawl!"

He explained again about budgeting as survival.

She repeated she could not, and her tone implied she would not do it. "No!"

Suddenly Ruthe blushed. *Ach-h, Kid, you're too much!* She scolded herself as she continued down the hall. *Keep your nose out of places it's not invited!*

Yes-but– Oh, admit it, her conscience prodded, *you've developed a lot of brass this summer; you're not nearly as afraid of people as you still make out to be. You'd love to burst into that apartment and start a miracle!*

A suggestion came in soft and intelligent-sounding, *Why not start another O'Brien-style miracle? They are lots of fun. Look at Ross's family. Good for everybody.*

Ruthe smiled at her smart and nimble feet as she marched them in a cute whirl and back down the hall. She pushed open the door that was slightly ajar.

Already out in the corridor though, her nose was assaulted by the now stronger odour of burnt food. At the door it stabbed her between the eyes.

But her mental picture had been fairly accurate. A nervous girl, no older than herself was straight ahead. Orange hair and freckles, and a cigarette shaking between her fingers was what Ruthe noticed first. An intelligent man with close-cut black hair, maybe in his late twenties, stood in a reasoning pose, dropping his arms in frustration facing the young woman.

Ruthe tried not to startle them. "Uh. Excuse me. Could I help in any way?"

"Oh," the man swung around with a jerk. "Everything is fine, thanks." He was already striding over to close the door as he spoke, "I'm sorry to have disturbed you."

"No, I was just leaving the building– but I've got time if you need help."

By his stare she knew he would rather be left alone. "Thank you," he said firmly. "We're okay."

She knew he was deliberately blocking her view, but Ruthe heard the bride whine, "What's the matter, Scottie? Too proud to admit we don't know how to play this game?"

"Honey!" he turned in a loud aside, "A stranger?"

"Why not?" she demanded. "You wouldn't accept my folks' help, and we know them well enough. So. We need an impartial counsellor."

Ruthe stood waiting, deliciously confident of a miracle. She had not had one for... *let's see how many days?*

With a reluctant sigh, and Ruthe guessed because he did not have the heart to be rude, Scottie drew slowly aside.

Flashing him a cheery smile, Ruthe moved further in. "You're just married?" she asked politely with a sweeping glance around the apartment. It had a simple, tidy look. The hide-a-bed and chair had old wool plaids tucked over them. It looked bare however. *On second thought,* she told herself, *It looks like a bachelor's place with things newly arranged.* Through the open bedroom door she saw boxes with feminine things scattered on the bed. In the kitchenette corner a crisp, misshapen thing lay on the broiler tray of the rangette, and a stack of dishes tottered in the sink. The strong burnt odour put knots behind her eyes and made them want to cross.

Ruthe decided to deal with that first. She went over to the cupboards and opened them, asking for foil. She found a roll, and quickly tore a piece and scooped it over the burned meat, balled it up, and turned to hand it to the young man, "Take that out to the garbage– like fast, will you?" Almost in the same motions she turned on the vent fan, and put the broiler tray under the tap with running water rushing over it. "What have you got in the way of flavour oils?" she tossed over her shoulder.

"I haven't the foggiest idea."

Ruthe found a bottle of vanilla and a tablespoon, she tipped some into the spoon, set it on an element and turned on the heat very low. "There," she spun around with a sense of victory, as a faint whiff of the sweeter scent rose.

"Well! Thanks!" the young woman was impressed. Her young husband was coming back in from the hall as she went on in a rush, "To answer your question, we're married almost a month. But we can't make ends meet. Or, at

223

least I can't. I have such a terrible luck with food– as you can see and smell. And Scottie won't hear of me going to work–"

"She pregnant," Scottie blurted out and quickly blushed.

"I don't care! Other married, pregnant girls do it!" The edgy, smoke-puffer turned on him, set to do fresh battle.

"Belle, you told me the doctor said–"

"Eh-eh. Whoa– th-er-e," Ruthe drawled soothingly.

Scottie bit his lip and looked down, obviously ashamed.

"Now then, I have no business policing a married couple's conversations, but you two seem to have reached what they call an *impasse*, and you need a mediator." Ruthe paused. "By the way, my name's Ruthe. You are Scottie, and you're Belle?"

"Isabelle." But Isabelle gave a perceptible sniff. Ruthe suspected it meant to indicate what she thought of her name. Personally, she thought it a paradox too, that this almost formal gentleman had the cute and informal name of Scottie, while this girlish bride had the old-fashioned highbrow name. *Better stick to main points*, she told herself.

"Okay. So you've found out some new things about each other, and it's hard to be objective when you've made a reckless commitment to love each other."

"Touché," Scottie winced. He eased himself down beside his wife in the same wide-armed chair.

Ruthe motioned Isabelle to move closer into the circle of his arm. She made a face, but obeyed.

Ruthe smiled, pleased she was such a good judge of character, while Scottie gave his wife a conciliatory kiss, and then a bit longer, while Isabelle softened and returned it.

"Isabelle, let's hear your side first."

She sputtered with pent up anger for a moment. As Ruthe expected, she began to feel that Ruthe would help her talk Scottie into her way of thinking, and plunged into her story.

"We met in April, at the swings near the kids' sandbox in the park. We fell in love." Here she digressed to describe the ecstasy of love. "When you've always felt like a misfit, and ugly, and un-together, well, to have some handsome man come along and make you feel like a princess, it just sends your heart racing. In my case, my imagination wrote the most beautiful scripts for all that would happen and what I could do to wow the world!"

Ruthe smiled dolefully. She knew about active imaginations.

"Scottie's in university and already has several degrees under his belt. I was all set to enter U of S this fall and major in Lit and Journalism. Then I got pregnant and sick until noon every day. That was not in my script. Well, my parents said they'd take care of it; not to worry. But Scottie here, he wanted to do the ol' honourable bit. Me? I was just madly in love and expecting miracles. So I listened to him and we eloped.

"When we told my parents they offered us some money to start us off, but ol' Scottie's a proud Scot." She mimicked him sarcastically. "I will look after my own family, thank you!"

"Hmm. I bet there are times though, when you're really grateful for his strong sense of responsibility, eh?" Ruthe asked gently. "You'll brag on it at your golden anniversary celebration." In her heart she identified quite positively with that old-fashioned pride. She wanted to add, "You both ought to have exercised it before you had intercourse," but she decided this was not the time.

"I suppose,"Isabelle conceded. "But! You can't imagine how fanatically scientific he is about everything! Including cooking and cleaning! He says I'm suppost to set myself good routines right from the beginning. Then it will all come easy to me!"

She tossed him a smouldering glance, "An' if that's not enough, Scottie's yearning to move out to a log cabin on a green meadow in the country. Yea-sure, he won't say it, but he's sorry he married me!"

Scottie was about to defend himself, but she raced on, "We can barely afford this crummy bachelor apartment on his salary, so how could we ever–?"

"Honey, that's not fair!" he objected.

He turned on Ruthe as if appealing to a person with a little more reason. "You've got to see this in perspective if you are to understand. About Isabelle working, for example, the doctor plainly said she has to relax through this pregnancy if she is to carry to term; why she insists on chain smoking all of a sudden when he warned her of the danger to the–"

"That's obvious!" she snapped. Isabelle saw that her last cigarette was only a wee short butt, and she quickly whipped out another one to light from the butt. "In this closet, who wouldn't?"

Scottie dropped more reserve as he grew desperate. He needed Ruthe to convince his wife that he was only trying to be a good, thoughtful husband. "Look, her doctor says she's got to stop smoking or she will impair the health of this baby. A disabled baby costs more. For Isabelle's sake I am sorry I am a poor man right now. I believe in the sanctity of life, and think if we put that first, the wherewithal to support our child, and us, will come later.

"About living in the country, since she brought that up; if we moved out right now, Isabelle would have plenty of space and fresh air and would not have to feel so cooped up all day. She would get better physical and emotional health for the baby's sake as well as her own."

"I don't mean getting outside! I want to get out with people! You've got such easy answers!" Isabelle pulled and lifted angrily at her loose white knit shirt to get fresh air under it.

"Did you, by any chance," Ruthe asked Scottie, "Grow up on a farm?"

"Not exactly. An old herbalist woman, found me, a deserted baby in the hills of Nova Scotia. She brought me up. Everyone down in the village thought she was daft, and maybe a sorceress, but she was good to me. She had me do a few chores in and around the cottage, and after that I could do as I pleased. Gram mixed her herbs for whoever asked, but she never needed money. She had different amounts buried in various places in the hills. We had a contented, idyllic life. Still, she urged me to get an education."

Scottie chuckled, still gazing into his past, "Like when I decided I must have organ music, even though I'd only read about it, she went down and bought a pump organ. It looked queer in that homely cottage on the hillside, but it provided us with hours of inner nourishment. I'd play and she would listen with her eyes on the sun setting over the valley."

He came back with a start. "Why do you ask?"

"Just a hunch," Ruthe laughed, her eyes twinkling.

Now Scottie seemed to think of her as a kindred spirit. "Ruthe, I've never farmed, but if I could buy a small one, I would–"

"Where on earth did you get all that money to go to universities the past seven years?" Isabelle wanted to know. "Out of your Gram's hidden cache? It's only after you get married and have to work that you're suddenly broke!"

Scottie's mouth was open to answer her, but Isabelle turned on Ruthe, adding sarcastically, "He majored in music, the humanities, and mathematics, but the only job he can land is as a lab technician with his favourite professor. Nobody can afford all his qualifications!"

"Belle-Honey. Why is that such a negative trait all of a sudden? You've been praising me for my education. I told you; that's how Gram tied up the money. Just for education. I've spent it. But in time my knowledge will create a good way to reap what has been sown."

He turned to Ruthe. "Gram always said a good education and my wits should get me anything in the world. I guess I dream too, I just call mine goals and realize they can take many years to come to pass."

She nodded. His answer helped Ruthe to understand him, but she was still puzzled. "If you've majored in music, maths, and whatever, couldn't you get into teaching or social work? Something that pays well?"

He sighed patiently. "I don't mind tutoring individuals who want to learn, but I'm not gifted for lecturing large, unruly groups. My psychology interests are more of a philosophic and research nature than public welfare. To tell the truth, I

226

studied maths and music simply because I find calculus and precision mentally stimulating."

Suddenly Ruthe's mind was screaming, *Brandt! This guy could help Brandt! Maybe better than Phyllis.* She saw a momentary snapshot of them sitting in Grosz'mama's home, talking casually.

Putting one knee on the nearest chair to steady herself, and with a knowing tilt to her smile, she asked, "How would you like to hear this positively brilliant idea I've just had?" As they stared back at her, Ruthe realized it was still coming. The idea was not fully formed in her mind yet. She just knew where it should end up.

She turned to Isabelle first. "Country life does not necessarily mean log cabins, crude facilities, and bears to fend from the front porch. Unless that is specifically what Scottie has in mind. But I've lived on a farm. Right now my family lives in a small town and I commute to the city. It's only half an hour's drive. Some farmers from our area do it almost every day too. We do our shopping here, or, I do for Mom, and so we end up with all the advantage of the city and of the country at the same time."

Scottie seemed to be restraining an exuberant, "See?"

"Back to my idea. We've been wondering what to do about Grosz'mama this winter. Grosz'papa passed away last year and she's been alone since. She's still well, mind you, and we drop in on her every day. But Mom's been talking about how it is not good for her to live alone another winter. Our dear Grosz'mama doesn't think she's as old as Mom makes her out to be, and doesn't want to impose on any of her children, nor does she want to go into a Home yet. All she needs is company, and that mostly at night. Anyway, we're on a lookout for someone to board with her. It occurs to me that this could be a married couple as easily as not."

Ruthe's mind raced on to other details. If she didn't tell them about her other city friends they could never report on her to her parents. Those secrets could remain as they were. Isabelle's smoking would not make a good impression at all. That would have to stop! Otherwise, what could be so bad about this couple? Best of all, there would finally be professional help, of sorts, for Brandt just in time before he dropped out of school.

To Scottie she said, "You could commute to your job here until you found a farm to buy and it was functional enough to support you."

"Oh, we couldn't impose on your grandmother," said Isabelle unsure of this plan but clearly tempted by Ruthe's enthusiasm.

Ruthe expected to sweep her along. She could see right through the young man's face, and kept working on him. Slyly she added, "Seems to me, Mr. Roth has land for sale. I don't know what he is asking, but Dad might. Oh yes,

Thiessens, just out of town, have talked of retiring and selling their place. Their barn buildings have gone to the dogs, but if you are willing to rebuild, the price may be reasonable."

Scottie held his breath, then looked gently but urgently at his wife. "Honey? What do you think?"

She shook her head and spoke slowly, deliberately, "I don't know... what... to think, dearest." She looked unsteadily into his eyes. "Guess it's what makes you feel complete, and I love you enough to be stupid and reckless enough to do it."

"Belle, if you don't think you could be happy–"

"Isabelle, you would bloom there, and you'd never be sorry."

Ruthe was suddenly aware of the time. "Hey, listen you two. Sorry to interrupt while you talk it over. Why don't you drive out on Sunday afternoon and meet my Grosz'mama? Look the place over. You don't have to commit yourselves this minute. Okay? Besides, Grosz'mama should have a vote too."

She gave them simple directions to Kleinstadt and to her Grosz'mama's house near the entrance of town. Then she was gone.

THIRTY-FIVE

Single, but a marriage counsellor! Ruthe laughed as she ran to the Rambler. *What next?* As she slammed the door at her side, her conscience spoke up with a gentle rebuke. Instantly she dropped her head on the steering wheel and prayed, *I'm sorry, Lord. I've let my summer's adventures go to my head. I'm no marriage magician. What I have done is only because You help me! I guess a little experience has made me conceited.*

She really had to be going, so she started the car, but conviction weighed her down like a wet gunny sack of potatoes. Her own ego had been in control of that scene.

A soundless voice piped up in the background, "But eh, it turned out okay, didn't it? You got another opportunity lined up, hot stuff!"

Ruthe heard it but pretended for a bit she had not. *Lord, here I thought my biggest problems were shyness and fear. Now it's pride.*

He depression grew as she parked the car and scurried into the SaskTel office. It would be a long shift. There was a wind blowing that threatened to bring an early winter.

She put her headset on by the hall mirror. *Lord, where exactly is the line between self-confident brashness and Your kind of poise? And, does this mean I don't deserve to have my hope for Brandt realized? Is it all going to fall through because I forgot to talk with You while I impressed that young couple?*

Between handling calls and small talk with other operators, Ruthe stared soberly away and did a lot more interspective praying.

It was still quite windy the next morning, but the sun was getting up in the wind-streaked eastern clouds. Knowing the time was soon upon her that she'd have to stick to indoor hiding places, Ruthe bucked the gusts and went out to watch the sun rise, all the while still thinking and praying. Great patches of pinks and mauves and blues shifted about on the vast outdoor canvas as she blurted out again her confession of doing good in the wrong attitude. Because of her old standby verse, First John 1, verse 9, she knew God forgave her, but repeated it until she sensed His forgiveness.

Her mother respected her privacy regarding the sunrise walks since a little scene long ago when Ruthe had to say why she went, however, when she came in, Ruthe was expected to come down to mundane things like setting the table, or brushing Sharri's long hair. Cheered some, Ruthe went directly to these duties and hummed along with the hymns sung on the various fifteen minute or half hour gospel broadcasts her Dad kept tuning to until they left for Sunday School.

Later, when lunch and dishes were finished, Ruthe wandered out into the afternoon wind and sunshine again. She spied about. Once sure no one noticed her, Ruthe was off on a sprint to Grosz'mama's house. Normally they all went over as a family when it was time for Sunday late afternoon faspa, or on holidays for the big noon meal. Today she wanted to be alone with Grosz'mama for a while, to prepare her, in case that city couple showed up.

Oh-no, Lord. I forgot to tell Isabelle not to smoke while she's here! Ruthe prayed anxiously as she ran. Her brain wave did not seem so good after all. Maybe it was best if the newlyweds did not show. *Dear God– I may've– really– messed up*, she choked with bursting lungs.

Private visits with her Grosz'mama had always been a treat for Ruthe. Her own secrecy had kept her away for months. Today Ruthe could tell by the way Grosz'mama poked her hair back under her black kerchief, then tied it again, that she had been having her afternoon nap. She apologized for disturbing her, "But I just had to have some quiet time to talk with you before others come," Ruthe explained in their familiar Low German dialect. As soon as she faced this beloved matriarch, words just came out in this language with respect.

Grosz'mama reassured her that it was all right, while she rocked demurely in her old rocker with the patchwork pads tied to its back and seat. They were so old, Ruthe hardly noticed them any more. "Sat die doch dol,"[17] she was urged.

Ruthe pulled an old wooden slat chair, painted brown, away from the table with the oilcloth cover, and sat on it sideways, hooking her heels up on the wooden rung between the chair legs. Grosz'mama had never laughed when one of her visionary ideas slipped out. Ruthe knew she would not flatter her if it sounded absurd, but neither would she make fun of it. In fact, it was Grosz'mama who had advised her when still a young girl, not to allow bad ideas into her mind. She put her elbows on her knees and tried to think how to begin.

Grosz'mama pursed her lips and rocked calmly and thoughtfully. Thinking time was welcome to her, and Ruthe knew instinctively that Grosz'mama would just study her lap and think, or pray, until either one had something to say.

As usual, Ruthe was ready first. "Grosz'mama," and she plunged into Low German, "Didn't you tell me once that you spend much of your time in this rocker praying for all your children and grandchildren scattered from B.C. to Manitoba? You pray about every bit of information they write you, right?"

The Old Colony Mennonite grandmother assured her with a nod and quiet response that yes, she did this, and, "Ekj laje aules en ons leewe Himmliche Foda seine Henj."[18]

Ruthe smiled, remembering that here God was always, *Our Loving Heavenly Father.* "I've been learning to do that too," she replied. "But last week I met a young couple and I felt I should offer them some help. I thought it was an idea from God. Only now when I've had more time to think about it, I wonder if I made a mistake. How can I tell when our Loving Heavenly Father tells me what to do, and when I have an idea out of my own silly head?"

Grosz'mama agreed that this was a hard one, and lifted her folded white cotton handkerchief to her lips and held it there while she stared into her lap, covered with her black Sunday apron, to ponder the question. Then she lifted her head to ask, "Kaust du, hast du frieheit, irjenz waut mea doa fonn ta fetalen?"[19]

Ruthe sighed and shifted her position. Nodding earnestly, she began to explain about Scottie and Isabelle, who needed a place in the country for the sake of their coming baby. "The man has a job in a laboratory at the university, but he wishes he could buy a farm. I told them they might find one around Kleinstadt, and if they were in a hurry to move right away, they might even come to board with you for a while." Ruthe paused, watching her Grosz'mama carefully. "Waut denk ye? Wud daut schaufen?"[20]

"Wuaromm nich?"[21] Grosz'mama said she was always ready to help anyone in need. If it was in her power to do something, God expected her to do it.

Ruthe's face was going to burst; she was grinning so happily. She felt relieved and thoughts that she had done the right thing came rushing back into her whole being. She felt so warm now that she stretched and peeled off her chocolate coloured, Sunday suit jacket, revealing a pretty floral blouse in pinks, mauves and greens that she had recently made from a remnant. Her grandmother admired the print and she willingly explained that she had made it on the new sewing machine, to help her mother figure out how to use it.

Suddenly they heard tires rolling in the gravel drive, and Ruthe stretched into a standing position to look out the windows over the kitchen sink. An old-fashioned car in shiny turquoise with a white roof had pulled up. It had multi-angled Cadillac fins at the back, only two wide doors, with only one very long window on each side.

Grosz'mama had got up and walked to the window, and exclaimed, "Die kua shient oba!"[22] She automatically tied her kerchief tighter under her chin as she went to the door, for she never answered the door without a head covering, in case a man was there. She obeyed her church's Bible teaching in that regard.

Ruthe laughed and expressed the opinion that it was quite an old car, just well cared for, as she skipped and hopped around the back and sides of Grosz'mama like an eager child waiting for a treat.

At the door Ruthe made introductions, hoping she had got the order the way the school textbook had said; "The younger is presented to the older, queen figure." She couldn't keep from grinning as she helped usher Isabelle and Scottie from the porch into the kitchen. As they politely helped her with introductions, Ruthe discovered that the couple's last name was Clarke. Still standing they made small talk about the old car. Isabelle made as if ashamed of it. Scottie commented, "Beggars can't be choosers," and, "If I take good care of it, that '56 Cadillac might be a valuable antique in another fifteen, sixteen years." Grosz'mama approved and told him so.

Isabelle, polite to the point of shyness, wore a mauve linen dress without a belt that looked a little too snug on her already. Ruthe's mind tried to connect Isabelle to Darlin' Bonne's Shop for a maternity wardrobe. Scottie looked quite handsome in his dark blue wool suit and tie. His short black hair showed off the attractive shape of his head.

Ruthe wondered only briefly if this couple found Grosz'mama odd in her Old Colony Mennonite garb, but Scottie treated her as a woman to be venerated and honoured. She smiled broadly again, *right; he revered his old Gram.*

Obviously, her grandmother was enchanted with Scottie's old world charms. Usually she was exceptionally shy and demure with men, but she told him he reminded her of one of her brothers who died young.

Scottie asked, "It was difficult to survive that pioneering era, wasn't it? What do you remember about it?" In halting, but clear and easy to understand English, Grosz'mama told him she was born here when it was still all North West Territories, not marked into provinces yet. She told of her childhood in simple farm buildings with roofs of thatched straw, and the danger of lightening strikes. Scottie led with questions, and her talk covered her education until age ten when the teacher confessed he had taught her all he knew.

Ruthe realized she had heard most of this before, but seeing how impressed Scottie was, made her swell with pride.

Isabelle listened respectfully too, but when Grosz'mama got to her diary and Family Record, and fetched it from her bedroom to show to Scottie, it occurred to Ruthe that Isabelle might find this boring and she ought to entertain her with other conversation. She invited the new friend to scoot up beside her on the old red and black cherry wood bench behind the oilcloth covered table. Their elbows on the table, they soon chatted about their favourite books, authors, dreams of travel and found they had common interests almost every time they changed the subject.

"I haven't experienced enough vivid life yet," Isabelle confided, "But I'd die to be able to write soul-stirring poetry."

"I've dreamed of writing novels," Ruthe reciprocated softly, then thought of Phyllis. *I've never said that before; how did she know?*

Just before three o'clock Ruthe heard Sharri and the rest of her family arriving through the back gate, and had a panic attack. *We haven't covered whether the Clarkes will move in or not!* The family trooped in with just a tap on the door, Sharri rushing at Ruthe with a piqued, "How come you sneaked out without telling me?"

Ruthe shrugged helplessly and introduced Sharri affectionately as her pet kitten, then her parents and Suzanne and Brandt to the newcomers, adding, "These are Isabelle and Scottie Clarke." Scottie rose and shook hands with each one, then graciously motioned her mother into the chair he had just vacated.

Her family stared openly. Grosz'mama often had visitors from far away when they arrived, but usually they looked ultra-conservative, or dressed in dark clothes. Ruthe felt ashamed, and with a quick glance at Grosz'mama filled the silence with, "They might be staying here until they find a farm to buy."

Scottie and Isabelle were busy looking at each other, so Ruthe expelled a long sigh of relief that she tried to make thin and inconspicuous, when she saw her Grosz'mama nod her head matter-of-factly.

Ruthe's mother asked sharply, "Es daut soo?"[23]

Grosz'mama answered carefully in English, "If dis nice couple would be so kind, to like to live wit me, I would be happy to give dem a home as long as dey need it, to start up a place of der own."

Isabelle and Scottie smiled at each other, and said in unison to Grosz'mama, with accepting nods, "Thank you," and "Just name the room and board, Madam."

"Too bad we've sold our old house," said her father, puffing up.

Ruthe said, "But they are looking for a farm, Dad. Isn't the Thiessen place for sale?" That set him off and running. Her dad ensconced himself just behind Scottie's left shoulder and began to tell him all about the Thiessen farm and his personal opinion of what it would take to fix it up and make it a worthwhile operation. Grosz'mama suggested the men might like to go to the living room, and the man never paused in his loud talk while he and Scottie and Brandt drifted into the next room.

Warily, Ruthe watched her family for signs of curiosity about how this couple happened to be here. Suzanne and Sharri vied to impress Isabelle with their sophistication and general knowledge, while their mother made digging remarks that were clues she was jealous of her daughters hogging the conversation with the new guest. She got up, however, when Grosz'mama and Ruthe did, to help put the kettle on and set the table for the usual Sunday faspa spread. In a sudden aside to Ruthe, she exploded hoarsely, "There. That will solve our problem about Grosz'mama for a while!"

It was not a meat and potatoes meal, but neither was it just a coffee break. Grosz'mama served good instant coffee, and with it huge trays of homemade buns and bread, many little dishes and saucers of jams and honey, peanut butter, real butter of course, and so on. Ruthe was asked to go down for a jar of rhubarb preserves, which would be served in clear little fruit nappie dishes. Ruthe noted that Isabelle stared with widening eyes as the table filled up.

Grosz'mama did not usually bake cakes or sweets other than cookies, but some of her other children had been by to visit in the past week, bringing a treat, so when she went to her pantry off the spare bedroom, she brought a bag of iced Long Johns as well as her familiar date-filled cookies, and the soft white cream cookies covered with marshmallow and coconut.

Ruthe had done a good share of visiting before, so now she focused on the table-setting and her thoughts, with only the odd parenthetical explanatory aside between her sisters' remarks. *Perfect. I think we did it, Lord!* she prayed. *They don't suspect I'm behind this. If they don't trust me, at least they trust Grosz'mama.*

Just how much they trusted and admired her self-reliance, the very thing she struggled with, came out momentarily when her dad announced loudly, "Well-now, you are city folks, aren't you? I can tell. Anyhows our Ruthe isn't faring too badly either. Only started working in the city this spring, but she's as sharp as any businessman. Why, she even swung us a brand new house."

Her mother moved to the doorway to answer him, but spoke for the benefit of the newcomers, "Ruthe's not stupid. She even had a good office job before graduating. The city may rattle you, Dad, but she's got a modern education and knows her way around with city folks."

Ruthe's face pulled back in shock, and she clutched at her hair. Scottie and Isabelle were both looking at her with amusement. Blushing she made a wry face and tried to get her father started on farming again, "What about the Roth farm, Dad?"

Moments later she could breathe normally again. *Lucky for me, this couple knows nothing of my other life in the city. I better keep it that way!*

As she continued to help weigh the table down with food choices, Ruthe could not help veering to the doorway to check on the topics of conversation. She often had worried that others would not know how to take the tactless things her dad was apt to say. However, she could soon smile again as she saw that Scottie had turned his attention to Brandt, trying to give him equal time. Brandt confessed that he was dropping out of school on his sixteenth birthday in a few more weeks. Scottie seemed to probe for his motives.

Ben Veer brushed that aside, "Brandt's dumb to be quitting. I keep telling him that. I know from experience it's hard to land a job with no education; only what can you do with today's youth? You can't talk a bit of sense into them!"

Next he asked nosily, "What do you do for a living?"

Scottie replied that he worked in a science lab, and went back to his conversation with Brandt. Taking a notebook from his shirt pocket, he made some quickly scratched signs, explained them to Brand and asked what this and this and that would make if they were treated thus and so.

Brandt, thinking this was a trick pencil game, cheerfully obliged with an answer.

"You're a genius!" Scottie told the thin, lanky teen. "I only came across that this past week at the lab, and we have all been stumped on it for days! We had our minds cluttered with too many other factors."

Noticing Ruthe in the doorway, he excused himself from Brandt, leaped up, and gripping her elbow steered her around the corner until they ended up in Grosz'mama's pantry. There he whispered, "He is a math genius, and wants to quit school!"

Ruthe tried hard to swallow a snicker. "I know. Believe me, I've tried to change his mind."

Scottie scratched his head.

She whispered back, "I bet you could motivate him."

"What's the real reason for quitting?"

"Reading disability." Ruthe made a twisted face. "I wanted to get him to a remedial specialist or psychologist, but Dad says none of his kids are going to be addled by a shrink! Brandt is smart; however, because he can't read and never tells the teachers he's stuck, he can't understand the exams."

"In that case, forcing him to stay in school isn't the best answer either," Scottie reminded her.

Sharri's voice was loud in the kitchen, "Where'd my big sister get to?"

"Go flatter him with more success," Ruthe advised, moving out with more buns, "He might stay in school to prove you right." Scottie's eyes were popping. "Should'a warned you about myself, eh?"

Humming a hymn, Ruthe bumped into Sharri, rotated her and steered her back into the kitchen. Next she winked at Isabelle, and whispered, "Plotting Brandt's education."

Brandt had always been the more silent one, suffering childhood diseases, rejection and loneliness by himself. Ruthe blamed his failure in school on the fact that he had missed so many classes in the first grade due to long illnesses. He had never had the chance to develop the basic skills of reading and writing. His teacher at the time made the mistake of feeling sorry for him and passing him on to the next grade. She had seen Brandt bottle up when teased until he broke out with another illness. The problem looked obvious; it was the solution that hid from her. Now she was giddy with hope for Brandt.

Their dad's attitude generally, and at the faspa was no help. "He's a slow learner, like me," he informed Scottie.

"Then, Sir, you have been fed a lie and you are passing it on to your son," said Scottie politely. "I'm convinced that Brandt is unusually intelligent. He just has some hurdles to overcome."

Ruthe smacked her lips even though she had not bitten into anything just then. *Thank You, Jesus!* she prayed jubilantly. The rest of the visit was a blur to Ruthe; she lost her powers of concentration.

That night however, Brandt stopped her in the middle of their bedroom-bathroom race to confide, "Know what? That guy? Over at Grosz'mama's? He's a whiz at mental figuring, and he says I have a natural knack for that new math. The one all the higher grades hate so much. He showed me a couple of problems, and they're easy once you know what all those different signs and letters stand for."

Speechless, yet grinning with a brimming heart, Ruthe stared. When Brandt saw her eyes filling with emotion and tears he shrugged and went on his way.

"Good things are going to happen to you!" Ruthe abruptly called after him as he shut the door to his room.

236

THIRTY-SIX

The Clarkes put what pieces of furniture were their own into storage at the home of Isabelle's parents', the Squires, and moved in with Grosz'mama by the end of that very week, with Scottie commuting to his lab job in Saskatoon.

Ruthe felt it only right that she pop in for quick check up visits the first few days, and to help Isabelle adjust to this dreaded rural life. However, Isabelle had cheered up considerably. She felt safe, she said, with Grosz'mama. The older woman invited her to work alongside her so their English conversations need not be interrupted while she did her household chores and cooking.

"Her baking and cooking all looks so easy!" Isabelle whispered to Ruthe, "I bet I can learn from your Grosz'mama." Sure enough, she hovered at the poised matriarch's elbows full of questions, so that Ruthe felt a twinge of jealousy. In her quiet, respectful way, Grosz'mama taught Isabelle how to make her Mennonite borschts, big brown bread loaves, thick sour cream gravy, and homemade ketchup from a big box of donated over-ripe tomatoes. These, Ruthe realized she had learned over all the times she happened to be there and helped.

She relaxed and smiled as she saw many other lessons slipped in that had less to do with food. Things like; the challenge of stretching creatively what small basics were in the pantry, organizing cupboards for efficiency, setting people-priorities first, and applying God's principles to common details in one's day.

Ruthe did not talk to Isabelle about not smoking. It was unnecessary. She never saw her new friend smoke after their first encounter in the city she assumed Isabelle had stopped on her own.

With each visit there, Isabelle became more talkative towards Ruthe, sharing plans of what she would do when her baby came, and when they lived in their own home. But Ruthe was not aware of any concrete steps to obtain a country place. Maybe Scottie never had time.

When he got back from the city about supper each day, the Veer family could count on Brandt taking off for Grosz'mama's. In a couple of weeks it appeared that Brandt was acting as Scottie's agent. He beat his dad to certain men down near the post office, to inquire of them about land for sale. It surprised their family. Normally he would have been too shy to return their "Good morning."

In time one of his inquiries led to a good deal. The Thiessen's shabby, run-down farm needed a lot of work, a new set of buildings, but it was only half a mile out of town and the asking price was reasonable enough to match Scottie's credit rating at his bank.

Isabelle got excited about designing her home from scratch. "So what if it takes a few years?" she asked as she came to see the features in the house Mrs. Veer, Suzanne and Sharri had bragged on.

Brandt hinted broadly to his family that he had offered to help Scottie with dismantling the old rotten buildings, "Since in two weeks I don't have to go to school any more." His parents scolding and ranting didn't seem to daunt him at all. Ben Veer threatened to go teach that Scottie Clarke a thing or two, but never carried it out.

The weathered grey barn was especially rotten and useless, so when the sale was processed and complete a few weeks later, Scottie let Brandt go ahead and tear it down board by board, while he was in the city. This appeared to condone Brandt's dropping out, however, Scottie assured the Veers that he was working on getting their son started in home schooling with himself and Isabelle, once the barn was down and the longer winter nights set in. They backed off and began to speak complimentarily about that smart young city slicker.

In the evenings Brandt and Isabelle crowded Scottie at his shoulders and helped him draw up plans for a new ranch-style home that could be added to later, and a modest dairy barn with some granaries. Grosz'mama hinted that a large vegetable garden could be profitable, and so Isabelle was eager to fit that into the farm and her life.

Ruthe was spacing her visits and getting back to her city friends, but she noted that Isabelle wasn't nagging Scottie for money, and yet she was continually chattering about lining up sleepers, crib bumpers and debating over cloth diapers versus disposable ones. She wanted to reward her patience, but hesitated to take Isabelle to Darlin' Bonne's Shop. Mulling it over she came up with a plan.

The next time in the city, Ruthe picked up an armload of remnants at the shop and took them home, making sure to take a receipt for a super fabric sale. The following day, her day off, Ruthe brought the bundle to Grosz'mama's with a cheery, "Well, I hope the canning is all caught up," dropping the materials in a tumbled heap on the table.

Isabelle shrieked and pawed through it, while Grosz'mama whipped her big white handkerchief over her mouth to hide her laughter and delight. She nodded deeply when Ruthe asked, "Grosz'mama, does your treadle sewing machine still work?" Then she got up to take the plants off it in the living room.

One squealed and bubbled with questions, the other watched with interest from the rocking chair, while Ruthe cut out– it appeared almost free-hand– some baby outfits, maternity smocks, skirts and slacks. All three wheeled the treadle up beside the table, then with a running patter, she showed off sewing tricks.

After watching Ruthe zip through the cutting and sewing up the first seams, Grosz'mama asked quietly, "Whereby have you learn't all dat?"

Ruthe replied in an off-hand manner, "Oh, I've picked up ideas here and there from friends."

By the time Scottie arrived at five they had finished a gingham maternity smock and two soft, towel-like baby sleepers, plus cut out a stack of printed flannelette diapers that just needed hemming. Grosz'mama willingly volunteered to help Isabelle do that the next day, and to stitch on some snaps by hand. Scottie was duly impressed as Isabelle showed him these things. When Ruthe gathered her personal things to leave, Isabelle begged her to come do this again. Scottie put his arm around Isabelle's shoulders and seconded the motion emphatically.

With beaming face, Ruthe promised to come again the next free day she could spare. Then, her hand on the door, she issued the invitation that had been simmering at the back of her mind, "So– last Sunday you were going to the city to assure your parents you were doing nicely; how about this Sunday? Would you like to try out our Sunday School and worship service at church?"

There was a full pause in the chatter. "We'll see," said Scottie.

"We'll talk it over," said Isabelle. "Maybe we should try it out, Honey, just once?"

Ruthe cheerily let it go at that, not having the heart to pressure them, yet she could picture new value added to their friendship.

Coming up the stairs from teaching her primary class on Sunday morning, in the fifteen minute period before eleven o'clock when everyone moved into the sanctuary to sit in the plank and slat pews, Ruthe saw that Scottie and Isabelle had just entered the foyer and were looking around reservedly. She hurried over to greet them with a warm, "Good morning!" Catching a few people, including Pastor Ewert, as they happened nearby, Ruthe proudly introduced her new friends.

Moments later Brandt came up from his youth class, and insisted he would show them a good place to sit. Others came to speak to Ruthe, so it turned out that she really did not get another opportunity to talk to the young couple the rest of the morning.

She did think about them during the service. Ruthe could not recall when she did not attend church, except when she had mumps or measles. Even such memories were faint. Sunday morning at church was the climax of her week. The hymns and sermons inspired her. After a week of city adventures the beautiful words and music had fresh meanings. She imagined telling the Clarkes how Pastor Ewert's messages, and the books in the three short library shelves at the bottom of the stairs had been her private Bible College.

In briefly snatched moments she tried to show her concept of God-matters to the Clarkes the following week, but there were other things happening in her life, so it wasn't until the Sunday after, when Isabelle and Scottie showed up for Sunday School as well as the worship service, that Ruthe got anywhere near discovering their reactions.

It was Thanksgiving weekend. Ruthe's family, sometimes other uncles and aunts and cousins, usually descended on Grosz'mama's house for a holiday like this. Isabelle had explained that the Squires always had their big Thanksgiving dinner on the Monday, so Grosz'mama invited them to join her clan for the Sunday noon meal. She felt there would be plenty of room, as none of her other children could come this time.

In a general milling before being called to the table, Scottie asked Ruthe a few questions about the denomination of their church, and its doctrines and practices. He sounded objective on one hand, but also honestly interested. Ruthe's heart fluttered with hope.

It surprised him that this church didn't have an organ, only an old upright piano, but the singing had impressed him. Isabelle chimed in with astonishment at the rich poetry and melodies in the hymns. And they had noticed the people.

Ruthe thought Scottie had directed his questions at her, but her father interrupted to explain and to criticize the congregation. She felt peeved that he was in one of his *I'll warn you about so-and-so* moods. *Dad, just shut up!* Then she reverted back to prayer in her head. *Lord, once he tells stories, he talks for the sensation of hearing himself. My signals don't get to him! You poke him please!*

Her one consolation, which she nursed, was that there did not seem to be any malice in Scottie's questions. He appeared to be doing methodical research into their faith.

But the impression Dad's giving isn't what the church and its people mean to me! Not able to contain herself longer, she used her dad's tactic, simply raising her voice, and presented a piece of her own views for contrast. They had already started into the turkey, and everyone around the groaning table hushed in surprise as Ruthe held forth, "Not everyone in a church can be tarred with the same brush. I, for instance, believe that the church is part of the Body of Christ, just as the Bible says, even if it is full of imperfect people. God is changing us, some maybe mature faster than others because they're more tuned in to the teaching of the Holy Spirit of God, but I think we should treat all the people with respect because we never know what God is doing deep inside anyone of them."

Grosz'mama, with a big nod, murmured an emphatic, "Yo, daut es soo," then remembering her English guests, said, "Yes. Dat is true!"

Invigorated by this affirmation, Ruthe went on, "Once we have the Holy Spirit living in and through us we should find a love welling up for the people around us. I find that I can love them in spite of their faults. I've got to love if I expect to be loved."

In a flick of a glance she saw that she had cut her dad down to size. He was getting red and would soon blow up. Ruthe felt hot and explosive herself. She had never dared such a thing before. Saying private, spiritual thoughts like that was not done in her family. Scraping her chair back, Ruthe fled out the door that was ajar from the cooking heat and pell mel into Grosz'mama's herb garden. Her mother called after her, but she had to put out this fire streaming from her eyes. *Why? Why, Lord, do I take it so emotionally? I'm all one raw, bleeding heart!*

She cried a while on Grosz'mama's handmade garden stool, which she found behind the tall, feathery and still fragrant dill, that had managed to sprout green tips after the fall frosts. Then she prayed some more, glad that the wide row of dried raspberry canes hid her from the highway traffic.

Ruthe had just about finished crying when Isabelle came out to look for her. She crouched and put an arm around her, "Scottie and I were wondering, are you okay?" Deeply touched because no one from her family ever came out to ask when she went off to work things out, Ruthe could only lean against Isabelle and sniff through fresh tears, "Thanks, for asking. I'm fine... I'm fine." But she was too choked up to explain herself. Then she pulled herself together and they went in, to prove she was fine.

The week that followed was a busy one in the city for Ruthe. Mr. Mueller's arson case came to court but ran into delays over lawyers or court timetables. Mr. O'Brien was upset because it could be spring before Ann's father would finish assessment and start psychiatric counselling, never mind treatment.

June's mother, Mrs. Johnson, on the other hand, had been committed to a psychiatric hospital for tests. Ruthe helped June to move her brothers and sisters to the Greystone, where she had already had them different weekends. Whether this was permanent was in question.

About this time June found a valuable antique collection of inkwells and very old glass bottles with stoppers while clearing out more rooms. June researched these at the library and made contact with some interested buyers. But it was Ruthe who had to make the final decision and close the deals. She had just deposited the proceeds, eight thousand dollars, wondering whom to give it to, when a couple of days later she received a bill for estate taxes that almost licked her account clean. Ruthe recognized that a miracle had happened and praised God for it, then forgot it. Only faintly in the back of her mind, did she realize she was beginning to take financial miracles for granted.

She didn't even see the Clarkes until a week later at church. Then she left right after lunch for the city, so they didn't talk at all.

It was Monday morning, as she was helping her mother with the laundry that Isabelle phoned and asked if Ruthe could come over. "I have something to tell you," she said. Ruthe threw in the last load, set the machine and ran over to Grosz'máma's with the wildest possibilities racing through her mind.

Isabelle looked very pretty in the new mauve gingham top they had made. The blue-green skirt was finished as well. "My, but that outfit makes your freckles sparkle!" Ruthe complimented, glancing around and at Grosz'mama.

The bustling woman in long brown dress agreed, "Isobel is salted with happiness." Then she went back to exchanging baked bread from the oven for unbaked loaves, smiling with a secretive purse to her lips.

"Well, what is it?" Ruthe begged, watching Isabelle cover the hot loaves with an embroidered cotton towel. "Has the doctor said you are going to have twins?"

"No, no!" laughed Isabelle, going to sit down. "I hope not yet. Don't think I'm up to just that yet! Although to hear Grosz'mama talk, it would be a great honour. I am tempted."

"Okay then. Tell me."

"Remember what you said a week ago yesterday?"

"No... What did I say?" Ruthe's mind was suddenly blank and her sense of weeks stretched out of proportion.

"You sounded off about what the Church meant to you. About God making us— no you, like Himself."

"Oh." Ruthe winced. Now she remembered. "Thanksgiving?"

Isabelle nodded and went on. "That started me thinking all week. Then yesterday in that Young Adult class, and all through the church hour, I tried to listen with your ears and see with your eyes." She blinked rapidly. "I found myself wishing I could be like you. That... that I could be close to God, as if we were united, like you'd said. I wanted my stupid old faults cleared up and erased, and to stop thinking about the people in my life and their bad habits all the time."

Now Ruthe was blinking.

"All afternoon, yesterday," Isabelle went on, "We listened in total silence to the radio programs that Grosz'mama likes. Scottie and I played chess, but I just couldn't concentrate. I kept thinking I really should have gone to the front as the pastor suggested at the end. But I was scared of what Scottie would think. You didn't know, did you, Ruthe, that he has always thought God was a myth that poor and lonely people had made up to comfort them selves? That the real creative power in the world is mother nature? Our hidden resources?"

"No. I didn't."

"I was afraid he'd say I was a silly– something or other– if I so much as suggested what I wanted to do. So I suffered in silence," Isabelle sighed. "Each radio broadcast seemed to say just what you had said. I envied you more and more!"

"And so?" However, Ruthe felt she must be coming to a happy ending because Grosz'mama sat down in her rocker, looking very pleased.

"Several times I was about to tell Scottie that I wanted– I had to be saved, or born again, or whatever. Then I remembered what he would say about nature righting itself. How prayer is the poor man's drug. An– I'd lose my nerve." Isabelle shook her head. "Want to hear something strange though? It turned out that Scottie had been feeling the same all that time!"

Ruthe smiled from ear to ear. She knew the ending.

"When we were getting ready for bed I was all set to tell Scottie that I was going to go ahead, regardless of what he said, I was prepared to go to church alone and be a martyr wife– when Scottie says to me, 'Hon, I don't know if you're going to like this, but I've decided that I need God; I'd like to know Him like Grosz'mama and Ruthe do.' Well!"

"Floored you, eh?" Ruthe grinned happily.

"Yes. I told him how I felt, and we knelt by that old brass bed and tried to pray. We told God we wanted to confess our sins and be born again. Then we went to bed, sort'a plain-feeling, sort'a happy, and sort'a unsure. What happens next?"

Ruthe and her Grosz'mama beamed at each other. Ruthe knew her grandmother must have prayed all day Sunday while this was going on. Both of them were very pleased at this news.

Ruthe came closer on the cherry wood bench behind the oilcloth table to hug Isabelle. It was the usual procedure to welcome a new sister in Christ at Darlin' Bonne's Shop, so it came naturally to her. As they made contact Ruthe felt a brand new fondness for this sister-friend. They were different in some ways, but they would be close, that she knew. She offered assurances; "Isabelle, you'll never be sorry in the long run, and with time, you and Scottie will grow very intimate with the Lord Jesus."

"Scottie wants to ask you some questions too."

"Okay. I have a shift later today, but I'll be back tomorrow to hear his story and questions."

She did as promised.

Scottie looked as frisky as a calf. Though a listener, he was quite talkative that day. He retold the events and his emotions of Sunday, and thanked Ruthe for her winsome personality. "That's what first attracted me to take a serious look at your faith. Plus, the generous gift of your time and sewing and fabric to help Isabelle, and Grosz'mama's warm hospitality. You two were my first opportunity to watch Christians up close."

Ruthe expressed surprise that he had not met any at the university. She didn't add that Ross had recently informed her that he had discovered several networks of Believers on campus.

"I did find one yesterday in our Assistant Prof when I shared my own news over lunch. I mentioned that perhaps I should have done more reading research first, and Alan said that in the Christian life one does not really understand the big truths until one takes the first steps of faith. He said to look up in the Bible, I Corinthians 2:14, 15, and 16. You know that passage?"

She thought she did, but Ruthe suggested they look it up. It was hard to break up this interesting conversation, and most of the evening was gone before they realized. However, Brandt sat pouting because Scottie did not even go to see how much he had done that day in knocking apart the old barn on the farm.

THIRTY-SEVEN

At their work evenings on the farm, Scottie learned that Brandt had never experienced this spiritual new birth. He had heard about Jesus as Saviour and Teacher all his life, but never taken a definite stand for or against Jesus. Scottie couldn't understand indifference if one knew the claims of Christ. He saw the impact this should have on the world. "Either you believed Christ completely," he later reported saying to Brandt, "or you deny He exists or has any powers. You can't disregard Him."

Ruthe's eyes and dimples sparkled for gladness to hear this.

Brandt told Ruthe later, "He talked to me like I was a grown up who could think and decide. So when Scottie asked me– sitting up on them rotten rafters– when I'd take Jesus, an' let Him have me, I said, 'Right now.'"

Her brother admitted to some nervousness that now he would be expected to go back to school, however he was cheered when instead a better plan was proposed.

Ben Veer's respect for the new farmer's old-fashioned manners and nebulous prize of higher education was growing. He went to the farm and helped tear down the buildings for a few days, talking like an expert until he had courage to ask Scottie to smarten his son up.

Scottie had, as Ruthe heard later, thanked him and explained that Brandt first needed to learn to read properly from a more specialized expert than himself.

"Got just the ticket!" Ruthe exclaimed when Brandt told her. "I met a high school teacher a few weeks ago who does such tutoring after hours. She's had a miraculous salvation recently, and is a powerhouse of energy. I could ask her to take you for two or three hours a week."

"For free?"

She thought so. By the next evening Brandt had passed this on, and Scottie came to Ruthe to set up an interview with Miss Shulton.

"In the meantime," he added, "I'll write the Education Department for permission to have Brandt take his grade eight with us. Isabelle can help him with composition, literature and history during the day, and at night I'll give him a hand with the maths and sciences."

"Your fee for all this?" Ruthe tried to sound light and teasing.

"The price of a farm labourer," Scottie grinned.

Brandt and Ruthe beamed at each other.

Once Scottie had met Phyllis and declared her, "Excellent, really excellent!" Ruthe began to take her brother along on Saturdays and drop him off at Phyllis' eleventh story suite for undivided attention.

When Ruthe came to pick him up, and taking care to be formal with Miss Shulton, she found Brandt blushing as his tutor raved about his potential.

Later on the highway, he admitted when Ruthe pumped him, "That woman is scary, she knows so much. She just... jus' vibrates! Her hair, her clothes, her talking, her actions... y'know what I mean?"

Nodding, pursing her lips to contain her smile, Ruthe asked, "So, did you learn to read any better today?"

"Yeah. I know all the phonetics now, and can sound out most words. It's not half so hard as I thought. Why didn't Miss Dyck tell me?"

"You were sick back then, remember? She forgot what you missed."

Isabelle had some of Phyllis' teaching knack. Brandt bragged at home at the table, "I remember more what these two women teach me in an hour, than in a year from any teachers of the past."

Ben Veer liked that line and repeated it all over town.

The Clarkes became well liked, not only by Brandt, but the whole Kleinstadt community. Of that, Ruthe was glad for she had seen them ostracize some families.

They first made friends in the church. The choir discovered a good director in Scottie when Bill became too busy. After stepping in a few Thursday evenings when Bill could not come, everyone took for granted that he would continue. It was a volunteer position, so no meetings were held, nor votes or appointment. Just understood.

Scottie improved the singing by teaching basics like reading notes, harmonizing, resonance, and good breathing. If Bill had known all this he had thought the choir did too. Ruthe, who attended practice when she could, appreciated these lessons because she had always thought of herself as a dimwit when it came to music. Brandt teased that maybe she had been sick at the time of those crucial classes.

He joined the choir when Scottie and Isabelle did, and was their discovered baritone. Though Brandt held back shyly, Scottie trained and persuaded him to sing solo verses occasionally.

Isabelle was asked to fill in for the pianist a few times, and when that teen left in January for Bible college, Pastor Ewert asked Isabelle to volunteer on a regular basis. Years of lessons from her mother, who played for chamber ensembles and soloists in the city, and accompanying when her mother practiced clarinet at home, made Isabelle a good choice for congregational singing.

Isabelle worked at memorizing the hymns and choruses used most often, and after a few months she was the best accompanist the church had ever had.

When the colder days of winter brought a couple of heavy snowfalls, Scottie and Brandt had to let up on their initial construction stages. The delays however, made more time for study and socializing.

The young couple was regarded as intellectual, but they gave that adjective a better reputation, for the people couldn't resist the soft-spoken Scottie and his way of hearing out their problems and views. Nor could they help but like the talkative, freckled, carrot-haired Isabelle, who wanted to be in on everything. She had made up her mind to like Kleinstadt and its mostly Mennonite people. They could not have kept her out if they had tried.

What is more, they were markedly loyal to Ruthe. It was Isabelle's loose tongue that brought things to her ears, she would not have heard otherwise. They praised and even defended her. While most of Kleinstadt appeared shallow and materialistic to Ruthe, the Clarkes discovered that a number thought Ruthe Veer was nothing but a mousy, shy girl who hadn't the wits or self-confidence to attract a good husband.

Ruthe had a subconscious feeling that her neighbours and acquaintances liked her better now that she was out of school. That is, until she guessed at the better publicity Isabelle was running for her. People stopped her on the street to ask how she was, and people in church asked her questions and seemed to hear her answers. Sometimes Ruthe glanced down at herself to see if she was wearing anything unusually attractive.

Suzanne made fun of Isabelle's *craze* about gathering baby supplies and collecting Mennonite recipes, that was, until Isabelle asked her for help in acquiring other families' favourite recipes through her girl friends. Suzanne began to copy some for herself, and acted as if Isabelle was her friend as well.

Ruthe mourned her long sunrise and sunset walks now that it was too cold to be outside unless moving briskly. When there was a storm brewing she spent less time in the city to keep her mother from worrying, so she seemed to have a little more spare time. She yielded to Isabelle's frequent coaxings to come by for chats. It seemed quite okay with her parents, in fact, they often wanted to go to Grosz'mama's then too. That didn't seem fair.

If she went just about her parents' bedtime, she got to go alone, and Grosz'mama trusted Scottie to lockup, so she retired to bed.

Ruthe took care not to refer to her city friends. Instead, to be safe, she steered discussions to truths from the Bible, which Scottie and Isabelle liked to draw out of her anyway. Ruthe found that she knew far more than she realized. Isabelle's praise was convincing too.

Sometimes the discussions slipped off to her family and coping methods. "Ruthe," Scottie would chide gently, "You really are hung up on needing your parents approval. With their own secrets and struggles to survive, which you have absorbed, they are not able to see outward to your needs and to help you much. Just cut the apron strings. You are a grown up now and a very nice person. You'll survive. For a fact, you'll shine much better once you separate yourself from them."

Ruthe shook her head, nervous at what all that implied.

Isabelle too, urged Ruthe to give herself permission to be all that was bottled up inside. "You are such a tight rosebud!"

Although she saw a kernel of truth in what Scottie said, and winced at Isabelle's comparison to a tight rosebud, just as Phyllis had, she felt deep inner wounds at their words. "Why, I thought I was very bold and daring when I popped into your apartment uninvited," Ruthe would retort lightly while in their presence.

"Yes-but,"Isabelle was quick with her answer, "You've never done anything as bold as that with anyone else!"

"Oh?" With wee silent prayers and forced self-control Ruthe resisted the temptation to brag on her other city adventures and friends.

Later, going home, or driving to the city the next day, her face would wet with tears, and her chin screwed around this way and that.

THIRTY-EIGHT

Back a few weeks earlier, at the time of the first snowfall, her windshield wipers slapped rhythmically at the slushy rain and big snowflakes while Ruthe sang cosily her favourite gospel song about the garden of prayer in her white Rambler.

> "...He speaks, and the sound of His voice
> Is so sweet the birds hush their singing,
> And the melody that He gave to me,
> Within my heart is ri-in-g-ing!
> And, He walks with me, and He talks with me;
> And He tells me – I am His own!
> And the joy we share... as we tarry there,
> None other– has ever– known!"

When she thought about the shortcomings and problems in the lives of her various friends, she could get depressed. When she sang and thought about her trustworthy and always-there Friend, she cheered up and was ready to tackle any new experience.

Ruthe tried to visit her friends frequently enough so they would not feel neglected, to keep current on their lives. This time she was on her way to the Greystone.

She had urged June all summer to invite her brothers and sisters over for weekends. Once she lived and worked at redecorating that big house, June only had time to slip home once in a while; she was always disturbed at the disorder and noise she found. At the telephone office one day, June had told Ruthe that she had managed to cut down on the panicky phone calls in the night. "When they fight I just threaten to cancel their weekend visit to the mansion."

"Wouldn't that defeat your purposes?" Ruthe had asked. "You want to get charge of them and be able to discipline them towards better behaviour, but if they stay away...."

June had nodded wretchedly. The role of motherhood was hard. Ruthe felt June did not know how to mix loving attention with firm discipline because she had not observed that in her own mother.

She did have an obsession for neatness and correct home decor. From kindergarten to grade four she'd had a school friend who invited her over and whose mother kept that kind of home. June grew up thinking that was how good people lived. By now the desire for tidiness and artistic arrangement was ingrained in her soul. Ruthe appreciated what that meant for the Greystone.

249

She also wanted June to be happy with her brothers and sisters, so when those weekend visits happened she tried to be around there to act as peacemaker and help June pick up some parenting tips.

Wesley, thirteen, had been sour and unmanageable while June lived at home. When she moved out, he began to take responsibility. To the best of his ability he made the other kids follow June's instructions. Ruthe pointed it out and praised him. However, sometimes he became too bossy. This got him into intense conflicts with Linnet and Byron. When they lashed back, Wes got upset and withdrew into pained silence for days at a time. "He could go like your mom," Ruthe warned June privately, "if you don't encourage Wes."

Linnet was a capricious and loud twelve. Her teachers called it social aggressiveness, maybe worse in the staff room. June had heard that they dreaded having her in class at all, and were relieved when Linnet played hooky. June begged Ruthe to talk sense into that girl.

Ruthe paid Linnet some special attention and took her shopping. She simply talked to the girl as if she were mature enough to have adult feelings, and asked her for her assessment of the family's situation.

Linnet hitched up her jeans, rolled her lips out in a pout, and gave her some angry, eye-opening answers.

Then, feeling it would be worth the risk, Ruthe confided how June felt and how much she and June longed to help. "Your sister has some dreams. She wants to train to be an interior decorator, and she wants legal guardian status so all you kids can have better futures." This giving of trust went quite a ways in winning Linnet over.

At the switchboard that evening Ruthe had another idea and went back once off work, to call a late night business session with June, Wes and Linnet. With a little flare for drama, she asked them to forgive each other, forget the past hurts and pledge to work together. She drove home well after midnight, praising God for another miracle.

But the six Johnson siblings needed more than one major change.

Byron was only a second-grader. School tests found him to be exceptionally gifted. He applied his high IQ however, to the art of being lazy. He deliberately tried to infuriate June and Wes, and anyone who would notice, with his "I couldn't care less," attitude.

I wonder if it means he does care– a whole lot? Ruthe mulled, but she had no idea how to prove or cure that.

Gilda, five, and Cheryl, three, were out-going and loveable simply because they were cute and often picked up and cuddled, even by total strangers. They were completely hedonistic. No rules applied, other than to be happy.

June was aware of her lack of patience with them and wanted to do better parenting. She sometimes slipped into a large community church, hoping to disappear in the crowd, and spied on the young parents with pre-schoolers to learn from their examples.

Dropping the kids off back at their mother's duplex for June the weekend before Thanksgiving, Ruthe met Mr. Baxter, their social worker. She expressed surprise to him, as if confiding in another professional, that he had not put Mrs. Johnson into psychiatric care. "June is handling a triple load, mothering her mother, as well as her siblings, and holding down a job, plus trying to squeeze in her own long range career plans. Seems to me it would be wiser to shift gears and support June."

"I haven't seen June in six months. I didn't know all that," the man answered. While Ruthe was filling him in on the Greystone and all of June's struggles, Linnet came back out on the sidewalk, leaned affectionately on Ruthe, and confirmed things in stronger language.

June was caught off guard when Mr. Baxter acted on that advice, and arrived with an ambulance two days later to take her mother away for extended testing at the university, just as she was delivering a hot hamburger-in-a-pumpkin casserole to the centre of the family table. While the younger kids dug into the only food they'd seen all day, she slapped together an overnight bag for her mother, and had a brief conversation with Mr. Baxter in which he urged her to take the children to live with her. "We can't pay you for foster care, but I've lined up some assistance for you. What else will you need?"

With a presence of mind that pleased Ruthe, June had said, "I sure would appreciate counselling for Linnet and Byron. They act up so much."

Mr. Baxter agreed to line up counselling with the Youth Centre, took the bag and hurried out after the ambulance.

When Ruthe pulled up in the circular drive the morning after Halloween, the snow was letting up. Just the odd flakes were falling. She saw a laughing Byron tripping lightly this way and that on airy runners, with an angry Linnet in hot pursuit but slipping on the snow-wetted grass. They circled around the huge tall blue spruces that stood as sentinels on either side of the wide round front steps, they darted between other green shrubbery near the grey stonework of the walls, out in loops over the lawn, back up and over the mortared terraces of slate and black rocks that formed the rockery border beyond the space and path between the kitchen exit to the berry garden and the back of the carriage house.

At first she just watched them run, thinking it might be a game, and wondering how three meals a day could make such an energetic difference, but once out of the car she heard Linnet swear and call her brother names, and when June appeared in the open door hollering for them to come in, Ruthe abruptly got involved by locking arms around Byron as he came whistling his body between her and the Rambler.

"Hey, are we playing Prisoner's Base? I got a prisoner!" she crowed while Linnet flopped on the grass behind her in exhausted relief.

Byron squirmed and wriggled. Ruthe tightened her grip and swooped him up so his feet were kicking in the air above his head. Gradually, making little grimaces in her struggle with the still busy boy, she walked up to the steps and joined June.

"Byron! I've told you and I've told you; leave those things alone!" June scolded. "They're Ruthe's and she can punish you as hard as she likes!"

Ruthe decided to withhold punishment until she knew what the crime was, but hugged her criminal to herself, until he tired, and allowed her to cradle him in her arms like a baby. Then she grinned at him and blew a kiss, knowing he'd squirm again if she tried to plant it on his face.

Linnet followed them inside and helped June recite all the things Byron had dared to touch and handle, even though they had both warned him that they were antiques, very valuable and terribly out of bounds.

They had no sentimental value to her, but Ruthe knew it was the right thing for their economic future to protect them. She looked around and realized that June had put away still more of the rare crystals and china, and ceramic figurines. She glanced at Byron, who seemed to be waiting for her to get angry, and then she glanced away across the gleaming red wood of the dining room suite. *Hmm? Could he be motivated somehow to take pride in looking after these things? Lord, he disregards them because June values them, right? What would buy his loyalty?*

Thoughtfully, slowly, Ruthe began to stalk about, carrying Byron. She heard Linnet warn June that an idea was coming, but she focused on glancing into the kitchen with its sword-sparkling black and white tiles, into the huge parlour with the old wine-coloured draperies, and down at the floral Aubusson carpet.

Just then, Wesley, preceded by Gilda and Cheryl, came down the broad turning staircase. The little girls walked tall and proud, calling out, "Look't me! I'm the upstairs maid!" their hands up to keep their new paper hats on. "No, you're for downstairs. I'm upstairs."

While Ruthe looked at them, Byron dropped his feet to the floor, ready for take-off. Ruthe managed to keep her arms looped around him and kept him loosely near her. He did not resist any more.

"Hey!" Ruthe shouted aloud, "I've got an idea!"

Gilda and Cheryl came running then, and Wes and Linnet moved closer too.

"June, let's call a family council and see if we can get ourselves some partners, okay?"

In a few moments they were comfortably sprawled in the plush carpet and couches of the master suite at the rear of the house. Ruthe made a speech, watching the expressions and reactions of the children until she had them in the kind of mood she wanted them to be. She told them how they were a special family of kids who had to help each other because they didn't have parents who properly worked at raising them. She praised June's concern and efforts for them. "And Wes here, you really want to keep everyone from being sent to individual foster homes, don't you? I see Linnet has shown how she cares about keeping your home neat and in order. That's wonderful, Linnet!"

Byron stayed out of Ruthe's reach but he was listening attentively. Cheryl was sitting on Ruthe's upper, crossed-over leg, reaching for her hands, and begging for another *donkey ride*. Gilda was clambering up the arm of the couch, up Ruthe's shoulder, and seemed to be aiming to sit on her neck. June came and lifted her away.

Nodding gratefully, Ruthe went on about how hard it is to love one's brothers and sisters sometimes, "But if we should ever be separated from them we'd sure miss them, wouldn't we?" The ones that did not nod right away she asked individually until she had ensured they understood the hidden threat, and had voiced a wish against it.

"So what's your Big Idea?" asked Byron abruptly.

"Right. I was just building up to that. You know June has a special deal with me; she gets free rent here if she does certain things in this house. We've got to keep it up in good shape, since it's really God's house, y'know."

"Is God your husband?" asked Cheryl innocently.

"No-o." Ruthe found herself on another tangent while she explained simply, who God was, and what a very important person at that.

Byron wanted to know, "How did this house ever get to be God's if He is invisible and lives in a sky home full of gold?"

Her voice grew mysterious as Ruthe explained that an old Irish woman had lived here for many years, who had been terribly angry at God. "Then a miracle happened, and she changed because she accepted His forgiveness and began to love God. Instead of passing her house on to her son and his family when she died, she made her will out to say this house was to be used to keep needy people who had no place to live. Since God is in heaven, she put me in charge of making sure His house is used that way. Only I know it really is still God's."

She shook her head solemnly. "Since this is so big I have to hire good servants to help take care of it. So far, I've found one, your sister, June. However, there's still lots of work–"

"You want to hire me!" Byron, exulted that he had caught on first.

Hesitation washed over Ruthe but she would finish what she had begun. She tilted her head sideways and considered Byron with an earnest study. "What kind of work could you do that would say, equal a week's rent?"

The young playground ruffian in tousled clothes shrugged, then gazed around the ceiling for ideas.

"Social Assistance has still not given me legal status as guardian," June reminded Ruthe, "Things are iffy yet. Don't promise...."

Ruthe motioned with a slight shake of her head not to worry. "I'm trying a different angle now."

Wesley's voice started out deep and suddenly became medium, "That lawn needs regular mowing and the trees watered. The rockery is full of weeds that need pull–"

"I was going to say that!" whined Byron, ready to cry. "Giv'me the gardener job!"

"Have you any experience?" asked Ruthe gently leaning forward.

"No, but I could learn." There was faint hope in his voice.

In her heart, Ruthe had planned to give Wes those jobs. She pointed out that a lawn of this size would wear her out for sure, and she had done some mowing of late. "Byron, why don't we pick five smaller jobs for you, Monday through Friday, with a chance to catch up on Saturdays if you missed one?"

He came closer to her.

"I saw how nimble you are on your feet. If June and I showed you which plants are weeds and you pull them out of the rockery one day a week– mind you, that's a summer job. We've got to think winter now, hmm? How about if you sweep the front steps clear every day? And the back ones too. Then there's garbage to take–"

Now Linnet became excited. She had seen a book in the public library on how professional maids clean. She would take it home and help with the regular cleaning inside, from room to room.

Wes was ready to volunteer for a list too, but just as quickly Ruthe remembered that he would have to be on babysitting duty whenever June was at work. "June needs you as deputy parent when she's away. Besides, with her shift work, and decorating jobs, you and Linnet may have to split some of the meal-making duties."

"For strangers?" Linnet gasped, "Or just for us?"

"At first you six, but when God brings us people who need a home temporarily, maybe more." Ruthe smiled encouragingly at this lively and maturing girl, "This is going to turn you into a fairly good cook, I bet."

June expressed concern that her siblings would not do quality work.

"Of course," said Ruthe to everyone in general, feeling reckless about trusting them, "if this gets to be a very busy guest house, and when I see that you are all doing a satisfactory job, I think it would only please God, the owner, if I give you some small paycheques for your work."

Until now Gilda and Cheryl had been content to be in the midst of a happy circle, but they recognized paycheque as a money word. Gilda wailed, "I thought I was the upstairs maid! Don't I get to do anything?"

"Me too!" shouted Cheryl.

"You shall have jobs," Ruthe agreed, but wanted some more thought. She asked June for some paper to make a chart, and settled into a thinker pose. She sent up a fast prayer for help in the silence.

"Ah," she exclaimed momentarily when the children got restless. "We have no waste basket emptier yet. Or a dish dryer. Or a table setter. Or a message-carrier. You know, in a big house like this, people don't shout at each other. If they want to say something to someone in a different room, or on a different floor, they write a note and send it by the messenger-maidens." Ruthe nodded firmly to convince the little faces gazing up at her. "If June wants to send a message to Wesley upstairs, could you take it without getting lost in this big house?"

Gilda nodded quickly. Cheryl, a little more cautiously.

Ruthe posed another situation; if Linnet answered the phone and it was for Byron, but he was outside sweeping the tennis court, could they run out to call him without shouting so all the neighbours could hear? "You might have to learn these jobs," Ruthe softened the impact. "You've never done them before. Are you willing to learn and obey?"

Suddenly Ruthe recalled the various antique dealers that had begun to phone and ask about items for sale. She turned on Byron, and stared deep into his eyes, wondering if he would bite if she offered him a super-big challenge. She took a breath. "You were here when that man from Britain came the other day, right?" (The boy nodded). "June and Linnet were worried before that you might break something expensive. What if I gave you a very responsible job; to memorize June's price lists, but also some careful answers, so that when these people call and June is not here, you can give them just enough information to make them interested, but not to give away prices until the right moment?"

June rushed closer to say no, but Ruthe raised her hand at her, and kept her eyes freeze-framed on Byron's, waiting for his response.

"I know what you're doin'," Byron said levelly, "You want me and June to be friends."

"You'd have to work on the same side, ánd we wouldn't let you touch any antiques or money until you prove yourself trustworthy several times over." Ruthe answered, not blinking in her stare-down. Everyone else was quiet.

"Some day I'll be a very smart businessman." Byron blinked. "With connections around the world." Very slightly he moved closer.

"Could well be," answered Ruthe smiling gently, "that some of those will be from back in these days." Shifting her position she added, "Twenty dollars if you have that list pinned by the phone memorized in a week."

Byron stepped up and pumped her hand, while Ruthe looked up at June. "Meantime, you and I will prepare him a little telephone sales handbook to memorize next."

Speechless with amazement, June shook her head. She was only beginning to understand what had happened here. In fact, Ruthe felt a little breathless herself. *Lord, what just happened? A miracle!?*

She recalled June's worry about whether they would stay or not. She turned to all five of the younger children again. "There is still one big problem that could keep you from living here for good. Your mother is not quite like other mothers, is she? She is sick and needs to be looked after. Really, it's best she is in that special hospital. You didn't put her there. You didn't make her sick—"

"That's what kids at school said! They said it's our fault!"

"Probably because they are scared it could happen to their parents. When people are scared they usually blame somebody. No. Mental illness is not started by kids, and it is not catching. Your social worker—"

"Mr. Baxter, yuk!" Byron made a face.

"So. Next time Mr. Baxter comes to see you here, you'll have to be polite and help him see that this arrangement is working out. If not, he does have the right to put you in different foster homes."

"He's not comin' for a long time," said Linnet. "He hates us."

"No," said June, "he's coming Monday to check us out."

"If you want to stay in this house with June, you all will have to behave so well in the next few days that Mr. Baxter will come and listen as you talk sensibly to him, just like I am to you now."

"You talk sense to 'im," suggested Gilda generously. The others agreed that Ruthe should talk on their behalf.

Just then the phone rang, and June quickly handed it on to Ruthe. It was Ross O'Brien, apologizing that it looked too much like a major snowfall to come use the tennis court. "However, we are having a pretty lively time here at our house; why don't you come join us for supper?"

Ruthe excused herself, knowing she was cutting it close to shift time again. Then she asked out of the blue, "Say, how is your grocery stock? Have you got room for June and her brothers and sisters? That's six more, y'know!" The Johnson kids squealed and argued as they piled into the Rambler, and Ruthe quickly delivered them to the full Ross home.

On Sunday evening she checked in at the Greystone again, in case June had terrorists chasing around and driving her insane. June was tucking the little girls in, back in her suite, so Linnet came down to meet Ruthe and chat with her for a bit. She raved about the previous evening at the junior O'Brien house. "It was like a whoopin' an' hollarin' wild west party! Or a circus!"

"Exactly Byron's speed, eh?" asked Ruthe.

Linnet added wistfully, "Their place is where to go when you get bored, but you better not be tired. I go berserk if they wind me up like a toy. I have to be alone to think."

Ruthe smiled and put an arm around Linnet. Silently she filed that insight; *I'll tell June, give her privacy space and keep her from wild crowds of peers.*

"Any more misbehaviour here?" she asked confidentially.

The young girl threw her head back absently to let her hair hang free, assuring Ruthe the kids had not been too bad. "Of course, we all got tuckered right out last night at the O'Briens' and this morning June wanted us all to go to Sunday School. That was new and different. Mostly we took naps all afternoon."

There was an unfamiliar note of discouragement in Linnet's voice, so Ruthe asked softly, "How about you? Do you like yourself better these days, Linnet?"

"Oh Ruthe! I love the grand room upstairs, all to myself, but it's so hard to be a kid, and a grownup all in the same body. I wish June could forgive me like you do when I get mixed up and say the wrong thing. I hate my guts more than she does!"

"Hey-y, hey, she's trying. June never got to be a young teen. She's just beginning to understand your feelings. I'm afraid older sisters aren't perfect. Give us a bit of time to learn too, okay?"

"Yeah, I know. And I hope the social worker lets us live with June. I don't want to live in a foster home with strangers! Can't you convince him?"

Ruthe didn't tell her that she had already talked with Mr. Baxter, or to be thankful they had got this far. Instead, she urged Linnet to join her in praying for this decision of Mr. Baxter's. June slipped in and joined them in the velvety parlour, listening quietly while Ruthe explained prayer to Linnet. They were just bowing to pray together when Wesley came out of some secret corner with a message for Ruthe.

"The blonde lady next door– she called and said your boyfriends want you to come meet their new girlfriends tonight, if you are free." Wes shrugged and turned away as if the meaning of the message was lost on him, but Linnet was full of giggles and questions.

Ruthe explained quickly, "They're really Cathy's ex-boyfriends. She just refers to them that way because it's easier than naming them."

Glancing at her watch and thinking a moment she decided; since they were over next door discussing Pastor Teaon's sermons, and since she didn't have an early shift in the morning, it might be all right to allow herself a visit for an hour, but first she would pray about Mr. Baxter with Linnet and June.

There was a chilly winter wind starting that night, so instead of dashing through the hedge path, she drove her car back to the street and up the next drive.

THIRTY-NINE

The O'Brien living room was ringed with guests, and Cathy and Muriel were walking in the ring with hot mugs and trays of sweet squares.

Graham was one of the first to leap up at sight of Ruthe, and he stood, straightening the drape of his suit pants until he had her attention and could introduce Grace Williams. Grace was an ash blonde with a golden tan. Graham using words like charming, and talented, explained that Grace sang in the choir.

Upon a few polite questions Ruthe learned that Grace had spent her childhood with her missionary parents in Java, but she had been left in Canada their last, and now this present term to finish high school and go to Bible College. Ruthe noticed she was lithe as an athlete, her speech gracious and her manners impeccable. "Are you still studying this year?" Ruthe asked.

"Oh yes. I'm training as a physiotherapist."

Ruthe told her that was great, and flashed Graham a sparkling smile to let him know that she approved of Grace, as she turned to Gordon.

Gordon had followed Graham's example to stand, but his introduction was very brief. "You'll like Stephanie. She reminds me of you." Then he sat down, blushing a deep red around his neck and ears.

Ruthe held out a hand of greeting to Stephanie, a dainty teen not much older than Joy. Stephanie had thick, straw-coloured hair swishing in a long, brushed mane down her back.

Lloyd sat on the other side of Stephanie and added, "Gord has been warming up to Stephanie who lives over the back fence from the Adams' place. It's uncanny how she's able to read his mind and help him say what he is thinking."

"That can be a handy gift," Ruthe answered.

There seemed to be a little space beside Gordon, so she sat down there, and putting her hand on his knee, said gently as if in an aside, though in this group they all heard and understood, "I'm glad for you, Gord. I think God will bless you both."

Gordon's face grew red too. He gulped and nodded vigorously.

Ruthe looked back across the room at Graham and Grace, "Hey, isn't our God great?"

Grace began to sing, "O Lord my God, when I in awesome wonder...," and everyone in the room fell in with her. Another hymn followed, and Mr. O'Brien came out of his den to sit at the edge of the room and listen. Chatting interspersed several other songs, and the time flew by pleasantly.

259

In the middle of another song, Ruthe glanced at the large window. Through the sheers she thought she saw something swoosh by. "Oh no!" she cried a moment later when she saw it again, "It's blowing snow outside!"

Usually Ruthe dreaded winter. For one thing, it was hard to walk or sit on a log to pray when it was so bitterly cold. She was not a winter sports person. The weather depressed her because it was so unpredictable, so colourless and limiting. Worst of all, she knew she would have to work extra hard at being cheerful and dauntless because her mother worried about her safety on the highway. Now she would have to account more closely for her travel time and whereabouts, so she would have to curtail her visits before and after her shifts.

As she peered through the driving, slanting snow that night, the Lord made a suggestion to Ruthe's mind; *Why not commit your travelling safety and health through the winter to Me? Why fret so much?*

She vowed to do that. Then wondered how hard it would be to keep.

FORTY

The dressmaking shop was Ruth's favourite and main place to drop in as the winter weeks rolled into the Christmas season. It seemed too long before the next time she was in the little green house, filled with activity, music, lots of colours, and warm friendships.

Three weeks before Christmas, Ruthe popped in and had just given Mrs. McPherson the rest of the afternoon off with an enthusiastic, "I'll be your relief receptionist until the girls lock up."

Betty was just seeing a client to the door and about to close it again, when her hand froze on the doorknob and she screeched– then screamed, so loudly there was a clatter and a running in from every corner.

Ruthe, the closest, had the best view to stand and stare as a tall man with brown wavy hair and burgundy parka embroidered in white and black, bounded into the doorway, swung Betty off her feet and squashed her in his arms in the most urgent hug Ruthe had ever seen.

Din and pandemonium reigned while Betty cried out, "Jim! Jim! Jim? Is it really you?" The man promised to rescue her and take her right home, as designers and clients clamoured to know what was going on.

Darlin' Bonne and Ruthe shrugged impishly, questioningly at one another. Baffled, they waited and watched while Betty and this man, who it seemed, was her own brother Jim, both acted rather berserk. They pounded each other's back, yanked at one another's ears, pulled back and hugged fiercely again. Minutes passed, mostly incoherent. Finally Darlin' Bonne raised her voice, commanding everyone back to what they were doing. Ruthe and Darlin' Bonne took an arm each of Betty and Jim and sent them downstairs to talk things out and get their story straight.

Hey, Lord, I hit it on a day of miracles, didn't I? Ruthe thought as she headed back to the wall desk to answer the phone. She cleared her little agenda for early evening, and looked forward to supper with this circle of friends.

Betty was scatterbrained with excitement, so they all rejoiced with her that she had prepared a large crockpot of sweet and sour spare ribs at noon, with rice in the steamer. The others set the table for she was darting about and forgetting what she was going for almost every time she crossed the kitchen. Betty was unable to eat as she and Jim told their story over the meal with all their being.

The letter Betty had written to her parents in the summer had never reached them. After a few weeks of no word they worried about her; they wrote and tried to phone nearly every day. More so after they got her July postcard saying,

Having a gorgeous time! Too busy to come home on long weekend. Why don't you drive up one Sunday or Monday? But Betty had forgotten to put her new address on it.

Then the school sent a bundle of Betty's unopened mail back. When the Oakes came to the nursing school and her apartment building to get to the bottom of this, the custodial staff had not seen anyone like her picture all summer. School officers were all on holidays. Completely distraught, the Oakes reported Betty missing to the police, who managed shortly to track down Sue, the girl who had been her roommate.

Frightened, Sue confessed that Betty had given her a letter to mail the morning she walked out with her luggage. However, she had lost it. "An' then— then, when I was moving out a couple days later, this guy and a kid, both with red hair, came to get her stereo and stuff. They acted as if she sent them." So went Jim's story.

"Oh, that's right, we sent the O'Brien boys," said Darlin' Bonne, "When we wanted to wire this place for music." Betty strongly seconded that.

"Why didn't the officer who came to talk with me," Joy was turning on Ruthe, "when you brought me, recognize Betty as one of their missing persons?"

"Guess they are human," was all Ruthe could think to answer.

Even the director of nursing, once located, insisted she was not accountable for the students during the summer.

"This fall," said Jim Oakes, "I stayed home from college and took up the search for Betty in earnest. I came into Saskatoon several days a week, and resorted to standing all day on a street corner showing Betty's picture to passers by in the hope that someone would recognize her face and tell me where she was or what had happened to her."

"Today someone did!" crowed Donnie and Joy in unison with Betty.

"Yes, praise God! Today a woman told me she had seen a young lady very much like that at Darlin' Bonne's Shop. She gave this address."

Throughout the telling, Jim and Betty had their arms looped over each other's shoulders, and when asked by the others what they would do now, Betty responded, "Naturally, we've phoned home already. And I've got to go home to console and reassure our parents that I'm okay. I feel awful about causing them so much heartache! I really thought they were avoiding me because I decided to work here. There was so much work here all summer too, that it was just a little nagging problem at the back of my mind. We've got to go square that away!"

"You did suggest a Monday outing to Rosetown more than once," offered Darlin' Bonne.

"I know, but I didn't want to embarrass the rest of you if they had disowned me... and other things came up we had to do."

Betty was sorely missed the three days she was gone. Then she was back with a big announcement for the girls. She had promised to come home for Christmas, and to bring Darlin' Bonne, Evelyn and Joy with her. "Mom and Dad insisted on it when they heard you girls have no home to go to for the holidays."

These three lit up at the prospect, especially Darlin' Bonne, who thought every Christmas card picture was turning real life. Donnie and Louise got envious and were about willing to forego their usual celebrations to go along for this old-fashioned farm-style Christmas.

Betty's happiness and the other girls' excited anticipation stirred up a secret agony for Ruthe. Driving to and from the city she tried to imagine such a wonderful reconciliation and new understanding between herself and her parents; it would not come. Meeting the Oakes when they came in for a day of shopping and to see the Shop, confirmed one thing in Ruthe's mind. Her parents were not as open to strangers and willing to forgive. They would not see the value of the Shop and its service to women and girls. *Lord, you know Dad would say rude things to Darlin' Bonne about her past as a prostitute. In fact, he'd tar them all with the same brush. Mom would be suspicious just because they are different from our Mennonite kind. I can give up dreaming for a miracle like Betty's, can't I?* However, the idealist in her could not stop pining for improvements in her own family relationships.

Darlin' Bonne still had recurring nightmares of aborted babies from time to time, especially when Joy got excited about young children she sewed for. In a subtle way that was similar, Ruthe found that much as she admired Betty, to see her so brilliant with happiness gave her a stab in the left side of her chest. Since Ruthe didn't confide this in anyone, she had to talk it out with her Friend on her drives home. Over and over she moaned that her parents wouldn't react that way. More than once she asked for grace to forgive Betty and not hold this against her. She could bury it for a day or two at a time, sometimes a week, then had to forgive all over again. Gradually the problem faded.

She did have that other happiness however, that came from having committed her health and safety in the winter to the Lord. When not focused on Betty, Ruthe was buoyed up over the fact that everything else seemed to be going well for her.

Because she had guessed that December would be a very busy month, both in Kleinstadt and in the city, Ruthe thought to do herself a favour by volunteering to work the night shift for someone else for the whole month. "All I have to do," she explained to various friends, "Is cut my sleeping time down to a few catnaps throughout the day, and presto– I'll still have enough time to do all the other things I want to do."

"Good theory," some retorted with a knowing lift of the nose.

Ruthe felt it was turning out fairly well. She took naps of course, but when she was awake she was so active she did not notice she was logging a huge sleep debt to her body. She hoped as a working person she might buy most of her gifts this year, instead of making little crafts as before. However, her father was laid off again, and her mother was complaining about where to get money for groceries and utilities, never mind gifts. The waiting period before her Dad's unemployment insurance kicked in bracketed over the month of December. When it came it would only cover a couple of months. So Ruthe turned her December pay cheques over to her mother in full, except for her travelling gas budget, and counted on her creativity again. She knew something that made her faith cheery.

June had sold for her, a number of antique furnishings and bought less expensive, modern suites for most of the rooms. Byron's memory and savvy with the collectors had proved a blessing more than once. As Ruthe had requested, June had also set aside a room for small antiques and interesting articles of less value, which might be suitable for gifts, or to sell eventually, when the right buyer came along. Right in that room, Ruthe had a delightful time picking out gifts early one morning for her city friends. She would sew rich-looking velvet patchwork bags at the shop instead of buying gift-wrap.

However, she couldn't make up her mind what the perfect gift would be for Isabelle and Scottie. She didn't dare give them anything from the Greystone because she would have to explain or justify the cost. Christmas would be at Grosz'mama's and all her family would see what she gave the Clarkes. "I suppose," she sighed, as she discussed it with June, "I could sew each of them a smart suit of clothes if I make a big production of it at home. With a story, naturally, about finding the material at a terrific bargain."

"Good thing you stocked that new house with a new sewing machine," commented June helpfully.

"Yes," laughed Ruthe, "Now that Mom has seen that I am a *born seamstress*, without her having to teach me, she is always coming up with a remnant she wants me to transform into clothing for somebody. She already has me lined up next Thursday to sew dresses for the girls as her gift to them. Oh, and one for me too!" She grinned at her own joke.

She watched as June examined the clocks with a practised eye. She looked again herself, at the stickers with descriptions and market values that June had painstakingly applied over the fall months. On an impulse she felt was inspired, she asked, "June? Is there something suitable for your brothers and sisters here? I want you to take it."

"Well, Byron has been nagging and hinting endlessly about that tin box of old metal soldiers," June conceded.

"Okay. And the others?" Ruthe had to coax a bit more, then June confided that Wes was rather partial to a certain French ormolu mantel clock, and Linnet had sighed over a diamond ladies' watch. Each was worth nearly a thousand though, and the watch needed to be taken to a jeweller for internal cleaning.

"Let's say they are from both of us then," announced Ruthe, settling it. "You can take along one of the less rare mantel clocks that Granny repainted and gilded, and sell it so we can buy nice gifts for Gilda and Cheryl too."

June was aghast, but Ruthe felt so good about being able to give gifts that were desired that she persisted and won.

Ruthe knew she could help herself to material at the shop to do more gift-sewing, but when a week before Christmas, her own expected sewing sessions had not materialized yet, she got edgy. Then Ruthe's mother handed back to her fifty dollars of her own pay for her own shopping. Delighted, and praising God, she decided to pick some jewellery boxes and china ornaments, and wool shawls from the Greystone for her family. It would save time. Their value was more than fifty dollars, but she could say that the receipts were confidential, and not turn them in to her mother as she usually did.

Rhythmically bouncing her hand on the wheel, she sang hearty praise choruses as she drove on the highway.

The twenty-third of December Ruthe still had not found anything special for the Clarkes, so right after her night shift she stopped at the shop, before Betty, Evelyn and Darlin' Bonne were ready for breakfast, to choose some suit and coating fabric, with matching lining and buttons and thread. At home she napped until nearly noon, then with her mother and sisters as well-entertained witnesses, she acted out a scene of astonishment at what she could produce if she read the instruction pamphlet that came with a pattern.

When Suzanne commented that she seemed to be doing what the designers at that special shop in the city were said to do, Ruthe retorted lightly, "Oh, nothing's new under sun. Anyone can learn to sew with flare. Nothin' to it!"

A fashionable winter coat in teal blue with expanding pleats fell together for Isabelle. So did a sharp looking navy pinstripe suit for Scottie. With shirt and tie, no less! The girls drooled and began to talk of dream outfits they wanted after Christmas, while Ruthe yawned uncontrollably and wondered aloud about catching sleeping sickness.

"Since you showed Isabelle how to make those sleepers," Ruthe's mother informed her, "She and Grosz'mama have made a stack of baby outfits and blankets and diapers." Ruthe heard a hint of jealousy.

Suzanne added, "Yea, she's big enough already to have her baby tomorrow, but Isabelle says she hasn't learned yet how to feed and change a baby. I told her; 'too late to practice now.'"

"Day before yesterday," said Sharri, "I took her my big doll to practice on. Right away Grosz'mama and Is'belle started dressing it in sleepers!"

Ruthe tried to show interest, but noticed that if she didn't keep active and chatty, she soon sat in a frozen pose and her mind dozed off for whole moments at a time. "Maybe my morning naps are not long enough...." she mumbled. When her nerves began to feel like thready little worms creeping around under her skin, she went back to bed.

Christmas Eve, in Ruthe's mind, was the climax of all the holidays. She stayed in the city in the morning until she had delivered her little surprises to her friends, and exchanged enthusiastic greetings with them. She made sure they all had a place to go to celebrate the next day. Darlin' Bonne, Betty, Evelyn, and Joy were nearly bouncing on their toes with anticipation of their drive to the Oakes' farm at Rosetown, as soon as they closed at six. Betty advised against eating fast food on the way as her mother would have a traditional ham with yams supper hot and waiting for them.

After that Ruthe had to go back to the Greystone to unload the gifts she had received. They in turn were wild to point out the parcels under the tree in the old parlour. "Look't! Look't, that tiny narrow one!" exclaimed Linnet. "It's jewellery and it has my name on it!"

Wes was very cool, and kept reminding his siblings they wouldn't get the expensive stuff of their dreams. Byron sided with him for a change, downright convinced that Santa was a hoax and that any gifts they might get from the Sally Ann were going to be practical ones as in past years.

Gilda and Cheryl were confused by these attitudes, but were giddy with hope. The gifts under the tree with their names on were wrapped in shiny foils and were big enough for at least one or two dolls. "That one," pointed Gilda, "Is big enough for a big Barbie doll carriage if the handle and wheels have to be put on afterwards."

"We go play wit a big, BIG family tomorrow," Cheryl informed Ruthe.

Ruthe bent down to agree and quiz the little darling, but Byron disagreed, "Naw, we've got'a babysit our Mom."

"We're doing both," said June to pacify, and prevent a quarrel. She explained to Ruthe that Mr. Baxter had called about taking their mother out of the sanatorium for a bit of a holiday, as most families did. She had agreed to take her, just for Christmas Day in the afternoon and evening, however, she seemed to regret it already for the discord it was going to sow among the kids.

Ruthe wished them well, wondering how she could make that turn out better, then paused at parting to lean her forehead against June's to pray for everything to go smoothly... for the mother and children to have some moments of true love together.

Once home, she slept the rest of the morning and into the afternoon, deliberately delaying in bed so as to be fully rested for the evening. After supper dishes, she, Brandt and Suzanne bundled up well, and went to the church to join the choir in carolling.

"I never want to miss the carolling!" she had trilled to Isabelle and Scottie when preparing them for this. "It's my supreme Christmas!" Ruthe was bubbly with pleasure that they were going to experience the essence of Christmas as she felt it.

Like most Christmas Eves she remembered, the atmosphere barely breathed in its reverent hush. The snow drifted down in large, furry flakes like gobs of damp cotton. A tender, downy coverlet dropped on everything. All week the temperatures had been low and their voices had tinkled like pinging glass when they talked or walked outside on the smart crunching, super-frozen snow beneath. Now, in a few hours, it was closer to 0 degrees and the air was more muffled and intimate.

A couple of choir men had brought their vehicles, one an open truck, and the other a large van. The choir first went to some out-lying farm and village homes to sing for widows of the church. Then back to Kleinstadt, to homes where they knew the carolling would be especially welcome and appreciated. Throughout, Scottie and Isabelle exclaimed in asides to Ruthe, "What a beautiful, peaceful night! Just like you said!" Or, "Look at the blue whiteness of the snow. See these big flakes coming down!"

Ruthe beamed and reflected their joy with satisfaction. Christmas was perfect this year. Deep in her bones she felt meek and looking forward to her sit-down job through the rest of the night. *Tomorrow can be an anti-climax for all I care,* she told herself, *let it roar all day at Grosz'mama's house; I'll crash on her bed for a nap.*

267

FORTY-ONE

The switchboard was busy at first, but by about two the public seemed to be getting to bed and the small handful of night operators were able to relax. Between infrequent calls, they drank coffee or hot chocolate and told stories, mostly describing family ways of celebrating Christmas, and favourite memories. As soon as the seven o'clocks arrived they hurried out to their waiting spouse or taxi, or in Ruthe's case, to her Rambler in the parkade on the corner. They cheered each other with comments about having done their duty and being able to enjoy their holiday now.

Ruthe looked forward to having a Christmas orange as she passed the breakfast table, and napping until it was time to load the gifts and go to Grosz'mama's for the big noon meal. The relatives that usually came had arrived the previous night at Grosz'mama's, who would have found, or made up beds for all. Isabelle and Scottie planned to be there until evening. The house would be wonderfully crowded and happy.

A block or three away from the office, one of the downtown churches broke into beautiful Christmas chimes. *Joy to the World*, she thought, so she rolled down her window to listen, and let the cold air stifle her yawns while she waited at the red light.

All at once a dishevelled-looking woman with her coat buttoned into the wrong holes, and carrying a tightly wrapped bundle, stumbled into the crosswalk in front of her Rambler, and right around to her open window. She thrust the white blanketed bundle into Ruthe's face, "Ere (hick)...Wo'd ya lika presen' la'ey-y?"

The light turned green. A truck directly behind them honked hoarsely, and like a frightened rabbit, the woman scampered at a tilt away behind her car, and in front of the truck!

The bulky bundle dropped onto her steering wheel, made it squeak a honk, and immediately the thing began squirming and churning mightily.

A baby? Stunned, Ruthe moved the bundle onto the seat beside her.

Why, the audacity of that woman! She...! Oh, I should get my hands on her! When she peered into her rear-view mirror and back on the sidewalk to catch that woman and ask some serious questions, Ruthe could not see a man or woman in any direction at this intersection. *Where did she go?*

The trucker behind her added to her confusion with his persistent honking, until with a door slam, he backed up and swerved past her.

Darting glances at the squirming bundle, Ruthe decided to drive around the block to see if she couldn't catch up to that drunk woman.

She started talking aloud, "Good Grief. What ailed her? Giving her baby away in such a drunken stupor! She doesn't deserve– Say, what if it wasn't even her own?!"

Dazed, eyes darting every which way, she let the car roll forward. As she turned the wheel around a corner the bundle burst open with all its activity, and there he was; not a stitch on him.

"Aren't you a Prince Charming in disguise!" she cooed at him, wide-eyed. "Just look at those silky black curls!"

He stared back through big round puddles of indigo ink. Then he opened his mouth to smile, and his smooth body shook as if he were laughing at her.

"Oh-h– you–!" Ruthe's heart melted and her right tire skinned the curb as she feasted her eyes.

Just as abruptly she was filled with hate for that miserable and stupid woman. *There are loving ways to give a baby away, but this is downright stupid! How could you give your baby away, or anyone's– while boozed up? On Christmas morning yet!*

The woman, it seemed, had vanished off the face of the earth. Ruthe circled around that one block and the other one on the other side several times, always returning to that particular intersection. Now she was alone on the streets. No traffic at all. A closed service station, plus a dumpy All-Day parking lot on one side, and a section of railroad switching tracks on the other.

Ruthe's first reflex was to go to Darlin' Bonne's with her unexpected problem and solve it from there. Then she remembered; they were at Betty's parents' farm, near Rosetown. At least an hour in the opposite direction from home.

Next she thought of taking the baby over to Ann and Ross's. Their house was full but they'd be quick to understand and help. Never mind; June and her brothers and sisters were there for the morning; it would not be fair.

Then it occurred to her that before she did anything else she ought to go to the police and report what had happened. they certainly wanted the woman's trail as hot as possible. Maybe they had heard from the baby's frantic real mother already.

Ruthe had grown so heated over the woman's nonchalant action that she let off some steam at the officer behind the front desk. His nameplate identified him as W. Heidebrecht.

"Take it easy, Miss. Let's call the emergency number of Social Services for instructions. It's just a new twist to the Doorknocker Foundling tactic."

While Ruthe tried to keep the wiggling baby bundle from squirming right off the desk, the officer, with the telephone receiver pinched onto his shoulder,

269

located a form pad and prepared to take down a description of the missing woman, and of course, the baby boy on his desk. To see him busy did calm Ruthe. She worked at controlling herself by cooing to her Prince Charming and focusing on him.

All she could remember, when the officer asked about the woman, was that she had worn a fuzzy beige coat with huge wagon wheel buttons done up into the wrong holes. Squinting into space to conjure up the image afresh, she paused, then added, "Her mousy hair was either terribly frizzy or done up in tiny wire rollers. Sorry, I was too surprised to look for details just then."

When she had convinced him that she couldn't recall another thing, and really did not know where the women went to, he suggested that they call Social Services again, and held out the receiver of his black phone. "Somebody's got to be on call," he muttered. An answering service finally answered, and said that Miss Schmidt was on call, and put them through directly to her number. Even then it rang ten times.

To the sleepy voice that answered, Ruthe explained crisply what had happened at the intersection.

"Th-there– this's never happened before, on a holiday. Not that I know...," Miss Schmidt mumbled. "There's no prec-ce... precedent–"

"You have no Doorknocker foundling category–?" Ruthe interrupted herself, "So what's the right thing to do this one time? I don't want to see this become a habit either."

"Goo– ques'ion. Our temp'ry 'oster homes are full's can be. Sides, people are all so busy... with fest-ivi-ties, an' all."

"Obviously," Ruthe bit back, now sure this woman was drunk.

"Look dear," Miss Schmidt yawned, "You sound responsible. Since our offices are closed, why don't you take 'im home? Bet you love babies, no?"

Ruthe must have growled assent, though later she couldn't recall doing it. *Of course I love babies! I want a house on a hill, filled with kids some day!* She wondered afterwards if she might have said that aloud. Yes, she supposed she could take him home and just tell the scene at the intersection as carefully as–
As soon as she let that idea into her head, she had a much bigger, better idea. What about Isabelle and Scottie? Hadn't her sisters said Isabelle wanted practice? Simply because this was bound to be temporary, this baby would make a stunningly dramatic Christmas gift to give those two. A vision of herself making a terrific entrance at Grosz'mama's and telling this poignant story played quickly through Ruthe's head.

The voice under the bedcovers at the other end of the line was whimpering, "...A splitting headache! I shouldn'a gone to that party. The Maternity ward nurses at City will give you a few spare diapers and things... out of storeroom. Tell 'em Maggie Schmidt sent you."

"Thanks Maggie. I'll just do that!" Ruthe put the receiver down rather firmly. The anger and disgust within was all washed away now that she had a plan. Still, the airtight sleeves and collar of her rust red coat itched and prickled her hot skin most uncomfortably.

"The gall of it all," said the solemn officer with the dark moustache sympathetically. "No one, not even a trained welfare worker wants to get seriously involved with a lost baby on Christmas Day."

Ruthe nodded, but now she didn't have time to stand and bad mouth others any more. "I'm taking him to our family gathering at my grandmother's in Kleinstadt, and I'm sure a young couple who are expecting a baby will be happy to look after him for a few days."

She was also tempted to tell him, now that her sense of humour was easing back, that her grandpa would have called his moustache a *cookie duster*, but a quiet voice in her conscience tapped her to let it go.

As she rewrapped the stark naked baby in his flannelette receiving and white outer wool blanket, her imagination saw vividly the baby Jesus, alive, in a straw-strewn stable, and then in a flash in her arms as she picked this one up. In that instant she was flooded with mixed emotions.

"Miss," the officer was saying in an attempt to cheer her. "Jesus once said, 'In as much as ye do it unto the least of these...,'" his voice trailed off hesitantly.

Ruthe looked at him through brimming eyes and nodded vigorously, but dared not speak. Her throat was knotted.

Back in her Rambler, Ruthe spent a few minutes confessing her upset feelings and reactions in prayer. She was ashamed of them.

Then she drove to the hospital for the diapers and baby equipment. Here the nursing staff was very sympathetic and as Ruthe left, they followed her to the elevator and told her what an angel she was for doing this.

She started for Kleinstadt again, nearly two hours later than her shift had ended, with the handsome Prince cooing and gurgling to himself in detached felicity. Fortunately, the car warmed very nicely, and though Ruthe felt hot and sticky, he was as content as could be, holding up a new bottle of formula and feeding himself. He kicked his aqua sleeper-covered feet and rolled his head to examine the details of his surroundings. His amused indigo eyes were especially bewitching. His expression implied that he had known all about this plot to get them together. Ruthe kept glancing at him. That she had been so stunned tickled him periodically, or so she told herself, for every little while he burst into little giggle-shakes with his plump little body, as if he were snickering.

"Oh-but aren't you adorable!" Ruthe cried again, and after a bit, again. Thoughts of adopting him crossed her mind, as did a primal yearning to have a husband and a whole bunch of handsome babies.

Lord, I know I promised You I'd never chase after anyone to get married; I'd focus on serving You, and leave it up to You to work out a wonderful husband for me, if You think that's best. But oh-h-h..., Ruthe tossed a frantic look over the flat snowy vistas that went for miles in every direction, *This morning I feel impatient for it!*

It would be going on ten before she reached Kleinstadt. The family would be gathered at Grosz'mama's for sure by then. So she mentally rehearsed a dramatic entrance and announcement there. *I've just got to pull myself together so I don't blurt out all my secrets,* she told herself firmly, as she pulled into her Grosz'mama's driveway behind three other cars.

"Maybe I'll sneak away and get more baby naps than you," she told her Prince as she nimbly wrapped him up in the blankets he had kicked off. Looping her purse and the diaper bag over her shoulder she picked up the baby and tottered from the sudden imbalance. In her eagerness and hurry she nearly slipped on the ice patch at the corner of the steps. Impatiently she banged at the door with the toe of her boot.

She had been seen from the kitchen window; the door flew open. "Oh my no! Rut-ie!" cried her visiting aunt from Alberta, with shock. "What have you there?"

"Hi, Auntie Justine! Glad to see you!" They had not seen each other in nearly a year, and her aunt must be thinking the unthinkable, so Ruthe added impishly, "You know, we can't really celebrate Christmas without a new baby. You didn't bring one this year, did you?"

Isabelle stood at the inner door to the cold porch. She hung the tea towel in her hands over her shoulder to lift the blanket and peek at the baby, while the aunt shut the outer door. "Aw-w, isn't he just darling!"

Ruthe began to beam immensely as she eased into the house and let Aunt Justine close that door too. "I call him Prince Charming."

"Scot-t-ie!" They could all hear the springs in the old living room couch squeak at her shout, as he jumped up and came hurrying to his wife's side. Absolutely everyone was behind him.

"Ruthe!" Scottie shrieked unnaturally, "Where did you get that?"

The mob crowding his shoulder cried, "Let me see! Le'me see!"

Smoothing down the blanket under the little charmer's chin, Ruthe held him out to Isabelle and Scottie. " I think truly great lovers and wonderful friends like you deserve the perfect Christmas gift." Ruthe liked her own flamboyance and her dimples twinkled in and out of her cheeks as she smiled and smiled.

They stared back incredulously and in unison.

To help them, Ruthe pushed Prince Charming up against Isabelle so she would have to take him.

"But-ah! I'll drop him!" she yelled in panic.

Scottie swiftly scooped his arms around her and under the baby. "No, Belle, you won't. However," he turned to give Ruthe a stern look. "This little lady is going to tell us what she thinks she's up to."

"Why," Ruthe teased, "It's simple. I've got you a Christmas gift."

"Hey, Ruthe," interrupted Sharri, suddenly appearing under her elbow, "We already brought along the ones you made."

"That's okay, Meitz. This is just a temporary one," Ruthe explained in a hushing way, putting her arm tight around Sharri's neck.

The others heard that of course, and realizing the moment had come to tell the truth, she quickly sketched what had happened at the red light early that morning. "I've notified the police and Social Services, and they are doing their best to find the real mother. It may take them a couple of days, but they will do their jobs."

"Meantime," she threw out her arms expressively, "This is a golden opportunity for two lovebirds to take a crash course in the care and feeding of baby lovebirds."

Everyone appeared satisfied, and the young couple was already lost to all but the winsome little fellow, who had kicked off his blankets again and was waving all his limbs happily.

Grosz'mama managed to get closer then, for a good long look. She touched his arm, he grasped her thumb, and letting him hold it a bit, she stroked him with her long thin and veined fingers. "Dis one is from a good home. He's not a crier from sickness or beating, she softly pronounced. "Not a new baby. Maybe six, eight monts."

Ruthe stood still and considered that he might have been kidnapped. Somewhere good parents had made him feel loved and content. They must be crying their eyes out today. She watched for a moment as Isabelle and Scottie cooed and explored him, and realized that when they had to give him back, they would weep a lot too. She sighed wearily.

Her parents and sisters, and the visiting relatives were all talking at once as they scattered to fill the rooms as before, and muttered, or said things like, "That woman didn't deserve her baby! They should've taken him away from her long ago!" And, "What an awful fright for poor Ruthe, to be accosted by a wicked, drunken woman in broad daylight! As I've always said, this world is being taken over by the devil!" There was some effort to ask her for more details, but they were already enlarging on the unknown parts with their own imaginations as they talked.

Scottie was the one with the most presence of mind, aside from Grosz'mama, who was diligently moving onward with Christmas dinner. In a few minutes he took charge of the show-off, spreading his blankets on the couch in the living room, and setting up the little guest of honour, so everyone could easily admire him. With a bit of propping the Prince sat upright and reigned with amusement. Sharri became the loudest, but all the cousins and adults joined in a coaxing for personal smiles from his highness.

Isabelle began a dizzy dither from the kitchen to their bedroom with the diaper bag, adding from her own supplies, and back into the living room to look at her baby. She was trying to organize a feeding, but since he had already helped himself to most of his bottle on the way, it really was not urgent.

Grosz'mama was convinced that Ruthe must be starved for not having had breakfast. She wanted to prepare a quick plate of sustenance. Saying not to bother, Ruthe still helped Grosz'mama to slide the turkey roast out for basting. The good smell got to her, and she volunteered to accept the test slice and the heart and liver on the side, which she could see were done, and which she would not have a chance to get at the table, as they were considered prizes. In a trice they were on a saucer, and handed to her.

They were hot so Ruthe blew on them, and ate gingerly with her fingers as she stood in the archway and checked the show on the couch. At one point Scottie raised his head, caught her eye, gave her a wink and a shake of his own amused face.

Ruthe turned, about to go for more food, when she yawned uncontrollably, and realized how utterly weary and detached she suddenly felt from everything. The noise of everyone talking at once pressed against her temples. All of life was suddenly revolting and she wanted off from it. Fearing she might collapse, Ruthe steered herself abruptly into Grosz'mama's bedroom at the back of the house.

Oh-h-ch. She was so sleepy. *I don't care to stir a cell.* Without another thought she let herself drop in a haphazard splash across her Grosz'mama's patchwork quilt-covered bed. Her body refused to feel. Her mind went blank. Like a dimming light, she was out.

FORTY-TWO

That evening the Clarkes took the gift baby to Isabelle's parents, and her younger sister, Jeanne. They stayed over until the evening of Boxing Day.

When Ruthe checked on them at her Grosz'mama's the day after, she heard enthusiastic reports of how the Prince had bought all those hearts completely too. So far the Squires had not showed up in Kleinstadt, but they had scheduled two visits in the immediate future.

Meanwhile the Prince reigned cheerfully as local neighbours and church friends heard and came by for a look. Even while Ruthe was there a short while in the afternoon, one family had not all handled the dark-eyed stranger and had some faspa, before the next car full of visitors arrived. Grosz'mama bustled about happily inviting everyone to pull a chair up to the table. It meant her dining table was full of dishes almost all day. Dirty ones were carried off and washed, but the centre of the table hardly got cleared until late at night, she proudly told Ruthe.

The Veer family was there the most, and acted as if they had part ownership of the baby. Ben Veer went downtown the first day the businesses were open again, where he stopped people in the general store and the post office to brag on Ruthe and the baby she had brought home for Christmas. He repeated his version of what had happened at the intersection to anyone who asked after his health or showed the least willingness to stand for a minute or two and listen.

Suzanne and Sharri made sure Isabelle knew what good babysitters they were, how much they loved children, and how experienced they were by citing an instance or two when they had handled little cousins.

Brandt grinned knowingly. Ruthe suspected too, he would get to babysit most after the holiday week and when his home schooling hours began again.

Anna Veer, their mother, thought of one thing after another that Isabelle did not have for the baby, so that she had her husband drive her over more than once a day, to donate to or show the new mom.

Ruthe felt it was all right to catch up on her sleep for a few days. She would take her sweet time about calling the authorities.

At last, when the statutory holidays were over, and Scottie was asking for an update, and the Social Services offices were open, Ruthe went to see Miss Schmidt in person.

The fish-faced, chinless Miss Schmidt scolded immediately, "You didn't leave me any phone number where I could reach you over the holidays!"

"Oh," said Ruthe, raising her eyebrows above her glasses in surprise, "Somehow I got the impression you didn't have pen and paper handy in bed, and that I was on my own with that baby until after the holidays." This drew attention to the older woman's unusually tipsy condition on Christmas morning, and embarrassed her. Ruthe wished she had been more tactful, but decided to go for frank bluntness now that she had put that foot forward. The woman reminded her of a nervous old teacher who cowered behind rules and traditions. For a split second Ruthe could see herself in similar shoes one day, *especially if I never slow down and don't try something new and daring once in a while.*

"One ends up in foolish situations at some holiday feasts," Maggie said lamely in self-defence. "It doesn't mean I'm out of character here in my office."

Ruthe simply blinked and politely told her all about the lovely Clarke couple to whom she had brought the strange baby. "They fell in love with him and are talking of adopting him if the opportunity should offer. We all refer to him as Prince Charming, he's very easy to take care of. In fact, he enjoys his admiring guests."

"There is bound to be a loving mother weeping for him," interrupted Miss Schmidt firmly, as if to cut short any thoughts of having good times with the baby.

"We're all saying just that!" Ruthe responded eagerly. "He just couldn't be so wonderful, if he hadn't had a fine home in the first few months of his life."

"Now then. We need to find temporary foster parents for him."

"Isabelle and Scottie will be more than happy to look after him as long as necessary," Ruthe volunteered as she had promised.

"Becoming foster parents is a long, involved process. We can't let just any–"

This time Ruthe cut her off, that tone scraping her the wrong way, "I thought you told me on Christmas morning that all your foster homes were full? Why not quickly process the Clarkes' application and make them foster parents? You wouldn't want to pass judgment until you've met them, would you?" She knew that last bit was a sharp barb, but this lady needed some prodding.

Suddenly Miss Schmidt was rattling off the qualifications of foster parents, and how their home had to be up to standards, and there were interviews and assessments to fill out. "I lose my job if I don't undo the error of letting you take that baby to an unprocessed home."

Ruthe pulled herself up straight in her chair and took a deep breath; "Scottie and Isabelle Clarke are building themselves a lovely new farm home just outside of Kleinstadt. Until it is ready they are living with my elderly grandmother; in my opinion a first rate home with cross-generational wisdom to raise a baby. My grandmother had eleven children and raised some of her grandchildren too. I count myself as one of those, during the years when my mother was in the hospital for some life-and-death surgeries. Presently, Scottie works at the university here in Saskatoon, but you will find Isabelle and my grandmother home all day, every day, and ready to show you excellent hospitality the moment you get to show up on the doorstep. They are waiting right now for me to call or bring them news of your coming. Meeting them should help you regain favour with your superior. If you've a better plan, please say so. Don't kill us with suspense."

Miss Schmidt looked down and shuffled papers as if checking for a schedule. Ruthe saw there was none. Then she looked up and said, "How about tomorrow morning? And do call me Maggie, please."

Ruthe grinned and got up. This was the perfect moment to exit. "Why thank you, Maggie!"

However, the next day Miss Schmidt took Prince Charming away.

Two days later, when Ruthe prowled those offices with a warm vengence, she met the social worker in the elevator. Miss Schmidt spoke eagerly to Ruthe as if to an old friend, telling her she had been quite impressed with Scottie and Isabelle.

"Yes?" said Ruthe coolly. "Scottie took time off work when I told them that you were coming the next day."

"Your grandmother is an exceptional saint of a woman. She should be canonized."

Ruthe smiled dryly, not sure what that last word meant, but the version she had heard the night before of that visit was of a prissy old bird. "This house is too small," she had snapped. "There has to be a separate bedroom for the boy, with a door, rather than those homemade curtains or dividers."

"My-my!" Grosz'mama had said, puzzled as to what that had to do with raising a baby. "My man and I managed good when we raised our children big. We did not have doors in our first house. Not when the first ones was small."

Miss Schmidt had tried to rephrase her words.

Scottie had understood the government guidelines she was to enforce, and had talked gently, professionally, explaining that they would be moving into a big sunny house in another three or four weeks, if they could finish the interior work as planned. He showed her the blueprints. "In the meantime, we'll try our best to make up for the lad's privacy."

Prince Charming himself had winked his long lashes at her, and very socially flashed his gracious dimples when she cooed at him.

"So why really, take him away?" Ruthe asked in a voice sharp as a knife.

"My hands are tied, Ruthe. I've got to go by the rules. Besides, the woman is due in two months! No woman can handle two–"

"No?" Ruthe didn't care to finish this conversation. She reached out and caught the open door of the elevator.

"Tell your grandma," Maggie called after her down the hall, "I'm coming back soon to buy more of that delicious raspberry jam."

Maggie, it turned out was a big cowardly softy at heart. In a few days she caught Ruthe at the elevators and tried to make up. "It's loyalty to my responsibilities that makes me afraid to trust my intuition," she confessed. What she didn't say, but Ruthe sensed, was that Maggie envied her open love of people and passion when she saw someone in need.

"So? You haven't got a home for the Prince after all?" Ruthe hoped she knew what Maggie was after.

"Oh, he's in a certified foster home."

"I recently read an article about two certified foster homes in this city that had too many kids and were abusing them."

Maggie changed the subject. "Richard Baxter was impressed with your suggestions."

"Huh?" Then Ruthe remembered the Johnson family. "So why does he leave them on the hook as to whether June gets permanent custody of her brothers and sisters?"

Maggie changed the subject again.

Ruthe felt she was an even bigger softie, for she allowed Maggie to worm herself into a friendship of sorts. Maggie Schmidt found out where she worked and how best to reach her if she ever needed to call. She answered the messages Maggie left for her at the clerk's desk. In a way, Ruthe decided to play along, hoping that Maggie would drop clues as to where Prince Charming was. When she told Isabelle and Scottie about this weird friendship, they also urged her to keep this contact open.

Back in Kleinstadt Miss Maggie Schmidt was bad-mouthed for a couple of weeks by just about everyone who had met the beautiful Christmas boy. But out of sight, he slipped from many minds. A few lives were permanently altered though. Isabelle, Scottie, Grosz'mama, Brandt, and Ruthe to name a few. Finding Prince Charming, or his mother, or anyone remotely connected to him seemed a lost cause after Maggie exhausted her usual channels. Eventually Ruthe even tired of prodding.

Maggie truly was not intuitive, she decided. *Everyone must see it all over me,* she told herself, *how the Prince stirred up new maternal desires and envies that tangle up my emotions in a whole skein of knots.* Socializing with the Clarkes, and helping them move into their new home shortly before Valentine's Day, just days before Isabelle's baby was due, Ruthe noticed, talk was nothing but of Prince, and the coming arrival. The more she tried to comfort Isabelle and persuade her that God would take good care of him, even if they never got to adopt him, and as they discussed and laid out things for the perfect little girl Isabelle was convinced she would have, the more Ruthe had painful swells of longing to have a good husband too, and to be able to adopt all kinds of unwanted babies and children.

Lots of them, Lord, not just one or two! She sighed often as she remembered that since age thirteen, she had been promising to leave her romance department to Him. Now she could not keep from dropping hints for the kind of lover-husband and home that would satisfy her.

"Hey, it's not that I have to have this Charming little Prince as my baby," she told her secret Friend aloud as she drove the highway to the city. "Thanks for that little loan of him, but he just symbolizes in my mind all the unwanted, unloved babies, and I yearn to gather them in my arms. Is that bad or good?"

FORTY-THREE

As their lopsided friendship developed Maggie realized how easily Ruthe jumped into people's lives to help them. She let Ruthe get involved in one or two of her cases. She told the younger, more intrepid friend about Sophie Keswecki, who loved children and ran a daycare nursery in a Ukrainian church. She specialized in abused kids, for it was across the street from an unmarked shelter for abused women. In describing Sophie, Maggie had said that whenever she had to remove children from a bad home situation she usually found out if Sophie had room for one more first. "She's such a gem; she even takes some home to her apartment for the night."

Ruthe decided that she would cultivate this Sophie's friendship and ask about Prince Charming. Perhaps he was in her hands.

Visiting the day nursery, Ruthe found Sophie very shorthanded, but yes, truly remarkable. "Mature, reliable women with enough energy for these long days are hard to come by," Sophie told her openly.

Without having to think or pray about it, Ruthe dropped her purse and coat, and pitched in to help out a few hours that afternoon. However, it was physically exhausting and she knew that her life was already too full to commit to doing this on a regular basis. She would pray for better ideas.

Watching each other and chatting between interruptions, the two got to know one another a bit. Sophie was twenty-eight, had experienced and loving attitudes about raising children, and was openly frustrated with longings for a good husband and a family of her own. Like Ruthe, she didn't care whose they had been first, or where they came from, a needy child was meant to be loved. Her motto was, "Children are priceless; it's an honour to be entrusted with them." When Ruthe described Prince Charming and his story, Sophie said he had been brought to her, and she had looked after him for four days before Maggie found another foster home for him. Though disappointed not to see him again, Ruthe admired this woman and wanted to be her friend.

Ruthe found herself confiding to Sophie, even on this first visit, things she had not told any of her other friends. Things like her desire for a good husband and children stirred up by watching newlywed friends and especially this beautiful baby boy over Christmas. Sophie understood and immediately shared more of her own passionate dreams; a house in the country, with a husband who loved children and took his role of husband and father seriously; they would adopt the most difficult and unlovable cases that could be found. Like stepping in front of a mirror, Ruthe recognized herself in that dream.

She promised to come visit Sophie more often. "Also, I'll see what I can do to round you up some more helpers," she said as she left.

A couple of days later, Ruthe mentioned to the girls at the shop that there was a paid position, and room for two or three volunteers at Sophie's nursery for abused and mishandled children. She raved about the good work of Sophie. Darlin' Bonne and the others watched for suitable young women, needing work, or something meaningful to do, and sent them over to be interviewed by Sophie.

The next time Ruthe stopped by to visit at the Ukrainian church, Sophie wanted directions to the shop to thank them in person. She had more caring staff. One had dropped out shortly, but she had hired one and another two were willing to help out just because they understood and loved children. They were good workers, easing Sophie's load, and Ruthe rejoiced with her. That night she stayed for supper.

Not long later, on a day in February that was suddenly warmed with a chinook wind from points west, Ruthe went for a simple window-shopping walk during a longer break in her split shift. The snow felt slushy under her boots and many people walked past her with their coats hanging unbuttoned and scarves trailing in the murky squishes of slush as they walked by. A background sound of trickling water was everywhere. The air tasted of a pleasant memory– *spring?* *No, hope,* Ruthe concluded. *Time for spring fever.*

Waiting for a walk light at an intersection, she turned her gaze up at the blue sky, hazy with wind-torn clouds, but stopped with a start at the roof line of the hotel across the intersection. There, clambering about and leaning on their tummies between the decorative outcrops were two little boys. No caps or jackets on at all. They looked like they had escaped from someone and were exulting in their freedom.

Noticing that someone had stepped past her into the street, she lowered her gaze enough to know she had a green WALK, and dashed over the street on a sprint, right up the steps of the Lord Nelson, and across the marbled floor of the foyer, never minding the clatter her hard-soled boots were making even on the red carpet runner. At the front desk, a uniformed young man stepped into her path. "May I help you?"

"Yes!" Ruthe panted. "There are two– little boys– up on the roof of– this building,– leaning over– having a good time. They need to be brought down– before they fall!"

The handsome young man with the square shoulders turned to the desk clerk, "Call the Fire and Police." Turning to Ruthe, "Wait here, Miss. I can get up faster alone." Then he whirled away and around a corner.

The clerk was dialing and talking briskly on the phone, describing what "this lady here" had just said, so Ruthe turned aside and noticed a rectangle of fat tub chairs in winter white upholstery. Breathing heavily, she stumbled to the nearest one and sat on the back. After a few moments she turned and went to the front of it to sit down properly.

How I got so winded from that short run, I don't know, Lord! Yet, she felt as if she had rescued those boys and they would be okay. She could calm down and leave soon. She had to be back at the switchboard in half an hour.

Ruthe was just rising again, when a police officer walked in. As he came in straight toward her, she saw, just past him through the glass doors, a large neon green fire truck back up towards the building. She had to explain again what she had seen, and repeat some parts so this officer could write it all down. She began to wonder if she had over-reacted and made a lot of work for others for nothing.

In moments, however, the uniformed security guard of the hotel came out of the sliding elevator doors with a boy in bright red sweaters and black pants dangling under each arm. A fireman in a shiny yellow coat came in from the outer door, so Ruthe brashly listened in while these three men, addressing the guard familiarly as Peter, discussed these two impish boys. She quickly caught on that they had caused trouble before, and they were known to belong to an escort who often used this hotel as a meeting point with customers. Sometimes she deliberately left her sons in the lobby, knowing that Peter liked boys and would keep an eye on them. Now this man, Peter, said, "Today I'm fed up with this situation! I'm calling Social Services to come pick 'em up."

The smaller little guy was squirming and wanting out of Peter's grasp, so Ruthe reached out and claimed him, and went to sit down in the tub chair with him on her lap. She distracted him by trying to get his name. Unfocused, or hard of hearing, he began to talk loud and with a lot of bravo, "I climmed a touzand trees, y'know."

His brother wanted to join him, and Peter let him go so he could stand by Ruthe's knees and chatter too. The older one was named Rocky, and he was proud of being four. Not to be outdone the younger one lifted three fat fingers and yelled, "I'm a-most TREE!"

"And what is your name?" Ruthe asked again.

"Brick."

"No, Brett," corrected his brother.

"Mama calls me a gold brick," the sturdy toddler said as if that settled it.

"Where is your Mama?"

"Out on biz-niz."

The officer tapped Ruthe on her shoulder, thanked her for calling attention to the boys on the roof, and departed.

Peter, the guard, asked Ruthe if she would mind staying with the boys while he made a phone call. She glanced at her watch and saw she had nearly fifteen minutes yet, so nodded.

A few minutes later he was back and drew another tub chair closer and was quickly involved in the lively conversation Ruthe was having with the two boys now filling her lap. The topics switched back from one to another with frantic speed. Ruthe suspected they would end up in Sophie's care before nightfall, and that Sophie would need to pay close attention to keep up with them. For the moment Ruthe allowed herself to enjoy the animated and scattered chat with these boys and with Peter, whom they regarded as an old friend. Then she sensed another dimension. Peter was eyeing her as if evaluating, calculating something.

Before she'd figured it out, Peter blurted in a low aside, "If you'd marry me we could adopt the tadpoles. The maternal one has offered them to me, gratis."

Ruthe ignored the last question asked by Rocky or Brett to stare in astonishment at Peter. He was taller and more handsome than Scottie even, whose looks she liked. He had broad shoulders, a smile that made her think of one of her favourite uncles, on whom she had dangled a lot as a child, but marry him just so they could adopt these characters? "You haven't asked my name yet!" she challenged, not sure what to make of his proposal, "You've got to be joking!"

"No, I'm dead serious." All smiles disappeared from his face. "I know it's weird that I want nothing more in life than to be a good Dad, and I've been watching for a person just like you."

"He wants to be a Daddy," Brick pointed frankly at Peter and said this as if he had just remembered this common fact. Ruthe felt that, tough, physical little creature that Brick was, planted so heavily on her lap, he still had picked up enough of Peter's quiet statement intended only for Ruthe, to know the drift.

Rocky had continued talking, describing some energetic scene he had seen on television, but now he stopped, aware that something else was going on.

Ruthe was flustered. *Lord, I can't say yes to a proposal like this, just for the sake of these boys, can I?* On the other hand, her inner eyes flew open with delight at the thought of marrying, and then adopting unwanted, even rascally kids like these. Just as she and Sophie had described. The idea was suddenly right up there, on par with earlier dreams in her life of being a missionary, or a writer. But to choose one on the spur of this moment would block out all other options. This called for more time. She found herself shaking her head, and trying to phrase a gentle 'no, thank you,' when Maggie Schmidt walked in.

"Ruthe Veer! Of all the people I know I should have guessed you might be in the thick of this kind of incident."

Suddenly Ruthe felt strong and in charge. She turned, "Hi Maggie. Let me introduce you to some brand new friends of mine. This is Rocky and this is Brett, or better known to those who love him, as Brick." Then she waved at the security guard behind her, "Perhaps you have met Peter?"

Maggie made herself gracious and friendly, shaking each one's hand, and ready to stand and chat. Ruthe twisted her wrist behind Rocky's head to see the time and moved with a start to get up as she gasped, "I have six minutes to make it back to the office for the rest of my shift. I was just using my long lunch time for a walk. Please excuse me, and let me run, okay?"

She slid the boys to the floor, and with a hand on each of their backs, crouched and said, "I sure liked meeting you boys, and I hope we can have more fun times together. You go with my friend, Miss Schmidt, and she'll let me know where I can visit you." She said that especially for Maggie's benefit.

Ruthe was too hurried to realize she had forgotten to say goodbye to Peter, but he followed her and caught her shoulder, "We'll get to visit again sometime as well?"

She smiled up at him impulsively, "Maybe. I'm sorry but I've got to run or my supervisor will tear me to shreds!"

The supervisor did approach her when she entered breathlessly, but only to ask if she would take a relief position on Information until the end of her shift. It was mostly routine work, she would be able to think, so she was grateful.

Her thoughts and emotions boiled and cooked like a cauldron making stewed soup of a cannibal all that afternoon, and on into the evening. What if she did marry Peter to adopt and raise kids? Perhaps she could insist on a period of time to get to know him first? Maybe it did not have to be Peter. Supposing God had allowed this to happen just to prepare her for such a possibility in the future with an even better man? In her headset she heard, beep-beep, a request for a number, she looked it up, and read out the number. Then she stared into space as she waited for the next beep-beep.

Lord, if I were to marry, what are the basic principles on which I'd base such a decision? What are the things I have to have in a marriage– things I can't ever do without?

Her responses memorized, the searches for numbers automatic, she could spend her thinking energy on herself. Ruthe made mental lists. She scraped lists and searched her heart and her memories for any Bible story or passage that might have a lesson that could be applied. She went back to making lists. Most of them were questions to which she saw no answers. She tried imagining a scene where she would tell her family that she was marrying a man like Peter, not because she had fallen in love, which she had assumed was a top priority, but because she wanted to make a lovely home and haven for unwanted kids.

When she pictured how her Mom would grab her greying head and exclaim all kinds of dire predictions of woe, Ruthe shook her head and closed her mind to that scene. She changed channels as if spooked by a horror movie.

Now her thoughts lighted on the idea of introducing Sophie and Peter to each other. Sophie would likely jump for such a proposal. Ruthe's nervous system sighed deeply, but instead of slowly going to wind down, it swung up to another intense high as she planned how she would visit Sophie and approach her with this idea. Yes, right after this shift.

They laughed about Sophie's adventure of feeding Rocky and Brick their supper in her apartment, and how tough and macho the boys tried to be, but how they lapped up every hug and kiss that Sophie gave so generously. They had volunteered to be her children "forever and fo-ev-ver," she happily reported to Ruthe.

Sophie asked a lot of questions about this Peter. That reassured Ruthe she was on the right track, until she became aware that she was answering, "I don't know," to almost every one. She didn't know his last name, or how to reach him, aside from calling the front desk of the Lord Nelson hotel.

Seeing Sophie willing to meet him and discuss this possibility of marriage, Ruthe jauntily lifted her shoulders and went over to the phone in Sophie's apartment and called the Lord Nelson. Hotel numbers she had memorized long ago. In her most business like operator voice, she asked how to reach the security guard who had been on duty that afternoon. She was given his home number, and learned as the clerk repeated his name, that he was Peter Green. With impish delight, Ruthe handed her scribbles over to Sophie.

"Or, shall I call him and invite him here to meet a better potential wife than myself?"

"I don't mind," said Sophie, pouring some freshly heated apple cider into deep mugs. She reached up into the cupboard and took down a third mug. "I've got enough cider here."

Ruthe grinned, dialed the number and made the invitation to come meet Sophie, who was looking after Rocky and Brett. "She might be interested in your proposal, if you are open to discussion on it."

"She's fallen for my little guys then?"

"Sophie's head-over-heels in love with them! Besides, she's been waiting for an offer like yours, while I'm too startled,... umm-m. I need time to work through what to think." Ruthe finished lamely.

It sounded like Peter was doing dishes while he talked on the phone, but he quickly asked directions to the address. The clinking and splashing of dishes stopped while he jotted notes. "Worth checking out," he commented. "I can be there in half an hour."

A headache had been creeping up on Ruthe all afternoon, she knew it was from the stress, and as she started sipping the hot cider it got worse and worse, despite how she exclaimed that this was a wonderful drink. One she had never had before, but she really liked the taste.

Peter arrived, and after she had introduced him to Sophie they got to talking and she kept her weary, aching head hung mostly over her mug, swizzling the cinnamon stick industriously. She missed whole segments of the conversation, saw she wasn't needed, and begged to be excused. Ruthe drove directly home to Kleinstadt.

A few days later when she felt better she called Sophie and learned that she and Peter were going steady with plans to announce their engagement as soon as their list of things that had to be a *Go* were met. Sophie eagerly named all the things they already had in common, and where they thought they would balance each other. When she had thanked Ruthe two, three times for introducing Peter, it began to dawn on her, *it could be me making these wedding plans!*

Exactly at that point the Evil One began to sneak in with hints that she might have made a big mistake in letting Peter go to someone else. She spent time when she was alone, trying to explain why it would not have worked, and just as quickly he brought positive points to her mind in favour of life with Peter. Sometimes she would sharply resolve to put it away out of her mind, and it would stay away too, for days or weeks at a time. Then, when she was tired, alone, and in need of a hug, in would zoom like a dart the thought, *If you'd snapped up Peter Green's offer, you'd have someone to comfort you now."*

Eventually she learned to recognize the thoughts upon first buzz or arrival, and swat them away like mosquitos that had to be squashed before they sucked blood from her and tortured her with a day long itch.

When Maggie Schmidt had to do something that made her squeamish, she now called Ruthe and asked her to do it as a favour. Just to take a message of bad news to a client, as a rule, but Maggie called it giving Ruthe's intuitive talents an opportunity. Ruthe realized she was being used, but she cared about people, and didn't mind meeting new ones, so she consented to most of the errands.

On Valentine's Day the Clarkes' little girl, Regina Esther, was born. The next day, Ruthe planned to go see them right after work.

Maggie met Ruthe during her lunch break and asked, "Could I send you to the hospital to persuade a shy, lonely Métis teen to give up her baby for adoption?"

Ruthe admitted she was going to see Isabelle and her baby, but wondered why Maggie would not do such counselling herself.

Maggie got excited. "The teen had her baby yesterday too! But now that she's seen her tiny baby– And Ruthe, it truly is unusually tiny, destined to be a midget all her life, the doctor says. Laura, fell in love with her baby and wants to keep it. I've got distraught adoptive parents waiting! Oh, please go persuade her to give it up again! If I go I could be seen as putting undue pressure on her."

Ruthe didn't want to put undue pressure on either, but making clear that she would just happen by to visit this girl and size up the situation, she agreed. In her heart she suspected that a mature and ready couple would make better parents than a mixed up, immature teen.

She had a perfectly lovely visit with Isabelle and her healthy baby with the silky orange-red sheen to her perfectly shaped head. But when Ruthe said goodbye and went down the hall to prowl around for Laura, things took a totally different turn.

She felt genuine compassion and concern for the lonely, frightened Laura with the dark doe-eyes and dark hair. A nurse who didn't know Miss Schmidt's plans invited them to come to the nursery to see the tiny infant in the incubator. The preemie was hardly longer than Ruthe's hand, had porcelain white skin, and a cap of tight black curls. Only by her tiny cries were they convinced the wee miracle was alive. Both lost their hearts to her, and when Laura begged Ruthe to help her keep her baby she found herself promising to take her side.

The next day, Maggie, her superiors and the adoptive parents were all upset with Ruthe. She tried to block out the conversations she had with Maggie and the one with her boss, Mr. Warrick. So long as Laura did not sign any papers, the law was on her side.

Winter was not quite gone, but the pressures drove her to try short walks off alone to pray where no one could watch her. She pondered on her ability to stand her ground; it had to be God's power at work in her.

Ruthe was extra busy for a while. She took responsibility for finding Laura and her baby Lois, an apartment, and a job. She was very pleased to end up with a fine basement suite in the home of a French-speaking, capable, and motherly landlady, who had children that could play with and babysit Lois, while Laura worked.

Networking through Darlin' Bonne's clients, she was able to get Laura a job as a window dresser for a large department store, and by planning a shower with the O'Brien sisters, they set Laura up as a self-supporting working woman, without ties to Social Assistance at all. That, Ruthe considered a triumph. It made her smug whenever she met Maggie.

Dr. Davie Pollock just opening his practice, agreed to Ruthe's appeal to be Lois' special doctor. He seemed to think with the two of them on her side, Laura and Lois would do famously.

Privately, to herself and to the Lord, Ruthe admitted Laura would never have survived on her own. It was only because she had rounded up her circle of friends and asked them to help out that it looked like Laura was going to grow up and do okay.

Lois was likely to be a miniature person all her life, but she already showed signs of thriving. Laura might need extra handholding, or counselling, as Phyllis Shulton told Ruthe to call it, and it was a long-term support commitment she was making to this new friend and her baby.

At the same time, Ruthe resolved that she would never settle for having children without a thoroughly involved husband.

She sighed deeply, *Sophie's way is better than Laura's, isn't it, Lord? Is that what my take-away from all this experience is about? Okay, I've got a new riddle for You; where then, is Your perfect 'husband' for me? Will I know him when I meet him?*

Another hard part was when visiting Isabelle and Scottie in their new ranch-style home, admiring their carroty-haired Regina with the deep blue eyes, not to blurt out what little Lois Delighette Weal, who had the same birthday, was able to do these days; focus her eyes, coo, smile, sit up, and read minds.

FORTY-FOUR

A while before Easter Gordon asked Ruthe to become his guardian. Somehow he had the impression he had to be adopted to get a surname, and since he and Stephanie planned to marry, he suddenly needed a surname to offer his bride. It took Ruthe time to figure out what Gordon was asking, and why he chose her. When she understood his motive, she felt touched and blinked away a mistiness, which helped to make her question more gentle, "Don't you just go to court and pay something like twenty-five dollars for a name you pick yourself?"

Seeing a crestfallen look coming over Gordon, Ruthe said quickly, "Tell you what, Gord, why don't we talk to Mr. O'Brien, or Mr. Newton? They are lawyers and can tell us what the procedures are."

When they brainstormed for suitable names they asked Stephanie to take part, since it would become her name too.

It was Mr. Newton who listened to their dilemma. He asked Gordon for all the information he could recall about his early life and the places he remembered. "I'll have these all checked out. It's best to look for the past just one more time before a leap into a name change. It may take a few weeks. If nothing is found, I'll notify you, Gordon, and help you apply for a name of your choice. Here in Saskatchewan it is quite simple and easy in English. You pay ten dollars and have it published in the *Saskatchewan Gazette.*"

Three weeks later Mr. Newton called Gordon and reported no finds in the research. He suggested that since Ruthe could read, she fill out the application on Gordon's behalf to save him the two hundred dollar lawyer fee. Gordon wanted the name Stephanie and Ruthe had combined after several sessions of reducing their first list. He became Gordon Franklin Woodbury, when Ruthe sent in the application and his fee.

He had discussed privately with Ruthe, how he ought to propose to Stephanie when his name was official. He wanted to know exactly what to say. At the time, Ruthe thought he was also on a bit of a fishing expedition for Lloyd.

The day Ruthe showed him the announcement of his new name in the Gazette, Gord got so excited he forgot the romantic plans Ruthe had helped lay for proposing to Stephanie. He took off on a jog across the back alley, then yelled as he entered the Rowntree's home, "Now I can marry you!" When Stephanie's mother appeared, he got flustered and asked, "Mrs. Woodbury?"

Lloyd, who had dashed after to witness the scene, entered in time to hear Mrs. Rowntree laugh heartily and say, "No, but the young lady who is eager to be Mrs. Woodbury is coming up with a pail of potatoes from the storage bin." Lloyd re-told the story often after that.

Graham's mother often invited the young men and their friends over to her home Sunday evenings, after the evening service. Not afraid of how the numbers varied, she would serve coffee, tea and juice, with scrumptious desserts with creams and berries. Since Ruthe tried to visit all her city friends on a roughly regular cycle, when it was time to visit these friends, she knew it was wisest to look for them, late of a Sunday evening at Mrs. McKenzie's cottage.

That's where she found them the Sunday after Gordon's breathless proposal to Stephanie. Grace and Graham were announcing their plans as well. Mrs. McKenzie called it an Engagement Party and served extra fancy cake with homemade ice cream.

Ruthe had already had a lovely day. The weather had become perfect for long, early or late-day walks again. She had just finished an easy shift. It was good to be alive and to have such interesting friends. After congratulating both couples, and some catching up, she sat back loose and comfortable, listening to the background street sounds of the evening outside the screen door, and in the foreground, to the pros and cons of having a double wedding. There was some teasing about Lloyd and Ruthe making it a triple wedding, but Ruthe put a blank, far-away look on her face as if she were listening to an angel chorus. Lloyd turned silent, and soon things fell back into balance.

While the others talked, Ruthe prayed silently, *You know, Lord, that I'm more open to marriage, but not to Lloyd, okay? Rather than being good Daddy-material, he needs one. A mother to help him know he is loveable too. I simply can't parent him and a bunch of kids on the side! Who would there be for me to lean on?* In a trice she realized she should always be leaning on the Lord, even when married. Still, she squirmed with reluctance at the idea of taking charge of a man who would often need to be shored up. *'Sides,* her face wrinkled a bit with distaste, *reminds me of how Mom has had to lead and guide Dad around.*

Ten months before, Grace's parents had gone back to their mission station for another four year term. There was no way they could come back for her wedding. Grace did not expect it. Lloyd's inheritance was now tied up in Bright City, but Ruthe suggested he pinch off enough to fly in the Williams.

Grace laid out reasons why it was out of the question. They accepted that.

Since Graham's only relative was his mother, theirs would be a very small wedding. "Okay, we'll invite friends then."

Stephanie had a family of eight and about twenty other relatives that just had to be invited, but Gordon had no one except for the friends in the room. "And that Adams couple," Ruthe reminded him.

When they explained to Gordon the difference between a single and a double wedding, he was all for it. "Just so's I'm not the only guy standing up there."

"That's how I feel," said Graham. "I want both you guys to keep me company."

"Fine. I'm big enough to be two best men at once," Lloyd offered magnanimously. "Is Ruthe going to be the matron or bridesmaid, or whatever?"

Quickly, Ruthe said, "Oh no. I never know my schedule more than two weeks in advance."

"Trade with someone!" the girls chorused. They persisted, even though Ruthe named several other girls from their church she had met or heard of, that she thought were prettier and better suited.

"How about the O'Brien girls?" Ruthe wondered how they could be overlooked while present. "Cathy brought you together, remember?"

Grace and Stephanie ganged up on her, promising to involve Cathy and Muriel, but wanting her to be in the wedding party too.

"You're our spiritual mother!" Gord tossed into the fray.

At that, Mrs. McKenzie rose, held out her hands to Ruthe and said, "Naow, there lassie, is a noble and true title y' can accept in the name of the Lord." Ruthe melted and nodded then, and Mrs. McKenzie cupped her face in gnarled but tender hands, to add, "Y're such a young lady, but you've brought maturity and common sense to the youths, an' it's only right y' bless and guide 'em on their day of vows before God also."

The others cheered, and then expanded Ruthe's title to include, Spiritual Mother, Representative of Absent Parents. Lloyd threw in 'Oracle of the Lord.'

"You're going overboard," Ruthe murmured and began to look for the right moment to rise and say her good byes.

Grace proposed that they splurge a bit and make the reception something special for all their Christian friends. Beaming blindly, his arm still around Grace, Graham said, "Girls, plan whatever you want. This little wedding is on Gordon and me."

Gordon's chest rose, "Yeah, don't worry; plan somethin' pretty."

The girls settled on a Saturday in early August. Then they started brainstorming in earnest with sketches and lists and room diagrams.

Ruthe began to giggle when she saw Gordon and Graham grow restless and ask about costs. She cut herself off though when she sensed Lloyd studying her admiringly. She looked at her watch and got up to say her good nights.

Even as Mrs. McKenzie held the screen door for her, and Ruthe went down the two cement steps sideways, she could still see Lloyd, with his arms up and his hands behind his head, smiling patiently after her.

FORTY-FIVE

Redecorating the Greystone had kept June busy all winter and past Easter. She has sorted, classified and arranged for the sale of many of the antiques that cluttered up the place. Correspondence brought a number of collectors from England who were thrilled to find oriental pottery, including some with Ming and Imari marks. One man was beside himself with the snuffboxes. Another two tried to out-bid each other on the Jacobite wine glasses. That brought a nice sum and Ruthe let June use that money to order more contemporary furniture and appliances. There were no other strays yet but the Johnson children, so at times Ruthe winced at handling so much money, but she was told some things needed to done, so she had new plumbing and heating installed, and all the rooms re-papered or painted on the upper floor, (June recruiting Ruthe, Wes and Linnet to learn by helping). June had learned to scrimp and make do with next to nothing during her years in school, and Ruthe was pleased to notice that June still shopped for the most economical way to get the best look possible. With her frugality she could make the money assigned to this go extra miles, for she said it forced her to think more creatively.

Ruthe often nodded with satisfaction when she thought of June. One day, praying for June and her charges, the enlightening thought came that interior decorating was a tangent she could have easily slipped into herself if she hadn't got *hooked* on working with people first. *If I hadn't crashed the shyness barrier, I'd probably be creative with things, right, Lord?* She noticed that June could talk to strangers, but she was always more comfortable if it was about antiques or decorating. Nor did June initiate spiritual discussions with others.

Word of mouth was giving June a professional reputation though, and she had begun to get requests from a few well-off families to give them decorating counsel. She pursued these as assignments for her correspondence course, and conscientiously did up before and after sketches and photos for her portfolio. It meant she was at home less, so Ruthe tried to drop in at the mansion to cover for her when she did not show up at meals, reasoned with the younger kids, and tried to teach and explain things to them that they had never been taught.

When Isabelle wanted help in papering her new bathroom, and to install a tub surround, Ruthe dared bring June out for a quick afternoon's work. In case any of her family were there, they made a pact not to discuss anything to do with the Greystone, Darlin' Bonne's Shop or any of Ruthe's other friends.

Grosz'mama was at the Clarkes, and June was happy to see her again. Ruthe's mother and sisters showed up later too. Since Isabelle had bought wallpaper for other rooms, Ruthe organized everyone to learn how to paper while June was there to teach them. It cut down on nosy questions, just as Ruthe had hoped, and it pleased Isabelle to get two rooms papered, plus the surround installed.

Thinking they were not being watched for a couple of seconds as they worked over the tub, June caught Ruthe's eye and mouthed, "Forgot." She pantomimed writing into her hand, "Linnet entered your name in a contest. They called." June flashed the holding of a receiver to her ear, "You won."

"What?" Ruthe mouthed back, even as they heard someone coming.

"Pool," June acted like a puppy, panting and paddling with its paws near its chin.

It was Sharri who spotted the mime. She wanted explanations. Her begging to know stirred up Suzanne and their mother's suspicions. It was tense work for Ruthe to get out of the situation.

Her family had become almost used to her irregular comings and goings. They accounted them to those stupid shifts that had no rhyme or reason. Especially since Ruthe admitted to often trading shifts as favours to other operators, she was the only one who knew what hours she really worked. However, incidents like these always raised fresh tensions.

If anyone were to get suspicious, Ruthe had thought it would be the Clarkes because they understood the many aspects of city life, and they seemed to understand her. She was semi-braced to swear them to secrecy and confide in them if they ever confronted her about the signs of her double life. So far they had not.

However, Sharon Rose remembered that big sister promise of a secret. It turned out to be the new home they lived in. Until now she had not mentioned the two huge brick and stone houses she had seen in the city, nor the rich-looking ladies that had hugged and kissed Ruthe as if they knew her, or the people in the convertible that paid the late evening visit. "If you don't tell me your secret," Sharri begged adamantly, "I'll tell about what I saw—"

Mrs. Veer was suddenly in the bathroom doorway. "What secrets does Ruthe have?"

Ruthe managed to fluff it off, but minutes later, when they could let go of the panels, June steered Sharri out and away. Trying to make up for her mistake, Ruthe figured.

"Not that I don't sometimes dream of involving Sharri in my adventures," Ruthe told June on their way back to the city. "I'd love to see her develop her precocious, vivacious personality like, say Joy, or Donnie, or Darlin' Bonne. There's no point in making her grow up too fast, but I can easily visualize her winning people like scented flowers woo bees."

293

"If she saw you in action, she'd soon be just like you," volunteered June.

"But what if I push her too fast and ruin her life? Maybe she could not handle the secrecy of this double life!"

"You don't trust your parents," observed June quietly, "Any more than I do my sick mother, do you?"

"Sure, I tr–" Ruthe felt a twinge of guilt. "Yea, but they don't understand!" Ruthe spoke still more slowly and thoughtfully, "Maybe you're right. Deep down I really don't trust them. Even with all their faults factored out."

"Why?" asked June simply.

Ruthe thought back. When had she started to distrust her parents? Was it when she discovered they didn't like, couldn't even be polite, to different races or cultures? No, maybe it was when she began to chafe at their criticising and picking apart relatives or people in church who had any titled position, or who gave a moving testimony. *Hm-m. That must be when I stopped telling them any of my thoughts about spiritual matters; it felt as if they dropped my precious pearls into the slop trough of a pigsty.* She wasn't sure she ought to dump all these thoughts on June though.

"Your little sister is going to be a carbon copy of you," observed June prophetically. Ruthe was happy to discuss this topic, so she left her hard thoughts until a private, a garden time.

Heavenly Father, she prayed later at dusk as she wandered around soggy patches by her favourite meadow and bush and felt the new grey pussies at each bud on the willows, *is it wrong to have such a separateness from my family? It isn't Your style, is it? I don't like it either, but You and I can't throw our relationship in the mud! Some things are just hopeless, and one of them is any chance of an ideal trust and understanding between my folks and me.* Resignedly, she dropped the matter again.

And what shall I do about Your Rose of Sharon? If I don't train her to love and serve You now, while she still adores and copies me, will I have any influence later? Before we know it she will be crazy for things, and then boyfriends...! Ruthe painted a sad picture.

June had said she understood her hesitation about confiding in Sharri, but a week or so later, before Ruthe had figured out how to go about it, she concluded that June must have given Sharri a few tips on becoming eligible for sharing secrets. The eight year old had a new attitude. She grew very jealous for her and vigorously defended her older sister whenever Suzanne made any unkind suggestions about her unaccounted for hours. Sharri became awfully fussy about how the household chores were done, taking extra initiative herself. Instead of nagging, she asked solicitous questions when she and Ruthe were alone together, questions that were meant to reveal her maturity and her loyalty. These tactics, recognizable as her own method, amused Ruthe. *Just how I advised Linnet*, she recalled with a smile.

The perfect opening came when Phyllis told Ruthe that she had helped Brandt catch up on reading skills and taught him a lot of other tricks for educating himself in whatever areas he developed interests. Furthermore, he kept hinting that he was needed on the Clarke farm for fieldwork, now that spring had fully arrived. Sharri's last report card had a note that she needed to focus her attention better, and to do her homework, so Ruthe suggested Sharri pick up with Brandt's tutor as he was done.

Phyllis was willing, but Anna Veer snapped, "She'll start chargin' us now."

There was a delay until Ruthe could come back with the answer, no, Miss Shulton would not charge at all. At that her Dad shrugged, "So long as it's no skin off my nose." Ruthe knew he felt pleased; Scottie and other men downtown had praised Brandt, but a direct compliment from her dad would be like pulling out a hen's teeth with tweezers.

As she drove Sharri in to her first Saturday morning lesson, a premonition told Ruthe, that if her sister were to become involved with her city friends she might soon have more trouble disciplining herself to do her homework. Feeling somewhat committed to continue in the path chosen, Ruthe decided to prepare Sharri. "This woman I am taking you to will show you how to study so that your school work can be a breeze. If you have the will power you'll be able to do it no matter how busy you get in other things. Y'know, like me." She emphasized the importance of keeping all that happened to them in the city strictly to herself if she wanted to find out some secrets. "I will not tell you all of them at once. You'll have to prove yourself trustworthy step by step, with little secrets first."

"Don't worry, Ruthe," Sharri promised zealously, "I'm very advanced for my age. You can count on me to keep my lip zipped."

Ruthe dimpled and giggled, "You *aula-douz*[24]."

Phyllis and Sharri took to each other immediately. Ruthe had told her older friend beforehand that Sharri loved secrets, so one that they discussed, pretending to whisper, but so that Ruthe should over-hear, was that Phyllis wanted Sharri's help in teaching Ruthe to be a writer.

The coffee table book froze in Ruthe's hand and her eyes magnified.

"Your big sister has lots of talents that she doesn't even know she has," confided Phyllis, raking long manicured fingers through Sharri's downy mass of light brown hair hanging down to the back of her waist. "You and I can work together to help her develop them!"

Clever, Ruthe smiled to herself as she left the fashion-accented apartment for her own Saturday's agenda, *Hmm, telling her that they are going to develop my talents, when Phyllis and I are working on Sharri's*

FORTY-SIX

A couple of Saturdays later Ruthe included Sharri in a short pop-in visit to her new friend, Laura Weal. Briefly she summarized beforehand what had happened to Laura and about her exceedingly little Lois.

Sharri was sympathetic but matter-of-fact. "Okay, I'll be polite. I know about unwed mothers. Y'know Rochelle's big sister? Heard about her? We have to remember, 'there, but for the grace of God, go I.'"

Ruthe turned to stare, "You're only eight! Or is it twenty-eight?"

"Eight and two-thirds."

Sharri was totally captivated by tiny Lois. She carried on just like the landlady's children, cooing and playing with her delicate limbs, ready to put her through all kinds of movements, much as she did with Regina Clarke. Lois' blackberry eyes sparkled responsively and shes reached up for more. Then Laura showed them some of the baby games they had discovered on their own.

Ruthe warmed with pride and assured Laura, "You're a fine mother!"

While Sharri airplaned the baby around the room, Ruthe sat beside Laura and asked pointed questions to determine just how well she was coping. It turned out Lois had had some longer crying spells at night. "I get tired, working all day, then I got to carry my baby most of the night too," the frail, pale young teen mother apologized. Once she had gone up and knocked on Mrs. Brisbois' door. But they were heavy sleepers or she hadn't knocked hard enough. Another night she had phoned to Ann O'Brien, who sent Marion over to spend the rest of the night, pacing with Lois.

"That's okay. Better to get help like that, then try to keep on by yourself. In other families there is a husband to take a turn, you know," Ruthe comforted her.

At home Ruthe watched Sharri closely. She chattered at the table in her artless, little-girl manner, about the reading drills with her tutor but made no mention of any other stops or people she had met. So in a few weeks, Ruthe added another surprise visit to their Saturday morning routine. She had a split shift, so she could spend two hours with Sharri before going back to work another three.

"Hi there!" squealed Darlin' Bonne as they entered the little green shop. She gave Ruthe an enthusiastic hug, then crouched to talk to Sharri, "You're her marvellous pet sister, eh?"

Betty closed in right behind her, "She looks like you, Ruthe."

Donnie bounced up from the sofa where she was sprawled, relaxing before her next client, and teased, "You should'a brought her long ago. We need to train a new designer."

"To sub for you," added Joy, coming down the hall. "Hey, you did bring us somebody new? How long can you stay today, Ruthe?"

Dutifully, Ruthe looked at her watch and reported that she must be sent on her way in an hour and a half, at three-thirty.

Sharri still hadn't said a word but her eyes were everywhere.

Darlin' Bonne knelt all the way down and hung her arms from the narrow shoulders of Ruthe's miniature. "Wow! How'd you like to be a dress designer, just like your big sister?"

"Aw," Ruthe moaned, embarrassed, "Don't go exaggerating!"

"You never told me!" Sharri now looked up, wide-eyed, "When? Do you really sew here, with these p'fessionals?"

She was going to laugh it off, but Darlin' Bonne laughed first, "Sharri-Darlin', Ruthe taught me!"

Sharri's grade three friends back in Kleinstadt all talked about shopping at Darlin' Bonne's when their mothers took them out of school for a day in the city. Those who had not been envied those who had. "Here we are," she said quizzically, "talking ordinary-like to these designer ladies?"

New clients arrived. After some cheerful small talk with them, and giving Sharri a quick tour of a sewing room not in use, Ruthe helped Evelyn show Sharri what she could do to be useful in quiet, unobtrusive ways, and when Joy came to warn her, Ruthe excused herself to go do the rest of her operator shift.

All the way home that evening, Sharri raved. She had trusted Jesus as her Saviour in Sunday School at age six, "But now! I watched how this Evelyn, and that Darlin' Boss-lady, listened to problems from women in deep trouble, an' always they could show how Jesus would be the answer to their problems! I think Jesus is far better than I ever dreamed, Ruthe!"

"If you'll keep it a secret I'll take you there again soon."

"Yeah, I want to learn to sew and to steer girls to Jesus!" Sharri cheered. "I won't tell anybody at home, but I think I better memorize more verses!"

In a few Saturdays, Sharri grew to be an anticipated help at the shop. Phyllis cooperated by dropping her off at noon, when Ruthe was tied up with her shifts.

Ruthe was too busy to have her career developed, so that plan seemed to go on hold. They did put their minds together to come up with something to account for the subtle changes Suzanne, Isabelle, and even Grosz'mama were noticing in their ever-smarter Sharri.

Then the learning sponge had an idea of her own. She sent away a magazine coupon to become a door-to-door salesperson for boxed greeting cards. She convinced her parents of her logic; if she went to sell cards to strangers, she would learn self-confidence and responsibility for her own money.

Their dad warned, "Don't let all that money burn holes in your pockets as soon as you pass a store."

Ruthe couldn't get over how easily they let Sharri walk off with an idea like that. She, herself, had to earn her every little privilege with much pleading and prayer, it had seemed.

Suzanne wouldn't say anything one way or another. She just slammed doors.

"I promise to bring all my money home," Sharri said, and Ruthe guaranteed that she or someone reliable like Miss Shulton would be with her at all times. Phyllis helped the scheme by buying an odd number of boxes of greeting cards each week, but Sharri seldom took time to go from door to door, except on Phyllis' floor of the apartment building. Sometimes the girls at the shop, or one or two of their clients would buy a box, so she succeeded without even trying.

Sharri found acting innocent at home easy, and she loved being treated like an adult in the city. She took great pride in her accomplishments and set herself new goals for talents and skills the way some folks collect stamps or rare coins. She was Phyllis' star pupil.

At the shop she first got to know fabrics and colours so she could go fetch supplies from the garage and get the right bolt on the first try. She entertained waiting babies, she helped customers choose matching accessories like buttons and appliques, she cut out the second pattern while a designer was sewing up the first piece of an outfit, in many ways she sped up the service and made things operate smoothly, just as Evelyn and Joy had done when they began.

Ever so softly Ruthe's conscience whispered about it being wrong to teach her little sister to be deceptive, but she was so busy going to work, checking up on friends, and driving back and forth, that even though the weather was fine, she just didn't have time for a quiet garden walk and talk with her Friend, sometimes not for days on end. Not listening for whispers, it was hard to hear them any more.

Phyllis added piano and voice lessons to Sharri's schedule, and advised her to get up early every morning to do gymnastic stunts to keep in top shape physically. Sharri's energy and brains were like a shot of adrenlin to the older woman; here was someone willing to take on her old obsession with learning. Phyllis had learned from her high school students that there are tremendous health and mental benefits in exercise, so she was eager to try, but found that her body balked against too strenuous attempts.

Sharri's school friends in Kleinstadt knew she was going to the city for special tutoring, but gaped at her graceful somersaults and bold comments championing their better teachers and school projects. They began to imitate her and see her as a leader. Ruthe became aware of this when she dropped by a science fair to see the display that Sharri and her friends had worked on. Sharri acted totally absorbed in the science project and the purpose of it, but two teachers and the school secretary stopped Ruthe to point out how her sister was a role model to her peers.

Ruthe reported this to Phyllis, who instructed Sharri not to waste her influence. "Use your popularity to get your friends to follow *your Leader*."

Sharri grinned a dimpled, blushing grin and shrugged her shoulders shyly, just like Ruthe often did. However, she took the counsel to heart and analyzed her friends with Phyllis, and plotted specific lines and projects for each one.

At Darlin' Bonne's shop Sharri was gradually helped to develop a fashion look that was distinctly hers. She wore her light brown hair in long, waist length ringlets, done with old-fashioned rag ties, so she could sleep on them and let her hair dry naturally overnight. She dressed mostly in free-moving A-lines now. Robin's egg blue, pink and white (often as dots) were her favourite colours, contributing to the fresh, sparkling and pure ingenue look she wanted to project.

Sharri said, "My school friends want to wear black. It makes them look older and dangerous!"

Darlin' Bonne answered, "Black is for sorrow and death and drama. None of which you should be beaming from your life yet."

A handful of city girls, clients of Sharri's age, met her at the shop and decided to go for pale, crisp pastel outfits like hers. It seemed to catch on. In a few weeks the shop reported a rash of other young clients coming in for this new look, including several from Kleinstadt.

All this meant that Ruthe had to appear to sew a lot of Sharri's new wardrobe at home, so it could be accounted for right before their mother's and Suzanne's eyes. The material was usually paid for out of Sharri's card money so that their middle sister could not accuse them of unfairness. Also, Sharri kept saying, "Let me try that! I can sew this myself!" After a while, it astonished no one to see her alone at the sewing machine assembling her own clothes.

In their hearts, Ruthe and Sharri knew Suzanne was smouldering. In the drives to and from the city, they sometimes puzzled on how to buy or make peace with her.

FORTY-SEVEN

One Saturday Ruthe had to work at the switchboard until nine in the evening. She returned to the shop to find that Sharri had surprised all the others, and herself, with a splendid idea. She had suggested a summer school for girls her age up to young teens– an intense holiday experience to learn poise and charm in social ways. By the time Ruthe got there they had been brainstorming a while and listed a number of nine to sixteen-year old clients who could benefit from such help.

"Y'see, Ruthe," said Sharri, hugging her waist and gazing up at her puzzled older sister. "The girls here manage to give those kids a few odd tips when they come in for an outfit; think how much more they'd learn if they got a crash course."

Darlin' Bonne crowded closer, eager for Ruthe's approval too. "Wouldn't it be fantastic? Think of the heartaches saved if they learn the secrets of a clean and happy life at that age!"

"Let's get Phyllis Shulton in on this!" cried Donnie and Louise in unison.

"Yeah!" responded Sharri excitedly, bouncing on Ruthe, "She knows all 'bout analyzing people and planning tactics!"

Since this wasn't one of Ruthe's ideas she was able to be objective and cautious. "Question one, how are you going to handle all this extra work? Where will you fit it all in?"

The mood turned slightly. With grimaces they all offered arguments; they could sponsor someone else, it could be an evenings-only commitment, or, how about closing down the shop for holidays?

"Maybe–" suggested Evelyn again, in a small but positive tone, "We have to get someone else, like a modelling instructor, to give them poise and grooming lessons during the daytime–"

"Right," said Betty, picking up the note firmly, "Your O'Brien loan for our start up here is paid off in a couple more months, so you'll have that income to invest until the registration monies are in. These girls could meet somewhere else during the day, and at night we'd be with them, around a barbecue, or swimming pool, or whatever, and teach them about living in Christ."

"That's it. We're still in business with this!"

"We've got it!"

At mention of the swimming pool Ruthe had an idea of her own. "In that case, let's use the Greystone!" She turned to Sharri, "Most kids would love a city

300

Ruth Marlene Friesen

holiday in a mansion, wouldn't they? Remember the place I showed you last week, where we popped in just long enough to meet June's sisters?"

"Would they ever!" Sharri hugged herself and twirled in a circle, rolling her eyes expressively. "Just being in that big palace will give the girls the Royal Treatment!"

"June's got it just about all fixed up and pretty now, but we haven't had many guests yet. We're to have that pool Linnet won in a draw for me, installed soon."

"Did Ross ever fix those grounds and the tennis court as he promised last fall?" asked Darlin Bonne.

"Not yet. University exams are almost upon him, but if I give Ross a deadline, I think I can expect him and his little elves quite soon."

"Wow-wh-ee!" Sharri went around the room, hugging each person.

The Easter season had just passed, so they admitted to each other that they would need to hurry if this were to be organized by the time schools let out. Louise got out some paper and wrote out the things they could agree on immediately.

After they had decided this course would be limited to girls ages nine to sixteen, who applied and paid a fee, Ruthe had a chilling thought; *Suzanne hears of this, and she will insist she has to take this course. Yet Sharri presumes she will help conduct it.* "We can't have Suzanne come and see you, Sharri, in a leadership capacity," she pointed out.

"Ruth-ee!" Sharri wailed instantly, "I've gota be there!"

"I know." Her arms were firmly, solicitously around her little sister, "But not as one of the organizers. If it happens that she wants to come, you may have to show Suzanne only the little sister that she knows and can understand."

"You mean, I'll have to pretend to take the course if Suz gets to come?"

"What better way to help those kids," asked Darlin' Bonne tenderly on the other side, "than to be one of them, Kitten?"

Ruthe nodded and sighed. This business of keeping secrets was making her very tired. She wished she knew for sure there was an end coming. This summer could be even rougher than the previous one.

Louise had a puckered face. "Hey, everybody. Do you think we could handle one batch of fifteen or twenty in July and another in August? Evelyn here has been checking the list of potentials and it is longer than the Greystone can hold. Ruthe, how many can you squeeze in?"

They hashed over the pros and cons and concluded that a month would probably do, and if they set up for it once, they could do it twice.

Who could they get to teach the girls what they wanted them to learn? Phyllis was suggested again, so they called her up. Ruthe had the receiver. Phyllis loved the idea. In fact, she had some girls in her school who needed that

301

kind of help. She had been casting about for something to do with them in the oncoming summer. "Why sure, I'd be delighted! A course in grooming, poise, diction, in etiquette, and wardrobe coordination? The whole bit? I'd love to do it! What is more, it will give me something to study in my free time."

"Personal maids to help the girls form these habits would be nice, and go with the lifestyle there," commented Betty in the background. Ruthe relayed that suggestion to Phyllis. In turn, Phyllis knew of an agency that provided excellent maids for jetsetters and high-class models in Montreal. These women were qualified hairdressers, some of them cosmetologists too. All very prudent and professional. She volunteered to make arrangements at her own expense.

As Ruthe hung up there was cheering. Sharri nearly came out of her skin, but it was late and Ruthe knew she had to break it up and get Sharri and herself home at a decent hour or there would be a scene. It was already past ten.

They did get a reaming out, most of it falling on Ruthe. "You know better than to keep a young girl in the city all day! Even with all your split shifts and overtime, you can't have worked all day long!"

"Yeah, there's laws against that," snapped Suzanne.

Ruthe opened her mouth to apologize and explain, however Sharri grabbed her arm and steered her to their bedroom, "Look, we don't have to answer charges like that. Not when everyone is so angry. Let's all cool down first."

Ruthe turned, her mouth open to speak, for she felt she ought to give some excuses, even if they weren't the major causes of the delay. Sharri kept talking and guiding her down the hall, and over a shoulder called back, "Have some compassion for women who work hard all day."

That made Ruthe giggle.

There was another flare up of angry charges when their dad came in still later, from his long day loading bales for a farmer, but he was very tired himself, so Sharri was able to diffuse the worst of it.

By breakfast the next morning it was a minor irritation to their parents, but not worth their full attention.

The Greystone was truly large. Ruthe, Darlin' Bonne and Phyllis soon toured it with the summer course in mind, and agreed on that.

June showed them the eight bedrooms on the second floor, and how she had divided the four bathrooms with solarium spaces between every two bedrooms into eight smaller but practical bathrooms. Now there was one for each. The rooms were empty, but freshly painted and papered in graduating colours of the rainbow. A swift, sweeping glance at the top of the stairs when all the bedroom doors were open gave a pastel prism effect.

With some discussion, they agreed that the rooms were big enough to contain twin beds in each, so Ruthe asked June to order these. That would provide space for sixteen girls at one time for the course.

The third floor was not completed, but they planned to block off a triangular corner of each of the three largest servant's rooms to create half-baths. There were already three bathrooms, albeit windowless and dingy. June promised to make them come to life. Twin beds would allow for twelve staff on this floor.

"The space around the opening of the stairs has room for a circle of lounge furniture," suggested Phyllis, so Ruthe added it to June's to-do list. She explained that she was about to start getting a small income from Darlin' Bonne's shop, but these costs would be recouped with the accomodations fee factored into the applicant's fees for the Charm n' Poise Course.

"That's twenty-eight rooms!" Darlin' Bonne counted gleefully.

When June reminded them of the large master bedroom and maid's suites down at the rear of the main floor, Phyllis and Darlin' Bonne joined Ruthe in insisting that they would get to stay. "There will be work for all you kids, and a chance to grow up from the responsibility," Ruthe promised happily.

Relieved, June assured them all the bedrooms on the second and third floors would soon be fresh and feminine with frilly sheers waltzing in the breezes, such as they already saw.

"Yes!" exclaimed Phyllis, "I love the gaily flowered wallpapers and the rainbow colours; like a crystal prism. You have perfect taste for making wholesome young ladies."

June blushed at her praise and said depreciatingly, "I was just trying to reflect some of Ruthe's personality."

Ruthe grew warm, and glanced around herself thinking, *Is this how I appear to an interior decorator?*

They came back down. The main floor plan revolved around the large oval dining table. To the right of it was the handsome old staircase winding slightly at the foot towards the front door.

At the foot was also the wide entrance into the parlour. Now its pink pearl walls were complimented with soft modern sofas in beiges and blues around a sculptured rug in muted green moss. Rosy golden accents in the chairs and lamps echoed the warm light that seemed to emanate from the huge painting of a prairie sunset beside the north window. Halfway past the stairs and still underneath the painting were a couple of room-width steps into a sunken section or family room. This room had french windows at ground level which had not been opened in years. Now pale blue sheers meandered in the breeze from the open doors and tempted one to go out to inspect the berry garden this side of the Chinese elm hedge.

Continuing through the family room, where the course organizers suggested several smaller tables seating four, and game boards, they came to the kitchen. It still had white and black tiles on the floor and smaller red and white tiles on the walls between the gleaming and chrome-like counters and the white upper cupboards. A sturdy oak work-island with sinks stood in the middle of the kitchen. A forest of plants, mostly herbs and violets, hung from chains at various heights in front of the generous west window.

A narrow maid's room with a small, windowless bathroom, was squeezed between the kitchen and the north wall. It had turned into Wes and Byron's bedroom. Peeking in, Ruthe knew that June had put in plain department store suites at each end. One bed had a red plaid spread, and the other one was rumpled and busy with black and grey spacemen glaring all over it.

Next to the kitchen and just before the rear exit door was the laundry room, with pantry shelves lining both walls. It had no window.

To the south side of the rear door was the spacious master bedroom and bath, which June had fixed up with three girlish bedroom corners in pink, green and blue with mauve, and long dividing privacy drapes, which were clasped back to the walls with large gold leaves. A large hassock and three beanbags in neon green and yellow fun fur created a meeting and play centre in the middle of the room that the Johnson sisters shared.

The deluxe main floor washroom was situated handily for guests from the big dining table, or the library, and a discrete distance from the parlour and family room. It came between the master suite and the den or library left of the front door, and had been lined years earlier in a dark burgundy ceramic tile. It would have been hard to take that all out, so June had simply cleaned it hard with toothbrushes, and hung soft velour towels in moss green and pale pink on all the brass bars. Ferns hung suspended over the pink and black marble sink, and June had found a way to put up more indirect white lights. Ruthe thought it looked quite avant garde now.

"This room, right by the front door," June confessed, "Was hardest to decorate."

Ruthe stepped in, recalling vaguely that it had glassed-in bookcases, dull red wing chairs, with even heavier red velvet drapes, a huge desk with a leather top, a marble fireplace cluttered with knick-knacks across the mantel and all about the sides and front of it. "Oh June!" she whispered in awe. "Where did all the dark stuff go? That window seat with the plants looks so inviting now! That fireplace– was it white marble with gold veins all along? And that mirror on top of the mantel does wonders!" Ruthe whirled slowly around, taking it all in. "That's right; we sold the bookcases and the old desk–"

June laughed proudly, "That money redecorated almost all of this floor."

Sighing contentedly, Ruthe said, "I don't mean to put down antiques, but I really like those straight lines of those new bookcases better. The honey-blond wood grain in there helps to warm up this room." Then she saw that the old books were in the new shelves. She was just wondering what to say about that, when June said, "I'm no great bookworm. I thought you might like to check over the books yourself to see if they express your personality and interests."

Ruthe joked about her lack of time, but certainly intended to sit down and go through all those books some day. Phyllis offered to help her, and they picked a tentative date and time.

Then they all moved outside to continue this evaluation tour.

They gazed at the fruit trees in the far left rear corner of the property. "What a tangled jumble of branches!" Darlin' Bonne exclaimed. But none of them knew what to do about them, so Ruthe put it to the rear left burner of her mind.

Keith O'Brien had been teaching Wesley and Byron how to systematically sprinkle the lawn since spring, and it was turning luscious and velvety, but the battle against dandelions had just begun. Phyllis suggested they experiment with salads and dandelion wines, or as potted plants to sell to motivate the boys to clear them out.

They agreed they might have to hire someone to give Byron lessons in caring for the rockery.

The raspberry canes needed trimming back too. Ruthe didn't allow herself to dwell on the thought that her parents loved the ones they found behind their new house, and would love to take charge of these too.

The friends turned away to a more inviting view across the unkempt and broken tennis court cement, the new kidney-shaped pool. It could just be seen, two meters down in an abrupt lower level of ground which sloped gradually up towards the left and the dozen or so gnarled fruit trees, which shared the ravine with them. The people who installed the prize pool had thoughtfully embedded some of their broken patio tiles into the slope behind the tennis court to make flagstone stairs.

Linnet was sunbathing in a white pool chair, and watching her sisters. Ruthe and her friends stood looking at them and the overall view, and discussed how the yard work seemed quite possible to do, and the mansion just perfect for the Poise n' Charm Course they were planning. Ruthe and June agreed to make the Greystone and grounds their area of responsibility, Phyllis would work out the details of the course, and Darlin' Bonne promised to get the modelling wardrobe made, and work on the spiritual impact events for the evenings.

After Phyllis and Darlin' Bonne left, and June went back to her work, Ruthe decided to go visit the pool-side girls. She found the stone stairs steep and had to stop to breathe a while before she could speak. "What ailed me– to say they sh– should put it down here?" she asked aloud.

Linnet and Gilda and Cheryl were happy to remind her of the big hole that had been left since the previous fall when a group of dead trees had been brought out, and one live apple tree had been taken to her Mom and Dad's house. "'Member? You had to pay extra to get all those crooked roots pulled out before them people could put in the pool?" said Gilda.

"Yea," said Cheryl with a hint of jealousy, "You got a FREE pool."

Linnet had been fairly smug, since she was the one who had entered Ruthe's name, and was getting use of it, with the proviso that she be super careful that her younger sisters would not drown in it. She did not like Cheryl's comment, so to prevent a quarrel, Ruthe quickly asked about the swimming lessons that June considered desperately urgent this spring. All three were happy to talk about the lessons, even to demonstrate them.

Finally, back up the steep steps, and seeing the broken court pad again, Ruthe wandered through the hedge to ask Keith about fixing it up. He was willing, but urged her to ask Ross another time, and offer the Mueller kids the use of the court and pool as a reward. Ann had too much pride to let the kids come without specific invitations. This might tactfully solve that problem.

The next day Ruthe went to Ross and Ann's home and explained the deal, with the added information about the Charm n' Poise Course to be offered at the Greystone. Ross promised to get it done by the end of June, but he was developing some pride too, and hesitated about the reward privileges. When a few moments later there was a comment about no student loan to live on during the summer, Ruthe decided to offer regular payment instead for services rendered. To herself, she added, *I'll just plan parties to invite them to.*

"Hey, Ruthe," Ross said suddenly, "Want a gazebo built as well?"

"What's that?"

"A small garden place to sit and contemplate. It usually has a platform and roof, sometimes a low lattice wall. Pillars with climbing vines. I'm suppost to draft a small building like that for a final assignment. If you can afford the lumber and stain, I'll be happy to actually make it for you. We'll see if my first architectural efforts are of any practical use."

"I'd be delighted!" Ruthe nodded and beamed. "That would be perfect for our outdoor modelling and photo sessions!"

"Just be sure you drop my name a lot, so I get a few more jobs like it this summer," Ross teased.

She guaranteed it, and began a mental list of people to tell.

"By the way," she asked, remembering the *help* she had seen in the big Gaelic Bible, "Are you raising your family on Granny's Good Book?"

Ann and Ross assured her they were, but Ruthe saw no sign of the huge Bible anywhere. They were interrupted by Sara, who asked a lot of questions about the course at the Greystone. Ruthe fed her hopes.

She had been right about Suzanne. In no time she had heard through school friends of the summer Charm n' Poise month, sponsored by Darlin' Bonne's Shop, and she was begging her parents for permission to register.

To be consistent with her image at home as a normal nearly nine-year old, Sharri begged her heart out as well. Their mother had a great sense of equality. All her children knew that and had often used it to manipulate her. Both girls poured it on, knowing that if one was refused, there was no chance the other would be allowed to disappear into the city for a whole month in the summer.

Neither of their parents could stand the whining very long, but they happened to meet Scottie before they decided. On his counsel, they gave in on two conditions; that each girl must pay her own way, and that Ruthe must check up on them to make sure they did not fall into sinful, worldly ways.

Suzanne complained that she had no source of income. Sharri took the wind out of that sail by offering to help her think of a way to earn some.

She did too. Sharri taught Suzanne to sew teddy bears, and then they went to visit all the families they could think of with newborns or young children. They sold as fast as they could make them.

Their mother still worried, and all three sisters made strong remarks meant to convince her this course would not teach them to strut and seduce men but rather to have good manners. The sponsors and teachers would be Christians. From then on, the number of close calls thinned down from countless times, to just once or twice a week when Ruthe had to blurt out, "Mom! They will be safe! Trust me!"

FORTY-EIGHT

Mrs. Veer had vowed to come along and see for herself when her younger daughters were to go to the city on the first of July. Then she learned relatives were coming from British Columbia; she would only get to see them at her mother's that Sunday afternoon. So it was up to Ruthe to drive her sisters in to the Charm n' Poise Course, but the fussing with their mother made her nerves jumpy. She resolved to drive off afterwards by herself for a good cry.

Lord, at least everything and everybody else was all set yesterday, she prayed, looking for comforting rays, *I'm grateful for that. There has to be a fly in every ointment, right?* Then she berated herself for thinking like a pessimist, just like her mother.

Suzanne caught her first glimpse of the large old building with its clinging gown of ivy, as Ruthe slowed and turned into the curving driveway. The velvety green lawns smelled freshly trimmed and the view of the gazebo, in an open space to the left, surrounded with climbing flowers and hanging full of pink azaleas hushed all three of them. Suzanne began to gush in whispers. Her respect for the opulence only increased when they entered the front hall to register arrival. "Ru-th-e-e!" she drooled, her mouth wet with saliva, "Have you ever seen such rich-looking rooms before?"

Suzanne tiptoed around the curved stairs, to the draped arch, and peered into the sunken family room. Then came back.

Sharri and Ruthe didn't answer any of her questions directly. They pretended to be awestruck like she was, and pointed out other beautiful details for her to note. "Look at this library! Oh-h, look at that long dining table!"

Phyllis came from the kitchen to welcome them. She wore a hostess gown with exploding red and gold flowers. Ruthe blinked at this stunning view of her intellectual friend. As arranged, she was politely introduced as Sharri's Saturday morning tutor, Miss Phyllis Shulton, who would be the Director of this course. She had Suzanne sign into a large and lovely guest book covered in white satin and lace, and welcomed them with promises of a wonderful time.

Then she gave them directions to their room on the second floor.

Ruthe thanked Miss Shulton, and followed her sisters up to see the room they were to share. "Mom said for me to check it all out, you know," she reminded them, and mentally wrote out the sweet and reassuring descriptions she would report at home.

In the room of medium blue swiss dot ruffles and white wicker, which Sharri had picked out two weeks before as their room, Suzanne sputtered and gasped, "Such lux-xury? For us?"

Sharri was delighted with the room too. Peeking and pointing around at things, she shouted for Suzanne to come see this, or "Hey, Suz, look't; our own private bathroom!"

Just then the hairdresser-cosmetologist assigned to them walked in. A petite, dark-haired woman with a lustrous pixie cut herself, she wore a smart white uniform coat dress. When Sharri asked if she was their maid, the young woman said, "Oui-yes, my nomm– Toni."

All her experience must have been with French-speaking models and personalities, Ruthe decided. The look of panic that Suzanne flashed to Ruthe at this discovery was priceless. Sharri saw no problem. She had asked Phyllis to assign a very French maid to her so she could learn some of the language as an aside summer project. She cheerfully returned Toni's introduction, "I'm Sharri, and these are my sisters, Suzanne, who's my roommate, and," she leaped to hug the arm of her favourite one, "Ruthe!"

Toni confessed in choppy English to being nervous, but at Sharri's warmth and friendliness, she motioned to the dressing stool by the very feminine, mirrored dressing table, and picked up a hairbrush as if to suggest she would like to brush her long, feathery curls.

Eagerly, Sharri sat down, then turning up at Toni, she said chummily, "How would you like to teach me some French?"

"Oui!" Toni beamed, "Ah-you-te-sh je Anglise?"

"Sure. You teach me some French, and I'll teach you some English this summer."

Suzanne crept up behind Ruthe. "Man, Sharri has nerve!"

"But she's got a new friend already," Ruthe returned in a low voice, "You can have friends too if you exert yourself."

"I didn't come to tackle French."

"I'm sure Toni will understand your English. The point is, be friendly and generous with yourself if you want to have friends."

"I know! Sharri gave that lecture when we went selling bears!"

Ruthe smiled to herself, and murmured as she motioned Suzanne back out the door, "Bet you'll hear it again out here."

She wanted to leave before she gave herself away, but Suzanne had heard about a tennis court and a swimming pool and now she wanted to see these. She wanted Ruthe to come with her, since she was as yet without a friend.

"Okay." Ruthe turned to wave goodbye to Sharri, who was busy trying to say a word with the right inflection.

Not to appear too familiar with the place, Ruthe looked around carefully before she guided Suzanne back down to the main floor.

She wondered if June had got back yet, when she saw Linnet waving from the kitchen and June in the background. They were unpacking groceries that had been delivered by a truck. Linnet talked a mile a minute about the terrific menus Miss Shulton helped her plan from magazines, and about how once she got her kitchen duties done, she could sit in on the Charm n' Poise sessions for free.

Ruthe steered her sister out as soon as she could without hurting Linnet's feelings, only to bump into another girl, about twelve, standing with her back to the wall. Giving Suzanne a hidden poke, Ruthe went up closer and introduced themselves to the girl. "Have you found the tennis court yet?" she added pleasantly, for conversation.

"No. I jus-it-was I... I–" stammered the girl. When Ruthe asked for her name, she gave it as Brenda. She looked relieved to have someone speaking to her, but was tongue-tied.

"Oh, then why don't you join Suzanne? She's on her way to look for it. I hear there's a swimming pool behind some trees, or down some slope." She pointed to the rear door, which stood wide open.

Brenda nearly tripped in her willingness to go. Suzanne tossed her head as if to indicate she knew more than this little nobody, and led the way to the short hall that went out into a sunny, park-like yard.

"One of my new tutoring students," said Phyllis softly, coming up behind Ruthe after walking Brenda's parents to the front door. "She's going to be dynamite when she finishes here. Very smart, but she has no self-confidence." Ruthe chatted with Phyllis about these expected miracles until another couple came in with a young girl, who was both shy and eager.

She went to the kitchen to sneak in a few minutes with June who had resigned from the telephone office to supervise the feeding of twenty-eight girls, six maids, Phyllis, and the Darlin' Bonne gang in the evenings. She had also taken on two decorating jobs for the summer, but they were only to require a couple of hours of consulting each day.

Linnet was wired with gratitude that Ruthe had suggested she get to take part in return for helping, and she now let her express it. "I don't mind," she chattered, "That June and Wes need my help to get the meals on and off the table. It's a small price to pay! And lucky me– I get to take it twice over! Thank you! Thank you, Ruthe!"

It was easy to be glad for Linnet and to expect great things to happen here over the next two months. Ruthe decided to cancel her private cry time.

As she got to the Rambler she saw Ross and Ann drive up in the familiar red Mustang, with a deliriously nervous Sara, and three other siblings, who came along to "see." She stopped to smile at them.

Sara soon squeezed out the single door from behind Ann's seat and dashed at Ruthe, "Guess what! Pansy sent me to press some flowers in Daddy Ross's Big Irish Bible, and I found this five hundred dollar bill! He said it was God's answer to my prayer. I can come to this modelling course after all!"

Ruthe praised God with her, and stood visiting with Ann and Ross, admiring the lovely gazebo and the beautiful grounds, and thanking Ross for the fine work on the tennis court. Ross in turn, thanked her for the seven new orders he had for such gazebos, and Ruthe warned him to get his "No Thanks" speech ready for the orders he would get when the parents came at the end of July and August to see their girls model in this gazebo. She teased him that he would get more than he could handle when classes started again.

"I'll just train my leprechauns to work assembly-line on our current orders," Ross tossed back, "We'll start a subsidiary business they can operate."

The rest of the week Ruthe deliberately stayed away from the Greystone, but phoned Phyllis and June daily for reports. She spent extra time praying specifically for the girls she had met, and the events planned. She knew on Sunday evening they had filled out personal profiles on themselves, and Phyllis and Darlin' Bonne had tried to get each girl to see a vision of the best person she could become if she worked at it.

Monday morning they began an intensive schedule.

At seven they were to have individual quiet time for prayer. Eight was breakfast. At nine Phyllis led a group Bible study and discussion on the topic VirtuousWomanhood. Evelyn Hargraves came in at ten to help Phyllis teach social etiquette, conversational skills and modelling. From eleven until noon, the girls could relax in the pool or on the tennis court.

After lunch, they had an hour's rest or free time, and another hour learning grooming from their hairdressers, also trained as makeup artists. Then another modelling session followed with a guest modelling instructor whom Phyllis had brought in. After that was more free time pool and tennis, however, they were expected to spend part of that dressing formally for the dinner hour around the great oval banquet table.

The sixteen girls had been divided into four smaller groups on Sunday, and right after the fine dinner they either planned or hosted a special event, each group acting as a sub-committee for entertainment, refreshments, or decorations. Monday evening they planned for Tuesday's party, and Wednesday they planned for Thursday's. Friday evenings the gang from Darlin' Bonne's hosted a surprise event. Each evening ended about dusk around the barbecue pit with singing, a

Bible story or testimony, and an invitation to accept Christ and let Him transform them into gracious new women.

Ruthe allowed time after that, for Phyllis to shoo all the girls to their rooms, and have a few last-minute chats with individuals who had questions, and then she called to get the day's news. News of Sharri was full of anecdotes and cute quotes. Each night, it seemed, two or three other girls announced decisions to join God's great big wonderful family. About Suzanne, both June and Phyllis only said, she was doing okay.

All the teens were to have their weekends free to go home. So, Saturday morning Ruthe came to pick up her sisters, and arrived early enough to stroll about and see for herself how things were going.

She found Suzanne first. A new Suzanne. In one short week her fourteen year-old sister had discovered how pretty she could be and how easy it was to impress anyone she took a fancy to, if she put on confidence. She had on something stunning with bold black and white diagonals and was practising show-off poses.

Oh-h dear Lord God! Ruthe stepped back and held perfectly still, *Just what Mom feared; a worldly, seductive daughter!* Panic cramped and twisted in Ruthe's heart.

Suzanne was vague and non-committal though when Ruthe tried to press her for a response to the evening sessions on inner development. "Aw, it's all right, I guess. Leastways, Mom and Dad don't have to worry about this being run by whores, or whoever. Those designers are straight and narrow, just a whole lot smarter than you, Ruthe."

She changed the subject while changing, unabashed, into Kleinstadt clothes, "Wish I could look like Miss Shulton. She's so polished and with-it. She's lived in Australia, and the States, and been around the world! Her clothes– la-de-da! They must'a cost a mint!"

Ruthe pursed her lips as she squelched the temptation to blurt out that Miss Shulton got them at Darlin' Bonne's and that she, Ruthe, had helped to sew some of those outfits. They were just fabric. Instead she moaned, "Oh, Suzanne, don't become...." She didn't finish the sentence because she knew Suzanne was not ready to listen.

Dear Lord, she prayed sadly, silently, while her sister went to gather her things for the weekend, *I had hoped Suzanne would finally develop an interest in You here, but it seems we're only feeding her vanity with all this luxury. I wish– we hadn't done it. What can we do about it now?*

While Suzanne packed her overnight case for the weekend, Ruthe went to look for Sharri. She hoped to find Phyllis, and did, moments later. Yes, Phyllis had noticed Suzanne's attitude and was concerned, yet she said gently to Ruthe,

"God doesn't force His love on us, remember? We may exude the fragrance of His graces but the final decision will be Suzanne's. And she must live with the consequences."

Nodding, but unhappy, Ruthe asked where to go find Sharri. Her heart was sinking straight down like a hammer heading for the bottom of the pool.

"At the pool," was where Phyllis thought Sharri would be. "Our pride and joy is genuinely interested in everybody and all over this mansion and the grounds. Ask Linnet."

Linnet said, "I saw her just a few minutes ago. Ask Gilda."

Gilda, coming in barefoot and in a wet bathing suit, was happy to tattle. "Sharri and her maid have a whole bunch of girls around beside the pool, and they don't let Cheryl and me splash– or make noise!"

"Here's Ruthe!" Sharri shouted joyfully, leaping up to meet her as she spied her older sister trying to navigate sideways down the flagstone stair path. "Guess what! Toni's a Christian now! So's Gina here, and Kim and Lucie!"

"Rea-l-ly?!" Ruthe gasped on the last step.

"We're having morning devotions here before all the parents come."

"Really?" still heaving, and not able to be more original, Ruthe landed with a plop on a spot of flickering shade a bit away from the pool's edge. She looked down the length of the pool and saw the elfin Cheryl in only pink panties, going from spot to spot along the edge and looking in. The group of girls she had just joined seemed to take turns yelling, "No Cheryl! No lifeguard!"

Apparently they had heard all about Sharri's older sister.

"Sharri ask learn Franche," said Toni shyly beside her, But she teash of Am-Friend, Jesu– who is worry for– no," she shook her head to erase her mistake, "Love me. Now I is happy for words! Scuse, too happy for describe!"

Laughing kindly, Sharri put an arm around Toni.

"Join us for our Bible study and prayer," invited Lucie.

"Gladly..." Ruthe paused as Cheryl, having noticed her, came up, turned around and plopped herself into Ruthe's lap. She cuddled the browning little girl close and waited for the others to pick up where they had left off.

Momentarily, Sara Mueller and Brenda Froese came down with the news that parents were arriving and asking for their daughters. The meeting broke up then, but Sharri generously promised the girls they would continue next week and for sure cover the topics they had asked about.

"Which were?" asked Ruthe, getting up still holding Cheryl snugly.

"Dying, baptism, and Heaven," answered Sharri.

As they filed after the others and headed across the lawn, Toni said to Ruthe, "Hope you not displease by mine friendship with Sharri. Suzanne says–" she stopped.

"What?" Ruthe's ears perked up. She tapped Sharri's back to make her pause on the tennis court, "Sharri, what has Suzanne been saying to Toni?"

"Ach, she's letting all this high society stuff go to her head. Suzanne is turning into a snob."

Inwardly Ruthe ground her teeth but turned to Toni and said warmly, "Now Toni, don't let Suzanne tell you any more rubbish. You are a very nice person and I'm glad you are here. Being a maid does not prevent you from being our friend. In fact, you are our sister in Christ. Do remember that, okay?"

She tried to talk to Suzanne about good manners on the way home, but it only got her sulking. The remaining three weeks at the Greystone, the middle sister grew more aloof from her older and younger sister, from everyone.

At the shop, during the next week, Darlin' Bonne and the young women decided they ought to close off the Charm n' Poise Course with a fashion show at the end of the month. It would give the girls stage presence practice, impress the parents, and the media could be invited to vote on the girl with the most charm and poise. A little fame might be fun and easy to arrange.

Sharri had already told Darlin' Bonne that lots of the girls wished they could take home the clothes they modelled as souvenirs. After some discussion, the designers agreed they could make another stupendous wardrobe for the sixteen girls coming in August if they threw all their free time into it, starting immediately.

Ruthe slipped in to watch more often now, and was there the night Darlin' Bonne announced the fashion show. "It's for your parents, but news reporters will be invited to pick out the girl with the most obvious charm and poise on the gazebo. Remember? Our shop is offering a two hundred dollar wardrobe to that wonderful gal! The rest of you may take home four outfits that you especially like from those you have been modelling in your sessions with Miss Shulton."

The girls went wild with speculation about who would win. Minutes later Sharri was the most popular bet among the girls. Phyllis had seen the most improvement in her protege, Brenda, but she confided that only to Evelyn and Ruthe, adding that the reporters would judge only by visual impressions.

To hear Suzanne at home on weekends, she was having a fantastic city holiday, and begged their parents to come see the fashion show. Ben Veer wanted to close his eyes to something so worldly, but at Sunday faspa, when Grosz'mama remarked that she would go if invited, they suddenly changed their minds and consulted Ruthe about her shifts, and if she would take them. "Besides," her mother explained, "Dad wouldn't know how to find that fancy place."

Ruthe sat in a still, cold sweat for a minute. Could she do this and not give any clue that the Greystone belonged to her? They were bound to read it all over her. In a quick prayer she threw herself into the arms of her dearest Friend, simply expecting Him to rescue her again. Then she nodded and agreed to take them, half expecting not to come back alive, half believing that she would see a new miracle as a matter-of-course. On the up-wave of this faith, she turned to Grosz'mama and invited her to come along. She accepted.

A few days later, Isabelle said she needed Grosz'mama to babysit, so she had to decline. Ruthe was disappointed. She had begun to look forward to the delight on her grandmother's face when she saw that lovely place.

It was a sunny garden party with stacking chairs lined up in semi-circles before the gazebo, and the young girls walked slowly, prettily through it, posing for photos, turning and showing off their lovely, demure and perfectly chosen clothes. The Veers were quite impressed with the scenery, and their defensive attitude relaxed visibly about the bad atmosphere they had expected. Ben Veer wandered off alone and came back excited to tell his wife about the neglected fruit trees in the back and the raspberry canes and strawberry plants on the other side of "This here palace." He handed his wife a few jumbo black berries, "Here. Try these sweet ones. Make you think of B.C., no?"

She scolded him for stealing, and made him sit down, while he mumbled, "Rich folk who can afford to waste fruit don't deserve it."

"They taste like the black ones at home," her mother said to her dad.

To avoid being caught smiling, Ruthe turned away, and missed what her mother thought of the berries, when she spied Ross with a notepad, taking orders for more gazebos from two couples. A third woman was moving into line.

The big surprise came when the reporters, some with TV cameramen in attendance, announced that Suzanne Veer had won their hearts. She was in a light blue brocade dress with puffy sleeves and skirt, looking so demure, quite old-fashioned and wholesome. She shot off shy glances, but also quite a bit of self-assurance. Her face was flawless, her hair turned just so. She was asked to go back into the gazebo and was photographed steadily for several minutes, while Darlin' Bonne stood nearby and reminded Suzanne to come to the shop soon for her two hundred dollar wardrobe prize.

Nervously aware that her friends were watching her, Ruthe, watched her parents as they showed astonishment, then pride. As they grasped it, Suzanne had just won a beauty contest, and it looked fair and square to them. She was going to get a year's worth of school clothes besides. Ruthe concentrated on keeping her mouth shut, and being on guard for all her secrets to explode in her face.

It seemed about over. Phyllis had made the closing thank you speech to everyone. The audience rose and gravitated to the buffet of elegant sandwiches off in the shade, where Cathy and Muriel O'Brien stood ready to pour tea, along with June and Wes Johnson who held out silver platers of sweets.

"Ladies, gentlemen?" Everyone swung around back toward the gazebo.

Brenda, the formerly tongue-tied girl, hopped up on the platform, and was swinging from a flower-twined pillar with one hand, and now called out, "May we have your attention for a moment, please?"

The guests quieted, staring at the pretty girl in burgundy taffeta. Her foot slipped for a second, but she caught herself and laughed lightly, more from sheer gladness, "There was one prize no one thought to hand out. We wouldn't even know what to call the title to give to the person who shows you how to be wonderfully alive! Free to be the most, the best, the fullest you can in Christ Jesus! I'm sure all of us who lived here this month will agree, the girl who deserves a million-dollar wardrobe, the one who has turned this place into a spiritual Chrysalis, is– Sharri Veer!"

The reporters had been packing up their cameras and notes, but now swung back into action with lightening speed as Sharri was cheered and pushed onto the dias of the gazebo, and Brenda hoped off like a sure-footed sparrow. A coterie of younger girls surrounded Sharri, with Phyllis and Darlin' Bonne laughing happily at this takeover.

"Oh-h-Lordy, Hallelujah!" Sharri cried out to her friends with tremulous emotions. "I love you all! We'll all miss each other, won't we?" She spread her arms and swooped them tightly around her shoulders in a grand hug meant to take in all of these girls. Then, she raised her voice to get the crowd's attention, and made a lovely thank you speech to Miss Phyllis Shulton, and the gang from Darlin' Bonne's Shop, and also the sweet and helpful personal maids, on behalf of herself and the other young guests.

Ruthe teared as the girls beamed at Sharri, some of them dewy-eyed as they recalled, she was sure, the precious, intimate times with her. Sharri had truly been the live illustration of all that this course was designed to teach them. They had caught on by loving and copying her. Right there, she suddenly knew that she had created far too much tension for herself by dreading her parents' discovery of her secrets, and moping over Suzanne's materialism, instead of rejoicing at the wonder of Sharri's lovely life and influence right here.

Ruthe started and turned. Joy had just tapped her arm. She whispered, "Darlin' Bonne says to tell you that next month we'll have in-house judging, okay?" Ruthe flashed her an understanding smile, full of all her best dimples and twinkles. She began to unwind.

Some minutes later the crowd was dispersing again, and she spied Phyllis introducing herself to her parents. Thankful that Phyllis was wearing a very classic, taupe suit instead of exploding colours, and dying to know what would happen, Ruthe moved closer.

Phyllis was telling them graciously how much she had appreciated Sharri's influence for good with the other girls. Her parents were flattered, but a bit tongue-tied, for they had never learned how to answer a compliment like that. Phyllis took advantage of this, and pressed further, "Do you think you could give Sharri permission to spend the month of August here as well? Then she can help us turn another group of girls in fine young ladies."

Ruthe's eyes popped as her dad, bursting with honeyed benevolence, answered, "Sure. Sure! Why not? Does a kid good to be of some use once in a while, no?" Her mother stood tall and gaunt, but beaming, as if she were being commended for inventing this very talented creature. She nodded a lot, but Ruthe knew her mother's hearing was poor and in a noisy crowd like this, she was only catching words and phrases here and there. Ruthe and her mother were both mortified as her Dad grabbed Phyllis' hand and added, "Tell y' what; if you folks is too busy to pick your apples and berries, we'll gladly take 'em off your hands for the loan of our little girl."

Phyllis smiled and exclaimed, "I'll be sure to suggest that. I think the owner of this estate might be quite willing to let you have some of the fruit."

Ruthe stepped behind her parents and allowed her face to go limp for a second with relief at how Phyllis had handled that for her.

Now Lord, when– how– do we organize this fruitpicking?!

317

FORTY-NINE

Suzanne complained some at home when she heard about Sharri going again, as Ruthe had been sure she would, but she had basically what she wanted from the course. She was on the TV news that night, which she went to watch at a neighbour's, and was looking for a Star-Phoenix so she could clip her picture. She had an appointment to get two hundred dollars worth of new clothes designed just for her, and Suzanne was busy planning what outfits she had to have so all the boys would be eating out of her hand when school started.

Ben Veer landed a temporary farmhand job the first week of August. It was across the North Saskatchewan river, but he still wanted that fruit, "from that there city palace."

Ruthe discussed it with her little sister when bringing her in to repeat the course. Sharri was more eager to talk about changing the name of the Greystone to the Chrysalis, but she agreed to persuade her new friends to help her pick the ripe berries. They would do it every other day just as Grosz'mama did with her raspberries.

Ruthe knew June, Wes, and Linnet would not have much time for jamming, so she brought the buckets of berries home with a pretty note that read: *The owner and staff of the Chrysalis* (this totally satisfied Sharri and made her happy) *are too busy to make jams. You may have these berries if you send back some of the jam you make.*

Anna Veer saw this as the far more official pact with the owner, whom she did not ever expect to meet, than the verbal deal her husband had made with that red-headed woman. She sacrificed her very best jars for the jams she sent back, and asked Ruthe to make pretty labels to go on the sides first.

The next weekend they brought home three big cardboard boxes full of red crabapples, and promised more when the larger apples were ripe.

Ruthe personally taught Byron how to pick fruit, clean it and make smart drinks with carbonated pop. The guests all loved this, and were all over him with thanks, so he adopted this as his special summer job. He read up on summer fruit drinks, and experimented, to hold his popularity. Nor did he allow Wes or Linnet to help him.

Bringing Sharri back to the Chrysalis one Sunday evening, she mentioned, "I think I'll go over to the O'Briens' next door."

The other girls were not returned from their weekends at home, so Sharri announced that she was coming too. "I want to meet more of your interesting friends." She really had only a vague memory of the Bright City men coming to

318

see their new house the previous summer, the eve of that rapturous moving in day. "You slept through most of their visit," Ruthe reminded her.

The men remembered the vivacious young girl well, and Lloyd declared her as cute as ever, though grown quite a bit now that she was nine. He asked, "Could I claim you for a little sister of my own?"

"Sure!" and she jumped up and dangled on his neck, lifting her feet from the ground, just as she did with her favourite uncles.

Ruthe kept her peace, since it gave Lloyd a chance to show affection in a doting, older brother way, but watched like a hawk. Later she recalled the sexual liberties of his past, and warned Sharri not to lead Lloyd on, or give him privileges of intimacy. "Old habits can come back in a flash!" she admonished.

Meantime, when Grace and Stephanie met the sparkling ingenue they invited her to their double wedding, only two weeks away and settled on a role for her. Sharri would be a candle lighter.

Ruthe had lost track. Were they at six, or at seven pairs of maids and swains in the party? She knew some friends had been added and others had dropped out, but she, nor Lloyd were allowed to decline or offer to step aside. It felt like a conspiracy to make a couple out of her and Lloyd. From the beginning she had determined to just do her official duties, and not do anything against her conscience. She would endure that much for these friends.

The following weekend Ruthe and Sharri accepted an invitation to see the brand new show homes that had been completed in one corner of the Bright city property. Lloyd had assurances from the contractors these two homes would be ready for his newlywed partners to move into when they returned from their honeymoons. Other large lots in that small wooded, development which was a part of the drivers training maze, would be sold later. The upscale looks were to compensate the residents for the novices driving up and down their streets.

A week later, the wedding day arrived, and Ruthe joined Sharri at the Chrysalis in the morning to dress up. While Ruthe was guarded and praying for the right words, should a crisis with Lloyd turn up, her sister was almost giddy with energy and happiness.

At the reception that afternoon, Lloyd was the witty master of ceremonies, and Sharri locked in on his sense of humour, retorting boldly to his comments. This created several running jokes. Ruthe, also at the head table on a dias in the rented banquet room, overheard guests at other tables ask each other, "Who's that girl anyway?" She began to feel a little ashamed of her overly wise little sister. In fact, she could mentally hear her Grosz'mama warning, "When you laugh too hard, somebody will cry soon too."

When Cathy O'Brien, who was also at the head table as a bridesmaid, caught her eye, glanced at Lloyd, then back at Ruthe and winked, she began to suspect that Lloyd was deliberately throwing Sharri those one-liners for his own subterfuge.

For several minutes Ruthe studied Lloyd who had gone back to the mike after an entertainment group sang. He was throwing out more one-liners about marriage, glancing at notes. *Lord, what did Cathy mean?* Like a gradual dawn, she saw how all this hilarity was a cover-up. His friends had beat him to the altar, and he was trying to be a jolly master of ceremonies. A wave of pity washed over her for that handsome man in the black suit– right now with an empty head and heart.

Many guests were rocking with laughter. Ruthe no longer pretended to laugh. She wished it was all over.

As the musical group got up to present another package of songs, Lloyd came back to sit beside her. "What's wrong?" he whispered, "My jokes make you sick?"

Ruthe turned slowly to look right into his eyes, but her own sad empathy was so near her eyelashes, all she could whisper was, "You're trying too hard. Why not honour them for their special day?"

Lloyd stared at her uncomprehendingly, stunned.

Ruthe shook her head slightly, "The Holy Spirit I know doesn't do 'roasts.'" Absently, she put her left elbow on the table, turned away and leaned her cheek on her hand as she tried to listen to the music. It didn't appeal much to her. *Oops, maybe I should sit up straight for the sake of the brides...*

She was startled out of her thoughts when Lloyd went back to the mike, and had a coughing spasm. He managed to croak, "Ruthe, wanna take–?" and he left the dias in a rush, handing her his notes.

What she did after that was rather a blur in her mind until a week later, when Lloyd invited her to his apartment along with the newlyweds, returned from two different national parks, to view the film of the wedding. He made a humble and gracious apology to her and to his friends. He was more like the Lloyd they knew and liked.

"Hey," Ruthe patted Lloyd's arm, "Stage fright can do weird things to a person. My mind is blank on it too."

Still, he sat with his hands over his face through the first part of the reception. Without the ambiance and table noise, it was easier to see how crude and secular his witticism were. Ruthe wished she were elsewhere, but when she became the MC she sat up and took notice.

Privately, she marvelled at how attractive she looked in her bridesmaid dress of warm creme chiffon. There was a spirit and presence that the faces nearest the mike seemed to pick up immediately. She had expressed sympathies for their host, then asked the guests if they would allow her to turn a corner and become more serious for a few moments. "Let me point out some of the good points in our newly founded Christian families. Signs that I think they will do well, even though newer statistics show that one in every two marriages will break up." Ruthe pointed out that, Graham was raised by a godly Christian mother, who had taught him to take his role as provider very seriously. Like Timothy in the Bible, he had learned the Scriptures since his youth and in the past year had dedicated himself to studying and obeying them more earnestly.

"Grace has godly parents who are missionaries in Java and have set a wonderful example by their great sacrifices and service to the Lord. She is committed to being a Christian wife, and knows where to go for wisdom when a misunderstanding or disagreement may arise." Ruthe urged them to walk and talk together with the Lord, and then they would never become a divorce statistic.

Then she turned to praising Gordon and Stephanie in a similar manner, and shared what gave her hope that they would have a lasting marriage. "If Jesus doesn't come to take His church up for that great seven-year-long wedding reception in heaven the next thirty to fifty years, they may well become elderly grey-haired saints of God, like Mr. and Mrs. Adams over there," and Ruthe pointed them out.

At that a mighty cheer and applause broke out from all the guests.

Ruthe looked away at the exit. *No sign of Lloyd. Isn't he coming back?* She glanced at his notes in her hand. She shuffled the cards, then put them behind her back. Next she looked at the table where the musicians sat, "Do you have another package ready?" she mouthed in a silent whisper.

They shook their heads.

She saw herself make as if to look at the notes again, then put them away once more, and said gently into the mike, "It looks like we have covered the basic program, but if any of you would like to come to the mike here, and give our honoured couples some godly advice, I think we can take a few more minutes for that."

The camera had caught Graham whipping a small notebook and pen from his inside pocket, and Stephanie asking Gordon for a pen and gathered up some unused table napkins. Mrs. Adams came first, and choked everyone up with her sweet, loving advice to forgive and not go to bed angry. Ruthe wondered why she had never taken time to become friends with that dear lady.

One by one others followed, until there was a line-up waiting for a turn at the mike. The cameraman had swooped around, catching various people wiping tears from the corners of their eyes. The advice giving, and the occasional sharing of what had gone wrong in others' marriages went on for another forty-five minutes. All that time, Ruthe stood nearby, and between each one stepped back to the microphone to thank and identify those who had not given their names.

Long before Cathy O'Brien, the last one, came up to tell the story of taking her boyfriends to Kleinstadt to meet Ruthe, just over a year before, Stephanie and Grace were snuggling up beside Ruthe on the black leather sofa. They thanked her for capping their wedding with such poignant sharing. "I've typed up all Graham's notes," Grace told her, "And we will treasure and review those oral gifts forever."

"I put my napkins in my Bible, and want to use quotes from them at our twenty-fifth and golden anniversaries!" said Stephanie.

There was nothing Ruthe could say in response. Her face was wet and her throat choked up. Yet through her tears she looked past them and saw Lloyd's embarrassment; she remembered it was not just stage fright that had caused her to block out her kind efforts at the reception.

She forgave Lloyd when he begged for it, and when he offered the excuse that he had never attended a Christian wedding before, she said tenderly, "I've never seen it done that way before either, even at a Christian wedding. I think in my stage fright I just said, 'Lord! Take over!' and He did."

"Yes but, you're constantly filled with the Holy Spirit, and have soaked up His Word," argued Lloyd.

"Not as much as I should," Ruthe shook her head, "I'm way too busy."

Somehow her relationship with him was a touch more formal when they met after that. If it weren't for Sharri, Ruthe thought, she might get all out of touch with that little clique. The newlyweds were gaining a new circle of married friends. Even Sharri noticed that she felt like an intruder, despite the glad surprise in Grace and Stephanie's greetings.

Lloyd was socially adrift. He was able to see his friends at work, and did not want to intrude on their marriages either. Sometimes he sought the Veer sisters out at the addresses of others he knew of, such as the O'Briens, the Greystone-turned-Chrysalis, Ross and Ann's home, he left messages at Darlin' Bonne's Shop, or chatted with Sharri while she was at Phyllis' apartment on Saturdays.

His attitude towards her was disconcerting to Ruthe. Always polite and courteous, he often went out of his way to keep her informed about Bright City's development and start of business. Some of his messages were to tell her of new men he had introduced to the Saviour. However, he never raised the matter of their relationship. Now, after their friends' wedding, Ruthe thought Lloyd was growing more complicated. Nor was she sure how to handle this. If he should ask for a date, she was prepared to refuse. She had settled that in her mind.

Then Ruthe realized that Cathy very much did like to discuss Lloyd. It opened up when Cathy, who was very womanly now, and spent almost all her time running the household for her father, and keeping everything going as her mother had, confessed, "I'm thinking and praying about love and marriage a lot these days."

Ruthe admitted she was too.

They talked for a moment about Sophie and Peter Green, about whom Ruthe had told Cathy before, who had married in the spring and now lived on a country acreage with Rocky and Brick, as the first of many children they wanted to have.

"So? Are you jealous?" asked Cathy, peering into Ruthe's clouded teal and gold-specked eyes.

"No," she answered quickly, then added thoughtfully, "In the depths of my inner being I know I want to hold out for a man wise and strong enough for me to lean on. Especially in spiritual things. I'm starting to weary of aloneness, though I still love my long quiet chats with the Lord - when I have them. I've read that sometimes God prepares us for what He's going to do in our lives by giving us a deep hunger for it. Well. I'm beginning to hunger for love and a precious friendship with a husband who has the same high goals and standards that I do."

"That's me too!" exclaimed Cathy, sitting down after wiping all her counters, "I'm ready any time."

"Now we have to watch out," Ruthe murmured, propping up her chin, "that our readiness doesn't lead us into leaping at the first temptation dangled before us, or, we might miss by a hair– maybe by a few weeks or months– the much better husband God has been preparing for each of us."

Cathy slumped together. "Meaning, we've got to wait all kinds of time? This is punishment for past sins, isn't it?"

At this, Ruthe roused herself to put a comforting arm around Cathy. "No. We're suppost to be busy developing a godly character and all kinds of virtues and good habits, just as you are doing now, Cathy."

"Why?"

"Because once you're married you are like a tea bag dropped into hot water. Only the flavour that was in there beforehand is what will come out." They laughed together.

Smart girl that Sharri was, she guessed that something unnamed was going on, and she discussed it with Phyllis.

One fall day, when Lloyd had to settle for talking to Sharri on the phone at Darlin' Bonne's, she asked him, in her own artless way, "Do you love my sister Ruthe?"

Lloyd had admitted that he did.

"Why don't you talk it over with her?" she had wanted to know.

"Cathy told me about Ruthe's vow," he had answered. "Besides, I saw how she handled Ross when he nagged her for a date. I'll wait it out."

"Waiting for what?"

Lloyd had moaned, "Maybe for her to fall in love with me and forget– Or, for me to become part of whatever she feels is God's plan for her life."

Later, in the car, telling Ruthe about this conversation, Sharri assured her it was all he had said, word-for-word.

"Listen, Pet. Lloyd's a nice guy. A gentleman. I'm glad for all God has done in his life. But I'm not, repeat, NOT in love with him. Until God Himself points out His choice for me, I'm not even beginning this vicious dating game. It eats up your time!"

After a moment to cool, she added, "Besides, y'see, Mietzie, I have this arrangement with the Lord. He's planning a marvellous romance for me. Just for the right time in my life. I've promised to concentrate on bringing lonely people to Him for love and healing, and to become worthy of the best man in the world."

She paused again. "I trust God's choices more n' mine."

Sharri had heard her adult sister expound on this tune with many variations. She looked up sideways with her dimpled, little sister smile, "I know, I know. He'll be better than all your friends rolled up as one. It's like Heaven, hard to describe."

Ruthe took it as a vote of confidence, and smiled as she stared up ahead on the highway. Then she smiled some more.

"Hey?" asked Sharri, "Are you seeing him already?"

FIFTY

Her city property returned to its previous routine after the second fashion show, and Ruthe wondered if she was discharging her duties regarding it as Granny had intended. Through the winter at least, it had been that large house June was decorating, and where the younger Johnson kids played frustrating games of chase; through the spring and summer, that glamorous city place where her friends had got away with running a fabulous fashion and manners camp, the place where little Sharri had shone like a star. Yet she had been the owner who gave permission to pick its fruit. Now, hearing from Sharri, and seeing how the young guests were thrilled to be there, Ruthe thought harder about how to turn it into a place for troubled girls to live. Should she tip off the police to bring 'strays' here? *It's not smart to leave it idle until next summer, is it?*

Although she didn't tell a soul, she started to have the odd daydream about living there some day herself, or a place of such size and grandeur. In her imagination she was supervising the happiness of her extended circle of friends without the hindrance of worrying about what her parents felt or thought.

The police, it turned out, didn't have to be tipped off. They were aware of the summer courses conducted at the grey stoned mansion, and also that it was quieter again. Within ten days they had delivered to the door, two runaway teens from Winnipeg, a prostitute who had been beaten up by her pimp, and a shoplifter, whose parents were not home.

Wes and Linnet called Ruthe, and she talked to the runaways for a couple of hours. One she persuaded to go back home. The other one was afraid of her abusive parents, so Ruthe arranged for Maggie to contact other social workers who would check out relatives in British Columbia that the girl thought would be safer. They sent her there, escorted.

The prostitute came on a different day. She allowed herself to be patched and counselled and took long naps until her bruises healed away, then she disappeared downtown.

The shoplifter, mixed up about life, responded gladly to Linnet's challenge to trust Christ for salvation and a better life. Linnet and Muriel introduced her to a good church youth crowd and got her into a Bible class. After a month, she moved back home to be a good example and witness for Christ, and was planning to go along with her new youth group on a missions trip to Mexico the next summer.

Others had started to say, *Chrysalis*, the name Sharri gave the Greystone in the summer. That gave it definition. Whenever Ruthe, or one of the young women at the shop, or Phyllis too, met someone who needed to start afresh, away from her current home, that person was taken to Darlin' Bonne's for a total royal treatment if it was not too late at night, then the Chrysalis for a place to stay. There June, or mostly Wes and Linnet, would provide essential meals and space. Eager to help, Linnet would clean around the guest, but let her retreat to think and pray and read until she was ready to talk. A few went to school temporarily from there.

That September Phyllis changed, Ruthe felt. At least towards her. It seemed to begin when Sharri told her elegant teacher-mentor about the noisy debate at home about her continuing to go to the city on Saturdays. Phyllis turned on Ruthe and gave her a lecture, meant kindly enough.

Feeling cut when she realized Phyllis' point was, "You distrust your parents because of past wounds and that's why you cannot bear to tell them the truth about your city friends and property." Much as she admired her sophisticated-looking but bookish older friend, Ruthe now wanted to go away to be by herself. If anything, the new Phyllis was tenacious about talking things through until they were resolved. This meant Ruthe could not get away so easily.

"So what's the solution?" Ruthe begged, deciding to go humble and admit she had this problem. Deeper down inside, she suddenly saw that she had helped Sharri get permission to continue these appointments because she'd grown to look forward to the writing lessons Phyllis had hinted at indirectly when she and Sharri were plotting to help her. Only now she was glancing at her watch for an excuse to leave; she could only take so much truth-facing at a time.

"Ruthe, you have all you need to solve that problem. You meet with the Lord often to talk over all your thoughts and fears. You've told me He answers your prayers. You have shown courage to do what He tells you to do. It will come."

She was glad she could use her odd shift schedules as an escape from conversations like this, but Phyllis' kindest dart lingered with her for hours and days afterward. She said, "Have you ever considered, Ruthe, that your deep interest in rescuing unloved and unhappy girls from their troubles is tied to your need to solve your own problems?"

"Yeah, I don't know why you're so afraid of Mom and Dad," said Sharri helpfully, "I'm not."

At first Ruthe was the main catalyst in each chrysalis transformation, but when she saw that she could not keep up, and with Phyllis' words ringing in her mind, she decided, *I'll fix that. I'll delegate the counselling work. But to whom?*

Once prepared to look for others, she observed how interested Muriel, next door, and even Linnet, right in the Chrysalis were in these troubled teens. She called a little meeting with them. Explaining her home limitations again, and that it appeared these temporary guests needed, mostly friendship, sometimes advice, she asked Muriel and Linnet if she could deputize them to help and counsel the guests between her own visits.

Muriel came and wrapped herself around her friend, "Oh, Ruthe. it's an answer to prayer! I was asking God for a sign I should get ready for a career in social work. I just know this is it!"

Ruthe was surprised to hear this, then again, she was not. It was all in keeping with who Muriel was becoming. Cathy had already said her sister would end up in social work.

Linnet had not considered such a career, but said she could feel along with these strangers when they felt angry at the world for picking on them, so she would be happy to give them some sympathy.

"That's great, Linnet," Ruthe turned and hooked a tender arm around the sturdy, strong-willed girl, "Except I see one little problem you will have to guard against. If you spend too much time commiserating with those girls about how they've been picked on and wronged, it will be harder for you or Muriel, or myself, to get them to change gears– mentally speaking– and help them to see that Christ Jesus is the answer. He's on the side of forgiving and forgetting those wrongs."

Linnet acknowledged that such a problem could surface, "But I'll watch it doesn't go that far," she promised.

"How about," Ruthe pressed gently, "You also make a goal of getting very close with the Lord Jesus yourself, read the Bible a lot, to know what He's like, and ask Him to fill you with a kind and gracious love that will bubble over and heal them? Then, when you must identify with their anger you can do it without it eating you up."

Muriel promised to go look for helpful books she and Linnet could study, and to share them with Ruthe when she had time, so they could all grow in counselling skills.

Ruthe glowed warmly. Her idea was so mature and wise. It had spawned more good ones. Holding out arms to combine them in a hug she said, "Let's plan on sixty-second prayer hugs whenever we meet or can slip off together for a minute, okay?"

For four days Ruthe hummed and floated through her life. Granny's wishes, no, God's will was being done with that big grey mansion after all on a continuing basis. How mysterious and marvellous of God to work this out over a year's time, building on one event after another. In this more worshipful mood, Ruthe got over the sting of Phyllis' confrontation. She decided that everyone needs a friend who knows how to wield a spiritual or emotional scalpel, and thanked God He had brought Phyllis Shulton into her life, but still, she avoided long personal chats with her without quite realizing it.

In fact, Ruthe was glad Phyllis came back to the Chrysalis a great deal of her free time to weed through that library of old books, and stock it with ones more suitable to the guests that were staying short whiles now. The teacher could not hide her special interest in any and all individuals who allowed her even a small wedge of involvement.

She noticed, as Ruthe had, that June could not do everything. She had landed more decorating jobs, so had given up her telephone operator job for good. Even so, they could not count on Wes and Linnet to handle full adult loads of responsibility, though they were doing commendably. Phyllis kept her eye on things whenever she was there, and stepped in to settle family differences, or deal with guests who gave in to old temptations.

To think, Lord; Ruthe prayed, *You give me a great big gift like this place, but You don't expect me to do all the work alone; You provide others! I can only begin to say an intelligent thanks.*

Ruthe gave up looking for people in need. They seemed to find her, or were brought to her. She just had to drop in at the Chrysalis (which she did more often now), and talk to whoever was ready for her there. Linnet usually met her at the door and reported on the guests with eager whispers.

There she often took them for walks outside, and used her garden analogy to explain to these new friends how a new life in Christ worked, but she observed that before a person really caught on, or was able to communicate personally and truly with her Lord Jesus too, that new friend had to confess all her sins and turn her back on every last one of them. Several girls failed to do this and were soon back in their old street ways. Ignoring just one area of one's life, not allowing Christ to cleanse and change them there seemed to create a handicap. Ruthe concluded that there must be an imaginary or spiritual boulder at the entrance to her garden of prayer, where one must confess everything before allowed further.

Each time she told one about this, her own conscience grew heavy, for what of her family life? Had she really passed that bounder and entered into the best part of the garden of prayer? Some of her guests never went as far as the orchard; were there parts of this garden she would never experience because she was still in the gate area? *Lord God,* she would moan silently, *I freeze into an icy panic at the idea of opening up and telling Mom and Dad what goes on inside of me! I'm even afraid to ask You to clear away the brick walls! But I want to see the more beautiful parts of Your garden. What will it take? Something drastic?* Ruthe maintained tension and braced herself.

FIFTY-ONE

Her parents expected her to help at home on her off-days with the housework, and in the summer time, with the gardening. Grosz'mama and the Clarkes wanted to see her a couple of times a week. City friends complained if they did not see her frequently enough. Besides that, fall and winter were coming on at a fast clip. That meant the daylight hours were shorter and the weather not pleasant for long walks outside. Hiding behind the furnace was quicker, but sometimes there was not even time for that as Ruthe tried to please everyone, and neglected her precious times alone with her best Friend.

One night, shortly before Ruthe's second city Christmas, she and Darlin' Bonne found a strangled native woman's body in the alley behind the shop as they took a short cut to see a neighbour that clients had said was sick. They reported the body right away of course, and were cross-examined four times about each detail. Without trying they soon had them memorized. But the perpetrator remained a mystery until late January.

A client at the shop mentioned something that caused Darlin' Bonne to see a connection between two odd clues. She offered this information to Sgt. Webster, in charge of this Homicide. It led straight to the man. The same man who had tried to strangle Darlin' Bonne the day Ruthe heard her scream.

Through this the police grew much more friendly and informal with the Dress Shop Gang, as officer Aubrey dubbed them. They even protected them from the publicity despite heavy media pressure about that key citizen help in finding the strangler. When Ruthe asked how they managed that, Ginter's face glowed a moment as he answered, "We told them what an excellent police force we have in this city. Took the credit ourselves, just to protect you gals."

Ruthe tossed back her head and laughed.

Time and again they called and asked for one or two women to come see some shoplifter, runaway or street kid. They tried not to interrupt the shop during business hours, but if June or Linnet were not at the Chrysalis, Darlin' Bonne's Shop was where they came next. Several of the officers came to be known on a first-name basis.

Charlie Brown, the Sergeant of the Morality Unit, with whom they had the most contact at the station, was a huge, likable man. He had twenty-nine letters in his last name and was the only one who could pronounce it, so he let the whole force call him Charlie Brown. Darlin' Bonne and all the others followed their example.

His desk assistant was Wally Heidebrecht; Ruthe could not recall that she had ever heard his proper title if he had one. He was a tall, dark type, skinny, in a loose uniform, with a black mustache under his nose. He was the one on duty the previous Christmas morning when Ruthe had brought in the baby thrust into her car window. They normally only met when they came to the station. However, they ran into officers Ginter and Aubrey almost every time there was trouble. If one was off duty the other was on. On occasion they had separate beats for the same shift, but converged on a crisis scene. They were good-natured and found Ruthe and her friends at Darlin' Bonne's amusing. At least she often felt they were secretly laughing at her. They seemed to enjoy their peculiar encounters, and they thought of them as nice, wholesome girls, and respected their compassion. But why telling belligerent girls about the love and forgiveness of Jesus Christ so often proved a charm baffled them. They were blunt about that.

If Ruthe tried to explain it, Aubrey would invariably say, "If it works we're not knocking it; carry on." They were rational men, they said, so it had nothing to do with them, strictly religious women's stuff. Ruthe hoped one day they would come around to her view, and that it was not for lack of knowing how to persuade them. She remained open and low-key and alert to any possibility.

These two men paid her a big compliment in December when they passed a hat in the police department to buy her a mobile car phone. One day, when both Aubrey and Ginter were on duty the same shift, they rendezvoused for a break in front of the shop as she was leaving, and placed this be-ribboned thing onto the passenger seat.

"What's this?" Ruthe exploded, so startled she was almost afraid. "What does this mean?"

While Ginter scratched his ear, Aubrey leaned closer and said, "Just a bunch of your friends celebrating your first anniversary as a city girl. Here we all signed this card."

"A year?! Not at Chris-stmas!" she stammered, as her mind swooped and swirled with more thoughts than she could think, never mind speak, "Back in spring– in, uhm?... In April is when I started—"

Ginter prodded Aubrey, "So– tell her it's from Santa. He over-slept in spring."

Aubrey turned and whispered loudly behind himself, "She doesn't believe in him. Shall I say it's from God?"

Then Ruthe broke up into a helpless accepting laugh. She made them install it and show her how to use it.

When Lloyd Sherwood heard about the phone he was mad at himself for not thinking of this gift first.

When Suzanne noticed it, and announced it to the family, everyone there was stirred up too.

Ruthe braced herself and stubbornly held to her story; "It's a luxury I feel I need; just like some folks think they have to have a TV. This was such a good deal, I couldn't say no."

"Okay, but I'm not paying no bills on that thing either!" vowed her dad. "You pay for your own long distance calls if you get a phone."

"Don't worry, Dad, it's in my name," Ruthe agreed. She didn't tell him that Cathy had calmed Lloyd down by suggesting he collect a gift of money for her from a number of their circle to pay the monthly bills for a while.

Unsatisfied, her mother continued to act offended some days after.

Ruthe decided it was her privacy and independence her mother was reacting to most. She felt like retorting, "So how do you expect me to confide in you when you don't show me the least bit of trust?" Instead she took her usual way out, and disappeared for a while to her spot under the stairs, and behind the furnace. Only God's comfort didn't want to come very easily. She felt that she had moved from silent implications to direct deceit. *But Lord! If I tell Suzanne it is a gift– she'll want to know more! And–* Her tears just would not blink away, and took forever to quit.

Later Suzanne whined that she ought to have a phone of her own too. In her room. Their mother snapped, "We can't afford to let all of you have the same expensive toys!"

Her first wound was still raw, but Ruthe swallowed this misunderstanding too and let it pass, for she couldn't bear to return the gift to the men who had meant it as a token of esteem.

It was these same officers, generous and loving to tease her, who upon delivering to the Chrysalis another homeless teen caught prostituting herself, told Ruthe about the notorious Lisa. "Saved this gal from the clutches of Lisa!" Aubrey crowed. According to him, Lisa was the highest priced, most popular prostitute in the city. "The slipperiest *Wanted* this hick town's got," said the officer who often compared Saskatoon to the big metros of Toronto and Montreal. Ruthe guessed intuitively that he was glad to be out of those crime jungles.

"Except," added Aubrey, as Ruthe followed him outside, "John Q. Public doesn't want us to put hookers out of business any more."

Ruthe let it be known that she did care. Not only about the immorality of prostitution, but about the suffering soul of Lisa. "I'm sure she has a heart that hurts with secret pains, probably greater than anything we can understand."

"Right!" roared Aubrey, "So she runs three Escort agencies and trains naive young teens from the bus depot to be hookers."

Another time it was Ginter, leaning a shoulder against a wall, who brought Lisa up again. "Y'know, gals...," drawled Ginter, the angular one with the diagonal mouth, "If we ever catch that sex-pot and put her out'a business we'll have to go on a three-day work week."

"Another time you said prostitution isn't illegal," said Ruthe. "Does she cause others to commit crimes?"

"She runs three escort businesses, and you know that's just a front for off-street prostitution. Charlie Brown swears he could pin her down in court for operating a brothel and pushing drugs if only she didn't hide her books so well. She gets involved in some aspects of her Johns' lives, and blackmails the ones who have things to hide from their employer or wives, or whatever. This Lisa is like the manager of a multi-ring circus." Then he fussed about having told her confidential stuff.

Another time, when Ruthe made a face over a stiff neck, Aubrey said solicitously, "Too bad you haven't made friends with our Lisa. I hear she is a great masseuse and reflexology expert."

Ruthe's eyes popped in surprise, but she began to suspect that they were egging her on to get involved in that woman's life.

Aubrey dug in with his teasing. "What? You didn't know a sinner can have the gift of healing in her hands? I swear, Charlie Brown has gone to her with a stiff neck. Guys at City Hall recommended her highly."

"Bu-ta!" Ruthe stammered, "I thought you were trying to arrest her, to put her away."

"Well sure. Running a floating crap game, and tying up public housing with speculation politics is against the law."

They had arrived at the scene of a suicide too late, and Ruthe was getting back into the car where she had made Sharri wait. It was a busy, full-moon Saturday night, and Ginter was working overtime. While the ambulance crew loaded, the two officers were taking a minute to lean against her Rambler and talk, their notebooks open, of course, ready to write up how Ruthe knew to be there. In a trice they got to talking of Lisa again, and how little work they would have if she was out of circulation.

"Haa!" Sharri gasped in a big exclamation, "That would be dreadful! Then you guys might have time to commit crimes– for excitement."

"Sharri!" the big sister scolded.

Ruthe had often wondered if a prostitute didn't feel sick with shame. She would. Their fresh reference to Lisa intrigued her. "What keeps you from bringing her in?" she asked, "She hypnotizes you when you get too close?"

Both Ginter and Aubrey guffawed loudly at that, so blushing hard, Ruthe fingered the phone beside her.

"Honestly," said Aubrey, trying to become serious, "You country gals are so innocent!"

Ruthe didn't bother to refute that. These men knew her well enough, she figured. They knew she really cared about the hopeless and unlovable ones, and she wasn't so naive any more; she had learned a great deal about city life and different types of folks in her first year and a half as a city girl. Aubrey had said so himself.

Ginter whistled and was already saying, "Ruthe, you'd love this sinner! Lisa's terribly wicked. Far worse than your Darlin' Bonne when you found her."

"Almost's bad's the devil," added Aubrey with suddenly a long face. "She's got income literally rolling in from several men of means. She is a good bookkeeper and blackmails whenever inclined, so they are all good boys and do exactly as she tells them."

Ruthe's intrigue grew. "So her real crime is blackmail?" If only she could meet Lisa and draw her own conclusions. Once more she asked, "Why don't you just go pick her up?"

"What makes our Charlie Brown so hopping mad," Ginter explained, "Is each time he lays a trap for Lisa she gets away. We only learn another hide-and-seek trick. Next time she uses another ruse."

Her new phone birred, so Ruthe excused herself to answer it. The officers lifted their notebooks and pens and moved back to their job, looking for witnesses standing about.

It was Joy, to say that Darlin' Bonne was still out on one call and Betty on another with the other car, and now she had another awfully urgent-sounding call. Plunging her hand into her purse, Ruthe came up with a pen. Quickly, she scribbled the address into her palm. "Close your door, Sharri."

Then she yelled at the officers as she let the car roll forward, "I'd love to meet Lisa if you can arrange it."

Aubrey saluted at her and Ginter's tall, lean body rocked with a laugh.

333

FIFTY-TWO

Early the next morning Ruthe headed outside to walk and pray even though it meant ducking her head into the wind and snow of a blizzard building up. Her mother had just worried about her driving in this weather. But there had also been another round of passing blame from one to another the previous evening. Ruthe had lost her temper and yelled, "Stop it! Stop always looking for someone to dump on!" She had said a few other things that had not healed or stopped the fray, and now she wished she could take them back. It was not how she was to be.

So many people hurt in our home and no one to sort them out. Lord, I can see through it; they yell because they hurt inside, but they won't accept help from me, and I hurt too much myself to shake any sense into them. Besides, Your Word teaches not to defend ourselves when accused. Ach, I don't have the courage! And no knight on a white horse is coming over the horizon to rescue us from each other. Oh Lord, will You ever feel sorry for us and heal our family? How come I can believe You could transform that terrible Lisa, but not us?

She was glad Brandt was doing so well in his studies with Scottie and Isabelle. He was turning into a fine, thoughtful young man. He had even started wearing suits to church, and she thanked Isabelle for it. She had to admit Sharri's popularity and interesting personality made her proud too. *One fantastic little missionary You got there, Lord!* she complimented her Friend. *But there's three others in the family, and it boggles my mind, to see what it will take to bring them around.*

In her honest dialogue she turned these matters over to look at them from another angle. Ruthe saw that her distrust of her parents was growing into an obsession. She had mulled this over many times since Phyllis had confronted her, and they had discussed it since. Now she was becoming convinced she did wrong in being so secretive about her city friends. If she had a major sin, this must be it. She sensed it was a hurdle she would have to face one day, but Ruthe just could not bear the thought of her secret roses, her friends, being disdained, so she closed her mind and conscience to it, and reaffirmed she had worthy reasons for her double-life. God knew it was best to suspend His rules in her case.

From time to time her family would press for frankness, as if she were up to some mysterious, no good, shameful thing. Her Dad tried to startle Ruthe into telling the truth by asking abruptly, "Where *did* this house come from?" at unusual times. She got so she expected this and would sigh sarcastically, "Out of the sky, on a white sheet." But then her Dad would lecture her on the sin of telling lies.

Her mother waited until they were working quietly side-by-side, then probed; what kept her so busy in the city so often? "Do you really have to work all that overtime Are you secretly saving to go away? Why don't you ever tell me what you are thinking?"

Ruthe simply could not believe her mother would understand, so she continued to use her well-polished evasive answers. "Mom, you know I'm a work-horse, just like you." And, "My thoughts are hard for even me to sort out, never mind explain them."

Sharri, of course, loyally did her part by interrupting dramatically whenever she saw such conversations going on.

A rougher crisis period came just after Christmas when Suzanne got her hands on the second annual Darlin' Bonne's Holiday Album. It was like a big, slick fashion magazine or sales catalogue, all in full colour, but more eye-appealing for the white spaces around the models, and brief, pithy descriptions, giving only the client's first name and three or four words describing the type of outfit made for her. Not only did Suzanne find pictures of herself and Sharri modelling some outfits in it, but one of Ruthe as well.

Ruthe cringed to think how it had slipped in, but it was a very unique design for a long-skirted, Italian-style wool suit in antique gold. Darlin' Bonne had copied it by looking at a sketch, and it had looked best on Ruthe in the end, so she had posed for fun, then told Darlin' Bonne to give the outfit away to the next client whom it fit, and who admired it, but could not afford it.

Afterwards she could not even remember what excuse she gave Suzanne, and concluded that she only got out of that tight spot because Sharri must have interrupted and clowned around. The scare haunted Ruthe's thoughts for days.

That winter was maddeningly long. Slow and deliberate in its cold pace. The tensions at home had a lot to do with it. Often Ruthe's imagination helped her escape by wondering about Lisa. Though she had problems, she considered herself to be much happier than such a person could ever be. What was Lisa like deep down inside? Was she satisfied with her kind of life? Did she have that gnawing emptiness that Ruthe kept picturing for her?

Besides that, she had been listening a lot to Isabelle, pregnant again and due to have another baby in February. Isabelle had decided that she enjoyed being pregnant and wanted others to notice and be open to discuss it with her. She discovered that Ruthe got strange moods too when spring was around the corner. They called it spring fever and often joked about how they would take off together and do foolish things once spring came.

Ruthe still spent some of her free time at the Chrysalis, talking one on one with the guests there, assuming there was no bad weather brewing. Muriel and Linnet were doing quite well, so she made herself spend a more reasonable amount of time at home.

She happened to be at the Chrysalis when a police officer, and then Aubrey brought her a shoplifter and then two runaways in succession. The latter had started prostituting themselves on 20th Street. The officers were hoping to get the girls out of it before Lisa found and started to train them.

"When are you going to introduce me to Lisa?" she asked directly, fully certain that businesswoman was not happy. *Bringing people to faith in You, is so much easier than it was two years ago. Lord, just help me to meet Lisa one time! It could easily be that she is ready, and has no one to talk to about it.*

Early one March afternoon, before the snow was all melted, as she was crossing the city's four lane 25th Street bridge, her phone birred. When she lifted it, it erupted with Ginter's deep, low voice, "Heya, Ruthe, Sweetheart– See that car passing you on your right?"

"Yes?"

"That's Lisa."

336

FIFTY-THREE

"Ah-h. Drives a Wildcat, does she?" Ruthe remarked, coming alive, and taking a good long look at the old dark blue sedan pulling past her. At the wheel was a long, thick mass of silvery blonde, Hollywood type hair.

"Yeah, 'the lady rode a tiger,' goes some song or poem, eh? Can you follow her and keep me posted on your phone? She'll recognize me if I get closer, but we're all itching to know her newest hideout address."

"Will do. Haven't seen her face yet," she promised eagerly, glancing in her rear-view mirror to locate Ginter. She put the receiver down beside her as the Wildcat picked up speed.

Gracefully Ruthe wove around a little yellow Lada ahead of her, and back in behind the big dusty navy blue car with the platinum blonde in the driver's seat. For a short distance she just followed her down the wide street towards the downtown area. Ginter stayed back a distance, and kidded her good-naturedly on her open line about her long awaited introduction to Lisa.

She thought she was doing a terrific job of looking absent-minded and dreamy, as if she took this particular way home at this hour every day, when suddenly Lisa twisted her wheel sharply to the left, in front of an oncoming car, into a back alley. Naturally, Ruthe had to stop for the long stream of traffic that followed that car; several others honked at her to let her know she shouldn't go that way.

She felt badly about losing Lisa, but Ginter assured her it was all right. Not to worry. "She makes crazy turns like that every once in a while, just in case she's being followed."

Ruthe had finished some grocery shopping for her mother and had intended to go home as soon as she picked up Sharri at the shop, but now she didn't want to give up. "If you like, I'll be happy to help you comb this area," she offered.

"Aw thanks, I was just trailing her for a bit of fun on my beat. I don't have a warrant along, and she's a stickler– one sec."

A moment later he was back on her line. "Sorry, got one from Dispatch. Got'a go."

While she brooded over whether to look around a bit, she roamed up one street of this little section between the river and the downtown business district. Then back up the next street. Most of the buildings were tall old ones, such as on the street where she had found Darlin' Bonne way back– "Come to think of it," she muttered, "It is the area."

Why would she live here? I'd have thought, being rich, she'd have a ritzy penthouse. Ah, but she has to have various hideouts, as Aubrey and Ginter have pointed out.

Ruthe decided to check out the back alleys. There was no room for drives or private garages between the houses, so anyone with cars had to park on the street, or in the back, entering from the alley.

Sure enough. The second alley she drove up, there was the muddy rear of the car she had followed a short time ago. The navy car was in a narrow lane between a high wooden fence and some dried up lilacs.

For a minute or two she considered going inside and talking to Lisa right away. *She'll become a Christian, and we could go over to the station and surprise Charlie Brown.*

Do be realistic! she had to scold herself, *You know you are to call Sgt. Charlie first. If you scare her off to another hiding place he's going to be so furious!*

But he doesn't know about this one. I'm the only one who has found this place! Ruthe argued with herself.

No, Ruthe. She recognized authority in that dear familiar voice as near as her conscience. *You must prepare for this meeting with Lisa.*

I should go tell Charlie Brown about this address?

Yes, and especially, she agreed, that she had to ask the gang at the shop to pray for this encounter.

Charlie was most grateful for the tip. He even suggested expansively that if she liked, Ruthe could come in later that night and be part of the stakeout. "It's usually fun," he said. "It's the one time I can feel like an actor in one of those sitcoms. Lisa has a new escape trick to show us every time, but with you there, the dynamics may change."

"I accept," she said smartly, unable to pinch her lips firm enough to keep them from smiling.

Still smiling and wondering whose side she would be on in the final crunch, Ruthe hurried home with her family's melting groceries. When asked where Sharri was, she truthfully exclaimed, "Oh no! I've forgotten it's Saturday!" and was able to use that as her excuse to race back to the city for the evening.

Sharri was at Darlin' Bonne's, and Ruthe went there directly. She told her friends that she was invited to be in on a stakeout to arrest Lisa, and that she wanted them to be praying for her the whole time so that she could tell Lisa of God's forgiveness without muffing it.

They shared her concern for Lisa and promised that at least some of them would be praying by turns until she came back or phoned. Betty and Sharri prayed with her before she left.

Ruthe drove off to the police station expecting miracles. However, she was quickly deflated when Charlie Brown informed her that she was to keep in the background until it was certain they had Lisa. "That won't work, Charlie!" she cried out boldly. "I feel it all through me. If you don't let me go in first, you'll just lose her again!"

Her mentally visualized plan was for her to go in, talk to Lisa, in her own way, of course, and then persuade her to come out and surrender to their custody. They could post a watch around the house to catch her if she frightened Lisa away.

Charlie Brown couldn't remember a single one of the other times she had given him good intuitive ideas. He swore violently as he waxed eloquent on his low opinion of her. How very little she knew about proper police procedure. He hated himself loudly for inviting her.

Taken aback, Ruthe grew rather angry herself and more articulate as she reminded this big, intense man in a white short-sleeved shirt, where his police procedures had got him with Lisa so far.

Wally sat on the corner of the Sergeant's desk, his long leg swinging, and listening with amusement and impatience to their bickering.

Two other officers sat in the wooden chairs, content to watch and rest their feet. They were not organizers.

Wally's detached impatience however, began to bother Ruthe. She couldn't tell right away why he got on her nerves. She felt like giving his swinging leg a sly kick. While she let Charlie have his go at foul oratory, her inner eyes opened to understand. *Lord, is Wally the Judas who's waiting to call Lisa and tell her when and how the rest of us are coming?*

He is? Ah-h-hm-m-m, Ruthe hummed to herself, pursing her lips just as her Grosz'mama did.

"Okay. Okay! You win, Charlie...," she pretended to yield very grudgingly. "But do yourself a favour, will you? Eliminate anyone who doesn't have to be in the know. Change the details again."

The huge, teddybear Sergeant was sour on the idea of the stakeout by now, and ready to quit. "Right now I'm ready to leave you behind," he growled, "But I wanted to watch you convert her. Aubrey and Ginter laid bets you can."

Ruthe grimaced a quick blush, but promised to do it his way if he'd just put it off one more night. "I've got this gut feeling that she knows, or is about to know, that we're coming."

"Me too!" While he turned to the matter of calling off the other men he had alerted, and talked to Wally, Ruthe engaged the two officers in casual conversation. She wished they were Aubrey and Ginter who were not afraid of

Charlie, but she had met these just days before and had questions, and a bit of information for them.

Charlie waved at them to get out, but she kept on talking and made only slow motion moves to leave, hitching her purse on her shoulder. Immediately though, Wally took the hint and slipped down the hall.

"Listen. Listen, you guys!" Ruthe hissed urgently as soon as she thought Wally was out of earshot. "Notice how Wally fidgeted and kept fondling that phone with his eyes?– He's your man. I'll bet you the two cents I have, he's gone now to call Lisa and tell her to relax, we aren't coming tonight after all."

Charlie's expression shrieked a soundless, "Wally?"

"Com'on quick," she urged, "Let's run over there before he gets back! We don't need an army."

For a split second Charlie bit his lip. With a push of his huge arms he shooed them out ahead of himself. She ran through the front door to her car, and the men, she assumed, went into the garage for theirs.

Parking at the front of the house she had found that afternoon, she sat breathing heavily, until the men arrived and placed themselves in the bushes and shadows. When Sgt Charlie Brown gave her a nod, Ruthe knew he had truly decided to try it her way.

Totally wet under her arms, Ruthe mounted the five or six steps and entered the building. She fought off a sudden case of nerves with desperate prayer.

The battered mailboxes in the front hall showed no clue as to which was Lisa's light-housekeeping room. Two of the three doors on the main floor had homemade plates. She looked up the staircase, sighing at the thought of checking every last door; *Lisa is likely to be on the last floor.* Beside the stairs was an old-fashioned elevator with an expanding metal grill gate. When she pushed the button the gate opened, but with embarrassing noise. *Lord, am I belling the cat?*

Stepping off the wheezing, scraping old elevator at the top level, she got a glimpse of a figure in tight designer jeans and a pale peach mohair sweater, disappearing down the stairwell at the other end of the hall. The white-gold hair rippling down the figure's back looked exactly like that in the old Wildcat that afternoon.

Got to make this trip after all, she gulped. Carefully, softly she followed about a flight of stairs or more behind, as she wound down.

Say, Lord? You're sure it's not just my wild imagination that's got me doing this? To be honest, my stomach thinks this wasn't such a great idea after all. I should not have made that fuss. Maybe I'm coming down with flu?– Oh no, what if I chase her into the cops' arms. They get what they want, but I don't get my chance to really talk with Lisa?

At one turn Ruthe caught sight of a plastic laundry basket the figure carried on her hip and gathered that Lisa was headed for some laundry room. *Lord, what do You want to happen next?* Lisa plodded steadily past the main floor. The stairwell ended in a dark, dank-smelling basement with cobwebs and hoarfrost on the walls.

By now Ruthe was much closer, half down this flight as Lisa went around a row of old broken and rusty lockers, and ducked to go through a low doorway into a smaller room. A short chain still swung that Lisa had pulled beside the single light bulb in the room. This cellar room had an old washing machine and the bottom of another wringer machine standing side by side. A couple of collapsible wooden dryer racks, such as her Grosz'mama had used before moving into town and getting electricity, sagged over the broken, cracked cement floor, and in a corner stood a small chrome table with a cut up and warped arborite top in a grey marble pattern.

For a full minute or two Ruthe stood in the doorway and simply watched Lisa as she pointed the hose into the bigger machine, turned open the water valve, and a rushing sound started in all the ceiling pipes. Then she dumped an armload of laundry from her basket onto the table and with a heavy sigh began to pick out the white and pale coloured articles, while the hose ran hot water into the washing machine.

Lisa was turning to drop the first pile into the old churner when she spied Ruthe in the crooked door frame. A frightened start spread over her smooth, sensuous face, then was put away firmly. "Wad'ya want?" she snapped, "This's a private laundromat."

"Lisa?"

"Yeah-h?"

"I've had quite a time trying to meet you!" Ruthe laughed, and hoped it sounded spontaneous and ingenue.

"Is that so?"

Despite the casual way she tossed her elbow-length mane, Ruthe saw tension in Lisa's hand muscles as she turned sideways to sort the rest of her laundry.

"Your landlord isn't the housekeeping type, is he?" Ruthe commented with a wry look glance around.

Lisa muttered a profane affirmative. Then she stared at her visitor, waiting for the next move. "Talk."

"Y'see, Lisa, from the first time I heard about you, and your reputation, I've had this strange conviction that you are dreadfully miserable and want out. Underneath your popularity with men, (and I hear you are financially astute), you are longing for just one person who would really understand you. One, who

341

instead of leaning on you, would give you a shoulder to lean on. One you could trust, feel safe wi–"

"What wise guy told you I'm lonely?" Lisa demanded, "Are you some kooky lesbian? Thanks, but no thanks!"

"God says to *let the mind of Jesus Christ* be in us, and since He is able to read everyone's thoughts, sometimes He gives me a peek into the feelings of others. I often feel misunderstood and so in my spirit I can identify with your pain." Ruthe got choked up with emotion, but added with new texture to her voice, "It really hurts, doesn't it, when the ones you most want to impress have their minds made up otherwise?"

"Listen, Honey," Lisa sighed like a tired, middle-aged woman who had been scrubbing all day. "I don't care what church you're canvassing or witnessing for, I've had my fill of religious crackpots when I was a kid. My old aunts pumped me full of being good, pure, and so on, so I'd be able to gather at the river. Hah. No thanks! I've survived city streets since I was twelve. I can look after myself. Bug off!"

"O–but I'm not talking about–"

Lisa turned on Ruthe again and added bitterly, "I've had a long, hard day. My plans for tonight have been cancelled, re-made, and cancelled again so often I can only do my laundry now in this @#$% @#$+*& hole! What a Saturday night. I'm too bushed to even watch hockey, so leave me alone, #@$%&@!"

"I'm sorry you're having such a frustrating day, Lisa. That bushed feeling? Well, I don't think it's just all physical weariness. You're sick and tired of living, aren't you? You're worn out from hating and hiding your real self. Right?"

Lisa busied herself stirring her clothes furiously in the washer with a long wooden spoon, and wouldn't look up or answer.

Ruthe moved opposite her on the other side of the machine. Her voice broke again, "Lis-a! Vicariously, I've been experiencing your emotions. I just had to come tell you; Lisa, there is a way out!"

She stared back at Ruthe with a long, blank face.

"You say you had religion crammed down your throat; I know others with the same complaint. It's too bad, but you are all missing the real secret that's close enough to touch you. Those who know God as a Person, one who is extremely kind and merciful, and as a Lover– are the ones who can savour the essence of generous living, the way it's meant to be!"

"I've heard all about 'God so loved the world,' and the 'old rugged cross,' and all that crap, but you're kidding yourself if you think you can know God. Like a lover yet! Ha! #$@#$!"

"Ah, but we can. I'm proof of that. If you like, I'll gladly tell you how, all I've learned about Him and His wonderful personality."

342

Ruthe helped Lisa guide her first load through the wringer rollers and drop them into the second machine, which was to act as a rinsing cycle, while she began to explain her friendship with the Lord Jesus.

Though they worked together well, Lisa appeared to ignore Ruthe. A bit of panic nipped as she wondered if she need go on. Then a swell in her heart confirmed that she would go on until Lisa got truly angry.

"Oh Lisa!" her voice broke again. "He only wants to love you! The Lord Jesus has waited so long for someone brave, or perhaps naive like me to come tell you. I wish you could be me for a while and taste this ...this relationship. He's so real! So alive! And ever so gentle. He longs to give you peace, and joy–lots of lasting joy."

Hands on her hips, Lisa stared with a cocked, critical expression. "Y'don't look nuts. Y'talk good English, y'gota be an actress hired to–" Lisa sighed deeply, "Or-r, do you really believe all that?"

She abruptly pushed the rest of her laundry to the back of the little table and lifted herself up to sit on it. "Why me, Hon? Tell me, why me?"

"Truth is, I don't know why God should love you and send me here to tell you. Nor do I know why He arranged history and time and places so that I'd be what I am, and know Him the way I do. I just know that from the time I first heard about you last year, I've felt positive that you weren't at all happy."

Ruthe thought of another tactic; "Say, let me tell you about some friends who've completely changed since they–"

"Somebody should tell you," Lisa interrupted, "That it's too late for me. Even if I move to Vancouver, or L.A., or Las Vegas, my reputation would go with me. No matter where."

Ruthe decided to skirt this warning. Forgetting to keep others' personal stories confidential, thinking only of the power of true testimonials, she told Lisa anyway about Darlin' Bonne; similar life-style, about Phyllis; who could not believe God loved her, and several others.

Lisa's expression hid her emotions well, but she listened to all Ruthe said about these people and their before and after stories.

Suspecting that Lisa liked to read stories too, Ruthe kept talking and her new acquaintance continued to listen when it was time to take the second load through the wringer and into the rinsing tub. She mentioned prayer again as if she went for walks and talks with the Lord every day.

"Y'mean, you hear His voice?" Lisa was suddenly alert.

"Not aloud. Like this urging to look for you; I just knew in my spirit it was what He wanted me to do. When we accept Christ as Lord and Saviour, God's Spirit is in us, and then we just *know* whatever He wants us to know, if we listen."

343

"Hm. When I was a kid I thought God talked to me."

Lisa began to pace. "What gets me," she exclaimed suddenly, "Is– I like you sort'a. And, why are my insides crawling... well, as if I am hoping this is the start of something?" She paced around and between the wooden dryer racks, her long white fingers and glassy red nails arranging clothes from her first load. Then all at once, she scooped an arm around Ruthe's waist and propelled her to the table, helping her to hoist herself up beside her.

In that moment Ruthe noticed that she was a little shorter and slimmer than Lisa, she re-noticed that this woman had a well-rounded feminine figure, and wondered what it would be like to be friends.

"Honey, let me get this straight."

Ruthe was about to remind her of her name, and remembered with a start that she had forgotten to introduce herself. "I'm sorry, my name is Ruthe."

"Figures. Okay, Honey, you're saying God told you He wants to chat with me like He does with you?"

"Well, I've prayed about you, and I like to think the Lord Jesus and I are close Friends and talk things over–"

"Even though I've hated Him for years? I've never done Him any favours, not even by mistake!"

Ruthe had to smile. "I've never done Him any favours either. He's so rich and powerful, I'd only embarrass myself if I tried."

The washing machine splashed away noisily with its continuous chunk-clunk, chunk-clunk, chunk-, but Lisa and Ruthe paid it no mind. Lisa wanted to know more, like how much Ruthe knew about her.

"Ahm, well, just that– that you are a well-known and clever," Ruthe paused, and decided to be truthful all through, "Prostitute. And, you know how to blackmail when it suits you." She paused again, "And the police are peeved that you always trick them."

"That's not half of it! Goin' just by what you know, do you honestly believe God can still love me? Is He blind?!"

"Under certain conditions, yes. In Isaiah 43:25, God says something to the effect that when He blots out our sins, He will remember them no more. But He does this only if you believe Christ shed His blood in your place, and if you repent, and really want to be rid of your sins."

"Of course, I believe He lived and died. I think I could even repent if I put one leg up, but I'm dead sure it's too late for me to change. I'm locked in. What's the use? You're looking at Hopeless Lisa."

Ruthe took a deep breath and came up with another tactic. "Lisa, would you be willing to turn your back on your present lifestyle– leave it for good– if God provided everything necessary and did the work of changing you? If you didn't have to lift a finger, or an eyebrow? You really wouldn't yearn for the old life?"

"Yeah, @#$% sure! That'd be a miracle on the scale of making a new planet with seven life-forms! But Honey, I keep tellin' you; it's too late for me. I'm too far into–"

"Good." Ruthe made up her mind to be deaf to pessimism. "The next step is to make a decision." First she had to convince Lisa that Jesus the Christ was able to change her all by Himself.

"No-o, I don't have faith like you, Hon. I don't know how to believe." Lisa tried to back down.

"It's simple," yet Ruthe groped in her mind for a way to define and explain how to believe. Then a new thought and words came, "How strong is your will power, Lisa?"

"@#$%&#, I'm stubborn. A real stinker!"

"Okay, let's use that first. Faith comes before understanding in spiritual matters. One must choose to believe in something you can't see to have faith. Later, God opens our minds to grasp how He did it. Faith is an act of your will, so let's try a tiny experiment; can you believe stubbornly for say, seven minutes, that God sent me bumbling in here to tell you He loves you? That He wants to change you?"

"Without letting up a second?"

"Without letting up one second."

It was time to rinse a load and throw in the last one. While they worked they both kept glancing at their watches. Ruthe thought for a moment about the girls waiting for her at the shop, and what her parents might say if she brought Sharri home around eleven. But Lisa soon stared into the distance and began to shake. Before five minutes were up Lisa hung herself on Ruthe's shoulder and sobbed, "Ruth-Honey, if He loves me so-o much, He must want to change me real-bad! It's a miracle you found me tonight, an' that we've talked this long. I'm goin'a let Him!"

Ruthe wrapped her arms around Lisa and they stood in the middle of that cold cement floor with the sudsy water splashing onto their feet. "Dear Lord Jesus," Ruthe prayed aloud, "Oh-but You're wonderful!" Then on, about Lisa's desire for change and praising Him for it in advance.

Lisa tried to pray too. She started out in the same way Ruthe had prayed, but slipped into the *thee* and *thou* English her aunts must have used. She lost her intention before she got to the end of a sentence. "Hon, I can't!" she cried out, "God's blocked off; I'm talkin' to the stinkin' air!"

"Stop thinking grammar, Lisa," Ruthe said, "He's heard all your thoughts all your life. Just tell Him how you feel and what You've decided to let Him do."

Lisa gripped Ruthe's arms tightly and tried again. Still blocked.

Then Ruthe remembered the people at the Chrysalis and how she had observed that all had to stop to repent and confess before they could mature to more intimate conversations with the Lord, before they ever sensed that He talked to them. "Hey," she suggested softly, "Try naming and confessing your sins as wrongs against God. I've noticed in some friends that Satan has a hold on them as long as they keep any of those secret, or don't want to give them up."

Lisa sniffed, then plunged into this new tactic. "Holy God of earth and heaven, I'm sorry for swearin' at You and my aunties. I'm sorry I said I hated Your guts! I'm sorry I ran away from home, and stole, and lied! And I @#$%@& all those guys! Oh God, it is wicked! You should hate me worse than I do! Please forgive me!" With jerking sobs her list grew longer and uglier.

It were as if Lisa were throwing up buckets of vile, foul-smelling vomit. Ruthe tried to breathe less, for there was such an acrid odour in the air. She closed her eyes tight, though she knew there was nothing frightening to see. She knew, and sensed Lisa knew, all this had to come up to be gone for good.

Finally spent, Lisa hung her weight on Ruthe. Trying to stand strong underneath, Ruthe could tell the heavier woman was beginning to feel different. Lighter.

Ignoring the odour, which was evaporating, Ruthe began to pray again, but reverently. "Heavenly Father, Lisa is awfully sorry, as You can see. Fortunately, You've promised that if we confess our sins and turn from our wicked ways You'll be faithful and just, or fair, in cleansing us. Lord, I know You are washing her whiter than snow right now. Quickly fill her with the brightness and freshness of Your presence too. Make the difference in her so obvious that we, and everyone else, will know You have done a miracle in Lisa!"

With that, she found her head grabbed with both of Lisa's hands, and stared into the jubilant, aware face of Lisa, which was framed by a full head and shoulders of platinum blonde hair that shone waxy bright under the sole light bulb. The next moment they were laughing and crying together as Lisa pressed her tightly to herself. "Oh Honey, now I am ever so glad God sent you bumbling in down here. Let's be best friends from here on, always, you an' me, 'kay?"

"Sure! You and me!" For a split second Ruthe wondered how much time this new friendship would take. She already had such a full timetable. Was it wrong to promise?

In that split second she also heard a faint cr-e-ak. Her ears strained to hear more. *Oh no. The men! They're not coming down here, are they?* She didn't know why she suddenly wanted more privacy.

Lisa had not heard anything in her excitement and Ruthe began to hope she had been mistaken. She managed to steal a glance at her watch while they embraced again.

–Nearly two hours? Charlie Brown must be wild!

Another depressing thought crossed her nimble mind, *what if Wally discovered our double-cross and has come to warn Lisa? Course not. Charlie would have intercepted him. Besides, Wally would never risk–*

"You know, Honey?" Lisa said out of the blue, "The cops've been looking high n' low for me for ages. Should I turn myself in?"

Because she had been worrying about Charlie and Wally, she didn't have an answer on her tongue. Ruthe stared.

Lisa went on, "K, so God forgives me– hallelujah, I not only believe it, but feel it too– only, somebody's got to pay the earth-time consequences. How about all the marriages I've messed up? When God forgives He doesn't undo all that #@$%&, does He?

Ruthe could have sworn that just around the doorpost a man choked.

Carefully choosing words, she explained that God's forgiveness blots out sin and guilt, legally or spiritually in His court of justice. "Making restitution can often heal some of the scars of our sin, but no, they won't just disappear. On the other hand, God has been known to pick up something evil, after it is turned over to Him, and make something beautiful out of it. I'm thinking particularly of human lives that seemed wasted at first. I don't know, Lisa, He might use you to share this experience in a prison and help others to be forgiven whom nobody else could persuade, and the Lord might just as well find ways for you to bring healing forgiveness to those you've hurt." She paused to lift the corners of her mouth for a quick smile, but they fell immediately back into earnestness. "That could be the most painful for you. They could be difficult to track down, some would refuse to listen, yet it might be worth it all for the sake of a few who would accept your help."

"Could be humiliating," Lisa sighed, "But if you hadn't come after me to hound me with God's love, I'd still be facing hell myself." She made a waving motion to evacuate the last wisps of fetid odours, which confirmed them to Ruthe, "Lots of hookers out there to hound yet!"

They sat on the table again, and got talking about how much Jesus suffered on the cross, and Ruthe forgot temporarily about the possible eavesdropper. They prayed together, praising Jesus for salvation and offering to suffer humiliation for Him.

At that Ruthe remembered Charlie Brown and mentally forced him to hold on a little longer. This discussion seemed vital to Lisa's stand as a Christian. Once they came out of here, there might not be time to clarify these points.

Lord, if Charlie has his way, I may only get to visit Lisa once a month in prison, and I might have to drive all the way to Prince Albert. How will I explain that at home? She was vaguely aware of long term facilities there, but not sure where else Lisa might end up.

The last load of laundry was still slopping about in the washing machine. It had been for more than an hour.

Ruthe was praying for courage and about to open her mouth to suggest they go to the police, when Lisa slid purposefully off the table and announced, "I might as well go to the police tonight."

"Now?" Instantly Ruthe felt foolish. "Why sure, why not?"

"Yeah, why not? They're open twenty-four hours. Fact is, they cancelled a plan to come get me tonight, would you believe? My informant said some outsider forced Charlie to change the date. You got a car? Bronson came and picked up his Buick at six."

"Sure. My car's out front." Ruthe giggled now with relief. "You're right, the cop-shop is open this time of night."

While Lisa knelt to unplug the washing machine, Ruthe stepped to the door quickly, and peered among the shadowy lockers. She thought she saw a masculine hand behind a rusty locker, steadying it in the right corner, but that was all. A shiver washed through her spine.

"...Let this soak overnight?" Lisa was saying, "Or do you think I might never be back?"

"What? Aw, leave 'em," Ruthe advised, now eager to go. "Let 'em rot. We know what those clothes stand for; if you go free I'll take you to Darlin' Bonne's for a new wardrobe."

As they went up the stairs together, Lisa empty-handed, said, "Hey, now I can go there and not be afraid of them convertin' me!"

FIFTY-FOUR

Four or five minutes later, they mounted the steps at the police station, through the front door, and straight to the front desk. Ruthe didn't know the man on duty, but Wally was hovering right behind him, and she knew, she just knew, he should have been off duty hours ago.

Lisa smiled at Wally, but said to the officer at the desk, "I'd like to see Sgt. Charlie Brown, please."

"He is out just now, but expected back any minute." The faces of the men were full of other questions. "Can we help you?"

"We'll wait for Charlie."

Her mind a whirl with questions of her own about how much to tell Lisa about this stake-out and what to tell Charlie, Ruthe felt a bit dazed and was glad that Lisa could be business-like about this.

"Would you ladies like to take a seat over there then?"

They sat down on the foyer bench near the door, and since they had been talking for over two hours, they just lowered their voices and continued. Mostly Lisa continued, for Ruthe was feeling more and more like a country bumpkin or a fish out of its element. But Lisa told Ruthe of some of her previous encounters with Charlie Brown, even how she had blackmailed Wally (who had just disappeared), into warning her of every stakeout. She asked if she ought to leave him out of this confession now.

"I have a feeling he's already in trouble with Charlie," Ruthe observed with a sigh, and plunged into a quick confession of her own. "I'm that stranger who bungled that stakeout Wally warned you of. I suspected him, and told Charlie to cancel his plans, and then asked if I could go talk to you."

Lisa turned and smiled warmly, as if she had figured as much.

The two men who had been part of the stakeout came by, grumbling to each other about lousy, wasted hours. Both turned to glare at the two women on the bench.

Charlie walked in from a rear hallway and went straight to the front desk and stirred up a cloud of paper while the officer informed him in a low voice about the two women that had asked to see him. Out of nowhere, Wally appeared at his elbow, but Charlie just growled a rude remark, and came abruptly to the foyer bench. Sounding brusque, or emotional, or, Ruthe couldn't tell what, he asked them to follow him to his office down the hall.

With a hoarse coughing spasm he sank with a thud into this old swivelling chair and shuffled papers to calm himself. When Wally reached in with a hot coffee, Charlie stretched for it eagerly. Wally was gone before Charlie asked, "You women want coffee?"

They shook their heads and Lisa plunged immediately into her confession. She stated her full name, "I'm Lisa Turnoff Starr, and I'm guilty of prostitution, living off the avails, using my three escort services as fronts for brothels and floating gaming parties."

"Too fast?" she winked at the Sergeant as he paused in writing down her words to raise an eyebrow, then went on, "The drug pushing and contraband was six times bigger than you suspected, although I was just a link for the Big Boys. A medium-sized cog in that oily Arabian machine."

Fascinated, Ruthe listened. It appeared Lisa was thoroughly familiar with all the charges he had tried to lay against her before.

Pausing only to gulp the strong-smelling coffee, Charlie scribbled while Lisa talked.

"The crimes you seemed to miss, were the loan-sharking and real estate speculations. Got a number of your boys and some of City Hall tangled up in that, and they don't even know it. Tonight I see how wrong it is to use people in those scams; it's all going to stop."

Ruthe stared at the larger than life Lisa. Before they had sounded like wicked sins, now they sounded like businesses.

Charlie scribbled in an unusually large handwriting, then when he had asked a few questions to settle the legal terms, and got some addresses, he hollered, "Heidebrecht!"

Wally came warily, and was instructed to type the confession for Ms. Starr's signature. He took it away.

Next the Sergeant grabbed his phone and dispatched three cars of officers to close down a mobile high stakes game.

"One more thing, Lisa. Where are your real books?"

Ruthe turned to stare as Lisa smiled, and shrugged with her open palms in the air, "Know the one landlady of mine with the savant son?"

The bearish man nodded apprehensively.

"Well, when I was afraid I couldn't remember things myself I told him. I sort'a filed it in his mind. Since I am the only one he ever speaks to, I knew the data was safe."

Just like Charlie Brown's, Ruthe's chin dropped in amazement.

"So you have no books?"

"None but the day books you've examined, Charlie."

"They're full of doodles!"

Lisa broke into a laugh, "And I'm the only one who can remember what I was thinking when I drew each one."

Ruthe's head swivelled left and right. *It was all so big and so simple?* she asked herself.

"Charlie Brown," Lisa asked candidly, as he leaned back and lifted his arm to scratch his neck with a yawn, "what're the damages? You goin'a arrest me?"

He grinned victoriously.

Suddenly Ruthe felt this was not going the way she had expected. Nor was Charlie showing any curiosity or surprise at Lisa's coming. *Could he have overheard...?*

She nudged Lisa, "Ahm-m, don't you think you should tell him why you are confessing all this?"

"Good question," said Charlie as if he'd received the nudge, "Why are you giving yourself up, Lisa?"

She smiled grandly. "Charlie, m'boy, you're not going to believe it could ever happen to me, but you asked!" She proceeded to give her own version of all that had happened down in the dank laundry room when Ruthe walked in to talk about God's love.

Ruthe beamed. It sounded far better from this full-figured beauty's point of view than when she had experienced it. Here she was this naive little Christian, full of the Holy Spirit, who had unwittingly, but obediently followed God's orders to help a desperate soul at the perfect time. Watching their good ol' energetic Charlie Brown, she saw that he believed every word. He avoided looking directly at her.

My, but You are wise! Ruthe told the Lord as she listened, *You saw to it that he is himself a witness to what she's saying!*

She suspected he was glad for Lisa, still, it looked like he hated to throw away all the work he had put into chasing her so long. He said as much. "What you've been doing is illegal in this city, Lisa. You know that. No one else has been so brazen, even after countless roustings. You've caused us–"

Ruthe interrupted, "She's just told you all of that has ground to a halt. Wasn't that the aim of your work? All your efforts?"

He looked at her then for the first time, and though he wouldn't speak, he smiled a weak smile.

"If Ruthe sticks with me my life's going'a be altogether different. With her for a friend, it should be permanent," Lisa told him sincerely. "You'll get to take some holidays now, Charlie."

At that they all smiled, even Wally, who brought in the typed confession for signatures.

"@#$%@+! If this's for real," Charlie volunteered impulsively, "You can count on me and the whole force to stand behind you!"

The atmosphere became one of mutual friends in a brainstorming huddle. What to do with Lisa over the weekend posed a problem. The rest would depend on the judge on Monday. Charlie did have several outstanding warrants for Lisa's arrest, so they agreed that he ought to put her in a holding cell over Sunday.

"There's no J.P. available this weekend," Charlie explained, "But I think I can swing a closed hearing with Judge Tomas first thing Monday morning, and old Tomas is known for his fair but unorthodox pronouncements. Anything is possible."

Wally was concerned that Lisa not be tried with lots of publicity. He suggested, "How about Ruthe signing an affidavit saying she believes Lisa's change of heart to be sincere, promising on her honour, that Lisa won't go back into busi–"

"No-way-Jose!" exclaimed Charlie, "We can't lay that on our Angel of Mercy! She's not God."

"But I will. I'm perfectly willing," Ruthe said, "Because I know God had done a miracle in Lisa's heart, and it's for keeps! I can vouch for His character even if I've known Lisa only a few hours."   ,

"And if Lisa ever fell out of God's good character, you'd be held legally–"

Ruthe would not let him go on. She shook her head and bumped Wally's arm, "Get me such an affa-david or whatever, to sign."

He left in a flash and Charlie Brown sat down resignedly.

However, Lisa was on a new topic. She looked from Charlie to Ruthe. "How far back do you two go?"

Ruthe blushed and gasped, "It's awfully late!"

Charlie leaned back and exaggerated a sigh, "Oh this little lady often brings in people to confess. We've met a few times."

"Just a few shoplifters!"

"She must tell them God won't forgive them unless they ask us to do so as well."

"She didn't tell me that," said Lisa, still pondering.

The affidavit came back fluttering in Wally's hand for Ruthe to sign. He also had a message to pass on; "Your little sister called."

With an automatic glance at her watch, Ruthe got up with a start. Leaning on the desk she signed, then said her good byes to Lisa and Charlie, and with brief assurances that they would see each other on Monday morning, she left.

Oh God, how will I ever explain bringing Sharri home after midnight? Please... please, come along and help me out of this!

She hurried to Darlin' Bonne's wondering how upset her friends might be with her. It was just after one. Most of them were slumped in the reception area,

Ruth Marlene Friesen

dozing, but as soon as she entered they lifted their heads and were awake with questions. Ruthe sat down and gave a very condensed version of the adventure with Lisa.

Even so, it was almost two before Ruthe and Sharri were on their way home. A crescendoing anxiety about their parents waiting up hit Ruthe. She had held it submerged in her subconscience so that she need not think of it, but all the way home she tried to get Sharri to help her work out a story to tell their mom and dad to explain their absence without telling the whole truth. Sentences from her long talk with Lisa bobbed up to the surface of her mind; those scenes did not want to be submerged yet to make room for this other problem.

Sharri knew their parents would be horrified to learn Ruthe was friends with a prostitute, but felt it should not be too hard to say and prove that Ruthe had done good rather than evil.

Ruthe insisted, she just knew they would take it wrong.

"Look what a great wonder the Lord did in Lisa tonight," Sharri roused herself from her sleepiness to counsel, "You talked her into believing when she thought she couldn't. If He did that for her, He can also put the right kind of answer into our mouths if we have to say anything when we get home."

Ruthe conceded that was true and tried hard to believe it.

However, the miracle was that one was not necessary. An aunt of their mother's, living a few miles out of Kleinstadt, had suddenly become ill early in the evening. Grosz'mama had wanted a ride there to sit up with her that night. Their mother had volunteered to do it with her. Their dad decided to go too—said the note on the table— in case the aunt died.

Brandt was staying at the Clarke's house as usual, and Suzanne was alone at home, breathing rhythmically like a pre-snorer in her bed.

Hallelujah! I praise You, Jesus! You are on my side! Ruthe squealed ecstatically under her breath, undressing while Sharri whispered repeatedly, "I told you so! Didn't I tell ya?"

They made up their sleep debt by taking a nap all of Sunday afternoon. Since their parents did the same, and Suzanne went walking up and down the one main street with a school friend, no one noticed.

FIFTY-FIVE

By nine Monday morning, Ruthe was back at the police station to see how things had gone for Lisa with the judge. She decided if the grand, energetic way Charlie Brown greeted her in the entrance area was a clue, and that his shirt sleeves were already damp under his arms was another, then he had been in very early and had good news.

"I take it Lisa's case was arraigned?" Ruthe had no time for preliminaries.

"Yep. Blessin's on you, Angel."

"So? What happened? What's going to happen?"

"I tried all yesterday, and from six to eight this AM, to find someone to testify against her." Then he rambled off on a tangent because none of the men brought in from the floating crap game would believe Lisa had really confessed. "Oh, and by the way, I lost my temper at Wally. He's resigned."

"Stop playing games, Charlie!" Ruthe was amazed at her display of impatience. "I happen to know you heard quite a bit in that dungeon on Saturday night. You were touched and you—"

"You knew?" His balding head turned so red, Ruthe stopped to rock herself with laughter. She actually had one over him now.

He tried to explain himself, "I swear, I'd never have believed her story otherwise! Not even from you." Sweeping his arm behind her back, Charlie motioned Ruthe along the hall as they talked.

Ruthe nodded vigorously and got herself under control. "I suspect God knew it was necessary for you to be there. Now, please come to today's punch line and tell me what the judge did with Lisa."

"Ah-well. Old Judge Tomas saw her first thing this morning and Lisa told him her version of Saturday night." Charlie stopped thoughtfully, "Would make a great evangelist, Lisa would. She preached the gospel clear as Billy Graham." Next he beamed from ear to ear, "But you would have blushed at the build up she gave you, Kiddo!"

Ruthe protested such a spotlight on herself, and Charlie said, "Now now. If it hadn't been for you and that spotlight, that bitch would be resting up for a media-picnic jury trial such as you can not imagine! I'd have seen to that, for the sake of justice."

Charlie shook his head, "To make a long one short, the old judge was quite impressed. He did remark that you were naive to sign that affidavit, as I tried to warn you, but he liked your confidence. Since she didn't deny the charges, or challenge any consequences; she confessed thoroughly and voluntarily,–" he interrupted himself for another aside, "Methinks some of the judge's buddies will be glad."

"So? After you vouched for her sincerity, then what?"

"Tomas gave her a conditional discharge. He fined Lisa the total of her bank accounts– wiped them out– and gave her an indefinite parole sentence."

"Life?" Ruthe gasped in sharp disappointment.

"Yep," Charlie started grinning again, "She's to see you at least every other day for an indefinite period. You're her probationary officer, Ruthe."

"Proba–? Hey, I don't even know what that means!" She stopped. "I bet I have you to thank for that, Charlie, eh?"

Charlie pretended to be crestfallen. "He asked my recommendation. I thought that's what you wanted." Then he brightened, "Come with me. Enough with public dialogue." Others were turning to stare at them as they passed them in the halls. "Ol' Tomas wants to meet you before you get to take Lisa home."

Home? The thought made Ruthe's stomach do a swooshing tailspin. *Not to Kleinstadt, I don't! That has to be to the Chrysalis.*

Tongue in cheek, Charlie Brown added as they marched down the street a few blocks to the courthouse, "Shucks. I'd hoped to putting Lisa away forev–"

"Lead on, please," Ruthe interrupted with a playful punch on his thick muscular arm. "I didn't know what I was getting into, but I'm not a quitter. I'll see this through, and Lisa and I will be good friends for many years."

They caught Judge Tomas on a recess, so they made their visit brief. He stared firmly and steadily at Ruthe as he asked her some personal questions to confirm Lisa's story. He gave her an application for Volunteer Probationary Officers, with a job description, a business card for the coordinator, and instructed her to go for an interview and get a date for a two-hour training session. There she would obtain anything else she would need.

Then he added a few words of advice, "The Supreme Being is capable of miracles, but human nature is human nature. To quote a proverb from the Good Book, 'A dog will go back to its vomit.' You have proven yourself very intuitive with people, according to this Sergeant, in a number of previous instances, but we always need to watch out for such as are used to a life of crime. This Lisa Starr may one day turn back, and disappoint you deeply."

Ruthe's expression was saying "No" though she had the presence of mind not to contradict him. Perhaps he saw that and stopped.

Next Charlie took Ruthe down other hallways to where Lisa waited. As they trotted down the echoing corridors, Ruthe thought of a funny thing. If only her parents could appreciate what an adult she now was. *Why, I'm legally responsible for a notorious prostitute that frustrated the police for years!* But she bit her lip hard as she tried to smile at her little joke.

Ruthe felt less amused still, when she saw Lisa in the daylight. She had been so absorbed with the redemption of her soul on the Saturday night, that somehow Lisa's voluptuous looks had not fully registered. As Lisa came at her with a big hug, Ruthe gasped in secret prayer, *Lord, what kind of babysitting proposition have I agreed to take on? You've got to help me!*

Lisa was relaxed and enthusiastic, "Praise God!" She was still in her high heels, tight jeans, and peach mohair sweater, which now, in the sunlight, looked too tight over Lisa's generous bust. Ruthe gulped and behaved shyly.

Charlie Brown accompanied them both to Lisa's bank a few blocks away, where, though he made it appear to be an ordinary, confidential business transaction on the surface, by showing the judge's documents to the manager, he got Lisa's account closed out and all in it transferred to the court. Charlie and the bank manager assured Lisa she was welcome to open a new account there, but she declined with a laugh.

Ruthe winced at this, for she had always thought of herself as one of the poorest folks around; now Lisa was even poorer. *I'll ask June today,* she murmured silently to herself, *if we don't have something left to sell.*

Back on the sidewalk, Charlie eyed Lisa carefully, "Any other banks?"

Lisa stood perfectly still, until Ruthe's questioning gaze caught hers. Lisa's glance flicked downward. She said, "As a matter of fact, yes. One in Sutherland, and one in Mayfair."

"Come," Charlie said briskly, "I'll give you both a ride," and he veered right towards the police station.

Between banks, in his police car, Charlie asked Lisa in a low, polite voice, "Do we need to visit that savant to ask him to regorge any other account numbers, or hiding places?"

Ruthe watched Lisa wince. "No. I recently combined most of my assets to invest in that real estate. The deeds are in this next one we are heading at."

When they came out of the third bank they were free to go, but the friendly Sergeant hinted, "Guess your new address will be Ruthe's Greystone mansion, or what y'may call it, eh?"

"I don't know," Lisa shrugged, "I'm starting life over with nothing but these clothes covering my birthday suit. I'm born again, y'know."

Ruthe assured Charlie that Lisa would live at the Chrysalis until the Lord showed her what to do next. As soon as they were dropped off beside her Rambler, had said good day to Charlie and were on their way, just the two of them, Ruthe told Lisa the story of Granny O'Brien and the mansion she had inherited. Then also of June and her siblings.

The stories encouraged Lisa to believe wonderful things would happen to her as well, but to tease a bit she commented, "So you're not a rich girl after all?"

"No," Ruthe answered strongly, "I'm quite a poor girl, and my family are not, repeat *not*– to find out about this mansion!"

It turned out that June was leaving for a decorating job at almost the same time they arrived, and Ruthe had a training class for a new operator skill starting at 11. They only had time to show Lisa to a room, and then Ruthe quickly took Lisa to Cathy's door and asked her to entertain and explain things to Lisa.

From the time they left the banks, Lisa had grown buoyant and liberated. When she saw the Chrysalis; "I gave up my hundreds of thousands to live here?" When she saw her room; "What demure beauty! I can learn to be a virgin in this!" When she met Cathy; "Do I get to move about in first-class circles? God is really treating me as if He has forgotten my past, and far better than when I tooted my own horn. But what do you gals do for sexual tickles?" Lisa talked non-stop, asking endless questions.

Cathy had picked up answering them at that point, sensing Ruthe's urgency to go. So waving at them, she turned, as Cathy called out, "Want me to take Lisa to Darlin' Bonne's right after supper so they can start on her Royal Treatment?" Ruthe thanked her heartily, promising Lisa to meet her there, then hurried away, comforted by Cathy's gracious hostess ways.

When she walked into the shop that evening, the girls were set back in astonishment as Lisa raved about their wonderful talents, this charming shop, and the cheerful, invigorating atmosphere. She had been there a couple of times as a customer, but had refused to listen to the personal message of the designers. Now she was totally on their side, emotionally high, and full of positive compliments. A great encourager.

If she's like this, Ruthe thought with sudden insight, *no wonder men enjoyed her company. She makes people feel special.*

It was a lively evening. Lisa brought a new ambience. She was amenable to the more modest necklines and hems, because she knew what deliberately provocative clothes were meant to do. She was alert to notice attractive details and pointed them out with glowing praise. Ruthe, also very observant, saw that Lisa presented herself with a good ol' country gal accent, but when she forgot herself a rich store of intelligence shone through.

When Darlin' Bonne muttered about a knotted shoulder muscle, Lisa soon had her lying down and worked her over like a trained masseuse, so that everyone's eyes popped.

"No telling what she'll add to our mix, eh?" whispered Donnie to Ruthe, who shook her head, suddenly at a loss for words.

FIFTY-SIX

When rushed with adrenalin, Ruthe knew to keep her guard up for the abrupt slump that would follow, sometimes a day or so later. She would come off a spiritual high, only to be exceedingly discerning and critical shortly after, and to dwell on the practical aspects that could go wrong. She expected this to happen to Lisa as well.

Lisa's high lasted three days. Sure enough, just as suddenly she withdrew into herself. She saw herself as a spiritual baby, absolutely ignorant of the plainest facts that the others knew and enjoyed, having been Christians so much longer. She wanted to catch up, but Lisa felt too far behind. She mourned all the wasted years of her life, and the things she had done began to truly revolt her.

Ruthe wondered if they had told her too much the night of her royal treatment, or, if she was right, that Lisa was so smart she just picked up on too many points at once. Maybe she was gagging on new truths. "But she's so hungry, spiritually!" she confided to the shop gang, and also Phyllis.

Phyllis thought she recognized herself in Lisa, and promised to help. Ruthe had already brought a Bible in an easy to understand paraphrase. A few days later, Phyllis brought Lisa an armful of Christian books to read.

While in this thoughtful funk, Lisa curled up in her pretty powder blue bedroom to read, or sometimes in the library on the main floor. She often said she was not the reading type, but she read hungrily, determined to learn what her life should be, what quality could she hope for, considering her past. She was afraid to make any new moves without knowing these things. The Paraphrased Living Bible fascinated her once she discovered that most of it read like a novel.

For those who sought her out and talked with her, Lisa was not hard to get closer to. Every day she quizzed June or Ruthe on what she was reading, or Phyllis, who made extra visits for Lisa's sake.

One day, as Byron tore past with Linnet in hot pursuit, Lisa remarked to June and Ruthe, "That brat is going to be a sexual deviant soon."

June gasped and left the room, offended.

"How can you tell?" asked Ruthe softly.

"He respects no one," Lisa sighed, "And he's confused about the difference between men and women." Ruthe worried for June, but Lisa would say no more except that she had seen many weirdos. "Can Christians have a sixth sense?"

Ruthe arrived late another afternoon and was amazed to watch Lisa and Phyllis and Linnet with heads together in a deep discussion. It was a lively comparison of spirit-filled Christians with carnal ones, with a Bible open to

Romans. An envious twinge made Ruthe realize that she had been avoiding Phyllis instead of spending time with her, *but somehow she's got way past me in Bible knowledge.*

When she joined them, Phyllis talked of moving up north to teach in the North West Territories the next year. A muscle in Ruthe's throat winced. In their weekly encounters over Sharri's lessons, Phyllis had urged Ruthe to try inspirational writing. She had allowed the intrepid teacher to take her through the steps of writing short stories in a manuscript form on her fine typewriter. Now, with Lisa in her life she could not see how she would ever find the time. Ruthe became aware that Phyllis was studying her face and posture.

"I'll promise to stay here another school year if you'll let me initiate you into a regular discipline of writing, whatever you want to try, stories, articles, a book, you name it, Ruthe."

Lisa began to egg her on too, "Do it! You got it in you!"

So Ruthe confessed that it appealed to her, but her life was so crowded, she could not picture making room for another thing that might absorb her much more than just an hour here or there. She mentioned the need to help Lisa grow.

Phyllis promised to meet with Lisa at least once or twice a week to discuss with her the basics of the Bible, and what God expected of her. "But now, dear Ruthe, will you promise to give me a similar block of time for your development's sake?"

How could she refuse? Two or three hours, usually late at night, somewhere during the week was an effort, but it was a start of a new thing in Ruthe's life. Like a little hidden seed deep under the dark earth it began to grow and stretch.

She had wanted to remind Lisa of her promise that first night they met, to make restitution if God did not send her to prison. Once she had the workshop for parole officers, Ruthe felt guilty that she could not report Lisa taking such steps. But Phyllis urged her not to put pressure on Lisa, and so she waited, and absorbed the bad news Lisa often had to tell her.

Two escorts from her agencies, which fell apart without her direction, came around to harangue Lisa for ruining their livelihood. One man had phoned from Vancouver to tell Lisa off for shutting down a very profitable drug line for him, (that day Lisa asked how to prepare for martyrdom), and an off-duty police officer met Ruthe at the door of SaskTel to berate her for uncovering the real estate speculation ring just when he was about to make a bundle. Like dropping a hot potato, Ruthe decided to cool it. Let the Lord prompt Lisa to make restitution when and how He pleased. It wasn't going to be fun.

Not too many weeks later restitution came to Lisa's attention through her Bible reading. She got an urge to go talk to certain people. Lisa went out looking for certain men, she asked appointments and apologized to each one in person, telling what God had done to change her. In a couple of cases she knew the man's family had been broken up because of her. Where the wife knew of her as the offending third party, Lisa looked for a tactful way to size up the damage. Then she asked Ruthe, and on occasion, Phyllis, to come along for moral support, and in case someone might be persuaded to trust Christ.

That positive outcome happened twice. Lisa's contrite, humble words opened up enormously emotional scenes. In the mop up they were able to help two women, three very hurt children, and one man return to his family, and all these trusted Jesus' blood to wash away all the shame and hurts of the past.

Lisa knew quite a few women in prostitution who needed a changed life as well. She went out to fetch them one by one, and she brought them to the Chrysalis, and to the Shop. The place seemed a bit crowded some days.

At first, Ruthe felt that as Lisa' probationary officer, she was suppost to watch her every minute, go everywhere with her. After she had handed in a couple of reports to Judge Tomas, she received a memo saying she could loosen her grip on her charge. Ruthe was glad. With a clear conscience she had time for some of her other friends again.

In particular, Phyllis was seeking her out, calling, leaving messages, and making sure Ruthe kept her promise to come up to her apartment once a week. Gradually, she got the hang of a writing routine, the rules of grammar and manuscript, and was beginning to have original ideas. Phyllis taught her how far she might dare go within the limitations of those writing rules. Instead of chaffing at the taskmaster Phyllis was, Ruthe began to enjoy herself, as if she were sneaking away to play in an arts and crafts store after the last security check of the night.

FIFTY-SEVEN

There were times when Ruthe admitted to her Friend in their very private garden walks, what she did not put down in her journals for then Phyllis might read them, though she solemnly promised she would never peek in those files, that she had collected far more friends in two years than she could keep up with. *Lord, I hope I'm not making a stupid mistake if I let some go. You'll have to show me which ones to keep in my life if You want me to help certain ones. I simply can't keep them all as first class friends!*

On the basis of that she spent a little more off hours around home in Kleinstadt. She had long ago observed that her parents were satisfied to accomplish just one or two jobs of physical exertion a day. That pace was too slow for the go-getter Ruthe had become. However, she discovered physical labour to be a rest when she was inexplicably exhausted emotionally or spiritually. She could pray and think while she weeded the garden or helped her mother put up some vegetable or fruit, then saunter off to visit Grosz'mama, or up the dusty road west to get to the Clarke farm. She got so she watched for opportunity to have such a day once a week, or after a crisis in the city.

An evening visit included Scottie and Brandt, and was different, but a morning or afternoon with Isabelle meant stimulating chatter while they sewed, painted, washed windows together, or whatever project Isabelle had set for herself that day. But the chatter was always on safe topics. A few corners had been polished and rounded off Isabelle's blunt personality by this time. She was never slow to speak her mind, but Ruthe found Isabelle to be a loyal friend, one who meant well and who respected her.

Both confessed to daydreamy moods in spring when the warmer winds came and whispered, "All things are possible!" before the snow was all melted away. They giggled over their spring fever.

Ruthe did not tell Isabelle about her city friends, but she shared freely about her habit of going for early dawn walks because she knew Isabelle would respond well, if she only would try it.

"Hah! Not me," her friend retorted without thinking of Ruthe's feelings. Isabelle was partial to sleeping in on mornings when Regina happened to do so, or Brandt got up quietly and looked after changing and entertaining her, so mommy could sneak in an extra half hour or so on her pillow. The idea of dressing early to walk outside and watch a colour show in the eastern sky, while praying, seemed just a bit much to Isabelle. "You wouldn't have time if you had a baby!" she exclaimed when Ruthe's early morning walks came up.

Ruthe shrugged. *I haven't got Phyllis' heart to force someone to something that I know they'll like.*

Isabelle sincerely desired to live as a good Christian. She thought her own relationship with her Saviour was so special that she wished her parents and her sister Jean would accept the Lord Jesus as Saviour too. She confided to Ruthe how she had tried to tell them about it, but they just set it aside as her religious experience.

The Squires tried to be careful when they came to visit Isabelle and Scottie, and their granddaughter whom they adored, not to come on a weekend. They felt they would be expected to go along to church.

God likes variety, Ruthe told herself, so she accepted variety in her friendship too, but she suspected Isabelle would have to change a little more before her family would come around.

Scottie and Brandt spent a lot of long hours in the spring and summer on the buildings and farmyard. The farm functioned self-sufficiently enough so that Scottie planned to quit his city job as soon as he obtained a small dairy quota. The place looked groomed.

"Just think, Ruthe," Isabelle exclaimed repeatedly, "Scottie's a pillar in the community, and can forget about being a lab go-fer. How these two years here at Kleinstadt have flown!"

Ruthe smiled with twinkling eyes at Isabelle, "Look at you, eh? Happily married, living in the country with no bears on the porch, handling your baby like a practiced mother, and growing plump with the next one!"

"All because you befriended us strangers."

Raising her face and hand upward, Ruthe said, "There's a compliment for You, Lord. Remember, I promised You the glory?"

Brandt was proud to be Regina's "uncle" and could change and carry her around as if an old hand with babies. He was the one who started calling her Reggie, and although Isabelle made a point of saying at church that their little girl's name was Regina, she and Scottie called her Reggie too, when they were tickling and playing with her. She grew fast, and in no time was sitting up straight on any eager arm, swinging her head around to look at everyone, making her carroty red curls bounce. By August, if anyone came closer to talk to Reggie, she broke into a broad baby smile, tipping back her freckled nose, and puckered up her lips for a kiss.

Uncle Brandt and others got to handle Regina quite a lot over the summer, for Isabelle had surprised herself and Scottie. She referred to herself as a baby machine, for they expected another by the end of December. This time she was feeling a little off of her energetic self and took frequent naps.

Ruthe had thought of her Grosz'mama as a very old lady, so it amazed her to find her at the Clarkes so frequently. Grosz'mama did not seem to mind being picked up by the Clarkes and brought out to the farm every few days to watch Regina, while Isabelle went to doctor appointments, or just napped. Grosz'mama had often told the story of how her parents had a set of twins, a boy and a girl, when she turned ten. "It was my duty to stop school, as I could read n' write so well as our teacher, by that time. My work was to wash diapers every day."

Through the summer and fall Isabelle often joked that she felt big enough, and heavy enough to be having twins. However, her doctor told her he found only one heartbeat.

FIFTY-EIGHT

"Listen to my heart beat," Lloyd said one bitterly cold January evening. In the telephone receiver Ruthe heard a muffled thum-thum-thum. She was stunned. What did Lloyd want to prove by this? *Is this suppost to be romantic?* After a long pause, Lloyd asked, "Ruthe? Are you still there?"

"Ahm... yes."

"What do you think it's saying?"

"It's unlike you to be so cryptic; why don't you explain it?"

"I guess I'm trying to say I like you." Another pause. "A lot."

"I thought we already were friends. Is this something new?"

A minute slipped by. "Ruthe, I didn't think you were totally innocent."

"Innocent, yes, I hope so. Ignorant, no." Ruthe sighed, "I probably have enough romantic feelings in me to blow up–" she grasped for a good symbol, "Bright City. But Lloyd, I know if I don't save them for the right person I can ruin my reputation and maybe my life. A few other lives besides. I'm prepared to wait for the Lord's guidance. I want the romance He's writing for me."

Lloyd remarked that this was great, and he wished everyone was so noble, then he said a hurried good bye and hung up. It was some time before Ruthe heard from or ran into him again.

Dr. Davie Pollock had made approaches too.

When Ruthe had discovered that Maggie had scheduled Laura for an abortion, and that Davie had been called in when the other doctor did not show up, and that he had delivered and saved Lois alive, it gave Ruthe a whole new respect for him. He sensed it when she lined him up to be Laura and Lois' regular physician.

Davie was friendly and full of compliments on how terrific she looked in her vivid blue shirt dress with the gold and black braid trims on the collar and cuffs, "Got to be silk, right?"

"No-no, just polished cotton. Oops," Ruthe said quickly, remembering Cathy's reminders, "I'm suppost to say thank you."

"Your hair looks thick and luscious with those natural curls tumbling down to your shoulders like that."

Ruthe couldn't help herself, she shrugged, "What can I do? Mom and Grosz'mama want at least one descendant to keep her hair long. Only my little sister and I have resisted going modern. Who can tell what she'll do yet."

"Speaking of family," Ruthe said, "I have to be home shortly. You asked me here to discuss Laura?"

364

Davie had been sitting-leaning against the front of his desk with his legs crossed at the knees. He now uncrossed them, pulled a chair up at right angles to Ruthe's knees and sat, leaning forward, to talk very frankly with her. "Ruthe, are you open to romance at all? You are a very fascinating person with a passion for people, but you really don't ever open doors for a 'relationship' do you?"

Ruthe opened her mouth, then closed it to smile blushingly at Davie. She liked his direct approach. She could easily be direct yet cheerful in response. Clapping her hand on his knee she said, "Dr. Davie, you are cute. You make something in me smile. So maybe the potential for chemistry is there. But–" she quickly took her hand back as she saw he was about to put his on top of it, "I'm complicated enough to look for other things to match up too before I'll open myself to romance. I have a secret deal with God; I'm to throw myself into helping people in need, doing the very things I want to be caught doing when He comes to collect me unannounced for the big wedding feast in Heaven, and without constantly on the lookout for a life's partner, and, He's to line up the right Prince Charming for me, and bring him into my life at the exact right moment, if that means I will serve Him better in a marriage than alone. I figure, Davie, that if I hold out for the very best God can dream up then I'll be sufficiently wowed to be satisfied the rest of my life."

The doctor had been watching her face intently throughout her inspired speech. "You knock me out!" he snorted softly. He added more reverently, "I bet much of the world will be wowed too." Then, with a wrinkled, puzzled brow he asked, "Do you get teased a lot about that –idealistic view?"

Ruthe sniffed up a laugh, "You were the first direct enough to ask."

"So?" she asked, trying to change the subject, "Any ideas to help Laura stay home and babysit Lois all by herself?"

"Hmm. If I'm not God's dream husband for you, am I good enough for Laura? I could marry her and she could stay home, except that Laura won't let me near herself without your permission."

Bright marbles for eyes, and unable to hold back the twinkles at the corners of her mouth, Ruthe leaned forward. "I love it!" Eagerly she gave him some very practical tips for winning Laura's confidence. Proceed slowly, was her key advice, "And be faithful! In fact, I will deliberately counsel Laura to respond slowly and to test your character, just as I might– in her shoes."

After two days off and staying in Kleinstadt, Ruthe found messages to call Laura back on the bulletin at work, plus two more when she got back from her break. She had meant to visit her after work. She found the same messages waiting for her at the Chrysalis. Joy, calling moments after Linnet and Byron gave her those, was tracking her down with the same message: *Call Laura Weal!*

She reached Laura still at work, tremendously relieved to hear from her. "Ruthe! Our doctor has asked me for a date! What shall I say?"

By Valentine's Day, Lois' first birthday, Ruthe had vicariously been on three dates with Laura and Davie. Laura gave her line-for-line accounts, and anxiously wanted to know what to do and what not to do. She was almost phobic about making another life-altering mistake.

Davie sought Ruthe out too. When they discussed Laura's intense reserve, she warned him sternly, "Whatever you do, Davie, no sex before marriage. Laura needs to see your gentle, playful side, as a human being, not just the Almighty Doctor."

By Easter Davie had persuaded Laura (after Ruthe told her it was okay) to visit his family, up north of Nipawin, and take along Lois.

Answering Laura's probing questions about requirements to look for in a husband, for being a good wife, and how to decide if a man was God's choice set Ruthe to a lot of thinking and praying on the subject. She got a clearer grasp of why the men so far in her life did not qualify.

Ross had been too immature. She wondered what Ann would do if he grew up one day, after all, and wanted a wife instead of a mother. That could still happen, since his attention was off himself now.

Although she admired Peter Green's noble goal of fatherhood and providing a home for unwanted kids, he lacked the spiritual depth she now realized she had unwittingly hoped for or expected. *Mind you,* she told herself and the Lord, *Sophie is all mercy and heart, so she is content. She wasn't looking for the depth of a Scottie.*

Davie Pollock lacked that too. Loves appeared to come and go easily for him. Ruthe hoped he would not tire of Laura one day and look for a fresh conquest. She feared Laura had not enough originality to keep Davie fascinated for years on end, but she did wish the security of marriage for Laura.

Lloyd? she asked her quiet Friend. Ruthe could not quite put her finger on why Lloyd was not her man, but she knew it more completely.

"What would make the perfect man for you?" Laura had asked before her Easter trip up north.

After a thoughtful pause, Ruthe answered, "I'm still becoming– but, right now I think he should be a man as strongly committed to Christ as I am, or more. He should be grown up emotionally, and have spiritual depth. By that I mean, all nine character traits of God's Spirit, and to think much deeper than just eat, sleep, and work. I want to respect him and be his loyal friend. I want to trust him with secrets. And, he should be a good father!" Ruthe stopped to smile mischieveously, "I think I'm going to end up with a great big wonderful family."

FIFTY-NINE

Someone Ruthe often studied for traits of a good husband was Scottie Clarke. Not for a moment did she consider taking him away from Isabelle. They were her happily married friends and she had no desire to come between them. They often invited her over, as they urged any one they met to come, for they had picked up Grosz'mama's hospitality.

People from the small town and surrounding farms and hamlets often came by in the evenings to the Clarke farm. Scottie led the men into the family room where they talked over both business and personal problems. He seemed to have an answer, or an outline for finding it, for anything from social perplexities, farm bookkeeping to civic leadership. Ruthe could not help but admire him when she saw him sitting in his favourite chair, earnestly listening to his guests and giving advice in that soft-spoken way.

Brandt sat in on most of those sessions, learning a thousand things not in his textbooks. Isabelle preferred to stay out of their living room when strangers wanted help. Scottie had taught her to respect confidentiality, so Ruthe would then stay in the kitchen with her and help in handling Regina, until Scottie waved them in.

There were times of course, when Scottie had no other guests, and she, like Brandt, was just part of the family circle. Ruthe had to accept some ribbing about her single state. Just as often, she could test ideas or opinions. Sometimes she got so relaxed she had to stop herself from blurting out, "Between you and some city friends my maternal instincts get played like a violin!"

Sometimes the conversations were very stimulating and set her to thinking long after she departed. Not always comfortably.

Pastor Ewart was also fond of discussions with the Clarkes. He said it helped him to sort out points logically, to express himself more clearly. So Isabelle thought nothing of inviting the Ewarts as well as Ruthe over after a Sunday evening service for coffee, which was a full table spread, like what her Grosz'mama called night lunch. Elbows on the table, they would get absorbed in some doctrinal or philosophical point and be talking until well after midnight.

Growing up with her parents' attitude, that church ministers were in a class to be awed as more righteous or wise, Ruthe found it hard at first to be herself when Pastor Ewart was present. With time she found him to be quite human and understanding, and Mrs. Ewart a very tenderhearted and shy woman, so she relaxed and talked honestly.

The pastor and his wife, Elfrieda, were impressed with Ruthe's grasp of Scriptures and how she gave herself with a reckless abandon to love and obey whatever she understood of the Bible's teaching. They praised her and complimented Ruthe until she felt quite warm and safe.

Brandt, always listening in on the same discussions, participated too, and Ruthe was pleased to think she saw signs of his steady maturity. For herself, but mostly for Brandt's sake she sometimes thanked God for turning her brashness in that apartment building into these precious friendships. *Must've been Grosz'mama's prayers*, she thought.

For someone a Christian only just over a year, Scottie had a remarkable understanding of human personality and how Christ's teaching integrated into every problem. Ruthe toyed for days with the idea of confiding in Scottie, and asking his help in bridging the gap between herself and her parents. Several times she was ready and willing, only there was never a perfect, uninterrupted moment to bring it up.

Once in a while, on a walk, Ruthe would entertain thoughts about telling her parents the truth. Soon her mind would seize up with fear, or she remembered something else she had promised someone– that had to be done first.

She was spending more Saturday mornings writing in Phyllis' apartment, taking Sharri's place, who had to curl up in a corner with a book. Phyllis had many projects for re-making people, but her main mission seemed to be to coax Ruthe into greatness as a writer. She made Ruthe sit at the typewriter and work. She might spend a few minutes with Sharri, then came to point out editing and plotting corrections, leaning on Ruthe's shoulders. Many of those mistakes Ruthe didn't make any more, so now she could lose herself in a story. The ideas flowed and her stumbling fingers gradually got faster and faster on the keys.

After a while Phyllis persuaded Ruthe to combine several short ones into a longer novel length that ran much parallel to her own city experiences. With all this tutorial drilling on plot motives, she began to see into her own sub-conscious reasons for actions, however, Ruthe still found it hard to cope with the truth. She often went away swallowing tears and thinking, *Lord, You are a much gentler counsellor!*

Phyllis means well, Lord, Ruthe defended her tutor. *She's such an encyclopedia of knowledge, and she believes she's helping me, and she is– really, she is! But did we forget salt? Where is the missing salt in all this?*

SIXTY

At Darlin' Bonne's Shop, months before Christmas, the new craze was making stuffed animals and dolls. Ruthe and Sharri spent some happy hours picking up this timely skill. The selection of antiques at the Chrysalis storeroom was nearly depleted, so Ruthe planned to sew up quite a few gifts this time. The sewing of these toys went over wonderfully at home, and bought peace. Together, or also separately, Ruthe and Sharri pretended to stumble on a pattern, then experimented at it until they caught on to thes basic steps. Then they adapted these patterns to make crowds of teddy bears, dolls and other creatures from a few meters of fun fur and what odd remnants they found at home. Their mother and sister were quite impressed and egged them on. "Try this cute one. Make this one, girls!"

From a bed heaped high with toys, Sharri and Ruthe chose gifts for most of the children they knew. When narrowing down the choices was hard, they put together two or three.

Suzanne soon complained that she needed another wardrobe; nothing fit right, or it was too old. Her mother's answer was, "I never owned so many clothes as you girls in my whole life! I used to have two dresses, both made of flour sack cotton. When one was in the wash I used the other one." The three sisters all gave each other winks and glances for it was an old song. To Ruthe's mind there was nothing to do but sew them each a new outfit or two, even if the muscles in her shoulders were knotted.

To ensure there would be a few surprises at Christmas the sewing sisters did their cutting and sewing in fits and spurts when the house seemed empty, usually around faspa time most afternoons. That was when Grosz'mama was most likely to have guests. It was convenient that Sharri could finish Ruthe's work."

Mrs. Veer didn't notice. Her mother had decided to accept an invitation for an extended visit with her other daughters and their families in British Columbia. She was packing to go right after Christmas. Anna was upset because– she didn't know exactly why, though she offered thin excuses. Mainly, Ruthe and Sharri said, (and Suzanne agreed), it was because their mother thought no one could look after her mother as well as she. She didn't like her routines messed up. She counted on her mother always being there for her.

Isabelle asked in her outspoken way, if their mother had grown used to thinking of Grosz'mama as too old to travel or do anything but be there. Scottie and Isabelle were rather pleased that she wanted to make the trip, and gave her enthusiastic support.

Ruthe wondered, *what could go wrong? Aunt Maria is coming to travel with Grosz'mama on the plane. Strangers might stare but surely would not offend the demure matron in Old Colony Mennonite clothing.* These travel plans made Christmas different. For one, Isabelle Clarke wanted to have the family Christmas gathering in their home, but Anna Veer pulled rank, "Ekj sei jedoch de elsta ajchte Dochta!"[25]

Ruthe comforted her friend, Isabelle, by whispering, "You'll get your chances yet. Probably far more than my Mom."

This was meant to make less work for Grosz'mama and Aunt Maria since they were packed before Christmas, and would leave on Boxing Day so as to avoid the rush of travellers going home the day after. But it made Grosz'mama conspicuous. They were all used to seeing her in her big navy blue apron with the tiny white dots, minding the turkey and meal preparations; now she was a guest, having interesting conversation in the living room with Scottie and her son-in-law, Ben. Ruthe and her mother were fussing in the kitchen, trying to make Suzanne and Sharri come in to do something too.

Isabelle was so big, all she could do was waddle about, setting cutlery and napkins on the table. She complained of backache and wished repeatedly that this baby would come soon. "Any day now, boy. You are welcome any day!" she murmured between asking Ruthe about the carolling the night before.

They wondered together about the Prince's second Christmas, hopefully in a happy home too, as they watched Sharri, Regina and Brandt have a great day full of playing with stuffed animals.

New Year's Eve was the holiday Ruthe had to work this time, and she was notified on the switchboard that Isabelle finally had to come into the city to have her baby. She hurried over to the hospital after her shift finished at two a.m., and discovered that Curtis Boyd had missed being the New Year's baby by arriving three seconds before midnight. He was a big, heavy baby with vim and vinegar in his cries.

The soft fuzz of hair on his head was a hot tomato red, Scottie reported, when she joined him by the nursery window. "I think our days of perfectly behaved babies are over," he added with a soft chuckle, "On to harder courses in parenting for Belle and me."

SIXTY-ONE

In a month or so Isabelle talked of wanting to be pregnant a third time, as she proudly informed anyone who showed the least interest. "Having babies is easy for me," she said. "Even Curtis, who is a bit more demanding– just like me– is a good challenge."

With no Grosz'mama to visit, Ruthe was at their farm a little more often that winter. Challenge and noise were key words.

At last a quieter time came. Scottie and Brandt had taken Regina along to go to the airport to pick up Grosz'mama one morning in March. Curtis was asleep on a quilt on the table. Ruthe was having a gab-fest with Isabelle while they waited for their beloved matriarch.

"Remember what we were saying Sunday night about being commanded to pray in faith?" Isabelle asked, "About getting answers when we pray specifically, according to God's will, and in Jesus' name?"

Ruthe nodded, "It works."

"Let me tell you a secret," said Isabelle dramatically, "I believe I'm pregnant again, and I've been dreaming of having twins. I want a boy and a girl who will both look like Scottie for a change." She stopped to make a wry face as she deftly tumbled Curtis back into his blankets. He had tossed them off and was rolling over towards the edge of the table, even while asleep.

"Ruthe, I've been praying about it, believing with all my might, and asking in Jesus' name, all of that. Now I'm more sure every day I will have a set of identical twins."

The guest tossed her hair away with splayed fingers and made a puzzled face. "I thought identicals could only be same-sex twins."

"Oh. Okay then, look-alike or fraternals is what I mean."

Isabelle launched into how these children would look and their traits. She wove in a description of how she had laid out fleeces the previous week to confirm it all.

"Someone once said this is the way novelists talk." Ruthe teased gently. "Are you sure you aren't pregnant with a fabulous story plot?" However, the expression on Isabelle caused her to halt the teasing. This young mother was dead serious.

"Isabelle," she said still more carefully, "Don't hurt yourself by telling anyone else. Kleinstadt is on a different wave-length than us dreamers and visionaries."

"Why? What kind of dreams have they killed for you?"

But Isabelle didn't have the patience for the answer. She quickly assured Ruthe that Scottie and she were the only ones who knew about this part. "He said maybe you would see it more objectively and be able to encourage or discourage me accordingly." There was pleading in the redhead's voice.

Ruthe looked thoughtful for a minute, *So-o, I've got to speak for God again?*

While she hesitated Isabelle added excitedly, "Want to know their names?" She sat back triumphantly, "I'm going to call them Evangel Gospel and Evangeline Grace!"

Gulping a laugh, Ruthe managed to say, "Hey, you're a poet through and through! Those... those are quite... um, Christian names, eh?"

Isabelle laughed too, but Ruthe could tell she was still waiting for a more enthusiastic reaction. "I suppose they'll end up with nicknames like Evan and Vangie."

Those were not so bad, Ruthe decided, and told Isabelle they were growing on her. "Sort of romantic and odd, like Prince Charming, eh? Once we get used to a name, and if it suits, then any name takes on the character of the person wearing it."

An awkward moment fell. Was Isabelle waiting for more? Ruthe prayed silently, *Now Lord, what can I say? Is she dreaming? Is this really from You? She could be awfully disappointed if You don't give her twins. Maybe You have promised to her. How am I to know?*

"Ruthe–" Isabelle said, after scooping up the waking Curtis and putting him blanket and all on the shiny off-white vinyl floor. "You think I'm... overdoing it? Off the beam?"

She began slowly, "It's perfectly possible that the Lord might give you twins in answer to your prayers of faith. He's shown me what I think might be visions and promises, and some have come true, so I can not dare to presume that you can't get them too."

"But? You're hesitating."

"Ahm-m. Since I haven't had this dream I can only concentrate on the signals that I've read about confirming God's will. I may get more excited once I catch your enthusiasm."

"Oh-but, Ruthe, I feel so sure of it myself!" Isabelle cried, "What other proofs or confirmations do you need?"

"One. If God answers your prayer, would it honour and glorify Jesus Christ, His Son? That's spelled out in First John."

"I just know it will!"

"Okay, I believe you. Do you have a specific promise from His Word to stand on? And, do your physical circumstances corroborate the likelihood of this... event?"

"Do I ever!" Isabelle responded, leaning down to hand Curtis a rattle, "Jesus said in John 24:14, *If you ask Me anything in My name, I will do it.* And somewhere in Matthew, *Everything you ask in prayer, believing, you shall receive.* Ruthe, I've done all that. My faith is big enough. Fact is, I've been thanking Him in advance, like that travelling singer suggested the other week. What's left to do?"

The station wagon drove up and they both rose from their chairs at the kitchen table. Ruthe was about to make a yielding, concluding statement when she remembered that Isabelle had not answered for the supportive circumstances. "What does your doctor say?"

"Dr. Pollock?" Isabelle was peering through the print curtains and announced, "Here's our Grosz'mama!"

"He says I'm quite capable of having twins. We can't check on Scottie's blood lines, but there were some twin cousins on my Dad's side."

Their little talk ended as Grosz'mama came through the door. Brandt followed, shouting over her head, "Here she is!"

Regina, stiff in her blue snowsuit, sat on his arm, wanted down immediately. Reaching for Grosz'mama's hand, she echoed sweetly, "Here she is!"

Curtis set up a confused howl as they gathered around the beloved old grandmother. "Hello Grosz'mama," Ruthe greeted her first with the usual hearty handshake, and then a shy after-thought kiss. "Woo ging daut fleajen?"[26]

"Goot. Goot!"[27] her grandmother pumped her hand warmly, then turned to Isabelle, who had picked up Curtis so he could see and be seen. She received Isabelle's greeting and kiss, and gave one to Curtis too, caressing his head. He curled away shyly to his mother for a moment, but when he heard Reggie say, "Come Grosz'ma. I show you my room," he suddenly threw his legs as if sensing the competition for attention.

Isabelle and Ruthe wanted to hear all about the three months in B.C. and let their Grosz'mama know how relieved they were that she had not decided to stay there. In some letters she had said her daughters were urging her to do that. Now they had to wait while the lady dressed in long black pleats and black apron, covered at the top with a lacy black cardigan, all buttoned up, went to see Regina's room. It was all papered in pink rosebuds and filled with white girls' furniture courtesy of her Grandma and Grandpa Squires.

Ruthe felt proud and loving towards the sedate back going down the hall, with the Sunday best black kerchief on her head. The long silk fringes and the bright red and pink and maroon roses embroidered in the back corner rested familiarly on Grosz'mama's back.

When Grosz'mama had admired Regina's room and come back into the kitchen to pick up Curtis and become better acquainted with this new grandchild, Isabelle teased, "Looks like this cross-country roaming makes you plump and rosy, Grosz'mama."

She smiled brightly with a bit of embarrassment, "Yah, ev'rywhere dey feed me so good. I might wey ten pouns mor'n when I left."

Scottie came in, after putting away the car and a quick look in the barn at a cow in labour. He put down two old, but well-preserved suitcases, tucked an affectionate arm around Grosz'mama and said, "We're so glad you count us as family too, and are with us again."

"Wal, I don't vant to wear out my velcome," she answered demurely. However, all could see by the happy beams on her face, that she was glad to be here, and that she hoped to be useful. Especially, since Scottie had told her on the way, she admitted, that Isabelle wanted to be pregnant again. Her other grandchildren were more grown; with this size she said she felt she could still be helpful.

From other conversations with her grandmother, Ruthe knew the fact that Scottie and Isabelle worked at a consistent pattern of family discipline impressed her. Also, that they openly worked at learning the Christian life. *Besides*, Ruthe thought, *how can she help but enjoy the respect, the compliments, and love they give her here.*

SIXTY-TWO

Phyllis was effusive about Ruthe's natural skill at noticing details, and writing dialogue. "All you needed was some help with good habits and tips for marketing. Keep looking up words and check your own spelling and grammar mercilessly. Eventually these little basics will become second nature to you, and you won't run into friction with editors. Practice will make your natural gift shine."

These compliments encouraged Ruthe, but she did not always remember to accept them graciously even yet, so she added with a self-depreciating little sniff, "...But I'm still weak on plotting."

Phyllis went over her story with the proverbial fine-tooth comb, explaining tiny things to tighten her writing. Moments like this made Ruthe appreciate Phyllis' thoroughness and perfectionism; others would have to crack the whip on themselves to learn this discipline. When buoyed with the action line, and Phyllis at her shoulder saying, "Yes! That's it!" Ruthe often blurted, "This is too much fun to be fair!"

She stopped looking for new friends, and dropped others that did not absolutely lean on her, so that she could slip over to Phyllis' apartment an extra evening when possible. Ruthe could tell her priorities were shifting.

"Sharri's worried the Charm n' Poise Course might not be offered again this summer," Phyllis confided, raising a new priority. "She understood you to promise last year, that you'd only skip one summer."

"I know." Ruthe replied. "With Lisa there, and funds low, and stuff...."

"She and I were planning a few improvements last Saturday, but she has seen how many guests Lisa keeps bringing into the Chrysalis."

"Yes, Sharri's after me to give them notice, but I don't know if I can get them all to move out for July and August. Some look rather shabby, and she doesn't think they'll fit in with the young set." So far Ruthe had no idea what to do about this. She didn't want to disappoint Sharri again, but she was stymied.

They took a mental head count; thirteen guests, including Lisa. A few of those behaved as if they had found a place to bed down and sponge up kindness indefinitely, with no sense of personal initiative.

Kindness was ingrained in Ruthe, so she urged faith in God to Phyllis, Sharri, and whenever they met, to June also, for money for groceries and utilities was low. Ruthe quoted what she had read about George Mueller feeding thousands of orphans by prayer and implicit faith in God. None could argue with that, even Sharri, the least patient. A day or so later, a freelance office decorating job that June had just finished over the winter brought in a sizable payment, and she willingly donated most of it for groceries. That eased things for about three to four weeks.

Just when the decorating money ran out, Phyllis gave Ruthe a cheque arriving at her address, for a short personal experience of hers. In tearful honesty Ruthe had written up that testimony. Phyllis had made her improve it over and over, then offered to mail it away for her. "My writing sold?" Ruthe screeched in amazement.

"Of course. It was excellent. The editor thought so too; read this memo." While Ruthe devoured it, Phyllis added, "Keep this up and you will manage to feed your guests without a problem."

A wave of utter weariness washed over Ruthe as she closed her eyes. She was tired of so much responsibility. All the expectations of her friends, which she felt bound to meet, plus, now taking up full-time writing? *How long can I live three lives at once, Lord?* she sighed. *Yet I haven't got the heart to choose one and cross off the others.* For a few moments she tried on in her imagination, a quiet writer's life. Then she decided abruptly, that since no one but Lisa was helping these poor girls come off the street and start living differently, she had better hang in there. *Sharri's summer course will be a one year flash-in-the-pan.*

Nothing seemed to change. If anything Ruthe's life got more crowded as friends laid expectations on her. Phyllis deliberately looked for her each week and insisted that she come sit in her book-lined study to write for two or three hours.

Lisa and Ruthe prayed together several times for a solution to the congestion at the Chrysalis, and Ruthe usually asked Phyllis to join her in praying about it too, before she could turn to the typewriter.

One day, she and Lisa were out looking for a married couple, bookkeepers, with an interest in real estate. Lisa was sure they would sublet some small apartments to which she could take her friends for the summer, when they passed the very house in the basement of which they had met around those old wringer washing machines. Both yelped when they saw a FOR SALE sign on the tiny lawn. They backed up and copied the phone number, then called from the first pay phone they saw.

It belonged to the very couple Lisa was looking for; they would sub-let the apartments if they had to, but would be happy to sell the building. It needed more renovation than they were prepared to do for their speculation purposes. Because of its run down condition and bad reputation the asking price was reasonable. Crowded into the dirty phone booth Ruthe looked at Lisa, who had the receiver to her ear. "You could be their resident landlady," Ruthe declared in a hopeful whisper, "We'd control the lifestyle standards."

"Yes!" Lisa shouted, her right arm raised high, "Yes!" She promised further contact, and they came out of the stiffling booth to talk.

Ruthe hated borrowing but impulsively was willing for this cause.

"The difficulty would be getting Charlie Brown and Judge Tomas to see it as a good idea," said Lisa. "I've been living clean a year now, but they'd be afraid I'd turn it into a brothel. They remember what kind of business woman I've been before."

"Let's not assume," said Ruthe feeling bold, "Let's go ask."

To their relief, the Chief Probation Officer, who had learned to appreciate Ruthe's positive influence on Lisa by her reports, and their police friends all voted confidence in them, and told them to go ahead. "They really believe in us! Hallelujah!" they sang.

Charlie Brown had only stipulated that he wanted a standing invitation to check out the place if he ever got worried.

"Any time!" Lisa offered generously. "I'll stick around and serve you coffee and cake." Laughter rippled as they recalled the unique slips she had given them in the past.

Bringing her regular report into the courthouse offices a day or so later, Ruthe met Judge Tomas in the hallway. He asked, "What is Ms Starr doing these days?"

Bright-eyed and in a warm, cheerful voice, Ruthe confided that she and Lisa were checking out the possibility of buying the old building where she had met Lisa. They would remodel it in jade marble and gold trims, then Lisa could be the encouraging, guarding landlady to a bunch of single, working girls, who would rent the light-housekeeping suites.

Ruthe saw the judge draw in his breath and his eyes narrow as if he smelled trouble in this idea. In an effort to convince him she was very involved in Lisa's life and well aware of everything she did, Ruthe quickly volunteered, "In fact, if we can ever afford to buy it, I'm planning to rent a room at this place. My parents do no end of worrying about all my highway driving at strange hours." She laughed faintly, "If I can just get them to trust me to live in the city. They are real scared of city dangers and temptations."

Judge Tomas replied to her breathless chatter with slow, measured words. "I have been very impressed with your thorough reports. You focus much on her spiritual development. Your observations implicate a lasting change in Lisa. This apartment idea could," he paused thoughtfully, "it could appear as a front for a brothel. However since you are right in the thick of it, and you have such high moral standards; and if you are going to be in the building yourself, I will give you my blessing."

He favoured Ruthe with a slow smile. "There's nothing quite like transforming something vulgar into something holy, is there?"

She tried her best to agree and thank him without getting gushy and any more than dewy-eyed as she shook his hand, then stepped into the Probation office with her report.

Lisa found, when she inquired at several banks and financial institutions, news of her transformation had got around; she had a fairly good credit rating. She was able to borrow enough to buy and remodel that old building without any loans from Ruthe.

Ruthe was secretly pleased that she would not carry any debt on her own shoulders. The Rambler she had paid off long ago, and the girls at the shop had paid off the one from Pearl O'Brien's art collection, but the operating expenses at the Chrysalis weighed her down. She bubbled with relief when she reported Lisa's successful loan at Darlin' Bonne's that night.

Betty squinted at her quizzically. "If you are so broke, on what are you spending all your share of the shop's profits?"

It was Ruthe's turn to look perplexed. "Huh?"

Darlin' Bonne jumped in, "Didn't you say that we should keep twenty percent for operating funds after salaries and the O'Brien loan was paid? And, if there was any gravy, to put your share in your old Greystone account?"

Ruthe leaped up to her feet. "You mean, the loan's paid off? We're out of debt? Free and clear?"

Betty, Darlin' Bonne and Evelyn had great fun convincing Ruthe that the loan had been paid off more than a year ago, and her half of the gravy, after expenses, had been averaging two to five hundred dollars a month since Christmas.

"Which account–?" Ruthe was confused, for she went in to ask about the balance so frequently.

Evelyn found the number on a deposit carbon.

For a full minute Ruthe stared at it, sorting details in her head. "Do you know," she said slowly, "This is the account I opened in that big brown Trust building downtown, when I met that lady to sell her the crystal. I forgot about it, and have never used that account after our shopping spree to furnish the new house for Mom and Dad. I thought I had emptied it." June and she both used the bank near the SaskTel building. It was from there they paid the mansion's bills.

"You should check this account tomorrow," advised Evelyn.

"I sure will! I can hardly wait!" Ruthe answered getting gleeful. "Our God of perfect timings even makes miracles out of our mistakes!"

It was April. The university students were free and Ross O'Brien was flattered that Ruthe approached him again, to work in partnership with Keith and his woodworking friends, to do the remodelling for Lisa's building over the summer months. "You can hire your Mueller sons if you need extra workmen," she said, "But Lisa and I have brainstormed up some unique features, so you'll have to tell us first if they are architecturally feasible."

After four more lively brainstorming sessions including Ross, some concessions and adjustments, the O'Brien company went to work. Lisa hoped to clear out of the Chrysalis by July 1, taking along her street friends, so they had a deadline.

They covered the old beige granite with a new smooth exterior. Using special tools to pre-paint the panels with a dark green jade marble, then coat them with a tough but clear resin plastic, they gave the whole house a polished, elegant look. All the trim was painted a brilliant, reflecting gold. The building shone in the sun.

Ruthe beamed proudly as she watched Glenn, Barry, and Christopher bustle about helping Ross and Uncle Keith with this job that made the front page of the newspaper. Even eight-year old Eldon scrambled about, fetching and handing tools, with a loud, "I can get it!"

"I predicted right," she murmured happily.

June helped Lisa order new furniture and to paint or wallpaper nearly everything inside. Ruthe learned new skills just helping them occasionally. New colours and new lighting features made tremendous differences. A big expense was the brand new elevator they had installed, and the jade-green broadloom on the stairs, with the brand new bannisters and spindle posts of brass. Cathy showed them where to order a stunning chandelier with the look of cut glass for the ceiling in the lobby.

It got a little hectic and crowded when the electricians came to put in the new furnace and heating system at the same time that Ross and his young crew were turning the damp, mouldy basement into a modern, well-lit utility room, and beside it, a beauty lounge.

The utility-laundry room was now a shiny white and yellow tiled place with up-to-date laundry facilities.

They repeated the jade effect on the rest of the basement floor, but the walls of the makeup lounge became a misty sea aqua. They built in a wall-length counter with mirrors and true lighting all around.

After a week of intensively cleaning every corner the last week of June, Lisa and Ruthe were ready to take delivery of the new furnishings for Moss Rose. They had meant to call it Regency House until they found another building so named. While transplanting some of the climbing roses from the walls of the Chrysalis, they settled on a rose's name as a tribute to Ruthe's secret garden images. This house of light-housekeeping rooms became the Moss Rose.

379

On Saturday morning Ruthe dropped Sharri off at the Chrysalis where she and Phyllis, and a crew of alumni from two summers earlier, tackled the cleaning and physical preparations for a new Charm n' Poise Course as fast as the current guests packed to move to the Moss Rose.

Lisa, in jeans and a white t-shirt, Ruthe, in beige dress slacks and an embroidered cotton blouse were outside the front door of the Moss Rose, waiting for the delivery trucks, and admiring several tall shade trees up and down the street.

Most of the suites were promised to their "butterflies" who were on their way that day from the mansion. Lisa had claimed the one at the back on the main floor. However, two suites on the third floor were still available for rent, so they went inside to Lisa's suite for bristol board and a black marker. Leaning on the left cement balustrade, beside the steps, they neatly hand-lettered a sign, *Lighthousekeeping Rooms to Rent.*

Ruthe had not yet raised the subject with her parents, of herself moving to the city. She promised Lisa she'd do that soon. Before Judge Tomas might ask why not. Therefore they agreed to cross off the s in Rooms.

Just then three cars pulled up and parked on the opposite side of the street. Ginter and Aubrey and six other men from the police force, dressed in casual clothes came sauntering over. "Good morning," said the gallant and charming Aubrey. "We got the day off."

"We've come to repay some favours," Ginter added helpfully.

Stunned and incredulous, Ruthe and Lisa stared.

"Aren't you expecting big trucks full of furniture?" asked one of the other men.

"Yes, we are," the women began to giggle, "No less than twelve suites of heavy beds and dressers."

"Hum-m," snorted Aubrey, "Quarter after nine; so where are they?"

Then, "As your introductory godfathers we have obliga–"

"Hey, you guys," Lisa choked, "Th-thanks!"

Ruthe nodded vigorously, "Sure good to have friends like you!" Just before her eyes filled up she caught sight of Charlie Brown and Wally walking up behind the group.

It was one of those overwhelmingly physical and spiritual days, that later blurred in Ruthe's memory because of repeatedly setting up similar pieces of furniture, but it had scenes that shone like a bright light whenever she thought over her life, especially that moment, because of the good will of those men.

SIXTY-THREE

Ruthe's mother always worried about her being on the highway so often at night. She set it aside as the fretting of a simple country woman, who feared the great unknowns of the city. Ruthe played down the dangers, and made sure never ever to report any near accidents, or to describe any unusual people she met. It was her way of protecting her mom from unnecessary worries.

After frequent prayer, and carefully plotting her words and timing, Ruthe asked her parents, "Would you like to come see a small light-housekeeping room in the city? I was thinking I could stay there whenever I'm working late shifts to save some midnight driving." She was startled at how gladly her mother jumped at the idea.

"All this time I've been worrying for you! Out of the blue today you finally think about my feelings?" Her mother nagged her dad to change out of his work clothes while she and Ruthe did dishes.

Ruthe and Sharri made faces at each other in puzzlement. All this time she had thought her parents wanted her to stay away from the city; now they wanted her to live there? *Did someone plant a seed thought in Mom's mind?*

"I've told you and I've told you," her mother added emphatically, while she bustled at clearing the table, "I worry about you when you are on the highway at night. I often wished you'd stay with relatives over 'til the next day at least–"

Opening her mouth, Ruthe was ready with her usual reply.

"Never mind they think they are better than us. Who else can we trust!"

Her Dad hitched himself around uncomfortably in his tighter *Klein Sindoagsch*[28] pants, and said, "Besides, when you waste so much time and gas driving back and forth you never meet a man you can marry."

"You want me to marry?!" She couldn't help the high notes.

"Well! Do you expect us to feed an old spinster?" He turned away muttering, "Supposed to be the other way 'round."

Going to brush her teeth and check herself in a mirror to see if she needed changing, Ruthe tried to absorb these shocks.

Lately she had been thinking she might be better off with less time in the city. Her fast pace was tiring her. Still, moving out could certainly give her greater freedom, and might become a bridge in her life, so she had to account for less and less of her time. The Chrysalis would be her first preference. She was in and out of there so often it had begun to feel almost like a second home.

And Lord, those Johnson kids are still rather wild; they need more supervision. But Mom and Dad would say I couldn't afford the rent of a place like that. How would I refute it without telling the truth?

The smaller suite with a shared bath on the third floor of the Moss Rose wasn't but four blocks from the telephone office, and it would certainly satisfy her parents for cleanliness in its present condition. Lisa wanted to give it to her rent-free. Knowing her parents' financial frame of reference, Ruthe had suggested, "My folks will think thirty dollars a week a suitable bargain."

There was a danger they would find out the landlady's past and since they warned Ruthe to avoid the company of prostitutes, such a discovery could have repercussions. *On the other hand,* Ruthe told her ever listening Friend, *they aren't likely to come by to the Moss Rose for more than a few minutes at a time, and that seldom; so how would they get to know Lisa at all? Besides, Lisa doesn't look so wicked.*

As the landlady they met that evening, Lisa was polite, but said very little, eyeing the middle-aged couple as a practiced character-inspector.

The Veers were impressed with the clean, classy looks of the building and the two room suite with quiet, restful blue and green and purple tones. "Good find," her dad declared. "Now just remember, the city is full of temptations. Satan will want to draw you into sin, so look out!"

"Don't make friends with worldly people," her mother warned, still in Lisa's presence. "If you talk with prostitutes, people will think you are one of them."

"You come home whenever you have a day off!" Ben Veer chimed in, hoping to get this lovely landlady on their side, assisting to keep their daughter from city evils. "You Ukrainian, or Hungarian? You understand, no?" he asked Lisa, his eyes on her full bust.

Lisa assured them that their daughter, Ruthe, could move in right away, and shook hands with her parents. Ruthe found only twenty-five dollars in her purse, so her mother made her dad pay the other five, and go to the car to get her overnight bag with extra bedclothes.

In a hurry to get them out of there, Ruthe quickly hung up her two extra outfits in the small closet, and threw her old pink fluffy housecoat across the bed, and was ready to go back to Kleinstadt.

Following her satisfied and talkative parents down the stairs, as they were afraid of elevators, Ruthe turned and caught Lisa's significant face and silent, "Wow!" Then a reassuring pat.

In the car, her parents declared, "That's a friendly business lady, even if she has red lipstick and blue eye goop like a painted woman." They argued about her nationality, something Ruthe had never thought to ask about. Judging from the cleanliness of the place, her figure, and her head of almost white blonde hair, her mother favoured Swiss or Dutch. Her father still thought Ukrainian.

The longest day of the year wasn't that far back, so when the next day Ruthe came off the night shift, instead of going straight to bed at her new rooms, she wandered over to the river and walked on the luscious lawns looking for new secret garden spots to be alone.

Sometimes she stayed in the city to sleep away the hottest hours, and walked at both fresh-after-sunrise and dusk hours, and was mesmerized by the shifting reflections in the wide South Saskatchewan river.

She had thought her parents predictable. Could they soften in other areas? What if she could solve it all by just explaining things to them in the right words? What were those words?

Ruthe wasn't used to so much time to herself, and soon felt compelled to go check on people. Back in Kleinstadt the next day when she brought Sharri home for the weekend from the Charm n' Poise Course where she was on staff, Suzanne wanted to know if she and a friend or two could use Ruthe's new city suite for an overnight party. Ruthe was about to say, "Sure," when their mother heard, and pounced on Suzanne to cancel such expectations.

They all went to bed grouchy.

"I want to learn to be single like you," Lisa told Ruthe a few days after she had moved in. "You handle it so well."

They had just discussed how Lisa now enjoyed time to read and think about spiritual things during the day, as well as the mornings when she helped tenants put on make up and fix their hair in the beauty lounge before they left for their various jobs. She had just admitted that there were moments when sexual fantasies came to mind, but she wanted to remain chaste like Ruthe.

With an earnest, deep breath, Ruthe confessed to wistful dreams and thoughts about a husband. "I don't know what God has in mind for me for sure, but it's almost as if He's saying to me, 'So what do you really think you need or want?'" In a long talk they agreed their cases were not quite the same, but they had the same Heavenly Father.

Lisa left for her suite, and Ruthe sprawled across the bed to think some more, when Phyllis Shulton knocked at the door. She carried in, when Ruthe opened the door, a heavy typewriter with a box of paper supplies on top.

"Sorry, Ruthe," she apologized, breathlessly, "I could not get the one I had in mind for you– My, this is nice!– I had to order it. Now that you have a private place of your own, I want you to start out with good, regular writing habits." She looked around, scanning the tiny kitchenette-bedroom arrangement for the best place to put these writer's supplies. "I should have thought of a small desk too."

Ruthe sat up and patted her knees, "How about if I put it right here and get comfortable against these pillows?"

Considering it only a moment, Phyllis shook her head, "No. You'll fall asleep; then you'll tend to get dozy when you mean to write."

"I only plan to sleep here when it's too late to drive home."

"Oh Ruthe! This is the perfect writer's garret! You've got to finish the novel you've started. I'll get you a desk soon, okay?"

Touched at this extreme kindness of her goal-oriented friend, Ruthe thanked Phyllis and set the typewriter up on the small kitchen table. Her previously begun novel lay on top in the box of bond paper, yellow seconds, and carbon sheets, so she pulled it out, rolled in a paper combination and set to work so that Phyllis had the reward of seeing her gift appreciated.

While she leaned forward in a dramatic scene paragraph, Phyllis slipped out. Ruthe noticed when the door closed, but kept at it, then began to sense a new freedom as she wrote for her own entertainment, rather than to please Phyllis. The story came alive, and two whole chapters flowed as fast as she could type.

The action stalled, and Ruthe woke to find her head hanging at a limp angle over the keys, her fingers poised but motionless.

The next day she was to be somewhere, but managed to write a couple of pages first. Ruthe could hardly wait to get back and sneak in another chapter. Or two! In fact, over the next several days she thought of several people she didn't really have to spend so much time seeing anymore. She noticed a subtle shift in what things were important to her, as she made room for this new love.

Isabelle called the office and left a message for Ruthe with the clerk; *When are you coming home? I've got exciting news!* She had an early shift that would be done at three, so she decided to go home right after work.

A hot July day became hotter when she got caught in a traffic jam surrounding a warehouse fire. It was the MacIntosh wholesale building near the railroad. The crackling flames attracted spectators, some of whom deserted their cars in the street to go look on the other side, where the lime-green fire trucks had congregated and men in glistening yellow rubber coats were shouting and moving about.

Mom will be jam-making, besides whatever Isabelle has on her mind.

She tried her car phone. Too much static to get through. Ruthe knew her mother was sighing for her this minute. Every direction was blocked for nearly an hour, so Ruthe sat in the sweltering heat and sighed too, wishing she had phoned Isabelle to say she'd come the next day, or at least taken a different route. As soon as traffic allowed, slipped up a side street and hurried up a different route to Kleinstadt.

SIXTY-FOUR

Her mother had been wanting her, but had finished the raspberry jam by herself. After half an hour of anxious questions and listening to Ruthe's vivid description of the fire and traffic jam, her mother pled great weariness, and went to lie down.

With an hour to supper, Ruthe walked over to see Isabelle.

"I've got twins! Since May!" Isabelle exclaimed to Ruthe. It's the second time I've got to stop nursing because I'm pregnant. Got a knack for having babies, don't I?"

"Don't you use natural planning?" Ruthe asked with a grin.

"Oh that. Last week Grosz'mama dropped enough plain hints; I pieced it together. Nobody else ever told me. Birth control pills are all the rage now. Grosz'mama says God turns every child into a blessing, whether you're ready or not. He provides natural ways...."

They were alone in Isabelle's vegetable garden, noting the progress of the rows of peas and other things coming up. Isabelle put an arm around Ruthe and said excitedly, "I'm really- really- having twins this time! My dream's coming true!"

Then Regina and Curtis were screaming in the sandbox.

This was summer. Her due date was in February again, a fall and winter away. Still, before the summer was done, Ruthe heard from various people in the church that Isabelle had told them she was expecting twins. They remarked, "She's so sure of it; what if–?"

Ruthe asked Davie Pollock about it the next time he called about Laura. He believed Isabelle was only having one baby this time. He saw no need for an ultrasound, though he promised to yield if she insisted on it. "Why do you think she has twins?" Davie wanted to know.

"She thinks so. Isabelle prayed for them, and is convinced. She's in for a big shock if it is all in her imagination."

"Okay. I'll send her for the tests," the doctor promised.

A few times Ruthe started to discuss it with Isabelle, but what with all the interruptions at church or in the Clarke house, they never got deeper than they had that first winter conversation about the dream twins. Ruthe felt torn between thinking she ought to warn Isabelle not to exert foolish faith, and wanting to believe that God admired His own for asking for bold miracles. *Lord, if Isabelle gets her twins then maybe I'll place an order for a custom-built husband. Okay?*

385

SIXTY-FIVE

The door to Lisa's suite was open. She waved Ruthe in to meet an old friend who had come into the city to see her. Emeraude and Lisa had started out together as hookers in Vancouver and helped each other out in those days. But Emeraude had moved quite a bit. "Now I'm the ol' Lady for a gang of crazies on motorbikes!" Emie bragged. "Mostly I sleep with Jonathan, the boss man."

Ruthe didn't say much. She just studied this new person. Emeraude was a tall, dark-featured woman with a sultry Spanish-like complexion. She said she was twenty-six but carried herself like a weary forty-six. Her dusty, dull hair tumbled down her back to her waist in a tangled, unkempt mess. The eyes looked dull and sad. *Her face*, Ruthe concluded, *makes me think of gooseberries.*

Emie, as she called herself, was taken with the younger-looking, calmer Lisa. Ruthe saw her watch Lisa with a parched and thirsty air as Lisa laughed and chattered contentedly, and moved efficiently the next morning in the beauty lounge, dressing the office girls' hair and encouraging them for their day ahead.

"What's y'er secret?" Emie held back Lisa's arm.

"I've found my last and only love; God," Lisa had told her. "He has forgiven me and given me a whole new outlook; He gave me Christ Jesus, His Son to live in me. The biggest and best secret of all time."

"What? Can God forgive our kind? N' change ya?"

"Hey, I'm proof," Lisa emphasized.

When Ruthe returned from work that night, the two women wanted to come sit in her small suite. Emeraude had watched Lisa all day, they said, and now Lisa wanted Ruthe's help to explain it again so Emie could understand. "I've tried it six or seven times, if once, Hon, and poor Emie says she can't get it."

Ruthe could hardly keep her eyes open after nearly two days and nights without sleep, so she let the talkative two hash it through once more. Silently, Ruthe begged, *Lord, please forgive me for thinking this suite was a good idea. Now I can't even excuse myself and say, 'I've got to go home.' Couldn't Lisa counsel Emie in her own suite? They have the same background.*

Late into the night Emie sat cross-legged on the econo loveseat in Ruthe's room, Lisa in a chair, and Ruthe slumped her head and neck against the wall above her bed after she had a few tries at explaining the plan of salvation and sanctification. She drifted away in a half-doze several times, only to wake and hear Lisa still trying to convey the spiritual riches a Christian has in Christ. *Lord, put the right brain cells into Emie,* Ruthe prayed faintly, *or connect the right wires so she can get this spiritual truth. Lift the fog....*

386

All at once Emie's sulky face lit up and glowed like a frosted light bulb as she grasped what God had done for her. She believed it. She was now His! An eternal child of the One, True, Father-God.

Before she had mainly mumbled in monosyllables. Lisa had done most of the talking. Now Emie wanted to describe her new feelings.

Lisa, glad for the victory at last, but seeing Ruthe's passivity, gave her a shove so she fell over onto her pillow and took Emie's hand and led her away.

When Ruthe tried to creep out to work early in the morning, she heard Emie down in the beauty lounge, cornering individual tenants, telling them the news. "Complete fo'giveness is to be had!"

In the afternoon she was still there, telling someone else that God had forgiven her, the worst sinner in the whole world. Ruthe had the grace to rejoice with her, and agreed with Lisa that their Lord better take all the credit Himself this time. However Ruthe said she had to go home to Kleinstadt that evening, not adding that her main purpose was to get a good night's sleep.

The third night Lisa and Ruthe took Emie to Darlin' Bonne's for the royal treatment. The atmosphere was filled as usual with the hum of sewing machines, their buzzing conversations, and the lively gospel melodies wafting about.

Of course, they came to Emie's wild motorcycle friends. She revealed that she was considered their sex goddess, but now she planned to stay here. "I don't care for that stale ol' life no more."

Ruthe's conscience stirred, *too bad those guys are beyond hope–* She stopped short. Had not Emeraude been as bad as they? Aloud she said, "Too bad no one's ever shown them this super-great life in Jesus."

Emeraude revolved slowly about to look at her. "Yeh! Y'know, this minute they're goin' roun' n' round, lookin' fer something' or someone, rippin' road up with them wheels. N' here, we got the answer!"

The seamstresses all agreed and said so. But Ruthe began to be wary. The Lord had provided the inspiration and nerve to get the notorious Lisa, and look at her! Even that long night of explaining to Emie had seemed hopeless, and her conversion was some inexplicable miracle. But those guys? She got chills. *Lloyd's little gang of juvenile delinquents was racy enough for this naive country bumpkin! I have not got faith to deal with that biker gang type!*

Yet, she could not bear to discourage Emeraude. In theory God's love included them and they should be told. She ignored her twinge of guilt for not volunteering, and urged Emie, "Talk to them first chance you get. "They know you well. If they see a change in you, they will believe you sooner." Just saying it helped Ruthe believe it.

It was all Emie needed. She was ready to run with the good news. It turned out they were not in the city yet. She'd been sent ahead by bus to find suitable quarters, and the men were to rendezvous with her at the river by the 25th Street bridge under-pass on Sunday afternoon.

All of the young women at the shop promised Emie that if she meant to meet them as planned, they would gather right here to pray for her. "We won't stop either," Ruthe finished fervently, "until you phone or come back with a report."

"Goodie! Goodie!" Emie cried, bouncing up and down impatiently in a new country print cotton dress, "I ken hardly wait!"

As they gathered at the shop for this special prayer meeting, Emeraude's excitement was infectious, and they made jokes about how the newspaper would look the next morning as word spread that a group of vile, brute men, carrying guns and knives and riding fearlessly on roaring motorbikes had been converted.

There had been a mighty summer thunderstorm with lightening and gutter flooding Sunday morning, but Emeraude was a ball of fire, confidently anticipating the joy that Jon, and the other men would have when they heard what she had to tell them. She whirled about in her Laura Ashley cotton print dress, with the lace V-bodice and the ruffled caps over the long sleeves. Emie crowed that Jon would hardly know her in this feminine outfit.

Lisa, Darlin' Bonne, and Ruthe wrapped their arms around Emie and prayed, then sent her off for her rendezvous just a few blocks away. As they waved her off at the front door, the sun was shining warmly on a sparkling green and wet world. They thought it a good sign.

As soon as they closed the door they fell to their knees and began to pray in earnest. For a start, they all prayed at once and aloud. Gradually, some voices died down as individuals paused to collect their thoughts and let the Lord show them what angle to pray about next. In a minute or two these voices rose and others fell softer or silent, waiting for direction in their intuitive spirits.

During such a pause Ruthe had what she thought might be a vision. It was like a flash look at a photo in which Emie was just a heap of cotton print. The instant she saw it, she began to flush with dread. Something had gone wrong. Or was about to, since Emie had only been away a few minutes. Ruthe just knew.

Ruthe grabbed Lisa's wrist beside her, and interrupted her praying, "Lisa. Quick. We've got to go after that poor girl! Something awful is happening!"

Together they whirled up, pushing each other as they got the door open, and dashed out to the white Rambler with flying steps.

Recklessly, Ruthe backed into the street with hardly a glance in either direction, while Lisa snatched up the phone to call the police. The dispatcher promised to have a squad car join them at the park.

At a riverside parking apron, Lisa and Ruthe jumped out and frantically scanned the gentle landscaped hills and flowerbeds twinkling with recent raindrops. They saw no one. But they heard shouting over the knoll straight ahead and beyond the massive bridge pillars. Both of them started at a run around a clump of ornamental shrub trees to better see over the top of the hill.

In a deeper dip beyond the trees, a sprint of three hundred metres ahead, stood six men with shaggy beards, tattered denim shirts and tight jeans. They stood in a semi-circle on the other side of Emeraude, facing her. A black and metallic spray of motorbikes lay strewn to one side.

One of the men, a huge husky black, with what Ruthe thought was a hideous mop of filthy hair, reached out and shook Emeraude violently and appeared to swear fiercely. At a sharp bark from the one with the matted red flames on his head, he backed up.

There was a terrific crack!

Slowly, limply, Emeraude crumpled backwards. As she reached the ground in an awkward pile of dark green and mustard yellow cotton print, Ruthe and Lisa had a clearer view of the leader. He stood arrogantly right behind the spot where Emie had just stood, facing their way. The aimed, smoking pistol was still pointed from his hand.

For a split second, Lisa and Ruthe stood frozen. Hearing what sounded like a burp of pain from Emie, and forgetting themselves and the dangerous men, they rushed desperately down the wet hill.

Racing two steps ahead, Lisa slid to her knees on the wet grass in clear sight of the stunned men, lifted Emeraude's head and frantically patted the colourless cheeks. The flat cheeks that so recently had learned to glow with that holy incandescence now were puffed and allowed tiny pink bubbles of blood to escape from the mouth.

Falling down on the other side of the twisted knees and body, Ruthe cried shrilly, "Oh Lord! Her message! Didn't she get her message out!"

A siren wailed downtown, heading in this direction. Then another.

"Shove off!" The oily and leathery-smelling men heard the siren and tires, and with sharp barks from their leader they leaped onto their bikes, revved and roared over the park to the rear lane by the river.

Seconds later the sirens and squealing tires came into the park and cut abruptly as they bounced onto the wet grass. Car radios crackled in the clean air.

Ruthe couldn't have cared less about the gang or the police. Hot tears for Emeraude streamed down her face. Her stomach felt as if it were sobbing too.

"Why'd she have to die? Why?!" Lisa was crying loudly.

Ruthe blinked through her sheet of tears to see if Emie's eyes were really dead. She couldn't see, but she knew it was true.

Yes, why? Ruthe wondered. Emeraude's joy had been so new, so fresh, so inspiring. *I hinted she should go.... Why her? Shouldn't it have been... me?*

Now she felt confused. *Would I really have been willing to take her place?* Dozens of questions swarmed in like vultures, thick and fast, without words.

Ginter and Aubrey came running up behind them. "@#$$%@! What's goin' on here?"

"Ruthe? Lisa?"

Trembling through to her bones, Ruthe erected herself on her knees. She found it almost impossible to focus her eyes. "They killed Emie, our friend– a'an all sh-e wan'ted to d-do was tell them-m.... Oh-h! Ohhhh!" she couldn't go on.

"Come'on away," said Ginter softly, taking her arm. "We'll look after your poor friend here. And find those rats."

Ruthe's legs didn't feel like walking. Lisa, led beside her by Aubrey, was sobbing and muttering angrily. Aubrey brought Lisa to lean on Ruthe, and excused himself to radio for help. The two clung to each other while Ginter tried to penetrate their shock with questions.

Feeling like her real self had leaped out of her body and disappeared, Ruthe answered mechanically. Yes, they knew that Emeraude was meeting her gang here as arranged, and the girls at Darlin' Bonne's had pledged to pray for her. "But when I had a sudden– what do you call them?"

"Premonition?"

"Yeh, suddenly I just knew that Emie was in big trouble. So Lisa and I rushed over here. But too late!"

Ruthe tossed her head listlessly as Ginter pressed for details of what they had witnessed. She described the shaggy-bearded men in denims and the pile of motorcycles nearby, and how one with long reddish hair held a pistol pointed at Emie, when she crumpled.

Lisa's version was the same, except repeated more choppily because she was still choking down sobs.

When the ambulance door slammed, Aubrey came back to their huddle and as Ginter indicated he had their account down in his book, said, "You two best be going home. Okay?"

Aubrey helped Lisa lean on himself, and Ginter put an arm around Ruthe. They led the two of them back to Ruthe's Rambler. Their hearts like deadweights, they said they would go back to Darlin' Bonne's.

SIXTY-SIX

Ruthe was sure she felt the worst. She had seen lots of problems in the last two years. Might God have made a slip? Had they sinned, or miscalculated, maybe? True, Emeraude had only been with them a few days, but her past did not make her any more expendable.

They were a quiet, forlorn bunch in the reception room. After Lisa and Ruthe had brokenly told them what had happened, there was nothing any of them could think to do but try to take it in. There was deep thinking along with the sniffling, fidgeting and questioning.

"We should have all gone with her!" Darlin' Bonne moaned.

Maybe we... Ruthe's thoughts trailed underneath her tossing and turning and tears, *we ought not to be telling people to let Christ clean and make them new... if it will cost them their lives. If I had not told Darlin' Bonne and Lisa about the Lord, they and the rest of us wouldn't be here, of course. But then Emeraude might be.... Oh, I'm sorry, Lord! This is a sick train of thought.*

A minute or two later Ruthe again found herself asking; were the things she, and the shop girls, had been doing were really worth the price of a life? Had she merely found a daydream in her loneliness, which brought a lovely psychological effect, and so far, fortunately, on all she had shared it with? Were her conversing and visits with the Lord a mental trick she had invented out of a desperate need for an understanding friend?

But Lord, she begged, *what of all those inexplicable answers to prayer? What of all these people I've watched turn into my spiritual roses; faithful, passionate, talisman, all those? They are real, aren't they? Oh, reassure me it was You! Remind me of the miracles of Phyllis, and... Lisa. Of the O'Briens. The house back home! How the Greystone became the Chrysalis! They did happen, didn't they? Lord-d! It's not just my body, the roots of my faith are rattling! Unless You come steady me, I don't know what'll become of me!*

At the same time, Lisa, who had become strong enough to have others lean on her, was clinging to Ruthe's arm and complaining brokenly that she just couldn't pray. "The words lock in my throat!"

However Ruthe was afraid to pray aloud what her heart was saying.

"Why, Ruthe, why?" Lisa begged over and over. "It was so pointless! If God planned it to His glory as we prayed, then why didn't she get a fair chance to tell those brutes her story first? Why, tell me why?"

She put a trembling arm around Lisa, "I'm sorry, I don'know," then collapsed on Lisa's shoulder and wept a fresh waterfall of her own.

Ruthe sensed Darlin' Bonne and the others hovering about, waiting for her to reaffirm confidently that God never makes a mistake. She used to say that so often; why wasn't she saying it now? Now she had trouble looking at them. Joy did try to say words to that effect, but they didn't have much influence. The rest were looking in astonishment at their natural leaders, and seeing them too weak to lead.

Feeling responsible, like the eternal older sister, Ruthe suggested with quivers, "Let's bring our feelings to the Lord in frank – honest prayer. We have to tr-ust Him to work out all thi-ngs togeth-er f-for good. E-ven if we fall into h-huge ink-hole."

A kernel of wheat has to die, drifted through some rear door in her thoughts.

However, when she tried to pray aloud she gagged. Her throat was swollen shut. Ruthe feared they were not going to have any spiritual break-through or answers until she'd had time to have this crisis out privately with her Lord in her secret garden of prayer. It could mean a number of sessions. She couldn't make these girls wait that long; they needed something right away to hang onto.

Again the idea touched the periphery of her mind; *A kernel of corn?... falleth into the ground..., and beareth much fruit....* In desperation Ruthe latched onto it, and told them to get out the Bibles and to re-read the only reference that came to her mind at the moment. The one where Jesus spoke of a kernel of wheat having to die to bring forth fruit. "I thought it applied only to Him, but let's see."

Bibles surfaced in a hurry, and they hunted through the gospels and a concordance until they located the exact place. It was in John 12, at verse 24. They had a brand new New Testament in the New International Version, just out, and it read, *"I tell you the truth, unless a kernel of wheat falls to the ground and dies, it remains only a single seed. But if it dies, it produces many seeds."*

Throughout her life Ruthe had heard sermons teaching this verse to mean a spiritual death to self or one's ego had to take place, so that Christ could make that person effective in life and witness. As she wiped her face, blew her nose, and tried to explain this parable, she began to see it applied also to physical death. Martyrdom stories always made her glad she didn't live in the Reformation. But this was present tense.

She bowed to stare at the words again until she absorbed them. Ruthe spoke out her discovery as it came to her; "One must be willing to die physically for Jesus' sake if necessary. In the depths of my heart... I know Jesus is worth such a total sacrifice... the Jesus I know and love. Only, I never expected to face it in my life time."

Joy offered, "Emie loved Him so much already; I don't think she minded dying for Jesus, did she?"

Lisa agreed, making a fresh effort to pull herself together. "She didn't flinch, even in those split seconds, facing that pistol."

"Maybe our question should be, then," said Evelyn, "Does Jesus mean that much to each of us– if we ever face a sudden violent death?"

Most of the girls hesitated and made comments like Donnie's, "Well-um. Depending on the circumstances."

Betty pointed out that her father didn't harvest any wheat, nor her mother any garden vegetables, until the old seeds had been buried, had rotted, and the new plants had sprouted and grown ripe. "Our mistake might be that we want God to give us the dead seed back as fruit. Like Emie's life back. Maybe we should just patiently wait with our whys for a while. We might see some great fruit after a season of growing."

With that thought Ruthe was able to get a grip on her emotions, and stop sniffling. She agreed with Betty, but was quick to add that this did not mean God expected each of them to die for their faith in a violent way. "We've got to sacrifice selfish motives and desires when they conflict with His plans for us. Then, if we are ever faced with such a crisis we will gladly die for Jesus."

"I simply can't picture those men being changed as a result of Emeraude's death," said Louise sorrowfully.

Ruthe couldn't either and said so, but she tried to pray aloud to bring everyone up to a more positive level. She pled with the Lord, "Do not let Emeraude's death be a waste. And, help us to trust You better than this!"

The police called and said they had sealed off all exits to the city. Every off-duty officer had been called in to search for this gang. The morgue was calling the coroner, and lastly, "Do you know how to reach your friend's next of kin?"

Lisa was quite certain that Emeraude had no relatives left in the world. With the girls nodding and whispering they would help, she promised to take responsibility for the funeral arrangements.

Sergeant Webster, of Homicide, knew them as good friends of the force. He promised to keep their names from the media under pretext of having to locate and notify the murder victim's next of kin.

Donnie turned the radio on. The local stations were giving a sketchy bulletin of the incident and warning people to stay in their homes. The city was sealed and to be thoroughly searched for a ruthless gang of killers on motorbikes.

Ruthe did not feel up to it, but was committed by a sense of duty to work her evening shift, from six to midnight. If she called in to book off, her connection to this murder could leak out. "I'm not a relative, and I'm not sick. Really, I have to go to work as if not at involved in this catastrophe."

"Darlin' Roo," whispered Darlin' Bonne, slipping an arm around her and swinging Ruthe aside, "you won't make it. You'll melt before your shift is up."

Instantly Ruthe's face grew red and swollen, and her eyes brimmed. "I know. So we'll ask God for a miracle– Just as if He's never missed onc-once before." She ate part of a sandwich and a banana, and went to work. From the lounge she called her parents to assure them she had got to work fine, and yes, she would lock her car doors, and head straight to her room at the Moss Rose after twelve. However, her mother didn't seem to hear that, and pled over and over with Ruthe to be careful. "Grosz'mama heard it first on the radio. She phoned us a few minutes ago."

"Okay, Mom, you call her back and tell her I'm fine, and I'm ready to be a kernel of wheat if that's what God wants." Her confused mother wanted to know what that meant, but Ruthe said goodbye and hung up. She didn't know why she'd blurted that, but expected Grosz'mama to sit in her rocker and figure it out.

The operators couldn't listen to radio or television in the toll room, but all were aware of the news and police warning. They joked quietly with each other that every parent was calling each child or relative to check on them and pass the time, for the evening was steadily busy on the switchboard until nine o'clock. Then the calls came more in fits and spurts, so they concluded that a good movie had come on the main TV channel. People were only placing calls during the commercials. It gradually became a "dead night." They had time to chat in the longer spells between calls.

However, Ruthe made sure after her coffee break to have several vacant positions between her and the nearest operator. There she could handle her calls with a routine drone, and between, stare down at the most frequently called numbers, to pick her soul into tiny pieces. She took a deep, critical look at her life; at her relationship with the Lord Jesus, whom she had considered her most intimate Friend, her values in life; what was she willing to die for? If she should die suddenly like Emeraude, was she satisfied with the life she had on record so far? The shameful truth, she decided, was, not really. She should have done more. At least more lovingly. Worst was the problem with her family was still unresolved. All at once she knew, *I should have dealt with this long ago!*

Between the calls that beeped into her headset, answering people automatically, ignoring the other operators, and staring deep into the distance, Ruthe confessed her shortcomings. By the end of the shift she was more or less at rest again in His love, however, she looked forward to long outdoor walks and talks. Then she would be at peace. For now, a soft little confidence was growing inside her that this afternoon's events would fit into His perfect plans in the end.

At long last it was midnight. She had survived, but assumed it was because her friends at the shop probably spent the evening praying for her. She would go to the Moss Rose, and if Lisa didn't meet her in the hallway to talk all kinds of hours, she meant to get some sleep. There was the funeral to plan with Lisa, and perhaps nosy questions from unexpected sources.

Ruthe got ahead of the other shift workers, and an elevator down all by herself. At almost a run, she hurried through the warm summer night air to the end of the block where she'd had to park her car by a meter, something she could afford to do Sundays and after six.

Br-ru-rum! Br-ru-rum-m! Br-ru-rum-m-m! Out of nowhere motors roared in a terrorizing ring around her! Some came bursting from the underground parkade at her side, and another swooped up from behind Ruthe right on the sidewalk.

L-Lor-d– He-elp! she shrieked soundlessly as a strong arm pinched her tightly to a hairy chest on one of the throbbing machines. *Is this happening too fast for the other operators to see? Aren't they out of the door yet? Oh-h, I was a witness! Now they'll kill me! Or use me as a hostage to get out of the city!*

Ruthe froze. Every muscle was wood. At the same time she was sopping wet with a cold, sodden fear.

395

SIXTY-SEVEN

The revving train of motorcycles tore down the otherwise silent street, sweeping Ruthe along like a scrap of material caught between their fingers. Her mind slipped a gear.

She gulped for oxygen as they made several low-angled and skinning turns.

Then, almost as suddenly as it had started they all killed their motors in a cloud of dust at a rear loading dock of a warehouse. She noticed some charred smoke and fire damage. She recalled the MacIntosh fire of two weeks earlier. It gave her a bearing; they were still right downtown, near the tracks. The police must be on Circle Drive.

Though she felt physically paralysed, her brain was nimble enough to tell her whole life's story in a breath; her childhood, school years, church life, and all her friendships gained in the last two years. *Lord! I think– You have another martyr– Sorry, I don't mean to be funny; I can't think. Pl-lea-se help me to die bravely! Help me!*

It occurred to Ruthe, as an abruptly passing thought, that she might be lucky enough to get Emeraude's message out before they pulled the trigger this time. *Okay, dear God. Give me the words that'll haunt them until they turn to You! Honestly, I don't mind dying. It doesn't matter that my family never understood me, nor if they never find out why I was killed, as long as You know. As long as I die pleasing You. Only, I wish I'd resolved that communications block with Mom and Dad!*

Alert with adrenalin from her fear, she took in some details around her after they pulled a string on a light bulb. She saw and smelled the men, with the background odour of charred wood and smoke, realized she was alone with them, and her mind flipped upside down. For some time, all she could think was, *JESUS, JESUS! J-E-SUS! Oh-h dear Jesus!*

"There," said the redheaded Moses as he picked Ruthe up under her arms like a child and seated her high on a grey wooden crate. It felt soft and crumbly on one side where flames had tenderized the slats. He stepped back. "We took a @#$ #$%*& risk stayin' an' waitin' fer ya."

The other five growled in accord.

"This aft in that #$#%@#+& park, I heard y' say, 'had the kid got her message through?' I hate all #$@% $%&#@ secrets, hear?" He crossed his arms authoritatively, "Yer t' say what her message was to have been. An' so help me, @#$%, if it wasn't a #$%@ #$%# good one, it'll be the last squeak out'a ya."

396

"#@$%@+* @#$%@&!" snarled the black giant behind him with vicious re-enforcement.

Every lung full of air she breathed was another cry for help, *Oh Lord, words! I need words! P-pl-ease, speak to them!*

Then she heard, "You-r old fr-iend, Emeraude, dis-cover-d a marvel-lous secret a few days ago." Her shaky and thin voice improved as she said, "She–she thought you fellas would be as thrilled as she was, and she could hardly wait to tell you."

"So?" the leader prodded.

There were spots of hot burning sensations in her neck and on her shoulders where her trembling nerves were knotted up and screaming with tautness. However, she sat ramrod straight on the crate and went on as surprised as they were at what she said.

"Emeraude found forgiveness for everything she had ever done. Love from God Himself. And peace. Oh, she got a wonderful peace!"

"Her?" the leader crocked in disbelief, "Emie? Found peace? Ha!"

Several of the other men, particularly the huge black man blocking the barn-like door, guffawed loudly.

"Yes. It shone right through her face. It was so real. Like a frosted white light bulb... y'know. I thought so at first."

The other men eyed her suspiciously. But their red-haired and bushy-bearded leader was listening, so they waited. Ruthe spoke more directly to him.

"Lisa told her all about what had happened to her just over a year ago. Emie was so impressed that by Wednesday night she decided to ask God for that too. You should have seen how excited she got when He answered! He told her that He'd been watching and waiting for her all her life, and if she was willing to turn from her past and follow Him, He would forgive her sins– completely forget them– and be with her constantly. She talked with God herself; how could she help but love Him back!"

"Emie never got excited," the leader said with a thick threatening note to guard what she said. "Nothin's scared her. Nothin' thrilled her. She'd seen and done everythin'."

"I thought she looked sulky and bored too when I first met her," Ruthe agreed, trying to remember this boss-man's name. "But didn't you notice a big difference in her when you saw her in the park?"

"We thought the Fuzz was baitin' us," muttered one of the men.

The leader turned sharply to hear that. Then he moved frightfully close, glaring at Ruthe, "Was she?"

"Part of some police trap?– No," she answered quickly. (*Right, Emie called him Jonathan*). "When Emeraude decided to tell you guys, and especially you,

Jonathan, about this wonderful experience she'd had, we... (that's our circle of friends), promised to gather at one place to pray for her. We knew you fellas wouldn't be easy to talk to, but we felt she had a better chance than we. While we were praying, I suddenly sensed that she was in terrible danger. Lisa and I followed. Because we were so worried, we called the police on my car phone."

Numbly he shook his head as it sank in that because he had feared a trap, and jumped to a conclusion, he had shot a girl. His girl. Every eye was on him. "Yer tellin' me that little bitch got on speakin' terms with God Himself?"

"There's hope for a @#$%@ like you, Jon," one of his men taunted.

"Yah-h!" laughed another, "If that #$%@ #$%@& could go to heaven, you an' me should be able'ta!"

"Shut yer faces!" shouted Jon, raising his fist and glaring around behind him, "I'm talkin'."

They pursed their lips and shifted back into the shadows.

He turned on Ruthe, "I'm not sayin' yer goin't live til dawn, but I want to know somethin' else. Why did she rate special? Why'd God forgive Emie? I tell ya, He sure didn't know that chick like I did."

"Ah-h-h, but–" Ruthe said slowly, hoping that disagreeing with him would not antagonize him more. "God did know her very well. He knows everything, sees everything, and is able to be everywhere. The only reason He forgave Emeraude was because she was ashamed of what she had done, and because she asked Him, and believed Christ died for her, just like the Bible says. You can be forgiven– if you asked and believed like that."

"Y' can't see God; how could she talk to Him?"

"It's hard to explain for those who don't regularly do it, but I've come to know the Lord a bit over the past couple of years. If you're patient, I can tell you what I know of Him."

Still having only slight advance control over what she was saying, she began at the very beginning, "God invented us. In a sense we're like Him because the Bible says He made man in His own image. That's all human beings. God wanted friends. Even heirs. But He didn't want us to love Him involuntarily, like birds or mice, so He gave us free wills. Not animal instincts. All of us decide what we're going to think, do, or feel, don't we? As a rule?"

No one answered, no one moved.

"Pity is, most of us have chosen to ignore Him. We all, from Adam and Eve down, have a natural bent to love ourselves and do our own thing. As you know, even your group has got to have rules, right? So God has a few for His universe and earth and people. From the time Adam and Eve disobeyed Him we've all been sentenced to death and distance from God. He's so holy and perfect that sin cannot be anywhere near Him. No more than a small patch of darkness can stay near this light bulb." She lifted her face for a moment to indicate it.

Ruthe was anxious to finish before this Jon character lost patience and decided to get rid of her, although she was more in the present tense, than in the near, or distant future. "Here's the exciting part," she went on. "God still loved us, so He devised a plan. All God's laws are irreversible so He couldn't say, 'Oh, it's all right; I'll forget it.' The penalty still had to be paid because sin cannot stand in His presence. So He came up with a greater law to swallow it up; the only alternative in the whole universe, substitution."

She took another deep breath and plunged on, "His Son, who was and is as perfect as Himself, would take on human life and die for us! It had to be someone both as holy as God and as human as us. Anyone else would only have died for his own sins as he deserved."

"We'll all die," said Jon with a frown, "He thinks of it as punishment?"

"Yes. Originally we weren't suppost to die. But physical death is only part of the sentence. We struggle along by ourselves in this life, and then spend eternity alone and in anguish too. Except for those of us who've chosen to let Christ exchange places with us. He rose from the dead with a new transformed body and He will live forevermore! So, we have all that our glorious Substitute has!"

"Y'mean– anybody? Everybody?" Jon was impressed. "@#$%#@, that's a blast!"

"Ahm-no. Just those who've made up their minds, or I should say their wills, to believe that Jesus Christ could and did substitute for them. Those who love Him dearly, and are becoming like Him."

"What if I don't care to be like Him?" Jon asked caustically.

"God respects the freedom of choice He gave us. If however, we choose our own way, we've got to remember the consequences will be to spend eternity dying for our sins in Hell. The Bible describes Hell as a real place, a great lake of fire, where the souls of the wicked burn forever without being so completely consumed that they ever stop suffering."

"I'd say that's torturing us for not choosing what He wants us to choose," Jon reasoned defensively.

The others nodded and agreed with mutterings.

"Ah-yes, but He made us. The world, and all natural laws are His. Everything that exists is His. That gives God ownership rights. We are in His ballpark and must play ultimately, by His rules, not ours."

The other men grew bold enough to ask their own questions, and now Ruthe was bombarded from all sides with demands to justify, or explain if she could, the faults of God. Why didn't God do something about all those countries slaughtering one another by the thousands? The Holocaust? The famines in

Africa? Social injustices even in Canada. Poverty, and so on. Could she disprove evolution? Would not sincere worshippers in other religions have their hopes fulfilled too? What would Heaven really be like? And where was that real description of Hell?

"I thought it was to be a grand ol' crap game or party around a nice, roaring bonfire," said the one they called Zoro. "Never did like organ music."

Ruthe explained that it was humanity's wilful sins that were the root cause of all wars and social problems. The laws God had set over nature for biological growth seemed to multiply them, as more people were born and chose self and evil; however, those laws were meant to multiply for good. "One day, Christ will return as the World King, to reign from Jerusalem, and there will be perfect peace and harmony for a thousand years. Justice and prosperity for everyone." She had forgotten her Bible at the shop, so she had to recite or paraphrase the passages she needed to back up her statements, but she was amazed at how clearly she understood these truths this night. Ones she had known separately now all lined up, and hooked into one whole piece.

The night's conversation was so long and complicated, she lost track of the subjects they covered. Ruthe hardly knew what she was saying until she'd said it. Then she forgot it just as promptly as they moved to another topic.

About three in the morning she lifted her hand to draw hair back out of her eyes and caught sight of the time on her watch. She felt she had told them all she had ever known, or thought, or heard on any spiritual matters in her whole life, and through it all with respect as if they were thinking beings of value. She felt dry and exhausted. There was a significant pause.

Jon broke it by kicking the rough crate he sat on and said, "Can't speak for them,... but I wish I knew God personal-like. If he's really like you describe Him, a guy's got'a be a @#$% @#$@ to ignore Him."

"Your right," Ruthe nodded fervently. "We can't even worship God as we ought, simply in gratitude for being his creations, never mind all His other undeserved grace and gifts to us."

All watched as Jon dropped his head and mumbled more softly into his beard, "I– I'm trying to say– I wanna change places with God's Son."

With a jerk Ruthe recognized what this meant, but cried inwardly, *Can this be true? Is this–? Oh-but, I love You, Lord Jesus! Thank You. Oh, thank You!* Where upon she found herself bursting with kindness towards this man who was so filthy and smelled of oil, grease, dirt and sweat.

"Here, Jon," Ruthe said tenderly, ready to touch him now and accept him into God's family. With one hand she patted the crate on which he had placed her and with the other she beckoned him closer. "I'll introduce you. Then you can talk to Him yourself, and tell Him all about it. All right?"

Nodding affirmatively, he leaned onto the old crate, hiding his face in his hands.

The other five watched carefully. Ruthe began to pray, but was so relieved to be able to pray aloud, and at this miracle, that in a minute she was crying. When she could not go on, she patted and stroked Jon's head until he began.

"Hello God. Can You hear me?" He paused uncertainly, then went on. He asked to be excused for not knowing how to pray, commented on the rainy weather and morning cloudburst, and then, "Ah-h-k!"

For a second Ruthe thought he had choked. However, quickly she saw he was realizing how God saw him. A liar, a thief, a ruthless lawbreaker, satisfying only his own evil lusts. Added to all that, he was now a murderer too, for he had shot Emeraude. Could God look down in love on such a man?

His shoulders slumped down as he begged God to try to forgive him. If possible, to help him forget the awful, awful thing he'd done. "God, I deserve to die! It's not fair You should do it for me, but if You can include cuss'd me with all the ones You died for back there one time,– please do! @#$%, I'm scared of livin' and I'm scared of dying! @#$@, I'm terribl' sorry, God! Try to believe me, okay?"

Another time or two Jon implored the Lord to undo the murder he had committed; to revive Emie in the morgue. Ruthe almost began to hope for this herself. Like a child, Jon promised to do absolutely anything to make up for it. Anything at all.

The whole area seemed to be charged with powerful cross-currents of both hot and soothing cool air. A mixture of garden fragrances and evil stenches swirled all around Ruthe. She half wondered if the worst odours didn't emanate from that tall black man at the door, but she was afraid to look that way.

She caressed Jon's damp, grimy head and whispered the promise from I John 1:9 to reassure him that God does forgive every sin that is confessed. After she had repeated this several times the comforting truth seemed to sink in, for his shoulders slowed and finally stopped twitching.

A few minutes later Jon raised a tear-drenched face. His beard was so dirty the tears made mud on his cheeks and chin. It reminded Ruthe of a garden puddle after a sudden spring shower. He shook his head dizzily and stared. "%&##, it's real. He did; He forgave me!" Jon turned to the others. "Jesus loves me! He forgave me and He's goin'a make a different man out'a me!"

Two of his gang inched forward. He got up and grabbed one with each hand. "You got to try this, Man. You haven't lived yet. It's terrif!"

Without further urging, they crouched over the crate on either side of Ruthe. Taking a deep breath, she suggested Jon pray with one, while she prayed with the other.

"Yeah. I wanna talk with God some more," Jon said eagerly. He put his arm on the back of his companion and greeted the Lord jubilantly.

When they were through these prayers and both the men had confessed their sins and promised to love the Lord, the three of them crowded around Ruthe to ask new questions. "What comes next? What do we do?"

She was discussing the importance the Bible should play in their lives if they honestly wanted to get to know God well, when two other men, who had been standing in the shadows, sidled up under the glaring light bulb and asked if they could join.

Jon took charge and made the men who had last come to pray introduce these two, "And remember, God only forgives what you confess and wanna be rid of, so list 'em all, or you'll feel miserable!"

Ruthe could see why he was the leader. Jon did things grand and thoroughly when he did them.

Only the huge, seven-foot black man was left. The one they called Harv. Throughout the night he had stood still as a statue, guarding the door. With arms crossed, he had watched and listened with an ominous silence. the last man had just finished praying and was describing his feelings of release and cleanliness, when Jon turned around to look for his right-hand man. "Harv-man, you–"

As the group's attention turned on him, Harve came to life. He tore the air with a terrifying cry, banging his fists on anything at hand. Before they knew what was up, he was upon Jon. An awful scuffle followed as the red man tried to ward off his fiercely slashing, and kicking black buddy. "@#$%@– you, Jon!" he roared, "don't y'see? She's lured y'all, every @#$%+*@ of ya into her trap! An y' @#$& fools fell for it!"

For a bit Ruthe struggled to wake up. This was like an early morning dream, and it must be high time to get up. Then she noticed his eyes. They were glassy and vacant. In spite of his energy, there was something about his rage, as if it was against something invisible. *Of all things; demon possession?* Immediately she knew, though she had never encountered it before.

A cold panic hit her again. As she reached in her fright towards Jesus, something slowly filled her. Something warm and strong like new blood. When it reached every part of her, she jumped off and down from the crate.

Harv had backed against the wall to catch his balance and breath. Slapping her hand firmly on his chest, she commanded with all she could muster, "Satan, in the name of Jesus, get out! Let Harv make his own choice with his own will!"

At that Harv emitted a high, unnatural scream, gradually changing in pitch to a long and pitiful whine. His legs crumpled and he slid down in front of her. Just as quickly, Ruthe dropped to her haunches to catch his head in her lap. His whole body rocked and shuddered so hard that she had difficulty in keeping her balance. He was a giant. Harv sobbed with high-pitched whistles for breaths.

After the longest time, during which the other men muttered low prayers for Harv, and Ruthe wondered if the Lord really had no good Christian man for this mission tonight, and still crying spastically, the black man began to tell them of his past. That he'd had god-fearing, church-going parents, and how they had taught him the very things she had been saying. He thought he had wiped them out of his mind, but they had come back. He had even learned to pray as a child, then he started keeping the wrong kind of company, and became ashamed of his mother and her old darkie-faith. So he had run from home. "I-I'm sure my heart-brok' Mama still sits up ever'y night to pray fer me!"

"You know, Harvey," Ruthe said softly, using the full name like his mother probably would, and continuing to massage the thick muscles in his neck, "I think your mother must be praying her heart out tonight. You just check! But now; you realize that Satan has left you, at least for the moment. However, he could be back. I suggest you ask the Lord to forgive you, promise Him you'll go back to tell your parents. Let the Holy Spirit take control of you right now. While there is hope. If Satan comes back and finds your heart unoccupied, he'll bring seven more or worse demons in; your last state will be worse than before."

"I never believed in spooks," he said woefully, "As a kid, I thought my folks super'tious cause they believe in the Holy Ghost, and demons and such like. Now I knows they's real! They's terribl' cruel!"

"Okay, so...," Ruthe coaxed, ready to move from this topic. "Why not come to Jesus now? He'll fill you with Himself, His Spirit, and then these evil spirits can't enter you again."

Harv nodded his head, then buried his face in her lap and prayed with wretched self-abnegation.

Ruthe's own sympathy dripped onto his head, and she worked her fingers apprehensively through his filthy, matted and kinky hair as his head rolled and writhed now on his right knee, just in front of her knees. She ached for his suffering soul.

She was too involved to analyze in more detail, but she noticed that the men appeared more compassionate towards Harv too. Several were around him, bumping and patting him with their hands. Finally God's peace settled on him, and he gained some composure, slowly.

They had a thousand new things to talk about after that. The hours whizzed by. Sunlight was beaming through the cracks of the outer shell of the building before they realized it must be daybreak. It was only then, that it occurred to Ruthe that she was dreadfully tired. More than all the tiredness she had ever had rolled into one. Her nerves burned with tension over every inch of her spine and neck and tightly locked legs.

She yawned a long yawn, and Jon saw too that the whole night had passed. He got up and offered to take her home, apologizing for keeping her so long. "You must've been raised a gentleman in your past," she said with a shy, accepting smile.

His mouth went into a lope-sided grin for a second before he said, "No. I'm turning into one now."

She was tempted to ask if he wasn't afraid of being caught by the police. They had not discussed giving themselves up yet, but oh, Ruthe yearned for sleep so much. *Lord, You show them what to do next,* she prayed, and got up from the floor, announcing the street address for the Moss Rose.

The other men said shy good byes to Ruthe, Harv promising loudly, I'm going back to thank my Mama right away!"

Jon put her on his motorcycle once more and took her to Lisa's apartment building. They coasted as quietly and inconspicuously as the bike would allow through downtown's soft, humid dawn by the river.

Ruthe felt wearier by the seconds, and realized more clearly how she had lived through this night only by the energy of her dearest Friend. By God's Spirit, Jesus had been in, around, and beside her the whole time. She would go for a walk tomorrow and tell Him so.

In front of the tall and narrow, jade and gold trimmed house, she slid off; Jon gave her a squeezing hug, and she promised, "I'll keep praying for you." Quietly, he rolled down the street as she stole up to her rooms.

Her digital alarm caught her eye as she stepped into the cool, dim bedsitting room. *Almost six? Whe-ew. A whole night!* She was undressing even as she closed the door. Her last waking thought as she lifted the corner of her bedspread, blanket and sheet all at once was, *I better grab that receiver off the phone.*

SIXTY-EIGHT

A thunderous rapping woke Ruthe. *Ou-u-wha–! Wha'now?!*
The bed creaked and Lisa called out, "Ruthe? Throw on a housecoat. The cops are with me."
Huh? The cops? What's goi–?
Bouncing upright onto the floor, Ruthe whisked her old pink Fluffy around her, and in the same motion hurried to the door. In the time she made the four long steps and opened it, she was so dizzy she was tottering.
Lisa caught her bodily and led her back to bed. "Is something wrong, Ruthe? We've been trying to find you all morning. We gathered last night that you were too tired to come back to Darlin' Bonne's when you didn't show. You needed to be alone a while?"
"Anything wrong, Kid?" asked Aubrey's voice, with real concern.
"Yeah, where've you been?" Ginter looked worried, bending past Lisa's head.
Ruthe rubbed her forehead and scratched her scalp, trying to place the day. "Wh-what time is it?"
Someone said, "Noon."
"Oh-wel-ll-l," she yawned enormously, the whole long night flashing before her, revealed in a stroke of lightening, also the alarm clock when she had stepped in, "That's about six hours. I've had less."
"Six hours!" Lisa was tenderly disgusted. "Honey, you didn't! Not another shift of overtime? But listen, I called, and they said you had gone at mid–"
"Receiver's off," observed Aubrey.
"Not overtime, Lisa. I was just kidnap–" Instantly she regretted that word. She tried to suck it back.
"Kidnapped?!" the word re-echoed. Both Aubrey and Ginter, who had been peering under and behind things, swung on their heels and came closer.
"Aw-w, sugar!" Ruthe moaned, using what Sharri had claimed as her swear word. "I should'a kept my mouth shut. I'm not awake yet. Ignore me."
"We have to report on this; business, not social," Aubrey pointed out sternly.
"Charlie Brown was real worried, not to mention Herr Sgt. Webster," said Ginter, towering over Ruthe again, "When we saw your car towed in and both we, and Lisa, found your number busy continually. The SaskTel boys said your line was off the hook. Everybody knows you never do that. You like folks to call whenever they need you."

405

"Oh?" she jeered, "Last night– this morning, rather, I must have had an inspiration then."

"K, Honey, tell us," Lisa begged, sitting down on the bed and rubbing Ruthe's back deep and firmly.

"Y'mm-mm. Oh-aw-right," she gave in, knowing that she would have to tell these particular people sooner or later. It would look much worse if later. "Last night, on my way to my car after work,–" Ginter had said something about her car just now. "Oh no. Oh-h-no-o-o!"

"What's-a-matter?"

"There's probably a ticket on the windshield this minute!"

"It's been towed to the pound," laughed Aubrey.

She stared, then felt absurdly giddy. "You mean, you guys...?"

"Naw. We've already paid your ticket." Ginter's usual grin cut across his face. "But when the tow truck brought it in at ten, our Sergeants began to spit gravel. That's when the real A1 hide-n-seek game began."

Ruthe's forehead wrinkled as she squinted at the officers and reached for her glasses, "Don't they trust you guys alone on duty any more?" she muttered. "How do I rate doubles?"

"Every man on deck, and in pairs, the boss man said," answered Ginter.

Aubrey urged her to go on, "On your way to your car?"

"Oh yes, our new friends from the park ambushed me, just as I–"

"They couldn't have!" shouted Aubrey in disbelief. "We had every street sealed. Every blessed exit!"

Ginter's face hardened with a righteous hate as he interrupted too to demand, "What did those @#$%@ (excuse me), do to you, Ruthe?"

"Besides paralysing me with fear, and giving me a fast ride, you mean?"

"Ride? Where? Exactly now," Aubrey persisted.

"Fraid I don't know the address, but we didn't try any exits to the city. I was too frightened when we arrived, and too sleepy when we left to take it down."

Aubrey insisted that surely she recalled some landmark for a clue.

Ruthe repeated what she had just said, adding that she would try to recall more when she could. She wanted to save that fire-damaged look to the building a bit longer, though she wasn't sure why.

While this was going on, Lisa had picked up the phone and dialled a number. She murmured into the receiver, "It's Lisa. Send Dr. Davie over to the Moss Rose fast. It's his friend, Ruthe. She–"

"I'm okay, Lisa. Honest," she argued. "They didn't hurt me at all. Davie doesn't have to come out here for me."

"Go on, Hon," Lisa hung up, ready to listen. "So what did they do?"

"Well. Their leader perched me on an econo-line pulpit and said he'd overheard me say something over Emie's body in the park about, 'did she get the message through.' He was intrigued by this hint of a big secret. So-o, he and his men vanished yet trailed us on foot to the shop. Later, they saw me go to the telephone office. They simply laid in waiting until I came off duty."

"Did they say why they shot Emie?" Lisa wanted to know. The haggard shadows under her eyes proved she had not slept all night either.

"They suspected, when she came up in such a new, friendly mood, and in a dress (of all things), that she had been sent by the police as a trap. When she wouldn't admit it, and kept talking so different, they decided to kill her and run."

Ruthe impulsively threw an arm around Lisa's neck, "Oh, Lisa! We should be shouting and singing! The Lord's done such wonderful things! Let's praise His name! Hallelujah!"

Lisa pulled back in shock. "You mean you weren't scared when they jumped you? Honey, you always–"

"I was scared all right. Let me tell you. I never prayed so hard in all my life! And, when they told me, that if the message Emeraude had been bringing them wasn't worth all their trouble I'd be...." Ruthe swallowed quickly. "However," she grinned happily. "God's grace and wisdom was great enough. The Holy Spirit took over and did a beautiful job. He put words in my mouth when I was too scared to speak, and a divine and tender love for each of them. I don't remember all I said to them but after a couple of hours, one by one, they all accepted Christ into their own hearts and minds, beginning with the leader!"

Aubrey and Ginter whistled.

Lisa cried, "How wonderful!" and in her excitement, she squashed Ruthe into her bosom. "Now we know that Emie's death was not without fruit! God knew all along what would happen, didn't He?"

"Yes. Though He sure tested my faith there quite a bit."

"That must be why we felt like staying together most of the night to pray for you." She added, "Betty was worried about how you were taking all this, so we prayed real hard that God would answe–"

"At Darlin' Bonne's?" Now Ruthe nearly shouted, "I knew you must be! I just knew somebody had to be praying!"

"Some dropped out about four, but Darlin' Bonne and Betty and I hung on until six. Sorry, Ruthe, we were all drained."

"That's okay. That's when we finished too!"

"Really?" Lisa squeaked in surprise. "Praise God! They all have the day off and opted to stay in bed. I did a few comb-outs downstairs, and was just going to bed when these guys came, wondering where you were. Can you believe it?

They were ready to go to Kleinstadt, when June urged us to try here first, or where you go for walks on the river bank."

"When their leader, Jon, brought me here on his bike," Ruthe explained, "I was so drained," she tilted back her head and felt the shooting pain in her neck and shoulders afresh, so she winced, "I just fell into bed. How I had the presence of mind to take off the phone– Well, I won't apologize for that after all."

With a fast tap at the door, Dr. David Pollock let himself in.

Ruthe expelled another huge, sighing yawn, "Look't what the wind blows today."

"What's up?" he asked, breathing richly and looking around at the officers and Lisa, and Ruthe.

Ruthe had been sitting on her bed with her Fluffy wrapped tightly about. Now she tucked her sheet, blanket, and bedspread around her knees for extra privacy. "I'm okay, Davie. Go back to work."

"Seems she's unharmed," admitted Lisa, rising, "Though I was real worried."

Ginter and Aubrey moved towards the door. "Check her anyway, and send us a report. Maybe you could give her something to relax, Doc," said Aubrey helpfully, "De' Angel had a rough night."

"Before you guys go," Ruthe pleaded, "Whatever you do, please don't let this leak out. Keep it under your hats, or badges, eh? You didn't hear a thing, right?"

"Course," said Aubrey, "Classified information. Until we find those characters!"

"Nearly forgot–" interjected Ginter, "Where are they today?"

They seemed to take it for granted Ruthe would tell the doctor all the details too, so she resigned herself, but she shook her head to cut down on words.

Aubrey snorted disgustedly, as he put his hand on the door, "Every law man was out last night after those killers, while you blithely sit down for an all night church service!"

"It wasn't so blithe!" Ruthe retorted impulsively, "I can't tell you where they are. I just suggested they go home and start making restitution. If they got past your exit barriers they're likely making trails all over the continent."

"You would!" groaned Ginter, "We should'a known."

"Shielding criminals from the law is an offense too, y'know," Aubrey cautioned.

Lifting her nose, Ruthe was ready to tease back saucily, but Ginter cried out first, amazed, "Have you forgotten your friend, Emie? You two are our material witnesses!"

"Yesterday you were all in pieces–"

"Exactly." Ruthe glanced at Lisa for support, "So if we want to forgive them with Christ's love there's nothing you can do about it."

Lisa agreed. "Emeraude died, but her death brought forth the fruit she wanted most. So soon too. 'Vengeance is Mine, says the Lord.' Our part is to love our enemies."

Tenderly Ruthe looked at Lisa.

Aubrey shook his head vigorously, "Uh-uh. Can't do that, my sweets. The Law versus the murderer. Justice gets the vengeance."

"But we're your only witnesses."

"So. You'd be subpoenaed, and you'd have to tell the truth in court," aswered Ginter soberly.

"Hmm," Ruthe muttered mostly into her shoulder as she leaned back, "Hope they never get around back here then."

"Sorry, gals. We get paid to hunt 'em. Better get back at it, eh, Bud? Webster'll want to know this stuff."

Davie let out a long, impressed whistle. "I believe I've stumbled on the city's top secret."

"You have, dear doctor," said Lisa with an awesome authority, "And I shall swear you to secrecy, or I'll have your tongue on a plate before you leave. Understood?"

He pretended to look horrified, while Ruthe begged him, as a doctor, as a close friend, as a Christian, all the reasons she could name, to keep everything he had already heard, and that which he was to hear, very confidential.

"On my word of honour," he replied gravely, "I shan't repeat a word, Ruthe." He nodded at Lisa, to make sure she heard his promise.

Lisa accepted and got up, while Ruthe sank back on her pillow, weary and believing him too.

Davie took her wrist and pressed his thumb on her pulse, "Sure must have been wild though," he murmured.

Lisa, who had just gone into the kitchenette corner of the room to heat some milk, sang out, "I'd have escaped, or died of fright!"

Ruthe could see he had a dozen questions on the tip of his tongue, so she made sure of his promise once more, and outlined the story she had just told Lisa and the officers.

"Whew," he said when she finished. He ran his hand over his dark head and down his neck.

Lisa handed Ruthe a cup of hot milk and a slice of hot toast and said solicitously, "Honey, you should book off work tonight."

"No-no," she answered quickly between a sip and a bite, "I'm not sick. I'll be fit as a fiddle in a couple of hours."

"Davie, tell Ruthe she can't go," implored Lisa. "She's got this thing about not being late, and never missing a shift."

He dimpled at Ruthe, picked up the phone and dialled *0*. While waiting for an answer, he said to her, "You need at least one day of decent rest before you crac– Yes, Operator, give me your top Cheese, or the Super in charge, please."

Davie turned back to Ruthe with a firm, professional push of his hand, "You crawl back under that blanket of yours and stay there."

"What kind of excuse will you give?"

"Yes. Chief Operator? Okay Madam, this is Dr. Pollock. I just want to notify you that one of your operators will not be in tonight. No, I have not admitted her yet to hospital, but it is a severe case of pernicious lassitude, and a functional dichotomy between her physique and fortitude."

Ruthe gave up. The idea of missing a shift suddenly sounded quite lovely. A luxury.

As he hung up, Davie said to Lisa, "I'm afraid we have taken Ruthe for granted. At least I have, what with expecting her at the hospital just about the time I see a need for her special touch on a patient, never mind calling her at all hours for advice on my romance department." He paused to blush pinkly. "Can I count on you, Lisa, to see she will rest?"

"Of course I'll pamper her."

Davie growled at Ruthe with a voice lowered by emotion, "Guess the world will manage somehow, until tomorrow."

Dropping a foil card with pills into Lisa's hand for Ruthe, he added, "Now Ms Veer, you take these and go to sleep, or I'll send an ambulance to fetch you where I can watch you myself. Do yourself a favour and make an appointment for a complete physical soon, with any doctor you like. Your heart is just a shade off beat."

She closed her eyes and made a face.

Lisa said goodbye to him at the door, then quickly came back to sit on the bed and ask just a few more intimate questions. They turned into another dozen.

Knowing Lisa would understand better than anyone else, Ruthe told her everything again, with more detail, this time including the scene with Harvey.

But yawns kept interrupting her. Her eyes lost focus for long seconds together, and the warm milk Lisa urged her to drink make her stomach feel warm and cosy and her head heavy. When Lisa noticed Ruthe had trouble finishing some sentences she made Ruthe take one of the pills and tucked the blanket up under her chin.

"I'll take the phone off again, and leave so you can sleep. Your body wants that debt paid back."

Ruthe heard no more.

410

SIXTY-NINE

Ruthe slept the rest of that day, through the night and into the next morning. She woke only because Lisa came in to gently shake her and say that Sgt. Webster was dying to see her and ask her some big questions; she could not put him off any longer.

Feeling relaxed and refreshed, Ruthe obliged. After showering and dressing, and a chat with Lisa over a bowl of cereal and a glass of fresh-squeezed juice, she went out to walk the few blocks to the police station.

Sgt. Webster, with Charlie Brown and another officer, allowed a few moments to inquire as to her health as they settled into chairs. When they began to quiz her in earnest, Ruthe realized that she owed Lisa a lot for the amount of rest she had been able to have.

She looked bright-eyed and quite the innocent ingenue, she thought, when she recalled that the building of her long, intense night with the bikers' gang had looked rather fire-damaged. "Could that help you any?" she asked.

They asked about the walls and what fixtures remained. She recalled the charcoaled wooden crate she was placed on, and the lone light bulb on a long dark cord. When they asked about smell, Ruthe stopped to consider. "Yes," she answered, "I believe there was a smell, like my grandparents had on the ash heap behind the outhouse on the farm."

With a nod and some rapidly barked commands, Sgt. Webster dispatched men to check out the MacIntosh warehouse that stood deserted after its big fire.

After a grilling that seemed to last all morning, he offered to take Ruthe to see if any other memories came to the surface. That visit shook her up visibly, for details of the long night's discussions and blurred into a fuzzy dream with her extra day of rest, but seeing the crates again, and the light bulb, and the cracks in the outer wood siding through which she had first caught daybreak's bright streaks suddenly made blocks of conversation come back with a rush. Her shoulder muscles even became taut in the same places. "If it were not for those crates, that one in particular," Ruthe said, pointing to a higher one, and those cracks, "I might be persuaded that I dreamed the whole thing up." She stood still and stared at the spot where Harv had caved in when she confronted the Evil One. She told of that scene cautiously, not sure how these men would hear it.

Sgt. Webster hunted for traces of the men or their motorcycles, but Charlie Brown, seeing Ruthe's tension, hinted to his fellow officer that Ruthe could go.

"No," said Webster, stopping his scribbling to stare at the ground outside the rear barn-like door, where bike tracks criss-crossed each other in a few spots,

411

but were mostly scuffed and obliterated. "I want to take the lady out for lunch and listen to all the conversations she can recall. There's clues here somewhere."

A while into this review in a nearby fast food spot, Ruthe realized there might be some detective value in rehearsing those talks and discussions, but she would have preferred to do it at Darlin' Bonne's. There were times when the Homicide Sergeant stopped her and asked her to go back and say exactly who said what and after whom. He seemed to want to memorize the whole script. Sometimes she could say, but often she shook her head and insisted, "Too much went on for me to register every word and detail of the night. I'm not even sure of all their names."

"So far you've named, Jon, Harv, and Zoro." He was especially heavy on the part where she had recommended they go back to make restitution wherever they knew they had hurt someone. She guessed he was hoping they would come back to confess to this murder, but Ruthe made clear that she had not urged it, and did not know if they would be that thorough in their new lives.

At last she sighed and hinted that she ought to go home to see her parents before she came back for her evening shift. "They'll be out of their minds wondering if I'm okay. I slept all of yesterday and never called."

"Lisa called 'em for you," Charlie reassured her.

They had talked over empty styrofoam the last hour and a half at an outdoor picnic table. Charlie admitted, "We must've heard your story about eight times by now, so—" he looked sideways at Sgt. Webster for a sign of quitting.

The distracted detective caught on. "Okay. I believe you, Ms. Veer. You have convinced me it happened as you said, and that you don't know where they are this minute. However," he guaranteed fervently, "Soon as I find just one of that gang, you, and Lisa Starr Turnoff, will go on the stand as my chief eye witnesses."

Oh-oh. Ruthe's mind switched into prayer gear. It would hit the papers and newscasts then. The fear of publicity brought her mind instantly to her parents, and her long-running double life. *Lord, I really mean to work on that, but I'm not ready for another crisis!*

She was dropped off by her car behind the Moss Rose, and made a trip to Kleinstadt, where she spent over an hour assuring her mother that she, and Sharri at the Charm n' Poise Course, had been perfectly safe the last couple of days in the city. "Besides, I hear the police have said that gang has left the city."

Right after work at midnight, she kept a phone promise to go to the shop and tell her friends about her adventures with the bikers. Lisa had told her how anxious they were to have her join them before they settled on a funeral date for Emeraude. They'd put it off for Ruthe's sake.

By now Ruthe could sum up that night in about an hour's time. For a change, no one sewed, all hands were still as they listened spellbound, and commented on the complete change in her confidence. She seemed more mature and wise than ever to them. Which made Ruthe nervous, for deep within she felt more vulnerable than ever.

As for the funeral plans, her phobia about the media, and thus her family finding out her connection to this drama, made her wish they had gone on without her the day before when Lisa had completed all the arrangements. When Donnie told her a couple of media people had been around the day before asking questions, and had figured out that Emie was a friend of the Shop, Ruthe became convinced that mobs of them would try to interview her, and her life would be over. Thinking about it made her freeze for whole minutes with panic approaching her terror on that first motorcycle ride.

"Ruthe-Darlin'! What's come over you? There's such contrasts here."

Darlin' Bonne and the others gathered round with sympathy but talked of puzzling after-effects.

To shorten the late night, Ruthe pulled herself together to get the decisions made. She would deal with her secret terror privately. "How about an early morning or dawn funeral? If Pastor Teaon and the funeral home don't mind?"

"Day after tomorrow?" Lisa asked, and promised to line it up.

"Yes. I've got a day off then, but I've promised to help Mom."

Ruthe was relieved the next day when Lisa informed her the early morning was acceptable to Pastor Teaon, and also the funeral home, which had already scheduled a different one for the afternoon.

At the dawn graveside service stood only the sombre young women who had prayed for Emie on Sunday afternoon, Officers Aubrey and Ginter, and one freelance journalist. Ruthe overheard that woman turn and make a remark to Donnie and Evelyn about being the only journalist up at this ungodly hour, so she made a studious point of keeping several bodies standing between herself and that woman, and as blank a face as possible.

Pastor Teaon said all the right things, but sounded alone. He invited farewell comments; Lisa responded with a few sisterly words addressed at Emie and promising to meet her in Heaven. When Ruthe saw the others glancing expectantly at her, she stepped behind Ginter's tall figure. She felt ashamed for spoiling it for the others.

Back at the shop for breakfast, when her friends pried, Ruthe admitted to being worried about being named in that woman's article. "My family will learn about my involvement, maybe even the... kid-... kidnapping from her, rather than me. I still don't know how to break it to them, even though I realized

Sunday night that it is wrong for me to live this double life. I promised God I would deal with it."

Darlin' Bonne wrapped her arms around Ruthe and prayed on the spot, "Lord Jesus, please give sister Ruthe peace and much wisdom over the next few days, so she can go ahead and do this hard, but right thing."

She was moved to tears, especially as the others came by to touch her and reassure her they would keep praying for her.

Ruthe had that and the next day off and spent them at home, helping with the garden, and the laundry and housecleaning, so that her mother could forget she had been absent and feel that things had returned to normal. She watched hard that first day for the right moment to break the news to her mother, but it just did not come. Her mother had the radio on every hour and every half hour, (hating the music between), to see if anything else had developed. In the evening Ruthe went for a walk to pray in the willow bushes, and resigned herself back to the idea that it was not meant to be.

Instead she found herself having an imaginary conversation with Emeraude, telling her how she'd got the message through to Jon and the gang.

The next morning, meeting local people on the way to the post office, Ruthe learned that everyone had heard of the murder of that woman in the park, and several wanted to know if she had gone to see the spot. This was tricky for Ruthe, since she had been the first there, with Lisa. Instead she said, "Oh, I'm not a great one for commemorating the scene of a tragedy. I've just been praying God will bring something good out of it, that's all."

By Friday, the fifth day after the murder the newscasters seemed tired of saying, "The police have no answers, and are still investigating. A handful of friends gathered for a seven a.m. graveside service yesterday, but no family has come forward." By noon there was no mention of the bikers' gang any more.

Ruthe went with her mother to Grosz'mama's for faspa that day. Her Grosz'mama wanted to hear the story from Ruthe's own mouth. So she outlined the story, playing careful tick-tac-toe with her words. As far as she could gather, a young woman who tried to leave a ruthless gang of evildoers on motorbikes, was shot by them. Maybe she tried to follow a more straight and true path, and if she had been used by them, they might have had their own way of dealing with quitters.

The elder matriarch with her ever regal calm sat in her rocker and expressed a quiet aghast at the wickedness, "Gott woat an jerajcht feaudeele."[29]

"Oba woat Gott den nicht fejäwe fe Jesus' seinshaulwe wan jane sikj-selfst bekjeare?[30]" Ruthe asked quickly.

Solemnly her Grosz'mama nodded yes, "Oba daut es wijchtijch, wan menschen een fonn Siene doot schlone waut Hee erschaufen haft."[31]

Ruthe returned the solemn nod. She was well aware of God's strong feeling against sin. However, in her personal walking and talking with Him, she had come to appreciate in balance, His tremendous love and willingness to forgive those who were sorry and would admit it. How could she remind Grosz'mama of that? Suddenly she recalled Manasseh from a sermon two or three Sundays earlier. The Bible said he was the most wicked man that ever lived. But he repented while he sat in prison and God forgave him when he cried out for it. Ruthe hitched her chair a bit closer and asked Grosz'mama if she'd ever read of King Manasseh in the Bible.

She had. Grosz'mama was willing to look him up and read about him again. So they did. Ruthe's mother sat quietly listening. When Grosz'mama had read the chapter aloud in her German Luther Bible, she looked up, right into Ruthe's eyes, which hovered close by.

"Jleewst enn dien Hoate, dee manna woaren sikj bekjearen?"[32]

Ruthe didn't know how to answer that question without giving away what she knew. However, she looked steadily back into Grosz'mama's eyes, and could not help it that her mouth began to smile ever so slightly. Just like her Grosz'mama, Ruthe tried to freeze her expression at the corners of her mouth, which twitched with a desire, a need to smile.

All at once Grosz'mama reached up and stroked Ruthe's head and down over her ear, murmuring softly, "Gott haft die oba enn wundaboa gloowe jejeft."[33] She sat back and began to rock, "Soo dan haw wie noch nicht daut enj jeheat."[34]

"Ekj weet nuscht fonn waut die woaren doonen."[35]

Ruthe was both frustrated and relieved to hear someone at the door, and her mother shooing her to go answer it. She scrambled to let in Isabelle, waddling, Scottie, carrying Curtis, and Brandt, leading Regina.

Now Ruthe was roundly scolded for not coming to see them in more than a week. "And what do you know of that awful gang murder?"

Her tact was to say that she had been far too busy to really to hear any newscasts, except the last day or two at home with her mom. "You fill me in, if you have any facts."

All three gladly recited what little they knew, and of course, in no time the children wanted attention, so Ruthe allowed them to distract her and to coo and talk to both Regina and Curtis.

Scottie tried to draw out Ruthe's personal opinion on the event, and she heard Grosz'mama tell him, "Rutee has faitt dat even such wicked men can be saved." That made her nervous for a moment, but Grosz'mama voiced no suspicions about how much she might know.

Next she threw herself wholeheartedly into Isabelle's craving for peanut butter and poetry, and her confidence that she was carrying twins for sure this time. The poetry piqued Ruthe's interest most, but she didn't know how to ask to see some, since she didn't have the courage to show off her own writing.

Isabelle confided that much as she longed to write poetry, she had nothing more profound to say than that she got these midnight cravings for peanut butter on roasted bun halves. "Brandt and Sharri both have said that this Phyllis Shulton has been urging you to write. What do you think, Ruthe, can you get an editorial session for me with her?"

As they were parting at the door, Ruthe congratulated herself. She began to see that others would drop the subject as soon as any little thing happened to them, but she would be the last person to forget the scary, exhilarating weekend. A part of her wondered if she would get mentally confused when old, and forget then; another part knew she always would remember those big angry men melting, transformed by the love and power of God.

She and her mother were in her Rambler, waiting for the Clarkes to back out first. Then Scottie came forward to her window at a little trot. He ducked his head down to her window, "Just wanted to say, we prayed for you on Sunday when we heard of that murder on the radio. We know how you tend to stumble into the lives of needy people. Isabelle even said she prayed for you when she slippered around at night, looking for miracle peanut butter to appear. Well, we're just glad you were safe and sound at work that night." Scottie patted her shoulder, "We'd feel awful if anything happened to you."

Ruthe just stared back into his eyes, motionless. "Thanks!" she whispered faintly, her eyes already watering.

She spent that night debating with the Lord, or rather, more with herself, whether to reward the Clarkes with the true story of how she had been involved with the bikers. They'd be impressed. In the end, she knew all it would do would impress them, and for all their loyalty Isabelle could not be trusted with secrets like that, if she couldn't keep her own about her dream twins.

A few days later, back at work in the city, and going to see her various friends as usual, Ruthe became fairly sure Sgt. Webster was having her followed. She was almost used to Ginter or Aubrey popping up, as they had done so often, but now she spotted other officers in her rear-view mirror several times a day. They were just there, and happened to say "Hi," when she came out of the SaskTel building, when she passed through Eatons, or the Bay, on a quick noon shopping trot; they were often on the doorstep of the Moss Rose, and the Chrysalis. Even when she felt it was time to check on her friends at Bright City, one was just coming in as she was going out. She mentioned this to Aubrey one day, but in the friendly banter, she realized afterwards, he had not confirmed or denied that she was followed by assignment.

Ruthe decided it would not help matters to become reactive. Then they might accuse her of taking food to the gang at some hideout, or knowing more than she had told them. Instead she prayed, *Lord, help me to live such a pure and exemplary life that anyone who studies me will be drawn to You, and give You glory and praise.*

On the other hand, she felt like she ought to write something in the way of a worthy epitaph for Emeraude.

The rest of the summer was unusually hot and busy with ordinary and mundane things. Ruthe now wondered if she had just such an overdose of excitement that now everything was a let-down. She made her rounds, visiting or checking on the friends she had made in the past, yet more and more she preferred being alone, and pounding at the typewriter in her Moss Rose room seemed a safe outlet for the torrents of words building up inside her.

The Charm n' Poise Course wound down again at the end of August with no outstanding scenes or notes, except that Sharri was more confident and had been treated like a young movie star. Ruthe felt as if they had drifted apart a little and now Sharri had no time to renew their relationship. *Or, maybe,* Ruthe weighed the matter, *Sharri is just copying the example I've set; becoming independent and self-sufficient, reaching out to help others.* She let it drift, for she was not sure of her own motives any more.

The hot weeks and months ticked by, gradually becoming fall, and Ruthe met no new friends to add to her secret bouquet of rare roses. She felt tired a lot, so concluded that it was just as well. When she wasn't rubbing an itch in her eyes, or catching up on sleep, Ruthe tried to sneak in an hour or two on her book. The more she watered it with her time, the more this secret grew, along with her pleasure at a very interesting plot.

The strange night with the bikers had left no physical mark, but Phyllis who was bold enough to hunt up Ruthe and check to see if she was really writing or avoiding it, confided to Lisa, who also was often near and was concerned about their evangelist, "Ruthe has retreated into her own private garden. I worry because I know what happened when I just sat and thought about my traumatic experiences." Phyllis turned back on Ruthe, draped over her typewriter, her chin on her hands, looking baleful and over-relaxed, "Please, Ruthe, confide in someone else if you prefer, but do work through those events."

Ruthe shook her head, wishing they'd go away before they peeked at the page rolled on the platen. she tried to put Phyllis off gently, "I'm okay, and the Lord is all I need just yet for sorting my thoughts and feelings."

She got a little provoked when Scottie Clarke noticed her moodiness too, and commented on it. She brushed him off lightly as well, but was touched that he and Isabelle cared about her even if they didn't know all her secrets. It comforted her that most of her friends cared. What she couldn't work out was whom to trust. Who could help her understand the mysteries she couldn't understand about herself? Or her parents?

Maybe all I need is some guts, she told the Lord, realizing intuitively that perhaps everything hinged on telling them the truth.

By fall, when new things were starting up again, Ruthe felt she had put the experience into its right perspective and could finally put it away like a book on a shelf. Most of the time it stayed there, closed. Only rarely did it jump down and flop open in front of her.

That winter there were a lot of snowstorms, so Ruthe often stayed a day or two at stretch in her rooms in the Moss Rose, just phoning home to reassure her mother where she was, and she threw herself into her secret novel. She knew Phyllis and Lisa had guessed, but they did not beg to read or discuss it, so she offered them no clues, and carefully hid her pages. No one should be able to snoop when she was away.

SEVENTY

Out of the blue, in the middle of February, just after the Sunday evening service at church, while most of them still stood visiting in twos or threes, and while Isabelle and Ruthe compared their current spring fever symptoms, Isabelle cried out sharply, "Sc-ott-ie!" With both hands she grasped a hat hook on the vestibule wall beside her.

Scottie made his way through a circle of olde women and swooped his wife up in his arms.

Ruthe overheard Isabelle tell him with clenched teeth, "Ahead of time, just as twins always are!"

"Okay, Belle," Scottie said, "I'll get you to the city. Fast!"

Ruthe saw a place for action and stepped in reflexively. She separated a swath through the staring people to the door. Her Rambler happened to be right at the foot of the outer steps, so without giving it a second thought or asking Scottie, she tripped nimbly down the cement levels and opened the right-hand door.

As Scottie carried Isabelle down, Ruthe noticed Brandt at the top step with Curtis on his arm, and Reggie playing peek-a-boo between his legs with another toddler, also in a snowsuit. "Brandt!" she yelled over her shoulder as Scottie backed in with Isabelle on his lap. "You look after the kids."

"Don't worry about us!" he shouted back, with quick understanding, "Grosz'mama and I will take care of everything."

Ruthe slammed her driver's door on herself, and instantly had the car started. She reversed, then spun down the slushy street. Ignoring the stop signs because she could see the few town streets were empty, she tore down the three short blocks to the highway.

"Scottie! We'll be too late! We won't ma–ke it! I can tell– it's faster no–w–w! Ow-wu-eh!" Isabelle's voice crescendoed in pain.

"I know, Darling. Just hold on. Ruthe's doing her best!"

She sure is! Ruthe answered in her head.

Once on the highway her car rushed on up to the higher speeds. Fortunately, she knew every curve and bend in this road. She pushed down the pedal harder. Soon she was passing three and four cars at a time, swinging back into her lane just in time. Next thing she knew she had to do it again. And again, from inertia, almost.

Twice, she nearly ran into an oncoming car. It was difficult to judge distances at these speeds.

419

Oh-h, Lord, she breathed tensely, *Let's not let Isabelle lose these twins, okay? She's got to have 'em!*

She glanced at her phone. "Can you use that?" she asked Scottie.

He reached a hand for the speaker, looking for the next step.

"Dial O and give her this number."

Scottie repeated them in as she called the digits, then he held it towards her.

Ruthe shook her head, "That's Dr. Pollock. Ask him to meet us in Emerg."

Scottie did. With Isabelle was groaning in agony, he fumbled putting it back, and the mike part rolled under his feet.

At a hundred and forty kilometres an hour, she had a strange sensation of her spirit detaching itself from her and watching them from the inky and sparkling velour of the night sky. In an effort to pull herself together she informed Scottie, "Should reach the city in another ten minutes."

He nodded, his eyes on Isabelle, who was panting and crying. Her sharp cries pierced both their hearts, and they smelled warm blood.

Ruthe leaned forward, concentrating tightly on her wheel, the road horizon, and her right leg tensed on the accelerator. A police siren joined them when they entered city outskirts. She knew there were many jokes about speeding to a hospital with a woman in childbirth, being held up by the police, and.... Now she couldn't recall any punch line.

Suddenly she remembered her car phone. Where–? Oh, it was under the seat. Scottie could not reach it over Isabelle's churning body. If she pulled over and waited for a ticket, it might be too late for Isabelle. *Listen, Lord, I have to stay ahead of those boys. At least til the hospital. Then I'll give myself up. Deal?*

"Hang on." With a dangerous squeal she veered left. It was the old trick Lisa had used, and came to her just as she saw a certain street coming up that she sometimes used to avoid the downtown lights. It had hardly any traffic at this hour, and connected with the wide Spadina Crescent that followed the river to the bridge. At the Twenty-fifth Street bridge she would have to ease back into heavy traffic somehow, but once on the other side, she simply would lean on her horn until up the emergency driveway.

It worked. The flashing cherry failed to take the turn and the siren faded. But when she crowded back into the bridge traffic another squad car appeared from nowhere to whine behind her. She screeched her brakes to a stop as the emergency doors opened.

But Isabelle had just gone limp.

"Sur-nough, he's here!" Scottie cheered with relief.

"Yeah!" Ruthe glanced inside and her eyes watered as she saw Davie shooing orderlies out with the stretcher. He was in his surgical greens.

420

Swiftly they laid the suddenly unconscious Isabelle onto the stretcher, and whisked her away. Scottie's dress shoes clicking fast after them.

Ruthe sat, just breathing whistling breaths through her mouth.

"@#$%@."

She jerked, startled. Aubrey's grinning face was up close against her window. Ever so slowly she opened the door.

"Look't what we have here!" he crowed.

"Our Angel de Mercy? I declare!" laughed Ginter. "Speeding? Ruthe, how you do drive! You should'a seen yourself!"

...*Think I did.* But she shook her head.

"Remember, Ginter," Aubrey was laughing almost too hard to talk, "My turn to send this in to the *Reader's Digest.* You cashed in on her the last two times."

"Huh?" Clinging to the car door, Ruthe pulled herself up and out. As she drew upright, a wave of dizziness sent her reeling against the car. A purple and roaring world spun around her.

When it stopped, Aubrey was holding her up with arms so strong and steady, Ruthe longed to crumple on him and rest a while. "Kid, you better sit down. Crime is a little hard on your physique, eh?" All at once Aubrey was gentle.

"You better rest a bit, Little Lady," said Ginter with his head cocked at an angle. "Fraid we'll have to take you in for questioning though. Too many squad cars involved in this chase to let you go. Sides, we haven't brought in a criminal in some time, have we, Aub?"

"Lead-where-you-will," Ruthe said passively. She ignored them while they consulted with each other.

Aubrey put her back into her car but shoved her over so he could sit at the wheel. Ginter disappeared to his own squad car, Ruthe guessed. She became aware of a damp spot on the upholstery, however, and knew Isabelle had bleed too much. As the minutes passed, she felt stronger.

At the station she explained about Isabelle and Scottie, what had happened at church in Kleinstadt, and how, at the speed she had been going she had not been able to reach her car phone from under Scotties' feet.

The officers and staff found the fact that Ruthe, of all people had been caught speeding very funny. She imagined this would be a locker room classic. They led her on a while about having to write a ticket, yet when she wanted them to hurry it up, they admitted they didn't plan to do that after all.

"So instead of standing ready to help Isabelle and Scottie, I'm here, giving you an excuse for an office party?" There was a sharpness in Ruthe's voice that chilled the laughter.

A phone rang, and abruptly a receiver was handed to Ruthe. It looked heavy and like an enormous shiny black thing to her. "Yes?"

421

"Ruthe?" asked a polite, low voice.

"Oh Scottie. How's everything? Isabelle's–?"

"I heard the police took you away from the doors. Are they holding you because of us? I'll pay any and all speeding fines; you know you saved Isabelle's life." There was real anxiety for her in his voice.

Ruthe assured him all was well, winking meaningfully at the friends about her as she said, "They were quite understanding when I explained the circumstances," But she was anxious to know about Isabelle, and should she say, baby, or twins?

Scottie told her that Isabelle was in Recovery. The whole labour was over in thirty minutes." Then, sighing, he added, "She doesn't know it yet, but the baby girl was already dead."

"Oh no-o! but the boy? There was one?"

"She hasn't been told yet, but yes, she did have twins. Ruthe, you remember how she counted on them?"

"I know." She was at wit's end for Scottie. "I wish I could have made it sooner. Was there really no way they could have saved the girl? The boy lives– for sure?"

"Yes, Evangel is doing fine. Don't blame yourself," Scottie soothed graciously. "You drove much better than I would have. The doctor says he will have an autopsy done to be sure; but he thinks Evangeline's respiratory system hadn't fully developed yet. She was younger." Scottie sounded so tired that Ruthe knew it was best not to pursue this conversation just now.

"All right, Scottie. You rest while Isabelle is sleeping. You'll have a big day tomorrow, when she finds out. Will the hospital let you stay with her?"

He assured her they would.

"Meantime, don't worry about the kids. Grosz'mama and Brandt will have them well looked after. The farm too."

"Yes, I'm sure of that. Ruthe, when I think, if we had never met you, I...." Scottie was about to cry, and that promptly brought her own floodgates wide open in empathy. She had never known him to get so emotional before.

"Hey-there. What are friends for? God ordained it." Quickly she finished off the call.

When she held out the receiver to whoever would take it, there was a silence bordering on reverence. Charlie broke it as he took the receive from her, "The world needs more friends like you, Kid."

Flustered, Ruthe left with hurried good byes, then drove slowly, agonizing in prayer, all the way home to Kleinstadt.

She gave the baby news to her parents, and when her dad asked if she had got a ticket for speeding, Ruthe simply replied, "They did notice me, but when I told them why, they let it go."

The next morning she was helping Grosz'mama feed the Clarke children so Brandt could get the barn chores done, when Scottie called from the hospital. Ruthe answered.

He reported that he had told Isabelle about the dead girl a little bit ago, and she was so stunned she was almost like a stone. "She won't speak or cry, Ruthe." Again, Scottie was on the brink of caving in. She allowed Reggie to interrupt and say hello to her Daddy.

Ruthe then urged Scottie to forget everything else for now and stay at Isabelle's side. Brandt was in the barn, and the children were being very good for Grosz'mama. "If you like, I can see about making some small funeral arrangements for wee Evangeline."

Scottie thought that was a good idea. "But I've given permission for an autopsy and it will be a few days before the doctor will want to release Isabelle, so set the date no earlier than Wednesday."

First she called up Pastor Ewert and related the details. He too knew of Isabelle's confidence that the Lord would give her twins, these two dream babies. He promised he and his wife would be praying for the Clarkes, and yes, of course, he would conduct the funeral.

When she called the undertaker in the next town, he was most under-standing, and said that such small coffins were specially ordered and quite expensive. She asked for measurements, which she could give to a carpenter. The man had a relative who had been counselled by Scottie, and knew they couldn't afford this very well, so he complied, but commented, "I'm surprised this has occurred to you."

"My Grosz'mama is here and remembers how it used to be done before your grandfather started your undertaking business," she explained.

"Ah-yes. He learned a lot of his tricks from those Old Colony ladies." Then he gave her some more pointers and tips, which she jotted down, and showed to Brandt who was listening nearby.

Brandt said, "I can build that little casket from leftover boards in the barn."

Ruthe had that day off. Though Darlin' Bonne's Shop did too, they were all away for a day at the Oaks' farm. She knew she could slip in and make a dress and maybe a tiny coffin lining for the wee dream baby. She checked to make sure Grosz'mama could manage if she was gone most of the day, and left, to make more arrangements, Ruthe told her.

She was glad to work all alone in the shop for a few hours. She needed to keep her hands busy so her mind would go forward instead of round and round in its thoughts. When she finished the padded satin casing and added a touch of pale embroidered lace, she made a long satin gown, the colour of old lace, trimmed with the same.

Having tidied up her snippings and left a note for the girls, she went next to a flower shop to pick out the daintiest straw flower arrangement.

All day, as she did these things, Isabelle was on her mind. Ruthe worried about her. Isabelle had come a long way since she had first met her. This had to be the biggest crisis of her entire life. She knew intuitively, that Isabelle had not left room in her mind for anything to go wrong with her dream babies, claimed with such stark faith.

She reflected on Isabelle's idealism, and idealists in general, as she sewed and went from place to place. Ruthe identified vividly with Isabelle's emotions of shock, disbelief, then anger, but she didn't know how she was going to convey it in a helpful way. Mostly she feared Isabelle would expect her to explain God's failure to come through.

Finally she sensed an attitude from above that said, *Now Ruthe you don't believe I'd let anything touch my precious children unless I was sure it could bring them to new depths of love and wholeness, do you? Especially if that person has asked for it?*

"No-o," she answered half aloud, "But I'm scared she'll turn bitter against You. This is too big for her. I don't know how to help her! What can I possibly say when I see her? I might break down myself."

Exactly what you should do, Ruthe. Cry with her so she won't feel so alone. It will break through the crust of ice she's building over her heart.

Right now? Will You come along please?

Knowing Isabelle loved poetry, she stalled by stepping into a card shop beside the flower stall, and tried to find a card or poem to put Isabelle's emotions into words. There was nothing close to it.

As she neared the nursing station on the maternity ward, two nurses looked up and recognized her. "Ruthe! Sure hope you've come to see Mrs. Clarke," the one remarked with feeling. "She's so withdrawn. Won't speak to anyone, not even her husband. Poor sweetheart."

"We've tried everything in the textbooks," said the other nurse. "Nothing works. I don't understand; she never got to know that baby, and she still has the other one."

"Oh, but they were custom-ordered babies," Ruthe answered with a sinking feeling. What if she failed too?

"Go ahead. Dr. Pollock was wishing for you earlier, and her husband has gone for coffee."

Ruthe nodded and turned in the direction they pointed.

Beat it, Satan. Scat. Sho-oo! Deliberately she worked at getting rid of the oppressor.

As she marched down the hospital corridor she allowed the pathos of the disappointed mother with dreams to flood her. Isabelle's soul cried out inside hers; in Isabelle's style and even some rhyme.

Softly Ruthe pushed on the door. Isabelle lay on the bed facing the wall, perfectly silent and motionless. *Maybe she's asleep,* she stopped, *I'll try tomorrow.* Then she noticed an eyelash flicker as though Isabelle sensed someone had come in, but she did not turn.

Hesitantly, Ruthe stepped forward and put her hand on the strong, freckled arm lying on top of her side. It would have looked relaxed except that her hand was clenched into a fist on the sheet in front of her. Ruthe whispered the words her imagination had just heard while she was in the corridor;

"Oh Lord, You said to ask in Your name,
and whatever I wished You would give.

Oh Lord! I asked for two more babies in Your name–"

Isabelle sat up. Her arms whipped around Ruthe's neck. She sobbed and sobbed. And sobbed some more. Right away, Ruthe gave in and cried too.

"Ru-uth-e," she said at last, "I didn't think anyone und-r-st-ood!"

Ruthe reminded her that she had known about the dream from nearly the beginning. "I also know it was not the usual dream, but a big step of faith for you, so the conventional comforts and Bible promises don't apply. The baby's–going back to Heaven– isn't nearly as much to you, as the fact that the Lord seems to have broken His word to you."

"He promised me, Ruthe! I had perfect faith!" A fresh gush of tears came. "He gave all right, b-but He held it out, and then snatched part of it back. It's not fair, Ruthe! It's just not fair!"

Isabelle became more belligerent and articulate in a rougher language as she gave Ruthe a piece of her mind about God.

Perched sideways now on the edge of the bed, Ruthe held Isabelle, hung her head in little nods and let Isabelle go on. What could she say to defend God? Besides, this poison had to come out sooner or later. She would rather she heard it than anyone else, even Scottie.

About then Scottie walked in with his coffee. He stopped as if his shoes had run into a low wall, but relief washed over his face to see Isabelle sitting up, energetic with pent up emotion, and finally letting it all out.

Together, Ruthe and Scottie pointed out that God is a loving Father who knows what is best for His family members. He loves them too much to give them anything to cause them unnecessary heartache, though some does come through sin or wrong choices. God must have seen her request as good in and of itself, so He honoured it. "But He also sees every day and moment of our lives; He knows what's coming," Ruthe crooned, "If we knew all God's reasons, we might as well take His place."

Isabelle's respect for Ruthe seemed intact, but she could not bring herself to agree, and gradually curled down on the bed, silent again.

Getting ready to go, Ruthe bent over Isabelle for her last comment, "The important thing is; talk openly and honestly with God. He's big enough to take your shouting and swearing, and when you are ready, He'll answer you honestly. Scottie and I care and want to listen and dialogue with you, but only the Lord will satisfy your questions."

SEVENTY-ONE

The weather had been mild. On Wednesday it turned bitterly cold again. Nevertheless, most of Kleinstadt came out for the funeral. Five local businesses closed for two hours in deference. People sympathized of course, because the Clarkes were well-liked, but many were curious. There had not been a baby funeral in town for ten years. Word spread this was an exceptionally pretty baby in the coffin.

Other wags said there shouldn't be a funeral for a baby born dead.

Ruthe was surprised to overhear two older woman talking with her Grosz'mama, about how many stillborn babies their husbands had buried in their gardens years ago on the farm, without benefit of a funeral.

"Was I wrong to assume we needed to prepare for a funeral?" she mused aloud in her grandmother's presence.

"Nä, dit'z goot, sea goot!"[36] said her Grosz'mama quickly. "Daut es fäl jesunda wan dee Mutta kaun sikj daut hoatje ut schedden, un nicht sikj festäakje."[37]

Later two other women in the church basement, preparing to serve the usual funeral refreshments after the burial, told Ruthe the same thing. Funerals help one to grieve and accept the death; otherwise it causes deep inner turmoil and damage. "You're a gud gurl for orga'nizin' dis for the Clarkes," said the one.

"Yes, they will thank you one day," said the other.

Ruthe and Pastor Ewert had agreed to set the wee coffin on a table in the vestibule so folks could have their look while they filed into the sanctuary. She gave the ushers the little folders to distribute, which the pastor had made up about Evangeline. It included her poem, which she had taken time to compose more completely after visiting Isabelle, and shown him when he and his wife came to see them at the farm. Mrs. Ewert had said she should read it at the funeral, but Ruthe was afraid she might not make it all the way through.

Then she went down to the basement to greet Isabelle's parents and sister Jean, and to discuss who would carry which of the children. Scottie and Isabelle both felt Brandt had to count as part of their family. She had forgotten to line up pallbearers, but Pastor Ewert tactfully suggested that Brandt carry the coffin in. Ruthe saw the Clarkes relax as if that settled it, so she made sure Brandt knew he was designated.

Two o'clock came. Pastor Ewert prayed with them and reminded them, "Tears are nothing to be ashamed of; they are most cleansing, and Psalm 56 says that God saves up our tears in bottles. They are very precious to Him. What is more, Jesus wept when His friend Lazarus had died, so He is weeping here too."

Ruthe went ahead in the line up to make sure the ushers had everyone seated, and noted with surprise that folks were standing along the walls with no place left to sit. She motioned Brandt to close the coffin, and carry it to the communion table in front of the pulpit. The Clarkes followed, with Isabelle pressed tightly against Scottie. His arm was wrapped around her in tender support.

As they did, a fact hit Ruthe with the force of a slap. They were no longer two happy friends of hers who happened to be married, have a little family, and to like her; Mr. and Mrs. Clarke were an older couple. Ruthe felt very single and young in comparison.

Isabelle's father, Mr. Squires, a tall man, with wispy orange hair, carried Regina in, with Mrs. Squires carrying the fussing, squirming Curtis. Jean, Isabelle's sister, looked like she would like to be elsewhere, maybe writing an exam.

Brandt sitting on the other side of Isabelle, turned around and held out his hands to Curtis, who seemed to leap eagerly into them. Soon he was quieter and gripping a couple of his Mommy's fingers.

Ruthe waited until Pastor Ewert took his place behind the pulpit, and in his familiar voice, full of compassion, implored all the congregation to come to Christ with their heavily laden hearts. An usher motioned her to a wee narrow space her Grosz'mama had made beside herself on the last pew. She slipped in.

They sang a hymn. It undid Ruthe's emotional grip. She wondered why she usually cried during the hymns of a funeral. The pastor prayed. Then he called her up to read her poem.

Already? Feeling suddenly damp and hot under her arms and down her back, Ruthe took her folded paper up and stood behind the pulpit. She had resolved not to look directly at Isabelle, but her first glance forward caught Isabelle's expectant gaze. With a great slippery lump in her throat, she began,

"Oh Lord. You said to ask in Your name,
And whatever I wished, You would give.
Oh Lord, I asked for two more babies in Your name,
To teach of Your love and the gift You gave."

At that, Isabelle buried her face in Scottie's shoulder and burst into weeping that echoed into the high ceiling of the sanctuary. Hundreds of eyes were on her, most of them growing wet in sympathy.

Ruthe had to blink fast to clear her vision, and swallowed at her lump some more. Now she felt compelled to go on.

"Oh Lord! I promised to give them both back to You,

Like Hannah, that saintly woman of Your Holy Word.
And now Lord, You've answered my prayer of faith:
You sent them both, and in every detail, cherubs.
But why? Why Lord? I cannot understand WHY
You'd take part of Your gift back into Your Hand!
Did You think I might take too great pride?
Or fail to lead them close to Your own side?
Was it that I be spared later agony in her life?
—I'm sure I would gladly have borne any knife!
Oh-h Lord! Your ways are higher than mine;
Let me put my trembling hand in Thine.
Dear Lord, keep me from a bitterness of soul;
Please take my broken heart and make it whole!"

Turning, Ruthe felt her way down off the platform and to her spot in the last pew. She was blinded with scalding tears, and tried to remember that Pastor Ewert had said not to be ashamed of them. Wiping her eyes with Grosz'mama's big white cotton handkerchief, she became aware that most of the congregation was blowing noses with her. A little out of sync, but together with her.

The sermon was short, yet snatches of it spoke to her tender heart. That was followed with another hymn and then Pastor Ewert dismissed them for the trip to the Clarke's farm pasture, giving brief directions.

Brandt had learned, and Ruthe relayed by phone to Scottie at the hospital, that there was a fee for burial in the cemetery, and after adding Grosz'mama's tip, Isabelle had described a little corner of their pasture which was wooded with white poplars and willow bushes, as the burial spot.

Putting Evangeline's body away for good was agony for Isabelle and Ruthe found herself helping to hold her up.

When that was done they had to go back to the church basement for the Ladies' customary faspa, where coffee, tea, (or just water), buns and cheese sticks were offered. The community used this time to visit and if they could find some words, they tried to offer condolences to the bereaved. Presence was understood to mean the same thing.

The Squires were not used to this, and though they had met only a couple of times in the past, of all these people, they only knew Brandt and Ruthe. Over the coffee and buns they talked mainly to her, and said how impressed they were with her poem. They had already picked up a few extra folders lying on the floor.

"Oh, it's not a real poem. I don't know anything about meters and stuff. I was just trying to sum up the anguish of Isabelle's heart."

They insisted it was wonderful. Then they asked her to explain other things about this church and the customs. She answered warmly as if it were natural they be here and be full of questions.

After they left her to say goodbye to Isabelle and Scottie and the children, Ruthe stood and watched as people filed by behind the chairs at the long table. Isabelle's face was screwed up with pain as she tried to respond politely to each one. *Hmm. At least Isabelle is not going to have to stay home, wondering how people will react if she comes into public again, because here she is meeting them.*

Scottie politely thanked each person for his and her sympathy.

Mrs. Ewert, the pastor's wife, stepped up to ask Ruthe, "How do you think she's doing?"

"She appears to be past hating God outright. I think she wants to demand an answer from Him, and it's hard to concentrate with all these people here." Ruthe paused. "When her wound heals, we'll have a different Isabelle. But that gash is very deep."

SEVENTY-TWO

Evangel came home a few days later. He was a tiny, dark-haired baby, looking much like Scottie. Almost as if he sensed his mother's sorrow, or perhaps his own loss, he was quiet. He slept through most of the night, and was sober and of steady gaze during his feedings.

"He's de egg-zat other-hand of Regina and Curtis," announced Grosz' mama, who was moving steadily from one thing to another in the Clarke household, trying to let Isabelle have her quiet spells. "One hardly knows dis baby's in deh' house."

In a few more weeks the spring thaws came and Ruthe thought everyone showed shades of cabin-fever as they came out to inspect patches of grass and other signs of spring. There was excitement and renewed outdoor activity all over Kleinstadt. In her more frequent visits, Ruthe tried to joke to Isabelle about the awful city slush on the streets, but Isabelle did not join her in their usual playful bout of spring fever. Her weeping jags had stopped but her soul was arid and cold.

One day she informed Ruthe that she was going to try to do without God again. "Sure, I had some nice times as a Christian, but I can manage just as well on my own. There have been times I guess He helped me, but how can I tell when to rely on Him? He's so unpredictable."

Ruthe prayed intensely each day for Isabelle even as she went about her city visits with friends, and to and from her job. She asked Darlin' Bonne's girls and Phyllis to pray for her as well, and even phoned Sophie and Peter to recruit their prayers.

About three weeks later, Isabelle told Ruthe she had not been able to do it. "The Lord has become such an intricate part of my life that I find myself praying to Him even when I didn't mean to."

Ruthe's response was, "If I didn't have the Lord to live for, I don't know what would be the point of living. Without Him everything is mechanical motions. Just bland existence."

Isabelle agreed, "My parents tell me they are trying out churches in the city now. I prayed for that so long! I guess it's not that God is wrong; I just don't understand why He let Evangeline die."

Ruthe's heart leaped. *She's growing!* There was hope for Isabelle if she could proceed from one truth to another in her understanding of God's ways. After the number of times Ruthe had told of her devotional walks and chats with the Lord, and Isabelle's retorts about needing her rest more, she was caught off guard

431

when Isabelle confessed that she had slipped away early a few mornings to sit on a log by Evangeline's grave, and talked bluntly with God.

Right on! Ruthe cheered.

As Isabelle's spirit slowly healed in the warmth of the sun and in honest talks at God on that dried birch log, as she called it, she began to write poetry. She had often complained before that she was not able to say just exactly what she felt. Ruthe's poem expressing her initial cry had opened the deepest vein she had, she told Ruthe, "Now the lines flow like crystal clear water from a pure mountain stream. And it works best if I start with 'Our Heavenly Father,'...."

Scottie confided to Ruthe that Isabelle had a secret tin bread box hidden somewhere, and she was filling it with her new poetry.

Ruthe didn't dare ask about it, but there were occasions when Isabelle would excuse herself, and come back a few minutes later with a page or two of very private verses.

At first they were bitter and chilly addresses to God. Gradually, they became quieter, and were addressed to Father-God, and later to, our Heavenly Father. There was one in which she suggested He might have taken this baby in answer to her other prayers for help in writing good poems, and for knowing Him more intimately. Maybe even to make her parents hungry for God.

Ruthe told her, "When God wants a tree to grow big and strong, He puts it out in the open spaces where the winds toss it, and the tree responds by sending its roots deeper. I'm no expert, but it looks to me like your roots are going down deep and strong into Him now."

Her own roots, meantime, seemed restless, searching and reaching to go deeper too. She could see she had grown a lot since high school days, but she longed to know still more about the Lord's ways and to have a greater power and influence in the lives of others, for His glory. Though her present lifestyle had many good features, it felt static and dull. She must be on the brink of change, but she hoped it would not involve as much pain as she had watched Isabelle go through this spring.

432

SEVENTY-THREE

A spiritual awareness with the most delicate sensations of life around her came over Ruthe as a part of her spring fever. She could see her whole biography like a panoramic-surround. Her eyes picked up exquisite beauty and colour, even if in blades of grass or new weed sprouts, her nervous system registered the emotions of others as vividly as her own, and she had colourful daydreams of things she hoped might come to pass. This spring she yearned for love and marriage. However, she recognized too, that she had built up such high ideals she could no longer settle for anything less. *What if I've become too idealist? Is that possible?* Ruthe mulled it over for a couple of days and decided, no, she preferred to stand by her high ideals. She would trust God, whose standards were even higher, to help her climb up instead of going further down.

Still, a tiny fear tapped at the windowpane of her spirit, *Won't I get any love and marriage then?*

It was ignored, for her heart also ached with a poignant passion for all the people suffering in many individual ways, all without Christ as their Friend. Dreams and visions for helping them flooded in on her mind, until Ruthe was distraught because of her inability to carry them all out. Some called for heaps of money, and some called for four or five times as many hours as she had in a day. Some days she was overwhelmed and berated herself as a stupid and foolish daydreamer. Other days, when she remembered to talk these ideas over with her Friend, she sensed a really big change coming over the horizon. The biggest dramas of her life were yet to happen.

What do You want me to do? she begged her constant Companion. *Will it start with another crisis and rescue?* Then she recalled promising to be a missionary as a child. *Are You sending me away as a missionary? That means Bible School first, You know, and I haven't any– Oh, sorry, I might be able to go on my share from the shop.*

Hey! Maybe I could go slumming in a big city out East? That would give me something meaningful to do between waiting for editors to decide about my book. Ruthe was almost afraid to think how she would cope if her story made friends fast and furiously. She considered insisting that it be published anonymously, with a foreword that gave all the glory to God. *Yes, if that's legal, that's what I'll do.*

Almost impishly, timidly, she sometimes added as a postscript to her prayers and thoughts, *Or, have You got me mature enough to meet that wonderful husband You've been preparing me for? So You can use us together to accomplish a great deal more than either can do alone?*

Phyllis discovered Ruthe's secret book about this time. She praised it highly, but also ferreted out each misspelled word and punctuation, suggested Ruthe throw out her chapter titles and divide some up. She even wanted some characters dropped because they added nothing to the plot.

Ruthe mourned them the most, but could see the need to re-write and heed all the other editorial points. All she could project was years of hard concentration and more ruthless re-writing. Ruthe simply did not have the time to do it justice in her stolen minutes and hours.

Phyllis strongly recommended a writing retreat.

"I've lived too close to poverty to let go of my job security for living from hand to mouth. What's more, it would mean another secret life, for how could I ever admit I was writing a book until it was published?"

Giving her a hug, Phyllis said very softly, "I know. The devil has you in a net and wants to eat you. Until you are liberated, happiness and your full spiritual potential is a prettily shaped cloud, drifting up high in the sky."

The words were like a dart and haunted Ruthe, echoing in her mind and thoughts for weeks. She told the Lord that she wanted to be liberated, but she couldn't seem to do it from inside the net. *Please, will You come from the outside and rescue me?*

One day in late March, as she sat at the switchboard and wistfully glanced at the high windows where a breeze played with the drapes, Ruthe was calculating how much time to the minute was left of her shift, when one of the supervisors startled her by plugging into her position and saying into her headset, that she could go to the Chief Operator's desk to take a personal call.

Operators were not allowed to take personal calls while on duty. All her friends knew and always left messages with the Traffic Clerk, or a supervisor. Whenever she got her next break she could check the bulletin for notes and go call them from the lounge.

"You're in trouble,"Daisy teased, "A police sergeant wants you."

Charlie, Ruthe decided, returning the friendliness, *He must have another girl for the Chrysalis. Only, he usually leaves a message.*

Picking up the phone on the big desk at the end of the huge room, she said confidently, "Hi-ya, Charlie."

"Hello. Ruthe Veer?"

Oops! Doesn't sound like Charlie.

"Sgt. Webster here. Not Charlie!" he laughed. "Sorry to bother you at work."

"That's all right." But she wanted to watch her answers; the supervisor shuffling schedules nearby had to be listening. "My mistake, Sir. What can I do for you?"

"Couple of minutes ago, a sharp-looking, well-dressed American walked in and asked for your address. Says he lost it. Says his name is Jonathan Astor. Seems a very polite business man, but these days, who knows, eh?"

"W-wat?" Ruthe gasped faintly.

"Wasn't sure whether you knew him or not. Do you–?"

"Listen," Ruthe commanded, "Is he still there? Right now? Of course I do! What are you doing with– I mean–"

"Hold it!" laughed Sgt. Webster, "I take it, you do know the man."

"Well, I don'know. I think-so...," Ruthe sputtered. A hundred questions were bursting in her head.

"He asked for the Homicide Sergeant. Seems to believe I'm a good friend of yours. Told him it was Charlie Brown you must've referred to, but Charlie's not in just now. I said I'd call and ask how you feel about seeing him."

Ruthe was about to blow up in a million pieces. "Sgt. Webster," she ordered with complete disregard for the supervisor and clerk. "I get off at four this afternoon. That's– in twenty minutes. I'll be over directly. Don't let him wand– Tell him I have to see him before he goes anywhere or does anything!"

"Sure thing, Ms. Veer. I'll tell him."

Oh-e-ew! Can it be him? It's almost a year. Has he changed so much they don't recognize him when he walks into the station? It has to be him! Oh, Lord, this isn't a trap set for me, is it? But I have nothing to hide from the police.

Ruthe knew Sgt. Webster still mulled over Emie's murder when he had time. Perhaps even knew more facts about the gang than she did, despite all she had told him about every leather jacket and every knee showing through jeans that she could recall. She had repeated the conversations of that night as verbatim as she could; it was a puzzle why Sgt. Webster had not been converted too by now.

Sure hope Jon doesn't confess to that murder before I get there, she worried as she put her headset on again and went back to her position. There she stopped herself with questions, *What? I don't want him to confess? Whatever ails me?*

Never had it been so hard to concentrate as she tried to contain all her scrambled thoughts, feelings, and memories, and still announce collect calls. Everything she thought she had carefully put away into the past like a book on a shelf was tumbling down on Ruthe.

As soon as she was relieved by the next shift operator, she raced off to the station and went panting, into the building.

A man with a huge smile hurried towards her. "Ruthe. Is it ever great to see you!"

Dumbfounded, she stared. Facing her stood a handsome young man of about twenty-six, in a sharp-looking brown suit with thin, orange pin stripes. A clean, genuinely eager smile shone from ear to ear on a smooth-shaven face. His hair gleamed in short, bronze-gold waves on top of his head. His big brown eyes sparkled with delight.

He stepped a little closer and took her limp hands into his, while her uniformed friends turned their backs and bent over their work. "Hey, I did as you said." He lowered his voice a bit more. "I went home and straightened everything out."

"Wo-onderful," Ruthe said, getting her tongue back at last. "I'd love to hear all about it!"

He flashed her an even bigger smile, "I've fasted and prayed long enough, and these guys are busy. I suggest we go down the street and look for a restaurant. We'll take it from the beginning, okay?"

Ruthe's conscience instantly noted that this was an invitation to a dinner date. But she wanted so much to hear all of his story. Ready to be rash, she accepted.

Jon walked like a gentleman beside her, leading her to a nice, secluded place in the dining room of the Bessborough, just blocks from the police station. They had a magnificent view of the river that she had never seen before, and they could watch the city light up on the other bank, after the sun went down.

Jon, or Jonathan, as he now wished to be called, began his story by revealing that he had been born into a well-to-do New York family. "My parents sent me to Harvard, but I was very restless there. I wanted something enormously challenging. Something to fill a nameless vacuum in my soul."

In his second year at Harvard he had concluded, after hearing some Marxists talk, that all the problems of the world were the fault of people like his capitalistic, establishment-conforming parents. Therefore, the one smart thing to do was to cut off all ties and be free of traditions. To Jonathan, that meant living instinctively, like an animal, doing exactly what he felt inclined to at any given moment.

"However, why just run with the pack, when you can be a lead dog?" he'd said when he boldly announced his intentions to his parents. He had bought a motorbike, rounded up a few friends on the road, and dropped his Business Administration studies. He had enjoyed planning activities with dare and danger, and treating drugs like chewing gum. Emie joined them, giving him more dramatic ideas, often topping his.

"How did your parents take all this?" Ruthe gulped. These details knotted up her shoulder muscles again, as she tried hard not to let the question into her mind, *Whatever would Mom and Dad say to me being friends with this man?*

"Dad disowned me. But my mother–" His eyes dropped guiltily. "If anyone ever died of shame, she did!" Jonathan's head rocked sadly, "She took a cerebral haemorrhage a few days before I got home last year. She clung to life until I was there. Mother didn't really regain consciousness, but when I took her hand, she squeezed it as if she recognized me. I swear she did. That night she died."

His father had been much slower to forgive. "I'd hurt him terribly by dropping out of Harvard. It washed up all his dreams that when I'd join him in his firm, we'd become really big financiers. As it was, he couldn't tell if I was a commie, a hippie, or a Charles Manson."

"Couldn't he tell you had changed when you came back?"

"I sure looked different! Before we left here, we had shaved and trimmed one another's hair. We buried our bikes, and we showered at the bus depot. And we sent Geoff to the Sally Ann for used clothes."

Ruthe's eyes were popping out as he added with a grin, "We separated, every man for himself, took buses, trains, whatever, to go home. I watched from across the street as those big police dudes brought you back to the warehouse; you have no idea how I prayed to know whether to confess right then and there, or not!"

Then Jonathan shrugged. "You'd said during the night, 'When in doubt, don't.' So I put it off until I knew beyond a shadow to come confess."

"Ah-h-ha." It was a sigh, a laugh, and a tremble, all at once. "So that's how the great escape took place! I had absolutely no clues to give the police, though I'm sure they had me followed for weeks afterward, in case I was bringing you food somewhere."

They laughed together.

"At one stop I bought a Bible to read," Jonathan went on. "It was staggering. Over and over it said all the things you had told us. Lots more besides."

Ruthe put down her water glass to speak, but Jonathan went on. "In trying to explain to my Dad, I remembered you sold me on Christ when you talked about your experiences and conversations with Him in such an open, honest way."

"Open? Honest?" Ruthe cried out with surprise, "Maybe I was transparent because I was afraid to be anything else, but that wasn't me talking to you. The Lord helped me with almost every word that night. I've thought about it lots, and to this day I can't recall half of what we covered that night! Just the outline, which, by the way, Sgt. Webster has memorized too."

"I'll tell you sometime then," Jonathan answered gravely. "I'll never forget what you said. Yes, I believe God helped you. You gave off light and power that was out of this world. Supernatural."

"Anyway," he went back to his story, "I sat down with Dad and told him everything I had done. The whole big sch-mess from beginning to end. Including Emie."

Ruthe was impressed. Such nerve to tell her parents all the past was beyond her reach. Eagerly, she asked, "Your Dad understood then? He believed it all?"

"Dad was stunned that I had sunk so low. But he understood then, and he believed I had really met God that night, and that I was truly changed. In fact, as he watched the changes still coming over me, he decided that he wanted such encounter with God too."

"That's marvellous!"

Jonathan lowered his voice again, and went slowly on, "Dad and I found ourselves on the same wave length at last. We began to communicate. Funny thing; we'd always thought of ourselves as total opposites but we discovered we were falling into– y'know, family love."

"Praise the Lord! That's just–" Ruthe paused to catch the past tense. "Oh. You said you *were*?"

He sighed, "I don't deserve exemption from sorrow or death, but I did feel terrible when he was murdered."

Sympathetically, Ruthe gasped.

"Drowned actually, by the crooks who had been blackmailing him for a certain piece of real estate."

"Oh Jonathan! I'm so sorry. What a shame!"

He nodded sadly, "Yeah-h, it was a blow. Just when we were finally getting along and respecting one another."

Ruthe reached out and touched his hand lying on the side of the table, noticing suddenly how clean and strong it looked. "Listen," she said, "We may not always understand what's happening, but God never, never makes a mistake with His moves. Not when it touches His own."

Jonathan looked back directly and steadily into her eyes.

"I've been saying that to all my friends for several years, but when Lisa and I found Emeraude dead there in the park, I caught myself wondering seriously, if that line was just in my head. If it was maybe the power of positive thinking, or my stubborn perseverance. But then God proved to me that night, that He is still Master of the universe, and that He," Ruthe slowed for emphasis, "does not– make– mistakes."

"You mean even murder comes from His hands?"

"No. He allows people to do evil as they choose, though at times He protects some Believers in Jesus, if they pray. On the other hand, He turns some evil, like murder, if it is given to Him in prayer, from ashes into beauty. If you study the book of Job you'll see, Jonathan, how Satan had to go to God for permission to bring calamity on someone. Later, God prospered and blessed that man twice as much as before because of the way he came through the testing of his faith. The Bible is full of such *ashes to beauty* stories. I guess our Heavenly Father lets troubles fall on those who trust in Him, when He knows these things will be turned into good for our character-building. Of course, some folks react wrongly to such troubles, and are a big disappointment to God in this goal."

"Doesn't He know our reactions beforehand?" inquired Jonathan earnestly.

"Yes, But remember, God gives us room to exercise our will."

"Ah– Ruthe," he moaned almost under his breath, "I wish He had not given me the freedom to kill Emie! When I think that perhaps there was not any other way for Him to get my attention than to let me do that terrible deed, to show me what a fool I was," he stopped to cover both of Ruthe's hands, "then I tremble before the awesomeness of God."

An involuntary shudder went through Ruthe. She did not know how she would ever return to normal living with that on her conscience. She drew in a hasty breath and comforted Jonathan, by explaining how Lisa and she had compared Emie's death to a dying seed in the ground, so that more of its kind could be created.

"That's good. I wish I could say that about Dad's death. It didn't bring anyone else to God. It was a waste. I didn't know at the time, but Dad didn't even have what they killed him for; he'd sold it."

Ruthe frowned. She didn't follow this.

"You see, when he disowned me and the heat from the crooks got too much, Dad went to the FBI. They advised him to go ahead and sell his business to his friend as he intended, but to arrange to keep up a normal facade for a while, and to pretend to make a big deal with the blackmailers for a trap. Dad's friend agreed to play along."

"So they caught them?"

"No, they got away. That's why I say, it was a terrible waste."

Jonathan now entwined his fingers and rested his chin on them with a sad conclusiveness. "Guess I could say my inheritance brought me back. I have nobody– nothing left, but some cold cash in the bank, and some stocks. I figured I'd better come back to confess to this dastardly deed and give you the money to do some good in the community."

An expression Ruthe was not in the habit of using popped right out of her astonished face, "You're kidding!?" As she did, she saw pleased satisfaction wash over Jonathan.

In a far rear corner of her mind she realized that he had meant to impress her. *Oh, you dummy!* she told herself, *What he wants— is me!*

Jonathan was smiling gently, and shook his head as if puzzled. "You know, on the way up here I realized, if Dad were alive I'd be so busy with making investments I'd be in the workaholic trap. I might've written a confession letter one day and sent it. As it is, I stopped at all kinds of places on the way, wherever

I recalled doing anything really stupid, and I made apologies. So maybe you're right; Dad's death is bearing fruits of repentance and good works in me."

Aware her face was an open book, and that tangled angles were being added, Ruthe tried to compose herself, and was unsuccessful.

"Strangely enough," Jonathan was studying her quizzically, "I stopped myself when I walked into the police station. As I asked for Homicide, I got to thinking; what if I wouldn't be allowed to talk to you once I was behind bars? They'll call you as a prosecution witness. So I just asked for your address."

Ruthe stared back, bewildered. *He held back for my sake? Lord, is this so I can talk him out of it?* Yet at the same time she was sure Sgt. Webster had figured out who Jonathan was. She glanced around the dimly lit restaurant, as it was past sunset, half expecting to see the Sergeant closing in on them.

"Your police, and the national RCMP still want me, don't they?" asked Jonathan, thrown off balance by Ruthe's confusion. "In every other town or city there'd be officers vowing to take me in. Y'mean, nobody in Saskatoon wants to lock up Emie's–" he lowered his voice, "murderer?"

"Oh they do!" Ruthe's tongue was back in gear. "I'm amazed Sgt. Webster didn't pounce on you! He's the one...," her voice trailed as her mind tottered under the onslaught of new thoughts that leaped at her, "Why the RCMP aren't escorting you, I don't know!"

"That surprised me too." Jonathan stopped to smile as the waitress neared and removed the dishes, and asked about coffee and dessert. When she was gone, he said, "Maybe God blinded them temporarily, like that army that came looking for Elisha in the Bible, just so we could have this short chat together."

Oh. So this is just a one-time chat? But what of the fall-out for me, if he goes to court? Flustered, Ruthe held up her linen serviette as if to examine it. "This sounds strange coming from me; I'm always urging people to get it all confessed and restitution made. Suddenly I'm swamped with a great desire to advise you against it." Ruthe hung her head and couldn't look up.

"You're suggesting I should not confess?" Jonathan sounded so astonished; Ruthe had to glance up at him.

Though she kept glancing away, she tried to explain, "Lisa and I, and God too, we've all forgiven you. Nothing would bring Emie back. You'd be prosecuted simply because– well, that's how the law stands."

Ruthe felt more miserable and ashamed by the second. This was all wrong. It was a sin. She must not talk like this! *How can I ever urge someone to repent in the future, if I hide this great wrong?* Suddenly a part of her knew that she had committed a sin for several years as well, in deceiving her family about her friends and activities in the city. It was almost as if God were leaning very close in front of her and saying in a firm, quiet voice, *Okay Ruthe, if you are so mature a Christian, dare you counsel a murderer to hide his confession just so you can keep up your charade?*

Her whole being knew her spiritual malaise had been building up to this for a long time, but she had averted her attention. Now her life was going to stop in its tracks until she dealt with it. Abruptly she was hot from the inside out, and seconds later, cold as if a huge barrel of ice water had been dumped on her. She gripped and held her elbows. *Lord, this is worse than that night with the gang!*

Jonathan asked again, "You don't want me to say anything about it?"

Much as she wanted to flee to be alone all night with the Lord and talk this out until she had peace, she tried to be civilized. "No-o. Usually I urge new Christians to confess everything. Christ commanded it. From my observations of Lisa's, and others' experiences, it's the right– really, it's the only right thing to do. Afterwards they have a tremendous sense of spiritual and emotional freedom, and often all their relationships are dramatically changed."

Ah-Lord, would that happen to me and my family if I–?

"Didn't they do an autopsy, or whatever, on Emie?"

Ruthe nodded affirmatively, but puzzled. It was a tangent from her train of thought. "They found a broken neck and a bullet embedded in her heart. Why?"

"I killed her!" He sounded raspy and ugly, "What's the first degree sentence up here? Life? I deserve death!"

Ruthe gulped, "We all deserve death in God's sight. True, murder is a big sin. Think how much Jesus loved us to forgive so much!"

"Then why are you upset about my confessing here?" Jonathan reached out and took Ruthe's right hand from her left elbow and held it gently in both of his large, strawberry blond-haired ones. Hot and cold washed through Ruthe as if she were all pipes and hoses.

She hung her head again. How could she explain her complicated double-life so it didn't sound petty? The effect the trial publicity would have on her family was silly compared to the importance of doing what was right. Now she knew it was wrong if Satan could use this secret spot to blackmail her like this.

Jonathan seemed to catch on. "Ah-h, I'd be creating problems for you? I didn't realize. I'm truly sorry. I should have stayed away."

"No, it's okay. I'll... I'll tell you everything. I need the practice." Like a rushing, babbling mountain stream, Ruthe poured it all out. Her secret city life, her friends and involvements with the O'Briens, the Greystone which became the Chrysalis, Darlin' Bonne's Shop, the Bright City boys, or young men, Phyllis, the brilliant teacher who was trying to make a writer out of her, Lisa, the prostitute, now turned into a unique landlady, and the Clarkes, whom she wanted to trust but dared not, the sister who was popular and the sister who always seemed offended, but how all these tied to her distrust of her own parents. Parents, who were not rich or very educated and intelligent, but to whom she felt a loyalty, maybe even love, only she didn't know how to express it because they never had said it.

And then Ruthe had tears and mixed feelings because she was telling all this to an almost total stranger, rather than friends whom she knew and with whom she felt comfortable.

"But why?" asked Jonathan.

Ruthe was sure he was trying to comprehend how she could make such a mountain out of a molehill. She cleaned her face with a tissue.

"I don't know yet. I think the Lord is trying to tell me. I need desperately to get away to talk it all over with Him, and to draw courage for my decisions. He is the one person with whom I have always been totally honest. Maybe He's just been waiting until I was up a tree and ready to face the music."

Jonathan took hold of each of her long, thin forearms, which were damp with cold perspiration, and drew her closer across the table. "Ruthe, it surprises me, and yet thrills me to think that God works so many years at purifying and polishing His Christians. I urge your own advice on you; throw yourself recklessly on the mercy of God, and confess whatever He points to as wrong. It may be get stormy, but after the clouds roll away you'll be glad you did."

Ruthe wanted to cry. That was exactly the encouragement she needed to hear. Only it needed to come from someone outside of herself. But this was a public place, so she slipped another tissue from her purse and turned aside to blow her nose. "You're right," she nodded. "I want to go home and work on it."

It had been about two and a half hours when they came out into the crisp spring evening air. Ruthe felt as if she had just got off from a long, long trip, and as she let Jonathan walk her to her car, she knew a bigger one was to come.

Since she wanted to go home to Kleinstadt, Ruthe gave directions to the Moss Rose, and assured Jonathan that Lisa would be happy to hear his story too, if he got bored. "And Lisa doesn't have my hang-ups to depress you," she added.

Jonathan slipped an arm around Ruthe and promised not to confess to the police until it was okay with her. Meantime, he would check in at the hotel where they had just been, and he would go see Lisa.

SEVENTY-FOUR

Ruthe struggled to concentrate on the highway as she drove home. Her head hurt so much. She didn't know where to start her thinking. Her mind was like a pot of raspberry jam at a rolling, foaming boil.

At home she realized she had missed going along to a special church service. She took a painkiller, and wrung a towel out in cold water. This she folded over her forehead and eyes after she had crept into bed. Whimpering, she begged God to clear up her pain by morning so she could go pray somewhere. "We've got to resolve this! Soon!"

She woke before sunup. Her headache was not nearly gone, but thinking of her urgent appointment in her secret garden, she got dressed.

Ruthe drove around to the farthest part of the Clarke's rear meadow by a narrow dirt road. It was only used by farm machinery in seeding and harvest; a more recent spot she had found, so her sisters could not be sent to find her. Nor did Isabelle wander to this bush. It was too far from their house. Their gentle Jerseys might happen along, but Ruthe knew she was likely to spend the entire day without anyone finding her. She had the day off, and had not promised anyone a visit.

First she spread an old wool blanket on the dew-damp grass by the mossy clover and buttercups on the east side of the clump of birches and wild Saskatoon berry bushes, where soft tweeting indicated that it was wake up time in the nests. On the discoloured blanket she threw the larger half of a torn and worn bedspread that she kept in her car for such times. Now the sun could bathe her as the sky filled with its light. Wearily she lowered herself on her comfort zone, arranging her Bible and a box of tissues beside her.

"I can't understand this awful tiredness," she muttered, as she did up her sweater, and then also her winter jacket against the wet chill. She yawned enormously several times.

"Now then, I don't mean to be rude," she prayed aloud, "As You can see, I haven't brought food or bedding, but I want to stay here until I understand clearly what You want me to do, and You give me the power to go do it. I'm not being difficult, Lord, I just mean business."

Ruthe thanked God that she could talk over her problems with Him, and that He knew her views and feelings, and all the other details too, much better than she did. The blush in the eastern sky bloomed rosy and grew broader and higher.

It confounded her that the Lord could bless her, with what she thought had been successful friendships and influence, when obviously, she had been

443

disobeying Him by her attitudes to her family. *Oh dear God, Your love and mercy is too deep, too high for me. How can You be so very patient with me? But Lord, if You want me to open up to Mom and Dad, and to Suzanne and Brandt,... oh-h, then You've got to show me how! Else I'll never manage it!*
Ever so tenderly her conscience said, *Are you ready to face it as sin, Ruthe?*
"Yes," she answered aloud. "Ye-s!" she cried out imploringly to the sky, where a deeper rose pink stripe gave some trees in the distance sharp black silhouettes. Hanging her head, scratching and pulling at her scalp, Ruthe confessed that she, a faithful pray-er and soul-winner, had sinned against her family and God. "I can't go on like this!"
"Please, Lord, I'm scared. This is why I'm out here; You've got to prepare me." Her panic grew as she thought about it, until it cut off the very communication she sought. Nothing profound came to her. A large space above the rose pink horizon turned mauve and blue, then lighter blue while the pink section crept higher and higher.
She depressed herself thinking what if she told her parents about Jonathan. *They'll rant and rave! They'll want me to quit my job and find something in Kleinstadt. Or, they'll insist I come home whenever I'm not working. They'll tell others here that I'm wicked and not worthy....* New discouragement dropped on her like a big net, and her hand was quickly into the tissue box.
The sunshine gradually warmed until it came to full strength, and the birds of this small woods, already alive with praise and worship songs began to swell with happiness and joy at simply being, or whatever they counted as their favourite blessings. They fluttered about and sang with all their might. Taking this in distracted Ruthe a few minutes, and when she looked back to herself, she had lost her train of thought.
She groaned, "I'm such a mouse before Mom and Dad!" Then she stretched out and rolled over on the cool, moistening blanket. She massaged her temples as tears welled in her eyes, "I'm bold with strangers; why is that?" Ruthe felt she wasn't gaining new ground; just wallowing in sad facts that she had long known.
Her eyes burned. Her head felt soggy and achy. A strong temptation came to lie still and nap for a bit. But she had made up her mind to settle this once and for all time; she forced herself to sit up, and to wrestle some more with her fears.
Time evaporated into the morning heat. She took off her jacket and tried reading her Bible, hoping to come upon counsel from her good Friend. She even tried for a minute to sing her old favourite hymn, *I Come to the Garden Alone*, but she choked on the third line.
Deeply dejected, she sighed, "Where is Your beloved voice?" and laid down. She was too exhausted to think any more, so she lay very still, her mind letting go, just breathing.

Like the drone of a fly coming and coming, an important truth quietly arrived: *I told Muriel to confide in her parents; look what happened– they all, every one of them, became Christians. Her mother, just in the nick of time too.* She knew that had been a wise move.

Ah-but, Darlin' Bonne told her mother and it– Ruthe stopped short as she realized that if her mother, Marie, had accepted her daughter there in the hospital, there likely would be no shop. Hundreds of women and girls would still be miserable, unchanged, and some dead.

However, June told her mother and now she's in a sanatorium, probably for life. True, June does have the kids in the Chrysalis, where she is giving them much better love and care than she could before. That made three cases where telling the truth had paid off well.

Betty Oakes came to her mind next. She had not meant to keep her whereabouts a secret from her family, and their anxiety was wonderfully erased when Jim found her. They were a very happy, communicative family. The other girls loved going to the Oakes' farm on a Monday.

When Ross had finally told his family, and herself, about Ann Mueller– *Hey, afterwards he became a new creature in You, Lord Jesus, and he and Ann got married after all.* Ruthe knew that would not have happened if he had not cried out for help and been honest.

She hid her face in her hands, *I thought my friends and experiences were unrelated adventures. You've been trying to teach me this all this time?*

Ruthe thought of Isabelle, probably serving porridge less than a mile from this spot. *When she gave in, she got a lovely home and family, with no bears to fend off after all. Now she's learning to walk and talk with You, and to write poetry. I can't even guess what good is yet to come for her.*

She gulped as she realized that Lisa was another prime example. She repented and turned herself in, ready for jail, and got paroled. Lisa faced the music in a number of people from her past, and has seen some fantastic miracles. *I was there myself! How could I have missed this vivid object lesson?*

What's more, Jonathan's been confessing since last year; see what it's done for him! The evidences from these examples overwhelmed her with conviction.

If I'm honest with Mom and Dad, Ruthe asked her Friend who seemed present again, *What's the best that could come out of it?* She decided that, leaving out all negative possibilities, she might get some of the love and emotional support she craved so badly. *This inner conflict would transform into peace, and maybe I could live one life instead of two overlapping ones. Perhaps Suzanne would be triggered to spill her secret torments too.* Mulling these and other likelihoods over she began to hope, and then to believe that she might have some miracles herself for a change.

Ruthe sat up and looked into the distance, not seeing scenery. *Whoa! I could go to the police with Jonathan too! What dirt can the reporters find on me? I'm nervous about the publicity– but only You know what good things could come out of that.*

Ruthe felt Jonathan was likely to end up in prison, but that he would do fine there, and that God had still a different man in mind for her. With this intuitive knowing, slipped in assurance that God would give her courage to be transparent, both at home and in the city. She drew in and expelled a satisfied breath.

Opening her Bible in the Psalms, her eyes now spotted verses that expressed her growing trust and joy in God. Also some which expressed His love and tenderness towards her. All she could do in response was to melt with humility and worship. *Why You deigned to bless all those others by me I'll never know!*

Flipping around in her Bible, her eyes fell on a verse she had once before underlined in Proverbs 4:18; *The path of the righteous is like the first gleam of dawn, shining ever brighter till the full light of day. (NIV)* She glanced up at the now too bright sun cresting above the now clearly green trees in the distance, all the subtle pastel shades of dawn having disappeared. All the world visible to her was bathed in vivid colours, many things radiating colour and warmth back up. Her jaw slacked, *You mean, if I'm dressed in the righteousness of Christ, my understanding, or light, is to grow like the dawning of a new day?*

She told Him resolutely, *I'm going home to tell Mom and Dad what kind of things I've been up to, no matter how hard it is! I want to see some miracles!*

He reminded her that she not only ought to confide in them but also let them help her. *Your proud, independent spirit, thinking you don't need them the way they need you, is what has built that brick wall in the first place.* Ruthe could not imagine what kind of help her parents would give her, but she decided not to pick on that point.

Rather, shedding fresh tears of relief at getting some answers, she prayed, *Oh Lord Jesus, what a marvellous Friend You are! No one tops You!*

Now she wanted to linger and take time for a long rest. She knew her life could take a fresh swerve and explode into all kinds of talking, more talking, and trips to the city. Times of tremendous excitement were coming. At that thought, all her tensions unwound, and she felt more exhausted by the minute.

Ruthe lay down again on her back, staring up into the fluffy white clouds against the light blue ten o'clock sky. *I'll just review an outline of all I should tell Mom and Dad...,* and she fell asleep.

SEVENTY-FIVE

About four o'clock Ruthe got at home to find the house in cool silence. Her sisters stayed after school, she suspected, for music lessons. After wandering around she found her mother in the vegetable garden.

Immediately, her mother scolded about how poorly the young plants were doing, and, "Nobody goes weeding when I send them! Nor did my iris bed ever get dug up when it should have been!"

"Yes, I did it." Ruthe picked up the spade nearby and showed how the soil was turned over and soft. "See here's my spade marks. The wind dried the darker dirt on top. That's why you can't see it now."

Her mother turned away muttering, and Ruthe panicked that she would lose her courage again. In the face of such negativism she had always cowed back and withdrawn. But she prayed for help and resolved to wait until supper time, so she would only need to spill her soul once.

As she made a salad for supper and helped her mother peel potatoes, Ruthe began to grow wet under her arms. Then she thought that Brandt might be a moral support, besides Sharri, but he was seldom home for meals, so she called Isabelle and asked if she could send him home for supper for a change.

Her stomach felt full of spouted potatoes, growing ugly, but she waited until all the family was at the table and they had recited their low German grace.

While everyone was serving themselves from whatever dish was nearest them, Ruthe announced, "I have something important to say to the whole family today. Dad, Mom–" she glanced at Brandt and the girls too, then rushed on, "I've been sinning against you. Particularly by my independence. I mean, my attitude that you needed me, but... well, I didn't need you."

She hesitated as she saw that they were all stopped in mid-motion and staring at her, startled. Her Dad, who was seldom at a loss for words would regain his tongue in a minute, so she hurried on, "It's been a big spiritual struggle for me. However, I want to confess some of the things I have been up to since– well, since I started working in the city. I don't know how this is going to come out, or how you'll feel about it, but I'm willing, if you'll forgive me, to try to co-operate with you as a proper, respectful daughter, and sister. So we can be the kind of family God intended us to be."

Suddenly she sat back, and years worth of tears brimmed over and she bawled like a scratched up two-year old. Sharri whipped a box of tissues onto Ruthe's lap and crept up beside her with her arms around her, cooing comfortingly.

447

Her mother came around the table and stood nearby, reaching for, but having difficulty in touching Ruthe. Between blowing her nose and wiping her eyes clear, Ruthe sensed that her mother wanted to make up with her, yet didn't quite know how. So she got up and gave her mom a hug. They clung to each other a moment, then Ruthe found herself shoved slightly back toward her chair. Her mom went back to sit in her own chair, red-eyed.

Her dad was choked up some, sputtering for words, "Wel-l, I don't know– I jus' don'know what to say! I've always said you should trust us more!"

"What's happened?" exclaimed Suzanne, "What's brought all this on?"

"Yeah, I missed somethin' here," said Brandt in a stranger's voice.

"I think I know!" said Sharri impatiently, "Just give her a chance. Ruthe will tell us what she wants to!"

Ruthe looked around at them over her tissues, one after the other, but zeroed in on her parents as she answered, "I gue-ess... I thought you wouldn't understand me. Or that you wouldn't let me go to work in the city any more and do the daring things I was–" she sniffed, "do-ing in the city."

"Like what?" her dad wanted to know.

Suzanne snorted but was alive with curiosity, "Yeah, what've you been doing that's so daring?"

"Well," Ruthe swallowed some tears and blew her nose again, "I rescued some girls from rape and strangling. On my grad night I rushed to the death-bed... um, of one of the mothers of those girls. I... I helped another one start a business, and I helped a prostitute to become a Christian.. .an-and, to fix up an apartment block. I helped a girl keep her baby when... when the Welfare wanted her to give it up."

"Can't see why you're ashamed of such things," her dad said, his interest in a good story kindled, "but what can we tell from a few words like that?"

"This's crazy," her mother said, wiping her eyes with a corner of her apron. "When you were born I prayed that you'd be a missionary. I often wondered why it wasn't happening."

Sharri now felt free to contribute, and piped up, "You've no idea how many people Ruthe has led to accept Jesus as Saviour! I've met some of these people and they all love her a lot! You should just see how much they fuss over her!"

Ruthe hooked an arm around her younger sister to slow her down some, but Sharri was eager to break news that she was bursting to tell. She turned to Suzanne, "Know that mansion that we were' at for the Charm n' Poise course? Well, Ruthe owns it! She's the one who donated it for that course. An' you know Darlin' Bonne's Shop? Her mom kicked her out because Ruthe led her to the Lord, so she thinks of our Ruthe here, as her Mom."

The gasps and exclamations came so thick and fast Ruthe could not keep up. Instead of apologizing and defending her actions, Sharri was turning this into a brag session. She tried to slip in comments to down play the greatness her little fan was portraying for her.

When her dad wanted to know more about the mansion, she shrugged, "I couldn't help it. Granny O'Brien left it to me in her will to use for rescuing other girls like the ones she heard about."

"Who gave you the money for this house then?" queried her mother.

"Okay, Mom, here's the truth. I told Granny O'Brien, who was sick in bed, that I wanted to build your dream house. She died right when you went on holidays, and left me a big cheque for your dream. I just decided to quickly have it built here as a surprise."

"Why couldn't you tell us that?" her mother demanded.

"Because–" Ruthe hesitated, "You always seem to see the worst in everything. Then I felt like I had to defend even my good deeds to you. I... I guess I just felt crushed and decided not to tell you." Tears began to flow again.

Brandt had been eating steadily while the others were distracted with questions and answers. Now he leaned back and stretched his arms up behind his head. "So? How rich are you, sister-dear? Can I trouble you for a loan to buy me a farm?"

"I'm not rich. I give things away almost as fast as I get them," Ruthe defended herself. "You know that what I earn at my job I share here at home."

Brandt grew kinder in his approach. "Actually, Scottie and me had figured out that you had a secret life in the city. We just weren't sure if we were seeing Dr. Jekyll, or Ms. Hyde here at home. Isabelle has been sure all along that you could do no wrong. She'll want to hear all these stories from you too."

"How come you never let me in on these things?" Suzanne demanded suddenly. "You always left me out!"

Ruthe was surprised. "Oh Suzanne. I always thought you had such self-cen–
...such moods, you weren't interested. Besides, you've never shown any interest in the things of the Lord."

"Some of us find it hard to talk about those things. It's hopeless trying to be like you! Everybody 'round here thinks you're so perfect. They're always bragging on you! I just want to be liked for me, even if I am different!"

"Suzanne!" Ruthe instinctively held out her arms to her sister as she did to anyone who show some honest transparency. "I don't want you to be just like me. You can be yourself! I was waiting for some sign that you cared about spiritual things!"

Their parents echoed the sentiment that Suzanne did not need to be a copy of Ruthe. Even though Ruthe felt they didn't fully realize what they were saying, she was glad they said it. It was the right thing for Suzanne to hear.

"Yea-but, Sharri has–!"

"Suzanne, it happens that Sharri has some traits like me, but she is her own person, and if you'll let us, we'll help you to find your full potential too."

It looked like Suzanne was beginning to believe her. "Really?" She still needed it confirmed strongly, "You'll be my friend?"

Ruthe felt exasperated, both with herself for not seeing this sooner, and with Suzanne. She got up and went around the table. "Stand up," she charged, "so I can give you a proving hug."

It was a disoriented supper. While some talked, other picked at the food. Then someone else waved a fork and launched into expression; all except for Brandt. He stowed away three plates full of mashed potatoes and smoked farmer's sausage, all the while glancing up to listen and register what he heard.

Ruthe knew the Clarkes would soon have a line-by-line account of this event, but she didn't care. She had a strange new sensation within her own being. The only image she could quickly compare it to, was that an ice block had moved, and a fast mountain stream was down, through and out of her. There was a sense of freedom and also of much hidden matter come to light. Like maybe an attic and basement spring housecleaning.

She told the family about witnessing the shooting of the prostitute the previous year. "Remember? The murder that was on the news so much, when the city was so fearful of that motorcycle gang?"

Her mother shuddered and began to drill her, "Did those men see you? Did they touch you?"

"They did come to see me later that night," she sighed, "As I came off work. They took me to their hideout, but God gave me strength and I was able to win them all to Christ." Here she felt a pressing need to focus on the positive, spiritual aspects, rather than physical descriptions. "All six of those men recognized they had sinned against God, and asked for His forgiveness. I told them to go home and make things right. They took it literally. Now one of them has come back to confess to the police in Saskatoon. He talked to me last night."

As she had thought, her mom wanted to know all about this man. "What does he look like? What does he do?"

"Mom, Jonathan is a handsome-looking gentleman. He wears a fine business suit, and comes from a wealthy background. He has good manners. He's not mean or cruel any more to anyone–"

"Yes-but," asked her Dad, "Is he as nice as Scottie Clarke?"

Ruthe considered and nodded, "Yes. You would like Jonathan too. In fact, you'd like all my friends, if you didn't make up your minds ahead of time to be afraid of them."

Her dad shocked her with his next speech. "Ruthe," he said slowly. "it sounds like you know more about hearing God's voice than I do. I used to be like that, but I got too busy trying to make a living. If you need courage to confess some sin somewhere, like to the police, I'll come with you."

"D-ad!" She was touched he would want to help in such a way, but she assured him, "I have nothing to confess to the police, Dad. I've long ago told them everything I knew. Now I just have to let Jonathan confess to the murder of Emeraude without worrying that it is going to upset my parents and family. If you don't make life rough for me, then it is all A-okay."

"Will you have to go to jail?" asked her mom, tremulously.

"No, no!" Ruthe answered quickly, "Though, if there is a court trial for Jonathan I might have to testify as a witness that I saw him shoot his girlfriend. That's all."

"Then he'll come after you!"

"No, Mom. You might hear about it on the news, and folks might talk a lot, but that's the worst that will happen."

Anna Veer was still not quite convinced and looked around the table for others to confirm Ruthe's words. Brandt spoke up and assured her, "She's right, Mom. And if he confesses, there is not even likely to be a trial. Just a lot of newspaper fuss over what a heroine Ruthe is. Can you stand a famous daughter?"

Their mother leaned back, more relaxed, "You're famous?"

Her dad quipped, "It wasn't so bad when Suzanne's picture was in the paper. We just have to help you kids not to get proud and have a swelled head."

SEVENTY-SIX

It was nearly nine when the dishes were finally washed, and the family discussion was dying down. Brandt had run off to tell the Clarkes all this news, and Suzanne and Sharri had to study. Ruthe decided that her adrenalin was so high right now, she might as well go into the city and tell Jonathan not to hold back any more. In fact, she worried the police might have picked him up already and that he was keeping silent for her sake.

She told her parents this was what she wanted to do, and they urged her to go get the matter cleared up.

On the way, she kept a tissue in her hand and frequently wiped away tears of relief as she drove. She was too tired to analyze it well, but she knew she was freed.

She stopped first at the Moss Rose, planning to pick something up from her room, and to phone the hotel to see if Jonathan was in. She found him in the front entrance of the Moss Rose, talking with Lisa. They quickly asked about her tear-stained face.

Ruthe spoke deliberately, "I spent most of the day in prayer, and the evening confessing my secret double life to my family."

She turned her face fully on Jonathan. "I'm free; you have my full blessing now to make your confession to the police. I won't hold you back any more. In fact, I'll go with you, if you like."

"Me too," said Lisa eagerly. It made Ruthe wonder how deep their discussions had gone. *They actually look handsome, side-by-side.*

Jonathan smiled that enormous smile of his and put a hand under Ruthe's elbow, and under Lisa's, "Let's go."

As they walked the few blocks to the station, Jonathan confided that Sgt. Webster had already paid him a visit the night before, and he had begged twenty-four hours grace, "Because you needed to work out some personal liberty of spirit."

She exclaimed, "You knew I needed twenty-four hours?"

He grinned. "Lisa told me last night, if you had gone home to pray about something, you'd be back with an answer in twenty-four hours."

Ruthe looked past his chest to smile guiltily at Lisa, and receive her loving smile. "Guess you have me figured out, eh?"

"Well, I spent my free time today praying for you too!"

By the time they entered the station Ruthe was feeling a bit giddy. She knew when she got over-tired she tended to talk with less inhibitions and tried humour more than otherwise. They found Sgt. Webster in Charlie Brown's office, both with their feet on the desk. Stepping into the open doorway she clapped her hands to startle them, and could not resist saying, "Lucky you, I'm bringing you something you have wanted a long time."

"Not," asked Charlie, lowering his feet, "another penitent soul?"

Sgt. Webster muttered something unclear and did likewise.

Lisa and Jonathan moved into the cubicle and made polite greetings.

The tall, balding Sergeant was immediately alert, while Charlie motioned everyone to sit down and hollered into the hall for another chair.

"Gentlemen," said Jonathan, ignoring the chair behind him, "I'm the guy who shot that young woman, Emeraude, about a year ago down by the bridge pylons. These two ladies were on the scene in viewing distance and can verify it. I'm afraid you'll also have to charge me with kidnapping this lovely young woman," he motioned with both hands, "But God in His infinite wisdom answered her prayers. She persuaded me to hate my own sins, and trust God's provision for cancelling them in His Ledgers. I've started over again with Jesus Christ."

"That how you see it?" Sgt. Webster stared hard into Ruthe's face.

"Yes, that sums it up." Ruthe blushed slightly, "He doesn't look or talk like the Jon of that night, but I'm sure it is the same man, and God has changed him tremendously!"

"You knew as soon as you laid eyes on him here in the station," accused the homicide specialist.

Ruthe lifted her head and drew a deep breath.

"How come you didn't stay here to make him confess right away?" Charlie Brown teased.

"Because... because I had certain fears to deal with."

Jonathan interrupted protectively again, "She did not prevent me. I could have. I was going to confess before I asked you to call her yesterday," he turned to Sgt. Webster, "But I was afraid you wouldn't let me see her at all once I was locked up."

Lisa spoke up, "Jonathan is a gentleman. He learned last night that Ruthe expected some flack in her own home if Jonathan's arrest were broadcast. He didn't want to hurt her, so he gave her time to work things out in her family."

Sgt. Webster turned piercing eyes on Ruthe, "Have you?"

"Yes," Ruthe answered with a humble sigh, and decided for total honesty again. "I went aside, to a private place to pray. I had a good session with my family tonight. Now I no longer need to live a secret, double life."

"She'll survive the fuss," Lisa said kindly. "Ruthe has a heart as soft as whipped cream, but she's as strong as the Twenty-fifth Street bridge."

"I know." Webster sounded kinder now too, but matter-of-fact, "You should write a book, Ms. Veer. Tell the world your version of the events. Your thoughts and emotions are the very soul of it all."

"Yep," prompted Charlie smugly, while Ruthe's chin was still dropping, "Beat the hacks to the punch. You've got a better story to tell than they."

"See?" Lisa came around Jonathan to wrap an arm around Ruthe, "Just as Phyllis has been telling you."

Ruthe stared from one to the other in the small room. This was not what she had expected to come up tonight. Yet it seemed like a nudge, '*Turn up this path next.*'

It was true that her family had received the breaking of her news much better than she had expected. In fact, she now realized, in a short while they would get used to this new information and things would get routine again. But if she took this new direction–?

She looked into Lisa's big, round, sky-blue-marble eyes. "What of my friends? What happens to them? What about the time it would take? I've been working on a book in secret, but it takes years and years!"

"It's just an idea," said Sgt. Webster briskly, "You work it out." He wanted to get back to Jonathan, and asked him, "You're giving yourself up tonight? Want a lawyer present?"

Jonathan nodded to the first question. "But I don't think I need a lawyer."

"Hey, Angel," Charlie raised his voice, "What lawyer would you recommend for your friend? He really ought to have one if you are to plea-bargain successfully."

"I only know Mr. O'Brien and Mr. Newton."

"O'Brien's semi-retired, right?"

Ruthe hesitated. "He's a Christian though, and would be more understanding than his former partner."

Charlie shoved a phone at her to call him. Which she did, and when she had explained briefly, Mr. O'Brien promised to come right down.

The officers decided to move to a larger room, and by the time they were settled there, Mr. O'Brien had arrived and Ruthe introduced him to the others.

The two sergeants excused themselves while Jonathan and Ruthe and Lisa told Ian O'Brien the basic story. He nodded with understanding, asked some questions, flashed Ruthe an interesting smile, and agreed to take the case. Then he went to the door and signalled the officers to return.

Together they reviewed and wrote out the details of that fateful day and night. Sgt. Webster left no aspect uncovered. Both Ruthe and Lisa spoke up several times to defend Jonathan and promote leniency.

Ruth Marlene Friesen

Though the Homicide Head was anxious to see full justice done, he finally explained that the outcome was in the hands of the judge. All he could do was proceed to the Prosecutor's office with this confession, which could expedite things. Then he wanted to hear from O'Brien.

"Criminal law is not my speciality," said the tall, grey-haired man quietly, "I am prepared to do some research and be thorough. In the meantime," he turned to Jonathan, "you are wonderfully fortunate to have these excellent women testifying both for and against you. They are the most unusual people I have ever met. I doubt that a full-blown trial will be necessary because of their testimony."

Jonathan nodded, "Yes, thank you. I know that, and am grateful."

Charlie tried to be helpful, "Arraignment is likely early tomorrow morning, but when there is no contest as in a confession, there is not likely to be a trial. Still, can you post bail?"

"I can handle it," Jonathan answered, turning to Mr. O'Brien.

Mr. O'Brien raised his eyebrows and glanced at Ruthe as if for confirmation. She gave him a slight nod to let him know that yes, she expected he could afford it. She was going on what he had told her about selling his father's business in New York, and coming to pay 'sorry money.'

It was after eleven when they agreed Jonathan had to spend the night locked up because no bond could be posted until morning. Lisa gave him a good night peck on the cheek, and promised to hold breakfast for him at the Moss Rose.

Ruthe moved closer, but wasn't quite sure how to handle her good night. She took his hand, then he laid his left one over both of hers, and they looked into each other's eyes.

"Thanks, Ruthe, for everything."

She nodded, "G'night, Jonathan. I'll be praying for you." Then she backed up and let Sgt. Webster guide him away.

As Ruthe and Lisa were about to leave the station, Charlie Brown stepped up to say something. He said, "Hey, Angel of Mercy, I'm impressed. I know your convictions run deep. Now you've worked out something that affected you to your core. I got'a say, before I was amused at your faith in God. To me, Jesus was just a historical man who had the misfortune to be crucified. It looked silly to me to watch people like yourself going around, believing He's alive and interested in folks today. But y'know, I've watched Lisa's metamorphosis here, and hearing you talk honestly about your fears, and how this Jesus-Invisible gives you courage to do things that scare you to pieces; @#$%@#, I think He must really be God after all!"

455

Ruthe heard this as a statement of faith. She froze a moment, smiled at Charlie Brown, blinked a bit, and squeezed his huge fleshy hand with her small, bony ones. "Thanks. I'm so pleased to hear this!"

Naturally she prayed, driving home in the clear, cool moonlight. Her energies were gone, and she berated herself for not phoning and staying in her city room, but she also praised God that the confession to her family was behind her and had gone so well. She knew attitudes would not all be transformed over night, however, now she had high hope that they would improve.

Then her thoughts drifted to Jonathan again. Ruthe had to admit that being near him made her tingle, more than Lloyd, or any other male creature she had ever known. At the same time a strong knowledge rose in her heart that this was not God's planned husband for her, and she was in great danger of being side-tracked if she got emotionally entangled with him. Considering her tender nature, and that this was a take-charge man, not used to "no" for an answer, Ruthe knew that she ought to flee like a panic-stricken bird.

Lord, what if I have to go through a court case with him? I'm willing to let someone else disciple him. But how can I sprout wings to fly out of this relationship? How fast can You deliver me?

Because she saw no way out, Ruthe didn't know if her dearest Friend took her questions seriously.

SEVENTY-SEVEN

The next morning, when she dragged herself late into the kitchen for breakfast, her mother greeted Ruthe with, "Sharri says that– that tutor lady, y'know, Miss Shulton? She's been after you to write a book. Why don't you do that? Then you won't have to work such crazy shifts no more."

"Mom, writing a book takes time. Lots of time." Ruthe tried to sound patient, all the while shushing up the feeling that her mother was trying to take over and run her life for her, with her limited knowledge. "It takes a lot of quiet concentration. I've been working on one. Even when it's done there is no guarantee it will make enough money so I can stop working."

"Well, you could take a holiday and try it. Why not go to visit Aunt Agnes in Ontario?" her mom persisted.

Ruthe opened her mouth, then let her jaw fall slack as she recalled years ago, when her aunt was still single and visiting them, she had confided her dream to write a book, and her aunt had been encouraging. Now she was married to a pastor and had a little boy named Billy, both of whom their family had never met. *Maybe Aunt Agnes wouldn't mind if I holed up for a month or two as their guest, and just wrote.*

Abruptly, Ruthe got up and started to clear breakfast leftovers. "I think I'll go talk it over with Phyllis today, and then I'll phone Aunt Agnes and see. Maybe that's not such a bad idea after all, Mom. Thank you."

Phyllis was thrilled to meet Ruthe in the halls of the high school, and particularly to hear of this plan. She encouraged Ruthe to go for the trip and the book project. "You've got your plotting and most of your rough drafts done," she pointed out. "All you need is some uninterrupted and steady hours to write your good draft and knit all the parts carefully together. I know you can do it, Ruthe! Getting away from this circle of friends who claim your time, even your job, it's all for the best!"

"But I don't want to end up sponging off my Aunt and Uncle for months and months; it's not fair to them," Ruthe reasoned.

"Listen, apply to cash in your company pension plan. Check that bank account downtown that you keep forgetting, and if you still need it, I'll be happy to deposit some into it for you." Phyllis coaxed, "Just think, if you pace yourself to do a chapter every day or two, a month is enough time to write the book twice."

Ruthe began to laugh giddily. "You think of every angle, Phyllis. This all came up so fast, but I want to pray and make sure I'm not running ahead of the Lord. Then I guess I'll phone my Aunt and Uncle and see if they'll have me."

Suddenly Phyllis grabbed Ruthe's wrists, "You've done it? I can tell! You've told your family! You no longer live a double life!"

Ruthe was surprised that it was so obvious, but confirmed that she was finally experiencing a miracle of her own.

She prayed all of her shift at work, as a constant undercurrent to all the calls she handled. Not the agonizing prayers of late, but more like the cheerful, confidential chats of her earlier teens. By the time she was done work, and went to drop in at Darlin' Bonne's Shop, she was ready to hint that she might be going away soon.

When they asked what held her back, she told them she didn't know what her aunt would say. Darlin' Bonne urged her to make the phone call right away, so they would know the answer too.

Her Aunt Agnes was pleased about Ruthe's plan to come, and all at once her Uncle Harold was on an extension. He sounded enthusiastic about getting acquainted; "We have a spare room. Just say how soon. We'd love to have a writer-in-residence!"

Ruthe thought she had to give two weeks notice at work and found it to be so the next morning when she checked with the Chief Operator. She resigned and applied for her pension deposits to be returned to her in a cashier's cheque. The clerk told her, her unused holiday pay would be in a separate cheque on her last day. Ruthe hadn't known that she had so much coming.

Her mom took a certain delight in having her suggestion work out for a change. As others heard of it and accepted Ruthe's decision, she grew more pleased, and said not a word about holding Ruthe back.

Jonathan, hearing about Ruthe's impending trip from Lisa as soon as he was released on bail, took it with huge disappointment. He met her coming out of the SaskTel building. Jonathan admitted he had looked forward to being in her inner circle of friends. "I would buy a car and offer to drive you to Ontario, but for the bail condition that I stay in Saskatoon until the judge has studied the case and is ready to pass sentence."

Ruthe's eyes narrowed as she wondered if he might be paroled into her care as Lisa had been. "Any idea what your sentence will be?"

"Ian O'Brien has been looking things up. He tells me I can expect a prison term, maybe ten years, cut to three with early parole because I accepted guilt."

She didn't tell him that rather than stay around to hold his hand, she was even more certain that it was time she moved on. Instead she assured him that her circle of friends would take him in and cheer him up. "Besides, there are many ways for you to obey and serve the Lord, right in Saskatoon. And in any prison too. I'm sure they need missionaries."

Over the next two weeks, between and after shifts, she dashed about to see all her city friends and break the news to them; she was going away and was not sure when she would be back. Most of them expressed regret to see her go, yet when reminded all agreed she had never had a vacation away from home. They wished her well.

Ross proudly told her he had written up an assignment on the jade and gold trimming he had done on Moss Rose, and had been commended highly by his professor.

Ann made frustrated, fretting comments about lack of money. Ruthe noticed, but ignored it, while beaming at Ross, "It's thrilling to see you discover the joy of accomplishment. You're really growing up!"

Ross glanced at his wife. "But I have to learn to be a good husband and provider yet," he said softly.

Ruthe stood up, just breathing a few moments, then answered quietly, "No one said it was easy, but keep looking in your Bible. I mean figuratively and practically, in both the heirloom one and the one you can read and understand clearly."

Ann came around from behind Ross suddenly and said, "I packed that antique away for safe-keeping."

Steadily, Ruthe looked into Ann's eyes, "Then you're keeping him from his inheritance. Don't complain, Ann, if you end back on Welfare. Granny was not insane when she tied up Ross' gifts in that old Book. Please don't fall for the sin of greed; I think you're being tested in your desire to be rich."

Ann turned to go get it.

Ruthe said her good byes quickly so as not to leave while Ann was out of sight, but giving Ross a hug, she whispered, "I'll pray for you all."

She put off seeing Lloyd until nearer the last day, although she asked Cathy O'Brien to break the news to him first.

On Sunday Jonathan showed up in the Kleinstadt church, slipped in beside Ruthe, and held the hymnbook for her. This caused a great stir in the small church. They couldn't understand why, afterwards Ruthe was so busy chatting with others, forgetting to introduce him around.

Isabelle invited all of the Veer family over for Sunday lunch, so they could get to pump Ruthe one last time. Even her parents teased her about the man in the brown and orange pinstriped suit with the nice, wavy golden-bronze hair. They did not want to believe her when she said, "He's Jonathan Astor who confessed to shooting that girl in the park last year. The judge is sentencing him in a month or two."

"But he looks so nice!" they exclaimed.

"He is," Ruthe insisted. "Even the police like him. Yet he confessed to impulsively shooting his girlfriend when he thought she had set him up with the police, so he is prepared to take his punishment."

Scottie leaned over and looked earnestly into Ruthe's face. "That man is a Christian because of your witness, right? He has the grace to be honest and take his medicine because of your influence?"

Ruthe grimaced and lowered her eyes in embarrassment.

Everyone grew quiet as Scottie reached out and lifted her chin, "It is a very noble thing; you ought not to be ashamed of it. The Bible says, 'he who wins souls is wise,' and I'm sure you have won more souls for Christ than we will ever hear about. What's more, they go out and win others. This Jonathan may become a great prison minister and soul-winner."

"But that's not me!" exploded Ruthe. "Almost every time the Lord has prompted me to speak to someone I've had to beg and lean on Him for courage." Tears trickled down her face as she said, "I'm not half as brave as you think. I'm a weak little softy with a heart of butter for people who don't know the joy of friendship with my precious Jesus!"

"Ah-yes," said Scottie, leaning back in his chair, "That is your secret. Success always boils down to a simple principle."

"I still want to know why you didn't confide in me!" wailed Isabelle. "I thought we were best of friends!"

Ruthe hedged, "I didn't want to hurt you!"

"Then let's go take this bucket of slop water to the garden," and the busy hostess steered Ruthe out the back door.

Recalling her pledge to be transparent, but not wanting to be unkind, Ruthe said with pain in her voice and eyes, "Isabelle, you blurted your own secrets to everyone in the community; how could I trust you with mine?"

In an instant Isabelle was in tears on her shoulder and they were making up, and learning from the truth.

The last week Ruthe was still remembering people she ought to say goodbye to, and give one more hug. People such as Peter and Sophie, who had added more foster children to their country home.

Peter predicted, "You'll have a fine husband soon!"

Sophie gave her what sounded like lovely promises, "Your turn's coming. I just feel it. In a year you'll have a great big, wonderful family."

Coming away grinning, Ruthe went directly to Laura and David Pollock's grand suburban home, to laugh and play with Lois, the chatty, nosy, acrobat, who was still only twelve inches high and wearing doll clothes, but socially savvy. Ruthe always did a double-take, thinking, *This wee creature doing gymnastic tumbles on my hand is the same age as Reggie Clarke!*

Davie was stretched out in his recliner in his stocking feet, while Laura dithered in the kitchen arch about serving something, and scolded Lois for showing off her somersaults and leaps. It was distracting, so Ruthe soon got to her farewells, but Davie got in a parting shot, "You were afraid to come to me for a complete physical; I hope you find another doctor whom you trust. Sweetie, you're taking your health for granted."

Ruthe's escape was to agree with him.

June and her brothers and sisters were hard to catch all at home at the same time, but she managed to entrust the care of the Chrysalis to June. "Just consult the O'Briens when in doubt. Lisa will help too."

As usual, June was distracted over Byron.

Eventually, Ruthe's conscience drove her to go see Lloyd at his Sales office in Bright City. She took the Rambler in first to Gordon to get it thoroughly serviced. He dropped what he was doing to handle it immediately. She met Graham on the showroom floor, and stood and chatted with him nearly half an hour. Finally, she asked directions and found Lloyd.

He took her hand, pulled her into his office cubicle and closing the venetian blind to the showroom, asked, "Should I stop hoping that the Lord has me in mind for your husband?"

Ruthe nodded sombrely, "Yes, Lloyd. I'm sorry it has taken so long for us to talk about this. You have wasted three years holding your breath for me, and Cathy is doing the same for you. I hope you can put me aside now and get on with God's true will for your future."

His lips trembled, he bit them, but Lloyd could not speak.

Ruthe ached for him. She stepped up and gave him a hug and said, "Allow yourself a good hard cry tonight. Tell the Lord how much you hurt, and then ask Him for His balm of Gilead, and for new direction."

She walked over the driving course gardens and visited Stephanie and Grace while she waited for Gordon to finish with her car. The McKenzies had recently adopted two little Italian girls, and Gordon and Stephanie expected a baby.

When she returned Gordon apologized about the long delay over the Rolls, but had finally received some parts from London, England, and some from London, Ontario, and would work on it whenever he had time.

Ruthe told him not to worry. She had no dreams for the Rolls.

There was no charge for the Rambler check-up.

Lisa was spending extra time with Jonathan while he awaited his sentencing. Ruthe had privately mentioned, that she felt the Lord wanted her not to get to close to Jonathan herself. "Are you up to comforting him and seeing he doesn't pitch overboard?"

"Fret not," Lisa had said, "I can manage a man."

Jonathan still sought out Ruthe whenever he could catch up with her, and she knew there would have to be one final good bye scene with him. Thinking about Lloyd made her resolve to make it a clean break so Jonathan would not pine away for her too long.

Aubrey and Ginter clearly were disappointed. Aubrey feared once she got into big-time slumming in those huge cities she would not return. She'd love it too much. But they wished her well and assured her the police in London would soon like her too. "We'll send word ahead," they offered, "D' Angel of Mercy is coming!"

Jonathan took both Ruthe and Lisa out for supper the last day that Ruthe worked in the city. She had already promised to spend the very last evening with Darlin' Bonne and the girls, where Phyllis was invited too, but she agreed to an early supper with him.

Her mind and emotions were separating and playing tricks on her. Most of the elegant meal Ruthe had weird sensations of watching the three of them from the ceiling or behind a large nearby green plant. They had friendly chatter, but she felt as if she were acting, not really in the things she said.

Jonathan, braced now to be a missionary in prison, asked Ruthe a couple of times for her address, "And you'll write me?"

She tried to be reassuring without making promises.

At the end, sensing Ruthe's discomfort over Jonathan's open mourning of her departure, Lisa took to patting her wrist and significant eye language to indicate, Jonathan would be cared for, not to worry.

Suddenly Ruthe got up, gave Lisa a great hug, then a quick one for Jonathan, said a few words that she couldn't remember when she got out on the street, and hurried away. She felt guilty, but did not go back.

The later hours at the shop were more pleasant, more like the many other evenings spent there. She savoured them, in case it was a long time before the next time.

At one point, Darlin' Bonne pulled her into another room and asked hoarsely, "Tell me honestly, you're not leaving because I brought up lesbianism a few weeks ago, are you?"

"No way!" Ruthe quickly assured her, "But I am praying often that the Lord will keep you from that temptation. Don't go there, no matter how much you miss a real mother's love, or feel wasted for a good, godly man."

"Yeah-h. Sometimes I feel so unlovable. I need a new miracle."

"Sometimes I do too, but our Lord is great enough, and cares enough to do something special for us. Let's both worship Him, and keep coming to Him until He does something good, okay?"

"Is that why you're going away?" asked Darlin' Bonne, drying her eye sockets on Ruthe's thin, bony shoulder.

"I can't explain it, but I think God has decided it's time to do something new in my life. He's heard the deep, deep cry of my heart. I almost wonder if this going away to write a book is just an excuse, but I promise to let you know after I know what happens next, okay?"

They sniffled together, and rubbed foreheads.

"Listen, Darlene Bonne Barrett, the Lord lifted you out of an ugly rut and started you on a new life; He can do it again if you ask!"

"Okay, Darlin', do it right now."

So Ruthe prayed aloud for their dear Lord to bring Darlin' Bonne to new heights in spiritual understanding and maturity, and the peace that should come with it. Also, to bring into her life someone whose love would be just like His.

A bit later the good bye hugs with each of the other girls were also rather wet as they weighed her down with gifts. There was a new wardrobe in a luggage set, and additional writing supplies from Phyllis. Ruthe had trouble seeing to drive home, but she sighed several times, glad these farewells had been done right.

Over Saturday and Sunday Sharri hung nearby like her former seven-year-old self, whining that she wanted to go along. "Send for me soon as school's out, all right?" Or a minute later, "I'll turn out rotten without you to guide me!"

Ruthe treated most of this playfully. She was afraid to promise too much because she really didn't know what God had in store for her, but a quiet anticipation was building inside, as she tucked last minute things into the new luggage and reassured both Sharri and Suzanne, of her love.

Sunday she focused on reassuring her parents, and Grosz'mama, that she would be fine, and would write or phone from time to time. With a map spread out before faspa at Grosz'mama's, Ruthe explained how she would break her trip up into stages.

Monday morning, before her sisters left for school, Ruthe put her luggage in the trunk of the Rambler, posed for photos as she got into the driver's seat, and waved good bye as long as she could see her family, which was nearly a block from home.

At the highway she adjusted her shoulders, *You wanted to take me farther to discover more beautiful roses in Your wider garden? I'm ready, Lord.*

<<*>>

463

Reader Survey

If you hate surveys, please ignore this section.

However, as any good writer, I aim to please my friends when I can, and would sure like to know what you like or don't like in this book. May I ask you a few questions? Reply only to the ones you can answer honestly. Email it to ruth@ruthes-secretroses.com   Or mail it to me at;

Ruthe's Secret Roses
Box 208, Hague, SK. S0K 1X0 Canada.

(Don't feel limited! Use the other blank pages, or different paper if you like).
1. In what ways was this book different or a surprise to you?

2. What did you like best? Which people did you identify with most?

3. What did you not care for or dislike? If you have figured it out, tell why?

4. What emotions or thoughts did this story stir up in you?

5. How do you think you may be affected by it in your future?

6. Do you know the Lord Jesus as your personal Saviour and Best Friend? Tell me more about your relationship with Him? Like when and how did it start, etc.?

7. What do you wish you knew that might help you be closer to Jesus?

8. Do your prayers get answered? Please tell of one or two of them?

9. The next book in this series will give Ruthe a romance like you've never seen before! As an author, it is fairly easy to develop any of the minor characters and make them the main personalities in a separate spin-off book of their own too. To which ones would you recommend I do that? (No guarantee, but it might influence me).

10. Check often at **http://Ruthes-SecretRoses.com** for updates. Better yet, subscribe to my biweekly ezine, RoseBouquet to follow my writing progress and adventures. To subscribe: mailto:RoseBouquet-subscribe@yahoogroups.com.

---

[1] translated from Low German; "Girl! Hold still!"

[2] *In The Garden* by C. Austin Miles (now in public domain)

[3] Afternoon tea or coffee break with baked goodies.

[4] I John 1:9 KJV

[5] I John 4:15 KJV

[6] I Thessalonians 4:13-18 KJV

[7] John 6:37b KJV

[8] James 1:5-7

[9] Romans 3:23 KJV

[10] Isaiah 53:6 KJV

[11] Kitten, used as an endearment.

[12] faspa is an afternoon tea or coffee break.

[13] scambled eggs

[14] Noon meal or lunch

[15] deep fried crullers

[16] a reference to snapped wires, and what does this mean?

[17] Now sit down.

[18] I lay everything in our Loving Heavenly Father's hands.

[19] Can you, have you freedom to tell any more about it?

[20] What do you think? Would it work out?

[21] Why not?

[22] That car sure shines!

[23] Is that true?

[24] "Old Box," an endearment for a child with adult ways.

[25] But I'm the oldest daughter!

[26] How was the flight?

[27] Good. Good!

[28] small Sunday, or less dressy.

[29] God will judge them fairly.

[30] But won't God forgive them for Jesus' sake if they repent?

[31] But God takes it serious when anyone kills a creature He has created.

[32] Do you believe in your heart those men will repent?

[33] God has given you a wonderfu faith.

[34] So, we have not heard the end of this yet.

[35] I have no idea what they will do.

[36] No, this is good, very good!

[37] It is far healthier if the mother grieves without hiding.

Printed in the United States
6140